ARISE THE DARKNESS

BOOK TWO

SHATTERED STEEL

BY
B.R. CRICHTON

Dedicated to the lovers of stories everywhere.

Cover design by Howard Vause
Edited by Ian O'Reilly
Book design by Guss Mortimer

ISBN-13: 978-0-9934894-2-6

FOREWORD

Five years, or near enough.

Far too long to wait for a sequel, I know, but life has a habit of getting in the way of writing and I am happy to say that almost all of that 'life' has been of the welcome variety. Anyone coming late to the saga will not have felt a thing, of course.

One of the great pleasures of writing is in seeing the characters come to life on the page. As the author, I know where I want them to go, but dammit they often have opinions of their own and I frequently need to tweak the story to align the plot with a protagonist's new direction. This is enjoyable but time consuming, and so I hope you will allow me to share with them at least some of the blame for the length of time it has taken to finish this book.

DRAMATIS PERSONAE

Abaddon: God sworn to the destruction of all worlds. (See *The Rage Within*)

Athusilan: Last of the Gods, dispassionate observer, and gatherer of tales of mortals for his *Book of Lives*.

Ganindhra: Fallen God, imprisoned upon his terrestrial throne in the isolated land of Lythuria.

Khalim-Shar: The Great Shar. A member of its kind that has been altered by the Daemon Elements left stranded in the world. (See *The Rage Within*)

Valia: Shar-hunter and warrior. Formerly called Lushara Bedein before fleeing Shol'Hara as a girl.

Marlon Padar: Shar-hunter and loyal companion to Valia.

Granger: Once an Emissary of the God, Athusilan, but banished to the mortal realm for rescuing the child, Kellan Aemoran. (See *The Rage Within*)

Acastes Fol'Denes: Korathean Heavy Infantryman turned Shar-hunter.

Kapaneus Paras: Companion to Acastes Fol'Denes.

Kekoa: Jendayan soldier sworn to ten years of servitude following the failed invasion that unleashed the Shar on the world.

Jon: Fletcher and Shar-hunter.

Abbil Musharit: Shar-hunter from Dashiya.

Elan Arellan: Last surviving Lythurian from before Abaddon's invasion. (See *The Rage Within*)

Alano Clemente: Ex-militiaman from Bal Mora. Caretaker of Lythuria turned Shar-hunter, and friend to Valia.

Rogan Fol'Brandam: Hatar (General) in the Korathean Heavy Infantry.

Raims: Captain in the Korathean Heavy Infantry and Rogan Fol'Brandam's right-hand man.

Bravik Fol'Gannity; Gilean Fol'Maddon; Morgarth Fol'Garras; Foaran Fol'Armen: Hatars (Generals) in the Korathean Heavy Infantry.

Casilda Clemente: Wife to Alano Clemente and caretaker of Lythuria.

Surilya: Kylyptian woman named in the journal of Gerasim Illaros, a Shar-hunter who died in the village of Depsing, where the first of the 'changed' Shar was found.

Dachen: Prince of the Eastern Kingdom of Tianpok. Second heir to the throne.

Sangye, Pemba, Yeshe, Tashimen, Kanchun: Eastern soldiers loyal to Prince Dachen.

Tsering: Eastern alchemist loyal to Dachen.

Adeyemi: Dark-skinned warrior from a land to the southeast of the Eastern Kingdoms.

Chapok: Prince of Tianpok and heir to the throne.

Jangbu: Personal bodyguard to Chapok.

Nirmaya: Young woman from Pashwar and leader of a fifty-strong band of women, the 'Sisters'.

Maidra: One of the 'Sisters', and lover to Nirmaya.

Starling: Young man from southern Korathea. At best, a thief and a miscreant.

Silman Fol'Ghealten: Captain in the Korathean Heavy Infantry.

Daelen: Korathean Heavy Infantryman and right-hand man to Captain Silman.

Ramash Suun: Leader of the 'Servants of the Arrival', a cult dedicated to readying the world for a returning God.

Masahara: Eastern servant to the Khalim-Shar.

Senji Dayivar: Commander of the Eastern armies loyal to the Khalim-Shar.

Belghutai: Speaker of the ruling council of Banihat.

Olgoi Kinbataar: Leader of the ruling *Conclave* of Ulan Balsaan.

Alisha: Eastern girl in the town of Bardiya.

Tau: Older brother to Alisha; a difficult birth left him with a limited ability to learn.

Dyansh: Friend to Alisha.

Unjen Yuddha: Captain in the Eastern army stationed in the town of Bardiya.

Commander Girvash: Commander of the Eastern garrison in the city of Baslika.

GLOSSARY

Anaki: The source of the Gods' power. Bead-like elements, little understood by the Gods themselves.

Ago-Camdi: *Fire-silver*, substance used in 'maddener' arrows that burn in moisture. Potassium.

The Akharran: The training complex for the Heavy Infantry within Kor'Habat.

Daemon Element: Anaki; the source of Abaddon's power. Some of these Anaki were cut off from their host at the time of his defeat.

Dam'Hara: Haram in charge of Shol'Hara.

Eastern Kingdoms: The 'Greater' Kingdom of Khumjang, and the 'Lesser' Kingdoms of Tianpok, Shibatsu and Lhaksang.

Hatar: A General in the Korathean Heavy Infantry.

Haram: A woman within Shol'Hara who bears children sired by worthy Heavy Infantrymen.

Hatiyara: Eastern war engine resembling a medieval ballista.

Heavy Infantry: Soldiers of Korathea. Centuries of selective breeding have produced and maintained a class of warrior far larger and stronger than any other.

Jendaya: Empire across the Adorim Sea, to the west of Korathea. (People – Jendayan)

Kodistai: Ruler of Korathea from his palace in Kor'Habat.

Korathea: Most powerful of the Western kingdoms; a much-reduced empire since the Jendayan invasion. (See *The Rage Within*)

Lamo Phenka: Eastern war engine resembling a medieval trebuchet or mangonel.

Lythuria: Last creation of the fallen God, Ganindhra. Geo-thermal plateau high in the Greater Cascus mountains.

Shar: Creatures unleashed on the world by Abaddon.

Shol'Hara: Complex within the city of Kor'Habat where the careful breeding of children suitable for training in the Heavy Infantry takes place.

Sparth: Long-shafted weapon favoured by Eastern soldiers, much like a medieval halberd.

Tianpok: Most northerly of the four 'Eastern Kingdoms' and home of Prince Dachen.

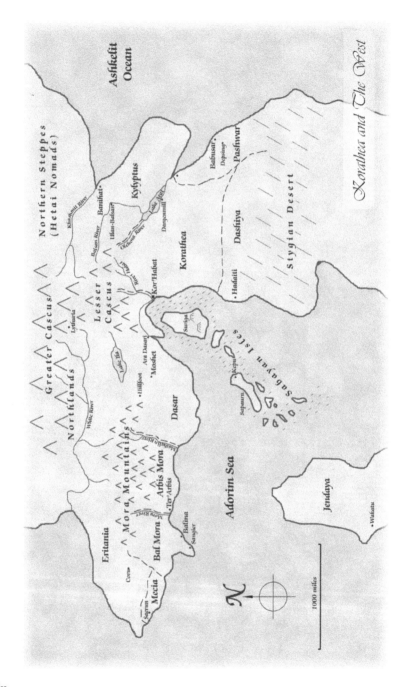

Korathea and The West

Ashkefit Ocean

Northern Steppes
(Hetai Nomads)

Kyfyptus

Banihati

Khan-Skatil River

Belgan River

Ithan-Badvar

Oktanea River

Dangenmill

Lake Aten

Korathea

Dashiya

Stygian Desert

Greater Cascus

Lesser Cascus

Lythania

Lodic Isle

Northlands

White River

Kor Hani

Kor'Habat

Hadaiti

Pashvar

Babusar

Depinay

Surnja

Ara Dasari

Moshet

Hillfoot

Kepu

Sabayan Isles

Dasar

Mora Mountains

Alabiha River

Arbis Mora

Ter'Arbis

Satnaru

Sajpaura

Batfma

Samjhar

Eritania

Mora River

Bal Mora

Mecia

Corus

Sagrun

Adorim Sea

Jenkaya

Wahattu

N

1000 miles

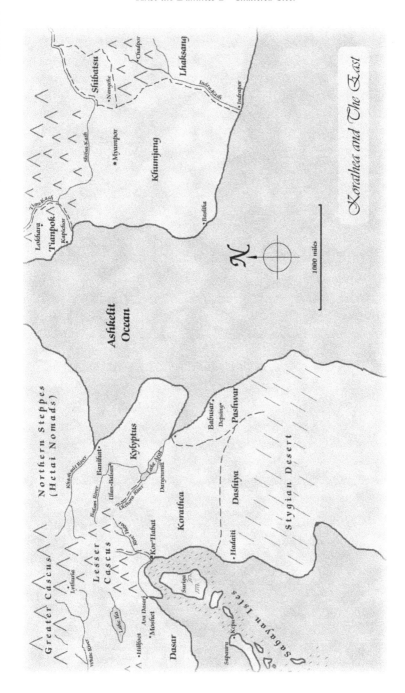

'Fire scatters shadow just as daybreak dispels night. But Valia's rising sun can only hope to chase the darkness away for a time, and for every dawn a dusk must surely follow.
Does steel remember the fire that birthed it?
Will it bend or will it break?'

From **THE BOOK OF LIVES.**

PROLOGUE

"Please, help them!" Ganindhra cried out, and his voice echoed within the hollow bole of the enormous tree

The fallen god could feel the carnage; sense the horror as it carried to him through a void that held no barriers. He could see within his vast mind the lights of the living failing in the dark, one by one in a distant place; a town called Ulan Balsan.

Ganindhra fought against his prison throne, thrashing to break free from the living wood that bound him to the soil and to life, but it held firm.

"It cannot end like this! The boy defeated him! Abaddon is dead!"

The Shar were deeper shadows against a dark background in that arena of souls, mindless evil wrapped in hateful night, eclipsing the dwindling glimmers of the living.

Was this to be his end? Doomed to watch the world being consumed as he withered?

Abaddon's final, spiteful victory.

"Help them, brother!" He called again. But there was no reply.

The lights were fading against the encroaching shadow.

"Athusilan!"

There was no answer to his call and still the battle raged. He watched the febrile minds, alive with terror, fall one after another.

But there was a mind standing proud of all others; it was one he knew. A tight knot of courage and persistence. There was fear there too, but it was a fear of failure more than of death. It was a mind driven by loss and the agonies of injustice.

Lushara Bedein; Valia, threw herself at the enemy with every vestige of anger and mettle she could muster. Her mind burned bright with fury as she fought, bringing Ganindhra hope; these mortals surprised him still. The clouds of violence masked her pain as she faced that deepest of shadows; and yet she was only mortal.

His hope faded. She faltered with exhaustion as the treacherous, creeping fingers of despair rose through the resolve that had carried her for so long.

"Not now," he sighed. "Have courage Valia, a measure more."

As if buoyed by his thoughts, Valia was a blazing torch again in the face of that torrent of darkness and despair. She burned the shadows away like a dawn and sent them into oblivion.

Ganindhra sagged, exhausted. Mortals had won this day and yet he could feel no joy for it. A new darkness beyond his reach was lapping at the door of his consciousness, and he knew that Valia and those who followed her would not find rest yet.

PART ONE:
SHADOWS FROM THE EAST
CHAPTER 1

The wine jug was empty, but the dark stains from careless splashes were still damp on the bedside table where it sat. Still more spilled wine had soaked into the floorboards overnight in a violent swathe that radiated from the upended cup.

Valia groaned as wakefulness assailed her with all the spite it could muster. She released the gold coin she had been clutching in her sleep and raised her hand to her face in a slow, measured motion, fearful that anything more sudden would bring added pain. She pinched the bridge of her nose, then felt the scars that ran across it and her right cheek. The flesh felt tight, even after all this time.

"Today is the day," she murmured through a parched throat. "I will tell him."

After a long moment, she sat up and swung her legs off the bed and was rewarded with a loud clatter as she knocked the up-turned cup across the floor. She winced, and forced an eye open, alerted now to the possibility of obstacles and traps lying in wait. She scanned the little room; it was typical of most of the inns she had stayed in over the many years she had spent travelling the continent. Runaway, mercenary, Shar-hunter; these rooms were as close to 'homely' as she had known ever since she had thrown off the yoke of Shol'Hara. A narrow bed that was barely large enough for her, a small bedside table, a chair and a washstand with a water jug and basin. Most of her belongings lay in a heap beneath the un-shuttered window and a welcome breeze blew across the room. Her armour was still grey with ash, untouched since she had dropped it where it lay, and her sword, she knew, was filthy in its scabbard; that would never have done in the past, but the health of the steel was the least of her concerns.

She stood and managed the two short paces to the washstand on unsteady feet, grateful to find the water jug full. She washed her face and hands, being careful around the burns on her knuckles and cheeks; painful little reminders of what had passed in Ul-an-Balsan only eight days ago. That stand against the renascent army of Shar that had gathered around a single member of their kind, was like a dream. Her own imprudent charge into a storm of searing embers to chase down that one Shar that held that single, all-important Daemon shard; the Element that made it more than its kin, was just an unreal series of fractured memories.

Victory. That she was alive at all was proof enough that they had won; that steel had emerged triumphant over claw. Yet she had felt hollow in the hours that had followed, and the guilty thrill that she had experienced on hearing that the Shar still roamed the Eastern Kingdoms confirmed to her that she had become the very thing that she had dreaded; an old soldier. Nothing to live for except the next fight; no plan beyond surviving the next encounter with the enemy. Spending days mired in the ever-dimming glow of past glories with no capacity to break a different path. This was what Gerasim Illaros, a fellow Shar-hunter for whom she held a grudging admiration and respect, had feared would be his own fate. The old fool had taken on one commission too many and ended up dead before he could free himself from the cycle.

Valia glanced at the journal on the rickety chair at the foot of her bed. She had carried it for a year since finding that first affected Shar, far to the south in Pashwar where she had earned the deep scars on her face. The book was full of Gerasim's innermost thoughts, right up to the final entry on the night of his death in Depsing. The knowledge that members of the Shar could change had come too late for him, and Valia reminded herself again of the dangers of hubris. His had been a career that had craved recognition and sought renown amongst the people he protected so ostensibly. His ways were not her own, but she had recognised hidden depths in the man even before she had pried into his private thoughts on the pages of the journal.

The guilty intrusions had given her something unexpected though; the name of a Kylyptian woman and a hint of purpose beyond the sword for herself. For a time, at least.

She dressed and tried to dispel the pulsating pain behind her eyes, using force of will alone. The pain remained, undiminished, and she was forced to reconcile the fact that she would have to endure it. A queasiness in her belly suggested that food might help, provided it was something plain. Sounds drifting up through the floorboards from the common room below told her that she would not be alone.

The inn had been renamed *The Shar's Folly*, in honour of the recent events and to acknowledge the fact that most of the Shar-hunters involved were staying here. Not being one to see an opportunity pass unexploited, the owner had held a ceremony to commemorate the re-naming, with large quantities of ale and wine being sold as a result of course. Valia could not even recall the original name. Whether or not the new title stuck was irrelevant as dozens of hunters remained to toast their achievement nightly, and to great excess.

From the angle of the sun streaming in through the windows it must have been near midday, and Valia squinted her eyes against the light as she descended the stairs. A cheer was raised that drove another spike into her skull and she held out a hand to silence it.

The ovation melted into soft laughter as she made her way to one of the tables. Marlon, her ever-faithful companion was there with his usual drinking companions and he pulled out a chair for her with a loud scrape that made her grimace. She heard him chuckle as she slumped into the seat and conversations were restarted around the room. The old scar on her back still itched and she wriggled against the chair back as much as she dared to scratch it. She blinked against the painful light and glared at Marlon for his lack of sympathy before raising a questioning eyebrow.

"What is that?" Valia asked in mild surprise.

"What is what?" he replied, scratching at the hair on his face.

"I thought you had simply been unmindful over the last few days, but that has a look of intent about it."

Marlon smoothed the growth over his cheeks and scratched at his neck. "A new look for my retirement." He smiled. "What do you think?"

Valia tutted softly, in no mood to be charitable. "It makes you look old."

He shrugged, looking a little less certain and searched the table for support.

"Rubbish." The rumbling, baritone voice of Abbil Musharit, the burly, (fully bearded) Dashiyan, came to Marlon's aid. "A beard does not age a man; it lends him grandeur and dignity."

Marlon nodded his thanks to his friend as Alano Clemente leaned forward. He smoothed the wisps of hair atop his balding head and fixed each of his companions in turn with a conspiratorial look until he was certain he had their attention. "I once served with a militiaman," he began, "whose beard was almost legendary in Bal Mora. It was rumoured that he kept a trained rat in there which, when he gave the command, would scurry from its cosy nest and attack anyone he directed it at."

"Was it true?" Marlon asked with a wry grin.

"Certainly not, but the rumour was enough to keep drunken brawlers in line. 'Do as the militiaman says, or else old Canello will set his rat on you'. You may laugh," he said over the doubtful guffaws, "but to a drunk, the thought of a rat running up a trouser leg with nefarious intentions is enough to focus the mind, and it broke up more fights than a bludgeon ever could."

"Thank you for that gem," Valia muttered. "So, you see, Marlon, not only can you look old, but you can also reek of rat's piss. Now, is there any food on offer?"

The Shar-hunter, Jon, banged the table twice and raised a hand to get the attention of a serving maid. The noise made Valia groan, but she kept her curses silent and locked behind gritted teeth. The young maid busied herself with filling a tray, while Valia scanned the room to see who was there.

Granger was sitting in a quiet corner, alone except for a silent Elan who could not rightly be described as 'company' since he spent most days uninterested in those around him and unresponsive when approached. The historian was writing in one of the many books he carried with him, no doubt recording recent events. He had interviewed every willing soul for their version of the battle that had seen the Shar defeated, and there had been no shortage of volunteers. Everyone was eager to have their names immortalised in the written word.

At a large table across the room, the eastern noble and his retinue of casual guards sat, aloof and dour. Their timely arrival on the battlefield just eight days earlier had been as welcome as the news they brought was troubling. The man had allowed them their night of revelry before informing them of the troubles in his own homeland the following morning. That was when Valia and her allies had learned that the Shar had not been wiped out after all, and that the Eastern Kingdoms struggled just as they had with the Shar.

This foreign noble wanted information only; not help with the Shar menace in his homeland, and so had spent several days speaking with the hunters in Ulan Balsan learning new tactics and methods of killing the beasts. Dachen, she thought he was called, had spent a full day with Granger, who had quizzed him without mercy about his home and he in turn was eager to hear what Granger could tell him. But he could not bring himself to speak to Valia. He had some half-witted cultural tenet that placed her and all other women into some sort of tier that was just barely above livestock, and he would never deign to ask for her advice. Granger had explained to her that it was customary in the East for all those of lesser social status to lower their heads wherever possible to be below that of their betters. This information was better than gold and she took extra care to stand as tall as she could in his presence. He could play those games in the Eastern Kingdoms, not the land she had shed blood to see free.

The maid arrived with a tray of bread, honey and dried fruit, as well as a jug of water, and placed it on the table next to Valia who managed a weak smile in thanks. Jon ushered the young woman closer and whispered something to her, flashing a glance towards the table of Easterners. She shook her head, giving him a doubtful frown before he produced a silver mark and slid it onto the table. The maid took only a moment to decide, and the coin vanished into her apron. Valia watched with mild interest as the maid sauntered across to the other table, pulling at the lace at the top of her blouse as she did so. Jon nudged Abbil in the ribs and cleared his throat, alerting the big Dashiyan to what was about to happen. The maid went around to the far side of the Easterners' table, to where a plump, surly man was seated. She put herself between him and the man beside him and placed a hand on the table. Then she leaned towards him, putting the open top of her blouse at his eye level and traced a finger over the top of his ear.

For a man of his size, he moved with surprising speed. He pushed back from the table, sending his chair clattering onto the floorboards and shouted in the Eastern tongue, waving his arms in frantic arcs as his fellows tried to calm him, scraping chairs back as they stood.

A shout of, "Yeshe!" was heard over the clamour as the man

stormed from the building. The maid retreated to a safe distance and retied her blouse as she hurried back towards the kitchens. Jon could not contain himself any longer and burst into raucous laughter, banging the table with delight at the mischief he had caused. The Easterners glared at Valia's table, and she managed an indifferent shrug as Jon's howls filled the room. Abbil was laughing too, but it was as much at Jon as at the prank itself. Alano managed to maintain his composure, allowing himself a brief chuckle at the Eastern man's expense.

"It gets him every time," Jon managed as he regained control of his laughter, wiping tears from his cheeks and breathing hard from the excitement. He was still chuckling when the young man, Kapaneus entered the room, glancing back out the door where he had evidently just encountered a furious Yeshe, on the way out.

"What have I missed?" he asked of the room in general as he made his way towards Valia's table. The Easterners were taking their seats again, directing several angry stares at Jon in particular.

"Just a little sport, Kapaneus," Jon replied. "Is Acastes in a better mood today?"

Kapaneus shook his head. "His ribs still ache, and he will not rest as he should, so his recovery will be a long one."

"And what was that young maid doing, slipping into his room last night?" the fletcher asked. "Polishing his sword for him? That won't speed his recovery."

"He is lucky to be alive at all," Abbil muttered.

"You can remind him of that when he gets here," Kapaneus said. "He is on his way now. I have been sent ahead to get his chair ready."

"Another faithful pet?" Abbil asked in mock surprise. "I would have thought Kekoa was up to the task, or do you share his scraps now?" He made a little yapping sound, which Kapaneus ignored.

The chair in question was a large, padded armchair with a slight recline that removed the pressure from Acastes' damaged ribs when he sat. He had taken the full force of a leaping Shar during the battle and only the heavy, plate armour had saved him from certain death. Kapaneus dragged the chair over to a space at Valia's table.

"Here? Really?" she groaned. "My head is sore enough as it is."

Kapaneus paused for a moment until Marlon motioned for him to continue. "Pay her no heed. The wine has soured in her belly and taken her temperament with it."

"Have you been yet?" Kapaneus said, eager to change the subject as he positioned the chair.

"Today," Marlon replied, directing the word at Valia as much as Kapaneus.

She nodded.

"I did try myself, but even following your directions could see no sign," Kapaneus said.

Valia washed down a mouthful of honeyed bread before speaking. "I promise; I will do it today. I need to speak with you anyway, Marlon."

Marlon was about to answer when the doors opened into the room and Acastes walked in with one arm held across his ribs and Kekoa at his side. He winced with each step he took but shooed away his faithful servant every time the little man offered help.

"Get off of me man, I am not a child," he barked, and was rewarded with a stab of pain for his bad temper. The servant gave Acastes a little more room and busied himself with clearing a path to the chair instead.

Acastes sat down with a long, staccato sigh, and leaned back into the chair. He was an enormous man as was typical of the Korathean Heavy Infantry, and the chair creaked under his great weight; a real son of Shol'Hara. Bred for war and trained in the Akharran of Kor'Habat from an early age, the Heavy Infantry were both feared and respected across the continent and beyond. He ran his fingers through his blonde locks, pushing the curls away from his blue eyes and looked to each of his companions in turn.

"The hero has arrived," he declared.

"The ego is undiminished," Valia muttered around a mouthful of food.

"Water!" Acastes ordered, ignoring Valia's comment, and Kekoa obliged by filling a cup from the jug on the table. Acastes took a sip, and threw it back at the servant, soaking the front of his shirt. "It is warm! Fate, man. What is wrong with your tiny Jendayan mind?"

Without a word, Kekoa scurried off to find cooler water for his master.

Abbil leaned forward and rested both elbows on the table, eyeing Acastes. "It is my view," he began, "that little man will put up with your abuse until his ten years of service are up, and then slit your throat in the night. It would do you no harm to show a little humility."

"I will show humility when he shows some common, bloody sense," Acastes replied. "What good is a servant that cannot think for itself?"

"He is a slave, and well you know it."

"I feed him do I not?"

"Please, gentlemen," Valia scowled. "You are ruining the genial atmosphere."

"Perhaps now would be a good time," Marlon said to Valia, gesturing towards the door. "Leave them to their *discussion*."

Valia sighed. "Very well. Let us get this over with."

"Should I ready the horses?" he asked.

She shook her head. "The walk will do me good."

Valia was already starting to feel better as the food settled her stomach and the fresh air cleared her head. Marlon walked beside her through the main gates, which for the first time in months stood open and busy with traffic. Farmers were returning to their crops now that the threat from the Shar was lifted, and the livestock that had filled the streets before now grazed in open fields. But there was a presence on the grassland that Valia would have been glad to be without. Ribbons of smoke curled into the sky from the encampment that had sprung up in a nearby field since their victory, where Rogan Fol'Brandam's Cavalry waited. A thousand Heavy Infantry were still expected to arrive soon; part of a force dispatched to deal with the Shar, but which had not arrived in time. That Rogan had not already departed for Kor'Habat and turned the Heavy Infantry around to return with him, was a worrying sign.

"Should I remove it; do you think?" Marlon asked.

"What?" Valia said, her attention pulled from the encampment.

"It itches now, but that will pass," he said scratching a cheek.

Valia laughed. "It is your face, Marlon. Do with it what you will."

"But you disapprove?"

"What has got into you? I do not recall you being so precious in the past."

They walked on in silence across the blackened stubs of grass where the fire had spread from the forest. Already, hints of green shoots were standing vibrant among the scorched clumps and Valia was reminded of Alano's words before the battle; '*The land forgives*'.

To their left, the scar of the bonfire where the Shar carcasses had been burned had been picked clean of its only bounty, the claws. Nothing remained of the beasts except the razor talons, and they were gathered as trophies and mementos or sold to collectors. Even without fire, the corpses would have rotted down to dust in a matter of days, leaving no bones as other beasts would. Further proof, if it were needed, that those creatures were not of this world and had no place in it.

They stopped at the edge of the forest. The scorched stumps had finally stopped smouldering, but the smell of burnt wood was still heavy and sweet in the air.

"I think this is where I went in,"Valia muttered, struggling to remember her charge into the inferno. A carpet of ash covered the ground and fine motes hung in the air, tossed on the gentle breeze; so different from how she remembered it. Valia walked on with Marlon behind as she recounted the chase in her head. Could that blackened stem be the same that had fallen beside her in flames? Was that fallen trunk, lying inert on the ground the same one she had leapt over when it had been alive with fire?

"This is more difficult than I had thought it would be," she said.

"Further this way," Marlon replied. "I remember that forked bough."

He led on over a shallow depression and under a large trunk held up by another tree, to a small clearing that Valia at once recognised.

"This is the place," she said. "There. The bolt."

She pointed to a charred stump where a steel shaft was embedded, and half covered with fallen branches. The huge bolt that had pinned the Shar to the tree long enough for Valia to take its head, would not budge when she tried to free it.

"This will need to be cut out," she said.

"Gerasim's bow," Marlon said, lifting the great hunk from piles of ash and debris. He took a moment to appraise the damage. "It did not fare well in the fire, but I believe it could be saved."

Valia was already down on one knee, searching the ground nearby. She found a claw in the grey ash and tossed it aside, continuing to search the detritus with careful fingers.

"It must be near," she said. "Come and help me."

Marlon placed the huge crossbow against a stump and knelt in the ashes. "Wait. Someone has been here already. Do you see the footprints?"

"Yes, Kapaneus has already searched,"Valia replied.

"No. Kapaneus searched for this spot but failed to find it. I cannot believe that he walked so close to the bolt and the bow and yet missed them both."

She followed the footprints with her eyes, trying to discern the path they followed.

"Such a strange and beautiful thing." The voice startled them both, and Valia reached by reflex for her sword before she realised that she carried none.

"Adeyemi!" she said in surprise, getting to her feet again. "That is your name is it not?"

The tall, dark-skinned man smiled from behind the gleaming Daemon Element he held between the thumb and forefinger of his left hand. In his right, a crude, broad-bladed weapon that she had seen him carrying on his back before, was held with a firm grip. The intricate scars on his arms and face were pale against the dark sheen of his skin, and the gashes on his cheeks that ruined the patterns there made Valia's own scars itch.

"What are you doing?" she demanded, suddenly aware that the only weapon she carried was a small belt-knife, and she knew that Marlon was similarly vulnerable.

"Such depth beneath the surface," he whispered in awe, his eyes fixed on the oval, obsidian bead.

"Please, let me have it," Valia said in a soft voice.

Adeyemi shifted his gaze from the Element to Valia, and his smile remained friendly despite the tension she felt. "Why should I give it to you? What power does it have?"

"None that you may wield. It is worthless."

He laughed. "And yet you kneel in the ashes to find it?"

"We want only to destroy it," Marlon said. "We believe it to be dangerous. In the wrong hands."

"And yours would be the *right* hands?" Adeyemi was still smiling, but his gaze had taken on a warier edge. "Why do you desire it?"

"We know of its origins, and the effect it had on the Shar," Valia said. She held out a hand. "Please, give it to me and I will see it destroyed."

Valia was acutely aware of the lie. She and Marlon had tried to destroy the Element they had retrieved in Depsing, the first they had found, but nothing they tried had made a single mark upon its glassy surface.

A sudden wistful look shrouded Adeyemi's expression. "I could never allow such a thing."

Marlon stepped closer to the man. "Do not be a fool. It can do you no good."

"I am told that it transformed a lowly Shar into something greater. Powerful magic indeed..." Adeyemi closed his hand around the Element. "Powerful enough, perhaps, to counter a lesser spell?"

Valia stared back. "A what? What are you talking about?"

Adeyemi only smiled in return. He raised the crude blade he carried and brought it down onto a charred stump, where it bedded in and stayed, freeing his right hand. He tugged at a cord around his neck, lifting a small pouch from within his shirt and worked it open with great care. Then he closed his eyes for a moment, dropped the element into the pouch and cinched it closed.

"Don't be a fool, man!" Marlon growled. "Give it to us and have it destroyed, or else risk this again." He waved his hand around at the ruins of the forest to make his point.

"I will keep it close," Adeyemi said, the warm smile still splitting his face as though they were exchanging pleasantries. He pulled the heavy weapon from the stump and made to walk past them towards the town. Marlon stepped forward to cut off his path, but Valia laid a hand on his shoulder, and shook her head.

"Not now," she whispered.

Marlon glared at the tall, dark-skinned man who answered with a bow of the head as he went by. After a moment, Marlon spread his arms wide in exasperation. "We cannot just let him take it."

"Neither of us is armed," Valia replied. "Enough blood has been spilt on account of that accursed Element, and I would not add any more of yours or my own to the sum."

Marlon took a few breaths to calm down before smiling. "This is not the Valia of old I see before me. Has age brought common sense in its wake?"

Valia sniffed and dusted the ash from her trousers. "Shut up, Marlon," she said, and began the short walk back to town.

Back at the inn, Granger and Alano listened as Marlon described their encounter.

"The way I see it," Alano said when Marlon was done, "is that he is doing us a great service by carrying it away. You should give him the other into the bargain."

Marlon shushed his friend, glancing around the common room of the inn. That he still held the first Element in his possession was not a fact he wanted known. There was no one else nearby but the conversation continued in muted tones all the same.

"I would sooner see them both destroyed," Valia answered.

"How?" Alano asked. "You have already told me that the hottest fire in a blacksmith's forge made no mark on its surface, and that it left its *own* mark upon the anvil when struck. What else is there?"

Valia exchanged a glance with Marlon and whispered, "They could be placed in a crucible of molten iron and cast into an ingot. Locked in iron, we can take a ship to the deepest part of the Ashkelit Ocean and drop them overboard. They will be out of reach for all eternity there."

"And I will be on hand to provide a settling infusion for when your stomach becomes anxious on the waves," Granger said with a wry smile.

Valia winced at the memory of her sea sickness on the voyage from Hadaiti so long ago. "Perhaps Marlon could bear this burden without me."

"Gladly," Marlon muttered. "I have the first, from Depsing, in my possession. It never leaves my care." He patted a breast pocket. "But there is also the matter of the second Element to deal with."

Granger held up a hand. "I am certain that they are not a danger so long as they remain out of reach of the Shar, and even then, I am doubtful as to whether they pose a risk. In the moments following Abaddon's defeat, the Elements sought only what they knew and found the Shar. They are most likely spent now; useless."

"*Most likely?*" Valia said with a slow shake of the head. "It is not worth the risk."

"What did he mean," Marlon asked, "when he said it held 'powerful magic' to 'counter a lesser spell'?"

Granger sighed. "His people are deeply superstitious. Perhaps he sees it as a weapon to use against his enemies."

"Could he really use it as a weapon?" Marlon muttered.

"Things do not have to be powerful to be used as weapons," Granger explained. "If Adeyemi believes that the Element can be used in such a way then he has only to convince his enemies of it. Belief has the power to build or destroy empires, if it takes root in the minds of enough people."

"What do you suggest?" Marlon murmured.

"We need to convince him of his folly," Alano suggested. "Perhaps the Eastern noble could be convinced to speak with him."

Granger nodded. "Adeyemi certainly follows the Easterners. I am sure they will see sense and speak with him."

"And if not?" Marlon asked, already certain of the answer.

Valia looked at each of them in turn. "There are enough hunters in Ulan-Balsan to take the thing by force if necessary; *they* will see our side."

Granger sucked air between his teeth. "That is a bold step."

"And one we would not wish to take, unless they fail to see reason," Valia countered. "By their own admission, their lands are plagued by Shar. Is it wise to send an Element into their midst when we do not fully understand the dangers?"

"More bloodshed," Alano groaned.

"It will not come to that," Valia said to ease the tension at the table. "But the threat alone should help persuade Adeyemi and his friends onto the correct path."

There was a general, muttered consensus from around the table.

"So," Marlon said, "we speak with this, *Dachen*, first."

Valia leaned back and rubbed her back against the chair to relieve the old itch between her shoulder blades. "It will not be me who approaches him. I swear, he hates every person with a pair of these." She grabbed a breast for effect. "He no doubt dreams of them at night only to deride them by day."

Alano laughed. "It is not only your breasts he hates, Valia, but your toes, the hair on your head, and everything in between."

"And you have done little to help sway his opinion of you," Granger chided. "You provoke him."

Valia sniffed. "I do no such thing. I will not '*lower my head*' and I will not bow and scrape in his presence regardless of their customs. If his arse was a little further from the ground, then I would not be asked to."

"This is what I am referring to," Granger said with a shake of the head. "But diplomacy is not your craft and there is no changing you now. I will speak to Dachen, and avert all-out war with the Eastern Kingdoms, which is what I am sure your sort of diplomacy would have achieved." He stood to leave as Valia rolled her eyes at the admonishing tone.

"I will join you," Alano suggested, scraping back his chair and standing with a sigh. "Valia. Marlon. I will join you for a jug of wine when the sun kisses the horizon."

Valia watched the two men leave, and they sat in silence for a long time. Finally, Marlon spoke.

"Do you think the man will see sense?" he asked.

Valia sighed and pinched the bridge of her nose. "I imagine so. If calm words fail, it is amazing how the threat of violence can shift one's position."

"We should be ready, in the event that the 'calm words' are not successful."

"Actually," Valia raised a hand to stop him, "I would sooner distance myself from this."

Marlon shrugged and scratched at the growth on his cheek. "Of course."

"Granger is always telling me that I take on too much and should allow others to share the burden. I know that you can be trusted with this task."

"I understand," Marlon replied, rubbing under his eyepatch with a gentle finger. "Once this is done, we can consider our next move. I was thinking of a nice easy escort service for merchant caravans. Perhaps we could get some of the Band together again."

Valia winced. She had been dreading this moment.

"I found something in Gerasim's journal," she said, watching for his reaction. "A reference to a woman for whom he had some affection. I believe her to be somewhere near Banihat and considered seeking her out to let her know about Gerasim."

Marlon shrugged. He had taken a copper mark from his pocket and was spinning it on its edge upon the table. He was watching the spinning coin with mild interest. "That sounds reasonable. Once the Element is in hand, we can leave. As it happens, we will need to journey there to take a ship if those blasted Elements are to be safely disposed of."

Valia hesitated. "I will go alone."

The coin slowed and fell from its edge, winding down with rhythmic certainty to a high pitched, clattering finale before it came to rest. The sound echoed from the walls of the common room.

Marlon had finally heard something in Valia's tone that told him to pay attention.

"There is no need," he said.

"I need to go alone," she insisted.

"I see." His tone was wary. "How long do you expect this to take?"

Valia sighed. "I do not know."

"And what am I to do? Wait here?"

"You can do what you like, Marlon. I am not your keeper." She immediately regretted her tone and held her hands out in a settling gesture. She stared at the ceiling for inspiration. "I'm tired, old man," she said at last. When he did not reply, she looked at him and found him looking back at her with that one, faithful, watchful eye that had seen every horror she had seen yet had remained steadfast and loyal throughout. It was a gaze that she could not hold for long, so she looked down at the table instead, and spoke in a quiet, measured voice. "I once asked Granger how many times my name appears in those books he keeps; those histories he writes. He told me that the instances were too numerous to count. It dawned on me then what I have become, and what lies in store for me if I continue this road. I am to have a *glorious past*." Her voice was anguished and bitter as she spoke the last and she forced herself to look at him again to see if he could understand.

"You have done great things," he muttered, "why wish them undone?"

"Would anything be different if they were?"

"So, you would have chosen another path?" he asked.

She sighed. "One person cannot change the world. I took up the sword to fight an empire I saw as evil, but I could topple a thousand empires, and still Mankind would drag itself back into the mire of greed and lust that first gave them dominion. Fighting injustice is like pulling weeds; unless the root is destroyed, more will spring up when your back is turned, and that root is the dark core of Man's soul that cannot be excised. The Shar do not belong here, and that has made it easy for me to stand against them and allay my doubts. Once they are defeated it could be called a genuine victory, but that is done now. There are no more battles worth fighting, and I have no more appetite for killing men."

"The Shar remain," Marlon said. "To the east."

Valia barked a bitter laugh. "The Eastern Kingdoms do not want my help and nor would I give it. They could burn and I would not piss on the flames. Not because I wish them harm, but because doing so would only delay the fires that would engulf them. Nothing I have done will change the inevitable."

"How can you say that?" Marlon muttered through clenched teeth. "You are a hero to thousands."

"A hero is only someone with the good fortune not to fall at the first volley!" Valia countered with more force than she intended. She continued in a more measured tone. "What makes a hero? At Hadaiti, I delivered a message; no more. And yet they call me '*Valia of Hadaiti*' as though I fell from the sky and laid waste to the Korathean armies with breath of fire. *Thousands* died that day, and each one of them stood with courage against all the might an empire could muster, yet they venerate *me*. I have killed; I have taken lives; I have survived through luck or Fate alone knows how, but I am not a hero!

"A widowed mother working all the hours of the day to feed her children is a hero. A mill owner whose own table is a little lighter on feast day so that his workers may celebrate with fuller bellies is a hero. The ruler who frees all slaves and gives legal right to dignity is a hero; but *not* me! I fight for causes that evaporate like mist at dawn. I fought the Korathean Empire; then I fight alongside Acastes and men I could easily have faced across the battlefield less than a decade ago. I *like* Kekoa; the little Jendayan has become a good friend and yet I would have done my best to part his head from his shoulders at Ara Dasari. Yesterday's enemies are today's allies and friends. How can I ever fight again, knowing that every life is a widowed wife; an orphaned child; a friend I failed to know?

"And through all of this, I only destroy. In building a glorious past I have given up the right to forge a future. I have been upon this world for forty-three years and in all that time I have not!

Built! A single! Thing!" She jabbed at the table with her forefinger for emphasis, then she sat back and calmed her voice.

"But I still have a chance to change. I think I have known this for a long time, and yet it took Gerasim's death to open my eyes to the truth. He almost had it, I could feel his need through the pages of that journal, but he failed to grasp it in time."

"What of friendships?" Marlon asked. "Are they to be buried with your past deeds?"

She leant across the table and placed her own calloused hand upon his. "No," she said with a tenderness she seldom showed. "There will always be a place for you in my heart, old man."

"Yet you still plan to leave alone." He pulled his hand from under her own.

"Marlon," she sighed, "I need time to find my way. I cannot fight any longer." She tried to catch his eye, but he was staring at the table. "I have no hatred left," she sighed.

He slid the coin he had been toying with across the table to her. "It is not gold," he said, "but I believe the sentiment is the same."

With that he stood and walked from the room, leaving an echoing silence in his wake.

"We should be safely inside the walls of Ulan-Balsan by tomorrow evening," the red-haired woman, Maidra said, startling Nirmaya from her torpor.

The gentle gait of her horse had Nirmaya swaying in her saddle, and she realised that she had been almost asleep. A breeze kissed the tips of the tall grasses of the Kylyptian steppe land and sent silent waves to buffet the road edge as they travelled, carried on a soft ocean of grass. The sky was a perfect blue, save for the streaks of icy clouds that rose from a distant northern horizon, and the afternoon sun poured its warm balm on the back of her neck.

"I will be glad of a mattress beneath me," she said, straightening in her saddle. She looked back at the long line of women on horseback; fifty-two in all, brought together for reasons just as numerous and bound in the sodality of the 'Sisters'. And of course, Starling.

"How long do you think we have before the Heavy Infantry reach the town too?" Maidra asked with a bitter edge to her voice.

"We have a few days at least, I would imagine. We have covered ground far quicker than they can," Nirmaya replied, not taking the bait.

"It was a mistake, leaving Kernhalt. You must know that," Maidra persisted.

Nirmaya sighed. "I was bored in Kernhalt."

"It paid a wage," Maidra grumbled. "Now we have been reduced to petty theft by that fool, Starling, and from the Heavy Infantry no less."

"We had no part in Starling's crime, and besides, that Captain Silman would have done far worse if Starling had not freed us with that dancing tongue of his."

"It was Starling's '*dancing tongue*' that had us in that vipers' nest in the first place," Maidra hissed. "He put us all in danger for his own personal gain, some of the Sisters are very unhappy with his presence here. There is talk."

"Every Sister has a right to voice their opinions. If they want him gone, then they only have to discuss it openly and a consensus will be reached. If they do not like the outcome, they are free to leave." She regretted the words as soon as they were out.

"Is that what you want?" Maidra snapped. "For me to leave?"

Nirmaya sighed and turned to the woman beside her. She furrowed her brow and added a childish pout to her expression. "Then who would keep me warm at night?" she cooed.

Maidra sniffed and straightened her back with haughty indifference. "Perhaps Starling could replace me."

"But his hands are so clumsy, and he does not understand the needs of a woman. Only you can do that." She winked and offered her best smile when Maidra made eye contact.

"Very well," Maidra said once her blushes had subsided. "But be wary of Starling, He would march you into danger on a whim if he believed there to be a few marks in it for him."

They rode on in silence for a long while before Maidra spoke again. "What are we doing in Kylyptus, really?"

"I told you, I was bored in Kernhalt," Nirmaya replied.

"But why are we following this merchant? You must know that Starling will seek to rob him. Why aid him in that?"

"Sometimes one must simply step outside to find a new opportunity, and Kernhalt was growing stale." She could not bring herself to tell Maidra about Dargenmill, nor how she had balked at the last moment and been left following this fool's errand to save face; and to allow her time to think.

"And what opportunity have we found...if we do not include theft from the Heavy Infantry?"

Nirmaya ignored the jibe. "Perhaps we can be of use against the Shar we have heard are gathering."

"I fear we are too late for that," Maidra countered. "That farmer we met on the road yesterday was very content to work past dusk in his fields. He claims the threat is gone."

Nirmaya glared ahead. "Good," she muttered. "If only Dargenmill would crumble too and bury Ramash Suun and his flock of Cultists." She did not realize that she had spoken out loud until Maidra answered.

"Insane fools!" Maidra leaned over and placed a hand on Nirmaya's arm, softening her tone. "It must be difficult; having lost your family to the Shar at such a young age. You should have been a hunter. You would have made a fierce one."

Nirmaya placed her free hand on Maidra's and returned a tight-lipped smile. "Thank you."

Starling arrived at Nirmaya's side with a wide grin. "I trust I am not interrupting a moment of tenderness, and if so, please carry on."

Maidra pulled her hand back and glowered at the man. "How auspicious your arrival is, Starling; we were just discussing the very subject of the common fool."

Starling winked at her, still with his broad smile in place. "Oh, Maidra, you should know by now that I am a very *un*common fool, and that your insults are like honey to my ears."

Maidra curled her lip back in distaste. "Honey to your...? That means nothing. Idiot!" She jerked her horse to the side and urged it into a trot to put some distance between them.

"Maidra's in a fine mood today," he said with a brightness that almost glowed.

"You know that she will kill you one day?" Nirmaya warned.

"No, no," Starling enthused. "She's warming to me, I'm certain. She never even reached for her belt knife that time..."

"That is because she knows that she could do the deed with her bare hands."

"Would you not defend me?" he teased. "In honour of what we once had; and could have again."

Nirmaya barked a laugh. "After what you did in that Infantry camp, allowing Maidra to squeeze the life from you would be a mercy." She shook her head. "What were you thinking? Stealing from the Heavy Infantry of all people?"

He waved a dismissive hand. "A few coins skimmed from the top of the chest. They will not be missed."

"You know that is not true. They will realise the chest is light, and they will know fine who to blame for the theft. Unfortunately, you have sullied the sisters with your actions and there are many who would have me send you away, or else leave you tied to a tree for Captain Silman to find when he passes by."

"Those voices will be drowned in the wine I will lavish upon them when we reach Ulan-Balsan," Starling replied.

"And if we find your merchant there? Will you rob him too?"

Starling managed a very convincing expression of deep hurt. "How can you think that of me? You know I am only acting out of loyalty to Korathea."

"Or what is left of it," Nirmaya muttered.

"Quite. And I would not relish seeing it diminished further. You do remember what I told you about that man, Dachen?"

"Yes, yes. Royal blood, spies, intrigue. All the fevered imaginings of your infantile mind."

"They are plotting something, Nirmaya. He is no common merchant, and I will prove it to you."

"By robbing him?"

"By confronting him," Starling corrected.

"And I am sure he will be delighted to see you again. The last time you met, you attempted to rob him on the road as I recall. How did that turn out?"

He waved a hand. "In the past." He stabbed a finger forward. "I always look ahead, to the future."

"A very short future, I fear. Starling," Nirmaya paused. "Be honest with me for once. Why are we here? Why follow this man across hundreds of miles on a vague notion that he may be something other than he claims?"

Starling sighed. "I was sick of Kernhalt and all the pressure and expectations placed upon me as the Governor's son."

"Poor little rich boy," Nirmaya teased.

Starling looked away and stared ahead at the unbroken horizon.

"Is that the only reason?" She asked.

"I had to get away," he replied, shaking his head. "I just wanted to do something different. I suppose that is why I am always finding myself in trouble; I am trying to break the mould I was cast in. I saw an opportunity to be involved at the start of something new. If he is a merchant after all, then what is he selling? Do you know that he made no attempt at trade during his short stay in Kernhalt? It must be something arcane, peculiar, and so, valuable. And, if he is not a merchant after all, and his motives are not commercial in nature, then that information itself will be worth something. It's exciting; you must surely feel it too or else you would not have come with me."

"You know why I came," she replied.

"I know," Starling nodded. "Dargenmill isn't going anywhere. You'll have another chance soon."

Nirmaya gave her head a shake to chase away the sombre mood that had come over her. "Let us hope that the Heavy Infantry allow us all to live that long.

Starling dismissed the idea with a wave, his swagger returning in a heartbeat. "Do not give them another thought. I can handle Captain Silman and the Heavy Infantry..."

"I will kill them all!" Captain Silman Fol'Ghealten seethed. "I will see them all dancing at the end of a rope from the walls of Kor'Habat, their entrails splashed in the dust below them! I will have them flayed for good measure and they will welcome the noose when it comes!"

The enormous captain of the Heavy Infantry clenched his fists on the desk in front of him and the sinews in his thick forearms worked like cables under the flesh.

"That will only draw attention to your error, will it not?"

Captain Silman glared at the clerk sitting across the small table from him; a diminutive man with short-cropped hair that had receded to leave an expanse of forehead, sun-burned and raw. A neat beard framed hollow cheeks, also reddened by the elements; this was a man unused to long periods outdoors. They were in the large command tent that Silman was using as they travelled north through Kylyptus. Every army travelled with an entourage of cooks, pot-washers and other hirelings, but this was one member of the retinue that Silman could have lived without. A clerk needed to oversee the spending that large forces were inevitably required to make when travelling in peacetime. This was not an invasion after all, and any supplies or services needed on the journey had to be paid for in full. It was the smug expression with which the little bean-counter regarded Silman that had the captain's anger rising, almost as much as the news of the theft itself. This would reflect badly on him, he knew, and could dash any hopes he had of attaining the rank of Hatar within the Heavy Infantry. Of course, leading a force of this size was usually entrusted to a higher rank than captain, but these were no ordinary times. The Korathean leader, the Kodistai, was lingering in the final throes of death with an intractability only possessed by the very old, and the Hatars were too busy circling Kor'Habat like vultures to venture this far from the seat of power.

"Then I will peg them out on these blasted plains for the ravens to feast upon!" Silman thumped the table with his fist, cracking the wood and upsetting an ink pot.

The clerk snatched his precious papers from the desk and clutched them to his chest, safe from the spreading ink.

Silman calmed himself. "That money will be returned to the coffers, every mark," he growled. "And you will never make mention of this again."

The clerk tidied the papers on his lap with fastidious care, not cowed by the captain's tone. "A report must be made," the clerk replied.

"You will follow my command," the captain stated.

"You over-reach, Captain. I am answerable to the treasury, and all discrepancies, temporary or otherwise must be reported."

Silman leaned back in his chair and regarded the little clerk with undisguised hatred.

"To what end?" he asked. "Will telling tales like a spoiled brat win you favour among your kind? You shuffle paper and tot up numbers while real men labour and bleed."

"Are we finished?" the clerk asked with a patronizing smile.

Silman glowered back. "We are done," he said.

Silman watched the clerk rise and walk out of the tent. Would the snivelling runt have spoken to a Hatar like that, he wondered? A soldier entered immediately after the clerk left, dressed in light-weight clothing trimmed with blue-green. He was a young, fresh-faced man not long out of the Akharran. His hand rested on the hilt of the huge, curved sword at his hip, but this was out of habit rather than eagerness to use it.

"We are ready to break camp, Captain," he reported. "The men will be ready within the hour."

"Thank you, Daelen," Silman replied as he cogitated.

The soldier hesitated. "Are you well, Captain?" he asked.

"What?" Silman muttered as he was dragged from his thoughts. "Yes. Yes, I am fine. Tell me, Daelen, what do you know of that clerk?"

Daelen shrugged. "Solinus? He is just a clerk." Then he smiled. "I know that he must have rankled someone in Kor'Habat, to be sent out here with us. Those clerks prefer soft beds and crisp linen to bedrolls on the ground."

"Beyond that, do you know of family; loved ones?"

"No, Captain." Daelen looked a little confused. "Would you like me to enquire?"

"No. No matter," Silman said with a dismissive wave. An awkward moment passed.

"If that is all?" Daelen said, motioning to the tent flap.

"You may go about your duties."

Daelen nodded and left the tent.

He was a useful man, Daelen; eager to please and quick to follow orders. His only fault to Silman's thinking was his almost fanatical loyalty to the Kodistai, which would need to be watched. Solinus the clerk, on the other hand, would need to be stopped from sharing Silman's mistake with his superiors. Out in the open plains, accidents happened all the time, and it would be a sad, but not devastating loss should the clerk find a viper in his bedroll, or stumble under the wheels of a cart.

The clerk was a problem that would have to wait, however. First, he had a coven of wenches to round up; them and that cocky young imposter who would beg for death before his own ignominious end...

As the sounds of breaking camp drifted through the thin tent walls, Silman stared at the spilled ink on the table soaking into the cracked wooden surface and dreamed of blood.

Dachen knew that he was tarrying here in Ulan-Balsan. The time was long past that they should be travelling to Banihat and then homeward across the Ashkelit. The journey so far had been useful in that they had learned much about the Shar and their habits, but more important than that was the knowledge that they could be defeated. The scourge could be wiped from the land and seeing these western Shar-hunters celebrating their great victory, brought Dachen hope for his own home.

He was yet to see the Shar gather behind an elevated member of their kind in his homeland of Tianpok, but should that happen, he would be ready.

"Adeyemi," he said as his friend approached. Dachen was waiting at the open gates of the town for the big, dark-skinned man to return from his wanderings. Adeyemi always appeared at his most content when walking long distances, exploring the land around him, filled with child-like wonder at every new vista.

"Friend Dachen," he replied, a broad smile splitting his face. Whorls of scars ran from his cheeks to his neck and vanished beneath his plain shirt, only to reappear on his arms in delicate curls and spirals. The cruel gashes on each cheek spoiled the finer markings, but the big man would never speak about it and so Dachen never pressed.

"The sun is setting, I was beginning to wonder if you had lost your way," Dachen joked.

"I found a meadow beyond that rise to the north where but-terflies swarm like a silent blizzard," he replied, eyes wide with excitement. "I stood amongst them and they lighted upon my flesh in their hundreds. It is a good portent, friend Dachen. I know it is."

Dachen gave his friend a tolerant smile. "It was a long way and you exerted yourself," he tried to explain. "The butterflies were drinking the sweat from your skin, Adeyemi. There is nothing more to it than that."

Adeyemi tut-ted. "You cannot see the signs presented to you because you refuse to."

"I do not see *signs* because there are none to see," he replied. "I am sure that the butterflies were very beautiful, but they were no more a portent of our future than the flies around cow dung."

Adeyemi laughed, his shoulders bouncing to the rhythm of his mirth. "One day you will see, friend Dachen. One day."

Dachen caught himself beginning to chuckle, so contagious was his friend's laughter. "I do not wish to spoil your good mood, Adeyemi, but the historian has asked me to speak with you. He believes that you have something of his."

Adeyemi's laughter subsided, although his smile stayed in place. "What is it that I have stolen?"

Dachen held up his hands. "He did not say 'stolen', only that you took an item from the battlefield that he would sooner see destroyed. For the greater good, he assures me."

Adeyemi shook his head and his smile faded. "Why destroy such powerful magic?"

"He assures me that this *Element* is powerless. I only agreed to speak with you about this out of respect for him. Granger is wise beyond his years; I can see that much in him."

Adeyemi clutched the pouch through his shirt. "Powerless, and yet they yearn to possess it."

Dachen sighed. "I have never asked about your past, Adeyemi, because you never volunteered to speak of it. But I know that whatever you carry around your neck in that pouch is a burden to you. Share it with me, won't you, friend?"

Adeyemi smiled again. "Thank you, friend Dachen, but I believe that the burden has been lifted. In time I will know for certain, and then the historian will have his answer. I cannot give it up now."

Dachen regarded his friend, trying to read the man's thoughts and motivation, but he could no more fathom Adeyemi's reasoning than a flea could leap to the stars.

Dachen shrugged. "Then our time here is almost done. Come and eat with us, I have instructed the innkeeper in the correct way to prepare lamb. His cook may yet get it right."

CHAPTER 2

Valia closed the door of the inn behind her as she left. The innkeeper had agreed to hold in storage what belongings she did not carry with her, and she was already beginning to feel a lightening of her burdens. The sun was yet to break the horizon and the town was silent; only a bleary-eyed stable hand joined her on the cobbled street, and she was certain that he would return to his bed as soon as she was gone. The young man held the reins of her horse and shifted from foot to foot in the morning chill while she tightened the straps of the saddlebags that carried all she needed. Her sword protruded from one of the bundles, but her bulky armour would remain in Ulan-Balsan.

The horse blew clouds from its nostrils as Valia pressed a silver mark into the stable hand's palm and nodded her thanks. He scurried off, no doubt thinking of the warmth of his blankets.

Valia looked up at a lightening sky. The stars were all but washed away by the coming dawn and soon the cold would be chased from the air by the rising sun. She led her horse along the cobbled street that would take her to the gates and beyond, hoping that the guilt she felt would fade along with the darkness. Marlon had not understood her reasons and she could not bear to have her mind clouded by any more arguments or protests from her other companions. She needed time to consider her future without their interference. The decision had to be hers and hers alone, but the need to sneak away like a thief in the night still needled her.

"You are leaving alone?" A voice startled her as she walked past the lumber yard. Her hand went to her hip by reflex even before she realised who it was. Kekoa was sitting cross-legged on top of a log stack, facing eastwards. His slight frame was straight-backed yet relaxed in practiced contemplation. He turned his sun-bronzed face towards her and smiled.

"Kekoa. What are you doing up there?" she asked, although she already knew the answer.

"The view is open from here. I come to this place to greet the sun each morning, although I am usually the only one who has stirred. Are you going on a journey?"

There was no point in lying to him; her saddlebags were proof enough of her guilt. "I am sorry, Kekoa. I should have told you. Yes, I am going to look for someone, and I need time to think," she replied. "Marlon does not understand, I…It is best if…I do not enjoy drawn out goodbyes."

"So, you do not plan to return?"

"I do not know," she said as the little Jendayan made his way down from the top of the stack "It can be difficult, I know. Especially when we do so of our own free will. It adds a burden of guilt that is absent when the choice is taken from us."

Valia looked down at him and cocked her head to one side. "How did you do it, Kekoa? How did you turn from soldier to servant without doubting your purpose?"

Kekoa pursed his lips and nodded, as though hearing a deeper question. "By seeing myself as neither," he answered.

Valia sighed. "You make it sound so simple."

"Does water from a quiet stream taste so different from that which thunders down the narrow gully? Water is water, despite its action, but it cannot control its destiny. We alone can choose whether to slumber as a mirror pond, or rage in waves against the cliffs. Both have their place in this world, and we must rely upon our own wisdom and conscience to choose which form to assume."

After a pause, Valia managed a sad smile. "I wish we had met sooner, Kekoa. I feel as though I have been hurling myself at those cliffs for an eternity. I could use your wisdom."

Kekoa returned her smile. "Wisdom is born from mistakes, of which I have made many. Greater wisdom still can be found in righting the wrongs of one's own past."

"You are still a good teacher," she replied.

"And you have a new life to forge?"

"I do," she agreed.

"Be watchful as you do," he smiled. "Cartwheels are quick to fall into old ruts."

She nodded as she considered what he had said.

"I suppose they do," she said at last. "But I am ready for something different."

"A moment, I almost forgot," he said, patting the pockets of his tunic until he found what he was looking for. He revealed a small book, which he offered to her. "A collection of words and phrases to help you further your studies, should you wish. Some pieces about our culture too, as you showed an interest."

She took the little book and flicked through the first few pages.

"Thank you," she said with genuine sincerity.

"It is yet incomplete," he added. "And the illustrations are limited by my own artistic failings, but if you enjoy learning about my society as much as I have enjoyed learning of yours…well, it is a start of a sort."

She nodded, tucking the book into a pocket within her coat, then there was a short, awkward silence as the parting of their ways loomed.

"Then I will teach you one more thing," he said. "*Ahui hohrai.* It means, be safe until our paths…" He held out both forefingers and laid them parallel. "Side-by-side? It is a rough translation," he laughed.

"Ahui hohrai,"Valia practiced.

"You speak as though it was your native tongue," Kekoa said swelling with pride. "My finest student."

"*Mahnui*, Kekoa," she said, laying a hand on his shoulder. "Thank you. Ahui hohrai."

Kekoa touched his chin with his fingertips and then withdrew his hand, palm upwards in silent farewell.

She turned and continued down the street as the sky brightened and found the gates already open and guards warming their hands over a glowing brazier. They barely acknowledged her as she left. She mounted her horse and rode south, avoiding the encampment of Heavy Cavalry on the plain. South would take her to a narrowing in the Balsan river and a bridge across it, then northwards to Banihat and a vague, but growing sense of purpose.

Rogan Fol'Brandam tossed the report onto the paper-strewn table and sagged into his chair. Behind him, the banner of his ancient family, a castle silhouetted against a low yellow sun, stood in proud defiance of the unwritten law that prohibited those symbols of the past; all were united behind the plain blue-green of Korathea. A gentle breeze blew through the spacious command tent, enough to lift the edges of the papers covering the surface in front of him. He weighted the report with a curved dagger and looked up at the rider who had delivered the information.

"So, you bring me news of..." he waved a hand at the paper, "nothing. No change."

The messenger looked uncertain. "Hatar?"

"The Kodistai still lives. He still lingers," He glowered.

"Some say that he has rallied, Hatar," the messenger said with a hopeful look. "On the day that I left, I heard that he had walked unaided by his physicians in the palace gardens."

"The last, frantic beats of a failing heart," Rogan muttered.

"Hatar?"

"How old is this news?" he said, in a louder voice.

"Seventeen days, Hatar, since I left Kor'Habat," the messenger replied.

"Then this news is stale already, and I waste time in this filthy hinterland," he growled. "What news of the Infantry?"

"They remain four days to the south," the messenger answered. "I passed another group, who could be here by evening."

"Oh?" Rogan raised an eyebrow. "What sort of 'group'?"

"I could not be certain," the messenger apologised. "I gave them a wide berth to avoid delaying my arrival here, but from that distance they appeared to be women. Fifty or so."

"*All* women?"

"As I said, they were far away," the messenger confessed. "But they looked well-armed and moved with purpose."

"Shar-hunters? A little late, perhaps." Rogan shrugged. "No matter. The Infantry is my main concern. The sooner they arrive, the quicker I can be done here and return to where I am needed. Send in Captain Raims as you leave."

The messenger stiffened at the curt dismissal but murmured his thanks and left the tent.

A moment later, Captain Raims entered.

"Is he here?" Rogan asked.

"He is, Hatar," the young Captain replied.

Rogan waited a few moments before spreading his hands. "Then show him in," he said in exasperation.

"Hatar." Raims pulled the tent flap aside and ushered a man in. "Olgoi Kinbataar, Hatar."

The man was dwarfed by Raims but made a good show of not being intimidated as he entered. He was an unremarkable man, typical of these northern grasslands; a slight build with black hair and a lightly bronzed complexion. This one had shrewd, darting eyes that Rogan recognised only too well from the politicians and diplomats of Kor'Habat. Their ilk, much like rodents, could be found in every corner of the continent.

"Would you like some wine, perhaps?" Rogan asked, leaning back in his chair.

"No, thank you. That will not be necessary," Olgoi replied.

"That will be all, Captain," Rogan said, pitching his voice for Raims to hear.

Captain Raims placed his right fist on his left breast in salute and ducked out of the tent.

"Will you sit?" Rogan returned his attention to his guest and gestured towards a chair.

Olgoi Kinbataar took the seat that was offered, an un-cushioned chair with a straight back, and cocked his head to one side.

"That young man will make Hatar one day," Rogan murmured. "When he learns to be decisive."

"Reticence is not usually a quality found in the young; why revile it when it shows itself?"

Rogan shook his head. "A hesitant man is soon lost on the battlefield, but then you do not have the look of a man who would know of such things."

Olgoi ignored the jibe. "I am intrigued as to why you have summoned me, Hatar," he said. "Or may I call you Rogan?"

"You may call me 'Hatar', Olgoi," Rogan replied. "Do not make the mistake of assuming us to be equals."

Olgoi grimaced. "I see."

"You are here because you may be useful to me," Rogan went on. "As a member of the Conclave here in Ulan-Balsan, I understand that you have some influence in the ruling council in Banihat."

"That may be true," he replied cautiously.

"Is it, or is it not?" Rogan pressed.

"As a Conclave member here, I have a proxy in Banihat with whom I communicate when important matters arise."

"Good. Have you communicated the fact that one thousand Heavy Infantry are days away from your gates?"

Olgoi hesitated. "They are aware," he said eventually.

"Then I will be blunt." Rogan leaned forward and placed his elbows on the table. "They are not here to deal with the Shar problem. If that were the case, they would have turned for home days ago. They are here to enforce protectorate status upon Kylyptus, and your people will be subject to the laws of Kor'Habat."

"With one thousand men? Bold." Olgoi declared.

Rogan managed a tight-lipped smile. "I admit that our armies are stretched and suffered much at Hadaiti and then Ara Dasari, but do not be a fool. The children of Shol'Hara swiftly become men, and I could bring a force down upon you that would cause the land to shake until your grandchildren are old and wizened. What I am here to offer is an opportunity for you and those of a like mind to make a great deal of coin from nothing more than free enterprise. Convince the ruling council to accept my offer, and you will be first in line to benefit from it."

Olgoi Kinbataar rubbed his chin, deep in thought. "What is your offer?"

Rogan leaned back again. "The Empire amassed great wealth at its height, and there is no shortage of gold within the walls of Kor'Habat. What the city and the land that still calls itself Korathea needs is meat and grain. Kylyptus has long been the larder of the east, and we would see your farmland increased along with production. You have unused grassland in abundance that could be put to good toil."

"A fine idea, but who would work those fields?" Olgoi asked. "One cannot simply snap one's fingers to plough new ground. We are a scattered people, spread thinly across the land."

Rogan nodded. "Kor'Habat is still awash with refugees from the Jendayan invasion. Their hands have grown idle and prone to criminality. Those who have not returned willingly to their own lands in the west will be forced eastwards into Kylyptus. I will see my city cleansed, and its grain bins filled again. You, for your part will welcome the incomers with open arms, and in return a share of the tax revenues will be steered into your own coffers;

and your own purse."

Olgoi smiled. "It is one thing to convince me, a businessman, of the sense in your offer, but quite another to convince the people to accept the Korathean yoke again. Could you not simply send your 'refugees' without the Heavy Infantry? We can do trade like any other, without reliving the days of the Empire."

"I will not be subject to the whims of politicians," Rogan riposted. "There must be no doubt as to where the produce flows. Without a leash, what is to stop you selling to the Pashwari or Dashiyans? No, my offer is not for negotiation; if your ruling council will not keep their people to heel, then they will be crushed. The Empire *will* rise again, and your choice, Olgoi, is a simple one; grow rich, or die. Kylyptus could not stand against Korathea in your grandfather's time, and it cannot hope to do so in yours."

Olgoi nodded slowly. "Then you leave me little choice. I will leave for Banihat in the morning to press your case."

"That would be wise." Rogan stood and turned his back on the Kylyptian. "There is another task that I require to be done," he said.

"Why not," Olgoi sighed.

"There is an individual who causes me much concern, a piece of grit in my eye that I would pluck out." He turned his head to keep Olgoi in his peripheral vision.

"Surely with the Heavy Infantry at your disposal, such irritations would be easily extracted."

"I would have this person killed, but I must distance myself from the act."

Olgoi chuckled. "I know of agents who might be willing to remove this person from your concern, for a fee of course."

Rogan turned to face Olgoi again. "I thought that you might. I have ten gold marks in that purse upon the table." He gestured to a small brown pouch. "I trust that will suffice to purchase the services I require. There will be a further twenty-five for you when the task is completed."

Olgoi picked up the purse and tipped its contents into his palm and smiled at the soft sheen of the coins. "Who, may I ask, has earned such ire?"

Rogan hesitated before telling him, ready to gauge the response. He spoke the name.

The Kylyptian's eyes registered surprise and not a little uncertainty, but the gleam of the gold won over the doubts that played across his face.

"A difficult target," Olgoi pondered.

"But not beyond reach," Rogan insisted.

"Indeed not, but a Shar-hunter has many dangerous friends close by. It will take some planning."

"I do not care how it is done," Rogan said, "only that it is done soon, and does not leave a trail to my door."

Olgoi tipped the coins back into the purse, and it vanished into his tunic. "I feel that we will have a very profitable future together."

"Then you should see it done," Rogan urged, and turned his back.

Alano ran down the cobbled street, breathing hard from his exertion under a hot, afternoon sun. He reached *The Shar's Folly* with sweat beading on his balding head and pushed the door open. He stomped in, fighting to catch his breath.

Jon, the erstwhile fletcher turned Shar-hunter glanced from his mug of ale to see who had made such an entrance. He put his back against the bar top and rested both elbows on the worn, wooden surface.

"Take your time," he called, "there is plenty of ale still in the barrel."

"The Easterners are leaving," Alano said through deep breaths.

Marlon and Granger, who were sitting at one of the smaller tables, exchanged looks. A few other hunters and residents were scattered about the room in small groups or else drinking alone.

"Then it is catching," Marlon grumbled.

"What?" Alano had his hands on his knees as he brought his breathing under control.

"Valia is gone too," Granger announced.

"What? When?" Alano straightened and made his way to their table.

"Sometime this morning, before sunrise," the historian explained. "She has left most of her belongings here in storage."

"I don't understand," Alano said, struggling to make sense of the new information. "Why?"

"Do not seek reason where there is none," Marlon growled back at him.

"Dachen and his escort left through the gates of Ulan-Balsan only minutes ago," Alano persisted. "Adeyemi was among them. We must act."

"And do what?" Marlon retorted.

"Gather the hunters! Give chase!" he exclaimed in frustration at their inaction.

"Half of the hunters are still sleeping off last night's wine," Marlon replied. "And the other half are already drunk again."

A loud belch erupted from Jon at the bar, proof that he could hear their conversation, and he raised his mug in appreciation.

"Acastes has Heavy Cavalry at his disposal," Alano persisted. "He will help if told what is at stake."

Granger gestured for Alano to sit, and he pulled a chair around to join them at the table.

"We know where they are going," Granger explained. "There is no need for confrontation yet."

Alano was beginning to feel foolish for his initial urgency. "So, we do nothing?"

Granger shrugged. "Give them their half day head-start. We can leave in the morning and keep them within reach until we arrive in Banihat. There they will attempt to acquire a ship to return them to the Eastern Kingdoms, where they will discover that sailors can be just as superstitious as Adeyemi. If rumours were to circulate around the docks of an evil talisman in their possession, they might find it difficult to secure passage. I believe that Dachen and Adeyemi will see sense and do what is right." He finished with a sly grin.

Alano leaned back in his chair, whistling a long, soft note. "That is a bold gamble, Granger."

"If it fails, we still have the threat of violence," he replied.

"Yes, and if the threat alone is not enough?"

"That is a bridge we will cross if we come to it," Granger said. "But I would rather not have blood spilled over something that likely, has no power. Ganindhra believed the changes inflicted by the Element would render it sterile."

The mention of the fallen god's name reminded Alano of the home he had left behind to come on this venture, and the wife who awaited his return. Lythuria lay nestled in the embrace of the Greater Cascus mountains far to the north, a haven of life in an otherwise unforgiving landscape. It had been Ganindhra's final creation, and by some convoluted sleight of Fate's hand, he and his darling Casilda had found themselves caretakers of a sort to Lythuria and its young inhabitants.

"Very well. So, we gather what support we can from the hunters here, and Acastes if he is willing, and leave in the morning," Alano agreed. "What of Valia?"

Granger looked thoughtful for a long moment. "Valia is at a crossroads and is best left out of this."

Marlon muttered something inaudible, and Granger rolled his eyes.

Alano wiped the sweat from his brow with a sleeve and took a long, deep breath. "Very well," he said. "I hope you know what you are doing."

Nirmaya kept a wary eye on the Korathean encampment as she and the Sisters gave it a wide berth on their way to the town gates. The tents looked as though they had been established there for some time with well beaten tracks running about them where the long grass had been trampled. A mounted cavalryman watched them from the edge of the encampment, but made no attempt to communicate, and they reached the gates unimpeded.

"If you are Shar-hunters, you are late," a guard announced from his position at the open gates.

"Is it true?" Nirmaya asked as she dismounted. "The Shar have been defeated?"

"It is true," he replied with pride, puffing his chest like a rooster. "We of Ulan-Balsan stood against an army of Shar and rid the land of them forever."

"How can you be so certain that you have eradicated them all? The Shar were spread from Pashwar to Eritania," she countered.

"Shar-hunters from every nation chased the remaining Shar here, where they gathered against us," the guard stated. "All that remains of their kind is ash and ill memories." He pointed towards a blackened forest of charred trees beyond a narrow strip of burned grassland. "It ended there, and it was Valia of Hadaiti who fought alongside us."

Nirmaya's eyes widened. "Valia of Hadaiti? Here?"

Starling stepped forward and smiled. "Then we owe you and your town a debt of gratitude. I trust you did not drink Ulan-Balsan dry of wine in celebration."

"There is wine aplenty," the guard replied, taking in the size of the group. "Although our inns have little extra capacity for such a number. Many residents have opened their doors to guests, and you are welcome to seek beds where they are offered. The inn named *The Shar's Folly* would be a good place to start. Or you may make an encampment in the field."

Nirmaya glanced at the field he indicated, right beside the Heavy Cavalry. "We will see what comforts the town has to offer," she said before leading her horse through the gate. The Sisters dismounted and filed in behind her and Starling.

"Valia of Hadaiti is here." Nirmaya's voice was an excited whisper.

"The 'Bitch of Hadaiti'... The 'Butcher of Hadaiti'; she has many names," Starling muttered.

"She is a living legend; I cannot wait to meet her."

Starling sounded less enthusiastic. "Perhaps in Pashwar, but I remember the remains of the Heavy Infantry trudging home to Kor'Habat, and the stories they told. She was nothing more than a brutal mercenary in their eyes."

"I should have expected you to be bitter, Korathean boy," she teased.

"I'm only saying that you should reserve your hero worship until you meet her for yourself," Starling advised. "Living legends seldom satisfy the expectations of their devotees."

"I wish I could have fought alongside her," Nirmaya went on. "If I had been older, I could have joined the cause."

"What would Maidra make of your infatuation, I wonder?" he enquired.

"Lift your mind from the gutter, Starling. You know it is not like that. Valia of Hadaiti was an inspiration to me after... after my family..." She faltered as the memory of claws and blood slipped from the dark pit of her mind where horrors writhed in midnight flesh. She cleared her throat. "And I knew that she had turned to Shar-hunting which made me want to be like her even more."

Starling laughed and stared at her. "You really are besotted, aren't you?"

Nirmaya tugged at her horse and upped her pace to leave Starling behind. They continued deeper into Ulan-Balsan along the main street, passing trading stalls and quaint timber structures until they reached a large, round stone building. A friendly resident directed Nirmaya along a side street that led to an inn with a freshly painted sign, *The Shar's Folly*.

The sky was dark by the time that all of the Sisters had found accommodation for the night; scattered through three separate inns and a dozen or more homes that had opened their doors to the influx of visitors, for a price.

Starling found Nirmaya and Maidra sitting at a small table in the crowded common room of *The Shar's Folly*. He pulled out a stool from under the table and sat down, helping himself to a large serving of wine from their jug.

"Please, help yourself," Maidra said over the noise of the bustling room, with a glower that Starling ignored.

"Thank you," he replied. "I shall."

Maidra bit down on her reply as Nirmaya leaned forward. "What have you learned?"

"In short, we are too late," he answered.

"Late for what?" Nirmaya asked.

"Almost everything, it seems. I have been speaking with a Shar-hunter who assured me that we missed the greatest battle for generations, and that is why it will be his name and not mine that graces the pages of history books for all time." He took a dismissive swig from his cup and refilled it from the jug. "Also, our eastern noble friend left this very day for Banihat, so at least we know that we are not far behind. Oh, and Valia of Hadaiti has vanished without a trace," he added. "Probably disappeared up her own living legend or some such."

"So, she was here?" Nirmaya insisted.

"Stayed in this very inn. Probably sat at this very table." Starling caressed the tabletop, voice falling to an exaggerated whisper. "Sipped from this very cup. I still *feel* her presence."

Nirmaya kicked him hard under the table. "You are behaving like an ass."

"Why don't you take your jokes elsewhere," Maidra hissed.

"Yes, Starling. Go and find a drunk to bore with your wit," Nirmaya added. "And try not to rob anybody while you're at it."

Starling stood with his hands raised in submission and a look of false hurt on his face, before snatching the jug from the table and ducking into the crowd with a shout of "Too late!"

Nirmaya sighed, just happy to be rid of him. Maidra placed a hand on hers and squeezed.

"The Shar are defeated," Maidra said.

"Do you believe it is true?"

Maidra nodded. "I do."

"Yet the madness they brought still remains."

"You speak of the Cultists?"

Nirmaya breathed a long, weary sigh. "I cannot erase what happened. Those I have lost will not be returned to me, and I will take little comfort in the knowledge that their cause will crumble in time."

"Enough," Maidra said, shifting in her seat to face Nirmaya.

"What is it?" Nirmaya asked.

"I have something for you," she said.

"Oh?" Nirmaya straightened a little, her interest piqued.

Maidra dipped into a breast pocket and took something out, hiding whatever it was in a clenched fist.

"What is it?" Nirmaya repeated with an impatient giggle.

Maidra looked serious. "This belonged to my great-grand-mother," she said. "It has been passed down my family, woman to woman for four generations, and I want to give it to you."

She opened her hand to reveal a plain, silver ring.

"I can't!" she protested. "This belongs in your family. You should give it to your daughter.

"I'm not having any children, Nirmaya," she scoffed. "Not me. You *do* know how babies are made don't you?"

Nirmaya laughed at the look of disgust on Maidra's face.

"This," she began. "I can't, I just can't. This is too valuable."

"It is only silver, and its value as a symbol far outweighs any coin it would fetch. 'Not bands of silver, nor bands of gold have strength to bind the heart'," she recited the line from a well-known poem. "I love you, Nirmaya. I want to spend my life with you."

Nirmaya took the ring from Maidra's palm with trembling fingers. She slipped it onto the third finger of her right hand and stared at it.

"It fits," Maidra declared. "Now you may never take it off!"

The threw their arms around each other, laughing like excited children.

"And I never will," Nirmaya said through tear-filled eyes.

They sat back and toasted their union, then dreamed of their future in comfortable, mutual silence. The noise of the inn washed over them, and they listened to the revellers who were engrossed in their own celebrations.

These were men still drunk on victory and wine, their stories yet to grow too old to tell again and again. Nirmaya almost wished that she had been there with them, standing shoulder to shoulder against the black foe, but she had seen Shar claws cut the flesh of those she once loved and a quiet, shrinking thought nestled in her mind, grateful that she had not.

CHAPTER 3

Olgoi Kinbataar had hoped for solitude on his journey from Ulan-Balsan to Banihat, but it was not to be. A curious fortuity had seen the inns of his fine town disgorge their guests into the streets as all eyes turned north-east to the capital. The Shar-hunters it would appear, had tired of their nightly revelry and chosen this day to take to the road for Banihat, where they hoped to press the ruling council for the bounties that Olgoi had been unable to cover from his own town's coffers. Of course, Olgoi would be an asset in that pursuit since he would vouch for the number of Shar slain, would he not? And so, he found himself in the custody of thirty benevolent guardians, eager to see him safely to Banihat.

And there was no sign of the hunter, Valia.

A dozen Heavy Cavalry joined them outside the main gate, with the enormous, golden-haired hunter Acastes at their head. The big man grimaced with every movement of his horse, and Olgoi remembered that the Korathean had been injured in the battle. At his side was the ever watchful Kapaneus and the meek and servile Jendayan. A most curious arrangement.

More curious still was the large group of women, only just arrived the previous day, eager to join the travellers on the road. Olgoi urged his elegant mount through the press of larger men and horses to better hear the conversation between one of the women and the historian named Granger.

"It is a free road, and you are welcome to travel it with us," he was saying. "I would be interested to hear what news you bring from the south, Nirmaya. Where have you travelled from, exactly?"

The woman, Nirmaya, nodded in thanks. "Kernhalt. It lies two weeks to the south-east of Kor'Habat, but there is little to tell. The town is in the heart of Korathea, far from the fringes where insurrection nibbles at the borders. I hear that the border with Dashiya is especially problematic."

A burly, barrel-chested man with a thick, black beard spoke up. "Perhaps if Korathea had respected that border in the past, the Dashiyan people would not be so eager to take back a little more than they lost."

Nirmaya laughed. "I have no sympathy for the Korathean loss of territory. I am merely reporting what I know."

"We will have plenty of time to discuss the south," Granger said to avert an argument. "What brings you so far north?"

The young woman exchanged a look with her only male companion. "Fools," she said with a smile. "I am, as ever, a slave to their whims."

"We are wasting daylight," growled the one-eyed man called Marlon, and he jerked on the reins of his horse, urging it onto the road.

By degrees, the throng formed into a drawn-out line of discreet groups of riders and pack-horses. Olgoi made his way to Granger's side, opposite the young woman, Nirmaya. He found Granger to be the most civil among the hunters; a man with whom he could converse on equal terms where acumen was concerned, whereas those of the sword looked down upon him for choosing a less intrepid life.

"I would be happy to travel alone," he said to Granger as they settled into a gentle pace.

Granger was staring at the ruins of the forest. "Please," he said, pulling his attention away from the bleak image, "you are no burden, you are a most welcome companion. Besides, the hunters hope that you will help them urge the ruling council to make good on the bounties. Most will need new employment now and are eager to settle all debts."

Olgoi stiffened. "I struck no bargain with the Shar-hunters. They must know that the coffers would not cover a full bounty for each Shar slain," he insisted. "I believed that they stayed for the greater good."

"Indeed, they did," Granger conceded. "And, as someone who did not kill a single one of the beasts, I will not argue either way."

"I heard tell of your heroics on the palisade," Olgoi chuckled. "You are too modest."

Granger dismissed the thought with a wave. "Driven only by terror, I assure you. The real heroics took part on the field below, and in the burning wood."

Olgoi nodded slowly. "And where is Valia?" he asked. "She has not been seen for a day at least."

Granger shrugged. "I am not certain, but I believe that she is ahead of us on this very road."

The young woman, who had been silent, showed a sudden interest in their conversation. "Valia is headed for Banihat?" she exclaimed.

Granger looked surprised by the excitement in Nirmaya's voice. "Yes. She is looking for someone, who was very close to a friend of hers. She carries bad news I am afraid." He studied Nirmaya. "Do you know her?"

Nirmaya shook her head. "Only by reputation. But I heard that she was in Ulan-Balsan and had hoped to meet her. I heard that you were friends; did you travel with her? Did you know her before Hadaiti? Is she as fierce as they say?"

"Slow down, slow down," Granger laughed. "I am losing count of the questions. Yes, I have known Valia since long before the battle at Hadaiti, although as she would tell you herself, the gulf between truth and invention of what happened that day is vast." He leaned towards Nirmaya and gave her a conspiratorial wink. "And yes, she is fierce. She is also tender and loyal, but she would tear my tongue out if she knew I had told you as much. So…" He tapped his sealed lips with a forefinger.

Nirmaya smiled. "Your secret is safe."

Olgoi leaned in. "Forgive me, perhaps I am becoming old or just unused to the ways of our southern neighbours, but I have never seen so many women travelling, armed as you are. What is your purpose?" He stopped when he heard a sharp intake of breath from Granger and recognised a warning when he heard it.

Nirmaya shifted in her saddle and sat a little straighter. "It is not only men who can wield a sword. Each of the Sisters is as good a warrior as any man."

"So, they have seen battle?" he asked.

"They…" she began and then faltered. "Most have worked as escorts for merchants at the very least. The governor of Kernhalt entrusted us with the security of his town."

"But not battle?" Olgoi replied.

"Not as such, no," she conceded. "But I would wager every mark I own on each one of them being capable of beating you in a contest of arms."

Olgoi laughed. "I do not doubt it, my dear. I have never been one for fighting, my skills lie in other fields. But I look at their faces and most are little more than children eager for excitement. A few are past their prime and would be better suited to sewing at the fireside, and yet they all appear to follow you. You should perhaps lead them home, to their fathers or husbands, before you lead them to their deaths. Playing soldier is a dangerous game."

Nirmaya gaped, staring at him. Granger groaned and brought his hand up to cover his eyes, muttering. Nirmaya was about to reply when a call from behind caught her attention. She favoured Olgoi with an acid glare before jerking on the reins of her horse and falling back down the line.

Granger whistled. "You are lucky that the hunters need to keep you alive until we reach Banihat," he warned. "You may well need their protection *after* that."

Olgoi shrugged. "She is just a girl who should return home to find a husband. A few children will dampen her fire."

Granger leaned over towards him and whispered. "I would keep that thought to myself if I were you. I have seen too much bloodshed of late."

With that, he urged his horse to a quicker pace to join Marlon at the front, leaving Olgoi to his thoughts.

The small group of a dozen Heavy Cavalry trailed at the rear of the group. Several packhorses carried the heavy armour, leaving the riders in the cooler, lighter travel garments that were favoured for journeys in peacetime. Kapaneus and Acastes were set apart by their civilian attire, since they were not of the Heavy Cavalry; Acastes having been given command over a small number in response to his pleas for help against the Shar. Of those who survived the battle, all had chosen to remain with Acastes until he released them, a fact that had irked Rogan Fol'Brandam, and so had seemed all the more delicious to Acastes for it. Acastes decided he would release them at Banihat and make a show of it.

"We should return to Kor'Habat," Kapaneus urged. "There is nothing else for us to do here. Your responsibilities lie in the city."

Acastes grumbled. "There is nothing there for me."

"There is *everything* there for you," Kapaneus insisted. After a moment of thoughtful silence, he went on. "A messenger arrived at Rogan's encampment yesterday."

"And what message did he bring?" Acastes mumbled.

Kapaneus shook his head. "I do not know."

"Has Rogan moved?"

Kapaneus shook his head again.

Acastes grunted. "No news, then."

"We *must* return to Kor'Habat," Kapaneus insisted. "This is taking us further from where we need to be."

"You may return at any time; you have my leave."

"What purpose would that serve?" Kapaneus hissed. "I have devoted my *life* to this."

"I never asked for that," Acastes replied. "You are worse than Kekoa."

"What?"

"Any fool who willingly gives up his own freedom on a whim was never worthy of it in the first place."

"This is not about *one* man," Kapaneus protested. "It is greater than you, or I, or Kekoa, alone."

"All the more reason for me to stand aside and let Fate have her way with us."

"Korathea will tear itself apart if the Hatars are left to act unchecked, you must know this." Kapaneus' comment was met with stony silence, and they rode for a few hundred yards before Kapaneus spoke again in softer tones. "I thought you were dead, Acastes. I thought you had died on the battlefield. Have you any idea how hollow that left me? To have come so far and failed?"

Acastes sighed, the deep breath giving him obvious discomfort. "I am sorry, Kapaneus, you did not deserve that. Let us see this done; the Element retrieved and destroyed, and then we will consider the future."

Kapaneus nodded, and Acastes went on. "I envy you, Kapaneus."

"We are on the same side, my friend, always," he insisted.

"But it is a side you were free to choose."

"And would choose again. Your time is coming, Acastes, embrace it or else it will crush you."

"It may yet crush me either way," Acastes murmured, then he brightened. "Enough of this! We should enjoy this journey, breathe in the air, and let the plains carry us where they will. Wine and women await us." He tried to spread his arms wide but winced as his cracked ribs protested.

"That is more like the Acastes I know," Kapaneus laughed.

"We should hasten our pace and catch up with the Easterners. That Element could easily be taken by force with the numbers we have. I am mystified as to why Granger did not suggest this sooner."

Kapaneus shrugged. "He feels that there could be a peaceful resolution in Banihat, so long as we keep them within touching distance."

"So now we follow the orders of a historian?"

"No, of course not," Kapaneus replied. "But he does have a way of bending one to his will. Keep him close, Acastes; you may need his judgement in the future. He is an especially useful ally." Then he smiled. "Not to mention a damned fine cook, which will make this journey a far more pleasant one than many in the past!"

The sun was casting the last of its amber light on the palisade of Ulan-Balsan when Captain Silman presented himself at the large command tent in the centre of the encampment outside the town. This tent was a far grander affair than his own, a manifestation of the owner's rank, but one day he might be similarly honoured if he could avoid marring his record. Captain Raims was waiting for him and nodded a curt greeting. "You took your time," he muttered. "What kept you?"

"Raims," Silman sneered. "You would not understand. I have a thousand men under *my* command, whereas you command nothing but that tent-flap. Now, will you lead me in, I believe the Hatar has important matters to discuss with me."

Raims glared at him for a moment before pulling the flap aside and stepping in onto the carpeted interior of the command tent. Silman followed and was at once struck by the opulence his own tent lacked. Thick carpets and cushioned chairs turned the canvas shelter into something grander even than his own quarters in Kor'Habat. The large desk must surely have come from the town itself, since it could barely have been loaded onto a cart, and he knew that Rogan Fol'Brandam had left Kor'Habat travelling light and fast. Nevertheless, he had certainly made himself comfortable since his arrival.

Rogan appeared from behind a heavy curtain at the back of the tent, drying his face and head with a towel. His head was clean-shaved except for the topknot that signified his rank, an honour that Silman would have one day soon, with prudence. The Hatar draped the towel over the back of a chair and sat down, throwing a booted foot up onto the paper-strewn desk.

"Captain Silman Fol'Ghealten," he said. "Thank you for joining us at last."

Silman thumped his right fist to his chest in salute. "Hatar. We travelled with as much haste as we were able."

"It is not the time taken for you to reach here from Kor'Habat that vexes me but the time it took you to report."

"Hatar, I felt it important to see the camp established."

"The soldiers under your command are capable of establishing camp without your oversight, Captain, and if you had thought to report to me first, I could have saved them the bother of getting too comfortable."

Silman could almost feel Raims smirking behind him.

"Hatar?" he said.

Rogan went on. "I will assume command of the bulk of the men, Captain. You will remain here with two hundred Heavy Infantry and hold your position until you receive further orders. The rest will leave at first light, under my banner."

"Hatar," he sputtered. "I do not understand."

Rogan banged the desk with a meaty fist. "I did not ask for you to understand! Only obey!"

Silman stood bolt upright. "Hatar. I will see it done," he declared as he felt his face flush. "Eight hundred Heavy Infantry will be ready at first light."

"Better," Rogan said, his composure returned. "You may

leave."

Silman saluted and spun on his heel, avoiding eye contact with Raims as he did so, and was almost out of the tent before he was called back by Rogan.

"One more thing, Captain. I will require your retinue as well. You have no need of cooks and smiths here. The town can provide you with the services you need."

Silman felt a lead weight settle in his belly. "The clerk, Hatar?"

"Most definitely. I tire of paperwork." He waved his hand over the papers covering the large desk.

"Hatar." Silman nodded and strode out of the tent.

He walked with purposeful strides through the Cavalry encampment, glowering ahead towards his own camp. When he reached his tent, only just erected by his two attendants, the young Infantryman, Daelen, was waiting for him.

"Anything?" the captain growled.

"A group of women did stay here," Daelen replied. "But only briefly. They left with a large group of Shar-hunters three days ago, possibly for Banihat."

"Thank you, Daelen. Were you discreet?"

"Very, Captain," he replied.

"Very good. Keep this to yourself, Daelen, and I will see you go far in the Infantry."

"Yes, Captain." The young man saluted, right fist to his left breast, as Silman ducked into his tent. The Captain stood in silence for a long time, the glow from an oil lamp his only companion. This paltry tent of his could be pitched inside the Hatar's and barely even be noticed, he thought.

He *would* be Hatar, and no amount of pedantry from a mere clerk would hold him back; no minor error in judgement would be used to crush his ambitions.

He turned and stormed from his tent.

In the dark, the men had gravitated towards the various cooking fires that had been lit around the periphery of the encampment. The orderly rows of low, ridge tents gave way to the more haphazard collection of shelters used by the supporting retinue. A young man was fussing with the packhorses and did not notice him as he walked past, and most others would be involved in preparing meals for the soldiers. The tent he was aiming for stood out from the others in that it was larger, and conical around a central pole, with ropes pegged out to hold up the skirts and increase the useful headroom.

Solinus looked startled as Silman ducked into the tent; the clerk was sitting at a small, folding table, pouring over a bound ledger by the light of several smoky oil lamps.

"Captain?" he started.

"Solinus."

"You could have sent for me," he said.

"I could have," Silman replied, not moving from the entrance. "But the matter could not wait."

"I see." Solinus closed the ledger.

"Do you? Do you see?" Silman was aware that his voice was trembling.

The clerk stood up and cast a wary eye around the tent, but Silman knew that the only exit was at his own back.

"Some days ago, I asked you for help," Silman said in a dangerous whisper. "Your discretion in a certain matter involving the theft of a few coins; coins that I will see returned."

Solinus spread his hands but did not reply.

"You declined to help, and now the Hatar has ordered that your services here with me are no longer required, and that you are to join him." He took a step closer. "You and your books of numbers will ruin me when that happens."

"It is only an error, the Hatar will understand…"

"No!" Silman blurted, before quietening his voice again and taking another step towards the clerk. "You see, Hatars are men of impeccable honour with flawless records. Only the finest will rise to the rank and you sir, are a burr in my boot on my march to the top."

He took two quick steps forward and Solinus backed around the table, putting the tent's central pole between them. A lamp, suspended from a hook nearby, cast harsh shadows across his fearful face.

"Show me," Silman urged. "Where is the documentation that points to my mistake."

Solinus licked his lips, and for an instant, his eyes betrayed his thoughts as they flashed towards the exit. He darted for the way out, but Silman anticipated his move and was already reaching for him. The clerks cry was cut off as a huge hand clamped over his mouth and jerked him back. Silman felt the little man's body quiver in his grip as he pulled him close. The shaking was soon replaced by terrified sobs that shook his tiny frame as Silman forced him face first onto the ground. He placed a knee between Solinus' shoulder blades and with his hand still clamped over the clerk's mouth, wrapped his other hand around to grip the back of the prone man's head.

"I gave you a chance," Silman hissed, before wrenching Solinus' head around with brutal force. Sinews ripped and bone grated against bone in a sickening crunch. Silman gave an extra twist to be sure and stood, leaving the paralyzed clerk to stare with dimming eyes at the roof of the tent, lips contorting as though desperate to speak.

Silman rifled through several neat stacks of paper and flicked through the bound ledger that the Clerk had left on the table. None of it made sense to him, although he was certain that to someone, his guilt would be laid bare on the page among the numbers.

He gathered every piece of paper he could find and piled them next to the body. Then he collected the lamps and emptied their contents, save for one, onto the heap, being sure to splash plenty onto the clerk. He stopped for a moment to look into the shocked, staring eyes, and he smiled. Then he nudged the slack head back over with the toe of his boot, so that it did not look as though someone had tried to wrench it from the shoulders; even a corpse can tell a tale, but not if he was careful.

He returned the lamps to where they had been and took the last of them with him to the tent flap. With a final glance around the now dim tent, he tossed the oil-lamp onto the corpse. The yellow flame splashed across the chest of the dead clerk and spread across to the heap of papers which curled at the edges as the blaze grew. Silman ducked away through the tents until he was far enough away to walk upright. He strode back towards his own tent, feeling lighter with every step. He did not notice the ashen face of Daelen, watching from the gloom at the edge of the orderly rows.

Finally, a cry of alarm went up, but by then the fire had taken hold.

Banihat was a city hewn from the rocks of the low cliffs that marked the boundary between the golden plains of Kylyptus and the turquoise waters of the Ashkelit Ocean. In stark contrast to Ulan-Balsan's buildings of timber and thatch, this was a city of stone and clay. Pale grey granite dominated here, from the neat, square cobbles of the streets to the blocks that made up the thirty-foot-high walls surrounding the city. Two and three storey buildings with small, shuttered windows were topped with tiles of deep orange that glowed in the mid-day sun. Twin piers reached out to embrace the incoming boats of the fishing fleets that operated in the clear waters, inviting them into the thriving docks. A vibrant market occupied the town square where traders vied for attention with songs and flourishes to woo the custom from those who passed by. Furs and fresh vegetables were displayed beside jewellery and farm tools in a riot of form and colour that defied order. A tall bell tower dominated the skyline to the west of the market; a granite tower topped with the famous Taaman Bell, a relic of a bygone age. Centuries ago, the great bell had declared the birth of princes and princesses to the land around the city, but those royal lines had been extinguished long ago by the greed of Korathea.

Valia stopped for a rest at the edge of the market and sat as she watched the shadow of the great tower creep out over the square. A group of children played nearby, joining hands to form a circle around a single, blindfolded child. They circled the lone child as they chanted in unison:

"Taaman-bell, Taaman-bell, speak to me.
I cannot hear the cries of your new baby.
Once for a daughter, twice for a son,
Three for plague so turn and run!"

On the final word the children scattered with the blindfolded boy in pursuit, arms outstretched and guided by the giggles and shrieks of his playmates. A few of the adults shooed them away from the tables as they fled, allowing the blindfolded boy to catch one of the smaller girls. The captured girl accepted her fate, and the blindfold, and took her place at the centre of a new circle for the game to start again.

Valia watched them play until the shadow of the bell tower was near the eastern edge of the market. She took Kekoa's phrase book from her pocket and flicked through it again, picking a page at random and practising the phrases she found there. She found a map, showing Jendaya to the west, with the city, Waka-tu, marked with a rising sun. Other images showed a sprawling city surrounded by rolling hills or dunes, cooking utensils and a humble dwelling, even a recipe for some sort of spiced dumpling. Despite Kekoa's modesty, the images were very good indeed, and Valia found a new level of respect for the man.

She flicked to the final page where she found a crude sketch; rough lines giving the foundation of an incomplete work. On one side she could see that he had formed the shapes of several

Shar, cowering and half engulfed in the shadows of a rift of some sort. On the other, the shapes of people, yet to be given fine detail appeared to be advancing on the Shar. At the head of the force was a giant, twice as tall as those at its back, with a sword raised, frozen in battle.

She stared at the giant and tried by sheer force of will, to extract detail from the rudimentary image. There was something that she felt certain was eluding her; something that she ought to know hanging just outside her understanding, tantalizing and elusive.

She touched the figure as though to stir it to life, but it remained inert, clinging to its secret.

It was with a tinge of regret that Valia left the city the following morning. She had not found Surilya in Banihat, but a chance meeting in a tavern had given her a clue as to where a woman of that name might be found. She took a ferry across the Khashmit river and onto the Northern Steppes where the sky truly dominated the land, pressing down on the horizon. Here, butterflies ruled, riding the gentle breeze across the grassy waves in search of the tiny blue and yellow flowers that reached up atop delicate stems to vie with the grass for sunlight.

Following the coast for a full two days to the east brought her to the first sign of human habitation since leaving the ferry. A large, low stone building with a neat, thatched roof stood not far from the wide, sandy beach. A stream was evident on the far side of the structure, spreading into a hundred, intertwined fingers when it reached the sand. The lazy sound of bells alerted her to the wiry-haired goats that were hidden in the long grass, munching through the vegetation. Each movement issued a gentle 'clonk' from the bells around their necks as they lifted their heads to watch her pass by.

As she neared the building there was the scent of soured milk on the air, and sure enough as she rounded the building, she found a woman kneeling and straining curds in the sunshine.

The woman looked up and saw Valia approaching. She stopped what she was doing and bowed her head for a moment before wiping her hands on the apron that covered her blouse and trousers, and stood up to meet her.

"I would tell you that you are too early, if you had hoped to trade with the Hetai," she said as Valia dismounted. "But that is not why you are here, is it?"

Valia was immediately struck by the woman's piercing blue eyes, set behind eyelashes as dark and full as the long hair that was barely tamed by the pale blue ribbon holding it back. Her complexion was dark and flecked with yet darker freckles over a proud nose, and Valia knew at once that she had found the woman she had been searching for.

"Are you Surilya?" she asked, already certain of the answer.

The woman nodded. "You should come inside," she said and made her way into the house.

Valia paused a moment before following her into the building, dread stirring in her belly.

A few moments later, Surilya stood holding the journal in her hands. She had recognised it as soon as Valia had revealed it. She stood with her back to Valia, facing a smouldering cooking range which held a variety of blackened pots and kettles. In the silence, Valia surveyed the living space, feeling awkward in the silence, an intruder in this woman's grief. The dwelling was far smaller inside than she had imagined but assumed that beyond the back wall was more space for either storage or animals. A steep stepladder led into a dark loft area where Valia could see beds and a small wardrobe. Everything was neat and spotless, from the weathered wooden table to the stone flags on the floor and every orderly item on the shelf beside the range.

"Were you with him?" Surilya asked at last. She turned to face Valia, holding the journal with a care verging on reverence.

"No, I was not," she replied.

Surilya nodded and closed her eyes for a moment of silent

B.R. Crichton

reflection, then placed the journal on the shelf above the range. "You must be hungry, and thirsty no doubt." She busied herself, filling a kettle with water and placing it on the iron bars above the fire pit in the range. Then she took some dark lumps from a basket, each the size of the palm of her hand, and quite flat, and added them to the embers before bringing the heat up with well-worn bellows. Soon, yellow flames licked at the kettle and she returned the bellows to their hook beside the range.

Valia leaned closer. "Forgive me, is that…?"

"Dung?" Surilya said as she turned to face her and raised an eyebrow. "Yes, it is. When last did you see a tree, or wood?"

"Ah. Last night, I found some driftwood on the beach," Valia replied. "But I take your point."

"The goats are very useful this far north," Surilya said. "I could not get by without them."

Valia drummed her fingers on the table. She had so many questions, but every one that came into her mind felt too invasive for someone she had only just met. Finally, she settled on one.

"Forgive me; are you alone here?"

"Alone? no," she replied. "I have one hundred and twenty-two goats. Danille comes twice a year from Banihat to take away the hides and cured meats I produce, and to bring what supplies I need. Also, the Hetai use this place as a meeting point for trade with merchants from the south; that happens each autumn, and again in early spring."

"Still, it must be hard." Valia said in surprise.

Surilya nodded. "My mother died shortly after I was born, and my father was not raising a princess. I learned what I needed to learn to be useful here, and it was a good thing too. He died of fever when I was fourteen."

"You were still a child."

"I do not pretend that it was easy," Surilya replied. "I cried myself to sleep most nights, and I cannot count the times that I almost lost hope."

Valia leaned back in her chair, trying to imagine the hardships faced by the girl, and remembering her own. The gnaw of hunger in the belly and shivering through cold nights under thin blankets, and worse than both, the dreadful uncertainty that there would be an end to either.

"We find strength when we need it, I think," Surilya went on, a distant look on her face as she recalled. "The first winter was the hardest; I had never known cold like it. The person we need to be is not always the person we are, and if we are to survive what Fate casts in our path, then we must adapt, or die." Then she smiled again and focussed on Valia. "But I survived. The kettle is boiling, I will make some tea and then see about a meal.

The tea was welcome, and the warm flatbread and goat's cheese even more so. Surilya had no wine to offer, but instead poured short measures of a strong spirit that tasted like a combination of seaweed and pain, and Valia did her best to heed the advice offered: "*Try not to let it touch your tongue.*"

Valia did not want to ask but supposed that Surilya was four or five years her junior although wisps of grey already touched her dark hair. Clearly, Gerasim had found a strong woman in her, a trait that heightened her physical beauty. They did not mention the old Shar-hunter again, and Valia felt it best not to bring him up unless prompted. The journal was there for Surilya to read if she chose to, and the news had been delivered; that should be an end to it and Valia knew that she should head south again in the morning.

They talked on into the night, comfortable in each other's company until they retired to the loft space where three beds separated by heavy curtains awaited. Valia had to stoop to avoid the sloping rafters and sank down onto the bed she was offered with a weary sigh just as soon as Surilya had prepared it. In the silence, the sound of gentle waves caressing the sand outside carried her away into a deep and dreamless sleep.

When she awoke, it was to a different rhythm; a slow, *swishing*, like the beating of a large wing encroaching on her gathering consciousness. She stretched the aching stiffness from her muscles before dressing with care under the low roof. Then she descended the stepladder into the kitchen where they had spent so long talking the previous night. A kettle steamed above the fire and Valia smelled the welcome scent of tea. She helped herself to a cup from a shelf near the fire and poured some of the hot liquid for herself, taking careful sips as she exited the house to find her host.

Surilya was not far away, swinging a scythe in lazy arcs, felling ranks of grass stems with expert precision on every pass.

"I did not intend to sleep so long," Valia said, glancing at the sun which was halfway to its zenith already.

Surilya stopped and leaned on the stem of the scythe. "A luxury of the unburdened mind," she replied. "I am glad that you find it restful here."

Valia pointed to the scythe. "Is that as easy as you make it look?"

Surilya shrugged and invited her to take it. Valia placed her cup in the newly cut stubble and accepted the tool.

"Keep the chine level with the ground," Surilya suggested.

"The what?" Valia raised an eyebrow.

"The blade. It is all too easy to dig the toe into the soil."

Valia nodded, adjusting her grip, and made a few practice movements over the stubble, trying to imitate what she had just seen, and then stepped forward for her first cut. The bright blade sang as it cut through a few stems on the first swing and then buried itself in the loam.

Surilya walked forward with a faint smile and produced a whetstone from her pocket. She took the scythe from Valia, flipped it over to bring the chine to chest level and honed the edge with practiced ease.

"Try again," she said, inviting Valia to take the tool again.

Not to be beaten, Valia accepted the challenge.

An hour, and many false starts later, she was able to make a convincing job of it. Surilya gathered up the stems that came to rest in clumps at the end of each cutting arc and tied them into bundles for storing. Valia's thighs and sides were starting to ache from the unfamiliar action when Surilya called for a break.

"You have not yet had breakfast, and it is almost mid-day."

Valia wiped the sweat from her brow and nodded, following Surilya back to the house, pleasantly surprised by the progress she had made with the scythe. The cool, salty breeze was most welcome after her efforts and they ate outside on a stone bench facing the sea. They had small, boiled potatoes, cooked in their skins and dipped in soft cheese and a thin, spicy sauce, all washed down with more tea. Then back to the scythe.

That evening, as they set about preparing the evening meal together, sharing tasks and talking about the day's labours, Surilya noticed the bundle of Valia's belongings that still sat at the foot of the steps that lead to the loft. She went to it and loosened the sword from its bindings as Valia watched. Then she carried it, still in its scabbard, to the range and lifted it high, going up on her toes to reach the iron brackets that were fixed to the wall there. She stood back and looked at it where it hung on display, glancing at Valia for her approval.

Valia nodded and managed a tired smile. "Thank you," she said. "I have been meaning to hang it up for some time."

"It can stay there as long as you wish it to," Surilya replied, returning the smile.

"Thank you," Valia said after a pause. "You are very kind."

Surilya gave a shy shrug. "Small acts of kindness cost nothing, but their return is beyond measure." She looked once more at the sword and then back to Valia. "But if you don't cut those carrots, we'll not eat before breakfast." She clapped her hands twice and set about stoking the fire.

CHAPTER 4

A deyemi stood at the end of the stone pier that formed the northern boundary of the harbour in Banihat. This was a beautiful city, the granite reminding him of home, although the architecture was far less grand. A tall bell tower was the single most striking feature, standing proud of all surrounding buildings. A pity then that Dachen was so eager to be away and had already secured passage on a small ship that would leave with the morning tide.

He loosened the top of the pouch that hung around his neck and peered inside in the failing evening light. The Element that was securely held within lay inert among the little seeds that had once filled the pouch to its top; now all that was left would barely cover the palm of his hand if tipped out. With thumb and forefinger, he pinched out one of the seeds and held it up against the deep purple sky.

How important were they now, those tiny seeds?

With a more powerful magic in his possession, how could they hold sway over his life any longer?

With a snap of the wrist he threw the seed into the water and lost it as soon as it dropped below the surface, swallowed by the immensity of the sea just as a single day is lost within eternity.

A single day. Each seed counting down what was left of a life. What subtle cruelty it was to be allowed to live but be given the vision of one's days draining away, to know with certainty when the last of them would come.

Adeyemi tightened the cord, securing the contents of the pouch and turned to make his way back into the city. Perhaps with what he had found, he could cheat death after all.

Dachen sat in the harbour watching an ochre sun rise from the Ashkelit Ocean until it became too bright to look at. Soon the tide would turn, and they could be on their way, homeward bound.

What sort of home would he find? A kingdom under his brother Chapok, the brother who had sworn to see him killed on his return, or had his father's health returned in his absence? He knew in his heart that King Gephal would not have survived for long after Dachen's departure; the years had whittled the man away to a spirit, barely tethered to a failing body. But the information he carried had to reach Tianpok if his home was to be saved. The knowledge that the Shadows *could* be defeated was as valuable as the methods they had learned from the Shar-hunters of the West.

"It could be you." Dachen was startled from his thoughts. It was Sangye, one of his warriors from Tianpok who had travelled with him this last year. He was leaning on the long shaft of his sparth, the gleaming blade above his head.

"What is that?" he asked.

"The prophecy," Sangye said as he sat beside his prince.

Dachen laughed. "Which one would that be; there are so many?"

"'*When the shadow casts its darkness from the north and the third King of that name passes from the world, cities will fall, and fires will burn high. Look to the west, for the sun shall rise there and bring with it a Saviour. And he shall turn you on your heads...*'"

Dachen nodded slowly. "That is one of them."

"Forgive me for speaking as I do, but I feel that I must take advantage of these last days when I may address you as an equal. Upon our return, I will call you 'Highness', and my tongue will be tied by custom. It was your desire that when in the West we call you by your name and forego the formalities that would mark you as royalty and endanger the mission."

Dachen sighed and motioned for Sangye to go on.

Sangye nodded, accepting the invitation. "I know that you and Chapok are not friends. This is no secret in Lokhara, although it is not openly discussed. I fear, as do you, that we are returning to a kingdom under Chapok, and not King Gephal, which would endanger your life, and by extension the security of the Kingdom. Chapok will not make a wise king." He paused to gauge Dachen's reaction to the last comment but was encouraged when the prince only nodded. "I truly believe that the people would sooner see you upon the throne, and Chapok will know this too. To return as simply the King's brother would put your life at risk, but to return as something greater; someone the people *believed* in and adored would mean that Chapok could not move against you."

"What are you suggesting?" Dachen asked.

"Make yourself the 'Saviour' of the prophecy. Make the people love you more; idolize you even."

Dachen stood, shaking his head. "I do not give those prophecies any credence."

"And yet, the *people* do." Sangye urged. "Listen to the words; *'When the shadow casts its darkness from the north'*; the Shar came from the north."

"Actually, they came from the west," Dachen corrected him with a satisfied smirk.

"No matter," Sangye waved away the objection. "They were first seen in the north and that is what sticks in the minds of people. *'the third king of that name passes from the world'*; Gephal the third." Sangye paused and his excitement was tempered when he spoke again. "I do not mean to make light of..."

"And I did not take it as such," Dachen assured him. "Go on, this is most entertaining."

Sangye continued in a quieter voice. "You can be that 'sun', rising in the west to deliver Tianpok from the Shadows. It will give them hope and Chapok could not act against you then."

Dachen sighed. "I thank you for your concern, but I will not hide behind the prophecies of lunatics when I next face my brother. If he sits upon the throne, then so be it. Besides," he added with a wry smile, placing a hand on Sangye's shoulder, "how would I go about turning people on their heads?"

The sound of hooves on cobbles alerted them to the rest of their party arriving at the docks. Adeyemi was with the other eleven soldiers and their horses, and of course Tsering, the aged alchemist with the mule that carried the sealed urns strapped to its sides. The contents of those urns had proved useful at Ul-an-Balsan, but all the same Dachen would be happier without them on board a wooden ship surrounded by water.

He could not help himself, he had to ask. "Are they sealed?"

Tsering answered with a gap-toothed grin and a laugh that did little to reassure him.

Did one need to be insane to be drawn to alchemy in the first instance, or did the task itself addle the mind?

Adeyemi came close enough to Dachen to speak without being overheard by the rest of the group.

"The Shar-hunters are here," he murmured. "And they are not alone."

Dachen looked down the length of the granite harbour with a growing sense of unease. Fifty yards or so away in each direction, the broad, cobbled docks were filling with dozens of armed men, mounted and on foot. Standing out from the gathering crowd, the armour of a dozen Heavy Cavalry shone in the morning sun. The dock workers and stevedores, seeing the gathering force, had started to melt away into warehouses and side-streets. Alerted to the sudden tension, the rest of Dachen's escort grabbed their weapons, stringing bows with practised ease or bringing sparths to bear.

"Hold!" Dachen barked. The Easterners held their ground, arrows nocked but not drawn and sparths held in defensive postures. "Do nothing to provoke attack."

He glanced up the street running perpendicular to the docks, contemplating all options including escape should the need arise, only to see that route filling with armed women and a man he had all but forgotten.

"Do you seek to rob me still, bandit?" he called out to the man who was lurking at the edge of the group of women.

"I wish only to talk!" A voice from the direction of the Cavalry on the docks. He recognised the man approaching as the historian, Granger.

"I misjudged you, historian. I was sure that I saw an honourable man in you," Dachen said as the old man drew closer. "Yet the company you keep suggests otherwise."

"Will you speak with me?" Granger insisted.

"We are speaking, are we not?"

"You know why we are here," Granger went on as he approached. "And we are willing to offer a fair price for it, if that is what you seek. We only wish to see a peaceful end to this."

"You would not have brought an army to this negotiation if you were indeed peaceful in your intentions. Nor a thief and his harlots," Dachen replied, glancing down the narrow street. The women had advanced with the bandit, Starling, skulking behind their ranks.

What kind of a man would be seen cowering behind his women?

Granger stopped a few yards short of the point of the nearest sparth. "I do not know anything about that."

"Then you should choose your friends with more care."

"You know what we want," Granger continued. "You must know that the Element can do you no good. Please return it to us so that it can be destroyed."

Adeyemi clutched the pouch that hung around his neck and pulled the crude impanga from its sheath on his back. He rested the broad, heavy blade on his shoulder. Dachen laid a restraining hand on the man's scarred forearm.

"Your land is safe now," Dachen said. "Let us return to ours. You told me yourself that the Element was useless; why bloody the cobbles over something that has no power?"

"We have to be certain," Granger replied. "At worst, there are those who might be willing to kill for it if they learned of its existence."

"Like your friends?" Dachen pointed to the force massed behind Granger.

"Wars have been fought over less; empires destroyed. Belief is more powerful than truth, Dachen."

Dachen looked behind at the Shar-hunters gathered there, then at the Cavalry and hunters ahead. Finally, he looked to the women standing in the street, brandishing their weapons as though it should induce fear in him.

He leaned towards Adeyemi and whispered. "Would you relinquish the Element?"

"I will not," he replied. "But I will not ask you to bleed for me." Then he smiled, that broad, infectious grin. "Do not seek to defend me. I will not die today, friend Dachen."

The leader of the group of women, the arrogant girl who had treated him with such discourtesy on their first meeting, stepped forward.

"Do as he asks!" she demanded.

Granger groaned and held up a hand to silence her, but Dachen's mind, which had been teetering on the cusp of discretion, toppled with that final nudge. Men, he could barter with, but not when they allowed their *women* to speak for them. *She* would not have the satisfaction of seeing him acquiesce to her demands. He drew his sword, and on cue his escort assumed offensive stances around him.

"No!" Granger protested. "This is madness."

The forces at both ends of the port edged nearer with a clatter of horseshoes on the granite stones as the tension in the air ramped up like a thunderhead filled to bursting and eager to rain blood.

"Sails!" A cry cut through the thickening cloud of dreadful anticipation from somewhere high upon the harbour walls. "Sails on the horizon! Dozens! Hundreds!"

Dachen lowered his sword and turned his head to the sea. There was nothing on the horizon but the hazy sparkle of a distant swell as far as his eyes could tell. But maybe a hint of a shape at the furthest extent of his vision; a tell-tale block of deeper brume that could be a sail. Then another; as his eyes attuned to the glare and dancing light of the indistinct skyline he saw another, and then more, and with glacial slowness a forest of sails inched from the brine to reveal a fleet of ships larger than he imagined possible.

"What is this?" Granger breathed as he watched the flotilla grow. "Do you bring war?"

Dachen stared in confusion at the horizon. "No," he insisted. "I know nothing of this, I swear it."

Marlon stood on the stone ramparts of the city walls, watching the ships approach. His beard had filled out over the past days and was no longer driving him to distraction with the prickling irritation that had plagued him earlier. He knew that it was a churlish thought but knowing that Valia disliked the beard allowed him a sense of satisfied defiance; when she returned, she could think what she liked.

All around him on the ramparts and the docks curious onlookers were gathering as they began to realise that the ships did not pose an immediate threat. These were not warships approaching, but a dispirited gathering of vessels ranging from three-masted barques to fishing boats filled with bedraggled, half-starved exiles. The larger ships clamoured at the mouth of the harbour while smaller boats beached where they could along the coastline and disgorged their pitiful cargoes onto the sand. Small clusters of people on the low cliffs grew to large masses in a short time and still the boats came.

Jon arrived at Marlon's side, pushing through the crowd to do so, with his hand resting on the hilt of his sword. He sucked air in through his teeth and then let out a long, low whistle. "What do you make of this?" he asked.

Marlon grunted. Memories of refugees fleeing a Jendayan invasion flooded back as he watched the dejected huddles gathering on the dock and on the distant beaches. People clung to loved ones, afraid to let go lest they be swept away by events outside their control. He did not need to be close enough to see their faces to know that they held the hollow stares of those who had witnessed horrors beyond their capacity to resolve.

"There is already talk of the fall of the Eastern Kingdoms," Jon went on. "That the Shar have chased them from their cities. There may be gold to be earned yet." He shifted his grip on the pommel of his sword, revealing the polished, grinning skull that adorned it.

Marlon shook his head. "They never threatened us like this," he murmured. "Look at those people, they have been forced from their homes in their thousands."

"We have beaten the Shar before," Jon said with a shrug.

"Where is Granger?" Marlon asked after a moment's introspection.

"I last saw him on the docks, still trying to talk sense into that crazy Easterner and his dark-skinned friend."

Marlon spun on his heel and pushed through the crowd, with Jon struggling to keep up as the press of bodies closed in the bigger man's wake. Back on the docks, they were jostled by crowds of dismayed easterners, fresh off the few ships that had squeezed into the harbour, as local militiamen barked orders in a language the newcomers could not comprehend. The militia were disinclined to allow the new arrivals to enter the city proper, preferring to corral them on the cobbled docks until the ruling council could give clear orders and formulate a plan. Many of the Easterners were clearly soldiers, carrying weapons that they looked ready to use at the slightest provocation and their anxiety was palpable.

At last, Marlon found Granger who was following Dachen and his escort at a distance while the Easterner was asking frantic questions of his dazed countrymen. The women were silent behind gauzy veils and kept their eyes averted, but the men babbled in response to Dachen's questions, some breaking down in tears as they did so. Marlon could only guess at what was being said in the eastern tongue, but he knew distress when he saw it.

"What is happening?" Marlon asked as he reached Granger's side. "Have you learned anything?"

"It is difficult to be sure," Granger replied, just as a fight broke out between the city militia and a group of eastern men attempting to push out of the docks and into Banihat itself.

A sudden shout went up, and every eastern man and woman turned towards the source and sank to one knee, heads bowed. The last to kneel were Dachen's escort, and they did so with reluctance as an elegantly dressed man, dripping with jewels and gold chains made his way across a gangplank towards dry land.

Only Dachen remained on his feet, and the hatred in his gaze could have melted stone.

Dachen watched as his brother walk onto the cobbled dock followed by four sparth-carrying guards. The lead guard's gaze was locked onto Dachen who recognised the contemptuous smirk as soon as he saw it.

Jangbu! How had that man found his way into Chapok's service?

"You keep poor company, brother," Dachen sneered.

"Will you not kneel before your king?" Chapok demanded.

"What have you done, Chapok? Have you brought ruin to the Kingdom already?" Dachen glared back at his brother. While the rest of his countrymen looked hungry and dressed in filthy rags, Chapok's lips were wet with the grease of a recent meal and his clothing looked clean and fresh.

"Do not dare to blame me for this. The Kingdoms have all fallen to the Shadows."

"And you simply fled?" Dachen was incredulous.

"Brave words from one who abandoned his home to follow a fool's quest. It was you who fled, Dachen. Now," Chapok leered, "will you bend your knee before me, and save your neck from the garrotte or does foolish pride still rule your mind?"

Dachen only shook his head, shifting his gaze between his brother and the guard at his shoulder.

"Perhaps Jangbu would relish the opportunity to bring you to your knees once again," Chapok goaded.

Jangbu smiled but no warmth touched the expression, the curled lips of a wolf.

Dachen glowered back at his brother. "You have no authority over me here. That privilege lies in the wake you left upon the Ashkelit Ocean."

"I have such authority, little brother," he sneered. "Over you, and your *escort*. They will enter *my* service now; you are alone in your pitiful defiance."

"The Shadows can be defeated," Dachen insisted. "But not by the likes of you and not while we show them our backs."

Chapok gestured east across the water. "Then by all means go. I will not mourn your passing, just as I did not mourn our father's."

Dachen lunged with a snarl, clawed hands desperate to close around the soft folds of his brother's neck. In a flash, Jangbu lowered his sparth and Dachen stopped just as the razor point pricked the skin beneath his left eye. Jangbu flicked the sparth to the side and Dachen felt the tug of flesh being cut. He raised a hand and felt the wetness with his fingers and took a step back, never taking his eyes off his brother.

"I will never kneel before you," Dachen hissed through clenched teeth. "A king is nothing without a kingdom and you have abandoned your birth right. You are not worthy of my loyalty." He spat onto the cobbles at Chapok's feet before turning on his heel and storming into the surrounding crowd, eliciting angry protests as he did.

Chapok smiled. "I will see your neck in a rope, brother," he murmured. "My birth right will be mine once again, and more besides."

More shouts, and the protests of people being pushed aside by the city's militia heralded the arrival of Banihat's rulers on the docks. Chapok smoothed his loose garments over his ample belly with bejewelled fingers and prepared himself to negotiate.

Serendipity was a curious thing, and Rogan Fol'Brandam considered the events of the past few days with something nearing disbelief. Upon reaching Banihat, he had found the city engulfed in a crisis that had tens of thousands of refugees from the Eastern Kingdoms filling not only the city, but the fields surrounding its granite walls. The ruling council in Banihat were overwhelmed, and the timely arrival of Rogan and his escort of nearly a thousand soldiers had practically been welcomed with open arms. Among the refugees were thousands of soldiers from the four kingdoms of the East, a force which could have conquered the city in a heartbeat, had that been their intention, and the Korathean offer of Protectorate status for Kylyptus had been embraced as the lesser of two evils. Liberation from their previous occupation had come because of Korathean withdrawal in the aftermath of the battle of Hadaiti when the Heavy Infantry were so heavily defeated. As a result, Kylyptians had little sense of national identity. Discussions with the fledgling ruling council had been short, with the Kylyptians eager to make the 'eastern problem' a

Korathean one.

He looked at the banner behind his desk in the spacious command tent and wondered at the fortuity of that too. The banner his ancestors had raised when Kor'Habat was young, when Shol'Hara was establishing the Heavy Infantry as the force it was today, had not been carried on campaign for centuries. But Korathea was changing, and old symbols would usher in a new age with fresh leaders anchored to a glorious past. There was a prophecy - not that Rogan put any stock in such things - that the Easterners clung to for hope; a belief that the sun would rise in the west and bring them salvation. His arrival at Banihat under the banner depicting a yellow sun behind a simple castle had stirred the deep-seated beliefs in many of these people.

Some even saw *him* as their saviour.

But, while the 'eastern problem' had helped in convincing the ruling council to accept Korathean rule again, the arrival of a displaced nation complete with a small, desperate army did give him cause for concern.

He was looking out from the high window which offered a marvellous view onto the ocean beyond the city walls. His were among the finest rooms in Banihat, as was only proper, and it made a welcome change from the drudgery of tented camps. He poured himself another cup of wine and turned from the window just as Olgoi Kinbataar was shown in by a towering Korathean guard.

Rogan sipped at the wine. "What news?" he asked.

Olgoi tipped his head. "Hatar, you are aware that the council awaits you in its chambers, along with many other interested parties? I believe that noon was the agreed time for this meeting, and the sun has long since passed its zenith."

Rogan took a long time to answer. "I have only just poured myself a cup of wine. I am sure they can wait."

"Indeed," Olgoi reasoned, "but their patience is being tested, would you not agree?"

Rogan took a slow sip from the cup, holding Olgoi's gaze. "You speak of 'patience', yet what progress has been made regarding our arrangement?"

Olgoi winced. "It has been chaotic of late; events have only gathered pace since my arrival here. I have made contact this very morning with one of those who might be willing to accept the task."

"'*Might* be willing'? You assured me that you had the contacts and knowledge to see this through," Rogan growled.

Olgoi raised both hands. "It is only a matter of time; I have no doubt. Your target is formidable, and the task must be carried out in such a way…"

"That it does not lead back to me," Rogan completed the sentence. "Your agent must have no knowledge of my involvement. Is that clear?"

"Of course." Olgoi bowed his head.

"Now leave me." Rogan turned his back on the Kylyptian and returned to the vista beyond the window.

Olgoi hesitated. "The meeting?"

"I will be there when I am ready. Do not press me for more."

The warning in his voice was enough for Olgoi Kinbataar, and he left the room with more haste than he had intended, favouring safety over decorum, and made his way to the chambers.

"At last, our Korathean overlord deigns to meet with us!" Abbil said, just loud enough for all to hear when Rogan finally arrived in the council chambers. The chatter quietened as all eyes fell upon the newcomer.

Rogan did not respond, instead he sat without a word and hefted a heavy boot up onto the large, circular wooden table around which they had gathered, and motioned for the council speaker to begin.

Belghutai Juchen was a woman of advanced years with hair that was more grey than dark. She wore her hair secured in a bun at the top of her head that pulled the skin of her forehead tight. This combined with her lean, sinewy frame gave her a severe look that was more than just superficial. Her success in business had seen her rise in power and prominence until the Korathean withdrawal from Banihat had opened the door to a political career. Her disapproval of Rogan and the disrespect he showed was evident from the tension in her body, but her face gave nothing away.

"I will call this meeting to order," she declared before the susurrus could become any louder. "Now that Hatar Rogan Fol'Brandam has joined us, we are to discuss the crisis that currently grips the city and forge consensus on what actions to take. I acknowledge King Chapok, son of Gephal, ruler of the eastern kingdom of Tianpok, and extend my sympathies to him for the grave situation that has befallen his home."

Chapok was flanked by a gaggle of advisors and aides, who hunched in their seats to keep their heads below his own. His guard, Jangbu, stood behind. As a royal guard, his first duty was to the safety of the King, and so his posture was a necessary indulgence.

Chapok gave a solemn nod in return before the speaker continued.

"I welcome Prince Dachen of Tianpok, reunited with his kin, sadly not in happier circumstances."

Dachen did not respond, but glared at Chapok from across the table, both fists balled in front of him. Belghutai registered the animosity that boiled in Dachen's eyes and moved swiftly on.

"Also joining us are representatives from the Shar-hunting community, who have worked so hard to rid our own land of the scourge. I recognise Marlon Padar, Abbil Musharit, Acastes Fol'Denes, Kapaneus Paras, Alano Clemente and Jon…" She waited for the Shar-hunter to offer more.

"Jon will do, my dear," he declared. "Any man in need of more to define him isn't trying hard enough."

A few chuckles rippled through the room, and Belghutai

sighed with the sort of tolerance a grandparent reserves for a small child.

"I would also like to welcome Elan Arellan of Lythuria," she went on. "It is an unexpected honour to receive such an... *unusual* guest."

Elan made no sign of recognising his name or the welcome and Belghutai cocked her head in agitation until Granger leaned forward to speak.

"Forgive my friend," he said. "He does not seek to offend. His experience of his surroundings is not as we would know it."

"Ah, Granger. The historian," she said. "I had not forgotten you. Tell me, is it a trait common to all of his people?"

Rogan banged a fist on the table, startling Belghutai from her pleasantries. "Is this why you have called me here? So that I may witness you enquire into the workings of the minds of animals? Look at his flesh; does that green hue not tell you that he is not a man but a beast?"

Alano placed a restraining hand on Jon's arm as the hunter tensed in anger and Rogan continued to speak.

"You tell me that you want to discuss action yet natter like fish-wives over this *pet*?"

Belghutai sat even more erect if it were possible. "It is important that all parties are acquainted, to better find a solution to this complex problem."

Rogan swung his leg down and leaned forward, placing his crossed arms on the table. "It is not a complex problem, but a re-markably simple one. A defeated King has crossed an ocean to beg for aid from a neighbour he despises. The only question should be: How much should he pay to retain the right to squat upon Korathean soil?"

He locked eyes with the king and awaited an answer.

Chapok showed no sign of taking offence; instead, he listened to the whispers of one of his aides and replied in fluent Korath-ean. "We did not abandon our wealth and will gladly pay for grain and meat."

"No!" Dachen said through clenched teeth. "We should be discussing our return to Tianpok, not the means by which we cower here."

"And I have already invited you to try," Chapok replied in the Eastern tongue.

"Then give me command of the armies," Dachen urged, slipping back into his native language. *"You can do as you please, but do not abandon our home to the Shadows."*

Belghutai cleared her throat. "I think it would be best if we were all to speak a common tongue. As we are not familiar with your own, I suggest we use that which we all understand."

Chapok continued in his own language, locking eyes with Dachen. *"I would have thought you would wish to remain here yourself in this barbarous land. Their women, like yourself, lack respect when addressing a King."* Then he offered an ingratiating smile to Belghutai and reverted to Korathean. "Of course."

"If I may," Granger volunteered, "I would like to take a moment to reflect on the position we find ourselves in. Perhaps my knowledge of the histories of our lands and those beyond could hold answers to our questions as well as possible solutions. It is after all, a *shared* problem."

Rogan grunted in censure but said nothing and so Belghutai motioned for him to continue. Granger stood to address the room, smoothing a creased shirt over his stomach.

"I have spent much of the last few days gathering the accounts of those who witnessed the events in the Kingdoms of the East. Some are contradictory; while others defy belief, and yet in trying to paint a picture of what has taken place across the Ashkelit, I have listened to the words of one whose testimony could never be held in any doubt; those of King Chapok himself." Granger bowed a little to lower his head at the mention of the King's name, and Chapok acknowledged the gesture by raising his chin. "The Shar have been in the East for almost as long as they have blighted our own lands; something that we here did not foresee and that is to our own great chagrin. To the north of here and beyond the steppe where even the Hetai nomads are loath to go is a land of ice and snow where life cannot be sustained. In the coldest of winters, the brine of the ocean itself turns to ice and bridges the Ashkelit, joining our two continents. The winter that followed the battle at Ara Dasari was colder than most. I remember thinking only of the cruelty of Fate for visiting such hardship upon the many thousands of dispossessed who had survived the Jendayan advance, only to find the elements turn against them before they had rebuilt their lives. I did not consider that it would allow the Shar to spread beyond this place."

"The Shadows did come from the north," Dachen confirmed. "We knew that they had come from here across the frozen ocean. We were able to fight them for a time."

"And then they started to change," Granger said. "At least, some did; two that we know of were changed by the events at Ara Dasari, imbued with the ability to become more than the others of their kind."

"But we have seen them defeated here," Dachen insisted. "It will be so in Tianpok also. We need only to stand against them."

"And your courage is a credit to your people, but I fear that the Shar that invaded your homeland are driven by something more terrible than we have seen here." Granger hesitated, taking care over how he chose his next words. He could not tell them the truth; could not expect these people to believe that he had once been an immortal Emissary. Marlon and Alano knew, and they were watching him now, willing him not to push the trust of his audience too far with tales of watchful beings on an unseen plane. "There are written accounts of a Shar variant known as the Khalim-Shar, or Great Shar. Their purpose was to lead their lesser fellows in battle, and I believe that is what has found its way into the Eastern Kingdoms."

Belghutai cleared her throat. "Tell me; from where did you

glean this knowledge? I consider myself well-read, yet I had never heard of Shar before, let alone this Great Shar you speak of."

Granger nodded before continuing. "The Jendayan Empire was the last place the Shar were seen, in the accounts of a forgotten war. Centuries ago, the people there were able to drive those last remaining Shar into a system of caves and collapse the tunnels, sealing them inside. Abaddon retrieved a few before his invasion of this continent, but knowledge of their existence elsewhere has faded from memory."

Marlon shifted in his seat, clenching a fist at the memory of their first encounter with the Shar in the mountains to the north of Arbis Mora. His brother, Foley had died that day, and his death had instilled a hatred for the Shar so intense that he could feel it like a knot in his chest that greeted him each morning and burned through every waking hour.

"Tales of this, *Abaddon* reached us too in recent years," Dachen muttered. "I would not have believed a word of them had the Shadows' existence not given them credence."

"And he would have destroyed your Kingdom had we not stopped him at Ara Dasari," Alano added. "He would have destroyed everything."

"His Shar do no less," Dachen retorted.

"No," said Granger, "I believe you are wrong there." He cleared his throat and continued as he found himself at the centre of everyone's attention again. "From what I have learned in the past few days, whatever leads the eastern Shar has a different aim, not merely destruction but dominion. Every account I listened to from those I asked told only of the people's terror as they fled the slaughter, with the Shar leaving nothing in their wake; all but one. A young fisherman who had been at sea when his village was taken returned to find his home burning and his family gone. Terrified, he turned his boat to the south and followed the coast to where he knew a larger settlement lay, desperate for answers and hoping beyond hope that he would find his loved ones there. When he reached the town, he found that it too had been sacked, but not abandoned. There were soldiers; Eastern soldiers camped outside the smouldering ruins, and Shar walked among them un-hindered."

"That is a lie!" Dachen spat. "No Eastern soldier, of any kingdom would allow it!"

Granger ignored the outburst and continued. "A young woman saw the fishing boat and ran towards the beach, shouting to the fisherman who was too far from shore to hear her words. The woman continued into the water, braving the breaking waves and began swimming out to sea, but she had alerted the soldiers, who gave chase. The fisherman battled against an unfavourable wind, trying to close the distance between himself and the fleeing woman but the soldiers shot arrows at her from the beach. He reached her just as her strength gave out and dived into the water with a rope around his waist to pull her back to the surface. An arrow had found her shoulder, but she was alive, and the fisherman managed to pull her onto his boat and let the wind push them to safety." He paused for a moment, to be certain he had everyone's attention. "She died soon after that and the fisherman headed north until he found the flotilla of ships that arrived here just days ago. Before she died from her wounds, she uttered four words; four words that the fisherman repeated to me. What she said chills me to the bone and tells of a terrible intelligence that only a Khalim-Shar could possess."

Belghutai was leaning forwards, her mouth agape as she listened. "What did she say?"

Granger turned to her and hesitated a moment before speaking. "'*We are being farmed*'"

Rogan burst out laughing. "So, the Shar have turned to farming now?"

Marlon nodded as the news sank in, ignoring Rogan's outburst. "It makes sense if you take the time to think about it. The Shar are trapped here now. If they are to have a future, they would surely seek to dominate us."

"Please," Rogan insisted. "This has gone too far. The Shar cannot dominate; when they stood together at Ulan Balsan the Heavy Cavalry crushed them."

Now it was Abbil's turn to laugh. "You entered the fight late, when it was already won."

"We finished what you could not!" Rogan said with a dismissive wave.

"You are like the young wolf," Abbil boomed, enjoying the sport of goading the Korathean Hatar, "coming to the kill to enjoy the spoils, but only after the stronger members of the pack have pulled the beast down."

Rogan laughed. "Our arrival was perfectly timed. I waited until the Shar were certain of victory and not expecting a new attack before I moved."

"Many men died while you waited," Kapaneus added in admonishment, and Acastes rubbed his healing ribs at the memory of his own brush with death.

"It is the burden of every great Hatar that he must sacrifice those under his command," Rogan lectured. "Victory is bought with the blood of *lesser* men."

"The blood of others is spent more freely by the cowardly," Kapaneus muttered in disgust.

Rogan waved away the comment as he would a troublesome fruit fly. "I will not debate tactics with such as yourself. The endgame is all."

"And what is your '*endgame*'?" Kapaneus asked, leaning forwards to put his weight on the table. Acastes made a quieting gesture, but Kapaneus went on. "What '*tactic*' did you employ at Ulan-Balsan to advance your aims?"

Abbil and Jon both started talking at once, hurling accusations and questions at Rogan as Belghutai tried to calm the room.

Alano, who had been deep in thought, cleared his throat and looked up. "'You do not slaughter the ox that pulls the plough'," he said over the noise of the argument, and all eyes turned to him. "It is a saying among the farmers of Bal Mora, and its meaning is clear, I think."

"As clear as Autumn mist," Rogan muttered.

"The Shar could live on goats and rabbit for as long as the land sustained them," Alano said. "But there is no flesh so sweet to the Shar as our own. They need us."

"Alano is right," Granger agreed. "The Shar need us to grow the crops that sustain ourselves and our livestock. They *could* slaughter us and have a feast that lasted a few years at most, or they could control us and aim to keep a steady supply of human meat at their claw-tips for millennia."

Rogan snorted. "All this. All of this from four words?"

"I *know* the Khalim-Shar," Granger replied. "It has a mind of pure malice; underestimate it at your peril."

Dachen banged the table. "We must return!" he shouted. "If the people suffer, we *must* act now!"

"With what, brother," Chapok sneered.

"Gather every soldier we have! Every man and boy able to lift a sparth or draw a bow, and sail east again!"

"You would not stand a chance," Chapok replied. "Our own soldiers stood against us; we are too few."

"Why!" Dachen asked. "Why did they fight alongside the Shadows? Is it because of the weakness they saw in you?"

"Once again, you utter words that would have you garrotted in Tianpok. I am your King!"

"Not here!" Dachen yelled, banging the table again.

"Soldiers from the Greater Kingdom of Khumjang, as well as Lhaksang and Shibatsu arrived at our border with an army of Shadows," Chapok replied in a calmer voice. "You should ask *their* Kings why they fought against us, if you are able to find more than mere smears on the floors of their throne rooms. If not for the courage of men like Jangbu, the toll would have been far greater. You see, brother, *he* was *there*."

Dachen slumped back in his chair, and silence fell on the room.

Granger was the first to speak after the lull. "People choose their sides for many reasons," he said. "Perhaps greed; perhaps promises have been made to protect their loved ones. We may feel, here in this room, that to side with the Shar is abhorrent, and it is, but people do not turn against their own without reason. Now, we know that there are survivors in the wake of the Shar advance, and if I am correct then they have been kept alive for a reason. I believe that reason is to supply food for the Shar."

"Then leave them there," Rogan muttered. "They pose no threat to us."

"Until the sea freezes again," Granger warned. "And the bridge between our continents can be crossed. Are you willing to take that risk?"

There was another long silence before Rogan spoke again. "I will send scouts," he said with a sigh. "A fast vessel should be able to cross the Ashkelit and be back before the winter has any chance of trapping us here."

"Winter comes early to Kylyptus," Belghutai warned. "Your scouts will need to make haste."

"I do not plan to waste a single day more than is necessary to find out the truth. I will assess the threat myself, and if it is a ruse," he looked to Chapok, "I will act accordingly." The threat hung in the air between them, Chapok managing a slight smile before Rogan stood. "This has taken too much of my time already."

With that, he stood and stormed from the room.

Nirmaya and Starling were sitting in the inn, '*The Weathered Barrel*', watching Elan at the next table in quiet fascination. The Lythurian was sitting with a bundle of arrows set on one side of the table, which he occupied alone, inspecting each arrow in turn with great care before placing it at the other end of the table so that the flights overhung the edge and were not deformed in any way. Every so often he would find an arrow that caused his brow to furrow the slightest amount and would set about re-whipping the fletches or point with fine thread. Occasionally he would make gentle passes over a whetstone to remove imperfections that only he could discern in the pristine arrowheads, and his silent audience would exchange shrugs and perplexed smiles.

A serving boy arrived with a jug of wine and placed it in front of Nirmaya. He was not yet a man but was already broad-shouldered and handsome with a winning, lop-sided smile, which he aimed at her. Her blush was not missed by Starling who stared wide-eyed at his companion until the youngster was out of ear-shot.

"You didn't. Did you?"

Nirmaya shrugged, smirking as she filled her cup and then his.

"He's just a boy," he scolded.

"Oh, I can assure you, he is very much *a man* now," she replied, enjoying Starling's jealousy.

"You're shameless. What would Maidra think of that I wonder?" he muttered, lifting his cup to his lips. "That is still her ring you wear, is it not?"

"What makes you think that Maidra was not there too?" she teased.

Starling choked on the mouthful, spluttering wine across the tabletop, but he did not get a chance to answer.

Elan did not flinch as Nirmaya and Starling did when the doors swung open and a furious group of Shar-hunters stomped in. Jon slumped into a chair beside Elan, gesturing to the serving boy who, knowing his customers by now, set about preparing a tray of drinks. Marlon, Granger, Alano, Abbil, Acastes and Kapaneus joined Nirmaya and Starling at their table, pulling chairs and stools from elsewhere in the room. *The Weathered Barrel* was quiet; most of the inhabitants of Banihat were busy at work, and the few Easterners who were inside the city were not drinkers, and so steered clear of the inns where wine and ale were the main draw.

Starling found the eastern people to be most frustrating. The fact that very few spoke even the most basic words of the Korathean language was a barrier in itself, and although a winning smile and a wink had usually been enough to thaw even the chilliest of foreign maidens, this had not been the case with the Easterners. The veiled women would not raise their eyes to meet his own, and the men growled at him whenever he showed too much interest. A pity really, since behind the gauzy veils they were a most delightfully delicate race indeed.

"What news, gentlemen?" Starling asked, sipping at his cup.

"Scouts," Abbil grumbled. "A nation is uprooted, and Rogan sends scouts."

"But that will take weeks," Nirmaya said, all mischief gone from her face. "Months, even."

"What did you expect him to do?" Jon said, inspecting one of the arrows that Elan was so preoccupied with. "In defence of the arrogant arse, it is not his problem but an Eastern one."

Elan took the arrow from Jon's hands and returned it to its place on the table, just as the serving boy arrived with two jugs of wine and six cups, and a mug of foaming ale for Jon.

"Chapok did not appear eager to liberate his homeland either," Abbil muttered. "It seems that his brother, Dachen was the only one born with courage."

Kapaneus declined to have a cup filled for himself, even as Acastes took a long drink from his own. "Does it matter?" Kapaneus asked. "Acastes, we should return to Kor'Habat; you know we must."

"And miss the opportunity to earn a few more marks in the East?" Acastes said in mock horror, his humour having returned as the pain in his side had faded. "How could you say such a thing?"

"They do not want our help," Kapaneus insisted.

"Then they are fools," Abbil added.

"They are proud," Granger said. "But a Khalim-Shar will take a unified force to defeat. Time wears mountains to sand, and it will be so with their intransigence. None of us is safe as long as a Khalim-Shar can walk the land; we must accept the burden even if it is not freely shared."

"How many of the hunters will work for free?" Abbil asked. "If the Eastern king does not want our help, he will surely not promise a bounty to secure it."

"Freedom is its own bounty," Alano replied.

"But does not pay for ale," Jon countered.

"What would Valia do?" Nirmaya asked, a certain breathlessness creeping into her voice, as it did every time she spoke that name.

"Valia is not here," Marlon muttered, his resentment of the fact made clear by his tone.

"Then we should find her," she said in excitement. "She came this way; didn't you tell me?"

"If Valia wanted to be here, then she would be here. She will not come if beckoned or bullied."

"When she hears of what has happened, she will come," Nirmaya said with certainty.

"You sound very sure of that, considering you have never met the woman," Abbil said.

Starling chuckled. "Does Maidra know that your heart flutters like a moth against the flame of Valia's name?" he teased with a little more venom than usual.

Nirmaya sniffed in response and buried her blushes in her wine cup.

"You must believe that she will return soon," Jon said to Marlon. "Otherwise why did you bring her armour with you?"

Marlon just shrugged and glowered at his wine. The owner of *The Shar's Folly* had not been keen to hand over Valia's belongings after being entrusted with their care, but the risk of facing Valia's ire was a distant and uncertain peril; Marlon had been far more immediate. "She will need them sooner than she thinks," he had said, and where the innkeeper might have argued against reason, he was unwilling to quarrel with a man who killed Shar for a living, especially one who was looming over him there and then, and so had given in after a short, principled protest.

Granger cleared his throat. "Regardless of Valia's absence, we do not yet know enough to act. We should be patient and hope that the scouts Rogan sends are favoured with good winds to speed their journey."

Jon banged his empty tankard on the table and waved to the serving boy for a refill. "Then we should take full advantage of the hospitality here while we wait." He lifted a fluted shaft from the table to inspect Elan's work with an admiring eye once again.

Elan took the arrow from Jon's hand and returned it to the table with no outward display of emotion.

"In all my years as a fletcher, I have never seen a man treat an arrow with as much reverence as you, Elan," Jon said, fishing for some sort of reaction. His eyes brightened as a fresh tankard arrived in front of him, and a fresh jug of wine was placed beside it.

"I doubt you have ever held anything in such high regard as you do a mug of ale," Abbil chuckled.

"You sound like my wife," he replied, wiping froth from his mouth.

"You have never uttered a kind word about that poor woman," Kapaneus laughed. "Why did you ever marry her?"

Jon winced. "We have all experienced a moment of madness, no?"

The little Jendayan, Kekoa, arrived at Acastes' side, bowing his head as he offered a small, fold of paper to his master. Acastes opened it to see what it contained. He raised an eyebrow and passed it to Marlon who read the message in silence.

"Valia has been here," he muttered. "She passed through several days ago and continued north according to this. The man who gathered this information believes that he knows where she is. A farm."

"You owe me a silver mark," Acastes jested. "The best

informants do not come cheap. According to that note, she was looking for someone. Anyone I should know about?"

"No," Marlon said quickly.

"Will we go to find her?" Nirmaya asked.

Marlon folded the note again and pushed it into a pocket. "No," he muttered. "Not yet."

Acastes broke the awkward silence, ordering Kekoa to refill his wine. The Jendayan lifted the fresh jug from Elan's table and filled his master's cup, bowing as he withdrew. Acastes raised the cup to his lips a moment before a crash of shattering pottery stopped him. He dropped the cup in alarm, splashing the dark liquid across the table as every hand went for whatever weapon it could.

"Elan!" Jon barked, having spilled his ale down his front at the sudden noise. "What are you doing?"

"Have you gone mad?" Acastes spluttered, looking at the mess on the table and floor.

Elan had returned to his task after knocking the wine from the table, and was rolling a shaft between his fingers, laying the whipping twine in perfect, touching turns.

Kapaneus was on his feet. "Wait. What is that?" He walked to where the shattered jug lay on the floorboards and found the flat base section that was still intact with a shallow pool of wine held in the remains. He dipped his finger in the liquid and rubbed it against his thumb, then sniffed at it. "*Black-root*," he said in disgust, wiping his hand on his trousers. "This wine has been poisoned!"

"What?" Acastes gasped, wiping his mouth across his sleeve to remove any drops that may have reached his lips. His gaze swung to Kekoa whose mouth had barely opened in surprise before Acastes had him by the throat.

"Stop!" Granger shouted, "It could not have been him. The wine was brought before his arrival with the message."

Acastes loosened his grip, allowing Kekoa to draw a few ragged gasps of air, but his gaze still held pure hatred for the Jendayan.

Kapaneus had rounded up the serving boy by the time Acastes had allowed his servant to slump to the floor and was holding the terrified youth by the back of his collar as he dragged him to the table. Starling was smelling the jug he had emptied only moments ago, his mouth suddenly dry and all colour gone from his cheeks.

"Is it…?" Nirmaya began.

"I don't think so," he stammered, but did not sound convinced as the serving boy arrived babbling at the table.

"I swear, my lord, the wine was paid for by another," he blurted. "I only turned my back for a moment to draw the ale and he was gone. I thought you knew him; I swear I know nothing of poison."

"Let him go, Kapaneus," Granger sighed. "He is only a boy; he would not do this."

"That is possibly true," Abbil said. "But then, who would?"

"Describe this person," Acastes ordered.

"I don't know," the terrified boy managed. "A man. Just a man…"

"Hopeless," Acastes hissed, turning away from the lad. His eyes fell upon Elan and he stared for a long moment before asking in a low voice. "How did you know?"

All eyes turned to Elan who was returning each arrow with great care to his quiver, as disinterested in his surroundings as ever.

"You knew that wine was poisoned," Acastes persisted. "How did you know!" He banged a fist on the table as Elan stowed the last arrow and made to leave.

"Leave him," Jon said. "You won't get anything from him."

"I could beat it from him!" Acastes threatened as Elan stood and walked away.

"He was probably the only one watching while the rest of us talked. Look, he and I had a clear view to the taps. I was too busy with our conversation to see anything suspicious, but Elan…?"

"Then he is the only one who can identify the poisoner," Acastes glowered at Elan's back as the Lythurian left the building.

"Then we should keep him close," Granger warned. "Not chase him away with threats."

"He is mad!" Acastes spat.

"He saved your life," Abbil said, raising a bushy eyebrow.

Acastes struggled for an answer but could think of none. "The sooner Rogan's scouts return, the better. This waiting will kill me as sure as any black-root." He turned and stormed from the inn. Kapaneus offered an apologetic smile before following and Kekoa, who had just about recovered from his master's assault on him, was close behind.

The days were simple and peaceful. At times, when she took a break from her efforts and the only sound was the whisper of gentle waves on the sand or the distant lament of a seabird, Valia felt as though she was the only living soul in the world.

This was a peace that she had never known before and there was something in the nature of the labour that carried her to each day's end with a sense of satisfaction. The callouses on her palms were still there, thicker if anything, but they had not come from wielding a weapon as they once had. That life felt as distant as the land beyond the horizon; extant yet remote.

She had been leading some of the sturdy goats back to pastures nearer Surilya's homestead, as a stubborn few were want to wander many miles in search of sweeter grass. The hollow, lazy sound of the bells they wore was enough to help locate them, and then a little gentle cajoling with a stick did the rest. It was late in the afternoon when she reached the building that had been her home for the last few weeks, and Surilya was stacking bags of flour and salt onto a shelf in the larder.

"You missed Danille," she announced as Valia entered the cosy kitchen.

"The trader?" she replied. "I thought he intended to stay overnight."

Valia went straight to the range and lifted the steaming kettle to prepare tea, gathering two cups with her free hand.

Surilya finished storing the sacks and turned, dusting her hands on the heavy weave of her loose-fitting trousers. "Usually he would, but he was keen to return to Banihat without delay."

"Oh?" Valia glanced up from her task.

"Don't bother with the tea," Surilya said. "I was able to get something a little more special from Danille this time. To suit your 'southern' tastes." She lifted two stoppered, clay jugs in triumph. "Wine, from Pashwar."

Without hesitation, Valia tossed the hot water from the cups into the sink and placed them on the table. Surilya, still holding both jugs, gripped one of the corks in her teeth and grimaced as she twisted it free. It came away with a satisfying pop, releasing the rich, spicy aromas within. She said something incomprehensible from around the large cork at the side of her mouth then cracked a goofy grin. Valia could not help herself; she burst out laughing at the sight, doubling over and weakening at the knees as she roared. She slumped into a chair as tears of mirth ran down her cheeks, giddy from the euphoric rush that had taken her. When last had she laughed like this?

By degrees, she got some measure of control over her breathing as involuntary chuckles still bubbled in her chest, eager to escape. Surilya had stopped her clowning and was able to pour the wine. Valia wiped her cheeks with a sleeve before lifting her cup. She closed her eyes and breathed in to savour the scent before taking a sip of the familiar liquid which she allowed to sit upon her tongue for a few, glorious heartbeats before swallowing. When she opened her eyes again, Surilya was regarding her with a sly smile.

"What were you thinking just then?" She asked.

Valia stared into her cup, at once sombre. "I was trying to remember when I last enjoyed wine like this. It has been a crutch of late; a way to fog the memory and cast a veil over those thoughts I would sooner not ponder."

Surilya lifted her chair and placed it beside Valia, then sat and leaned close. "You do not need to tell me if you choose not to but know that I am here to listen if you need a sympathetic ear."

"Thank you," Valia replied. Then she brightened. "What news did Danille bring from Banihat?"

Surilya leaned back with a dismissive wave. "Let the south stay in the south."

Valia made to take another sip of wine and paused. "There is something you are not telling me."

"It does not matter here."

"What 'does not matter'? Surilya?"

Surilya sighed. "Kylyptus is to be ruled from Kor'Habat again. But," she said as she saw Valia's widening eyes, "it was not taken by force. Banihat has willingly accepted protectorate status to help manage the refugees."

"'Refugees?'" Valia asked, her wine still hovering beneath her lips.

Surilya looked disinclined to speak further on the matter but forced herself to go on. "There is conflict in the East. Danille claims that many have fled."

There was a long silence, and Surilya glanced up at Valia's sword, which hung above the cooking range. "Do you want to take it down?"

Valia leaned back and considered the news. Finally, she took a sip of wine and smiled at Surilya. "No. No I do not." The truth of the statement surprised her; the words could surely not have been uttered by 'Valia of Hadaiti', and yet they had come unbidden from a part of her that was not burdened with the compulsion of responsibility. They were the words of Valia Lushara, the woman behind the mask of scars and fury, stripped bare of all but potential.

Surilya leaned forward and placed her hand on Valia's cheek, her thumb tracing the line of the scar left by the Shar in Depsing. "When the meadow thrush leaves the nest, it roams the wilderness for many years until it finds a new home. Once that home is made, it stays for the rest of its days."

Valia closed her eyes and pressed her cheek into the warmth of Surilya's touch, unashamed and uncaring of the scar. She placed her own hand on Surilya's and brought it round to kiss the palm and fingers.

"I am home," she breathed. "I am home."

CHAPTER 5

Winter came early to Banihat and tightened its icy grip as Shar-hunters and Infantrymen waited for word from the east. Most sought the warmth of taverns and inns and jugs of warm, spiced wine, drawing into ever tighter huddles against the chill and the dark. For all their advancement, humankind was not so different from the animals of the forests and plains. Cold still had them gathering for the warmth they could share and to lift their collective spirits, compelled by primal forces they obeyed without thought.

But for Elan, a man whose phantom soul danced on the knife edge of oblivion, there was no such urge. His wraith-like cognizance had found a new fascination and he pursued it with callous efficiency.

Blood dripped onto the fresh snow as Elan pulled the arrow from the dying man's chest. A final wisp of warmth escaped from between quivering lips, turning to mist in the icy air. Elan squatted down beside the body and stared into glassy eyes as though trying to read the fading mind within.

Including the would-be poisoner from *The Weathered Barrel*, this was the fourth man he had killed since he had arrived in Banihat in the summer. Now, fresh flakes of snow were starting to fall, settling on the soft, black cloak that covered the failed assassin. This one had thought that waiting until the early hours of morning and creeping into the inn to find his sleeping victim would give him a greater chance of success than his predecessors.

He had been wrong.

The first assassin had been sloppy. His initial mistake had been to allow Elan to see him emptying the small pouch into the wine jug. Any number of crimes can be perpetrated in a busy common room, but villains would do well to look out for the quiet, vigilant man in the crowd. His second mistake was in returning to the seedy inn from where he had been recruited to crow about his success before his task had been completed. Discovering who had employed the man had been a simple matter of waiting and following. It had been the leader of the ruling Conclave from Ulan Balsan. Olgoi Kinbataar for his part had also been careless, returning to the same inn time and again to recruit one of the many thieves and cut-throats that frequented the place.

Perhaps now that a fourth had failed, Olgoi would change his approach, and in some small partition of his fractured consciousness Elan knew that he would need to be alert to that. This had become a strange obsession for his abstracted mind. A small spike of something he may once have called curiosity needled at him too; why would Olgoi Kinbataar want to kill Acastes?

The winter was colder than any Valia had experienced for many years, and she was grateful for the comforts of the sturdy farmhouse. The loft where she and Surilya slept extended partly over an enclosed barn of sorts, where over a hundred goats sheltered from the worst of the weather and as a welcome consequence, warmed the room above with their body heat. Valia did not even notice the smell of damp animal hair and dung anymore, not that it had ever been offensive, and she marvelled at how simple the solutions were to life's hardships when one put down roots. A winter on the road could be grim, and she had avoided travel whenever she could when the snow came, but it had been difficult to avoid at times during her old life as a Shar-hunter.

Here, a welcoming stove and warming drink were never far away.

She smiled to herself as she considered this, having just awoken to the gentle sound of goats bleating below and the soft *clonk* of the bells they wore. She moved her hand under the heavy blankets to where her bed met Surilya's, trying to remember when they had moved them together the first time for the warmth that they could offer each other, and found the adjacent bed empty. More than fending off the chill, the closeness had banished all feelings of solitude that had remained a stubborn part of Valia for as long as she could remember, the human touch bonding their spirits further. Their embrace was not one driven by lust, but rather the joy of affection shared, given and accepted in equal measure without condition. She sighed, knowing that Surilya was most likely feeding the goats or spreading fresh straw beneath them, but wished that she were there to share those first languid moments of wakefulness instead.

She sat up and thought about preparing tea, but instead pulled the furs that topped the blankets from Surilya's side to her own and curled up beneath them, enjoying the guilty pleasure it brought.

At last she threw off the covers and forced herself to sit up again and this time she followed through, searching the floorboards with naked feet for the fur-lined leather slippers that Surilya had made for her. The stone floor below could suck the heat from unwary toes in a heartbeat, so she was grateful to find the soft shoes at her bedside.

She reached the kitchen table and found a plate warming beside the range, its contents covered with a linen cloth. Valia smiled as she lifted the cloth and found a fresh scone, still warm and moist and begging to be covered in butter. She ate every crumb, washing it down with hot tea sweetened with honey. With a care that bordered on reverence, she lifted the leather thong over her head, staring at the gold coin suspended from it for a long moment before hanging it from a hook above the stone sink where a plain apron hung. What would Truman think of her now, she wondered, hoping that he would have found solace in her new happiness. Then she washed her face in a shallow basin, rubbing the last remnants of fatigue from her eyes.

The sword above the range caught her eye and she stared at it for a long time, trying to find some affinity that she must surely have once felt for it, but recognised none. Its blade could be rusting in its scabbard for all she knew, but she did not care and had no desire to oil the steel of that relic as she once had.

The rhythmic crunch of approaching boots in the snow outside signalled Surilya's return. The door opened and a vision in fur wreathed in a cloud of steaming breath stomped in, shaking snow from heavy leather boots.

"I would have helped had you woken me," Valia said, filling a cup with steaming water. She wrapped a clump of dried tea leaves in a square of linen and pressed them into the cup with a small spoon to draw.

"You looked so peaceful. I did not have the heart," Surilya replied as she shook herself free of the heavy coat she wore. "I see you found your breakfast. I must admit, a part of me had hoped that you were still in bed and I could have eaten it myself."

"No such luck," Valia replied with a smile. "I will make it up to you though. Your tea will be ready by the time you fight yourself free of those boots."

Surilya slumped a little and groaned. "I forgot to check the fox traps."

"Let me," Valia volunteered. "You should warm yourself."

"No, I will be back before you would have had a chance to dress properly anyway," she replied with an admonishing smile, reaching for her heavy coat again.

"I will keep your tea warm," Valia offered by way of encouragement.

"Your kindness fills me with gratitude," Surilya said, looking at once dejected and amused. "Where would I be without you?"

"Checking fox traps?"

"Indeed."

Surilya shrugged her way into the heavy furs and after a final, theatrical glance at the warm fire that had eluded her, she opened the door onto the icy world beyond and trudged out, leaving Valia to shake her head and chuckle.

She fished the little linen bundle from the cup, squeezing the fragrant amber drops from it between the spoon and a thumb. She placed the cup beside the glowing range to maintain its warmth, and sat down to open Kekoa's book, rubbing her back against the chair to ease that old itch.

She smiled at the memory of the little Jendayan and the tangling of Fate's whims that had thrown them together. She went again to that final page and the incomplete drawing of the giant leading the army against the Shar. Kekoa had captured so much of the narrative of the scene, yet with very little detail. A true artist could transport the spectator's mind into their work, and even here with these sweeping outlines she sensed the roar of the battlefield, the rush of the moment.

The giant remained a mystery and so she closed the book and forced herself out of her chair.

The water bucket was low, so she poured what was left into the large pot that was kept warm by the fire and slipped her feet into her boots. Rather than battle with the laces, she left them untied, knowing that she was not going far. The snow all around was their source of water during the winter, and there was little point in walking beyond their own front door to find it. Pulling on her own coat she ventured outside, careful to shut the door behind her. Her breath steamed in the dry air and the cold nipped at her legs where the boots and coat failed to meet and only a linen nightgown protected her skin.

No matter, she would be done in a few moments.

Valia scooped up clumps of powder in a bowl and pressed them into the bucket, using the underside of the makeshift scoop to pack the snow down. A bucket full of snow tended to melt, leaving a pitiful amount of water by contrast, and so she worked to crush the air from the powder. A few large flakes floated down in the still air, landing with a chill whisper on the soft drifts. Surilya's tracks snaked away to the east following the coastline and vanished over a gentle rise where Valia knew the nearest trap was set and marked with a tall stake. Foxes were drawn to the farmhouse by the mice that were in turn lured by the warmth of the shed, and the snowy burrows were a tell-tale sign of fox activity. The thick, white fur that allowed the foxes to survive the icy steppe was just as valuable to the people who lived alongside them and was an important source of income too.

Her fingers were cold and numb already but Valia knew that she would be in the warm again soon, so she did her best to ignore the raw air.

Then she heard it. Or had she felt it through the ground?

Something was approaching.

She straightened her back and looked east as a heavy front edged in from the sea, obscuring the water with a haze of falling snow.

A boat faded out of view in the murk almost as soon as she had discerned its shape. She began to trace Surilya's steps, following the deep depressions of the footfalls as she pulled her coat around her.

"Surilya!" she called out.

No reply. But the trap was a hundred yards away at least in a shallow depression and the snow had a way of deadening sound.

She picked up her pace, taking long strides in snow that was so deep in places she had to wade through it. She felt the powder filling her loosely fastened boots as she forced her way up the gentle slope.

Finally, she saw her. "Surilya!" she called out again in relief.

Surilya stood up and held a dead fox aloft by the tail in triumph, only the ruffled, bloody fur at its neck marring the perfect whiteness.

Valia laughed through heavy breaths, and Surilya laughed too, shaking her head in puzzlement.

"What are you doing out here dressed like that?" Surilya called as Valia almost doubled over to steady her breathing.

Valia was still laughing and shaking her head when she straightened again.

That was when she saw them. Dozens of liquid black shapes, loping through the deep powder, unmistakeable in their form.

Valia's belly turned to ice, a deeper cold than the winter air.

"Surilya!" she screamed. "Run!"

Surilya turned to see what Valia had, and for a moment she froze. Then she dropped the dead fox and ran, stumbling in the deep snow as it dragged at her legs. She fell, disappearing for a moment before struggling upright again. Valia ran towards her even though she knew it was futile. The approaching Shar cut through the snow like salmon in water and the first reached Surilya's back unhindered.

With the slowness of an unfolding nightmare, Valia saw the creature rake its claws across Surilya's ribs as it passed; slicing through the furs that had protected her from the cold but could do nothing against the razor talons. Blood sprayed onto the pristine snow as she fell, her eyes fixed on Valia's.

Valia screamed; an animal sound that rose from her primal core, a venting of despair and fury that shook her whole body. A small part of her remembered the sword above the range in the farmhouse, but she knew it was too far away to be of use and the thought was swept aside by a wretched wave of hopeless sorrow.

She felt her sanity slip from her in that moment.

She ran at the nearest Shar and hurled herself at it, driving her fingers into its spongy hide as she screamed, inviting oblivion to take a measure of fury with her. She tore at the tacky flesh even as her own felt the cold bite of claws. The screaming of her senses did not register the blow to the head that brought the blackness, and her last vision from the cold ground was of heavy boots standing, untroubled in the snow.

Granger walked with gloved hands clasped behind his back, crunching through fresh snow atop the battlements of the city of Banihat. This was proving to be the hardest winter since the year of the battle at Ara Dasari. The sky hung like a grey lid over the city, pressing the cold upon it. The top of the Taaman bell tower was lost in the low cloud, silent, as it had been for almost two centuries. The tower had been built when Kylyptus had been a kingdom, by the ruler, Taaman to declare news of the birth of his heirs. For generations, the bell had proclaimed the arrival of his descendants to whomever was within earshot, and in darker times had been ready to warn travellers away. During a time when a plague was wiping out whole villages, the bell had been ready to warn those outside the walls should the city itself become infected. Three peals of the great bell would serve as warning to anyone approaching the city. Mercifully, it was a measure that was never needed. There was even a children's rhyme about it.

He nodded a greeting to the pair of soldiers who huddled over a glowing brazier and was more than a little tempted to join them in their island of heat. But he pressed on in the knowledge that the walk would do him more good than the temporary warming the fire offered. After all, his stomach had swelled with the inactivity of the past months and he knew that a man of his age was better served by gentle exercise. He chuckled at that thought; his age could be measured in millennia, yet in his new mortal form these were surely his twilight years. As an Emissary of Athusilan, he had been immortal until a single transgression had seen him banished to live and die as a common man. A sad smile replaced his mirth as he remembered that the 'transgression' had a name; Kellan Aemoran. But in saving Kellan, Granger had set in motion a sequence of events that would ultimately see the end of Abaddon's reign of terror.

"And I do not regret a single thing," he announced to the

empty battlement. "A year of life and love as a mortal is worth ten thousand years of your insensate existence."

He wondered for a moment if he was being arrogant and that his life was not important enough to be added to the Book of Lives. Was an Emissary *really* watching from an unseen remove as he had done, he thought? No matter.

He reached the south wall and turned to follow it, looking out over the pristine whiteness below. The eastern refugees had all long since moved further south to escape the bitter cold of northern Kylyptus, living rough in tents. There was talk of heading for Kor'Habat, but that city was as unwelcoming as an adder's nest, with mistrust and power games winding up tensions that the thousands of refugees, not to mention the soldiers, could easily trigger. Chapok's gold would buy a welcome for some at least, but the King had shown little interest in holding his people together and many had talked of staying close to the coast and nearer to home, perhaps in Pashwar.

Only Dachen had remained in Banihat, with a few members of his escort still loyal to him, determined to await news from Rogan's scouts. Adeyemi stayed too with the Daemon Element still in his possession, but it was surely as safe with that man as with any other.

Granger found himself at the east wall sooner than he had expected and soon spotted the clearing in the snow atop the ramparts where Kekoa would sit, cross-legged each morning to greet the sun, even when the dawn was obscured by a blizzard. He walked on until he reached the end of the wall where the harbour opened out to the ocean and leaned on the granite rampart to stare into the grey murk that hung over the water.

"You look thoughtful again, Historian." The voice startled Granger.

"Adeyemi, I did not hear you approach." Sure enough, the big, dark-skinned man was placing his feet into Granger's own footsteps, avoiding the tell-tale crunch of fresh snow.

Adeyemi followed Granger's gaze to his feet and realised what he was doing. He smiled. "I apologise, friend Granger. Sometimes I do things without realising."

"Old habits, yes?" Granger watched for a reaction, but the broad smile never wavered.

After a long silence Granger spoke again. "Adeyemi, as a historian I have travelled to many places; seen more cultures than most." The subtle lie was so easy now. "I know of your home and its great architecture and literature. I know who you are. I know what you do, those marks on your skin tell me as much."

Adeyemi raised a finger to the delicate whorls that scarred his cheeks and traced the lines of the cruel gashes that had ruined the pattern. "No longer."

"But why, Adeyemi? Will you share your story with me?"

Adeyemi leaned with one elbow on the rampart beside Granger and peered over to the rocks and foam below. "Perhaps you already know more than I am comfortable with you knowing."

Granger ignored the threat. "It is not all darkness in your life. Would you not want that known?"

"Known by whom?" The smile had faded. "Those who know me now know as much or as little as I choose. To all those before, I am dead." It was a brief flash of anger, and the smile returned.

"You cannot escape the past, Adeyemi, it defines you. I can see that you have tried to forge a new path, but you are still placing your feet in the footprints of others."

Adeyemi glanced back at the depressions in the snow he had followed unconsciously. "Old habits. I would look to the dawn for portents of what is to come, but the future, like the horizon is occluded and murky." Then his expression changed to one of puzzlement as he looked out into the gloom of low, grey cloud and fog over the ocean. "Ships?" he asked. "Yet more refugees?"

Granger peered out over the water, as huge shapes coalesced from the murk. Ghostly forms, grey with frost took shape as though birthed from the fog itself. The ships crept forward in the still air with the rhythmic splash of oars floating across the water, barely discernible. With a growing sense of dread, Granger strained to make out the strange shape that stood out at the bow of the lead ship. As the apparition took form, he came to recognise what stood on the ice-rimed prow. His throat went dry and his belly turned cold. "Alert the soldiers," he whispered in horror. "Sound the alarm, we're being attacked!"

The first ship surged into the harbour and dragged its hull along the granite pier of the northern edge, shattering oars that had not been ejected in time. Standing erect atop the bow, the Khalim-Shar raised an enormous trident above its black head with a long, sinuous limb. It crouched to brace itself against the heaving of the vessel and screamed an ear-splitting war cry to its kind, a sound that echoed in the docklands and cut through the icy air with a blade of deeper cold. The Shrill call was followed by dozens of black shapes leaping from the ship and landing, cat-like on the snow-covered cobbles of the docks. They swung their wide maws this way and that, using the ring of eyes that circled each of their heads to take in their surroundings. Each eye was a glistening jewel of obsidian in the writhing, midnight flesh, dominated by a large pair above their bony jaws. Excited chittering and bestial shrieks joined the sound of the tortured hull rasping against stone.

"Form ranks!" Rogan bellowed from horseback as the Heavy Infantry hurried down the narrow streets that led to the harbour. "Seal the docks! I want ranks at every exit! Where are the archers? Why are those ships allowed to enter un-harried?"

As more ships slid into the harbour the Heavy Infantry arrived at their designated positions and tried to form an orderly defence, splitting into small groups of a dozen or more to block the myriad lanes and alleys that fed the city. Several Shar had already made it into one of the lanes that led from the back of an abandoned fish market at the northernmost part of the harbour, and a squad of twenty Heavy Infantry arrived to stem the flow just as another ship began disgorging its cargo onto the docks. The front rank of ten men locked shields and formed a low barrier while the ten behind them held their shields higher and angled back, just as they had been drilled to do from childhood. But this was neither a volley of arrows nor an advancing army of men and the first Shar to meet them simply leapt the barrier.

"Guard the rear!" an infantryman bellowed, but it was too late.

Too slow to turn, the rear rank fell apart as the Shar slashed at their legs, cutting tendons and smashing bone where the armour was weakest at the joints.

"Hold the line!" another yelled, but his rallying cry was drowned by the screams of his comrades. The next two Shar found easier targets with the shield formation in tatters, and too little room for the Infantrymen to swing the huge, curved swords that they favoured. In seconds, the twenty men had fallen as more and more Shar flooded the docks and made for the city...

Dachen, and the five members of his escort who had remained loyal to him, rounded a corner a moment after the Infantry at the northern end of the docks had succumbed. Dachen widened his stance on the snow-covered cobbles and welcomed the familiar feel of the sparth in his grip again. Swords were all well and good, but the long shaft of a sparth kept the enemy at a comfortable distance.

"Pemba; Tashimen! Maddeners!" he shouted.

The two archers did not hesitate, selecting arrows from their specialized quivers and shooting them at the approaching Shar. The 'maddener' arrows had proved to be a potent weapon against the Shadows in Tianpok, and not for the first time Dachen felt vindicated in his decision to bring an alchemist with him to the West. Lilac flame erupted from the wounds a heartbeat after penetrating the black flesh of the two nearest Shar. The creatures shrieked as they stumbled in their frantic efforts to shake the arrows free, crashing into their fellows as they did. Another two well-placed arrows had a gout of fire and smoke bursting from the flanks of two more Shar.

"Sangye, Yeshe, Kanchun, with me!" Dachen called on his remaining three sparth bearers to join him as he charged the stricken Shar. "Take their heads before they can heal! It's the only way to stop them!"

Yeshe was breathing hard from his exertions already but moved just as quickly as his leaner counterparts to take advantage of the crippled beast.

The long-hafted sparth was perfect for fighting Shar, with its lengthy cutting edge at the end of an eight-foot pole, the enemy could be held at a safe distance or else cut down with the heavy blade. As the burning creatures thrashed in mindless agony the four soldiers set about ending the torment, hacking heads from writhing bodies as more arrows found their mark.

An onrushing Shar evaded the arrows as it darted into the street with powerful thrusts of its hind limbs, to leap at Dachen as he severed the head of one of the shrieking creatures. Just in time, he brought the point to bear and pushed the sharpened butt of the sparth downwards. The long, pointed blade bit into the Shar's chest, and Dachen pulled on the haft, feeling the butt bite into the cobbles as he did so. The speed of the Shar carried it over Dachen's head in a wide arc, skewered on the sparth's point as the prince stumbled backwards. The archer, Tashimen was too slow to react and the Shar crashed into him, sending him sprawling. The sparth was ripped from Dachen's hands as he fell, and he felt a sharp pain run up his arm as his elbow cracked against the cobbles. He rolled over in the wet, trampled snow, trying to put the pain from his mind, but aware that his right arm was now useless. He looked up as the Shar recovered, shaking the sparth free a moment before Pemba placed a maddener in the side of its head.

Lilac fire illuminated its wide maw from within as it shrieked and bellowed smoke and steam from between the hard, bony ridges of its jaws. A flailing claw caught Tashimen in the throat as he struggled to escape the creature and he went down again, clutching at the wound with blood spurting from between his fingers. Oil splashed from his quiver as he fell, and the maddeners were scattered on the slush-covered stones. Kanchun arrived at Dachen's side to help the prince onto his feet as another Shar got through untouched. The sparth bearer swung his weapon at the creature, biting into its shoulder but not killing it. The Shar rolled away as the fire in the mouth of the first began to subside.

Tashimen was still and lay in a growing pool of blood where he had fallen. The tips of the maddeners were now smoking as the oil that had covered them dispersed in the slush, then one by one each point was engulfed in a flare of blinding lilac fire. The Shar with the wounded shoulder was only distracted for a moment by the flames, but it was enough for Adeyemi to strike from above. The big man leapt from an open window and brought the blade of his crude impanga down on the Shar's neck. The head fell away and the body was left to writhe on the cobbles. Dachen watched it die too as he stumbled away with Kanchun's help.

"Pull back!" he shouted, wincing at the pain it caused him. "There are too many!"

There was no way that Pemba would be able to keep up with the number of Shar now entering the street, and his quiver of maddeners was looking light already...

"Can you run, friend Dachen?" Adeyemi asked with deep concern etched onto his face.

"Yes," he replied with a curt nod and cast a glance at Tashimen's bloodied body. With a curse, he turned to leave. "Pull back!"

Pemba used his last three maddeners to cover their retreat, before he too turned and ran.

Rogan bellowed at his cavalry from the saddle of his own

horse, urging them to form up for an assault along the harbour. His orders were reinforced by the sharp blasts from a signaller on their own horse nearby, the horn echoing around the stone harbour. Just as they had done on the field outside Ulan Balsan, the Shar would fall against the might of the Heavy Cavalry. The Shar would be crushed beneath the huge, armoured warhorses or else fall to the swords of the riders. Anything still moving in their wake would be dealt with by the gathering formation of Heavy Infantry that would follow. From their position at the southern edge of the docks the Heavy Cavalry had a clear run of fifty yards before they would meet the first of the Shar. They would clear a swathe all the way to the northern pier, allowing the Heavy Infantry to take control of all routes to the city where the defences had failed.

"Captain Raims, has the Infantry been positioned?" he asked just as the last of a sixty-strong Heavy Cavalry company formed up.

"They are moving now, Hatar," the Captain replied.

"Good," he said, then turning to face the gathered Cavalry he shouted, "On my command! Show no fear and the day will be ours!"

The horn sounded and the Cavalrymen roared in fervour.

"For Korathea!" Rogan roared. "Charge!"

Hurrying down one of the many lanes accessing the harbour, Marlon, Abbil and Jon arrived at the backs of the Heavy Infantry just as a black tide of Shar punched through. The lead Shar reached Marlon first who swung his sword as he sidestepped. The blade all but severed a forelimb, and he deflected the next with his shield, spinning into the next attack. Abbil finished the first Shar with a clean cut through its short neck with his heavy, two-handed sword. Jon deflected the raking claws of another with his shield and split the talons with the tip of his blade as he countered. The Shar screamed as its claws flopped, useless at the end of its limb

117

and Jon gave it no time to recover, moving in for a killing blow before the wound could knit.

Marlon deflected another cruel swipe but was knocked back into the body of the Shar that Abbil had just beheaded. He stumbled backwards and hit the cobbles rolling, knowing that to lie there would see him dead in seconds. Seeing that he was vulnerable, a Shar charged at him. With a roar, Abbil lunged, inflicting a deep wound in its lower back, and giving Marlon the heartbeat he needed to get to his feet. He rose just in time to see another, moving at speed towards him, and spun as it leapt, aware that he could never parry such momentum. He timed it to perfection, cutting into the Shar's shoulder as it passed, but the impact ripped the sword from his grasp as the steel stuck in the tacky flesh. The wounded Shar stumbled away, taking the sword further from him even as another leapt. In the moment that the Shar was in the air, two arrows sprouted from its head, throwing it off balance and Marlon was able to duck beneath the scything claws. Elan added another three arrows to the enraged Shar's head from his position on the rooftops, giving Marlon time to retrieve the sword that had since fallen from the shoulder of the rapidly healing beast. He took the head from the first before turning to the second even as another arrow struck home. Sparks flew from the cobbles as his blade passed through the Shar's neck, leaving the body to twitch on the stones, claws clutching in spasms like dying spiders.

He stood, breathing hard, and looked towards the docks where ships were edging in under a weak shower of arrows. There had been no time to organise a decent defence.

Then Marlon saw a figure in the chaos, standing proud of all others. It was a Shar, there was no mistaking that, but where all others moved on all fours, this one stood erect on hind legs that were longer and slenderer than its fellows'. The long, powerful forelimbs were still tipped with black claws, but grasped in one of those huge talons was a trident the length of two men. Even with its hunched posture it towered above all others. It strode forwards, leaning on the huge trident like a shepherd on a staff, shrieking and chittering at its army. Then it stopped and swung its head towards him. The round, obsidian pools of its dominant eyes fixed on Marlon with a cold stare. For a heartbeat it froze before lifting the trident to point directly at him. He was suddenly aware of the Element, wrapped in linen in the tunic beneath his armour. Marlon had not felt pure fear for a very long time, but now, under the assiduous gaze of the Khalim-Shar, his courage faltered.

Then something out of view, further south along the docks stole the Khalim-Shar's attention, and Marlon was freed from the thrall. He gasped air into his lungs as he realised that, in his moment of terror, he had stopped breathing, and shook off the feeling of dread that had clouded his thoughts.

"There are too many of the bastards!" Abbil was shouting. "We must retreat!"

At that moment, a loud clatter of hooves announced Acastes' arrival. He pushed past Abbil towards the oncoming Shar, steering his mount away from the slashing claws and leaning this way and that as he reached to make each stroke count. Kapaneus arrived a few heartbeats later, on the back of a wild-eyed stallion to protect his friend's flank and for a moment the pair held their ground.

"Pull back, you fools!" Marlon yelled as a fresh wave of midnight forms broke into the street over the bodies of the slaughtered Infantrymen.

"More Infantry are coming!" Acastes declared. "Hold your courage."

Sure enough, the sound of rapid marching feet echoed down the narrow street from behind them. At the same time, the Shar that had been bearing down on them a moment ago turned and slunk from the street back towards the docks.

Marlon, Abbil and Jon watched as forty Heavy Infantry marched by to seal the street again. The soldiers dragged their dead comrades aside with no outward sign of empathy and formed an eight-deep rank across the street.

The relative silence was suddenly shattered as Heavy Cavalry charged along the docks with the defiant roar of men. Then the deafening screams of Shar and horses overwhelmed the brash voices. The Cavalry were only visible for a moment as their speed and momentum carried them by, but their panic and disarray were in no doubt. Marlon ran forward to see what was happening and even the narrow view afforded to him from his position in the street showed a scene of utter carnage. Horses rolled with shattered legs and thrown riders struggled to rise, dazed, before the Shar fell upon them. That wave of armoured Cavalry that had passed a moment ago was suddenly countered by a surge of black shapes, throwing the men and horses back like flotsam and smashing them on the stones of the harbour.

The new ranks of Heavy Infantry lurched back under the weight of the Shar offensive. The men held for a moment before dozens of Shar burst through, scattering the defenders as wind scatters autumn leaves. Once their ranks were broken, the Infantrymen fell to the onslaught with barely any fight at all, screaming as claws found gaps in armour or as limbs were simply torn away. Those who found the space to wield a sword were engulfed by the sheer number of Shar flooding into the street and vanished under the black swarm.

"Elan, some cover if you will!" Jon shouted, hoping that the Lythurian was still poised above them as he turned to run.

The series of arrows hissing through the air as the men and riders retreated down the street signalled Elan's continued presence, but his bow could not offer anything more than a distraction. Shar screeched in frustration while their tormentor harried them from his elevated position allowing the fleeing men to open some distance between them and their attackers.

Marlon almost collided with a dozen militiamen who came running out of a side street into his path.

"Regroup in the square," the first managed through heaving breaths. "They have broken through."

"We hadn't noticed," Jon replied, but his dark humour was lost in the sound of Acastes and Kapaneus clattering by on horse-back.

The city square, which was situated in the southern half of the city at the end of a wide avenue leading to the main gates, was filled with terrified people clamouring at the steps of the council chambers. News of an attack had spread like flames in dry grass and the people were wild with fear. At the top of the broad, gran-ite steps and behind a protective line of grim-faced militiamen, Belghutai called for calm.

"Return to your homes," she shouted over the uproar. "Lock your doors and secure your windows until order is restored."

A hail of questions and demands drowned her words.

"Please! Remain calm," she called, but already there were those intent on fleeing, bundling hastily packed belongings up beside children and the elderly on the backs of carts. At the far side of the square a fight broke out when a startled horse caused a cart to collide with another. Men shouted over the din, desperate to corral loved ones in the press of bodies. Women heaped blan-kets around the shoulders of children against the cold. A small boy, separated from his family, cried as he shuffled through the slush and the forest of frantic legs, searching for a caring face.

Strong hands plucked the boy from the path of a skittish pony and lifted him to safety.

"Hello there," Alano said with a warm smile. "Where were you off to?"

The little boy sucked on his bottom lip, wide-eyed, but did not answer.

"Where have you come from, little one? He asked. "Where is your mother?"

The boy wordlessly looked down at the hilt of Alano's sword.

"This was given to me by a very good friend, called Dimas Malmotti," he said, baring a little of the fine steel. "A funny name,

121

that, isn't it? It has kept me safe for a very long time, and I promise it will keep you safe too. You sit on my shoulders and we will see if we can find your family." He hoisted the boy up onto his shoulders and turned this way and that for the child to see.

"Turgen!" a voice sounded out above the clamour. "Turgen!"

Alano turned towards the source as a woman with tear-streaked cheeks burst through the crowd.

"Mama!" the little boy shrieked, bouncing with excitement.

Alano lowered him into his mother's grateful arms and ruffled his dark hair. "Stay close to your mother, little one," he said.

The woman bowed in thanks and vanished into the throng.

"Alano, the horses?" Granger asked as he hurried to the man's side.

"Saddled and ready. The pack-mules too," he replied. "Have you spoken with Belghutai?"

Granger shook his head, surveying the crowded square. "I could not get near her. This is only a fraction of the population; most have stayed in their homes."

Alano scowled. "Doors will not save them, no matter how sturdy their locks. I will urge these people at least to move towards the gates. How much time do we have?"

"Not nearly enough," Granger replied. "Good luck."

With that he hurried away again.

Granger made his way through the narrow streets flanked by shuttered windows and locked doors. A few families were making their way to the square, eager to leave the city, but most put their trust in granite walls and the Heavy Infantry to keep them safe and remained indoors.

Granger reached the base of the bell tower breathless, only to find the wooden door firmly locked. He sagged before casting his frantic gaze around until it settled on a steel-bladed shovel leaning beside a door. The wooden handle was cold and damp in his hands, but he ignored the minor discomfort and swung the shovel at the door. A splinter of aged wood flew away, giving Granger fresh hope he attacked it with new vigour.

A young man gave him a suspicious look as he hurried by with a bundle under each arm but said nothing. Granger hacked at the brittle planks around the lock until he was certain they were weakened enough. He put his shoulder to the door and thumped against it, relieved to hear the timber crack under his weight and it creaked open on rusted hinges. A final push had him stumbling into a dark and dusty little room whose only feature was the stairwell leading up from it.

Granger took a deep breath and started climbing.

Alano reached the gates only to find them closed and a large crowd of people arguing with the militiamen there.

"Open the gates!" he shouted to the militiamen.

"We have been ordered to bar them," one replied. "The city is under attack."

"And the enemy is already within the walls," Alano protested. "Sealing off the exit only traps the people within."

"We have orders," the militiaman repeated.

"To do what? Hold the gate against an empty road?"

A brief look of uncertainty passed over the militiaman's face before he set his jaw and stood a little taller. "It is not my place to question orders."

"But it is your job to *take* orders." Starling forced his way to the front of the gathering throng of people desperate to leave the city. Behind him, Nirmaya and dozens of Sisters were on horseback, with bundles strapped to the animals' flanks and a few pack-mules in tow. Starling held his hand out, palm down. "Do you know what this is?"

"I do not," the militiaman replied, regarding with indifference the large ring that Starling wore.

"It is a Governor's seal, you fool," Starling barked, remembering the glee he had felt when he had first stolen it from his father.

"And you are standing in the way of an agent of Kor'Habat!"

"You are no Governor," the man replied, although he looked a little less sure.

Starling looked around as he laughed, still holding up the ring he had stolen from his father, the Governor of Kernhalt. "We have a sharp one here, folks. But disobeying the orders of a bearer of a Governor's seal is just the same as pissing up the leg of the Governor himself."

The militiaman swallowed hard and looked to his fellows for support. He came to a decision.

"Is the road clear?" he shouted, keeping his eyes on Starling as he did so.

A voice from the barbican floated down. "All quiet on the road."

He hesitated for a moment before saying, "Open the gates."

"You have chosen wisely," Starling said with a bright smile, and was the first out of the gate.

The granite stairs wound ever upward, illuminated by occasional, narrow slits in the stonework. Lamp holders stood empty as they had done for the last two centuries, but Granger's eyes had already grown used to the dim light. He stopped for a moment to catch his breath, cursing the stupidity of politicians and his excess weight in equal measure. He started up the stairs again, the burning in his thighs and lungs vying for his attention as the effort took its toll on his ageing and neglected body. He pushed both to the back of his mind and pressed on, making a mental note to take more exercise if he survived the day.

At last he reached the top of the stairs to find a trap door above his head. He reached up and pressed on it and cursed as it refused to budge.

"The Sisters and I will stay and fight," Nirmaya declared as the inhabitants of Banihat streamed past her out of the gate and onto the road.

"Have you fought Shar before?" Alano asked.

"No, but we will not falter," she insisted.

"That is good, your courage will yet be needed if these people are to be protected. If the Shar take the city there will be nothing to stop them following these people onto the road."

"You want us to run with them?" she said in distaste.

"I want you to *protect* them," Alano corrected. "How many Sisters follow you?"

"A little over fifty, every one proficient with a sword."

"And they will be tested in time. Will you do this?"

"It still feels like running," she protested.

"Nirmaya, look around you. We are *all* running. Please!"

At last, Nirmaya nodded in agreement and called out to the Sisters who followed her through the gate to join the column of fleeing people. They formed a thin defensive line on each flank that would not have held a single Shar, let alone a horde.

Granger reached the trapdoor again, having descended the stairs to retrieve the nearest lamp holder. The strap-ironwork was as sturdy as it had been two centuries ago, with only a dusting of rust on its surface. He stabbed at the wood at the hinges of the trapdoor using the pointed base of the lamp holder until the rotten planks gave way, then he heaved them upwards. The planks came apart in a shower of dust and snow which rained down on Granger as he struggled through the gap at the top of the steps.

It was cold at the top of the tower, engulfed in cloud and exposed to a biting wind that he had not been aware of on the ground. The stone tile roof was intact, and only windblown snow had settled on the flagstones around the huge bell, but it was slick and icy underfoot and so he took a moment to steady his footing.

The bronze bell hung from a headstock of iron supported on a pair of granite bell frames which all looked as sturdy as the day they were set in place. He searched for the hammer and found it in a cradle against one of the main pillars. The huge hammer was icy to the touch and heavier than he had imagined and for a moment he doubted that he would be able to swing it. Shifting his grip closer to the head made it easier though and he turned to position himself for the strike.

Now, how did that child's rhyme go?

Once for a daughter, twice for a son,
Three for plague so turn and run.

A horn sounded below.

He set his feet wide on the slick stone and swung the hammer as hard as he could.

Rogan watched with disbelief as his Heavy Cavalry crumbled on the stones of the harbour. Their initial surge against the Shar had come to an abrupt halt when the creatures moved as one against the mounted soldiers. The front rank of horses was cut down, throwing riders to the merciless claws and crushing jaws of the Shar. Then the force of the black wave hit the following ranks, tossing horses back and engulfing their screaming bodies. The gleaming armour was ripped away to expose soft flesh beneath, feeding the frenzy of blood lust that drove the Shar onward. A tall figure strode with purpose along the harbour in the wake of the unfolding destruction, but it was not a human figure; this was a Shar...

The form was different yet unmistakeable, a lithe body on powerful hind legs, broad shouldered with long forelimbs. It leaned on a huge trident clasped in its right claw, as it held its head up high to regard the scene through a multitude of eyes. The creatures wide mouth held the same cruel grin that was set into the visage of every Shar, yet every shriek that sounded from it held greater complexity than he had previously heard from its kind.

It was giving orders.

This was a leader.

"Captain Raims," he ordered. "Sound the order to rally, we will regroup in the square."

Captain Raims relayed the order to the signaller and followed Rogan towards the square at speed.

"It is the call to rally," Abbil managed through heaving breaths. They had almost reached the square when they heard the horn ring out across the city.

"If they have any sense they will rally in the square," Marlon replied, unable to gauge the direction from which the sound was coming. "Barricade the smaller lanes and concentrate their efforts."

"It's moving," Jon shouted, as he ran. "They have abandoned the harbour."

Sure enough, the echoes of the frantic blasts were shifting in an invisible landscape that only the ear could discern.

Then a new sound. A bell.

It pealed out with a deep, sonorous echo that filled every crevice in the city.

Then again, before the first had died, a warm, liquid sound that could almost be felt on the skin.

A third, adding a new layer to the rebounding tones of the first two.

"The Taaman bell," Marlon shouted as they jogged into the crowded square. "Someone is sounding the bell."

"But why?" Abbil puffed, coming to a halt at the edge mass of people.

The echoes died away until only the frantic horn could be heard over the chattering people.

Then the bell pealed again.

Dachen and his escort reached the stables to find Tsering, the aged alchemist, already waiting beside a loaded packhorse.

"The city is lost," he said. "Make for the gate as fast as you can, and we will meet you on the road. Pemba and Kanchun will go with you and take our horses. Sangye and Yeshe will stay with me."

The bell was still ringing; three peals, and then silence, again and again. What it meant, Dachen could not be certain, but people had started coming out from behind locked doors and staring up into the murk towards the bell tower as though the answer would be etched there in the leaden clouds. It was a signal they all understood however, and the streets were becoming ever more packed with frantic city folk desperate to leave with as much as they could carry.

Screams from the direction of the port were becoming louder and more insistent as the fighting edged nearer.

Adeyemi, Sangye and Yeshe watched as the others vanished into the throng.

"What now, friend Dachen?" Adeyemi asked.

"We will buy them what time we can. I am certain that the Koratheans will make a stand in the square. We can join them there and have a clear route of escape if it is needed."

"You cannot wield a sparth with that injury," Adeyemi warned, pointing to the wounded arm that Dachen was holding in his other. "You should make that escape now."

Dachen grimaced. "I have one good arm yet. Are you ready?"

Adeyemi grinned and gripped the pouch he wore suspended from his neck. "I will not die today, friend Dachen."

"I envy your confidence," Sangye muttered, but tapped the butt of his sparth on the wet cobbles and indicated that he was ready and turned to Yeshe. "Are you sure you can keep up?"

The stout man scowled but did not answer.

"This way," Dachen ordered, and led them down a narrow lane in the direction of the square.

Granger dropped the iron hammer and barely heard the ring of the steel against stone. His fingers were numb from the cold and the punishing vibrations that had stung with every strike, and in his ears, the sound of the bell still reverberated.

A few unsteady paces had him on the first step of the long descent, and he hurried down the dizzying stairwell, hoping that his message had been understood. Belghutai had put her trust in the Heavy Infantry when she had told people to stay in their homes, but Granger knew only too well that the city had been lost the moment the first ship had entered the harbour.

The city had to be evacuated. It would be too late for most, but if the triple peal of the Taaman bell had spurred even a few to make it to safety, then the risk would have been justified.

The excruciating pain of warm blood rushing back into frozen fingers brought Granger to a stop. Flexing his knuckles brought fresh waves of pain from every joint, and it took a long moment for him to regain control of his breathing in the gloom of the stairwell.

He set off again as the pain subsided, taking care not to misstep in the darkness, knowing that a fall on the steep spiral would not end well. His eyes had grown accustomed to the dark again, and he turned away from the occasional slits that allowed light in through the curved walls, not wishing to ruin his vision. It was not only weak light that seeped through the gaps, but sound too, and screams of terror echoed around the city. He could not tell how close those sounds were, or indeed, which direction they came from, but they injected an urgency to his pace that had his thighs burning and knees aching.

At last he saw the pool of weak light that signalled the door at the base of the building and sighed with relief. Then his blood ran cold as a Shar skidded to a halt in the slush at the broken door and turned its head to regard him with glassy, black eyes.

Granger froze and stared down at the creature.

Acastes and Kapaneus reached the square ahead of the re-treating Heavy Cavalry, to find it packed with terrified people loading carts and pack-mules with as much as they could carry. That infernal bell had fallen silent again although its triple peal had spurred more people into the streets leading to the square.

"Move, you fools!" Acastes bellowed at the mass, but he was just another voice among thousands calling out in fear, anger and panic. The main, southern exit from the market square was a choked bottleneck of desperate families, clinging to one another in a tangle of interlocking cartwheels and skittish horses.

A frightened man nearby looked up at Acastes from beside an overburdened pack-mule. "The road is blocked; we are trapped here," he shouted.

From his elevated position, Acastes could see a denser throng at the southern edge of the square where a wide road lead to the gates.

"We can use the side streets," Kapaneus said to his companion. "Work our way around."

"If they are not blocked too," Acastes murmured.

They forced their way to a street that vanished into the warren of alleys and lanes. The narrow, cobbled arteries that would otherwise feel cosy and quaint now felt bewildering and claustrophobic. With the low cloud and uniform granite walls all around them, it was not long before they lost their bearings.

"This lane," Acastes urged, wheeling his mount down a lane that ran off a small courtyard.

"No, it curves around to the north. We should go back to the last junction and take the left fork," Kapaneus shouted.

"It was choked with people," Acastes protested.

"Then at least we would know we would be heading in the right direction."

"This way," Acastes insisted, and pressed on into the lane.

With a frustrated grunt, Kapaneus followed.

Granger fell back into the stairwell, and kicked the door shut as the Shar slashed at him. Claws shattered the edge of the door, scattering splinters as it swung shut. He jammed his foot against the base and braced his leg, knowing that it was a futile effort. The heavy wood shuddered as the Shar hammered against it, sending painful jolts through Granger's leg. The top hinge exploded under the onslaught and the door sagged inward, slowly at first and then crashing down on top of him as the bottom hinge was torn from the rotten timber.

He tried to lift the door, but it came thudding down again with a force that drove the air from his lungs as the Shar landed on it. He could see the black shape through a crack in the boards; a glint of light reflected from an obsidian eye. The slender tongue slipped out from between black lips, tasting the air and savouring what it found there. The Shar chittered in excitement.

Granger could not move. He closed his eyes, waiting for the cold sting of claws in his flesh.

The door shuddered as claws scrabbled against it, then the weight was lifted, and the timber was heaved aside.

He waited, hoping that death would be swift.

Nothing.

He opened his eyes to see a dark face above his own, but not the one he had expected. A wide smile broke out across Adeyemi's face when he saw that Granger was not harmed. The large blade of Adeyemi's impanga was glistening black in the dimness. On the flagstones beside him, Granger could see the twitching claws of a beheaded Shar. The spasms that animated the body slowed as he watched, until it lay completely still.

"Can you walk, friend Granger?" Adeyemi asked.

To his great relief, Granger realised that he could. "Walk?" he replied. "My dear friend, I could dance a jig!"

"There is nothing to be done now," Dachen said from the street outside. "We must leave the city."

Olgoi Kinbataar's eyes widened with fear when he saw Acastes' horse bearing down on him. For a moment, he was sure that the Korathean had discovered his attempts to have him killed.

"Kinbataar!" Acastes shouted. "What are you doing, man?"

"Some personal effects," he replied, patting the strap of a large satchel that he had slung over his shoulder. "Of sentimental value. I could not leave them."

"Do you know a way out of this blasted labyrinth?" Acastes demanded.

"I do. You are going the wrong way."

Acastes held out a hand and Olgoi accepted it. He almost yelped as the huge man hoisted him up with minimal effort, to straddle the horse behind the saddle. The soft jingle of gold coins as the satchel bounced on his back caused Kapaneus to raise an eyebrow, but there were more urgent matters at hand.

"Turn back," Olgoi said, and then gripped the straps on Acastes' armour with bloodless knuckles as the huge horse lurched into motion.

Olgoi licked his lips and his hand found the slender blade he carried at his hip. He glanced back and saw Kapaneus right behind him and hesitated. A nearby scream had him withdrawing his hand from the weapon.

"Turn here," Olgoi said, and Acastes steered his mount into the lane, revealing a crowded road at its end.

"How far are we from the gates?" Acastes asked.

"Two hundred yards at least," Olgoi replied. "Midway between the market square and the gates."

"At least they are moving," Kapaneus said as he pressed ahead on his horse. There was a slow drift of people and carts across the narrow view of the main road as they headed towards the gates. Curses were being shouted at those who slowed the rest with their over-burdened carts and animals. The desperation was clear in the jostling press of bodies.

Seeing Kapaneus moving ahead, Olgoi laid his hand on the

handle of the slender knife again. If he were to act, it had to be now. His heart was racing as he pulled the blade from the leather sheath and his hands were shaking. He had never killed a man before; a goat when he was a child, but that had made him sick to his stomach and plagued his dreams for weeks afterwards.

The blade was clear of the sheath and the gap in the armour beneath Acastes' arm was right in front of him. He placed the wavering point on the top edge of the strap joining breastplate to back-plate and took a deep breath.

No.

Not now. Kapaneus would find him, regardless of the confusion in the city. Even if Olgoi slipped into the mass of fleeing citizens, Kapaneus would hunt him down. A wise man waited for the perfect moment, and this was not it.

Olgoi returned his knife to his hip, just as they joined the throng of terrified people making for the gates.

Marlon and Abbil heaved another cart onto its side across one of the lanes leading from the square. The paltry barrier alone would do little to slow a Shar, but at every entrance the hasty barricades were being doused in lamp oil. Fire had driven the Shar from the forest in Ulan Balsan, and perhaps it would hold them back here. A militiaman arrived with a small barrel and smashed it over the side of the upturned cart.

"More wood!" Abbil bellowed. "Build them higher!"

The market stalls around the edges of the square were being broken up and dragged into place as what was left of the Heavy Infantry and Cavalry prepared to defend the square at the only route into the square that was not yet blockaded. A few bloodied Infantrymen staggered into the square having survived the running battles that had swept through the streets from the docks so quickly. There were screams echoing around the city from those who had left it too late to flee or else were being attacked in the false sanctuary of their homes. A few citizens arrived to find their way blocked and were dragged over the barricades by the militia-men building them.

The first fires were lit before the last of the civilians were out of the square and the crackling of the burning wood set off a fresh wave of panic in the crowd.

"Jon! Bring that cask of oil over here, man!" Abbil shouted as Jon lifted a small cask from the back of an abandoned cart.

Jon placed the cask on the ground and knocked the bung into the barrel with the hilt of his sword.

"Get a move on!" Abbil urged.

"It's ale!" Jon shouted back, and lifted the cask to his mouth, letting the brown froth wash across his cheeks. He held the cask out in Abbil's direction.

"Now is not the time for ale!" the Dashiyan growled.

"It's always time for ale!" Jon replied.

"You are a madman!"

"I have learned that there are two things that one should nev-er attempt while sober; marriage and battle."

Abbil just shook his head as a militiaman arrived with a torch to set the barricade alight.

"That is all that we can do," Marlon panted. "Time to go."

Jon cast his gaze around the square. "Have you seen Elan?"

Marlon shook his head. "Not since we reached the square, no."

"That one has a way of looking after himself," Abbil assured him. "To the gates."

The last of the ships to enter the harbour did so in a more measured manner. They navigated the wreckage of the scuppered vessels to dock in the city without the carelessness of those that had led the attack. Senji Dayivar was the first to set foot on the cobbles, walking down the gangplank with careful steps. The rock beneath his feet was unnerving in its solidity after so long at sea, but that was not what brought him to a halt after his first few paces on land for several weeks. The grisly carnage on the stones was sickening.

He had put from his mind the horrors he had witnessed in Khumjang and Tianpok; but seeing this fresh slaughter, smelling the tang of iron in the air, brought them flooding back in a bloody wave.

Horses lay butchered on the cobbles, shattered legs contorted at impossible angles, their entrails unravelled and steaming in the chill. The bodies of huge men lay everywhere, dismembered limbs still encased in plate armour that did not protect them against the Shar. He had heard tales of the great size of the Korathean soldiers and had scarcely believed them until now, but where he had once thought of them in awe he now saw that they were just men, as fragile as his own people.

Smoke was rising in the south, within the city walls, and there were sounds of fear and battle trapped beneath the blanket of low cloud. The echoes stirred the pity he had thought buried in a heart heavy with sorrow.

The soldiers made their way from his ship onto the docks, and he gave them a moment to reacquaint themselves with solid ground before calling for them to form ranks. Leaving them to wander about the bloody aftermath of the battle would do them no favours. They were greeted by the skeleton crews who had piloted the initial ships into the harbour. Their relief at having survived the reckless manoeuvres used to land the Shar was clear in their expressions, but none would look upon the massacre that had ensued.

In moments, the two hundred men who had sailed with him had assembled in neat rows, a small forest of gleaming sparths above their heads. The heavy, winter cloaks they wore were open at the front, revealed the armour beneath; thick leather discs overlapping those below like fish scales gave good protection against most types of weapon whilst remaining lighter and more flexible than steel plate. Lighter scales covered the arms and legs, but none wore helmets, only fur-lined hats to protect them from the cold. Other ships had since docked and still more soldiers disembarked and set foot upon this foreign land. They would likely not have to do battle today, as the Shar had done the butcher's work for them, but soon they would be called upon to fight for this new order.

The towering figure of the Khalim-Shar strode with purposeful steps along the edge of the harbour towards Senji and his men. The creature had changed even since they had set sail only weeks ago, much as it had been doing by degrees ever since it had first appeared. He noticed that it walked upright with more ease than it had before, and its short hind quarters were longer than he remembered, making its gait less awkward. It still leaned on the huge trident for support, but the hunched back look less of an affliction than before and more like its natural posture. The forelimb not clutching the trident extended as far down as the creature's knees and razor claws gleamed in the dim light.

Senji tried not to look too hard at the thing's flesh as it drew nearer; the constant flux that roiled upon its surface was not easy on the eye, or the stomach. He concentrated instead on the eyes. The dominant pair, common to all Shar were still there and he saw his face reflected in them when the Khalim-Shar stopped a few short strides away.

"Senji," the Khalim-Shar said in a rasping voice.

"Khalim-Shar," he replied, bowing low.

"The city is taken," the creature said. "The final resistance dwindles, and victory is assured."

"Yes, Khalim-Shar," Senji replied.

"Your soldiers will secure the city and those still within it," the Khalim Shar hissed. "Let the people of Banihat know that they have a new master. They belong to *me* now."

"Yes, Khalim-Shar," Senji said again. Then he saw a figure, high up on the wall at the southern end of the harbour. Strange that someone should be standing there, watching when all others would either have fled or else be trying to hide. The man, if it was a man; it was difficult to tell from such a distance, was carrying a bow. Senji recognised the motion of an archer putting an arrow to a bowstring and watched as the figure raised the bow to shoot.

A heartbeat later, Senji realised his mistake in standing watching as he did. Some deep-seated instinct spurred his muscles into action before conscious thought could muster, and he dodged to one side. He felt the touch of rushing air pass his cheek before the arrow buried itself in the chest of one of his men. The stricken soldier fell to his knees and crumpled forwards in the stunned silence. Senji touched his cheek in shock and saw his fingers come away red. The Khalim-Shar leaned close and its tongue lashed out to caress the fresh wound and taste the blood.

"Good," it breathed. "There is fight in them yet."

Senji recoiled in horror and looked back to the wall, but the figure was gone.

The last of the Heavy Infantry had retreated to the southern exit from the market square and were throwing everything that they could onto a hastily constructed barricade.

"Get oil!" Rogan shouted from his horse. "Does nobody have oil?"

Another arrived with a small, wooden cask that he upended on the pile of broken carts and tables.

"Pull back!" Rogan urged. "Make for the gates!"

The barricade was lit, and the last of the survivors staggered down the road towards the gates. Some were being helped by their comrades, too badly hurt to manage alone. Every one of them was blood spattered and dazed. The Heavy Infantry were not accustomed to being routed, and the sting that every man felt to his pride was worse than the pain of their wounds.

Fewer than a dozen Cavalrymen and barely twice that number on foot remained, such was the ferocity of the Shar attack. Almost a thousand men lost in a morning.

"There are still people in the city," Captain Raims said, still clutching his blackened sword as though he meant to liberate them alone.

"They are beyond our help now," Rogan replied as they drew near the gates.

"There are reinforcements at Ulan Balsan," Captain Raims began.

"They will not be enough," Rogan barked. "Our best hope lies in calling for aid from Kor'Habat.

They reached the gates just as the Lythurian was descending the steps that led from the top of the city walls. The strange, green-tinged man paid them no heed as he exited ahead of them and accepted the reins of a horse from one of the Shar-hunters who had gathered outside. The historian and Valia's companion were among them, as was the eastern noble and some of his men.

"Move, you fools!" Rogan shouted. "That barricade will not discourage them for long."

Then Acastes rode past, with Olgoi Kinbataar clinging to him like an infant to its mother.

Typical that they should survive the day when so many more worthy men had fallen, Rogan mused.

CHAPTER 6

The people of Banihat had not had time to plan their escape. Some had grabbed whatever valuables they could, but most left with the clothes they wore on their backs and the loved ones they clung to. None had planned for a night exposed to the elements, in deep snow and freezing temperatures.

That small purse of coins snatched from its place on the high shelf could not be burned for warmth against the gathering cold. That silver candle holder with gold inlay could not be eaten when morning came and with it the hunger from a night shivering in the dark.

It was a sorry spectacle; thousands of people digging into the snow drifts to shelter from the wind. There was no wood to be had since trees were sparse this far north, and what there was lay frozen under deep snow. A few fires had been lit with the wood stripped from carts where it could be spared, leaving only those parts vital to their function. Fights had broken out already over the right to burn whole carts. Why should one man's children shiver in the dark while his neighbour has a cart laden with sacks of wool? Why should a man burn what was left of his livelihood to warm the fingers of one who failed to plan? These were the arguments of the desperate and the frightened, the animal urge to turn inward and protect one's own at the expense of all others.

"Those fires will only give away our position," Acastes

muttered. He was standing on the road at the northern extent of the refugee procession with Marlon, Alano and Granger. The glow of a sentry lamp could be seen a little further up the road and again at regular intervals around the encampment.

"If the Shar want to find us, they need only follow the road," Marlon replied, kicking at the muddy slush at his feet.

"We have covered barely five miles," Alano said. "Why do you suppose they did not give chase?"

Granger shivered, drawing his coat tighter around his shoulders. "The Khalim-Shar knows that it does not need to hurry. We will be slow, and it can consolidate its position in Banihat. If what they say of the East is true, then its aim is not our destruction but our enslavement."

"Perhaps if we reach Ulan-Balsan ahead of them, the Shar can be held at the river," Alano said. "They will not cross open water and the bridge to the south can be held with a minimal force."

Granger shook his head. "That river is frozen, mark my words. "Our best option is further south. We should cross the Olchora ahead of them and watch the mountain paths to the west."

"The Olchora?" Acastes whistled. "That is a long way to travel with several thousand hungry refugees. The people of Ulan-Balsan will swell their number further. No, we should make a stand at Ulan-Balsan; we have beaten them there before."

"No," Granger replied. "This is not the same. The Khalim-Shar is a different opponent altogether; more cunning and ruthless by far. Besides, their number is far greater this time. Marlon, how many would you estimate? Marlon?"

Marlon was staring north. "What?"

"How many Shar would you estimate attacked the city?"

Marlon sighed. "I could not say; five hundred or more, although I did not see every ship into harbour. I do not know."

"You seem distracted, my friend," Acastes said. "Staring up that road will not hold them at bay."

Alano placed a hand on Marlon's shoulder. "It is not the Shar that fills your thoughts though, is it, my friend?"

"I need to go back," Marlon murmured.

"What? Don't be a fool," Acastes sputtered.

"She was north of the city according to the information I gathered in the city." Marlon groaned. "She may not even know that Banihat has been taken. I should have gone for her as soon as I learned…"

"It is not your fault, Marlon," Granger insisted "Valia will hear about it, and she will not be so foolish as to try and take the city back alone." He smiled, betraying a small doubt that yes, she might well try such a thing. "She will cross the Khashmit far to the west of Banihat and head south to safety. Do not worry about Valia; she is resourceful, and no fool."

Marlon was shaking his head. "No, I must go back. She is in danger."

Acastes shivered. "The Steppe in winter is not a place to enter on a whim."

"Even more reason to seek her out."

"And where would you begin looking? That place is vast and barren, even the Hetai Nomads can go months without seeing another clan."

Marlon took a long time to answer, and when he did it was barely a whisper. "I can feel her pain."

Acastes shook his head and muttered under his breath but Alano stepped closer to Marlon. "I will come with you," he said.

"I cannot ask that of you," Marlon replied.

"Then do not ask. All the same, I will come with you."

"You have done enough, old friend. Go home to your wife."

Alano shook his head. "Casilda is less safe now than when I joined you. Everywhere is less safe. Valia has never failed me and I will not fail her now."

At last, Marlon nodded.

"If you are looking for an army to follow you, then you will find one here," Alano said, casting a glance back at the encampment that extended along the frozen road.

"No," Marlon said. "A large force will only draw unwanted attention. I will accept your offer, but any more would be a hindrance. We will leave at first light."

"We will continue south then," Granger said. "And cross into Korathea to the north of Lake Arat. I cannot say where we will go from there, but we will leave word. If Rogan Fol'Brandam has any sense he will send the Heavy Infantry to cover the mountain passes of the Lesser Cascus. But this winter is cold, and I expect rivers to freeze where they would flow in milder years, so there may be more crossing points for the Shar than expected."

"We should return to Kor'Habat," Acastes declared. "That great city will not be so easily taken. Let the Shar throw themselves at its walls."

Korathea is more than just a city," Granger cautioned. "You would gift the Shar the whole of the east of the continent, *all* of Korathea's lands. You would be reliant on Dasar to feed the city once stocks are low."

"True words," Alano said, "but the final decision will not be ours to make. We need the Heavy Infantry, and we will be forced to march to their drumbeat."

Marlon grunted.

"Then tomorrow I will go and find the only person who can change their tune," he replied. "But first; sleep."

At the first sign of a lessening in the darkness, Marlon was awake. He gathered his pack and picked his way through the ghostly landscape to where Alano was already busy at one of the many clusters of animals, saddling his own mount. The horses had been gathered for warmth and covered in blankets where they could be spared. No snow had fallen overnight, but a twinkling of frost covered the huddled forms that lay in the shallow depressions in the snow where the people of Banihat had made their icy beds.

Marlon's joints were stiff and painful with the cold and it was a relief to work some blood into his limbs after a short, restless sleep.

"It is not too late to change your mind," Marlon murmured so as not to rouse those who had found the comfort of sleep. "The warmth of Lythuria must be a tempting prospect."

"Casilda's father used to say that, 'a comfort is no comfort 'til discomfort's burr is held.' When I feel the warmth of home again it will be all the more welcome."

Marlon threw the saddle over his horse's back and paused to regard his friend for a moment. Then he shrugged and continued fastening the flank strap and girth. Next, he loaded the pack mule in silence, double checking that all Valia's armour was there. She would need it when he found her.

Clouds of breath fogged the air as their horses shivered, eager to be moving. The snow that had been trampled to a muddy slush the day before had re-frozen, creating a treacherous landscape of hardened ruts and patches of slick water ice. They walked their mounts north along the road to where two sentries stood huddled, sharing a blanket around their shoulders. Their breath billowed in the still air, illuminated by the sickly lamp that burned at the end of a pole.

Abbil was there too, hunched into a fur-lined cloak beside his horse, and Jon, pacing back and forth to keep warm.

"I hear that you are going back to find Valia," Abbil challenged and Jon ceased his pacing to listen in.

Marlon shrugged and grunted an acknowledgement.

"Do you know where to look?" Abbil asked.

"North of Banihat last I heard," he replied. "She may not know that the city has fallen."

"How do you know she yet lives?"

"She lives," Marlon said with hesitation.

Alano stepped forward. "We hope to find her before the Shar spread northward. If we are fast and stealthy the Shar will never know that we have been, and we will re-join you south of the Olchora."

Abbil nodded. His dark eyes sparkled in the lamp light. "It is a good plan. We should leave without delay."

Alano glanced at Marlon before speaking again. "We felt that a small force would have a greater chance of going unseen."

"Four is a small force," Abbil replied, his beard shifting to suggest a grin somewhere beneath.

"There is no need for…" Alano began.

"Valia of Hadaiti risked her life to keep my land free when the Korathean Empire came to take it. There is not a Dashiyan who stood upon that battlefield who would not risk their own for hers in return."

"And you, fletcher?" Alano said to Jon. "Would you not prefer to turn south."

"To where?" he replied, blowing out clouds of hoary breath. "To the warm embrace of my loving wife? Ha! I'll find more warmth out there." He nodded northwards.

Alano looked to Marlon again, who swung his leg up over his saddle and shrugged. He shook his head, knowing that to argue would be a waste of his breath, and mounted his own horse.

They travelled in silence as the gloom lifted. The cloud was not as low as it had been the previous day and the rising sun managed an intense glow on the horizon which warmed their spirits if not their bodies. They broke from the road after a while and headed north-west, away from Banihat, travelling for an hour before turning north again to find the Khashmit River. The snow was not so deep here, and the horses did not have to kick through knee-deep drifts as they had done nearer the road. The wind had scoured the landscape to reveal withered flags of defiant grasses, brown and brittle above the frost.

They spoke little as they travelled, and it was past midday before they reached the river. The land took on a subtle slope, leading down towards the wide, wandering ribbon of the Khashmit.

In a land of gentle undulations, the river was only discernible by its absolute flatness, as both were white with snow.

"We should let the horses drink, and feed a little," Alano said as they reached the river's edge.

"Will that ice hold us?" Abbil muttered. "It is not natural to walk on water."

Alano chuckled, "Your rivers may not freeze in Dashiya, but I assure you, a frozen river such as this could hold a herd of cattle."

Marlon dismounted and set about clearing the snow to find the water's edge, then started cutting a hole in the ice with a small hatchet. The ice was hard and brittle and razor slivers flew as he worked. He was a full hands-width down before he broke through to the water trapped beneath. Soon he had widened the hole enough for the horses to drink, then he filled his own water skin with the clear, chilly liquid.

"We should walk the horses across," Marlon said, looking up from the hole he had made.

They started walking, crunching over the thin layer of spindrift on the ice. The river was perhaps fifty yards wide at this point and they were halfway across when Alano spoke, his voice an urgent whisper.

"What is that?" he hissed. "Downriver. Left bank."

Marlon placed his hand on the pommel of his sword. It was strapped to the side of his horse along with his round shield.

"Riders," he said, relaxing a little.

The three mounted figures were little more than smudges against the unyielding grey of the snow and cloud, but they were heading right towards Marlon's party. The riders fanned out as they approached, and it was soon evident that they were armed.

"Are those Dachen's men?" Alano said. "I recognise those weapons; the sparths."

The sparths that two of the riders were carrying were unmistakeable; long shafts with an elongated cutting edge at one end.

Marlon grunted, unsure. Then he saw the dark forms of two

Shar, fifty yards behind the riders but moving with swift sinuous strides down onto the frozen river. Marlon was about to shout a warning when he saw one of the riders turn in his saddle, and on seeing the onrushing Shar, showed no sign of panic.

"Shar!" he spat, pulling his sword free and lifting his shield from his horse's flank. He slapped the horse on the rump, sending it whinnying to the frozen bank of the river. Jon, Abbil and Alano did the same, scattering their horses and the pack mule as they prepared to face the Shar.

When the riders were fifty yards away, the Shar passed them, claws tearing splinters from the ice in their eagerness to attack. Alano sidestepped the first lunge, swinging his sword as he spun away. The Malmotti blade, forged by the great master swordsmith himself, sent a twitching forelimb skidding across the ice as the Shar screeched in pain and anger. The second Shar swung at Abbil, who managed to parry the blow with his sword but failed to inflict any damage. Jon circled the Shar to attack it from behind when an arrow struck his left shoulder above his shield, piercing the leather armour and slicing across his flesh. He roared in anger, hurling a curse at the bowman. Marlon was rushing to Abbil's aid when he saw the bowman nock another arrow as he drew nearer. He crouched as he moved, trying to cover as much of his body as he could with his shield. An arrow thudded into the leather-covered oak but did not make it through. The archer was nocking another arrow as he rode past and turned in his saddle for another shot. Marlon rolled and the arrow skittered past him on the ice.

Alano ducked the scything blade of the sparth that the rider had swung at him, slipping as he did and landed on his hip with a painful thump. The sparth bearer pulled on the reins to come around for a second charge, but he was too eager, and the hooves slipped beneath his mount and horse and rider crashed onto the ice. Alano was quick to take advantage despite his painful hip, and he kicked the sparth from its owner's grip even as the man tried to free his leg from beneath his thrashing horse.

The injured Shar had reached its severed limb which lay twitching on the ice. It pressed its stump to the black ichor of the dismembered limb and waited while the writhing flesh knitted again. Alano saw it begin to recover use of the limb and left the fallen man on the ice. He rushed towards it, seeing it turn its head to fix its dominant eyes on him. The Shar took two steps and then leapt forward. Alano dived onto the ice, rolling onto his back as he did, sliding under the Shar and driving his sword upwards. The blade opened the creature's belly the full length of its sinuous body, exposing writhing black gore within. The Shar screeched and flopped onto the ice, struggling to rise. But Alano was not about to allow it to heal a second time and he was upon it in a heartbeat, taking the head off in a single stroke. The body convulsed and then was still.

Abbil was being pushed back by the second Shar, and two deep gashes across the chest of his leather armour were proof of the creature's intentions. Alano sheathed his sword and picked up the fallen rider's sparth. He charged at the Shar, piercing its flank with the point and knocking it onto its side. Abbil sidestepped and removed the head with two strokes before it could recover. A quick nod of thanks, and then they turned their attentions to Marlon.

The second sparth bearer was charging at Marlon with the point of the long weapon held at chest height. Behind Marlon, the bowman had nocked another arrow and had started a slow canter forward.

Marlon fell and rolled as the sparth bearer reached him, swinging his sword at the horse's fetlocks. The horse went down screaming as the sword bit, throwing the rider onto the ice. The sparth was thrown from the attacker's grasp and Marlon was on his feet in a heartbeat. Dropping his sword, he ran towards the sparth and the onrushing bowman, scooping up the long weapon and hurling it in one fluid motion. The sparth struck the bowman in the chest, sending him tumbling backwards and the arrow arcing wide of its intended target. He hit the ice and did not move again.

The winded rider meanwhile had recovered and stood, drawing a short sword from his hip to face Marlon. But Jon was already behind him and hacked upwards into the man's armpit where the armour was light, all but severing his arm. He screamed as he fell to his knees, dropping the weapon he had held for only a moment.

Marlon looked all around to make sure there were no attackers waiting nearby. He took long breaths as he looked around. Alano ended the torment of the injured horse by cutting its throat with a regretful shake of the head. Abbil dragged the other rider across the ice to join his injured fellow.

Abbil dumped the man on the ice. His leg was broken, crushed beneath the weight of his horse when it had slipped and fallen, but he was otherwise uninjured. He was jabbering away in a language that none of them understood, but begging was a universal tongue, and this man was clearly pleading for his life. The other collapsed forward as his blood loss sucked consciousness from him and he lay face down in a growing crimson pool that steamed in the chill air.

"Easterners," Abbil said. "That armour is the same as Dachen's men; and those sparths."

The man's eyes brightened. "Dachen? Dachen!" Then more incoherent babbling.

"This one is done for," Abbil murmured as he kicked at the foot of the unconscious man. "But what shall we do with our chatty friend?"

"Oh, I have more ideas than you could possibly imagine," Jon grimaced, loosening the straps on his leather pauldrons to inspect the damage.

"Kill him here," Abbil said stepping forward.

"Wait," Marlon cautioned. "He may have information."

"I wish you the best of luck getting it from him," Abbil replied.

"Take him with us," Alano suggested. "Let Dachen interrogate him when we meet the others again."

"He will give away our position at the very first opportunity," Abbil protested.

Marlon looked all around at the barren landscape. "Where would we hide?"

The injured man's eyes darted from one to the other, trying to follow the thrust of the conversation. He spoke and earned a sharp crack on the back of his head from a furious Jon, who held up the leather shoulder armour. The arrow had passed through by a full hand's width, glancing across the front of his shoulder which was bleeding freely, although it was the punctured armour that occupied his concern.

"Look at this!" he shouted. "These were new last winter!"

"Take him with us," Marlon said.

"His leg is broken," Abbil growled. "How will he travel"

"We have two extra horses now." Marlon motioned to the two horses waiting on the ice. "Splint his leg."

"With what? I see no trees; no branches," Abbil replied.

Marlon picked up the sparth dropped by the man and laid it against the dead horse. Then he stamped on it, breaking the shaft under his boot.

"With this," he said, kicking it over to where the man lay propped up on an elbow.

Jon picked up the stick and held the ragged, splintered end up to the man's face. Then he spoke in the manner of a man trying to make himself understood by foreigners by speaking loud and slow.

"Do you see this?" The man stared at the broken shaft as Jon waved it under his nose. "If you give us any trouble, I'll shove this up your arse!"

The injured man understood the spirit of the threat if not the exact details and lay back to allow his lower leg to be splinted. In the end, two more sections of the sparth were used to make a brace, securing the crude support with strips of blanket from under the dead horse's saddle. The man had screamed when Marlon pulled the limb out straight but had soon receded into a torpid silence behind a face drained of blood as the leg was bound.

"We should move," Marlon said when their prisoner had been lifted onto the saddle of his horse. "If these were scouts, they will be missed, and I would sooner find shelter tonight."

His companions nodded in agreement and gathered the horses.

They travelled north for a time before turning eastwards back towards the coast. The only information that Marlon had gained pointed to a farm to the north-east of Banihat somewhere near the ocean, but that would need to be enough.

"Why does he stare at me like that?" Olgoi muttered.

He was walking beside Granger who was leading his horse along the slushy road. An elderly man sat on the horse, holding his infant granddaughter bundled in a blanket in his arms. Most of those who could, walked, allowing the very old, the very young, or the injured to travel on horseback. Nirmaya and her Sisters were on foot, strung out at either side of the dispirited caravan, self-appointed defenders of all who had escaped Banihat. Even Dachen and his men walked beside their mounts which carried the despondent shapes of the exiled.

"Hm?" Granger murmured. He was exhausted from a cold, sleepless night followed by the relentless march.

"The Lythurian. He has been looking at me that way for some time."

Granger followed Olgoi's line of sight and found Elan on the other side of the road with eyes fixed on the Kylyptian.

"I am not sure. Does it make you uncomfortable?" Granger asked, having long since given up trying to explain Elan's behaviour.

Olgoi was silent for a while.

"Do you think he wishes me harm?"

"Why would he? Have you wronged him, or someone he cares about?" It was a rhetorical question, but Olgoi almost choked on his response.

"Certainly not," he protested.

Granger laughed.

"Elan has a gentle spirit; he would do nothing to cause you injury." Then a mischievous smile played across Granger's face. "Unless…"

Olgoi's head snapped around toward Granger in alarm, but the historian just laughed.

"You have a cruel sense of humour, historian," Olgoi muttered when he realised that he was being mocked. "And this is no place for japes."

"Of course not. I apologise."

They walked on in silence, and when Olgoi turned back to keep an eye on Elan, the Lythurian was gone.

Olgoi swallowed hard. "Do you suppose Rogan will return soon with the Heavy Cavalry, and reinforcements?"

"I do not expect to see Rogan again until we reach the Ol-chora River, if not Kor'Habat itself," Granger replied.

Rogan had ridden ahead with what was left of his Heavy Cavalry to alert the people of Ulan-Balsan, but Granger doubt-ed that the safety of those people was paramount in the Hatar's schemes. What remained of the Heavy Infantry had also been ordered to forge on ahead of the Banihat civilians who had no hope of matching that pace.

Ahead on the road, Acastes was doing his best to charm one of the Sisters and appeared to be making some headway given the way she was laughing at his jokes. Kekoa held the reins of Acastes' horse with its injured rider; a man whose foot had been crushed by a cartwheel in the panic at the gates of Banihat. Kapaneus was just behind, leading his own horse which carried a skinny young boy and his little brother; both youngsters engulfed in the same blanket.

"That man never leaves Acastes' side," Olgoi observed.

"Kekoa?" Granger said. "He is Acastes' servant, bound to him by an oath of Jendayan honour."

"No, the other one," Olgoi replied. "Kapaneus."

Granger shrugged. "They hunted Shar together for a long time. They share a bond that runs deeper than ordinary friendship."

Olgoi did not answer but Granger could tell that Kapaneus' presence bothered the man. Or perhaps it was just a general malaise that he sensed; a natural response to the trauma of war and seeing all he had held dear ripped from him.

Olgoi heeled his horse to go faster, as though it would see him in Ulan Balsan any quicker.

Nightfall saw them arrive at a small farming village. The inhabitants were still loading carts and pack animals with their belongings. These people had received fair warning from Rogan earlier in the day and had the luxury of time to gather what they needed. There were not nearly enough roofs to give shelter to all, but the grain store offered a bland meal that even Granger could not enliven. Fights broke out over the price the farmers demanded, and accusations of hoarding were aimed at them for daring to keep the bulk of what they had for their own families.

Granger knew that it would not get any easier until they reached the town of Ulan-Balsan and the supplies it held. Hunger could turn neighbours against one another when its claws scraped at an empty belly.

Marlon watched the sun setting on the third day of his search. They had met no more scouting parties, but they needed food and water and the horses were no better. There was nothing with which to light a fire to melt snow; they had tried lighting bundles of dead grass, but it was frozen and icy, refusing to take a spark. He was wondering how the Hetai nomads survived out here in winter and was beginning to doubt their existence when Alano spotted what looked like a settlement on the horizon to the north.

"The Hetai?" Abbil suggested.

Marlon only grunted in response, and Jon gave the prisoner a warning glare. The Eastern man nodded in silent assurance that he would be no trouble.

They approached with great care what turned out to be a cluster of five conical tents in the gathering darkness, but there was no sign of life.

Worse than that, there were signs of a slaughter.

The butchered remnants of some sort of animal lay all around; only mounds of thick hair soaked in frozen gore remained. The area in the centre of the group of tents was stained too. The wind had done what it could to scour the blood from the snow, but a blurring of its edges was all that had been achieved.

"There is no one here," Jon said as he emerged from one of the tents.

Marlon bent down at the edge of a tent and plucked a small knot of hair from where it had become tapped against a ground anchor. He knew that it was human. This was not the coarse hair of a hardy goat but the delicate strands of something once washed and combed.

"The Shar have been here," he said, letting the wind blow the dark locks from his fingers.

"If they have already moved north, then…" Alano left the rest unsaid.

"No," Marlon breathed staring northwards. "They came from the north."

The low sun had revealed something to him with its dying light. When fresh snow is packed underfoot it hardens and resists the action of the wind that would otherwise scour it away, leaving tell-tale lumps to betray the footfalls. Cast into stark relief by the dying light was a trail of raised prints stretching northwards across the barren landscape, unmistakeably Shar with prominent claw marks still evident in the hard-packed crystals of ice.

"There must have been dozens of them," Alano breathed.

The wind hissed in reply, driving a haze of spindrift across the endless, barren landscape.

CHAPTER 7

The surface of the Balsan River was frozen into a broad strip of pale grey. Streaks of drifting ice crystals danced in spirals on the strong breeze, swirling around the weary legs of the people of Banihat as they approached Ulan-Balsan. In warmer conditions, the pitiful column of refugees would certainly have had to endure the thirty-mile trip south to the bridge where the river narrowed; the cold had at least offered this one, simple kindness and shortened their journey.

To the east lay the forest that had burned in the decisive battle of the previous spring. The ashes had long since washed away from the charred remains, leaving cold black pillars that jutted from the frozen soil like monuments to a long-forgotten tragedy.

The wooden palisade of Ulan-Balsan was plastered with driven snow, evidence of the siege it had endured from the ferocious north winds. There were no storms on the horizon today and a low sun had offered a little cheer if not warmth. Dozens of militiamen and townsfolk had left the protection of the town to offer what help they could to the thousands debilitated by cold and hunger.

Captain Daghur of the Ulan-Balsan militia spotted Olgoi and Granger and waited for the men to reach him as the throng shuffled past.

"Welcome back to Ulan-Balsan," Daghur said without

enthusiasm. "We were concerned that you would not make it this far."

"Word has reached you then?" Olgoi said, accepting Daghur's arm and continuing towards the gate.

"Hatar Rogan Fol'Brandam passed through here several days ago," the captain said. "He told us what has happened in Banihat. How many are with you?"

"A little over four thousand," Granger said. "Can Ulan Balsan accommodate them? A day or two to gather their strength."

Daghur nodded. "It will be done. Most have already left with the Hatar's Heavy Infantry for safety. Those who have remained have had time to prepare. There is food and shelter in the town, and we will make room as we can."

"Thank you, Captain," Granger said. "But we should not linger any more than we must.

Daghur offered a tight-lipped smile. "Captain Silman would have you leave immediately, but a day or two to regain your strength can do no harm."

"Silman?" Olgoi said.

"Heavy Infantry," Daghur replied with obvious distaste. "He arrived with a thousand soldiers just after you left in the summer. The Hatar, Rogan Fol'Brandam took most of those to Banihat before the winter, and then most of what remained when he passed through again, heading south."

"Are there no Infantry left in the town?" Olgoi asked.

"A dozen, no more," Daghur allowed a smile to play across his face. "And Captain Silman is livid. He has been ordered by Rogan Fol'Brandam to escort all the civilians of Banihat and Ulan-Balsan as far as the Olchora River."

"With a dozen Heavy Infantry for protection? He needn't have bothered," Granger muttered, then he quickened his pace. "Now, my stomach is turning on itself with hunger."

By nightfall, every house and storeroom, cellar and stable was full. Most homes had been left empty; furniture stacked and all that could not be carried had been stored against the day that the owners could return. There was ample food for the sudden influx, and the grateful refugees lay down with full stomachs for the first time in what felt like an age.

The Shar's Folly was full, and the innkeeper was delighted to see so much coin crossing the bar top for the first time since the start of summer. Every table was taken, and fresh casks of ale and wine were tapped for the new customers.

With the inn's cook being among the first to leave the town, Granger had inserted himself in the kitchens and could not be budged. He muttered the likes of "this is living," and "hollow existence without food?" as pots boiled on the range, filling the common room with delicious aromas. He crushed herbs between his palms and breathed the scents in, adding a handful of sprigs to the stew. Bread, cheese and cured meats had taken the edge off the travellers' hunger, but the main course was only just reaching readiness.

"We should not wait here too long," Kapaneus said to Dachen as they watched Acastes regale a group of drinkers with some tale or other across the room.

"No, we should not," Dachen replied.

"A day, perhaps."

"The horses will not replace their lost weight in a day," Dachen warned.

"We are better prepared for the journey now," Kapaneus replied. "Leaving Banihat was chaos."

"That it was," Dachen sighed and massaged his right elbow.

"How is your arm?

Dachen shrugged. "The dressing that Granger prepared is helping, and the spur-root infusions he makes me drink certainly ease the pain. It is not broken, for sure, yet he insists I rest it."

Kapaneus chuckled. "He has many talents, that historian. I would take his advice if I were you."

"I will. And I am grateful for his help."

"Just wait until you eat his food..." Kapaneus said, leaning close.

"I only hope it smells better than this poultice." He raised his injured arm a little and wrinkled his nose in disgust. They laughed, both aware of the sour aroma that escaped from beneath the dressing.

They sat in silence for a while before Dachen spoke again.

"I find it strange that we had a quarrel at all."

"You mean the Element?" Kapaneus asked. "That conflict is not resolved yet."

Dachen sighed. "Adeyemi is a strange one, but he is my friend."

Kapaneus nodded. "I understand." He paused before continuing. "Who is Jangbu?"

Dachen snapped his head around to face him. "He is nothing!"

"Clearly," Kapaneus replied with a wry smile as Dachen's hand moved, unbidden, to the scab beneath his left eye.

Dachen jerked his hand back down and took a few calming breaths. "He is of Khumjang," he said in a quieter tone. "How he came to be in my brother's company, I neither care nor desire to know."

"Khumjang?" Kapaneus said. "The 'Greater Kingdom'?"

"There are some who call it that," Dachen scoffed, "but I believe greatness comes from the measure of its people and not the size of its lands. They call Tianpok a 'Lesser Kingdom' and yet our archers are famed for their skill, our wool is sturdier than any that those southern lands can boast, and our horses are surely more surefooted. A 'Lesser Kingdom' indeed!"

Kapaneus laughed, feeling the tension ease. "I will not make that error again, I assure you."

Seeing the Easterner fall silent again, Kapaneus asked, "You lost men in Banihat?"

He nodded. "Tashimen; a good archer, very brave."

"What became of the rest of your escort? There were twelve

at least."

Dachen shrugged. "Chapok ordered them to leave my service; five refused. I was surprised to see Yeshe return to me; I was sure that he was gone."

"They disobeyed the King?" Kapaneus mused. "They must be very loyal."

"They are. I argued with them over this for a long time, but they would sooner join me in exile than serve under Chapok. Tashimen paid for that decision with his life."

"I am sorry," Kapaneus said, hearing the note of regret in the Easterner's voice. "And Adeyemi?"

"Adeyemi is his own man; he owes his allegiance to no-one. He stays with me through friendship."

"Loyalty and friendship can be difficult to explain at times." Kapaneus said, glancing in Acastes' direction. "Perhaps they are one and the same."

Dachen flexed his elbow a little, then nodded towards the big man, "What story is he telling them?"

Kapaneus cocked his head to pick out the words from the hubbub and smiled. "Ah, yes. I remember that; a Shar we were tracking in Dasar one winter. I had ventured out onto what I had thought to be solid ground to head it off and keep it from entering a dense wood. Unfortunately, beneath the thin layer of frost was a quagmire of cold, sucking mud. I became quite stuck, as did the Shar that Acastes had flushed towards me. Of course, Acastes himself fared no better when he followed and became bogged down despite my warnings."

Dachen chuckled. "What became of the Shar?"

"It lost its head, although both Acastes and I both lost a good pair of boots that day." Kapaneus cocked his head and listened a moment longer. "He is more heroic in this telling though."

"A good story is one that grows in the memory," Dachen noted.

"I'll drink to that!" Starling declared as he arrived with a jug of wine in one hand and a cup in the other. Nirmaya was with him and they were already swaying under the influence of too much wine. Kapaneus shuffled along the bench he occupied, and the newcomers flopped down into the space. Starling made to fill Kapaneus' cup from the jug, but the man placed a hand over it.

"Not for me, Starling," he said. "I would sooner keep the few wits I have left."

Starling shrugged and held the jug up to Dachen who shook his head.

"Well this is a cheery table is it not?" Nirmaya slurred as a serving boy arrived at the table carrying a tray laden with bowls of steaming stew.

Kapaneus began taking bowls from the tray. "You have had a long journey, and the wine has gone to your head. I suggest a good meal and an early night."

"Are you really a prince?" Nirmaya asked with a giggle, paying no attention to the meal placed in front of her.

Dachen clenched his jaw and took a deep, calming breath. "I am the second son of King Gephal of Tianpok, so yes, I am a prince."

"You don't seem happy," she said squinting at him, "If I was a prince, I think I'd be happy." A hiccup punctuated the statement.

"If you were a prince, you'd be a man," Starling said.

"Oh yes," she replied, then doubled over in silent laughter, punctuated by sharp squeaks with every intake of breath.

Dachen was shaking his head when Kekoa arrived. "The horses are stabled, Kapaneus," he said, bowing his head, which for some reason only intensified Nirmaya's laughter.

"Thank you, Kekoa. Sit and eat," Kapaneus replied, "I saved you a bowl of stew."

"I should eat in the kitchen," he said with a glance in Acastes' direction.

"No need. Sit."

Kekoa nodded and joined them on the bench, pulling the

bowl towards him and breathing the aroma in.

"Are your men taken care of?" Kapaneus asked, distracting Dachen from Nirmaya who was still giggling to herself.

"Yes, it will be a squeeze, but we have space in a house near here," Dachen said. "I will join them soon. I might have stayed to eat with them, but the historian's reputation for cooking had to be tested."

The door was flung open with a crash, and the chatter subsided as Captain Silman walked into the common room. He scanned the crowd until his eyes settled on Starling. "Do not let me disturb the festival atmosphere," he said with a sneer, and started a slow, measured walk towards Kapaneus' table.

Starling brightened when the big man approached, throwing his arms in the air. "Captain Silman!" he declared. "Welcome."

"We meet again, little man," Silman replied. "Are you reduced to a single wench now? What has become of you?" He shook his head in mock sympathy and smiled.

"Don't be like that," Starling replied. "Have a drink. Oh, and if you find yourself short of coin, I am sure I could spare a few marks for you."

Silman's smile slipped. "Do not bait me, boy. The road south is long and treacherous, and we will travel it together."

A huge hand landed on Silman's shoulder and spun him round. He reached for the dagger at his hip, but Acastes already had his own blade drawn and held high. He tut-ted in warning. Kapaneus was also on his feet with a throwing knife poised above his right shoulder. The room fell silent.

"Why are you harassing these weary travellers, Silman?" Acastes asked in a casual tone.

"Acastes," Silman sighed.

"Ah," Starling smiled. "I see we all know each other then. Delightful."

"You are normally seen skulking around the Akharran," Acastes remarked, ignoring Starling's quip. "What brings you so far from your home comforts?"

"Duty, Acastes," Silman sneered. "Something you would know nothing about. I might have known you would be the sort to surround himself with thieves and harlots."

"Oh? How so?"

Silman pointed at Starling. "Were you aware that your companion is in possession of a stolen Governor's seal?"

"Really?" Acastes smiled and raised an eyebrow. "A *Governor's* seal, you say. Starling, is this true?"

Starling held out his hands in surprise. "What? I have no seal."

"See, he has no seal," Acastes said, never shifting his gaze from Silman. "Now we will move onto your second, and in my eyes more offensive slur; apologise to the lady."

"What?" Silman spluttered.

"I believe you named her a harlot," Acastes said. "Apologise."

"Yes, apologise to the harlot!" Starling declared with much glee, spilling wine on his trousers as he did so.

"You play a dangerous game, Acastes," Silman warned, ignoring Starling's joy. "I have soldiers here who could end you and your merry band."

"Yes, I heard that you had *a dozen men* under your command, very impressive," Acastes mocked.

"The last I heard, *you* commanded a sycophant and a slave."

Kekoa stirred in his seat. "In war, the lesser enemy is your friend. Avoid engagement that weakens you both against the greater threat," he muttered.

"It speaks," Silman sneered. "Acastes, tighten the leash on your *pet!*"

"I think that Kekoa has a point." A new voice joined in from near the kitchens.

"Granger," Acastes said without turning. "If you are able to discern meaning from his ramblings then you are welcome to try." He lowered his knife a little as the tension eased.

Granger walked further into the common room. "You may

have your differences but the Khalim-Shar is a far worse enemy than either of you could be to each other."

Acastes cocked his head in thought for a moment and returned his knife to his belt. Kapaneus relaxed his stance but kept his blade in hand.

"This is not finished, Acastes," Silman murmured as he pushed past and made for the door.

Acastes watched Silman stomp through the door before turning to Kekoa.

"Go and check on the horses or something," he ordered.

Kekoa slipped from the bench and bowed without a word before hurrying from the room.

Acastes took the vacant seat and pulled a bowl of stew closer. "I hope this was worth the wait," he muttered and raised a steaming spoonful to his mouth but Kapaneus caught the big man's wrist before he could eat.

Acastes sighed and returned the spoon to the bowl.

"It is quite safe," Granger assured him. "I prepared it myself."

"It would only take a moment's inattention for someone to slip a poison into the pot," Kapaneus replied, pulling the bowl towards him. He sniffed at the stew and tested a little on his tongue. "You spice this so heavily it could mask any poison."

"Life is too short for bland food, young Kapaneus," Granger lectured. "And I assure you, it is fine."

Satisfied, for this meal at least, Kapaneus pushed the bowl back to a grateful Acastes.

Dachen was still watching Starling as he leaned back in his chair, shaking his head. "Your crimes catch up with you, young Starling. One day your luck will desert you."

Starling raised his cup in a wavering, sardonic toast and slurred, "I do not rely on luck, my friend."

"Then I hope that you do not rely on your companions. Your bodyguard could not stand if she tried," Dachen noted with a nod towards Nirmaya, who was slipping deeper into a drunken fugue, leaning ever more on Starling for support.

"Is it true?" Kapaneus asked. "Are you a thief?"

Starling puffed himself up. "I am an artist!" he declared.

"Does your 'art' involve taking that which does not belong to you?"

Starling chuckled. "If the occasion calls for it."

Acastes took a large mouthful and grunted. "There is much of it about," he muttered around his food. "Tell me, Dachen, has Adeyemi come to his senses yet? Will he allow us to destroy the item he stole now that he can see the danger it poses?"

"Stole?" Dachen raised an eyebrow. "I was led to believe that it was simply found in the forest."

"Valia slayed the beast," Acastes warned. "It is hers by right."

Dachen spread his hands and cast his gaze around the room. "Then, where is she? If she has a claim, then she should be here to make it."

"She already did that, before you sneaked away to Banihat. He would not listen to reason then, why should he listen to reason now?"

"I am afraid that Adeyemi has grown attached to it," Dachen replied. "Besides, Granger assures me that it is without power."

Granger grimaced and leaned forward to speak, but Acastes began before he was able.

"Then perhaps I should simply take it from him," he said.

"He would kill you if you tried," Dachen warned.

"Hah!" Acastes scoffed. "I was trained in the Akharran with the Heavy Infantry; Korathea's finest men. I do not fear the rusty blade of Adeyemi."

"Then you are an arrogant fool," Dachen replied.

Acastes banged his fist on the table. "I have bested better men than him!"

"I think," Granger said, rising as Kapaneus tried to calm his friend, "that it is time to turn in for the night. We are all exhausted from our journey, and I would sooner continue this discussion with a clear head."

There was a general murmur of assent around the table, and even Nirmaya managed to sit upright, just in time for the fiery-haired Maidra to arrive at her side, glowering.

"There you are!" she snapped. "I have been looking every-where for you."

"She was here," Starling offered.

"I can see that, you buffoon!" She glared at him as she helped Nirmaya to her feet. "What did you intend to do with her? Get her drunk, and then what?"

"I assure you, my intentions were purely honourable," he slurred, but Maidra was already walking away with Nirmaya under her wing.

Acastes leaned over and slapped Starling on the leg and said, "No luck tonight, little man." Then he drained his cup and left.

Starling had a vague awareness of his companions leaving and managed a few curt parting greetings. The common room was beginning to empty now, as exhaustion took its toll on the travellers. People dispersed to the various dwellings in which they had found shelter, and soon Starling was alone at the table in a room that felt more spacious than it had before.

"Will no-one drink with me?" he shouted to the emptying room.

He shrugged at the low murmur which answered him and emptied the wine jug into his cup; the cup remained half empty. He sighed, and took a mouthful, swirling the wine over his tongue to draw out what flavour he could with his dulled senses. A moment later, his cup was being filled from a fresh jug, and Olgoi Kinbataar joined Starling, sitting on a chair across the table.

Olgoi smelled his own wine and closed his eyes to savour the aroma, then took the most delicate of sips that hardly had his lips wet. "From the foothills of the Mora Mountains in Northern Eritania," he said. "The innkeeper has always held a cask for me. A more refined complexion, I am sure you will agree."

Starling regarded the newcomer with a quizzical eye before taking a large mouthful of the wine. He swallowed, then smiled. "Mmm, clompexion," he murmured.

Olgoi allowed a moment of silence before speaking again. "I could not help but overhear your conversation. Forgive me, but I believe you could be an individual with a certain, how should I say it, skill, which I may require."

Starling took another mouthful of wine and forced himself to focus on Olgoi before the man continued.

"It would require your utmost discretion and I could pay you most handsomely, but," a look of doubt crossed Olgoi's face, "perhaps I misjudge you. It would be exceedingly difficult."

Starling leaned forward. "How handsomely?" he asked, suddenly lucid.

A smile touched Olgoi's lips. "I had not misjudged you, after all." He leaned close and explained to Starling exactly what he wanted him to do.

Marlon paused at the door of the cottage. It was a large, thatched building with shelter for animals at one end. Whatever livestock had been kept there had been slaughtered, leaving only their blood-stained hair frozen into the ground. The thatched roof had been partially burned but the flames had failed to take hold in the snow.

He stepped inside.

It was cold. His eyes took in the neat kitchen. A chair lay on its side but otherwise there was little sign of disturbance. There was no sign of looting; the shelves were full. He walked to a step ladder and climbed the first few rungs. Two beds pushed together and piled with blankets and furs.

"Was she here?" Abbil asked, startling Marlon.

He stepped down and turned to face Abbil, then his eye moved beyond the Dashiyan. He strode past without a word to the range and reached up to where a sword hung on a pair of brackets. He took it down and held it with a care that bordered on reverence.

"She was here," he said.

"Marlon," Abbil began in a sympathetic tone, but could not put his thoughts into words. Instead, he straightened a chair to the table in the awkward silence and brushed a little of the snow from the table that had blown in through the damaged roof.

Marlon surveyed the kitchen, still holding the weapon in his hands. Something caught his eye above the stone sink. He placed the sword on the table and walked over to where a hook held a woollen apron, and a coin suspended on a leather thong.

He lifted the coin from the hook and stared at it.

"Marlon," Abbil said again.

He stuffed the coin into his coat and strode to the door. He pulled the tarnished blade from its scabbard as he crunched through the snow to where the injured eastern soldier sat on his horse.

"Where have they taken her?" he shouted, lifting the cold steel to the soldier's neck.

The terrified man lifted his bound hands in defence and began babbling in his own tongue.

"Marlon!" Abbil shouted.

"Where is she?" he shouted again, pushing the blade closer and pressing it against the man's neck.

The injured soldier squeezed his eyes shut and began to mewl like a child.

"Marlon!" Abbil shouted again. "She is gone."

"No! She lives!" Marlon yelled back over his shoulder.

"She is dead! Look around you."

"No!" Marlon screamed, pulling the soldier from his saddle.

The Easterner landed on his splinted leg and howled in pain.

"Where have they taken her?" Marlon bellowed, pressing the sword against the man's throat.

Abbil pulled Marlon back. "She is gone, Marlon!" he yelled.

"Kill this little man if it salves your pain, but it will not return her to you."

Marlon pushed him away and took a few heaving breathes. "She. Is. Alive!"

"Marlon!" Alano's voice reached them from the near distance. He was standing on a flat piece of ground fifty paces to the north-east.

Marlon glared at Abbil a moment longer before stomping away to see what Alano had found. Abbil watched him leave before turning to the groaning soldier. He shook his head and followed Marlon.

Alano was staring at a patch of ground still red with frozen blood. Jon was nearby but his back was turned, staring out to sea.

"A goat..." Marlon whispered.

"There is no skin or hair as in the barn," Alano said. His mouth was dry.

Marlon clenched his teeth and turned to face Alano. "She lives," he glowered.

Abbil arrived, shaking his head. He dropped to one knee and reached down to touch the bloody ground.

"Was she here?" Jon asked.

"She was," Abbil replied. "I am sorry, friends. This blood must be hers"

Jon swore an oath under his breath and sat down in the snow, not willing to look at the stain.

"We should mark this spot," Abbil declared. "Valia of Hadaiti will not be forgotten."

"Nor will she be mourned," Marlon growled. "Not until she is dead."

He strode back to the horses. The injured soldier did his best to crawl to safety, but Marlon showed no more interest in the man.

"Please, come with us," Granger begged one more time. He was standing at the wooden gates of Ulan Balsan watching the stream of refugees make their way onto the road south.

Captain Daghur smiled.

"There are too many people here who will not leave. I must stay."

"They are emboldened by a past victory over the Shar," Granger insisted. "It will be different this time. You have spoken to them?"

"You know that I have."

"It will be far worse when they attack again," Granger urged.

"You do not even know for sure that they are coming. Perhaps they will stop at Banihat. Perhaps they will pass this little town by..."

"You know that is unlikely."

"Nevertheless, my duty lies here with the people of Ulan Balsan."

"They are stubborn," Granger replied. "Have none of them listened to what their fellow Kylyptians told them about Banihat? There is no way to defend against what is coming."

Daghur slapped the paling at his back. "Our defences are good. What comes, comes."

Granger groaned. This argument was old, and he could see that Daghur would not be persuaded to change his mind. There were too many people unwilling to leave their livelihoods behind and the captain's sense of duty tied him to the town and its foolhardy inhabitants.

"Then good fortune, Captain," Granger said, offering a hand. "I hope that Fate is kind this time; she can be a cruel mistress."

Daghur smiled and took the offered hand. "Perhaps I have a part yet to play in your histories. Have a safe journey and give my regards to the South."

Granger gathered the reins of his horse and joined the throng on the road, falling into step beside Dachen's party who were also leading their mounts.

"You could not convince him to leave?" Dachen asked.

"I could not."

"He has a strong sense of duty and will not abandon his home so easily," Dachen nodded his approval.

"It is suicide and you know it," Granger replied.

"There are many kinds of death," Dachen murmured.

Granger sensed the Easterner's mood and changed the subject.

"How is the elbow?" he asked.

Dachen flexed the limb a few times. "Much better. I had feared it broken. The dressing you provided has helped greatly."

"A simple concoction of gild-lily roots and ground yellow-stone, and it was the least I could do after your timely arrival below the Taaman Bell."

"It was Adeyemi who killed the Shar."

Granger turned and nodded to acknowledge the dark-skinned man. Adeyemi offered a wide smile in return.

Granger also noticed the old alchemist, sitting astride the sturdy pack-horse with the clay urns strapped to its sides. Tsering was murmuring to himself, his facial expressions shifting through a wide range of emotions as he did so. He laughed out loud and then returned to his mutterings as though chiding himself for the outburst.

"Tsering has remained in your service, I see," Granger said.

"I am not sure that alchemists *serve* anyone," Dachen replied, then leaned over and whispered, "I am certain that he is a little mad."

They both glanced back at the alchemist who was giggling again at something.

"Just a little?" Granger replied.

"All the same, I am grateful for his presence." Then Dachen called to one of his men. "Pemba, a maddener if you will."

"They are not prepared," Pemba replied.

"The arrow alone will be enough," the prince said.

The soldier nodded and fished an arrow from a quiver on

his horse's flank. He threw it across the gap and Dachen plucked it from the air then held it out for Granger to inspect. The shaft and feathers were not unusual, but the tip was quite striking. Four razor-sharp fins bulged out from the shaft, curving to meet at the tip to form a tulip bud-shaped cage. There was room within the blades to hold something the size of a fingertip.

"This is a 'maddener'," Dachen explained, "and those urns contain *Ago-Camdi*; the best translation I can offer is 'fire-silver'. A curious substance: when Ago-Camdi meets water, it burns with a fierce heat and will sear flesh in a moment."

"Water?" Granger asked, feigning ignorance. He knew how the maddeners worked; had seen them used against men in the wars fought in the Eastern Kingdoms centuries ago and witnessed the agony they caused and fear they could spread among an army. "And yet they burn the Shar."

"There is water in their flesh just as in ours," Dachen explained, unaware that he was speaking to a man who understood this better than he himself did. "When not in use we store it under oil to protect it from the dampness of the air. Even Pemba's quiver contains oil when his arrows are charged, but I am always more comfortable when it is sealed in those urns." He glanced back at Tsering.

Elan was suddenly at Granger's side. He took the arrow from his hands and ran an appraising eye over it. Dachen was about to protest but Granger placed a hand on his arm.

They watched as the mute Lythurian inspected the elaborate point and then ran gentle fingers down the length to the fletching. He took a small pair of clippers from a belt pouch and snipped away at a section of bulky thread. The clippers were stowed in the pouch only to be replaced with a fine-bladed knife which he used to pare down the quills of the feathers. Then he re-whipped the fletchings with expert speed and precision, all whilst walking along the slushy road.

The arrow was passed back to Granger, who handed it to

Dachen. Dachen inspected the fletching then tossed it to Pemba who was glaring suspiciously at Elan. But Pemba's face brightened when he inspected the arrow.

"This is excellent work," he exclaimed, looking up from the arrow to where Elan had been, but the Lythurian was already walking on ahead and paid no heed to the compliment.

In the warm shadows of a vast hollow tree, Ganindhra brooded, bound to his throne.

"You have grown sullen, brother." The voice startled him.

"Who is that?" he demanded, trying to turn.

"And forgetful," the voice continued. "Do you truly not know who I am?"

"*Athusilan*," be breathed.

The visitor walked around the living throne so that Ganindhra could see him.

"Brother!" Ganindhra cried before gathering some decorum. "What are you doing here. It is forbidden."

"By whom?"

"It was agreed."

Athusilan smiled. His hair was white but his skin smooth, and his eyes burned a bright blue as they always had. "And how many remain who made that pact?"

Ganindhra sagged a little, softening his gaze, and took a long look at Athusilan. "You look well, brother."

"I look as I have always done." He shrugged.

"I am fading, Athusilan," Ganindhra said after a short silence.

Athusilan nodded. "I sense it in you."

"The *Anaki* allow me to wither yet rob me of death. And those same Elements have unleashed Khalim-Shar on this world."

"Abaddon was a fool," Athusilan said. "The *Anaki* make us what we are. Using a part of himself to create what he did was madness. None of us understand the *Anaki* enough to control them."

"He understood better than any."

"He was wrong to pry into their secrets and you were right to attack him for it," Athusilan replied.

"I thought you were bound to remain neutral in all matters," Ganindhra chided.

Athusilan half turned away. "I choose to remain apart; that does not mean that I do not recognise folly when I see it. Whatever he did, delving into his own substance gave rise to the Daemon when you struck him down. He should have died, but he endured. The *Anaki* should have left him then but they remained tethered to him, doing his bidding."

Images of the swirling black mass of *Anaki* Elements that formed the Daemon flickered in Ganindhra's mind.

"And some of those Elements remained here when Kellan Aemoran defeated Abaddon," Ganindhra muttered.

"The 'Mad One's' legacy is still strong on this world." Athusilan mused, then asked, "How is my Emissary?"

"You will know better than I how Granger fares. Do you not have *another* Emissary watching his every move?"

Athusilan smiled. "Indeed. I was wise to banish him here."

"You made him mortal." There was a bitter edge to Ganindhra's voice, but it was not for Granger's loss, it was envy for what he himself did not have.

"You grow weary." Athusilan stated.

Ganindhra stared at the floor for a long time before replying. "I am much diminished. I did not see the Jendayan army approaching until it was too late, such was my distraction. The People I created here were all but destroyed. I failed to protect them." He slumped in his throne.

Athusilan nodded. "It has been recorded in the *Book of Lives*; they will not be forgotten."

Ganindhra chuckled, but it was a mournful sound. "And I am cursed to remain here and be a part of each tragedy."

"Is it not your wish to persist?" Athusilan asked.

"I become less every day; it is a terrible fate, to wither without the release of death. And what of you, brother? Why do you *persist*?"

Athusilan looked perplexed. "It is my duty to gather the stories. To allow great deeds to be forgotten would be too terrible. That is what was agreed; it is my bond. I persist because I must."

"So, tell me then; why have you come," Ganindhra asked. "To lend assistance?"

Athusilan shook his head. "I must remain an observer as I promised I would, but you called out to me during the battle at Ulan Balsan. It has been needling me; why did you call for my aid when you knew that I could give none?"

Ganindhra took a long moment to answer "We are the last, brother. I am alone and fading into madness or worse. We have made so many mistakes in the past and I am fearful that we are making another."

Athusilan laid a hand on Ganindhra's gnarly shoulder. "Stay strong. I will always be watching you."

He stepped back and smiled at Ganindhra, holding his gaze until a blinding, narrow ellipse opened at his back and engulfed him. When the bright opening closed, Athusilan was gone, leaving Ganindhra to blink away the afterimages from eyes that were never meant to know weariness, alone in the gloom and echoing silence.

Senji Dayivar approached the circle of soldiers and forced his way through to the centre of the crowd. There in the clearing was the last soldier yet standing against them in Ulan-Balsan, defiant in defeat. The man was exhausted, barely able to hold his sword. His leather armour was bloody and his faced was bruised; one of his eyes swollen shut. An eastern soldier jeered and Senji silenced him, pointing his own sparth at the man in warning. Two Shadows circled the survivor within the circle but had refrained from attacking.

"What is your name, soldier of Ulan-Balsan?" Senji asked.

The soldier swayed and placed the tip of his sword on the ground for support, leaning on the hilt. He spat blood and stood as erect as he could manage. Senji had been relieved to find this town all but deserted; the slaughter in Banihat still sickened him when he thought about it. The memory of the woman, Belghutai, haunted his dreams; dragged naked into the square where she was torn apart by Shadows

After a long pause, the man spoke. "I am Captain Daghur of the Ulan-Balsan militia. You have no place here. Leave, and take your demons with you."

Some of the Eastern soldiers laughed, and Senji held up a hand to stifle them.

"You have fought well, Captain Daghur, but the battle is done. Lay down your sword."

The soldier turned his head this way and that, taking in the overwhelming force around him. "The battle," he slurred, "is not done yet."

With that, he lifted his sword and charged. Senji swung the long haft of the sparth, knocking the sword from the man's failing grasp before he was close enough to use the weapon. Then he swung it back to crack against the captain's temple, knocking him unconscious. The two Shadows lunged.

"Wait!" Senji shouted without thinking. The Shadows stopped and regarded him with their unreadable obsidian eyes. He swallowed hard, unsure now if he had over-reached. "He can work."

The Shadows shifted their stance and the eastern soldiers dispersed at Senji's back.

The Khalim-Shar had arrived.

The huge creature strode into the clearing and stopped in front of Senji who struggled to hold its gaze.

It made a high-pitched chittering sound in its throat and flexed its clawed grip on the enormous trident it carried.

"Good," the shrill voice grated. "Very good, Senji."

The Khalim-Shar tasted the air with its tongue, then turned and strode away. Senji exhaled at last and sagged against his sparth.

They should rest. He did not know when they would move again.

CHAPTER 8

*A*lisha works the treadle with her foot and spins the wool-clad bonnet to a blur between her knees. She presses the surface of the tray against the soft wheel and feels the dull shudder as the silver is stripped of imperfections.

"Gentle pressure, butterfly," her father murmurs, not looking up from his own task. "Keep it moving; always moving."

"Yes, papa," she replies, rolling the surface back and forth, side to side.

She glances up to see her father, polishing the horn handle of his newly crafted walking stick, his injured leg still held out straight before him between broad splints.

"Why are you spending so much time on that stick?" she asks.

"The change that cannot be overcome should be embraced," he replies. "This stick will become part of me in time."

"You have been working at it for over a week already."

He smiles.

"Time spent creatively is never time wasted."

"Polishing this tray feels like a waste of time," she grumbles.

"It will make a lovely wedding gift for someone soon," he assures her.

"Why trays?" she asks. "Why do brides get trays, and not jewelry or clothes; or a good kitchen knife?"

Her father chuckles.

"Clothes would be nice, and a kitchen knife would indeed be practical. I do not know when the tradition started, but I can remember your *grandfather telling me that the marriage and the tray were one; both need care and regular polish to prevent them tarnishing with age."*

"I think it's silly," she mutters. "A tray."

"Silly it may be, but the town of Bardiya is built on the trappings of that tradition. Silver is in our blood. The largest mines in all of Khumjang."

There is a long silence, broken only by the mellow hum of the spinning polisher.

"Were you afraid when the mine collapsed?" she asks. Her eyes do not wander from her task, but she can see in her peripheral vision her father lifting the stick to inspect it.

"I was afraid that I would not see you, or Tau again," he replies, getting to his feet with the aid of the new stick. "But I never gave up."

"I'm glad you don't have to go down there anymore," she says.

"Sometimes we need to go to dark and dangerous places to find beautiful things, butterfly," he replies, leaning over her shoulder and turning the tray to reveal a mirror polish. Her own reflection fills the silver surface with her father's gentle smile behind. "And other times, great beauty is found closer to home."

Alisha worked the treadle with her foot and spun the wool-clad bonnet to a blur between her knees. The morning sun chased the winter chill from the workshop with streaming rays of gold that painted the dust and fibres in the air. She flipped the tray in her hands to inspect the surface and brown, serious eyes looked back at her. She wrinkled her nose and stuck out her tongue at the reflection and then returned to the task

Light flashed on the wall to her right as she worked to polish the new tray. She glanced at her older brother and smiled.

"Don't you smudge that with your fingers again, Tau," she warned. "If you've been eating honey again…"

Her brother grinned back at her before returning his attention to the dancing light on the opposite wall. He had always loved to use the shiny surfaces of the silver trays to throw sunlight to places it could not reach alone. That was what Tau did best; he brought light and laughter, despite his curious condition.

His had been a difficult birth, so her father had told her, and Tau had been left with a slow mind as a result. Slow, and utterly devoid of malice.

She heard the creak of the workshop door and turned to see Dyansh, standing in the doorway. He had his hands on his hips in a pose that suggested a great feat had been accomplished on his part.

"Well?" Alisha said.

"Who was up before sunrise to finish his chores so that he could take the boat out?" he declared.

"Surely not *Dyansh*," she mocked. "*He* would more likely be found drooling into his pillow when the sun was at its peak in the sky."

"Ha!" he replied. "Wrong! Hey, Tau, do you want an apple?"

Tau nodded and put the silver tray down, readying his hands to catch the fruit that Dyansh had pulled from his coat pocket. Dyansh feigned an underhand toss, and Tau clutched the air in front of him with awkward hands.

"These apples bruise easily, and I am a terrible thrower," Dyansh said, walking towards the other boy with the fruit safely in his grasp. "Enjoy it."

Tau took the apple with a broad grin and returned to his chair to devour it.

"Apples, at this time of year?" Alisha said, allowing the polishing wheel to slow and stop.

"One of the perks of rising before Cook, is that she is not there to guard the barrel," Dyansh smiled in triumph. "Besides, what would be the point of owning the best Teahouse in Bardiya if I couldn't share a few apples with my friends."

"You hardly *own* it," she replied. "Your uncle owns it now."

"Only until I come of age," he insisted. "Next year it's mine, and Uncle Giranth can go back to Baslika and run his own affairs."

"What if you are forced to become a soldier, like the older boys were?"

Dyansh shook his head. "Uncle Giranth says that the war will be over soon," he replied with certainty. "Tianpok has fallen and soon the soldiers will return home."

"How does he know that?"

"He thinks he knows *everything*. He thinks that we are indebted to him, just because father was brave enough to stand up against…"

"Hush!" Alisha silenced him and glanced at the open door for a long moment before giving him a withering glare.

"Sorry," he murmured. "At least you have kept this place."

"It is Tau's now," she said, "but that won't last long. It will be taken away in time, unless mother re-marries, and nobody is that foolish."

She glanced at the horn-handled walking stick that leaned on the bench where her father had left it.

"Or if you marry," Dyansh suggested.

"No thank you," she muttered.

"You take the veil next year, then you can marry. If Tau cannot run this place, then you can."

"You mean 'my husband can', I will never own anything except a stupid tray."

"*I* would never do that," Dyansh said and then quickly lowered his face to hide his reddening cheeks. "I mean, when I marry, I would never treat my wife that way." He lifted his head again and declared. "I would let you own whatever you wanted."

"You would '*let me* own whatever I wanted'?" her voice took on a dangerous edge. "'*Let me*'! How very gracious of you to *allow* a woman to anything at all."

"That came out wrong," he said, raising his hands in defence.

Tau laughed at them both, his chin wet with apple juice, and Alisha allowed herself to deflate a little. "It's not your fault," she said at last.

Dyansh lowered his hands. "Are we still going fishing? The tide is out. We need to dig for bait."

Alisha cocked her head and looked back at him. "You will *allow* this? How kind. How could I refuse."

She walked past him with an airy grace and out of the workshop door. Dyansh rolled his eyes and gestured for Tau to follow.

Alisha lowered her gaze the moment she was outside on the footpath. A few short strides led her to the cobbled lane that skirted the house and the adjoining workshop, and then onto the wide, main street. She greeted one of her neighbours; a middle-aged woman sweeping the dust from the cobbles in front of her own house. It would never do to have a dusty street outside one's own gate; people would talk. The woman nodded back and returned to her task without a word. Alisha could remember when the woman had been loquacious to the point of nuisance, but that had been before her sons had been taken away to war. There was a hole in Bardiyan society once filled with brash young men, confident and eager to embrace the future and make their mark. Now, they were gone, and no one knew when they would return, if they retuned at all. Their conscription into the Khalim-Shar's army had bought her town a place in the new order; their loyalty would protect those they loved, but a mother's sorrow was the inevitable charge of war.

Dyansh and Tau caught up with her and matched her stride, but unlike Alisha, they kept their heads high, and Dyansh greeted the men they met in the street. The veiled women kept their eyes down and their heads bowed, their gauzy shrouds twinkling with pearl and silver.

"Going fishing, Dyansh?" one man asked as he walked past them.

"I saw razor gulls circling yesterday," he replied. "Yellow-gills must be here to breed, and they will be heavy with roe."

"Save me some," the man called as he receded. "I will pay you better than any fish merchant will!"

Dyansh waved and they carried on along the street which followed a gentle slope downwards towards the harbour. A hum of chatter floated along the street, carried through the well-kept houses to either side. Then, a sudden, oppressive silence alerted Alisha to the fact that something was awry

A Shadow had emerged from a side street twenty yards distant and now blocked their path. Alisha glanced behind her and found Tau a few yards behind.

"Cross over, Tau," she urged with a flick of her wrist.

Tau stared, wide-eyed, but he had understood the gesture. They all crossed the street while the Shadow regarded them with black eyes which glinted like a dark jeweled crown around the low dome of its head. The largest of the eyes, the pair above its wide mouth, followed Alisha and her companions, but the Shadow made no move towards them.

Alisha shuddered at the sight of the creature. Its ever-crawling flesh made her own skin itch and she was relieved when they were safely around the corner out of its sight.

"I hate those things," she muttered as Tau huddled close to her. "Where is the other one?"

"They will leave us well alone," Dyansh assured her, and offered Tau a wink and a smile.

"What about Rishut?" she asked. "Did they leave *him* well alone?"

"Rishut was a fool and a thief," Dyansh replied.

"We never used to execute thieves," Alisha argued. "And it was only cheese. His family are poor, and his father is too sick to work."

"He should have asked for help."

"Maybe he was too proud."

Dyansh hunched his shoulders and walked on. "But he should not have died like that," he said at last.

Alisha's dreams were still stalked by blood and screams, chasing her to uneasy wakefulness night after tortured night. She shivered and hurried her pace.

"Mother says that we are to embrace the new ways," Dyansh added. "Even those we do not like." Then after a pause, "Father did not agree."

Alisha pursed her lips and hooked her arm through Dyansh's on one side and Tau's on the other. "For what it's worth, Dyansh, I believe our fathers would have been of the same mind," she said, and pulled them both down the road with a spring in her step.

They reached the small harbour where Dyansh kept his boat moored; a small vessel with a single sail and room enough for two, or three at a stretch. He climbed down a limpet encrusted ladder to reach the boat which sat at a slight list on the mud. The cobbled docks held a small market which had quietened from the height of the early morning bustle, but it still attracted a small throng to the various stalls.

Alisha listened as a few muttered curses floated up from the boat as her friend clattered about looking for his bait buckets. Tau whimpered and pressed himself into his sister's back; the Shadow had followed them and was fifty yards away where the road entered the harbour.

She squeezed his hand and stared back at the shadowy creature. A black tongue darted from between wide lips to taste the air, and Tau shrunk a little further into Alisha's protective embrace.

"It will not harm you," a voice startled Alisha, and she cast her eyes down at once, lowering her head as soon as she recognized the speaker.

The portly figure of Captain Unjen Yuddha sauntered across the deserted dock towards them from where he had been hidden among the shoppers of the market. The whip he carried was secured to his belt in a tight coil; with two Shadows to enforce order on the town, there was no need for any other weapon.

"Oh no," Alisha groaned.

Dyansh appeared at the top of the ladder with a filthy rope

clenched in his teeth as the tubby soldier drew near.

"Going fishing, Dyansh?" Captain Yuddha asked in an amiable tone, hands clasped behind his back. His darting eyes flashed between Alisha and her friend.

"Yes, Captain," the boy murmured, lowering his head in respect for the soldier.

"What have you there?" the man asked, nodding towards the rope.

"Bait buckets, Captain, and a spade."

"Ah," Yuddha smiled and rocked back on his heels. "I remember doing the same when I was a boy. Enjoy it while you can though, you must be what, fourteen? You will be a man next year. Time to put away childish things and take on the new responsibilities that come with age."

"Yes, Captain," Dyansh said, scratching his arm.

"Have you considered joining the town guards?" the captain asked. "Bardiya needs strong young men like yourself in the garrison. What do you say?"

Dyansh managed an awkward shrug in reply.

"Listen," the captain said in a quieter tone, leaning in towards the boy, "I am sorry for what happened to your father. The soldier, Mohanish, was well reprimanded for his actions that day. It was a difficult time; big changes always are, but we should put it all behind us and move forward. '*You can no more change the past than lick your own behind*', as my grandfather used to say," Captain Yuddha laughed.

"Yes, Captain."

"The future is bright for those willing to take it; for those strong enough," Yuddha said. His eyes lingered on Tau for a moment before turning on Alisha in the awkward silence. "Enjoy your fishing."

With that, he turned and walked away. Alisha breathed a long sigh as she watched the man recede, and then glanced to where the Shadow had been watching them. It was gone, which in a way was worse.

"Come on," Dyansh glowered, pulling the buckets and spade up on the rope. "let's get to the beach before the tide turns."

The smell of salt.

Layers of stench heaped upon the musty brine, each telling its own lurid tale.

Valia's mouth was sour with the taste of stale blood and her tongue was dry and sticky. She was greeted with a wave of nausea, but her stomach felt empty and a dry crust crackled on her cheeks as she grimaced. The halting awakening of her senses brought new discomforts with every passing breath. She was cold to her bones and her muscles ached, too drained to shiver. The creak of damp wood and a rhythmic splashing told her that she was on a large boat or ship. She could feel the vessel lurch in time to the sounds and realized that she must be on a galley of some sort, propelled by oars.

A ship!

Why did it have to be a ship?

She moved a hand up to her chest to search for the coin.

It was gone.

A flood of memory assailed her, causing her whole body to stiffen. She tried to open her eyes, but they were dry and viscid. At last her eyelids broke the seal revealing only darkness punctuated by blurry shafts of dusty light from narrow cracks above.

"Hush," a voice beside her soothed, and she realized that she had cried out a name.

Surilya!

A fist tightened in her chest, crushing her heart.

Cold and darkness took her once more.

CHAPTER 9

"Look, there is another," Starling said, pointing upriver.

"Hmm," Acastes managed, and shrugged. "Once again, you state the obvious."

They watched as a huge log bumped and floated its way over the shallows of the ford.

"It's unusual though, wouldn't you say?"

Acastes tossed a pebble into the water. "Loggers have always used the river to move timber. They move it to the mills on Lake Arat. It is only a day's ride from here."

"A day and a half," Kapaneus murmured. "Although the biggest mills are a good bit further down the lake."

Starling shook his head. "Not this early in the year. They wait until the spring melt raises the water to keep the logs from jamming in the shallows."

"These *are* the shallows," Acastes insisted. "I see no log jams."

The three men were keeping watch at the ford, where the water was only knee deep on a man. They had crossed here some weeks ago with the refugees from Banihat and Ulan Balsan. The water was ice cold but was only frozen at the fringes with an ever-thinning crust. Winter had eased its grip the further south they had travelled, with this river crossing being the last great discomfort for the thousands who had waded across. Some of those people had continued south, deeper into Korathea, perhaps intending to go as far as Pashwar or Dashiya; others had turned west towards Kor'Habat and the safety of its mighty walls. Captain Silman had also been delighted to shake off the refugees and had turned west towards Kor'Habat. There had been no news from the north since they had crossed the river, and the scouts sent had not returned.

"But further upriver there are other barriers," Starling mused. "And ice."

"Perhaps the loggers are taking advantage of the Shar's absence," Kapaneus suggested. "Starting the season early."

"Then they are in for a surprise," Starling muttered.

"We are wasting our time here," Acastes complained. "Shar will not cross water such as this, even if it is a ford."

"But the Eastern soldiers might," Kapaneus reminded him. Knowledge that men fought alongside the Shar was as unsettling as it was inexplicable.

"The Shar will cross in the mountains where the river is narrower," Acastes said.

"Where the loggers are working." Starling stated as the log floated past. "Someone should warn them."

"Word will reach them," Acastes said with a shrug.

"Before the Shar?"

The three men exchanged glances.

"It would not hurt us to send a small party upriver," Kapaneus suggested at last.

"It will not be me," Acastes insisted, tossing another stone into the chilly water. "Who would be foolish enough to head back into winter?"

"I will go," Adeyemi volunteered.

The largest tent in the encampment was crowded, with room to stand only, and still there were those forced to peer past the tent flaps to see inside. These were the people who had chosen to stay and watch the Olchora; Dachen with his meagre escort, as well as Nirmaya and some fifty of the Sisters, also twenty Shar-hunters still eager to fight, and Acastes with his companion Kapaneus. Granger had remained, and Elan was present in his way, but Olgoi Kinbataar had stayed too which surprised all who knew him. Granger had fully expected Olgoi to make for Kor'Habat with much haste, and yet he had stayed to watch the river.

"You are eager to seek out discomfort," one of the hunters joked.

Adeyemi offered a wide smile. "I see those forests rising with the mountains and would relish the chance to explore them."

"Thank you, Adeyemi," Olgoi replied, "but if you are to carry a message to the loggers, then perhaps someone should accompany you; a more familiar face, if you take my meaning."

The dark-skinned man's smile only widened, and his shoulders bounced with silent laughter.

"Who will do this?" Olgoi asked. His eyes settled upon Starling and remained there.

Starling flinched under the gaze. "Me?"

"Thank you, Starling," Olgoi said. "A selfless offer indeed. You are light on your feet and are well suited to keeping pace with Adeyemi."

"No, I…" Starling began to protest, but a long and meaningful stare from Olgoi had him sagging. "Very well."

Granger watched the exchange with interest.

"Thank you, both," he said.

"Have we had word from Kor'Habat?" Dachen asked.

"None," Granger replied. "although it may be some time yet. Even a swift rider would be hard pressed to be back here before the middle of Spring."

"If ever," Acastes snorted.

"Surely, they will not allow their lands to be swallowed," Dachen insisted.

"They will remain in Kor'Habat and vie for position as the Kodistai's health fails," Acastes said. "He could be dead already."

"We do not know that," Kapaneus replied. "There is yet time

for us to return. Perhaps we all should."

"We agreed to wait here for Marlon's party," Granger replied.

"Pah! Those fools are dead," Acastes said.

There was a murmur of agreement around the tent. "We cannot hold back the Shar alone," one of the hunters called out, which was followed by more muttering.

"None of you has been forced to stay here," Granger called out before the dissent could gather impetus. "But we agreed to wait for Marlon. It is not our intention to face the Khalim-Shar alone and that is why we have taken the position we have while we keep watch. Marlon could not abandon Valia, and we should not abandon him."

At the mention of Valia's name, Nirmaya stood a little taller. "I will wait for Valia. Who else has the courage to stay?"

The Sisters present exchanged looks and nodded to one another.

"And what if she is dead, girlie?" a hunter sneered. "I want her to return just like you. I have fought at her side, *unlike* you. But we must accept that she is almost certainly dead. You saw how many Shar attacked the city."

"Will your courage hold when the Shadows come?" Dachen asked Nirmaya. "Stories of heroism are easily told and listened to more readily yet. They burn in the heart and give cause to dream; but the Shar are a nightmare. Their flesh crawls under the gaze and sickens the stomach. They do not rely on courage when they attack because they are mindless and will keep coming long after your grit has turned to dust."

"You know nothing of me!" Nirmaya fumed and Maidra laid a soothing hand on her shoulder.

"I know enough," Dachen replied.

"We should not fight amongst ourselves," Granger pleaded over the growing susurrus.

"I will stay," Dachen said, holding Nirmaya's acid glare.

Slowly, all present acceded to remain at the river and wait for a little longer.

Valia awoke shivering in the cage, a thin blanket her only protection from the cold. The bodies pressed against her on either side offered some warmth but if this was to be their new home, as it appeared it would be, then she doubted many would survive for long.

They had spent weeks in the hold of the ship, fed a daily ration of thin soup and starved of light and hope. She still felt hollow, resigned to die and prepared to endure whatever indignities she must to reach that goal. There were groans from within the wooden cage she shared with the seven other prisoners, all men save for Kalie, the Hetai girl who had cared for her in those early days of her captivity. Most of the prisoners were from Banihat, whose fate she had learned of in woeful, whispered accounts.

Valia had been too numb to care.

The ship had made it as far upriver as the north-western end of Lake Arat, where it moored. Stumbling into the bright light on legs cramped from inactivity, their ordeal only became harder. They had walked in groups of eight, linked by chains joining heavy wooden pillories that clamped around the neck and one hand of each prisoner. Thus, they had walked for weeks, one hand free to eat what little food was offered or to steady them when they stumbled. They ate in chains, slept in chains and defecated side by side like animals. The wood rubbed at the shoulders and neck as well as the wrist of the secured hand. It would have been impossible to sleep with the wooden devices in place if not for the exhaustion that overwhelmed Valia at the end of each day. Those who could not go on were thrown to the Shar, while the soldiers who escorted them looked on with disgust, horror, or for some, a perverted grin.

These were Eastern soldiers, of that she was certain, but she could not understand their alliance with the Shar. This could be what Dachen had come to warn them about, but that man, as her life before her capture, was meaningless now.

Into the forests and foothills of the Lesser Cascus Mountains they had walked until they arrived at this place on the northern side of the river. The pillories had been removed, and Valia still remembered the agony of moving her left arm again after so long being clamped up beside her jaw. Here, they were instructed to cut heavy branches and drive them into the ground to construct the cages that they now occupied. The soil was cold, but not frozen, insulated as it was by the thick layer of pine needles dropped by the tall, arrow-straight trees that dominated these gentle slopes.

The air was still bitterly cold.

In another cage a man woke and at once started weeping. Valia did not cry; she could not. She felt nothing. She could see perhaps ten cages in all, although she could not see beyond the rise where the soldiers had their tents; there could have been more. The soldiers had started a fire and were gathering around it in the dawn light. Valia reached out a hand between the bars, trying to feel some heat from the distant flames, and a Shar was suddenly beside the cage, chittering and scratching at the ground with its claws. Valia pulled her arm in and watched the Shar slink away to circle the other cages.

"If it is outside the cage, it is food for the Shadows," a soldier called out from the nearest fire. He had a heavy accent but spoke Korathean well. He laughed and returned his attention to the fire.

"What are we doing here?" Valia murmured.

Beside her, Kalie stirred. The swelling around the younger woman's eye had reduced overnight and had changed to a deeper hue of purple. The prisoners had all endured daily suffering, but at night, in the soldiers' tents, Kalie endured so much more. Valia threw her blanket over Kalie's own and lifted it to the woman's chin. The younger woman shivered and curled up a little tighter.

One of the soldiers was making his away from cage to cage, rattling the bars with the butt of his sparth, eliciting more groans and cries of alarm. When he reached the cage that Valia occupied he kicked the wooden post nearest Kalie's head.

"Up!" he barked. "You must cook now."

She was up in an instant, shaking the sleep from her head.

"Yes Aanga," she said, scurrying across the ground to the door. She ignored the protests of those she disturbed in the cramped cage and pushed at the hinged side of the cage. The ends of the poles scraped across the needle-covered ground until there was enough space for her to exit. She pushed it shut behind her and stood, mindful to keep her head lower than the guard's as she did so. The soldier stepped up close to her and cupped her chin in his hand, lifting her face to his to inspect the eye. He grimaced at the sight before a call from near the fire ended the inspection.

"Go," he said, and Kalie hurried off followed by the guard, Aanga.

"Look, we could escape at any time," one of the prisoners murmured. "Our bonds are cut, and the cage can be opened..."

Another prisoner hissed at him to be quiet. "The Shar would cut you down before you could get clear."

"At night, then."

"The Shar do not sleep."

"I will not die here."

"You are a fool."

"Coward!"

Someone began crying.

"I have barely eaten in days. Why are we here?"

"Another night of cold and I will surely die."

"Hush!"

A different guard was striding from cage to cage, pulling open the crude doors.

"Get up!" he barked. "You smell worse than dogs! You will wash!"

Goaded with threats and kicks, the prisoners exited the cages. Two had died in the night and the corpses were dragged out for the Shar. The sound of tearing flesh and snapping bones needled at the prisoners' backs as they were marched down the gentle slope through the tall trees to the river. An enormous pool had formed beneath a short section of rapids in the Olchora, where the water rested clear and tranquil before continuing its journey to Lake Arat, and the sea. Further upriver, the steeper ground rose to meet the Lesser Cascus, hidden in cloud.

"Strip, and wash!" a guard shouted.

Apart from Kalie, who was still in the encampment preparing food, there were only two women among the prisoners: Valia and a sturdy woman perhaps a little older than herself. The Eastern guards giggled like children and elbowed each other, flashing glances from one woman to the other. The older woman was hesitant, squeezing her blouse at the neck and staring at the water.

"Strip! And wash!" The command was repeated.

Most of the men had already started making piles with their clothing on the dry pebbles beside the pool. Valia undressed, holding the eye of the guard who had given the order until she stood naked in the chill air. Taking Valia's lead, the other woman had also begun undressing. At last, Valia turned and walked into the water, leaving the guard to hide his blushes behind boyish bravado.

The water was cold and Valia found herself taking short, sharp breaths as she plunged into the river. The scar between her shoulder blades itched like fury, as did her cheek when she splashed her face. Soon, her skin was numb with cold and she scrubbed at it to shift weeks of grime until her fingers no longer worked.

A shout alerted her to a commotion a hundred yards downriver. Someone was trying to escape. Whoever it was had simply allowed themselves to be carried with the gentle current until he had thought himself far enough away to swim. The splashes had alerted the soldiers and now a mounted archer was making his way along the river's edge to round up the escapee.

Soon the shivering man was stumbling back upriver across the rounded stones with the mounted soldier at his back.

"Dress!" the soldier Valia now took to be the leader shouted. "You will eat now."

In their absence, Kalie had made a large pot of porridge. It was unseasoned but thick and Valia devoured the contents of the bowl as if it had been the sweetest honey. Her stomach ached for more.

"You are still hungry?" the leader called out. "Eat more! You will need to be strong."

The prisoners hurried back to the fire where Kalie spooned out more of the porridge. She filled Valia's bowl with a little extra and offered a small smile.

"My name is Garutan," the soldier said as the bowls were filled. "And I can be a good master. See how I fill your bellies when you obey my commands?" The prisoners watched while they ate. "I have a task to complete and will require your labour for it. You will cut down trees and prepare them for their journey downriver. When you do as you are instructed, I will extend great kindnesses to you." He gestured to the large pot. "But if you disobey my orders, I will treat you accordingly. There can be no escape from here and I urge you not to attempt any."

The would-be escapee was dragged into the clearing, his elbows bound behind his back so that his shoulders were contorted at a painful angle. He was forced onto his back and three soldiers held him down, one gripping the man's head between his knees. Garutan pulled an iron rod from the coals of the cooking fire and made his way to where the prisoner struggled on the ground.

"Obey me, and I will extend great kindnesses to you," Garutan repeated. "Disobey me…"

He brought the glowing end of the rod down and laid it on the eye of the prisoner even as the frantic begging began. The hiss and sizzle of the boiling eye was quickly drowned out by a blood-curdling scream. Garutan withdrew the rod before the man could gulp down another breath, and the second cry was far weaker than the first, breaking down into feeble sobbing.

Garutan held the smoking tip of the rod up for all to see. "If you should try to escape, the Shadows will feast on your flesh. But I am a reasonable man and will give a warning first. Disobey me or try to flee and I will take an eye. Disobey me again and the Shadows take the rest." Then he spoke to the soldiers still holding the stricken man. "Dress his wound, I want him working in two days."

Garutan dropped the iron rod at the side of the fire, surveyed the prisoners and nodded. "Now, to work!" he shouted.

"We have been wandering these wastes for weeks now," Abbil grumbled from behind a beard heavy with ice. "How much snow must we endure?"

"You're right," Jon agreed. "We should be heading south."

"She is not dead," Marlon muttered, hearing the conversation. His own beard was covered in frost where his breath had frozen.

"Very well, she is not dead," Jon replied, "but have you considered that she may be *not dead* further south, where it is warmer? Because I can assure you that all sensation in my bollocks has gone south and I would dearly like to find it again!"

Marlon grunted in response.

"He makes a fair point," Alano added. "If she has been captured, they would not remain here."

"And if she is free, where better place to hide?" Marlon countered, smoothing the beard that covered his cheeks.

"Pah!" Abbil laughed. "Valia; *hide?* Have you lost your mind?"

"Marlon," Alano said, "every single camp we have found has been devoid of life. That last settlement we found had precious little to add to our supplies. We are running out of food; the horses are exhausted, and you have to accept that we could be wasting our time here."

Abbil drew his horse alongside Marlon's and placed a hand on his friend's shoulder. "There is nothing here. We have seen no sign of life in weeks. I am sorry, Marlon. You know that I would ride into fire and back for Valia, but she is not here."

Marlon grunted and hunched down deeper into his coat.

"What do you think, Gobby?" Jon said, turning to the captured soldier.

The man looked startled for a moment and then started babbling in his own tongue until Jon waved him silent again.

"Do you see? Even Gobby wants to go south..."

Marlon scanned the frozen horizon. It was said that this steppe land held nothing but wind and sky, and feeling the bite of the air, surrounded by a land that never rose to meet the eye, he was inclined to agree.

"We will make for the Lesser Cascus," Marlon said at last, "and use the forests for cover, then follow the Olchora until we find Granger and the hunters."

His companions sighed with relief.

Marlon searched the northern horizon one last time before urging his horse south.

Starling steered his mount through the trees, using the river on his right to guide him. Ahead, Adeyemi preferred to travel on foot, his long, sinewy legs carrying him with ease over the boulders and stumps that littered the river's edge. The sun was low on the horizon when they stopped to make camp at the end of the first day, and Starling was hungry. He started gathering wood for a fire while Adeyemi cleared what snow there was from the little depression where they had chosen to spend the night.

It took some time, but when the fire was lit, Starling rummaged through the saddlebags for their supplies. "Should we have the dried beans tonight, or would you sooner save them for tomorrow, the next day, and the next," he joked. "What I mean to say is, we have beans."

"I like beans," Adeyemi replied with a smile. He had found a small orange beetle and had coaxed it onto his hand. He watched in wonder as it climbed over the tip of his thumb.

"Nobody likes beans that much."

Adeyemi laughed as Starling put the pot over the fire to boil. "Be sure to make enough for three." He teased the beetle back onto a mossy rock and watched it crawl away.

Starling raised an eyebrow. "Unless you have invited the insect to dinner, you really do like beans," he said, adding another couple of handfuls of the hard, brown kernels.

"We are not alone," Adeyemi whispered.

Starling spun his head in alarm, scanning the trees for threats.

"It is Elan," the dark-skinned man went on. "He has been behind us all day."

A shape detached itself from the shadows of the forest and suddenly Elan was walking towards them, carrying a brace of white-furred hares.

"And he is most welcome," Starling declared, scrambling to his feet. "Would you care to exchange some of that game for these lovely beans?"

Elan dumped his pack at the edge of the clearing and sat down without a word. Then he set about skinning the hares with swift, practiced ease.

He did indeed share the meat, or at least did not protest when Starling helped himself from the skewers, and soon they were resting by the fire staring into the glowing coals. Adeyemi was holding the pouch he wore around his neck, squeezing it to feel the contents.

"What is so precious in that little bag?" Starling asked. "Apart from the Element of course."

Adeyemi raised his eyes at the pointed question and smiled after a thoughtful pause. "If I told you, would you try to steal it from me?"

Starling rolled his eyes. "Once again, you delve into the past to hurt me. We are allies now; you and I."

Adeyemi smiled, and then started to laugh, silently at first but growing in intensity.

"Why is that so funny?" Starling asked over the laughter.

"You can paint a donkey gold, but underneath, it is still a donkey," Adeyemi said when he had calmed himself. "Excuse me."

With that the big man rose and walked down towards the river. Starling shifted onto a higher rock to keep the man in view, but it was dark, and the moon was yet to rise. The faint silhouette against the river showed that Adeyemi was removing something from the pouch. He held it up and regarded it for a moment before throwing it into the river. The Element? No, whatever it had been was tiny; too small to have been the Daemon Element.

Adeyemi turned and Starling slid back down the rock into the shallow depression, knowing that he had been spotted.

When Adeyemi returned Starling was already under his blankets. "I was watching to be sure you were safe from wild animals, or worse."

Adeyemi laughed. "Were you indeed, Little Bird? Were you indeed?" The intricate scars that swirled across Adeyemi's cheeks and down the side of his neck were stark against his dark skin in the dim light of the glowing coals. So too were the slashes that ruined the patterns.

"Tell me about your homeland," Starling said to change the subject. "You speak so little of it."

Adeyemi stopped laughing. "What would you like to know?"

"Where is it? How far away? What is it like? Are the girls pretty? Why did you leave? Do you have a family? The usual things," Starling replied.

"You want to know if I miss my mother's smile?"

A sudden image flashed unbidden into Starling's mind:

A mother's smile forced through lips that were bruised and bloody.

Mama is alright, baby. Don't cry.

He shook the memory away, chasing it back to where he had hidden it for so long.

"I am only curious," Starling said at last, averting his eyes.

Adeyemi nodded, perhaps sensing a shift in his companion's mood.

"My homeland lies to the south and east of the land you call the 'Eastern Kingdoms,'" he said. "Many days on foot, I could not tell you, although you could not mistake your arrival. The humblest dwellings glitter with quartz, pressed into the walls in whorls and waves, multi-hued in the sun." A wistful look clouded his eyes. "In the dry season, children collect red 'rattle seeds' and string them onto necklaces in the shade of great *Mukamba* trees. There is a bee; small and stingless, that produces the sweetest honey you will ever taste, if you are brave enough to climb the cliffs where they build their nests to retrieve it. The songs that dance across the fields as farmers tempt seedlings to the surface. Can singing draw sweetness from the soil? I think so. The first rain brings yellow blossom to the tips of the *Mukula* trees and with it a scent that cannot be forgotten." He breathed in as though he could smell it then. "The women?" He opened his eyes and glanced at Starling. "The women would break you like a dry twig, Little Bird."

Starling smiled, ignoring the jibe. "Do you miss it?"

Adeyemi stared into the glowing coals. "The allure of one's homeland is not easily washed away; like red dust in a cracked heel, it lingers."

"Why did you ever leave?"

"Why do the grey deer leave the fertile plains to calve on the stony plateau?" Adeyemi replied. "Forces compel them."

"Forces?"

"Go to sleep, Little Bird," Adeyemi said, shuffling down onto his bedding.

"Yes, very well," Starling replied, seeing that the conversation had been ended. "Sleep well then."

He huddled down unto his bedroll, pulled the blanket up to his chin and watched Elan do the same.

That night, Starling watched Adeyemi fall asleep. The big man held the pouch in his hand with a grip that did not ease, clinging to it as a man clings to life.

Starling put it from his mind; it was too soon to act in any case.

There would be time enough for that...

Valia swung her axe, falling into a slow rhythm. Each stroke ended with a dead thud of the broad blade biting into the base of the pine. Wood chips littered the forest floor where she worked, nibbling away through decades of growth to take away the tree's strength. Soon it would fall, and the stem would be denuded of its branches and sawn into lengths ready for floating on the river. Men were busy at another fallen stem with huge saws, working in teams to drag the flattened steel back and forth through the timber. It was dangerous work. No one could be quite sure which way the log would roll when the cut was complete, even with the wedges and stones used to hold them in place. Already today, one man had been crushed to death when a log pinned him against a rock, and two had died the day before when a tree had not fallen in the expected direction.

The Shar, of course, were quick on the scene to devour the broken bodies, but Garutan could only see his workforce dwindling, and was quick to beat anyone he deemed to be responsible. He carried a long, flexible stick, as thick as his thumb that he used to lash the prisoners whenever he witnessed a perceived transgression. The stick broke the flesh and left angry welts where it didn't, and every prisoner worked a little harder if they felt his eyes upon them.

The man who had tried to escape on that first morning in the river had recovered enough that he could work. He was sullen and resigned as he labored and seldom spoke to his fellow prisoners, even when they rested or ate. Valia paused to watch him for a moment. He was wearing a dirty rag around his head which covered most of the wound where his eye had once been, and he was hacking at the branches along a recently felled stem. Perhaps feeling her eyes on him, he glanced up at her with an expression that showed no emotion before returning to his work. She wondered how long he would survive. He was a ghost already.

A sudden, searing pain brought Valia back to her own reality as Garutan struck her across the back with the stick.

"I did not call for work to cease!" he yelled. "You will not stop until instructed!"

Valia lifted the axe again, her back burning with pain, and for a moment imagined using it on Garutan. But it would have been a short-lived show of rebellion as either the bowmen stationed around the forest or the ever-present Shar would cut her down a moment later. The thought was a sweet one, however, when all else was bitter.

She returned to work, swinging the axe with calloused hands, chipping ever deeper into the heart of the tree, weakening the stem with every stroke. She felt a strange affinity with the pine as she laboured. They were not so different; tall and proud yet worn away by manifold abuses contrived to break the back of the most resolute spirit.

This tree would fall soon, and so would she. It was inevitable.

The burning welt across her back awoke the old itch between her shoulder blades where a scar still lay. She dared not stop to scratch it though. A wetness told her that she was bleeding, but there was no time to tend the wound now; perhaps Kalie could dress it later.

As though sensing her thoughts, Kalie arrived carrying a bucket of water and a ladle.

"You are bleeding," she said, putting the bucket down and carefully lifting Valia's shirt at the back.

"It will heal," she replied, turning and grasping Kalie's hands in her own.

"I will dress it," Kalie insisted.

"If Garutan sees, you will have your own welts to worry about."

Valia took a drink from the ladle and pushed the bucket into Kalie's arms. "Go, quickly."

The young woman did as she was told, picking her way over stumps and boulders to deliver water to the other prisoners and Valia returned to work. Not far away, a team of men was using long, stout levers to roll a processed log into the water, heaving against the weight in unison to bump the massive stem over the mossy boulders. It splashed into the river and all but vanished under the surface for a moment before settling in for the slow journey east, drifting with the current down towards Lake Arat.

A call went up; there was some activity downriver that was getting everyone's attention. Valia saw that the other prisoners had stopped working and so felt safe enough to do so herself. There were people making their way upriver towards their camp; more prisoners by the look of them. Thirty men or more, chained together in groups with the hateful pillories around their necks and wrists, were being escorted by as many soldiers and the unmistakable shapes of several Shar.

These soldiers were different though. Their western features and mis-matched armour marked them out as possible mercenaries. One caught her eye and she lowered her head out of reflex, hating herself for cowering as she did. She lifted her gaze again, but the man had passed her, and was joking with his fellows.

Valia watched as the prisoners filed past, exhausted and bruised. One of the prisoners' eyes widened when he saw her, but he said nothing as he went past, and it took her a long moment to pull a memory from her clouded mind.

"Daghur," she mouthed to herself. The Captain of the Ulan Balsan militia was scarred and filthy, but she remembered him, and it was clear that he had recognized her.

That evening as the light faded, they made their way back towards the encampment. Valia could see that the new arrivals had already built their own cages and were awaiting their fates in huddled clusters within the crude enclosures. Kalie was stirring a large pot by the fire. Soon she was spooning the bland porridge into bowls as the prisoners filed by. They sat on the cold ground and ate without talking, eager to fill their bellies. Valia was staring into her empty bowl when a figure shuffled closer.

"Valia of Hadaiti," the man murmured. "How were you taken?"

Valia glanced sideways and saw that it was Captain Daghur. "Does it matter?"

"I suppose not," he whispered. "Ulan Balsan has fallen."

Valia only nodded.

"What opportunity is there for escape?" he murmured after a pause.

"None," she stated. "Do not attempt it."

Daghur paused again. "We will speak again."

"Wait!" Valia hissed as he turned away. "Who are those men? The soldiers."

"They come from Dargenmill," he replied. "They are Suun's men."

"Suun? The cult leader?"

Daghur nodded, then he shuffled away leaving Valia alone with her thoughts.

Kalie was serving a fine-smelling stew to the soldiers. They leered at her and exchanged jokes that neither she nor Valia could understand; perhaps it was for the best. Garutan was entertaining the commander of the new arrivals in his tent, and Valia could see, through the open flap that there was wine on the table. She could not recall the taste of wine and yet her mouth watered for it.

Kalie ducked in with their meals. Garutan grabbed the Hetai woman around the waist the moment she had placed the bowls on the table and pulled her onto his lap. She allowed herself to be manhandled even as he squeezed her breasts for the entertainment of his guest. Lewd laughter erupted from both men at whatever comment Garutan had made. The tent flap was pulled shut as Kalie managed a last, wistful glance outside.

Valia balled her fists until they ached and tried to block out the sounds of laughter from within the tent. She cursed her impotence as they were herded to their cages leaving Kalie to her fate. At least in the cages a little solitude could be found, but Kalie would find none yet. Valia felt hollow as she lay on the ground, scraping the needles into a pile beneath her. A Shar slunk by, a reminder that they were under constant guard should anyone try to leave their cages. Exhausted as she was from her day's labour, sleep would not come. Even clamping her hands over her ears could not block out the noises from the tent, nor silence the scream in her head that had started the instant she had watched Surilya die.

It was late when Kalie was pushed into the cage by one of the soldiers. She was shivering as she collapsed with her back to Valia on the bed of pine needles. Valia threw their shared blankets over Kalie's balled-up figure, and without speaking, pulled her close for warmth. Sometimes words held no value.

B.R. Crichton

CHAPTER 10

The tree made almost no sound after the initial creak from the base. Only the gentle hiss of air passing through its needles preceded the crash as it hit the ground across the river. Valia and the prisoners had cleared the area around their encampment and were now fashioning a rough bridge to the southern bank. Two trees lay side by side across a narrowing in the Olchora which would give easy access to those trees over the water.

"Strip those branches!" Garutan ordered, although several prisoners were already busy cleaning the stems.

Daghur joined Valia in the icy water, pulling the fallen branches to the bank. They hauled the sodden limbs to where they would be stripped of needles and used to straddle the two stems. They did not possess the means to make boards here in the forest, and so stout branches would be used to form the walkway.

"I know how it will be done," Daghur muttered at Valia's side.

Valia hushed him. "It is impossible. The Shar cannot be evaded so easily."

Daghur went on anyway. "Do you remember a few days ago, a tree was felled into the river?"

"I remember the lashing that Garutan inflicted on the fool that made the error; he may yet die from his wounds." Valia replied.

Daghur winced at the memory of the wretched man, held

face down and spread-eagle above the ground by a rope around each limb, and Garutan's frenzied attack with the switch. The man had howled himself into unconsciousness. "We need to do it again."

"What?" Valia hissed as she waded back out into the water.

"The tree must still be stripped of branches and cut into lengths," Daghur said. "It is difficult and slow to do so in the water, which is why it angers Garutan, but if another tree is felled into the water…" he paused as a soldier walked by, then went on in a quieter voice. "A man could hide beneath a large enough cluster of branches, and simply drift until far enough away to swim to shore."

"The Shar?"

"The Shar will not know. They are wary of water."

"When your absence is noticed, they will hunt you down," Valia said as she worked. "You could not stay in the river for long, it is still too cold. No, it is a foolish plan."

"Then we could fight!" Daghur hissed, then he glanced around to be sure he had not been overheard.

"With what?" Valia sighed.

"Axes, machetes, our hands. They give us weapons every day."

"There are fewer than a hundred of us; mostly too exhausted or terrified to fight, against fifty soldiers and a dozen Shar."

"Then you must help me," Daghur persisted.

"To escape?"

"I will bring help."

"To what end?" she replied, angry now. "To attempt rescue? Even if you succeed, it will be a futile gesture. Who would come to our aid?"

"I have to try."

"You will be killed."

"I was ready to die in Ulan Balsan; given myself to it," Daghur hissed through gritted teeth. "Every day granted to me since is a gift I should use to avenge my people. What happened to your fire?"

Valia rounded on him but stopped herself short of lashing out. Instead she grabbed a branch from the water and pushed past him to the shore.

Daghur followed, dragging a branch of his own. "Please help me," he insisted, quieter again. "All I ask is that you allow a tree to fall into the river."

"I will be beaten, at best," she replied. "If they suspect that I am part of your scheme I will lose an eye. You will also be made to suffer when you are caught. For what?"

He shrugged off her protest. "There is a tree downriver with a bent top. It is weighted towards the river and you may not even be punished at all if you draw Garutan's attention to it. Just be sure that it is you who fells it. I will be sure to be in the team who tidies up."

"So simple," she murmured.

"Amongst the branches I can slip under water, then a cluster can be released to obscure me."

"Garutan will be furious with the delay," Valia said, shaking her head. "Your death will not be quick."

"Slavery is the slowest death," he replied. "Will you do it?"

Valia dragged another branch to the shore as she considered his plan and her part in it. The one thing that infuriated Garutan the most was delay, and losing workers slowed their progress further. She considered that after the beating he had meted out had left one of their number crippled, he may temper his punishments in future.

"I will do what I can," she said at last.

"Thank you, Valia," Daghur whispered. "Thank you."

A knock at his door startled Rogan Fol'Brandam from a shallow sleep.

"Come!" he barked, sitting up and throwing his legs over the edge of his bed. He was in full ceremonial dress of polished breastplate with blue-green trim and all the finery that went with his rank. This was how he slept now, snatching brief spells of rest whenever he could.

"Hatar." It was Captain Raims. He wore a look of deep concern.

"Is there news, Raims? Is he dead?"

"No, Hatar," Raims replied.

Rogan grunted but was a little relieved that he had not missed the Kodistai's passing. He wanted to be there when it happened; dying men were known to show great favour to those near them in their last moments, when fear began to bite. Rogan might need the boon of being at the ruler's side when that time finally arrived.

If it ever arrived.

"Then what is it?" Rogan asked, smoothing the topknot on his head.

"It was suggested that the town of Dargenmill may not have been warned of the Shar attack," Raims said.

"Word travels," Rogan replied. "They will know."

"It was suggested in the presence of the Kodistai," Raims went on, "by Hatar Bravik Fol'Gannity. He claimed that you were remiss in abandoning a Korathean town, whilst already in the field."

Rogan stood and grabbed the water jug from beside his bed and hurled it against a wall. "Bastard!" he yelled. "Why Dargenmill? Why no concern for the towns in the South?"

"Hatar Fol'Gannity felt that Dargenmill held certain strategic importance and that it was the most likely to be attacked next."

"Dargenmill holds no strategic value. At best a message should be sent ordering the town to be evacuated," Rogan seethed.

"Hatar, I informed them that you had in fact dispatched Captain Silman to carry out that task," Raims said calmly, ignoring the outburst.

Rogan shook his head. "What? Did I?"

"No, but Captain Silman has not yet returned to Kor'Habat.

He will still be on the road, and a message could be sent to intercept him. No-one needs to know when the order was given."

Rogan laughed. "Raims, you devious bastard."

Captain Raims stood a little taller.

"I will send a messenger within the hour," Rogan said, striding to his desk. "You will go far, Captain. You will go far."

"Hurry, Alisha," her father urges as he leads the way into the workshop. He walks with a pronounced limp, using his stick to take the weight from his rigid knee. "The first cocoon has already started to open."

Alisha climbs onto the stool and then onto the workbench where she kneels and leans towards the window. Four gems hang from the lintel at the top the frame, gleaming metallic in the morning light.

"See, that one," her father says in a hushed voice. "It has started to split."

She watches the cocoon pulsate with emerging life as the pristine capsule begins to open. Each is the size of her thumb, perfect spirals of translucent crimson. She can see now that the textures she had observed through the gossamer carapace were those of the creature within.

"Three years," her father breathes. "Do you remember when they first arrived, my butterfly?"

She nods her head.

"You were only seven then," he concedes. "And you were quite transfixed by the caterpillars. Your mother wanted me to kill them of course; they ate the kale in her garden, but how could I begrudge such magnificent creatures a few leaves from our table?"

She watches the butterfly wriggle free from the casing. It pauses to recover from the effort.

"It's tired, papa," she says. "It is breathing hard."

"It is not breathing as you know it," her father replies, observing the subtle palpitations. "It does that to fill its wings. They have been folded into the cocoon for so long, like one of your dresses, pressed at the bottom of the drawer, full of creases. It will not fly until the wings are dry and smooth.

The wings spread further with every passing moment. Crimson wings, impossibly large, unfold in front of her eyes. Long, blue pennants unfurl at the back of the glorious butterfly as it soaks in the warmth of the gentle, spring sunshine.

"It is going to be a dry spring," her father whispers.

"How do you know?"

"The emperor butterfly knows," he replies, nodding towards the insect hanging from its ruptured cocoon.

"How does the butterfly know?"

"It can sense change."

"What change?"

"The change that is all around us, all of the time. The rising and setting of the sun; the march of the seasons. In days of old, people believed that the emperor butterfly could control the seasons, but in reality, they sense the changes that are perhaps too subtle for us to feel, and then force a different change upon themselves. Change happens by action or inaction, the true gift is in knowing which is ours to control, and which we must embrace."

"How do they do it?"

"It is a mystery," he smiles. "But farmers have used the emperor butterfly to decide which crops to sow in the spring for generations. If the cocoons remain sealed, they sow barley, if the butterflies emerge it is a promise of a dry spring and they sow rye." He nods his head. "This year, they will sow rye. The butterfly bides its time; it must wait until the moment is right."

She watches until the butterfly tests its wings, opening and closing the delicate membranes, revealing the mottled purple and blue undersides.

At last it drops from the cocoon and catches the air, flickering crimson and blue in the sunshine. Her breath catches as it rides away on a tender breeze, to begin the cycle again.

Alisha put her elbows on the workbench and leaned towards the window.

The emperor butterflies had returned. Or rather, their

caterpillars had scaled the wall to find shelter under the window lintel again. Five perfect jewels awaited their moment. This would be their second year in their cocoons if they did not choose to emerge this spring. The ragged leaves of the kale in the vegetable garden outside told their own story, and the fact that she knew it had irritated her mother made Alisha smile.

From the workshop window she could see to the path that led to the front door of the house and her attention was dragged away from the cocoons by the arrival of Captain Yuddha.

Her chest tightened at the sight of the portly man. What could he be doing there?

Her mother opened the door and Alisha watched as the woman lowered her head, fussing with the veil she had clearly fitted in a hurry whilst at the same time smoothing her dress with the other hand. She could not hear what was being said, but very soon, the captain had been ushered indoors and out of sight. This would set tongues wagging and her mother would no doubt be delighted with the attention and jealousy.

A flash of light alerted her to Tau's presence in the room. He was using a polished tray to reflect ripples of sunlight onto the ceiling and was transfixed by it. She decided not to distract him from his happy pursuit.

She slipped out of the workshop and hurried down a narrow lane that would avoid going past the house. If she was in trouble, then she was in no hurry to find out why.

She made her way to the Teahouse on the edge of town where Dyansh lived, and then skirted around the building to the large barn at the rear. If he wasn't fishing, he could usually be found there.

"I was sure you would be asleep in the hayloft. Are you still trying to get that old thing to work?" she asked.

Dyansh looked up from the machine he was working on and smiled.

"It will work well enough," he replied. "I want it looking its best when I sell it though."

"It's in pieces!" Alisha protested.

"But they will go together easily enough. See that carriage over there?" he asked, pointing towards a pair of large wheels on either side of a rusty axle. "All I need to do is position it under the blades and bolt it on. A perfectly serviceable five-bladed plough."

He pushed the collection of blades and rods, and it swung away on the chains he had supporting it from a rail high up in the roof space. He stepped out of the way before it could swing back and hit him.

"Who is going to give you money for that?" she teased.

"You wait and see," he replied, showing her the stiff brush in his hand. "The steel is good under that layer of rust. Look at the edge on that." He tried to point out the polished edge along one of the plough's blades but cut his thumb as it swung.

He winced and sucked at the little wound as she laughed.

"How did you manage to lift it up on those chains?" she asked, shaking her head in wonder at the array of tools.

"I used a block like this one," he said, holding up a system of chains and pulleys. "Do you want me to show you how?"

She stared back at his hopeful face.

"Actually, yes," she said at last. "Why not?"

It turned out to be very simple, and with her curiosity piqued, they spent a long time looking through the collection of tools that Dyansh had inherited from his father.

"Was that his sparth?" Alisha asked.

Dyansh nodded and lifted the long weapon from its place on a rack.

"I oiled the blade today," he said, his voice growing distant. "Father always said that steel was a living thing; it needed to be fed, or it became weak."

Alisha looked through some of the other items on that section of the wall.

"Is that a bow?"

"Yes," Dyansh said before a look of mischief crossed his face. "Want to try it?"

"I wouldn't be allowed," she whispered in excitement.

"Who would know?"

"Let's do it," she hissed with a furtive glance towards the door.

Dyansh strung the bow and retrieved a pair of arrows from the rack. A few moments later they were standing at one end of the barn, staring down its length to where a haybale was propped against the far wall. A small, red rag was tucked behind the twine for a target

"Now," he said, standing behind her, "the secret is to keep your arm straight, and the elbow of the drawing arm high. Yes, that's it. Bring your hand right up tight to your cheek. Keep your head up. Breathe in, and release."

The arrow hissed though the air and thudded into the haybale a hand's width from the rag.

"Woah," Dyansh said in surprise. "We will call that a lucky shot. Try again."

Alisha sniffed as she accepted the second arrow. "'Lucky'?" she said with a warning look. "we shall see."

The second arrow struck the bale a hair closer to the rag than the first had done.

"Are you certain you have not done this before?"

"More arrows," she said, staring at the haybale at the end of the barn. "Get me more arrows."

Dyansh pulled another four arrows from a dusty quiver and handed then to her.

"Keep your elbow high," he reminded her as she aimed. The arrow struck a little high this time. "Who are you thinking about while you are doing this?" he joked.

"No one in particular," she said, nocking the next arrow. "I did see Yuddha earlier, at the house."

The arrow struck high again.

"Yuddha?" Dyansh asked. "At your house? Oh no."

"What is it?" she asked, raising the bow again and drawing the string back to her cheek.

"It's probably nothing," Dyansh replied, shaking his head.

A little low and to the left.

"Tell me," Alisha urged as she nocked the final arrow.

"I overheard some gossip in the Teahouse the other day," he said watching her draw the string back. "Some women were talking. They mentioned Captain Yuddha."

"Yes," she murmured as she aimed.

"It makes sense, after all. Your mother is still a beautiful woman. He is looking for a wife."

The arrow struck the center of the rag and pinned it to the bale like a bloody ribbon of flesh.

Alisha dropped the bow and hurried out of the barn, leaving Dyansh to stare in disbelief at the arrow in the haybale.

She had calmed herself by the time she reached her home and opened the front door. To her great relief, her mother was alone in the kitchen at the large wooden table and was busy kneading dough with what looked like an unnecessary degree of violence.

"There you are," her mother chided without looking up from her task. "Where have you been? It is nearly supper time."

"I am sorry, mama, I did not realize. Can I help you with cooking?"

"Where is your brother?" she snapped back, pounding the dough even harder. "Where is that useless boy? Two days in labour with that child and this is what I get. He almost killed me; you know. What have I done to deserve this? Such a *useless* child."

"It's not his fault, mama," Alisha said, wringing her hands.

"And you; what have you been doing? You are almost a woman; soon you will take the veil and yet you still play like a child. I get no help here! You were supposed to sweep the street outside the gate today. Ghita swept her side and now we look like a family of Indrapor peasants!"

"Sorry, mama," she said and set about tidying the sink.

Her mother placed the dough on a shelf and covered it with a cloth and then turned to look at her daughter with an appraising stare.

"You are not so pretty," she mumbled.

"Mama?"

"Go and find your brother!"

Alisha hurried from the room, confused by her mother's temper. Perhaps Dyansh had been right and she was to marry Captain Yuddha, but Alisha would have thought that such a union would have pleased her mother.

Tau was in the workshop, dusting silver trays that had gathered no dust.

"Tau, dinner time," she said with a smile.

Her brother grinned back at her and followed her back to the house. When she opened the door, her mother was drying her eyes with the corner of her apron.

"You think this is easy?" she asked, at once angry again.

"Mama?" Alisha asked in confusion.

"Serve the meal," she demanded before muttering half to herself, "You will see. You will see."

They ate in silence. Alisha was aware of her mother's glare but could not for the life of her think what she had done wrong. She winked at Tau whose wary eyes wandered from his mother to his sister and back again, no more able to understand the mood than Alisha was.

"Tidy the plates," her mother said when they were finished.

Alisha stood and collected the dirty dishes and took them to the sink.

"Leave those," the woman snapped. "Just go to bed. Leave me in peace."

"Yes, mama," Alisha muttered in confusion, and left the room to make ready for bed.

CHAPTER 11

Valia heard the loud crack even before she felt the jolt of the switch striking her back.

Then came the searing pain.

"Fool!" Garutan shouted as he struck her again, this time hitting an elbow pushed back out of reflex.

The tree that Valia had been working at, the one with the bent top, had fallen into the river just as she had intended. She had drawn Garutan's attention to the danger and then cut away more than she should have on the side furthest from the water, ensuring that it would not fall onto dry land.

"It is as I said," she protested as another blow landed on her shoulder.

Garutan stomped away, shouting for prisoners to abandon their work and wade into the cold water to deal with the mess.

Valia breathed a sigh of relief. Garutan appeared to have accepted that the error was inevitable and had vented enough of his anger to punish her no further.

It was awkward and slow to de-limb the tree in the river, but a group set about the stem as instructed. Daghur was quick to make his way along the length of the tree to put himself among the upper branches. He hacked at them with his axe, stacking what he had removed on a secure branch.

Valia tried not to watch him as she walked along the tree

above the water but cast occasional glances to where he worked as she set about the larger boughs on the lower stem. He had three other prisoners near him; she could only assume that he had drawn them into his insane plan too as they worked together to form a dense cluster of floating branches.

She glanced at the nearest guards and they showed little interest in the work being done, even Garutan had disappeared from the worksite, and Valia began to wonder if Daghur's plan might actually work.

She dragged a large branch to shore; these heavier limbs could be cleaned further on dry land before being deposited in the water to float downriver. The thinner, higher branches were of less importance, and while it was preferred that they not be floated with the bigger timber in case they choked the river, they were often left to the current to save time.

The nearest guard, who had been sitting with his back to a large stump, started to take an interest in a muffled argument at the top end of the tree. Something was wrong but Valia could not hear what was being said. The guard stood and peered towards where Daghur was working.

What were they doing, drawing attention to themselves like that?

Valia swung her axe at a branch and allowed the shaft to slip from her calloused grip. The heavy axe splashed into the water below.

"Bollocks!" she shouted, and the argument ceased.

The guard walked towards her as she made an exasperated gesture with her hands.

Aanga, she thought his name was, pointed to the waist-deep water where the axe had fallen. "You get!" he said.

She held up her hands in resignation and slipped down into the water. It was cold and delving into it with her arms only soaked more of her clothing, but at least the guard had been distracted. He shook his head and strolled back to his stump.

Valia climbed back onto the tree and set to work, as much to chase the chill from her flesh as anything else. The argument had started again in hushed tones at the other end of the tree. She was tempted to make her way there to silence them, but she neither wished to draw extra attention to the squabble nor implicate herself in their foolishness.

The group went silent, and from the corner of her eye she saw Daghur slip into the water behind the huge bundle of branches they had accumulated. The others exchanged guilty glances and continued to work. It was normal to have to enter the water to work at the underside of the tree if it was jammed and unable to roll and so the guards took no notice.

The cluster of branches broke free from the main stem and sat motionless in the dead water of the downstream side of the tree. With painful slowness, the branches inched away from the three remaining men; the guards had not yet noticed the missing man.

Valia thumped her axe into the stem to secure it and dragged another branch to the bank. The guard's eyes were on her and her nerves jangled as she wondered if he suspected anything and if she was betraying her thoughts with her actions.

It struck Valia that trying to act as though nothing was awry was in fact the hardest thing to do when every movement or flicker of emotion felt manifestly contrived.

A muffled shout from the top end of the tree got the guard's attention and Valia turned to see what was happening. One of the other men was swimming after the cluster of branches with awkward strokes. He ducked under water to try to conceal himself, but he had been long since spotted. He resurfaced before reaching the branches, gasping for air in the icy water.

A call went up and three soldiers ran along the riverbank and drew level with the man in the slow current. One of the soldiers nocked an arrow and aimed at the fleeing man. The escapee ducked under the water again before the arrow could be loosed.

The bowman waited, watching the surface of the water. The

man resurfaced after a few seconds, still short of the branches he was chasing, and the bowmen released his arrow. The shaft struck the water just short of the man's head and vanished under the surface. He cried out and rolled in the water, exposing the arrow which had struck his shoulder. Still the soldiers paid no heed to the drifting branches.

Garutan arrived, shouting furious orders at his soldiers. After a brief exchange one of the western soldiers waded out into the water to help the struggling man, who was now trying to claw his way to the bank with a weak, one-armed stroke.

The branches picked up speed as the current took hold.

Daghur was going to make it!

The injured man was dragged, weeping from the river.

"Please, please," he begged. "Don't take my eye."

Garutan squatted beside the distraught man and twisted the arrow in his shoulder. The man screamed in pain before resuming his frantic pleas.

"I have information if only you don't take my eye," he wailed. Garutan twisted the arrow again and the man howled.

"I was trying to bring him back, I swear," he said once he had stopped crying out. "I was not trying to escape. I was afraid you would blame me. I was trying to bring him back." Garutan exchanged a few words with the soldiers nearest and then held a quiet conversation with the man. Valia could not hear what was being said, but the man pointed to the other pair at the top end of the tree and was nodding with the eagerness of a man who believed that he would be forgiven if he revealed all.

The cluster of branches vanished around a bend in the distance.

Eventually two guards came towards her and Valia's heart sank. She pulled the axe from the wood where she had left it and waited for them.

So, this was to be her last stand. So be it; she would die, bathed in their blood.

"You move!" Aanga ordered. "Out of way."

Valia loosened her grip on the axe and the soldiers shooed her out of their way. The other two men who had helped Daghur were being called back to the bank. They exchanged worried glances but made their way along the stem until the soldiers could escort them at sparth-point to the camp.

"Work!" Aanga shouted at Valia once the soldiers were gone.

She realised that she was still holding the axe in numb hands and set back to working on the branches.

She saw a Shar dart across the log bridge that they had made a few days earlier, where it vanished among the trees of the south bank. It re-appeared moments later, following the edge of the river. On her side of the water, another Shar mirrored the movement of the first. Daghur would not be free for long.

As the sun went down at the end of the day, the prisoners made their way to the encampment where a cooking fire smoked. Kalie was at a large pot stirring the bland food they ate every day, but her eyes were fixed on the pot and did not offer the usual welcome she reserved for Valia most evenings.

In the clearing where the prisoners usually sat for their meal, three men lay stretched, spread-eagle. Ropes around their wrists and ankles secured the men to stakes driven into the ground. A soldier was kneeling at each man's head, waiting for the prisoners to gather and watch.

"Kneel!" Aanga ordered and the prisoners dropped to their knees.

Garutan emerged from his tent with a look of fury on his face and every prisoner lowered their head. He stopped by the fire and warmed his hands before speaking.

"Do you remember our first day here?" he demanded. "I told you what the punishment was for attempting to escape. I demonstrated it to you."

Valia glanced at the man who had lost his eye, but he did not flinch.

"I told you then that I would take the eye of any man who tried to escape." Garutan continued. "I would have thought that you would understand that this punishment would extend to anyone aiding another to escape."

Valia felt her face flush but kept her eyes down.

"One of your number is missing," Garutan said. "He thought that he could simply float away. That man has either died from the cold in the river or else been taken by the Shar that followed him. I told you that there was no escape, and now you see that this is true." He retrieved the metal rod from the coals of the fire and approached the man with the bloody shoulder. The man began to struggle but the kneeling soldier secured his head between strong knees.

"If you disobey me or try to escape," Garutan said, "I will take an eye."

He brought the glowing tip of the rod down into contact with the screwed-up face of his victim. The sizzle of flesh was drowned out by the howl of agony that emanated from the bound man.

Garutan returned the rod to the coals for a few moments while the injured man sobbed and the remaining two begged.

"If you should aid another to escape," Garutan said withdrawing the rod. "I will take an eye."

Again, the awful scream that ended with the pitiful sobbing when the deed was done. One of the kneeling prisoners vomited on the ground.

"If you know of a plot to escape and do not tell me; I will take an eye."

The third man was screaming before the glowing metal had reached him, but the result was the same; an eye seared and boiled from its socket, in punishment for defying Garutan.

Garutan threw the rod onto the ground in anger. "Now I have one prisoner dead and another three who will not be fit for work for some time. Do you see what you have done? No food for any prisoner tonight. Throw it in the river!" He stormed off to his tent as two soldiers pushed Kalie out of the way and lifted the large pot from the fire with a post. They vanished from sight, but splashes could be heard shortly after as the food was discarded.

Valia had lost her appetite anyway.

Garutan was brutal with Kalie that night. The muffled screams from his tent told of the venting of his anger in the most cowardly of ways.

When at last she was pushed into the cage, Kalie could barely move. Valia pulled her close and the smell of rape and blood burned in her nostrils. She could taste it and it had the tang of death.

Fury at her helplessness; fury at Garutan's brutality; fury at her own pathetic fall chased her to a fitful sleep plagued by dreams of shadows and futility and wasted lives.

"Did I not say that we were too far south?" Abbil grumbled.

Marlon surveyed the river. The Olchora was too deep to ford this far south. An enormous log eased its way past them on its way to Lake Arat.

"The loggers are back," Marlon murmured.

"Do we follow the river and hope that the ferry is in a better state of repair than when we last crossed there," Abbil asked, "or north to where the river narrows? I do not relish the prospect of swimming."

"Where would Valia go?" Marlon whispered to himself.

"What do you think, short-arse?" Jon asked of their prisoner. The Eastern soldier's leg was still bound but over the last weeks he had been able to put more and more weight on it. He was lucky not to have lost the limb to infection. His hands were tied now, and Jon led his horse on a long tether to ensure he did not try to escape.

After a short, unintelligible sentence, Jon nodded. "I'm with duck-legs here. What he said."

"There will be more settlements to the south," Alano reasoned.

"We could do with the supplies, and they could do with the warning."

"Valia, Valia," Marlon muttered, scratching at his beard. "Where are you?"

Gaining height again will only lead us onto colder ground, and I was beginning to feel the touch of spring," Abbil said. "South, I say."

"I agree, our aim now is to find Granger as soon as we can." Alano added.

"South it is," Jon said with an affirming nod.

Marlon tugged on his horse's reins and steered the animal upriver.

"Or north," Jon said, rolling his eyes and then muttered to the prisoner, "He's worse than my bloody wife. Prettier though."

They rode in silence for a while until Abbil's mood was too sour to hold back. He slowed to allow Alano to draw alongside him.

"This is ridiculous, Alano, you have to try to talk sense to the man. How long will he wander the wilds looking for a dead woman?"

"He is convinced that she is alive," Alano replied.

"That does not make it so," Abbil hissed back. "I am as heart-broken as any of us, but Valia is dead. We found her belongings, saw the blood. She was the bravest, most fierce woman…no, person that I have ever met, but everyone dies, Alano. Even Valia of Hadaiti."

Alano stared at Marlon's back. "All the same, I cannot desert him now."

Abbil scowled behind his beard.

"Wait," Alano hissed.

Up ahead, Marlon had dismounted from his horse and was gesturing for the others to do the same even as he crept forward.

Alano and Abbil followed while Jon helped the injured prisoner to hobble to cover. Jon waved the tip of his sword in front of the man in warning. The man nodded in timid understanding.

"What is it?" Alano whispered when he reached Marlon who was crouched behind a moss-covered log.

Marlon pointed upriver and Alano squinted into the distance. "Shar!" Abbil whispered.

"I see it now," Alano said. "Is it alone? What is it doing?"

The Shar was slinking along the southern bank on the outside of a gentle bend in the river.

"What is that?" Abbil said, pointing.

Something was floating down the river towards them, and the Shar was keeping pace with it.

"Is that a body?" Alano whispered.

As it drew nearer, they were able to discern the shape of a man clinging to something beneath him. It was a cluster of branches, and it was barely enough to keep his body from the water.

"Fetch a rope," Marlon ordered. "We can pull him to safety; the Shar will not cross after him."

Alano slid back to where the horses were standing and took a length of rope from the pack-mule. He grabbed a sturdy lump of wood from the ground and tied it on as he made his way back. By the time Alano reached the fallen log again the drifting man was much closer, and so was the Shar. It spotted him from across the river as he ducked down. It shrieked; a sound that sent shivers down the spines of the men.

"Throw it," Marlon said, seeing the rope.

Alano stood with the loops in his hand and suddenly he saw another Shar on their side of the river only yards from their own position. For a moment he froze.

Marlon sensed that something was wrong and pulled his sword from its scabbard just in time to see the Shar glide over his head. Alano dived to avoid the raking talons and landed in the river.

The Shar turned as it landed, skidding over mossy boulders until it faced Marlon and Abbil. With the log at their backs they were forced to stand their ground. It chittered and tasted the air with its black tongue before lunging towards Marlon. He deflected the blow but lost his footing on the wet ground and went down in an awkward heap among the rocks.

Abbil bellowed as he swung his sword to deflect the next attack. He kept his feet planted on the mossy surface, afraid he would slip if he dared move and braced his lower back against the fallen tree. It was a defensive stance and he struggled to counterattack. The Shar sensed this and returned its attention to Marlon who was struggling to his feet.

Jon burst from cover several yards away with a shout and hurled his sword at the Shar as it prepared to lunge at Marlon. The blade bit into the creature's flank and stuck there as the Shar shrieked in rage. It leapt over the tree and turned again to face them, carrying Jon's sword with it.

Abbil and Marlon stumbled away from the log as Alano spluttered to the bank. The Shar climbed onto the log and tasted the air. It shook its body and Jon's sword slipped from the ever-shifting flesh, landing out of reach.

"Watch your step," Marlon warned. "These rocks are like ice. Spread out."

Alano was shaking with cold but his Malmotti blade was free of its scabbard and held ready. A scrape of hooves broke the brief silence.

"The bloody prisoner!" Jon cursed.

But the Eastern soldier was not running away. He erupted from the undergrowth on horseback holding Valia's sword high in both hands. The Shar lunged as he brought the heavy blade down and the steel cut into the creature's head. The weapon was wrenched free from his bound hands but the Shar stumbled and raked at the weapon, desperate to shake it loose. Alano did not give it time, moving in quickly to take the head from the stricken beast.

Across the river the other Shar slashed at the water and

shrieked as its fellow died.

Jon stared in disbelief from the prisoner to the twitching, headless form on the ground.

"What the…? What do you think you are doing?"

The Eastern soldier was staring across at the other Shar, trembling and pale. The Shar glared back and slashed at the water one more time before turning and loping upriver again.

The soldier began to weep, covering his face and muttering into his hands

"What are you bleating for?" Jon asked. "It's dead. You helped kill it."

The man slumped in his saddle and Jon helped him down before he could fall. He was talking slowly but that did not help Jon to understand, although his distress was evident. He stared at the running Shar until it vanished from sight and then turned to Jon and spoke again, shaking his head with sorrow.

"I have no idea what you are saying, Stumpy," Jon said, pulling his belt knife free. "But I think that you've earned this." He cut the man's bonds.

The soldier rubbed his wrists, nodding in what Jon took to be thanks before sitting on a rock and burying his face in grubby hands.

"The rope," Marlon said. "Quickly before he drifts any further."

Alano had the coils in his hands again and picked his way across the rocks to catch up with the drifting mass of branches. His second attempt had the rope land across the body of the man who was able to grasp it with weak fingers.

They gathered at the bank as the floating mass drew close and Alano, already soaked to his skin, waded in to help the man to safety. At last he was out of the water and slumped against a rock. His skin was blue, and he shook in spasms that made him groan. Marlon threw his own coat over the man's shoulders and tried to rub some warmth into his flesh.

"How long were you in the water?" Marlon asked. "How did you come to be there?"

The man struggled to lift his head and Marlon helped him onto his back.

"Daghur?" Marlon gasped. "Is that you?"

The man tried to speak but a bout of painful shivering stole his words.

"It *is* you," Marlon said in astonishment. "Fate, man, what are you doing here?"

"They came," Daghur managed though lips cracked and blue. "Ulan Balsan is lost."

"The Shar came?"

Daghur nodded, then a shaking finger pointed to the Eastern soldier. "And them," he said with unbridled hatred. The Eastern soldier was so deep in his own sorrow that he did not notice the accusation. Daghur's eyes started to close as his chilled body failed him. The shivering stopped, and he relaxed against Marlon's embrace...

Suddenly Daghur's eyes snapped open and his icy fingers clamped around Marlon's wrist with surprising strength.

"Valia!" he forced the name out through clenched teeth. "They have her."

"What? Where? Who has her?" Marlon said, pulling Daghur into a more upright position.

Daghur sagged against him, his breath shallow.

"Damn you, man," Marlon shook the dying man. "Where is she?"

But consciousness had fled from him and his slowing heart was beating its last. Marlon laid Daghur on the rocks and rose, staring upriver.

"Get the horses," he murmured.

Valia knew that something was wrong the moment she awoke. Kalie was cold to the touch.

"Kalie?" she murmured in the gloom. The young woman did not stir.

Valia tried shaking Kalie's shoulder but it was stiff.

"Kalie," she whispered, knowing then that the woman had died in the night. Sweet, caring Kalie, who had nursed her wounds from Kylyptus to Lake Arat, and her soul ever since.

Why do men do these things? Valia felt hollow; cored of all emotion and yet sickened with loss. A stale, greasy taint left behind in a pot long emptied of any sweetness. She pulled the blanket closer around her and held onto Kalie's body for a few moments more. Had Valia ever thanked her for the care she had shown?

Too late now.

A guard rattled the bars of their cage with the butt of his sparth. Valia rolled away from Kalie's body and crawled to the door. She pushed it open on its crude hinges and stood in the cold morning air. She watched as her cage emptied, leaving the still body under the blankets they had shared. The guard prodded the body with his sparth and shouted something. She did not know what.

She walked towards the small tent at the edge of the encampment which held the axes and saws that they used each day. A guard stopped her and signalled for her to lower her head. Every morning they had formed a sullen queue with heads bowed while tools were allocated, but not today. Valia was already forming a plan in her mind. The guard gestured again for her to lower her head, but she stood tall. He took a step back and brought the point of his sparth down level with her chest, shouting something; she did not know what language he had used and did not care.

Let him summon Garutan to punish her. Let him come.

She glanced over her shoulder and saw Garutan striding from his tent, still fastening his armour. He went instead to the cage where Kalie lay dead and held a heated exchange with the guard. She could hear nothing but her own blood rushing; felt nothing but her heart drumming for vengeance in her chest.

Let him come.

She could take this sparth from the soldier in front of her, or else the felling axe that lay a few strides away and split his skull. Bowmen would cut her down in moments unless the Shar reached her first, but Garutan would die, and that was enough.

The guard shouted again, and his voice was like a whisper in a hurricane. She looked down at him, daring him to strike her and the acid in her gaze had him taking a step back. She glanced again to the cage, but Garutan was returning to his tent.

Valia's bloodlust simmered on but Garutan remained unseen.

She had been foolish. For too long she had toiled under the false acceptance that any act of defiance would be futile.

Not so now.

There was a purpose to her life again, and that singular goal was the killing of Garutan and anyone else who stood by him. It would be her final act, but so be it. She laboured through the day with the new-found comfort that her ordeal would all soon be over and that she would have her victory before the end.

She did not see Garutan for the rest of the day; he remained in his tent, and that night as she lay down on her bed of pine needles, there were no sounds of revelry from within. No matter, she would see him soon enough and when she did, he would die, and she would continue to kill until she herself was slain.

Her final vengeance could wait.

CHAPTER 12

"How many soldiers are there?" Alano asked.

"Forty or more," Marlon replied. "It was difficult to tell. They are spread across both sides of the river. Bowmen too. And mercenaries."

"Mercenaries?" Alano asked.

"They are not Eastern," Marlon replied. "Not from their armour."

"How do they cross the river?" Abbil said.

"A log bridge, level with the camp."

Abbil grunted. "And prisoners?"

"Eighty or ninety, perhaps more. They were mostly working on the south side of the river; the camp is on the north and cleared of trees and cover."

"What about Shar?" Jon was cleaning his nails with a belt knife.

Marlon nodded. "I counted six, but I could not be certain at that range."

"You were wise to keep your distance," Alano said. "If the Shar had caught your scent on the air…" he left the rest unsaid.

"That place will reek of human sweat and fear," Marlon replied. "I would not be noticed."

There was a long silence. The call of a meadow lark floated across the river.

At last Alano asked. "Did you see Valia?"

Marlon stared at the ground. "I did. She does not look well."

"How so?" Jon asked.

"I cannot say. Perhaps she is merely exhausted."

"Very well," Abbil said. "We should return with reinforcements and take the encampment by force."

"No," Marlon said without hesitation. "There is no time. We should make our move in the morning."

Abbil laughed. "Four men; against forty?"

"Or more," Jon added.

Abbil nodded and pointed at Jon in acknowledgement. "*Forty or more*, and six Shar at least."

Marlon balled his fists. "There must be a way."

"Yes, there is," Jon said. "Fetch support. Bring the rest of the hunters with us, perhaps Acastes and a few of those Heavy Infantry fellows. I'm in no hurry to meet the Soul Keeper, if you get my meaning."

"There is no time," Marlon muttered.

There was a long silence while Marlon clenched and unclenched his fists in agitation and the other three men traded worried looks. Again, the trill of the meadow lark punctuated the silence.

Alano cleared his throat. "Perhaps we could use the river against them."

"How so?" Abbil leaned forward.

"Divide their forces; separate the prisoners from the soldiers."

Marlon nodded. "The prisoners will fight, when they see that they have a chance for freedom."

"You cannot know that," Abbil countered. "They may simply flee."

"You said that there was a single crossing point." Alano said, and Marlon nodded. "Could it be destroyed?"

Marlon shrugged. "Difficult. There are two trees, each thicker than a horse, side by side. We could not easily shift them."

"We could burn them."

"The wood is yet green."

Abbil interrupted them. "We should keep an eye on our little friend," he nodded towards the prisoner who was sitting against a nearby tree, more withdrawn than usual. "Perhaps you were premature in cutting his bonds, Jon..."

Jon glanced at the sullen man and shrugged. "He does not appear keen to run off."

"But he could warn the enemy if he gets wind of what we are planning."

"So far, we have planned nothing," Marlon growled.

The meadow lark called again and Alano cocked his head.

"If we attack before dawn, we could kill a dozen as they sleep," Marlon went on. "Rouse the prisoners and arm them."

Alano rose to a crouch and edged towards the river with a puzzled expression.

"Even then," Abbil argued. "we would be hopelessly outnumbered."

"What is it?" Jon asked, seeing Alano's confusion.

Alano turned back to the group. "A little early in the year for a meadow lark to be calling for a mate, wouldn't you say?"

"What?" Jon replied, shaking his head. "So, the bird has needs; what of it?"

Alano squinted at the distant trees across the Olchora and then relaxed. He stood and turned to his friends with a smile. "You will want to see this." he said.

Marlon, Jon and Abbil joined Alano where he stood and gazed across the river.

Standing on the southern bank was Adeyemi with his impanga raised in salute. Beside him, stood Starling and Elan; Starling was waving with both hands while Elan simply stared.

"It looks as though the odds have just been halved," Abbil laughed, slapping Marlon on the shoulder.

"Yes indeed," Jon murmured, "and we're still all going to die."

It was a pleasant, spring morning when Kapaneus rushed through the encampment to the large command tent at its centre. He pushed the flap aside and stepped in.

"Acastes! An army approaches!"

Acastes almost spilled the wine he was holding. "Under what banner?" he demanded, lurching to his feet. "From what direction?"

"From the west, and they carry no banner, but scouts say that they are Eastern men; six hundred at least," he replied.

Acastes paused. "Shar?"

Kapaneus shook his head. "Only men."

"How far?"

"A few hours at most," Kapaneus said. "They will be here before midday."

"We need every arm that can hold a weapon ready to meet them. How many can we muster?"

Kapaneus almost laughed. "You are joking, of course. Fewer than a hundred, and half of those are Nirmaya's Sisters."

Acastes visibly sagged. "Then we may be about to find out their worth." He lifted his armour over his head and allowed Kapaneus to help with the straps that held the gleaming cuirass to the backplate. He grunted in protest when Kapaneus hauled on the leather. "Careful, man. I need to breathe."

"It is a mystery," Kapaneus muttered, "How these bindings have grown shorter over the last weeks. Perhaps a little less wine and a little more exercise would remedy that."

"Very amusing," Acastes retorted. "Now, hand me those grieves. I can manage from here without the sauce."

Kapaneus paced while he waited. "If we ride out to meet them and take a position on the high ground, we could disguise our numbers by spreading out along the skyline; let them believe that we are a larger force than we are."

Acastes grunted as he pulled his steel vambraces onto his forearms. "That will work for precisely as long as it takes for them to engage us."

Kapaneus was not listening. "*West*," he murmured.

"What?"

"Why would they be coming from the west?"

"You can ask them," Acastes said, pulling the large, curved sword from its scabbard to inspect the edge. He pushed it back home with a metallic rasp, "when we meet them."

A few hours later, Dachen and Sangye joined Acastes and Kapaneus as they rode down from the crest of a gentle rise towards the Eastern army.

"You think that they have come from Kor'Habat?" Kapaneus asked.

"Sent by Chapok?" Dachen murmured, shaking his head. "He had his chance to kill me."

"We will remain vigilant," Sangye reassured the prince.

The large force had stopped and formed loose, defensive squares on the plain. Two riders had broken off from the formations of foot soldiers and was approaching the centre ground.

"Do you recognise them?" Acastes asked.

"Yes." Dachen nodded. "The one at the front is Tsomo, the baker's son. Further back in the column is my cousin Pema and Uncle Rinchen. That one is Korchen; we shared a wet nurse." He paused a moment, then snorted. "Of course, I don't recognise them!"

Sangye laughed out loud.

"I meant…" Acastes began to protest but gave up. They rode in silence until they stopped a few yards short of the riders. Neither man was openly armed.

"What is your purpose here?" Dachen asked in Eastern tongue.

"We are seeking a prince of Tianpok," the man said. "I am Lhoma, of Myampor. This is Tenzin, also of Myampor."

Tenzin nodded an acknowledgement.

"There are no princes here, Lhoma of Myampor." Dachen

placed the butt of his sparth on the ground and leaned on it.

Lhoma nodded. "It is said that Prince Dachen remained outside the walls of Kor'Habat to take the fight to the Shadows, while his brother cowers within."

"Speaking ill of a king could have you garrotted, Lhoma of Myampor," Dachen warned. "You should be wary."

"It is said that Prince Dachen faced the Shadows at a town to the north and defeated them," Lhoma said.

"I heard there were many people in that battle," Dachen replied.

Tenzin leaned in close to his friend and murmured something in his ear. "It is said that Prince Dachen has a scar beneath his left eye; a gift from Jangbu, Champion of Myampor," Lhoma suggested, touching his own cheek.

Dachen felt his eye twitch. "Many things are said, Lhoma," he retorted. "But there are no princes here. Take your army and continue your search elsewhere." Dachen pulled on the reins of his horse and turned his back on the pair.

"We are an army without a leader," Lhoma called out. "A People without a homeland. Everything but life is lost, and life is nothing without pride."

Dachen stopped and Lhoma continued in heartfelt tones. "The Shadows destroyed everything that mattered; turned brother against brother with false promises. Fear and greed have ground us to dust and scattered the smut in the wind. Behind me are the last, free vestiges of a people ready to fight to retake what was taken. People of four kingdoms; Khumjang, Lhaksang, Shibatsu and Tianpok, all searching for a leader to follow. All hoping for a man worthy of being king."

Dachen turned to face them again. Lhoma was out of his saddle and approaching Dachen with hands outspread. Sangye angled his horse to protect the prince.

Lhoma dropped to one knee and lowered his head. "I pledge myself to your service, Prince Dachen of Lokhara. Give me your trust and I will give you my life. *When the shadow casts its darkness from the north and the third King of that name passes from the world, cities will fall, and fires will burn high. Look to the west, for the sun shall rise there and bring with it a Saviour. And he shall turn you on your heads."*

Tenzin was kneeling too now with his head bowed.

"What just happened?" Acastes murmured, unable to understand what was being said.

"I think," Kapaneus said, "that we have just got ourselves an army. Look."

Every soldier on the plain had gone down on one knee. Men of four Kingdoms were pledging allegiance to an exiled Prince in a foreign land; a man they hoped was a saviour. Dachen stared at the soldiers in front of him, and the hundreds beyond, and dared to believe in a prophecy.

Alisha watches her father take the tray from the high shelf. His right leg is stiff, and he leans on the horn-handled stick for support. The tray is tarnished and scratched, its edges beaten and misshapen, but this specimen will never be sold. He sits beside Tau and lays the tray on the forming anvil, placing a leather mallet in his son's hand.

"Use the form below to shape the silver," he says, and Tau starts tapping the tray with the soft mallet. "Be gentle or the metal will split, it will stretch with patience."

He continues to watch Tau for a few moments before withdrawing in silence. The boy's brow is furrowed with furious concentration as he works the edge of the tray.

Her father sinks into his chair at the workshop's window and sighs.

"Will Tau ever learn to work silver as well as you can, papa?" Alisha asks in a hushed voice.

Her father shakes his head.

"Tau does not have the capacity to learn as you and I can."

"Then why do you still teach him?"

"Because it makes him happy, I suppose."

"Is Tau happy?"

"I believe so, butterfly," he smiles.

Alisha pauses before speaking again.

"Sometimes it makes me sad," she murmurs.

"What does."

"Tau. He will never learn new things; he will never grow up; not in his mind at least."

"Is that so terrible?" her father asks. "Tau is trapped in his own innocence. He will not grow as you will, but he is content within his world. Tau cannot change, but that alone should not be cause for sadness. There are many who can change but will not, and those people are more worthy of your sorrow, and your pity."

They sit and watch the boy work at the silver with the leather mallet. The tray gets no nearer to being worthy of being sold bearing the family mark, but Tau looks at ease and brimming with purpose.

Surely that is enough.

Alisha leaned over the side of the little boat and trailed her fingers in the water. The gentle slap of the swells on the hull had lulled her into a dreamy half-sleep.

"You have not said much today," Dyansh said, pushing the tiller to hold the boat's course. "Is your mother still acting strange?"

"My mother has always been a little strange," she murmured.

"*Stranger* than usual then."

"Yuddha has been back more than once this week," she said. "My auntie has been there too, as well as some of the older women. This is what they do, isn't it, before a marriage? The women gather to make sure that everything is done correctly; that there is no *impropriety* on the good captain's behalf?"

"No *what*?"

"I heard one of the women saying it as I left the house today."

"Ah," Dyansh said with a knowing nod. "Has she told you yet?"

"She tells me nothing. She has become very cold and distant. Perhaps she feels that I will get in the way of her new romance."

"'Romance'," Dyansh said, "That is a word I had not associated with Captain Yuddha; or your mother."

"Don't be rude," Alisha chided, but she could not hide a coy smile. "Some things are best not considered."

"What will you do?" Dyansh asked.

"What *can* I do?" she shrugged. "In the summer I will take the veil, and then I will find a husband of my own I suppose."

Dyansh made a fine adjustment to the sail and then stared up at the clear, blue sky.

"How far do you think this boat could go?" he said after a long silence.

"What do you mean?"

"It could follow the coast, south to a different town. I am sick of Bardiya."

"A new town with the same problems," she replied. "The Shadows are everywhere, I am told."

"Across the ocean then, with enough food and fresh water, we could cross to Pashwar in the West."

She sat up and stared at him.

"'*We*'?" she gaped. "Are you insane? We would be caught, and you would be garroted. I would live the rest of my life in shame."

Dyansh stared out across the ocean.

"Tomorrow is the new moon," he said. "Who will the Shadows feed on this time?"

"It is over a thousand miles across the ocean."

"The prison is empty," he went on. "Who will they deem 'unworthy' tomorrow?"

"Take me back to shore!" she demanded. "Never speak of this again."

"I'm sorry," he muttered, pushing the tiller hard and hauling on a rope to change the sail's angle.

"This kind of talk is forbidden," she warned. "You know this. What has got into you?"

Dyansh glowered at the horizon. "It is a year ago to the day since Mohanish killed my father," he said at last.

"Oh, Dyansh," Alisha said, reaching for his arm. "I am sorry. How could I have forgotten. I have been so caught up with myself lately."

"There is no need," he replied. "It's not your fault. But Mohanish still struts around town without a care. He comes into the Teahouse and treats us like less than dirt. Sometimes he says the food is off and refuses to pay his bill, even when he has emptied the plate. My father wanted no part of this '*new order*', and neither do I. Some days I just want to fight back."

"They would kill you," she cut him short. "You mustn't."

"It will get worse, Alisha."

"You don't know that. You can't," she insisted. "Give it a few days and these feelings will pass. Sometimes I feel the same, but you must be strong."

The boat cut through the water on the stiff breeze and soon they rounded a small headland bringing the town into view. The enormous headframe that sat above the mineshaft on the southern edge of Bardiya dominated the horizon. Alisha tried not to look at it.

"Are you sure you want to go back?" Dyansh asked at last. "We could take a trip to Hollow Cove if you like. We should make the most of this; once you have taken the veil, I will not even be able to greet you in the street."

"No," she sighed. "I have work to do. Tau cannot manage on his own."

"He will need to learn."

"He can polish well enough, but his hands are too clumsy for engraving, and he leaves the patina on for too long."

"Have you asked Sujnay Ahaju for help," Dyansh suggested. "Sujnay was a good friend of your father's, and he is a good man. He helped me a lot."

"Hmm," Alisha mused. "Perhaps."

The docks were quiet when they slipped into the stone

embrace of the harbour. Most of the larger fishing vessels were out at sea, but the market was deserted. Vegetables, fish and spices still lay on the tables under the bright awnings, but there was no sign of life. Only the gentle slap of water against the side of the boat and the distant cry of a gull broke the silence.

"Where is everyone?" Alisha asked.

"I don't know," Dyansh replied, steering the boat to bump against the timber pilings that lined the stone of the harbour. He tied up to a steel ring, leaving enough slack for the ebbing tide, and helped Alisha to the ladder.

"I can hear voices," she said when they were both on solid ground.

They hurried from the harbour and up the gentle slope towards the centre of Bardiya. Further along the road figures hurried up the hill ahead of them.

"What's happening?" Alisha asked, an edge of fear entering her voice.

Dyansh shook his head, quickening his pace.

They reached the back of a crowd which had gathered around the central, cobbled square, and craned their necks to see what was happening.

"This way," Dyansh urged and pulled Alisha towards the town hall. They climbed the wooden trellis that led to a flat-topped canopy of stone copings which gave them a clear view of the square beyond the crowd. On any other day, someone would have scolded the children for climbing on the building, but today their attention was elsewhere.

A few soldiers patrolled the edge of the square, keeping the thousand-strong crowd back. They all carried whips, coiled in their hands except for the soldier, Mohanish. He cracked the whip over the heads of the townsfolk, forcing them to duck and push back against those behind. He grinned as they yelped in fear, relishing the power he held over them, backed up by the two Shadows that prowled on the cobbles of the town square.

The stones were spotless; scrubbed clean of the gore that had washed over them at the last new moon. Alisha chased the remembered images from her mind and glanced at Dyansh. Her friend's eyes were fixed on Mohanish and his breath was short and shallow.

"Dyansh!" she hissed, pulling his gaze from the man who had killed his father.

A moment later a shout went up from the far side of town, where the houses gave way to open grassland. A caravan was approaching on the Baslika road to the south-east. They watched in silence as a dozen mounted soldiers with their sparths pointing skyward led two wagons into the square. A pair of Shadows brought up the rear, tongues darting at the nervous townsfolk who backed away from the edge of the street.

The lead wagon was an ornate carriage with curtains drawn across the little windows. The body was held on wide leather straps that cradled and protected whoever was inside from the jostling of the wheels on the road. By contrast, the wagon behind was far cruder in design and function. The driver of the second wagon sat in front of a large iron cage, open to the elements and crammed with a dozen or more prisoners. The caged men and women gripped the bars for support with filthy hands as the cart bounced over the well-swept cobbles.

The wagons came to a stop side-by-side, and one of the soldiers who had already dismounted, hurried to the door of the carriage. He opened the door and stepped back. A moment later, a man in flamboyant military dress stepped out onto the narrow running board. He took a moment to take in his surroundings before stepping down onto the cobbles. His leather armour shared the fish-scale design of the other soldiers but was trimmed with red and gold. He tossed the red cape from his shoulder revealing a jeweled dagger at this hip.

"Commander Girvash!" Captain Yuddha beamed as he hurried across the square to meet his superior. "You were not expected until later in the day. I will have refreshments brought right away." He lowered his head when he was close and gestured towards the town hall.

Alisha and Dyansh gasped as one and shrank back against the wall.

"Thank you, Captain," Commander Girvash replied. "It is an easy journey from Baslika, the road has been well maintained through the winter months. An easy day."

"It is reassuring to have the garrison so close, should it be needed," Captain Yuddha agreed.

"Is it, 'needed' Captain?" Commander Girvash raised an eyebrow.

"Not at all," Yuddha said, "Bardiya is a peaceful and productive town. The mines still yield silver in abundance, and the soil cannot help but produce a bounty in grain. Please, come and take tea with me."

"I shall, but first I have an announcement." He looked around at the gathered people and paced across the cobbles. "People of Bardiya! I have come today with a gift. I know that many of you will be anxious with each new moon as you wait to discover who will be chosen to fulfil your obligation to the Khalim-Shar. It has been easy for us all whilst our prisons have been full, and I know that the burden of choosing who gives the least to your community is a heavy one. You must remain productive; both in your fields and in your homes. The old and the sick have no place in the Khalim-Shar's plan, and nor do those who would rail against this new order." He paused to regard the people around him, but none would meet his eye. They stood with heads bowed and eyes fixed on the ground. "Behind me is your share in the bounty of men's weakness. The village of Kirkut chose rebellion over productivity and sought to evade their obligations to our ruler, our God! Eight men I bring you for eight new moons; eight sacrifices to spare you the choice from among your own. Seven women, to be given to those soldiers most deserving in the eyes of the good

Captain Yuddha. You see, when a man's heart is turned against his ruler, he is better off dead as he will only ever *take* from his society; he is a parasite upon it. But a *woman* can remain beneficial as long as her womb is fertile."

"Fools!" one of the prisoners shouted from within the cage. "Don't you see? You are no better than sheep to them!"

"*Those* are the fools!" Commander Girvash shouted, pointing at the wretched prisoners. "Societies change through the ages. Those unwilling to embrace new ways are ground beneath the ever-rolling wheels of progress."

"Two sons I have given you!" the man raged. "Two sons and a broken heart. Where are my boys now?"

"His sons are part of the glorious birth of a new age!" the commander replied for the town to hear. "As are yours, people of Bardiya. Their loyalty has bought you your freedom; do not squander it so lightly."

A soldier had opened the cage and the prisoners tumbled out, chained together by a series of iron collars.

"You are food for the Shadows! Nothing more!" the prisoner shouted again. "Rise up, people of Bardiya! Rise up before they feast on *you*! They are insatiable!"

The soldier silenced the man with a blow to the head with the butt of his sparth. The prisoner collapsed, dragging those nearest to him down onto their knees.

"Weakness," Girvash went on, "is not to be feared but cleansed! This nascent order will see us strengthened under the watchful eye of our new God and those in his image. I would urge you all to embrace this change if you have not done so already or be plucked from the herd and expunged as you would a deformed lamb. Take them to the barracks and secure them!" The last was directed at one of the soldiers, who used the point of his sparth to force the prisoners out of the square towards the buildings where the soldiers were garrisoned.

Yuddha fell in at the commander's side as he strode towards

the town hall. Alisha and Dyansh shrank back as the soldiers approached, but the men paid the children no heed.

"Take one of those women for yourself, Yuddha," Commander Girvash was saying as the crowd parted to allow them through. "I understand you have never taken a wife."

Yuddha glanced up and saw the children above the doors and smiled to himself.

"Thank you, Commander," he replied as they passed under the stone canopy, "but I already have someone in mind."

Valia awoke after what felt like a blink of the eye. Gone was the leaden ball of hopelessness and loss that had chased her to fitful sleep ever since her capture. There was a blessed simplicity to knowing one's struggle was near an end, and that all pain would soon cease.

She followed the morning routine without protest; allowed the abusive words to wash over her. She accepted her ration of porridge from the only other woman in the camp now, who had assumed Kalie's kitchen duties without a word.

What was her name?

It did not matter. Not now. What use was a new friendship this close to the end?

Mere distraction.

She sat cross-legged with the other prisoners and ate her food, tasting nothing. The axe she took from the supply tent felt light in her grip, and when she ran her calloused thumb along its edge the sound of keen steel filled her senses.

Valia watched as a pair of Shar crossed the log-bridge onto the southern bank of the Olchora, followed by a pair of Suun's soldiers. She joined the sullen throng of prisoners as they crossed the bridge interspersed with Eastern guards. She fell in step behind the one-eyed man; Garutan's first lesson to them all. The man turned as he walked and fixed Valia with a gaze that held neither spark nor spirit. Perhaps he too was resigned to his own fate. He turned away and trudged on, thin and wasted of body and vigour.

More soldiers crossed the bridge and spread about the fringes of the large clearing in twos and threes as the prisoners settled into their tasks. Another Shar followed the last of the prisoners across the bridge and at last Garutan showed himself. He stood beside the cooking fire on the other side of the river, warming his hands.

Valia had returned to the place where her previous day's labour had ended; a felled tree which needed to be stripped of its branches and cut into manageable lengths. She set about stripping the lower limbs from the stem while one of the recently disfigured men dragged them away, his wounded face wrapped with a grubby rag. She cast the occasional glance to the north bank where the encampment had been established. A dozen soldiers remained on that northern bank, with Suun's men and their eastern allies forming discrete groups. The woman who had assumed Kalie's duties was washing bowls in the river when Garutan barked an order at her. She abandoned her task and hurried back to the tents. She stood with her head bowed while Garutan spoke, and then hurried away into the cluster of tents.

Garutan stood at the fire with hands stretched out above the coals for warmth.

A short time later he shouted something that Valia could not discern, but she could hear impatience in the tone. He shouted again, and then gestured to one of the soldiers. The sparth bearer nodded and strode along the path that the woman had taken. Garutan returned his attention to the fire.

Valia worked with one eye on the encampment.

Garutan was becoming agitated. He shouted again just as Valia noticed a ribbon of smoke rising from the tented area.

A cry of alarm and flames leapt as a fire took hold. Some of the soldiers on the southern bank abandoned their posts and ran for the bridge. Garutan was bellowing orders while men dropped their sparths and ran to the river with buckets to douse the spreading fire. Valia watched as the soldiers crossed back to the encampment and started to follow, gripping her axe with both hands.

A Shar leapt into her path and tasted the air with its tongue. A high-pitched chitter emanated from its throat and its flesh seethed. An arrow was suddenly protruding from the side of its head and an instinct that Valia had thought forgotten took over her actions. She spun and stepped to the Shar's side, bringing the heavy felling-axe down on the creature's neck as it recovered from the impact of the arrow. The Shar crumpled, and Valia finished the task with two more strokes, leaving the writhing, twitching body to thrash its last. Most of the soldiers were across the bridge by now, adding to the throng and confusion, but a few had remained with the prisoners. A bowman had just enough time to pull an arrow from his quiver before two shafts struck in rapid succession. He fell without ever seeing who had loosed them.

Another Shar ran at Valia, leaping when it was near enough to attack. She dropped to the ground and rolled, swinging her axe with one hand as the Shar passed over her. The axe-head hacked a gouge into the Shar's shoulder, and the stricken creature crumpled when it hit the ground. Valia wasted no time in getting to her feet and finishing the job.

"Fight! Fight for your lives!" A figure charged from the trees, urging the stunned prisoners to turn on their captors. It was Starling, and the slender blade of his sword flashed in the morning light. The prisoners stood, stupefied for long moments, their mettle long since eroded by fear.

"Fight!" Starling shouted again.

With an animal cry the thin, one-eyed man hacked at the back of the nearest guard. His axe failed to penetrate the leather fish-scale armour of the Eastern guard, but the impact knocked him to the ground. The prisoner swung at the guards unprotected head, smashing through his skull with ease. Blind fury drove him on to strike again and again, spraying blood and gore across the slick rocks. An archer ended the attack with a well-placed arrow, but the prisoner's actions had spurred others on to fight. Before the bowman could nock another arrow, he was set upon by three prisoners. He screamed as they cut him down with their hatchets, hacking at the arms he had thrown up to defend himself. Moments later, he was dead.

The head of a Shar tumbled into the clearing and Adeyemi fell upon a startled soldier. The dark-skinned man slapped the sparth aside with his crude impanga and hacked downwards into the man's neck.

A sparth bearer rounded on Starling and advanced over the boulders. Starling took a step back and felt his foot slide on the moss-covered rocks. The soldier swung the long weapon in a wide arc that Starling only just managed to get beneath. The long edge of the blade passed over his head as he ducked, but he lost his footing, falling back among the round boulders. The soldier saw his quarry stumble, and pounced, twirling the sparth in his grip to stab downwards. An arrow struck the attacker's shoulder as he leapt and the point of the Sparth struck the rocks at Starling's side. Starling had his face shielded with one arm but stabbed upwards with the sword in his other in a desperate attempt to defend himself. The soldier fell onto the sword point, his weight driving it down until the hilt butted against Starling's chest. The soldier's face jarred to a halt a finger's breadth from Starling's own, and the two men stared in shocked silence for a few, dying heartbeats.

Adeyemi pulled the corpse from Starling with one hand and dragged the young man to his feet. He took a moment to bring Starling back to his senses.

"Come back, Little Bird. We are not done yet!"

A quick smile, and he was off again, bounding across the rocks with a sure-footed ease. Starling slipped with his first step, but struggled on towards the bridge, desperate to shake the image of those dying eyes from his mind.

Shar screeched and men shouted as the prisoners turned on the guards. Hatchets became weapons and the prisoners fell upon the soldiers who were quickly overwhelmed. In moments, there were no soldiers left alive on the southern bank and those who had crossed only moments ago were hurrying back in disarray.

A Shar leapt onto the backs of a group of prisoners who were hacking at a screaming soldier with their hatchets, cutting two down with razor talons. Valia was quick to attack it, hurling her axe at the beast. The heavy blade struck the Shar's head and lodged in the oozing flesh. The Shar was knocked back and it lost its footing. Hatchets bit into the flailing limbs as the prisoners struck. They were beyond fear now and their screams of fury could not be separated from the screams of the Shar as they took it to pieces with their tools, dismembering the creature with delirious savagery.

A call went up from the northern bank near the encampment and those soldiers still on the southern bank ran for the crossing point. Adeyemi reached the bridge before them and ran onto it. He stopped a few strides along its length and turned, standing with feet spread wide. In one hand he gripped the pouch he wore around his neck, and in the other, held his impanga. The soldiers would have to go through him, or else swim to get back across the river. He roared as the soldiers approached, and the first two went down before they reached him as an unseen archer picked them off with well-placed arrows.

Valia paused beside a dead soldier to retrieve his dropped sparth and at once recognised the arrow in his chest. Lythurian.

Elan.

One by one, the soldiers fell from the bridge as arrows struck home. The few who reached Adeyemi were no match for his strength and skill with the broad blade he wielded. The nearest soldier stabbed forward with his sparth, but Adeyemi swatted it aside and gripped the shaft. Then he drove it back at the soldiers, causing several to tumble into the icy river. Four soldiers remained on the southern bank now and found themselves trapped between Adeyemi on the bridge and Valia on the bank. Two of them turned to face Valia as their fellows stepped onto the bridge to face Adeyemi. Valia raised the sparth over her shoulder with one hand and hurled it like a javelin. The heavy, pointed blade struck the soldier in the chest and knocked him off his feet. He landed on his back and blood erupted from his mouth as his last breath was forced from his punctured lungs.

An arrow felled the next soldier before Valia had reached him, and now only one remained on the bridge with the body of Adeyemi's last victim floating away in a crimson cloud below. The last soldier glanced back at Valia, then back at Adeyemi grasping the bloody impanga in his dark fist. He dropped his sparth and chattered in his own language, holding his palms up in surrender. Valia grabbed the shoulder straps of his armour and lifted him up. Then she pulled him towards her and drove her forehead into his face. The crunch from his breaking nose was audible above the fighting in the encampment. Valia dropped the limp body into the water and pushed past Adeyemi without a word.

There were screams from the encampment now as the soldiers who had formed up at the bridge were set upon from behind. Valia could see Garutan shouting orders at his dwindling force.

She needed to be the one to kill him.

Garutan was calling his men back to defend him in the chaos. Against the backdrop of blazing tents, Valia could see Marlon attacking the soldiers with a fury she had not witnessed in him before. He was holding nothing back as he threw himself into the fray. His sword and shield were wet with gore, his bearded face red with blood and rage. Alano danced among the enemy with the Malmotti blade in his hands, never still for a moment, every movement a continuation of the last and a precursor to the next. Then she saw Abbil and Jon facing off against a Shar in the glaring light of the flames, as she pushed on to the north bank of the river to add her weight to the fight. She took up a sparth from the ground and hurled it at the defending soldiers which knocked one of them backwards with the force it carried. Then she lifted a sword, dropped by one of Suun's men, and attacked the defensive formation. Someone called her name, no more than a whisper in a hurricane, but she was too caught up in the tempest to pay it any heed.

The defensive formation around Garutan crumbled under the weight of the attack and the remaining soldiers broke formation in panic. Elan was now on the bridge, targeting any soldier that still held a weapon, and suddenly, the battle was over.

The soldiers ran, leaving their commander undefended. Garutan bellowed a curse at them as they fled, then fell to his knees and held his hands out in submission. He glanced around for a moment, taking in the carnage that lay everywhere and then laughed, perhaps realising that his encampment had been overrun by so few. He looked up when Valia came to stand in front of him, and his shoulders sagged. Valia punched him in the face, feeling his nose crunch under the weight of her fist. He fell backwards and did not move.

"Valia!" Marlon's voice reached her at last. Like a long-forgotten memory heard in a fading dream. "Valia!"

He was suddenly in front of her. "Valia," he said again, dropping his sword and shield. His eyes were wet with tears as he put his arms around her and drew her into an embrace. "I knew," he murmured. "I knew."

She was certain that she ought to feel something now, but Valia felt only numb.

"I knew that you were alive," Marlon said. "I cannot tell you how, but I knew."

He sat at Valia's side, staring into the fire.

The surviving slaves were either seated near the fire or else picking through the remains of the burned tents. The diversion had worked but had destroyed much of what the newly liberated slaves could have used. Two soldiers were kneeling nearby: one of Suun's men and an Eastern soldier. They were joined by pole across their backs around which their arms were hooked and tied by the wrist at the front. Their commander still lay unconscious on the ground.

Jon stopped poking about in the ashes of what had been the commander's tent and walked past the fire.

"I'd better go and get Sparky," he announced. "I left him tied to a tree. I wouldn't want him to be abducted by squirrels now."

Valia watched him stride off into the forest and then returned her gaze to the flames.

"Why did you leave without a word?" Marlon asked at last, scratching his bearded cheek.

"Did we not have words?"

Marlon stopped scratching, conscious that he had grown the beard to spite her. "I know, I need to shave this off. Lately it has been easier to just let it grow."

"Do as you please," Valia murmured.

Marlon dipped his fingers into a pouch at his hip and retrieved a gold coin strung on a strip of leather.

"I found this," he said, offering her the coin.

Valia took the gold mark and turned it over in her hand. "It should buy enough wine to celebrate our victory when it comes."

She tossed it back to him.

"Valia, you have carried this coin since Ara Dasari. This is Truman's token. Have you forgotten? Have you taken a blow to the head?"

Valia shook her head as she stared into the flames. "My mind is clearer than it has ever been."

Marlon sighed and put the coin back in the pouch. "I also found your sword, and I carried your armour with me against the day that I would find you."

She nodded, remaining silent.

Elan sat beside the fire with a bundle of arrows he had

retrieved and set about repairing the fletching. Valia watched his expert hands work.

How could a man who had lost everything find contentment? Or was he hollow just like her? A broken mill, still turning in the water's flow but inside was nothing but shattered gears and decay.

Jon returned with an Eastern soldier in tow. The man was not bound but was rubbing his wrists as though he had been. Valia was on her feet in an instant, reaching for the sparth that leaned against a nearby post. She strode towards him with murderous intent, lifting the sparth as she approached. The man saw her and backed away, babbling in fear as he did so.

"Wait! No!" Jon protested, putting himself in her way. "He is with us. A prisoner."

"Then why is he not bound?" Valia demanded.

"He's tame, he's..." Jon began before turning to the easterner. "Why are you not bound, Blossom?"

"Because he is a traitor." The voice came from the commander.

Valia looked from the terrified man behind Jon to Garutan as he shifted on the ground. His face was smeared with dried blood and he winced from the pain of the broken nose she had inflicted earlier.

His hands were tied behind his back, but he forced himself into a sitting position and spoke in his own language for a moment. Jon's prisoner babbled back in panicked tones and Garutan responded with words that he spat like venom.

"What are you saying?" Alano demanded, seeing their prisoner crying and imploring as Garutan scowled.

"His loved ones will pay the price for his treachery," Garutan sneered. "He knows this."

The man was openly weeping now, collapsed onto his knees with tears flowing down his cheeks.

"What did you say to him?" Alano pressed again.

Garutan laughed. "We all made a choice." Then he turned

back to the distraught man and spoke again in the Eastern language.

"Enough!" Valia shouted. She threw the sparth down and paced back and forth. "Marlon, a knife."

Marlon took a dagger from his hip and tossed it to Valia. She caught it and approached Garutan.

"On your knees!" she ordered.

He managed to kneel and Valia stood in front of him, staring down. "Now, pay attention."

She stepped away to the front of the other two prisoners and held the dagger for them to see. "I know your name. Aanga."

The eastern soldier looked up with a terrified expression. He swallowed hard.

"You understand me. You will answer my questions, or you will die," she threatened. Aanga nodded. "Why did you bring us here? Why do you need these trees?"

Aanga stammered "I, I, I, we need, need wood for build…"

"Build what?" she demanded.

Aanga's mouth worked silently and he shook his head.

Valia drove the dagger into his throat. She twisted it with a sickening crunch before pulling the blade free. A gout of blood erupted from the soldier's ruined windpipe and his eyes went wide with shock.

The second soldier cried out and tried to pull free of his bonds, but he remained tethered beside the dying man. Aanga coughed and spasmed as his body tried to rid his lungs of blood.

"Valia! No!" Alano shouted. "This is wrong."

She turned to face him; his hand was on the hilt of his sword.

"Do not," she warned.

Marlon was on his feet and Jon put himself in the middle, holding his hands up for calm. In the silence, Aanga gagged and bubbled his way to an undignified death while the other soldier sobbed and tried to pull away from the slumped form beside him.

"Let's all calm down," Jon urged.

"This is wrong, Valia," Alano pleaded. "We should question them, yes, but this is murder, plain and simple."

Valia turned back to the prisoner kneeling on the ground. He had slumped a little to one side under the weight of the body still tied to the pole. He was pleading for mercy through tears that flowed down his cheeks and mixed with saliva. He smelled of urine.

Valia went down on her haunches in front of him and held the dagger close to his face. "Are you afraid?" she asked.

The man nodded, crying like a child.

"Why do you need these trees?" she whispered, labouring every word.

The man began to shake his head and Valia raised the dagger a little. He quickly stopped shaking his head "No, no... the trees are for, they are going to Dargenmill. Yes. Dargenmill."

"They are going to Dargenmill?"

He nodded. "Yes. Yes. Dargenmill."

"Why," she asked.

His hopeful expression slipped a little. "To build. Suun. For..." he babbled

"You do not know, do you?" she said

The man began to panic. "For...for...Ramash Suun. To build...for..."

Valia stabbed him in the throat, twisting the blade as she had before. He thrashed against the bonds, fists white and eyes wide with terror.

"This is murder! They have surrendered!" Alano shouted, pulling his sword from its scabbard. Marlon did the same and turned on Alano.

Abbil too, had his sword free. "What are we doing?" he called out to everyone, "This is not why we came here."

Valia stood and walked towards the gathering. "Would you fight me, Alano Clemente? Would you fight me for the lives of these murderers; these rapists; these *Shar-collaborators*?"

"It is not for you to judge them," he replied.

"Is it not? Then who should they stand before?" she asked. "You? How would you judge them?"

"Not like this," Alano retorted.

The soldier was still at last, and Valia turned to Garutan.

"Valia, I warn you," Alano began and Marlon stepped in front of him.

"Would you fight a friend?" Alano said with a sad shake of his head.

"Would you?" Marlon replied. "Valia? My sword is yours, but you are putting me in a difficult position."

"It is your choice," Valia murmured. She returned her attention to Garutan and walked towards him.

"Do not let her do this," Alano urged Marlon, "for her own sake."

"Valia," Marlon cast over his shoulder, keeping his eye fixed on Alano. "Take some time to think. You have suffered much lately."

"Lie to me once," she said, voice dripping with menace, "and I will take an eye. Why is the wood going to Dargenmill?"

"I was simply ordered to come to these forests and cut down trees and float them down river for timber," Garutan replied. "I do not know why they need it."

Valia grabbed a fistful of hair to hold his head steady and pushed the dagger into his eye. He screamed as she levered the blade, pulling the punctured eye from its socket.

Alano lunged forward but Marlon was expecting it and swung the flat of his sword at the man's midriff. Alano deflected the blow but came up against the point of Abbil's sword at his throat. Alano froze.

Garutan's howling eased a little and he slumped. His eye hung from the socket by a thread of gore and rested on his cheek. Valia gripped the ruined eye and ripped it from his face. He screamed again, and she threw the gobbet into the fire.

"What has she become?" Alano whispered.

Abbil shook his head, urging his friend not to move.

Valia squatted beside the panting Garutan, who was dribbling with fear and agony. "Why. Does. Dargenmill. Need. Timber." She spoke each word in a calm, quiet voice.

Garutan groaned and Valia gripped his hair again to lift his head. "Weapons," he slurred. "*War engines.*"

"War engines?" she asked. "For what purpose?"

Garutan focussed with his remaining eye and managed a weak smile. Then he laughed. "To smash the walls of Kor'Habat."

Valia considered this for a moment before she leaned close and whispered. "This is from Kalie." Then she stabbed him in the throat and left him to drown in his own blood.

"You had never killed before today."

Starling managed a half smile. "Did it show?"

Adeyemi smiled back. "There is no shame in that, Little Bird."

Starling was leading his horse near the front of the procession. A little over sixty prisoners had been freed but there were not nearly enough horses for them all. Even with the mounts they had captured, most had to walk, and so the injured were carried on horseback.

Starling made to speak but remained silent.

"What is it, Little Bird?" Adeyemi asked in a soft tone.

Starling hesitated. "Does it ever become easy? I watched Valia today and felt sick to my stomach, yet she did not flinch. That man I killed today; that man who fell onto my sword. His eyes…" He trailed off.

"Killing should never be easy," Adeyemi said. "And yet if your cause is just, then your conscience should remain unworried." He chuckled. "When I met you, you were a bandit on the road, yet you felt no compunction until now? That sword you carry is not a trinket."

"The threat of violence and superior numbers have served me

well until now. I have never needed to use it in anger. Of course, I am trained to. My father is a provincial Governor no less," he said with mock pride. "And he insisted on my being trained by the masters of the Akharran themselves. I have skewered more straw-filled manikins that I care to remember. None of them bled, and none of them looked into my eyes as they died."

"Death comes to us all," Adeyemi replied. "That you witnessed that man's passing at his allotted time should not burden your heart."

Starling glanced sideways at the big man to see if he was being toyed with, but Adeyemi was not laughing, he was holding the pouch he wore around his neck.

"Allotted time?" Starling said, eyeing the pouch in his grip. "Is that what befell those three men? Valia merely witnessed their passing at their allotted time? You will have a hard time convincing Alano of that."

Adeyemi laughed. "Friend Alano is a farmer at heart. He does not have a warrior's temperament."

"Do I?" Starling asked.

Adeyemi offered him a wide smile. "That remains to be seen, Little Bird."

Marlon led the party into the encampment on the field beside the Olchora river. The injured were helped from the horses and Marlon asked that tents be made available for the rescued prisoners, and for Valia, but it had already been arranged.

"Welcome back," Granger greeted him with a warm, vigorous handshake. "When the scout told me of your approach, I could scarcely believe it." He shifted his attention to Valia, who arrived moments later. "Valia, you cannot imagine how relieved I am to see you. We feared the worst." He tried to embrace her, but she was stiff and unresponsive.

"Thank you, Granger. Where can I wash?" she replied.

"Of course," he said after a moment's pause. "You must be exhausted. A tent has been prepared for you. Kekoa will take you to it, he was extremely excited to hear that you were coming back."

The little Jendayan was already there, gesturing for Valia to follow.

Granger shot a perplexed glance at Marlon as Valia walked away. "Is all well?" Granger asked.

Marlon sighed. "We need to talk."

They found Acastes already in the command tent with Kapaneus. Acastes was nursing a cup of wine and eating a bowl of nuts he cracked with his teeth, one by one. Marlon informed them of what they had learned during the search and after Valia's rescue, including the information about the war engines.

"How is Valia?" Granger asked after Marlon had finished his report, sensing that something was amiss.

"She barely speaks," he said. "She is distant; withdrawn. I cannot tell you what she has experienced because she will not tell me."

"And Alano?" Granger asked.

Marlon shook his head. "Has not spoken since the morning of her rescue. I reacted harshly, I…"

"You did what you thought was right at the time. Alano will understand that," Granger tried to reassure him.

Acastes leaned back in his chair. "If you ask me, Valia was too soft on those bastards."

Marlon turned his head to face the big Korathean. "Well you were not there, and I did not ask you."

"Now just a moment…" Acastes began, but Marlon cut him off.

"You look well fed; camp life clearly suits you."

Acastes stood as Kapaneus stepped between them to calm the brewing dispute. "This will not help. We do not need new enmity at a time like this."

"Kapaneus is right," Granger said. "We need unity now, not petty squabbles."

Marlon scratched the flesh under his eye-patch and groaned.

"I am tired. The last few months have felt like years."

Kapaneus placed a hand on Marlon's shoulder. "Sleep, a hot meal and a jug of wine, in any order you choose will restore you, my friend."

"Perhaps. But first, what has happened here? There are more tents than I expected to see."

"Men loyal to Dachen," Granger explained. "They arrived here a week ago. They tell us that all is not well in Kor'Habat. The refugees are living in squalor outside the city walls and the Hatars are unwilling to let Eastern soldiers in."

"The Hatars will use this as an excuse to seize power from the Kodistai," Kapaneus said and shot a knowing look at Acastes.

"I thought he was dead," Marlon said.

"He is still stubbornly *dying*," Acastes snorted. "As he has been for quite some time."

"Well, if what we learned from that slave-master is true, then he may yet live to see his city walls crumble."

"Hah!" Acastes scoffed. "Those walls are invulnerable. Kor'Habat has never been taken by a hostile army; with or without *war engines*."

"Such arrogance caused the downfall of the Korathean Empire," Valia declared from the entrance of the tent. "I was there; I saw it."

"Valia, you should be resting," Granger said. "Is your tent comfortable?"

"My tent is fine," she replied, walking to a small table and inspecting the map that was unrolled there.

"Would you care for some wine?" Acastes swirled the last dregs in his cup before swallowing what remained.

"How soon can reach we Dargenmill?" she asked.

Kapaneus exchanged confused glances with the others in the tent and shrugged. "Three weeks perhaps. Why?"

"It is time to put an end to Suun's madness. Those cultists have become a threat."

"We will be leaving for Kor'Habat as soon as we are able," Kapaneus assured her. "'Wait for Marlon', that's what we agreed, then go to Kor'Habat."

"Kor'Habat can wait, it is time to take the fight to the Shar, starting with Suun."

Kapaneus shrugged. "Suun's cult is misguided, I will grant you that much, but it is a stretch to say that they are 'a *threat*'. A few lunatics, that is all."

"I saw his men aiding the Eastern soldiers, unconcerned by the Shar that guarded us," Valia snapped. "We sit on our hands while the enemy is gathering allies."

"And we should consolidate our position where we are best suited to defend it."

"You have an army," Valia insisted. "Why will you not use it? They are building war engines to use against us."

"*Dachen* has an army," Kapaneus corrected. "We have twenty hunters, fifty Sisters and the word of a slave-master. They could be strengthening their palings with that timber for all we know and yet you talk of '*war engines*'."

Granger stepped in as the conversation grew heated. "Could we agree to send scouts to Dargenmill?"

"Every day, they grow stronger," Valia scowled. "We should strike now; raze the town to the ground and send the Khal-im-Shar a clear message."

"There will be women and children in Dargenmill," Marlon murmured.

Valia slammed her fist on the table. "There were women and children in Ulan Balsan and Banihat!" she yelled.

"And you would slaughter more innocents?" Kapaneus snapped back.

A voice from the tent opening broke the tension. "I heard that you had returned, Valia, but I had thought that it would be a happier occasion."

It was Dachen. Kekoa slipped in behind him and made his

way to Acastes' side. The Korathean held out his wine cup and the Jendayan dutifully refilled it. Acastes accepted the wine without acknowledgement. "Valia would use your army to attack Dargen-mill," he said.

"I heard," Dachen replied, "from halfway across the camp."

"Your thoughts?" Acastes asked.

Valia straightened to glare at Dachen.

Dachen nodded. "I agree with Valia, for what it is worth," he said, drawing surprised looks from everyone there. "I have been to Dargenmill and seen the madness in Ramash Suun. It has been a year since our paths crossed, but he spoke of building an army even then, to fight the Shar-hunters when the time came."

"Ravings," Acastes declared.

"No doubt," Dachen replied, "but he is organised, and clear in purpose. Your wars left many people homeless and without hope, it is little wonder that they flock to a man who offers change; something new."

"The Shar are feared wherever they are found," Acastes argued. "No sane person would ally themselves to a cause that would aid them."

"Then you do not understand people," Dachen replied. "When you shatter everything that a man knows, and tear away all that he holds dear, then he will follow any cause that promises to give more than it takes. Shelter, security, a sense of togetherness from a shared cause will win hearts."

"The fellowship of the wretched is found in the lowest of places," Kekoa murmured.

Acastes scoffed. "Every time you speak you make a little less sense."

"Dachen and Kekoa are correct," Granger said. "Suun and his followers are the result of a war that raged without a care for the damage left in its wake."

"And if it is true that they are working on war engines to use against us," Dachen added, "then we would be wise to act before their work is complete. I have interrogated the prisoner you took on the steppe, Marlon, and I believe that many of my kin will side with the Khalim-Shar in return for the safety of their own families."

Valia nodded. "We are in agreement then."

Acastes sighed. "I will come too," he said and Kapaneus threw his hands up. "But if there is no sign of 'war engines' being built I will have no part in any attack."

"Then rest well," Valia murmured. "We will break camp in the morning."

Marlon watched Valia as she pored over the map while everyone else left the tent. He opened his mouth to speak but stopped himself before he had uttered a word. With a final, worried glance, he turned and left the tent, and Valia to her thoughts.

The morning was crisp and clear, typical of late spring. The call of meadow buntings eager for a mate and the buzz of insects awakened from the torpor of winter should have been the only sound.

Instead, the field hummed with the breaking of tents and the loading of pack-mules.

Alano found Granger strapping leather satchels to the flanks of a waiting mule. "Still filling those books with stories, Granger," he said, alerting the older man to his presence.

"Ah, Alano," he replied, "I have not seen you since you returned yesterday. And, yes, I am still gathering tales. The memory is not what it once was, so if I have any desire to share them..." He patted one of the satchels.

Alano smiled at Granger and nodded. "This is where I must leave them," he said at last.

"I had feared as much," Granger said as his shoulders sagged. "Can what passed between you not be mended?"

Alano shook his head. "There is more to it than that. I had told myself that if I could ensure that Valia was safe, then I could return home knowing that I had not deserted a friend."

"And yet you appear unsatisfied."

Alano's eyes searched the ground in front of him before looking up again. "Valia has changed, Granger. There is a bitterness there now, a callousness. I do not fault Marlon for defending her as he did, but he of all people should have recognised what she was doing for what it was and helped me to sway her from her actions."

"You feel betrayed?"

Alano managed a sardonic smile. "A little," he said. "A great deal. Most of all, I am sad that a friendship has ended in such a way. It is not what I had hoped for. I thought her dead, I truly did, but Marlon knew, he *knew* that she was alive. Despite all the evidence to the contrary he carried a certainty with him, always, that she was alive. When we learned that she was being held in the forests, Marlon showed no surprise. I do not share their bond, and perhaps I should not be surprised."

Granger nodded. "I understand. But you have been away from Casilda for too long already. Valia will come to appreciate your sacrifice for her, in time. You should make your peace with Marlon and Abbil before you leave if you can. It will ease your mind."

Alano shook his head. "I cannot yet. I am sorry."

Granger sighed. "I understand."

They stood in thoughtful silence for a moment before Granger spoke again. "Warn people wherever you see them, Alano. Let them know what we are facing. The day may yet come when every man, woman and child from Dasar to Mecia will be called upon to fight. Spread the word."

"I will do that," Alano said, embracing Granger in farewell. "Stay safe and write good things about me."

"Always, Alano." Granger replied. "Give my warmest regards to Casilda, and the children."

Alano nodded, then turned to leave. He stopped, and half turned back. "Granger, look after her."

Then he left and gathered his belongings, making ready for the long journey home to Lythuria.

Captain Silman arrived at Dargenmill a little before sunset. There had been nothing he could do to lift the spirits of the twelve men under his command over the past weeks and he felt disinclined to try. They had been so very close to home; a few short days from Kor'Habat when word had arrived that he was to travel to Dargenmill. Dreams of ale and women had turned sour with that curt message. Although the order had come from Hatar Rogan Fol'Brandam, Silman could feel the hand of his old rival Raims, in this. That bastard would pay in time.

Incredible as it seemed, the Kodistai was still alive, and the Hatars were circling his bed to curry favour with the old man as he stubbornly clung to life.

Silman would be Hatar one day though. This was just another discomfort he had to endure until he could be the one to give the orders.

Dargenmill at least offered some short-term respite.

A fresh paling had been erected to enclose new buildings that had been built outside the old gates. The town had expanded, and very recently by the look of it, with much of the timber used yet to be greyed by the sun. The militiamen who met his small party regarded the dozen Heavy Infantrymen with suspicious eyes and one whistled to a larger group within the town for support. Silman was the only one on a horse, but a half dozen pack-mules laboured under the weight of equipment as they trudged through the mud.

One of the militiamen noted the mud clinging to the Infantrymen's boots and spoke with a wary smile. "The spring thaw is most welcome, but the mud is not."

Silman glowered at the group of men now blocking his path in the gateway. He could see fresh cobbles within. "And we would be rid of that mud all the sooner if you stood aside, Militiaman!"

The man did not budge, but rather glanced over each shoulder to be sure his fellows had arrived at his back. Emboldened, he went on. "What business does the Heavy Infantry have in Dargenmill?"

"What business?" Silman replied. "Since when do the town militias of Korathea question the sons of the Akharran? Stand aside."

The man stood his ground, although he shifted his stance and fidgeted with his gloves. "I am under order to question all who come to Dargenmill."

"And I am a captain in the Heavy Infantry and choose not to answer you," Silman barked. "I have spent many weeks fighting through ice and snow, and you are all that stands between me and a comfortable bed and a warm whore. Stand aside! Do not make me ask again."

The militiaman placed a hand on the sword at his hip and took half a step back to both give himself room and bring his fellows closer to his back. He swallowed hard.

"Let them pass, let them pass!" A man was making his way towards them from within the town, jumping muddy puddles in an attempt to keep his feet dry. He was middle-aged with a clean-shaven head and a look of manic energy about him. He had his simple brown robes hitched up in both hands to spare the hem from the mud.

Silman watched him approach. The young soldier, Daelen, stopped at the side of the captain's horse and nodded towards the town. "Eastern soldiers, Captain," he murmured.

Silman looked beyond the hurrying man and saw that the soldier was right.

"Welcome, welcome," the man said, bursting with enthusiasm and breathing hard from his exertions. "Please forgive me, I saw you approaching from my position on the temple, but of course, it took me some time to get down." He slipped a hand behind the horse's cheek piece and led the huge animal past the militiamen. As the man picked his way across the mud towards the cobbles,

Silman surveyed the burgeoning town. There were armed men wherever he looked, but none wore the matching armour of an organised militia; a mixture of every type of leather and mail was on display.

The Eastern soldiers stood out, not only because of their smaller stature than most, but because of their fish-scale leather armour. They showed no hostility beyond wary gazes but that did not settle the feeling of unease that was stirring in Silman's belly. Perhaps they were merely part of a larger group of refugees.

"Magnificent, is it not?" the man leading his horse said, pulling Silman's eyes away from the watchful soldiers.

"What?" he replied and was suddenly struck by the man's piercing blue eyes.

"The temple. Is it not magnificent?" The man stopped on the cobbles and gestured with his free hand towards an enormous building. "And so close to readiness!"

The massive structure was webbed with scaffolds and ropes as timber and stone were hoisted up high to the masons and carpenters at the top. It was terraced, much like the Kodistai's palace, with each successive layer a little smaller than the last, rising in giant steps, themselves linked by flowing stairways.

"What is it?" Silman asked.

"Why, it is the temple to the returning God, of course. The first of many." The man beamed with pride.

Silman glanced back the way he had come to gauge his best route of escape.

"How rude of me," the man went on. "My name is Ramash Suun. Come, please, we have much to discuss."

Room was made in an inn called *The Happy Wastrel* for the men, and after a long soak in a steaming tub, Silman made his way to the common room feeling fresher than he had done in weeks. It was good to have light clothing on again after so long in armour. A young serving maid ushered him towards a small, private room. She looked nervous; frightened even, but perhaps his size was what caused her to be so jittery. He leered at her as he walked by, unable to remember how long it had been since he had had a woman.

"Wine," he demanded, and she scurried away with his eyes following her. Oh, he would have a woman tonight.

"Already taken care of, Captain," the cheerful voice of Ramash Suun declared as they door swung shut on silent hinges.

Inside the wood-panelled room, Suun was sitting alone at a small table with a large jug of wine set upon it. He stood and gestured to a free chair. Silman slumped into it while Suun filled two cups.

"Your arrival is most fortuitous," Suun said, full of enthusiasm. "I have been meaning to go to Kor'Habat for some time now, especially since the news came, but it has been so busy here."

Silman drained his cup and put it down with a pointed nod of his head.

"This is a truly exciting time," Suun said as he refilled the cup.

"How so?" Silman asked, not sure what to make of this little man. He was aware of the cult that had sprung up after the battle at Ara Dasari almost a decade ago and had heard of this Ramash Suun too; a small group of madmen, he had been assured.

"My Order has been waiting for eight years and the time is finally upon us," Suun said.

"Your 'Order'?"

"The *Servants of the Arrival*," Suun said, wide-eyed with fervent righteousness.

"Cultists?" Silman sneered.

Suun leaned back and shrugged. "I blame myself. I was so caught up in the cause that it was some years before I thought to name it. 'Cultists' seems to have stuck with those unfamiliar with our cause.

Silman put his cup on the table. "What exactly is your, '*cause*'?" he asked.

"To prepare the way, of course." Suun was full of fervour

again, his blue eyes shining from behind a swarthy complexion.

"For whom?"

Suun laughed and offered Silman a kind smile. "How much do you know of the history of our world, Captain?"

"I know some." Silman replied, a little confused.

"Do you know of the Gods?"

Silman shrugged. "I know of the legends. The myths and children's stories."

"Myths? Children's stories?" Suun looked sad for a moment before brightening. "But you know now that they were true!"

Silman shifted in his chair. The horrors of Ara Dasari had planted a seed in the minds of all who witnessed them that perhaps there was far more beyond their world that they thought possible. A glimpse of a larger, more terrifying universe.

"Why did you choose to come here?" Suun asked.

"I was sent." Silman replied. "To warn the people of Dargenmill of an invasion of Shar, and possibly Eastern armies."

Suun chuckled. "The Gods guide us in ways we cannot fathom."

"What?"

"You were sent, indeed, but not by whom you think," Suun smiled.

"I was sent by Hatar Rogan Fol'Brandam," Silman said. "Who, despite his own opinion of himself, yet falls short of full deity."

"Oh, the Gods have ways and ways," Suun muttered.

"Suun," Silman said, getting angry now. "I have come a great distance to warn of imminent danger to the people of Dargenmill. I was sent by a Hatar of the Heavy Infantry, and I will be leaving as soon as my message has been delivered."

Suun nodded. "I believe you were *meant* to be here."

"I tire of this," Silman snapped, pushing his chair back with a loud scrape.

"Wait, please," Suun said, pushing his own chair back. "There is someone you should meet."

Silman paused as the little man rose and made his way to the far side of their private room. Suun tapped on a wooden panel and glanced back at Silman.

"Do not be alarmed," he said, then tapped again on the wood.

The panel creaked back to reveal darkness beyond. A small chamber or a tunnel, Silman could not tell.

"This may surprise you," Suun said, "but I urge you to remain calm and listen to what he has to say."

Silman was eager to drink more wine and find a whore for the night; perhaps that serving maid would oblige for a few marks, but his curiosity was piqued by this new development and, so he waited.

Ramash Suun stood smiling at him from the dark opening, unconcerned by whatever lay beyond in the shadows.

Then the darkness shifted, and Silman's belly turned to ice. A Shar detached itself from the gloom and prowled into the room with a sinuous ease, silent but for the scrape of black claws on the floor. Its flesh crawled and oozed, and the creature tasted the air with a darting tongue.

Silman stood, knocking his chair over and tried to cry out, but his throat was dry. He choked and backed away, reaching with shaking fingers for a sword that was not at his hip as the Shar regarded him with obsidian eyes.

"You are in no danger!" Suun called out. "Please, remain calm."

As if to emphasise Suun's words, the huge Shar stopped and eased itself into a strange sitting position, like some sort of enormous dog.

"What is this?" Silman manged at last, edging towards the door that would take him back out to the common room.

"Proof of the sincerity of my offer," said a new voice from the secret opening.

Silman paused as the newcomer entered the room. He was from the Eastern Kingdoms, from the look of him, and dressed in a simple brown robe that reached the floor. He had dark hair and darker eyes, and a smile that made Silman want to run almost as much as the Shar had done, a predator's delight in the curve of his lips.

"Who are you?" Silman managed.

"My name is Samut Masahara, and you are Captain Silman of the Heavy Infantry. Tell me, how was your journey?" His accent was subtle and his command of the Korathean language was flawless.

"Long, and cold for the most part," Silman managed at last.

"Then you must be tired, forgive me," Masahara apologised. "I should have allowed you more time to rest."

"What is this?" Silman asked again.

Masahara regarded Silman for a moment. "A strong man such as you will also need a woman tonight; the serving maid you were admiring perhaps?"

Silman flinched. "The serving maid?" he repeated, narrowing his eyes.

"Yes, Elindre, I believe, is her name," Masahara said, pulling another chair to the table and helping himself to the wine.

Ramash Suun stepped forward from the secret doorway and leaned towards Masahara. "Elindre is to be married later in the spring, I do not think that…"

"For 'The Order', Ramash," Masahara cut in.

"Of course," Suun replied.

Masahara went on. "She is a Servant of the Arrival and as such will do as she must to seal the bargains we must strike."

"Do you know what that is?" Silman asked, pointing at the Shar with a finger he struggled to keep from shaking.

Masahara looked surprised. "Of course, Captain. That is the dawning of a new age."

"Have you seen what they can do?"

"Have you seen what *men* can do?" Masahara retorted.

"They massacred the people of Banihat," Silman said,

incredulous.

"They massacred the…" Masahara took on a look of confusion. "Did you witness this?"

Silman's mouth worked but he did not utter a word.

"No?" Masahara teased.

"Nearly one thousand Heavy Infantry went to Banihat, and I saw what remained, limping south again. The Eastern Kingdoms are no more, their people scattered or dead."

Masahara laughed and gestured for Silman to sit again. "The stories from the Eastern Kingdoms are fanciful at best. Have you actually seen the slaughter, with your own eyes?"

"I saw what was left of my fellow Infantrymen; listened to their accounts."

Silman sat at last but waved away the offered wine.

Masahara sipped from his cup before continuing. "When a foreign force invades a land, the people have to make a choice; capitulate or fight. Where they choose the latter, the invaders are bound by their expansionist ideals to use force against those who chose to bear arms against them. Capitulation leads inevitably to the erosion of culture and pride from the host, but this is the way of men is it not? The people of the Eastern Kingdoms made their choice and those who chose *wisely* are living as they always have, albeit under a different banner. Banihat? The only slaughter was of those who met their new ruler with weapons held high in defiance." He leaned forward. "This is the way of any new order. Capitulate or fight."

"What Masahara is trying to say, Captain," Suun said, "is that when a God comes to exercise dominion over a world, it is better to meet him on bended knee than with a shield wall."

"The Khalim-Shar is coming, Captain Silman," Masahara said from behind his wine cup. "Stand against him if you will, but you will die; you know that he is unstoppable. Accept him as your God and ruler, and you too can share in the power he will bestow upon you. For why else do men strive for power if not to inflict their will upon others? You yearn for the rank of Hatar do you not? Not for the glory it will bring you, but for the power it will give you over your fellows. All men crave it, whether they admit to it or not."

"How do you know these things?" Silman asked, uncomfortable with the way this man was laying his soul out bare before him.

"I know the workings of the minds of men, and I can read your desires like ink on parchment," Masahara replied with a measured smile. "You desire it and much more. You can have so much more."

Silman glanced from one man to the other. "What do you want from me?"

"To bring peace." Masahara put his cup down. "Conflict leads to death, and you will be asked to end a conflict. A time will come when you are called upon to act in the interests of lasting cessation of all wars, forever."

"End a conflict?" Silman swallowed hard. "And what will I get in return?"

Masahara reached across the table and added more wine to Silman's cup, then held the Captain's gaze. "The Khalim-Shar will give you Kor'Habat."

CHAPTER 13

The journey to Dargenmill had taken a little over three weeks. Of the six hundred men who had sworn allegiance to Dachen, only a quarter had horses. Those on foot marched without complaint, covering thirty miles or more every day. They were camped in a woodland, a day's march from their destination; here they would recuperate for a day or two before moving on the town.

Starling was lying in the shade. The trees were in full leaf now and the pale green of the young shoots was further enhanced by the golden light dripping through them. This was, indeed, his favourite time of year; the winter frosts were a fading memory and the heat of summer lay in an indistinct future. Spring was that glorious land bordered on each side by uncomfortable extremes. He lay dozing and wishing that the wine had not been abandoned. Valia had decided that any unnecessary loads were to be left behind.

Wine! Unnecessary? Even the wineskin he carried held only the memory of an aroma.

He opened one eye as he sensed a presence nearby.

"Hello, Olgoi," he sighed.

Olgoi glanced about. All around him, soldiers lay, resting.

"Try not to look so guilty," Starling mocked.

"You have not done it yet," the man hissed back.

"I will, in time," Starling replied. He closed his eye again and made to resume his nap.

Olgoi sat beside him on the ground. "We had a bargain."

Starling made a show of struggling up onto an elbow. "And I will fulfil my part. Why are you so impatient?"

"You spent several weeks with him in the forest, did you learn nothing then?"

"I learned that he guards that pouch like life itself," Starling replied. "This will take time and finesse."

"You assured me that you could do this."

"I can, I can. But do you see him here?"

"I know, he is scouting ahead with Kapaneus," Olgoi conceded. "But time is running short. He will return and soon after we will march on Dargenmill."

"And the other half of our deal?" Olgoi whispered, glancing about. "It must appear…"

Starling rolled his eyes. "It must appear to him that Acastes is the thief," he mimicked.

"Yes, that is vital."

"You never did tell me why," Starling said.

"That is because you do not need to know." A nervous smile touched Olgoi's lips but there was a tension in his gaze that suggested this matter was more urgent than his easy manner suggested.

"Thank you for your clarity." Starling lay back down, and after a moment he heard Olgoi shuffle away. He moved a hand to a belt pouch and felt it. Inside was enough dried spur-root to put a horse to sleep. Now all he needed was the opportunity to use it.

He lay a while longer, considering his options before getting up to take a walk. Part of him wished that he had never accepted Olgoi's challenge, but a greater part of him remembered the gold that had been promised.

He made his way up the gentle slope until he reached a level area encircled by the remains of an ancient wall. Moss covered blocks lay scattered between the trees that had long ago reclaimed the ground of whatever had stood here. These ruins could be found all over the continent; their purpose long forgotten. Even their very substance was being swallowed by the soil. At the centre of the circle of rubble were two tall, stone monoliths, twice the height of a man and as slender as his thigh. Between them, a flat stone slab lay on a block that created a waist-high platform, covered in a deep litter of leaves and mulch.

He was startled to find Nirmaya sitting alone on the other side of the slab.

"You have been avoiding me," he complained, and hopped up onto the slab, trying to hide his fright.

She did not answer and so he lay back on the slab

"What do you suppose went on here all those years ago?" he mused. "Human sacrifice maybe." He made a strangled sound. "*Deflowerings*, perhaps?" he added with a lascivious grin.

Nirmaya groaned. "I could do without your wit right now, Starling."

He slipped from the slab and sat beside her, pressing a shoulder against her own. "Would you like to talk about it?"

"No, I would not," she snapped back at him.

Starling nodded and sat in silence, waiting.

"I mean, what would you do?" she said at last, and he smiled to himself.

"Have you spoken with Valia?"

"Fate! No," she replied. "She was surly before. Now she is beyond reach. Even Marlon and Granger keep their distance."

"You should. Talk to her, I mean." he said. "It could help."

Nirmaya sighed and buried her face in her hands. "I have been putting this off for so long. I do not even know how I feel any more. How do you think she will take it?"

Starling chuckled. "Nirmaya, it is not your fault. You are responsible for your actions alone. Just clear your head *before* we march on Dargenmill."

She nodded and placed a hand on his. "Thank you, Starling. I will tell her."

He patted her hand. "Good girl," he said. He braced himself for her ire, but her mind was already elsewhere, and his patronising comment went unnoticed.

He did not have the heart to attempt more sport with her and so stood and wandered off to be alone with his machinations.

Adeyemi and Kapaneus made straight for the command tent when they returned just before nightfall. They found Valia, Marlon, Dachen, Acastes, Abbil and Jon waiting.

Valia lifted her gaze from a map as they entered. "What did you find?" she asked.

"Welcome back, Adeyemi; Kapaneus," Dachen said before either man could answer. "It is good to see you both safely returned."

Adeyemi accepted the welcome with a smile and a nod, then he turned to Valia who was ignoring Dachen's pointed censure. "It is as we feared. The slave-master was not lying."

"War engines?" Acastes asked. He was working his way through a bowl of nuts, but paused his constant crunching for a moment, and brushed the shells from his clothing.

Kapaneus nodded. "While Adeyemi remained hidden, I entered the town under the guise of a mason seeking work. They are building a temple to rival any building I have seen outside of Kor'Habat."

"Why a temple?" Acastes looked puzzled.

"The cultists or, *Servants of the Arrival* as they call themselves, truly do worship the Shar." He shook his head in disbelief.

"Madness," Abbil grumbled.

"Indeed," Kapaneus continued. "And they have an army."

"How many?" Valia asked.

"Thousands," he replied. "Five thousand according to one boast."

"They outnumber us ten to one," Jon murmured.

"Eight to one, at most," Abbil said with a dismissive wave and a roll of the eyes.

"Not well trained for the most part," Kapaneus went on. "I witnessed their drills and they are not skilled fighters, but they are well armed. The town has swelled to three times what I remember."

"We will attack fast, and hard," Valia said. "We will burn those war engines and anything else that will take a flame."

"What about the soldiers?" Kapaneus asked

"No," Marlon replied, "we target the war engines only and leave before they have their boots on."

"Better to kill them now," Valia growled.

"There will be innocents in the town as well," Marlon persisted. "Burning everything in sight will only end in unnecessary death."

"I did not put them there," Valia murmured.

"The war engines," Dachen said, eager to avert a new argument. "Describe them to me."

Acastes chuckled and cracked another nut.

Kapaneus screwed up his face as he tried to describe the unfamiliar weapons. "Most under construction. There were several that looked like huge crossbows, but each limb was the length of two men."

"*Hatiyara*," Dachen said nodding. "A crossbow, yes, but using the tension of coiled ropes to propel a shaft large enough to cut a horse in two. Anything else?"

Kapaneus nodded. "A wheeled device with a long arm suspended from a cross-piece." He tried to use his arms to mimic the contraption."

Dachen recognised at once the device that Kapaneus was describing. "'*Lamo Phenka*'; a raised counter-weight, when released, can turn the arm with such force that boulders are thrown like pebbles. With that catapult," he warned, "they can bring down walls."

Acastes scoffed but Valia was already asking another question.

"Town defences?" she asked.

"The town has expanded most noticeably to the south, and the paling with it," Kapaneus said. "We saw no gaps nor obvious weaknesses. The gate is a simple double-hinged design. It opens inwards and is secured with a batten the size of a man. We won't break it down with what we have, and it is under constant guard."

"And yet they let you walk in, look around and then leave again?" Jon said.

Kapaneus laughed. "They even tried to recruit me."

"Perhaps we could open the gate from within," Jon suggested.

"Someone would need to get into the town again," Kapaneus said shaking his head. "Then move around unnoticed at night, with those guards." He looked doubtful.

"It is possible," Adeyemi said with a shrug.

"If you are volunteering," Acastes said, munching on a nut as he discarded the shell, "then please leave that Element with me. Better that than deliver it to the Cultists."

Adeyemi gripped the pouch he wore and gave Acastes a wary smile. "You still covet that which you do not hold."

"I would take it if I wanted it," Acastes laughed.

"You would try," Adeyemi warned.

"I can get in," Nirmaya said from the tent opening. "I could give you access to the town."

The tent fell silent as all eyes fell on Nirmaya.

"What makes you think that?" Valia asked.

Nirmaya hesitated for a long moment, her mouth suddenly dry. "Because Ramash Suun is my father. I am Nirmaya Suun."

"What?" Valia said, incredulous.

"Although I have not seen him for many years."

"And you only tell us this now?" Valia said in exasperation. "Why would we trust you?"

"She could inform Suun of our plans!" Acastes warned.

"I do not owe him my loyalty," Nirmaya replied.

Valia glared at her. "Well?" she urged.

"I was fourteen when it happened, not long after the battle at Ara Dasari." She spoke quickly at first, to get the words out before they could be bottled up again. "I was on the road to the north of Babusar in Pashwar, travelling from a successful day at market. My father was a sheep farmer, you see, and we had struggled during the occupation. Since the Koratheans had withdrawn, things were getting better and for the first time that I can remember, my father was smiling. My mother was there too, and my two younger brothers were asleep in the cart. They were twins; identical, so many people could not tell one from the other at times. I could, of course, little Danesh had a tiny blemish just here." She pointed to the corner of her left eye. Her hand was shaking when it returned to her side as the memories came flooding back.

"The Shar attacked without warning. Little Danesh never even woke; he never had the chance. Rimu did. I still remember the way he screamed. I remember how my mother fought; and I remember how my father did nothing." Her voice became distant. "I told myself that he was frozen through terror, and perhaps that was true. I believed that the horror of watching his wife and sons die is what kept him rooted to the spot on the cart. But something changed in him that day. He could not accept that such horror should be visited upon him in vain. He wanted to believe that there was a reason behind it. That belief was the root of this *cult* he leads. I can only imagine his followers suffer a similar delusion. I left soon after and took up the sword. I have not seen him since."

The tent fell silent. Kapaneus placed a hand on her shoulder and bowed his head. There was a moment of shared sorrow for a childhood lost.

"How can I be certain that you will not betray us to him," Valia asked.

She shot at acid glare at Valia in return. "I hate the Shar, more than you can imagine," she replied. "And I hate what he has become. I will do this, because if there is any redemption to be had for him, he needs to have his world shaken again."

Valia held her gaze for a long moment. "Are you certain that you can do this?"

Nirmaya set her jaw and nodded without hesitation.

"Very well," she said. "We will begin preparing for the attack."

The command tent emptied as Starling approached. Nirmaya walked past him and nodded with a tight-lipped smile.

She had told them.

He spotted Adeyemi and Kapaneus and held up the two bowls he was carrying. "You must be hungry."

"Did you know?" Kapaneus asked, nodding towards Nirmaya's retreating form.

Starling shrugged. "I did."

"You did not think to tell us?" Adeyemi said in accusation.

Again, Starling shrugged, and shook his head. "Why would I? She is not her father." He held up the bowls again, "Granger has been working all afternoon on this. I don't know what it is, but…" He left the sentence incomplete and smacked his lips and rolled his eyes to show his approval.

The bowls were accepted with mumbled thanks, and the two men walked off to enjoy their hot meals. Starling watched Adeyemi walk away.

"Sleep well," he muttered, then went to his bedroll to wait for darkness.

The strong aroma of Sulphur fills the workshop despite the open window.

"The depth of patina depends on how long you leave the paste to do its work, Butterfly," her father says, placing the graver back in its holder. "You left it a little too long that time, but it is an easy task to cut back to clean metal. Just not too often." He smiles at her and winks.

"But how can you see how dark the silver has become if the paste is covering it, papa?" she asks.

The silver tray on the workbench has an intricate butterfly etched into the surface; dark lines bring out the detail against the shine of the uncut silver.

"That is the art," he says, applying the pale paste with a cloth and wiping away the excess, "to see below the surface; to know how the metal is changing even though much of it is hidden from you. And then," he plunges the tray into a basin of water and rubs the engraving with a soft brush. After a few moments he removes the tray and dries it with a towel, holding it up to catch the light, "knowing when to stop."

The butterfly looks alive on the mirrored surface and from behind it her own face looks back at her through wings of silver.

"Get up child! You cannot sleep all day!"

"Sorry, mama," Alisha muttered, squinting against the bright light that streamed through her window as soon as the shutters were thrown wide.

"You need to dress smart, your auntie is coming today," her mother insisted, fussing at the open wardrobe.

"Why would I need to dress smart for Auntie?" Alisha asked, sitting up.

"Don't argue, child!" she snapped back. "And don't embarrass me. Captain Yuddha is coming to the house for tea."

Alisha wrinkled her nose in distaste.

"Show some respect!" her mother snapped. "And don't embarrass me!"

She threw a dress onto the bed and hurried from the room, pushing past Tau as she went.

"Good morning, brother," Alisha muttered.

Tau stared back at her.

"You have some porridge on your chin," she pointed to the same point on her own face and then back to him. "Porridge."

At last he dragged his sleeve across his mouth and stood for inspection.

"That got it," she smiled, and then lay back again with her hands behind her head. "I cannot wait for this wedding to be over. The sooner she marries Yuddha the better for us all. How jealous her friends will be, married to a Captain. *Yuck!*"

Tau was still staring when she got out of bed and walked to the bedroom door.

"A little privacy, brother," she smiled, and pushed the door shut.

At last she walked into the kitchen to find her aunt already at the table drinking tea. The woman had a way of always looking down on Alisha even when seated.

"Good morning, Auntie," Alisha said with as much warmth as she could muster.

"Alisha," the woman sniffed in response.

Her aunt had never married, which was of no surprise to Alisha since even a veil could not obscure the permanent scowl on the woman's face. Dyansh said that milk curdled if she so much as glanced at it, and that even the Shadows were afraid to look at her.

"Alisha, get more wood," her mother demanded. "But do not sully your dress."

"Yes mama," she said, making for the side door that lead to a little, covered courtyard. She filled a small crate with split logs and turned back towards the kitchen, hesitating by the door.

"In the summer, I would hope," her mother's voice floated out to her.

"Have you told her about the wedding yet?" her aunt asked.

"Not yet. She is yet to take the veil; she would not understand."

This was ridiculous!

Alisha strode in and dumped the logs beside the fire.

"I am not a foolish child," she declared, placing her hands on her hips and glaring from one woman to the other. "You can tell me, you know. I know that you are marrying Yuddha so there is no need for the big secret."

The women stared at her in shocked silence for a long moment before a spiteful grin settled on her aunt's face.

Her mother started shaking her head.

"You stupid girl. Captain Yuddha does not want to marry *me*," she said at last with an edge of bitterness in her voice. "It is *you* he wishes to marry. In the summer as soon as you have taken the veil." She looked her daughter up and down. "Although I cannot understand why."

Alisha stood frozen in horror.

"What?" she managed to say before her legs took over and had her running from the kitchen. She barely noticed the startled captain as she rushed past him on the path, her eyes were misty with tears and her mind awash with confusion. She ran as fast as she could, not sure where she was going but desperate to put as much distance between her and the house, and with it drive a wedge between herself and her newly discovered fate.

She found herself at Dyansh's barn and burst through the door.

"Alisha?" he said in surprise, looking up from the large plough he was working on. "What is it?"

"I can't do it, I can't do it," she sobbed, running into his awkward embrace.

"Do what?"

"They want me to marry Yuddha," she cried.

"What?"

"I thought he wanted to marry my mother, but he wants to marry me, and she has said yes."

"But you can't marry yet," he insisted. "You have not taken the veil."

"In the summer," she said, shaking her head. "I will marry him in the summer. They have planned everything.

"So soon?" he said.

She nodded in response and squeezed her eyes shut, regaining control of her breathing.

"We must leave," she blurted. "We have to go."

"What?" Dyansh replied, still reeling from the news.

"Just like you said," Alisha urged, standing back but keeping his hands in hers. "We can take the boat, to the south or even across the Ashkelit to Dashiya. Will you still do it?"

"I thought you didn't want to," he said.

"Will you do it?" she demanded.

He nodded at once.

"We have time though," he said. "There is the rest of spring to make plans and prepare. We will need food for sixty days at least, and water. Alisha, it will not be easy, but we can do this together."

"Yes," she agreed, wiping the tears from her cheeks. "We have to do it. We have to leave, you were right."

She squeezed him in an embrace again, feeling his hesitant arms close around her, and the knot of fear in her belly softened to be replaced by a calm resolution to be free.

Starling woke before dawn. Sleep had become elusive since they had freed Valia and a man had died by his hand. A queasy knot had settled in his core the moment he had stared into the doomed soldier's eyes, and it had not shifted since.

He had been alerted by movement in the camp but was relieved to see that it was only Kekoa making his way to the edge of the wooded area to greet the sun, a ritual he performed every morning.

His heart was beating fast already. The guilty weight of the Element in his breast pocket gave him a tinge of regret rather than the triumph he should have felt. Stealing it had taken all his stealth and guile, even after Adeyemi had devoured the food laced with the spur-root. He remembered how his hands had trembled as he reached for the pouch, fear and curiosity vying for dominance in that moment of glorious thievery.

Apart from the Element, all that the pouch had held were a

few dozen golden brown seeds, each not much bigger than a pin head. The seeds, he had left, while the Element had been spirited into his breast pocket where it now rested, burning at his conscience.

His final act in the brilliant crime had been to place a few fragments of shell from the nuts Acastes enjoyed so much on Adeyemi's blankets, placing the blame at Acastes' door and not his own.

Olgoi would be pleased, and hopefully pay up in full.

Adeyemi would be furious, but would no doubt get over it.

No, that too was a lie.

He lay in the darkness and tried to savour his victory, irritated by the stabbing itch at the back of his mind that could only be named guilt. He pulled his blanket up to his chin and closed his eyes. He must have fallen asleep because he was suddenly awoken by a furious roar that echoed through the woods.

He sat upright, chasing the sleep from his mind and threw the blankets aside.

Adeyemi!

He pulled on his boots and ran through the camp in the gathering light.

"Where is it?" the big man roared as Dachen and Pemba attempted to calm him.

"It has been stolen!" he shouted, searching through his blankets until his eyes fell upon something in the gloom. He lifted something small between thumb and forefinger. "Acastes!" he spat before pulling his impanga from the sheath beside the bed and striding towards where Acastes was stirring under his own blankets.

"Get up!" Adeyemi yelled. "Get up! Return what you have stolen!"

Starling's hand went to his breast pocket before he could snatch it back down.

Acastes rolled over and placed a hand on the sword beside

him. Adeyemi kicked it away and struck Acastes on the side of the head with the flat of his impanga.

"Where is it!" he bellowed again.

Kapaneus was on his feet with his sword in hand. "Adeyemi!" he shouted. "Stop this madness!"

Acastes was dazed and struggling to stand when Adeyemi pressed the impanga to his throat. Kapaneus lunged with his sword but Adeyemi deflected the point of the blade before it reached his chest and kicked Kapaneus in the midriff. The smaller man landed flat on his back, knocking the breath from his lungs.

The momentary distraction was all Acastes needed to roll and reach his weapon. He came up in a crouch with the huge, curved blade before him. "Put your weapon down or I will kill you," he threatened through clenched teeth.

Adeyemi attacked, moving with such speed that Acastes was forced back as the crude impanga rang against his Korathean steel. Kapaneus had recovered and swung at Adeyemi with his sword. Adeyemi snarled as he stepped inside the stroke before it was completed and punched Kapaneus twice with his free hand. The blows were so quick that Kapaneus was already falling from the first when the second landed. Then Adeyemi stepped close to Acastes even as the Korathean tried to turn his defensive stance into an attacking one. He kicked the sword from Acastes' grasp, and punched him in the face.

Acastes stumbled, trying to grapple with the furious man, certain that in a test of pure strength he would win. Adeyemi twisted and rolled Acastes over his shoulder as he would a sack, smashing the larger man to the ground. Before he could recover, Adeyemi had him in a choke hold that had the larger man gasping and losing strength with every heartbeat.

"Where is it?" Adeyemi hissed into his ear.

"Stop!" a voice called out from somewhere nearby.

"You stole it!" Adeyemi growled.

"Adeyemi! No!" It was Dachen.

Kapaneus was coming back to his senses and fumbling with his sword. "I'll kill him," he cursed, drooling blood as he stood.

"Kapaneus, stop!" It was Granger this time appealing for calm. Kapaneus paused.

"He *will* kill you," Granger warned. "You cannot win this."

Kapaneus looked in desperation at Acastes as Adeyemi choked the life from him and snarled. He threw himself at the dark-skinned man. Adeyemi saw the attack coming and dropped Acastes' limp body to meet it.

"Stop!" Granger shouted again, but Adeyemi had already leapt. Kapaneus was too slow; he felt his sword being knocked from his fingers and saw the lightning speed with which Adeyemi spun and brought the impanga scything towards his head. The last thing he saw before closing his eyes was an arrow. He heard it hiss past his ear towards Adeyemi, but even if it struck, it would not alter the path of the impanga now.

Strange how a man's thoughts quicken in the moments before death.

But death did not come. Kapaneus opened his eyes to see the impanga, stopped a hair's breadth from his left ear, still held in Adeyemi's fist. The dark-skinned man was staring at the taut bundles of bone and sinew that was his own forearm.

"Elan!" Granger shouted. "Everyone, stop!"

The arrow had grazed Adeyemi's arm and left a deep gash across his scar-patterned skin.

Kapaneus sagged and looked beyond Adeyemi to where Acastes was struggling onto one elbow.

"What are you doing?" Acastes rasped through a throat raw and painful.

"I need it back," Adeyemi breathed.

"What?"

"The Element."

Acastes looked confused. "What? I don't have it."

"You took it," Adeyemi said. "I know that it was you."

Acastes tried to laugh, but it turned to a cough instead. "You are mad," he managed at last.

Starling saw Olgoi appear on the other side of the clearing. The eager expression he wore quickly faded when Acastes got to his feet.

Jon stumbled into the clearing, still pulling on his trousers. "What have I missed?" he asked.

Adeyemi lowered his impanga at last and turned to Acastes. "You have killed me," he said, and walked away into the forest.

Elan retrieved his arrow from where it had struck a tree some way off. He wiped the point on a small cloth and inspected the fletching while he walked towards Starling. He stopped a few paces short and looked up, seeing Starling as though for the very first time, studying his face. Starling swallowed hard.

"Good morning, Elan," he said, but the Lythurian just walked away.

"Reminds me of my bloody wedding over here," Jon said. "Only, there are fewer edged weapons." When he got no response, he scratched his groin and sniffed loudly. "Mind you, I wish I'd slept through that as well," he murmured, then walked away into the trees.

Nirmaya turned at the sound of rapid hoofbeats behind her. It was Starling.

"What are you doing here?" she demanded.

"Support," he replied, slowing his horse to match speed with her own. "Of one sort or another."

"You cannot follow me into Dargenmill," she said.

"Why not? Two travellers are just as likely as one."

Nirmaya chewed on her bottom lip. "I need to talk to my father."

"It would be my pleasure to meet him too," Starling said with a smile. "It's about time I met him, don't you think? Us being what we are."

"What?" she said in exasperation. "We're nothing. There is nothing between us. You…Oh, you're unbearable."

Starling laughed. "I'm sorry." Then he grew more serious. "You may need help, that's all."

"I do not need help to confront my father," she retorted. "The gates? That is a different matter."

"Have you any idea what you have volunteered for? It will be dangerous; you could be killed. *We* could be killed. You're right, I've changed my mind."

He feigned hauling on his horse's reins for a moment and then gave up. "He won't stop. I did try, I suppose I will have to come with you now. Besides, the mood back there has turned sour." He felt through his tunic to the Element beneath the cloth. He could not return it to Adeyemi; not now, not after seeing what the man had almost done to Acastes and Kapaneus.

Acastes *and* Kapaneus!

Giving it to Acastes was also not an option, after his brush with death at the hands of Adeyemi.

He considered giving it to Marlon, but *he* would probably tell Acastes anyway, and Valia, well Valia would most likely simply gut him for sport.

"Oh yes," Starling said, sitting high in his saddle and looking around at the countryside. "I need a break from *them*."

They rode in silence for a long time

"What did Maidra say?" Starling asked.

Nirmaya did not answer, and Starling did not press her. The fiery-haired Sister would doubtless have been furious.

"She understood," Nirmaya said at last. "What did Camille say?"

"What do you mean?" he asked as she smiled at his startled expression.

"I am not blind, you know. I have seen you sneak to her tent in the dark. She is pretty. You make a nice couple."

"Don't," he muttered. "It was just a bit of fun. Fate, I think she's besotted."

"And who can blame her? You really should seek your father's blessing and marry."

"I doubt my father would be happy to see me again. I stole his governor's seal after all…"

"He has forgiven his only son many times before if I recall correctly," she teased.

"Only son?" he replied. "He'll have others. Trust me; Kernhalt will be bursting with his little bastards."

Nirmaya pressed her lips together, sensing a change in his mood.

"You said your mother died when you were young."

"She did not simply *die*," he murmured. "She was taken from me."

Nirmaya waited for him to elaborate, but he steered the conversation elsewhere.

"How will you open the gates?"

"I don't know," she replied. "I will think of something."

"They will be guarded, and even if you can distract them you will not be able to move the batten alone." He shook his head. "This is a terrible plan."

"Valia will approach the town after two nights. On the morning of the second day, the army will attack as soon as the gates are open, one hour before sunrise."

"And if you fail to open the gates 'one hour before sunrise'? What then?" Starling asked. "Valia assaults the town anyway? She has lost her mind if she does. An army ten times the size of what she can muster, ensconced behind a defensive paling. It would be suicide."

"Then I had better not fail," Nirmaya said, at last making eye contact with Starling.

"*We* had better not fail," he replied before puffing out his cheeks and exhaling.

Once they were on the main road, their progress was easy. On either side crops flourished in the warmth of spring, reaching up towards the sun in myriad shades of green. Farmers worked the land without a care for what had happened in the East and further north in Kylyptus. Distant wars could not take precedence over the need to feed their families. Sheep and cattle grazed where crops were absent, and trees rose in clusters in defiance of the tamed land around them.

Towards evening, the land began to fall in gentle waves towards the vastness of Lake Arat, the far shore of which was a distant haze on the horizon. Seated amid the stunted trees of Lake Arat's forested shore was the town of Dargenmill.

"It has indeed grown," Starling murmured. "And look, there's the temple."

Nirmaya could not have missed the enormous stone structure rising above the rooftops around it. Layer upon layer of granite terraces rose towards the incomplete upper levels with sweeping arches and stout pillars pushing the temple ever higher. Each level was linked by wide, curved stairways that flowed from one terrace to the next. An intricate scaffold engulfed the upper levels in a web of poles and ropes from where a persistent ring of steel on stone carried across the plain to the travellers.

Nirmaya heeled her horse without a word and continued towards the town.

The ground grew muddier as they descended the gentle slope; the lowlands always being the last to dry after the spring thaw.

They were greeted by two guards, dressed in non-matching but well-maintained leather armour, while another two lounged within the open gates.

"What is your business in Dargenmill?" the first guard asked in a friendly tone, placing a gentle hand on the nose of Starling's horse.

"We are travelling from Kor'Habat to Pashwar," Starling lied, dropping down from his saddle. "Where we are to be wed."

This drew a sharp glance from Nirmaya.

"You should do so here in Dargenmill," said the second. "Why wait? And soon this will be the greatest city ever built. You will boast to your grandchildren that you were among the first to enjoy its burgeoning glory."

"Thank you, sir, I will think on it. Can you perhaps recommend an inn in your fine town? Or should I say, city?"

The guard laughed and shrugged. "For now, suit yourself, but I can recommend *The Gilded Throne* if you enjoy fine wine. My cousin will make you feel at home."

"Wine, fine or otherwise, would be most welcome. Where will I find *The Gilded Throne*?"

The guard pointed along freshly laid cobbles. "Follow this road until you pass the temple, then turn left and you will see it there. Tell Sammick that I sent you."

"Your name, sir?" Starling held out a hand in greeting.

"Just Mal, to my friends," the guard replied, taking the offered hand.

"Thank you, Mal. I will make sure that there is a jug of wine in the common room with your name upon it when you next visit your cousin."

Mal stood back as Starling mounted his horse. "You are very generous," he replied and saluted with a fist to his left breast.

Starling smiled and nodded and urged his horse through the gate and onto the cobbles. "Well aren't they a friendly bunch," he murmured after exchanging brief greetings with the other guards.

"They have an idiot's glee, that is for sure," Nirmaya replied.

They followed the road as instructed, and Starling exchanged pleasantries with several people along the way. A few clusters of Eastern soldiers could be seen here and there and other soldiers in assorted armour formed small groups on corners or outside buildings. They passed through the newly built section of the town to the older, more worn buildings. The cobbles assumed the gentle furrows of a well-worn thoroughfare with puddles in places and a few muddy potholes. The buildings were the same mixture of stone and timber, never more than two levels in height, with neat thatching that was dark grey on the older buildings.

The temple loomed ever closer on the right side of the road, but Starling's eye was caught by something else in a large court-yard that had the look of a market square about it.

Row upon row of dozens of huge, wheeled timber structures that could only be the war engines that Kapaneus had spoken of. Their design was as varied as it was obscure, and Starling strug-gled to imagine the functions of each different type. Coils of rope lay everywhere in sizes that ranged from the thickness of a man's thumb up to a stout arm. Intricate lashings held beams in place against others or formed woven nets large enough to hold a horse. Within the square, men who looked to be of Eastern origin worked among the contraptions, directing others to hoist or hold enormous timbers.

Starling puffed out his cheeks. "I once spoke to an Infantry-man who had fought at Hadaiti against these things. He lost both legs that day, and every friend he had." He flinched at the thought. "These cannot leave here."

They rode in silence until they were level with the temple. It was even more impressive up close.

They turned left onto a similarly cobbled road and sure enough, *The Gilded Throne* came into view. A large board bearing the painted image of a grand, yellow throne upon which sat a grey rat, declared that they had reached their destination. A boy rushed to take their horses as they dismounted near the door.

"Take care of them," Starling said as he tossed a copper mark into the air.

"Yes, my lord," the boy replied, snatching the coin from the air with a grubby hand and hurrying away down an alley at the side of the inn.

They entered a bustling common room, filled with evening drinkers and labourers enjoying mugs of ale after a day's work.

"Take that bench in the corner," Starling suggested. "I'll get some wine and something to eat."

Nirmaya hesitated.

"I'll ask about your father, if you like," he added.

Nirmaya nodded.

"Go and sit," he urged. I can deal with this."

At last she made her way to the bench he had suggested, and Starling ambled towards the bar counter.

"You must be Sammick," Starling said to the bearded innkeeper, who smiled at hearing his name. "Your cousin, Mal assured me that yours was the finest inn in Dargenmill."

The innkeeper's smile slipped a little. "Second cousin, once removed," Sammick corrected. "But he is right about my inn." The smile returned to its full splendour.

"My friend and I are looking for a room, a meal, and a jug of wine, Sammick," Starling said, making a show of taking his coin pouch from his hip. He dropped it on the counter with a heavy thud. Glancing back towards Nirmaya he added, "Separate beds."

His expression must have betrayed his thoughts since Sammick placed a jug on the counter with a wry smile and whipped the cloth cover from its top. "Never mind, eh, lad. A few cups of this and you just never know..."

Starling offered a doubtful expression in response which had Sammick shaking his head in sympathy.

"What's on the menu?"

"Fish stew, roast hare, or rack of lamb" He recited, although the extra emphasis he placed on the final dish left Starling in no doubt as to what was recommended, and almost certainly the most expensive.

"Lamb rack it is, sir," Starling replied to Sammick's obvious approval. "How much do I owe you?"

"I can start an account if you like," Sammick replied, eyeing the pouch of coins as Starling returned it to his hip. "Here on business, are you?"

"Always," Starling replied. "Of one sort or another."

He gathered the jug and two cups and turned to leave the counter. Turning back at the last moment he asked.

"Oh yes, where might I find Ramash Suun?"

Sammick shrugged. "The temple, most days. Or else in *The Happy Wastrel*; an inn nearby. Although I don't recommend *their* wine. Costs more than it's worth. Now, some folk are happy to pay it, but I would hate for you to leave town with a poor opinion of us."

"That would never do," Starling replied with a wink and a smile, then he went to join Nirmaya in the corner.

The fourth tier of the temple was all but complete and the final two were well under way. To the East, the sun had yet to break over the horizon where Lake Arat blended with the distant shores of Kylyptus. The lake, of course was part of a border soon to be erased. All would be united under the coming God.

Ramash Suun inspected the baffling array of ropes and pulleys used by the labourers to haul the blocks of stone from ground level to their final resting place in the temple's walls. Already it was the largest building in Dargenmill by some margin and the fourth level terrace offered a view of the entire town and surrounding area. He loved this time of day; before the masons and their apprentices arrived, before the sounds of hammers on stone filled the air and the shouts and calls of two hundred men vied to permeate the spaces between. Ramash Suun took these moments to savour the journey. The Khalim-Shar was coming, of that there was no doubt, and Suun's faith and patience that had been so tested in recent years, had held fast. The stone beneath his feet was solid testament to that.

"A shame that you will not complete it in time." Suun recognised the voice of Masahara and turned to face him. He lowered his head and murmured a greeting.

"Boats will arrive one day hence, carrying the Khalim-Shar and his army," Masahara continued. "All hands will be required to prepare for the next stage of his great plan. Your, *offering* to him will have to wait. That is why you have built this, is it not? In the hope that he indulges you in some way?"

"I do not seek to gain his favour," Suun replied, keeping his tone respectful, "only to show due reverence. The Order wishes only to offer itself as a supplicant to him. Every true Servant of the Arrival does this without thought of personal advantage."

Masahara stepped forward and brought his face to within a finger's width of Suun's. "*I* will rule at his side, *not you*. It was promised to *me*! What use does the Khalim-Shar have for piles of stone?" He stepped away and spread his arms wide to take in the rising temple. His calm demeanour returned, and he smiled. "Perhaps he will allow you to keep it, but you will never be near the true seat of power at his side."

Suun bowed his head again. "That was never my intention."

Masahara turned and strode away, descending the sweeping staircase to the lower levels. Suun sighed and walked from the open terrace through a wide doorway and into the room within, where stone cobble gave way to wooden boards beneath his shoes. One day soon this would be a dining hall for those Servants who would choose to dedicate their lives to the Khalim-Shar's service. Fireplaces set into each of the four corners of the room would make this place comfortable even in the harshest of winters and warmth would fill both body and spirit. He walked through to what would soon be a kitchen and closed his eyes, trying to imagine the sounds and smells that would fill the empty room.

"I was told that I would find you here."

Suun turned and squinted against the light from the doorway. The silhouette moved further into the room and his eyes were able to make out the details of a young woman. Her face was older than he remembered, but there was no mistaking who she was. His hand moved, unbidden, to cover his mouth, but not before a sharp gasp had escaped.

"Nirmaya?" he managed through trembling lips.

"Father." The reply was cool but, in that moment, he could hear nothing but his daughter's voice, see nothing but this woman who had been a child when they had parted.

"My child," he said, moving towards her on unsteady legs. "You have returned to me at last."

His steps became surer as he drew closer to her and at last, he was able to throw his arms around her with tears of joy rolling down his cheeks.

He felt her return the embrace and when they parted, he saw that her eyes were wet with tears too, even though she tried to fight them back.

Ramash smiled. "Nirmaya. You always were stronger than me, but sometimes you should let those tears go."

Nirmaya wiped her eyes before the tears could fall. "You have been busy," she said, looking around the grand room.

"*So* busy," he agreed. "But never happier now that you have come back to me."

"I have had a long time to think, father," she began.

He hushed her to silence. "It does not matter, child. Time heals all. You left a child but have returned a woman."

"*You* left *me*, father," she growled. "And time will not bring mother back, nor Danesh, nor Rimu. Have you forgotten them already?"

"I could never forget them," he replied in shock.

"Nor protect them!" she spat.

Ramash stared at her for a long time, trying to form words that the naivety of youth could grasp. "Nirmaya, your mother's passing opened my eyes. We are but frail, brittle beings with no permanence except in memory and deed. There are higher callings that can bind a life to a greater purpose and give it meaning. This temple will be the seat of the returning *God* who will reign supreme across the world, and we can all bask in his radiance."

"*God?*" she sneered. "The Shar are worse than vermin!"

He lashed out before he had a chance to think, striking her

cheek with his open palm. "Nirmaya!" he called out, already racked with regret. "Forgive me. Please."

She lifted her face to glare at him, still holding her stinging cheek. "I came here to try to bring you back from the edge of the abyss," she said through gritted teeth. "But I see that you have already fallen."

"Nirmaya, forgive your father," he cried.

"I don't know who you are," she replied and turned to leave.

He grabbed her arm and held onto her. "Stay, please," he begged. "Tomorrow the Khalim-Shar arrives here. You will see for yourself that I have been working for a cause that casts our own lives under its great shadow; renders all other things insignificant!"

Her eyes went wide. "The Khalim-Shar is coming here?"

"Stay, and see," he urged. "Be here for the new dawn. He comes with an army, thousands strong. The righteous will not be stopped."

"You are mad," she whispered, and tore her arm free. "My father is dead."

He watched as she left, and for a moment he almost followed her. He stopped himself and tried to concentrate his mind on the preparations that would need to be completed before the following morning. If one was to dedicate one's life to a single, world-changing event, then all other distractions must be put to the back of his mind. The sacrifices that he had made and would continue to make would help to shape the future of the world. Now was not the time for sentimentality.

Now was not the time for weakness.

Nirmaya found Starling eating breakfast in the common room of *The Gilded Throne*. She slid in next to him on the bench and leaned close.

"We must leave. Now," she whispered, casting her eyes about for eavesdroppers.

Starling's porridge spoon paused halfway to his mouth. "Why?" he asked.

"The Khalim-Shar is coming. Tomorrow," she hissed through clenched teeth.

"What?" he replied, returning the spoonful to the bowl. "How do you know that?"

"I spoke with my father, this morning."

Starling leaned back in his seat. "What about the gates?"

"Forget the gates!" she replied a little louder than she had intended and glanced up to be sure she had not been heard. She lowered her voice. "Forget the gates."

Starling sighed. "We must destroy those war engines. When Valia arrives at dawn tomorrow…"

"Are you insane?" We need to leave now or else have the Khalim-Shar's army at our heels all the way to Kor'Habat."

Starling waved away the protest. "We will be far from Dargenmill by the time any army arrives here; done before the sun rises fully."

"How? How do you plan to open the gates? This was a mistake."

"Listen," Starling said, leaning in close. "After you went to bed last night, leaving me alone in a strange town I might add, I took a walk around. I may have strayed into an inn or two to get a feel for the place."

Nirmaya rolled her eyes. "Yes. And?"

"I made the acquaintance of a merchant; a purveyor of lamp oil who let slip the whereabouts of a large quantity of his stock. I suspect that a few barrels of oil could create quite a diversion near to the gates. Enough to give us access to them perhaps."

"The oil is valuable; it will be guarded," she countered.

"I have enough spur-root to ensure that any guards have a good night's sleep."

"Why would you have spur-root?" she asked, voice laced with suspicion.

"Not important," he said quickly, dismissing her question. "What is important is that we can draw the guards away from the gates for long enough for us to open them."

Nirmaya chewed on her bottom lip in thought before looking up at him. "This is not you," she said, shaking her head. "Heroism is not your style. What aren't you telling me?"

"Firstly," he replied holding up a forefinger, "that hurts. And secondly…" he raised another finger beside the first and hesitated. "I don't know. I just know that this is important. I can't explain it. People are dying, Nirmaya; people *will* die. You're right, I'm no hero. I have always looked after myself first, second and third. I'll still be leaving the saving of the world to others, believe me, but…" He hesitated. "It feels like the right thing to do; isn't that enough?"

She placed a hand on his. "Tell me what your plan is."

He returned her gaze and nodded. "This is what we will do…"

CHAPTER 14

Senji Dayivar approached the Khalim-Shar and dropped to one knee.

"The soldiers are setting camp, Khalim-Shar," he said with head bowed. "The boats are ready. We can begin the crossing to Dargenmill tomorrow at first light."

"No," the Khalim-Shar replied with a voice that made his skin prickle, a high-pitched metallic grating. "I feel an urgency. The *Anaki* call to me."

"Khalim-Shar?" Senji dared as a shiver washed over his body.

"I will have them as I have had all others, then I will be complete." The Khalim-Shar stood facing the expanse of Lake Arat, holding the huge trident it favoured in one hand. Two strange protuberances had appeared of late where shoulder blades would be on a man, but Senji could not fathom their purpose.

The Khalim-Shar drove the butt of the trident into the ground and turned towards him. "We will leave now."

"Khalim-Shar, the men are not yet rested..."

In a heartbeat, the Khalim-Shar had its terrible face level with Senji's own. "I will have the *Anaki*!" it shrieked and Senji fell backwards onto the ground in terror. Had he gone too far?

A massive, clawed hand planted itself to either side of his head and the Khalim-Shar brought its dominant eyes to within a hand's breadth of his own. Senji dared not move; he dared not breathe as he awaited the Khalim-Shar's next move. The area between its eyes writhed and twisted until a black, glassy marble emerged from the tortured flesh above him.

"I will have them all!" the Khalim-Shar hissed and Senji stared in horror at the ever-shifting hide and the dark jewel within.

Senji watched the oval bead vanish back into the ooze before the Khalim-Shar stood tall again. "See it done," it said before snatching the trident from the ground and striding away.

It was a long time before Senji dared breathe again and when he did it came in frantic, chest-heaving gulps. What had he done? What path had he agreed to travel to protect his beloved Dohna? Would she forgive him if she knew?

He stood and dusted himself down before turning towards the growing encampment to break the news to his men.

They would see little rest tonight.

Starling strolled down the cobbled street that led from the gates into the heart of the town. The large square that held the war engines was close to the gates, which meant that, should he and Nirmaya open them as planned, Valia and her small army could reach their target in moments.

The sun was dipping below the horizon, throwing a final splash of coral hues skyward, while labourers were finishing their tasks and making their way to various inns and taverns to toast their efforts amongst friends.

He counted around fifty war engines of varying designs and at different stages of completion. Carpenters and smiths had spent the day under the supervision of Eastern engineers, cutting and shaping enormous pieces of timber and steel and linking them with a dazzling array of pins, hinges and hemp rope.

Each completed war engine had been wheeled into place in the square to form orderly rows. He watched as a small team of horses was tethered to one of the enormous crossbows to have it hauled into position. The wheels clattered over the cobbles until they came to rest in one of the shallow depressions that ran the length of the old market square. These shallow furrows were common and used to drain the square in wet weather. They worked well in place of chocks to keep the engines in place. The drains ran parallel to one another at a spacing of around six paces, and fed into a larger ditch which, Starling assumed, made its way to the lake eventually. Once the horses had been untethered, the ropes were coiled and placed against the wheels until they would be needed again.

Starling considered those furrows and a more detailed plan began to take root. Perhaps they could work to his advantage.

He was getting ahead of himself. There were many things to do before that.

His pace quickened, and he made his way towards the small tavern he had happened upon the previous night. It was hazy with pipe smoke and dust and smelled of hard labour. Indeed, most of those who were there looked fresh from the day's industry, with sawdust in the hair and knuckles streaked with ingrained grime.

Starling ordered a jug of wine from the tavern master and took it and a cup to a seat with its back to a nearby table. He poured himself a cup and waited.

"Young Starling!" The exclamation made Starling smile.

He turned to see who had spoken and feigned surprise. "Lucerna! My friend, forgive me. I did not see you there."

"I thought that I had insulted you last night," Lucerna joked.

Starling laughed. "Not at all, dear fellow. But I see that you have company."

Lucerna gestured towards his two companions. "Please allow me to introduce Infelicis and Victus. We have been discussing a new business proposition."

"A pleasure, gentlemen, but I should allow you to finish," Starling apologised.

"We are done," Infelicis insisted. "Our business is concluded and we are toasting a bright future."

Starling leapt to his feet. "Then I insist upon you doing so with my wine."

Starling topped up the cups on the table. The two men, Infelicis and Victus were young, even younger than Starling, and he wondered whether the shrewd trader, Lucerna had given them a favourable deal or used his experience against them.

Either way it did not matter. What mattered now was that Lucerna had remembered Starling as being a man who was *free* with his wine. And '*free*' he would be.

"Tell me, friends, is lamp oil your business?" Starling asked.

"It is now," Victus replied with a proud grin.

"Our father is a weaver, and his before him," Infelicis added.

"But our father would see us stand on our own feet rather than follow in his footsteps," said Victus.

"Dargenmill has grown, and with it the demand for lamp oil," Infelicis went on.

"And Lucerna has assured us that he can provide enough for our needs."

"And, the finest quality," Lucerna added.

Starling glanced from one to the other as they spoke. "Well that is wonderful news. A budding enterprise indeed. Remember this moment; this is where it all began, gentlemen." Starling raised his cup in a toast and watched as his companions drank deeply as he sipped.

"Allow me to fill your cups!"

So it went for an hour or more until all three traders were quite tipsy.

"Tell me," Starling said. "How does one secure such a valuable commodity from common theft?"

Lucerna waved a hand. "I have it under guard until tomorrow when the contracts are signed. Then it is up to these young gentlemen."

Starling laughed. "I remember a few years ago, I was moving a small shipment of silk cloth from Dashiya to Kor'Habat. A single cartload; a dozen bolts as I recall. Well, I recruited two guards from Hadaiti to escort myself and the consignment for the duration of the journey. More wine?"

Starling went on spinning his tale, filling cups before they could become empty and drawing the men into his confidence. It was too easy.

"In the morning," he said, reaching the end of his story, "I found them both, wrapped in purest silk, fast asleep on a bed of manure!"

The three men burst into laughter.

"Two bolts, ruined," Starling lamented to the delight of his companions. "But I learned of the power of Dashiyan wine, and that is a lesson best gained early in life, and no mistake."

"Dashiyan wine is the least of your worries," Lucerna declared. "My men developed a taste for *rakshi* whilst on a trip to Hadaiti some years back. The pair of them would drink until they could not stand and then sleep for a full day. Have you ever tried it?"

Infelicis and Victus shook their heads.

"I have smelled it," Starling replied, screwing up his face. "And I swear, it burned the hairs in my nose."

Lucerna laughed. "That is what I thought! And yet all three of my men took to it like puppies to milk!"

Starling shook himself. "Gentlemen, I have had too much wine," he slurred. "I wish you luck with your endeavours. I hope to see you soon."

He turned as they bade him farewell and stumbled from the room, leaning on the doorpost for support on his way out. His steps grew steadier as he distanced himself from the tavern until he was striding down the street with purpose.

He ducked into numerous inns and taverns until he found what he was looking for in a small, dimly lit establishment off a narrow alley.

"Do you have the head for it?" the innkeeper asked, looking

him up and down.

"I would surprise you," he replied with a wink.

The innkeeper looked doubtful but reached under the bar all the same and retrieved a large, stoppered bladder.

"Everything on the floor leaves with the sweepings in the morning," he warned as he handed over the drink in exchange for a few copper marks. "And *anyone*."

"I will not be drinking it here," Starling thanked the innkeeper and left.

In the dark of the alley, he unstopped the bladder and tipped the powdered spur-root into it. The strong smell of the rakshi reached his nose and he held it at arm's length as he replaced the cork. A quick shake to mix it well and he set off again in the direction of the warehouse district.

Timber structures, large and small, formed what was the warehouse district in Dargenmill. Starling could only see one building with a guard stationed at its door, one of the smaller structures with a closed set of double doors that filled one end.

"Are you Lucerna's man?" Starling asked, swaying a little as he approached.

"Who wants to know?" came the brusque reply.

"Well, I do," Starling chirped back. "I'm from the buyers. I mean the buyers sent me to... they are with Lucerna now."

"Make sense man," the guard grumbled. "What do you want."

"It's a celebration," he said, holding up the bladder of rakshi, happy to play the cheery imbecile. "To celebrate."

"Congratulations," the guard snarled. "Enjoy your party, but I'm working, so piss off!"

Starling laughed. "But you are invited. Not to the party, the inn, they are still at the inn," he slurred. "No, you are not...you need to stay here, but you can also... this is for you for."

Starling offered the bladder to the guard.

"From Lucerna?" the guard shook his head. "That doesn't sound like him."

"Oh, no," Starling replied. "It's from the buyers. Should I not have... are you not allowed... sorry."

"What is it?" the guard demanded. "Wine?"

"So sorry. My apologies. It is from the buyers, Infelicis and Victus. They perhaps did not ask. I will return the rakshi."

"Rakshi, you say?" the guard said, suddenly interested.

"Perhaps they did not ask," Starling repeated, turning to leave as he mumbled an apology.

"Now, now, there's no need for that. Bring it here. I would not like to sour the deal by offending the buyers. They meant well, and that should be appreciated."

The door opened, and another guard exited the shed.

"What's going on?" he demanded.

"Young lad here has brought a gift from Lucerna's buyers," said the first. "A shame to send him back with it."

"Lucerna don't tolerate us drinking wine on duty, Stultus. You know that," said the second.

"It's rakshi," Stultus murmured through his teeth.

The newcomer's eyes widened. "Rakshi?"

Stultus nodded. The other guard looked uncertain; he swallowed hard before speaking again.

"A little wouldn't hurt, I'm sure," he reasoned. "On account of it being from the buyer."

"Wouldn't want to sour the deal," Stultus urged.

"Yes. No. Sour the deal." A moment later the gift had been accepted and Starling was retreating up the road to find a quiet place to wait.

Nirmaya stayed in the common room of *The Gilded Throne* for a long time after Starling had left. He had been full of the thrill of the caper when he had set off, which she was not surprised at in the least. Mischief was his motivation for rising from his bed most days. She was perplexed by his indifference to the approaching Shar army however, and she worried that he either did not believe her, or worse, that she was wrong to have believed her father.

The common room filled with patrons as the sky darkened, and soon it was alive with chatter and the sounds and smells of food being served.

The cool night air was a welcome change as she found herself wandering towards the temple again. A few lamps cast an umber glow on the sweeping stairs while a few more gleamed from within the wide windows of the lower levels.

Perhaps there were artisans still at work this late.

She stared at it, wondering at her father's tenacity. If only he had been so dedicated to his family!

Then two men emerged from the second level and hurried down the wide stairs. Huge men.

Heavy Infantry.

She watched for a moment before stepping into a shadowy doorway. The man in front was talking in urgent, hushed tones as the second hurried to keep up with him. They drew closer as Nirmaya pressed her back against the door and squeezed her eyes shut, certain that she would be seen. Their heavy footsteps started to fade, and she opened her eyes.

Foolish! She had no need to hide; she was as free as anyone else to walk these streets by night.

Nirmaya exhaled and breathed again as her nerves settled.

She edged out from her shadowy hiding place and looked back up to the doorway on the second level from where the soldiers had emerged. Shadows moved against the walls within. She ventured closer to the stairs that led up the exterior of the first level and paused to listen.

"You waste time and manpower on this, Suun," someone was saying. "Others can grasp this and yet you cannot."

She was sure that it was an Eastern accent she heard.

"Symbols such as this can rally the masses." Her father. "I will not be deterred by anyone but the Khalim-Shar himself."

"He demands nations, not trinkets!"

"This will unite us; it is no mere token. A beginning; a centre."

A laugh.

"This is my life's work, Masahara. The culmination of everything I have achieved. Nothing I have done before this has any value to me."

Nirmaya tensed; her whole body going rigid. She did not wait to hear the response but turned away and strode back down the street.

"We'll see about that," she hissed under her breath.

They led their mounts through the trees in the darkness. There was no moon and all that lighted the way was what little starlight could penetrate the canopy of leaves and needles above.

Their gentle footfalls were wind in the leaves; a subtle hiss as they approached their target. Valia had brought with her every soldier with a horse. A hundred and fifty Eastern men, the Hunters, and most of Nirmaya's Sisters.

It was vital that the attack was fast, and over before the defences could properly muster.

Dachen drew alongside Valia. "You trust this girl to open the gates?" he murmured.

Valia did not reply.

"What will you do when she fails?"

"Those war engines must be destroyed," she said.

"You will attack a fortified town anyway?" He shook his head. "Not with my men. They are not yours to command. You will be left with a few dozen Hunters and a band of *women* who have no business on a battlefield."

"'No business'?" she asked. "I have seen men fail. Our fate should never have been in your hands alone. You think that the strength of your arm gives you the right to dominion; to keep your women behind veils with heads bowed? Yet you crumble when tested. Your homeland is lost, *Prince*, let these women fight for theirs."

Dachen made a dismissive snort and slowed his pace, allowing her to move ahead. He found Adeyemi in the gloom and made his way to him. As was his way, Adeyemi was the only one without a horse.

"You have been as sullen as she," he whispered. "Are the omens poor for the night?"

"Why do you make sport of me, friend Dachen?" Adeyemi replied.

"I am sorry, my friend," he apologised. "You are still lamenting the loss of the Element. You know it held no power?"

"You *know* this?" Adeyemi challenged.

Dachen shrugged. "I know that you are master of your own destiny; you have always been. Even before you found that thing, you were always so certain. Do not doubt yourself now."

Adeyemi chuckled but it lacked the glee that he normally radiated. "Oh, I will not die tonight, friend Dachen; I will not die tonight. But soon."

Dachen could not make out his friend's expression in the darkness, but he could sense the dejection in his voice. *Time*, the prince thought. *Time mends all ills.*

Starling waited in the shadows of an alley, watching the small warehouse as stars wheeled overhead. A militiaman had strolled by earlier but had been too engrossed in a tuneless whistle to notice the young man.

He heard footsteps approaching. Peering out from his hiding place, he was relieved to see that it was Nirmaya, and not Lucerna coming to check on his wares.

"Nirmaya," he breathed as she went by.

She flinched and ducked into the dark alley beside him. "Is it done?" she asked.

He nodded. "I hope so. It has been two hours at least, and not a sound."

They waited in silence for a few, tense moments before Starling exhaled. He pointed towards the shed where the lamp oil was stored. "Let's go."

They stepped out from the alley and walked towards the timber building, casting the occasional glance behind to see if they were being watched. Their tread became softer as they approached the door. Starling pressed an ear against the wood and listened. He glanced at Nirmaya and shook his head. The only sounds were drifting over from the inns and taverns far away from the warehouses.

He pulled the door open a little way and listened again before peering within.

He chuckled and opened the door wider.

Nirmaya followed him in and saw the forms of two sleeping guards in the lamplight. One was on his back on an empty handcart while the other was slumped against a crate in the corner of the building.

Dozens of small casks were stacked in a neat fashion against one wall. Each carried a proud little brand, burned into the cask head with Lucerna's name.

"Help me with these," Starling urged as he started loading the casks onto an empty handcart. "Twenty ought to do it."

Nirmaya lifted one and felt its weight. "There is something I have to do."

"What?" Starling hesitated. "Where?"

"The temple," she replied.

Starling continued loading the cart. "You won't burn it down with that. It's made of stone!"

"There is timber there that will burn," she replied. "I can damage the scaffolds too."

"The temple is not important," he hissed. "Those war engines are all that matter. Who cares if you do a little damage to the temple? It will be repaired."

Nirmaya did not answer.

"This is about your father isn't it?" Starling said, placing the final cask on the handcart. "This is just your way of getting back at him."

She covered the cask in a blanket and wrapped her arms around it to support the weight.

"Very well," Starling groaned. "Leave the war engines to me. But you had better be at the gate when you are meant to be. The horses are saddled and ready."

Nirmaya nodded and left Starling alone with the sleeping guards. Starling lifted the handcart and was pleased to find it well balanced. He wheeled the cargo out of the shed and offered the guards a final, sorrowful look before closing the door on them and trundling away with his loot.

Most of the taprooms were closed by the time Starling reached the edge of the market square where the war engines rested. A drunkard finished urinating in a doorway and managed an indecipherable stream of gibberish before staggering away down the road.

Starling surveyed the war engines. At the edge of the square was a row of crates and heaps of coiled ropes, piles of timber off-cuts and tools. There was enough clutter to disguise what he was doing. A militiaman was ambling along the far side of the square and Starling ducked low and waited until the soldier was gone. He unloaded a single cask of lamp oil and placed it in one of the shallow gutters that ran the length of the market down towards a larger drain. He turned it until the stopper was at the bottom and pulled the cork free. The clear oil glugged out into the gutter, and Starling watched as it oozed along towards the first engine. The wheels were positioned in the depression and the oil stopped at this first obstacle before seeping around it to continue to the next.

He smiled to himself and went along to the next gutter to do the same.

There were eight in all, and when the first of the casks was empty, he added another. Every piece of timber, every strand of rope that lay in the shallow channels was soon soaking up lamp oil. The final few casks he upended in the huge coils of rope and piles of timber.

He glanced at the stars and decided to retreat to the shadows for a little longer. It was still too early to open the gates.

Nirmaya hurried down alleyways and side-streets to reach the temple unseen. A woman carrying a bundle like this in the early hours of the morning might have raised suspicions and she could not trust herself to talk her way out of a confrontation. A series of stone steps linked the various tiers at what she considered to be the back of the temple. This was the side furthest from the main street and looked to be where the masons dressed the stone before hoisting it into place. Her arms were burning now with the effort of holding the cask.

Damn him and his temple!

The stone of the lower levels gave way more and more to ornate timber the higher she got, with the top two levels under construction being predominantly wood.

She put down the bundle with a relieved sigh and massaged her aching arms and shoulders. Then she unwrapped the blanket to reveal the cask. She glanced about in the darkness but saw no-one and so pulled the stopper free and poured the oil onto the blanket. She pressed the blanket against one of the supporting beams before splashing more oil onto as many wooden surfaces as she could. She soaked the ropes and hoists too until the cask was empty, then she lifted a lamp from a pile of tools and knelt to light it.

The spark from the flint striker was blinding in the dimness, and the lamp lit on her third attempt.

Nirmaya paused to steady herself, taking long, slow breaths. She searched her feelings, strangely curious to find if there was any doubt at all in her mind. She found none. This was the right thing to do and was the least that her father deserved.

She only had to wait until the time was right.

The view from the top was beautiful, even in the starlight. Lake Arat shone like a black mirror, throwing reflections of the constellations up at her.

She squinted into the distance. Lights danced on the lake.

Not reflections, surely.

She strained her eyes, trying to discern shapes on the horizon. Ships!

"What are you doing here?" the question rang out like a bell in the dark silence.

She spun, reaching for her sword. "Father?"

"Nirmaya?" he said, softer now. "What are you doing here?"

Her heart pounded, and her breath came short and fast. She glanced at the distant lights on the lake, and his eyes followed her own.

"He comes!" Suun breathed. "He comes with the dawn!"

He looked back at Nirmaya. "Do you know what this means?"

Nirmaya backed towards the steps she had used earlier and Suun advanced.

"The Khalim-Shar is coming! You will bear witness to his arrival," he declared.

"Be quiet!" Nirmaya hissed, fearful that her father's ravings would attract attention.

"The Servants of the Arrival will welcome him," Suun went on. "You will witness a new age dawning!"

"Be quiet!" Nirmaya repeated as Suun reached the oil-soaked timbers.

He smelled the air before running a finger down a sturdy timber joist. He held the finger to his nose. "What have you done?" he whispered. His look of concern was slowly replaced by one of calm disappointment. "Oh, child."

Without thinking, Nirmaya hurled the lamp at the boards under her father's feet. It shattered and spread fingers of flame across the floor. She did not linger but turned and ran down the steps, heedless of any obstacles that could trip her in the dark.

The oil from the lamp had splashed onto Suun's robe and in moments he was engulfed in flame. The ropes and timbers flashed alight as the flames spread, and Suun screamed in agony, desperate to pull the burning wool from his skin.

Nirmaya ran as fast as she could, tears streaming down her numb cheeks. She did not know in which direction she was going; she did not care, she only wanted to get away from her crime. Her father's screams followed her into the night and chased the little girl from her soul.

Starling smiled in what he hoped was friendly incomprehension.

The two Eastern soldiers who had found him had their sparth points lowered and were chattering away at each other in their own tongue. One of them tapped the toe of his boot into one of the oily gutters and narrowed his eyes.

"Ah, just a little spillage, I assure you," Starling tried, hands held up.

The soldier shouted something and jabbed his sparth at Starling's chest.

"Easy. Easy," Starling said, lowering his hands in defence.

A distant shout caught the soldiers' attention and Starling glanced towards the temple. Flames were taking hold on the upper levels and the fire waved in lazy arcs against the stars.

Too early! It was too early!

He nodded in the direction of the temple. "You really ought to see what that is about."

Then he turned and ran. For a moment he was sure that he would feel the point of a sparth at his back, but when he dared to glance back over his shoulder, the soldiers had abandoned the chase.

He ran down a side street with the aim of coming back around to the square and charged headlong into three soldiers coming the other way. He landed on the ground in a heap on top of one of the soldiers.

"Bloody fool!" the soldier yelled.

"The temple!" Starling blurted. "They're burning the temple!"

The soldiers exchanged quick glances before heading away at speed and leaving Starling to catch his breath.

He wasted no time when he reached the market square again. He hurried down the row of casks and struck a stream of sparks into each gutter as well as the piles of material he had emptied the last casks onto. The oil took a flame with alarming speed, and in moments, eight lines of flame had stretched across the square to set ablaze the rope and timber that had been absorbing the oil for the past hour.

"Too soon, too soon," he cursed under his breath as he ran towards *The Gilded Throne*.

Shouts were ringing out in the night by the time he reached the stables at the back of the inn. There was no sign of Nirmaya.

Starling cursed. He squeezed his eyes shut as his mind raced, then he grabbed at the reins of the waiting horses and hurried from the stable.

"Where are you, Nirmaya, where are you?" he murmured as he hurried down an alley that he hoped would take him near to the gates. Two soldiers ran past him in the other direction but paid him no heed as they hurried to the growing cacophony at the square.

This was all going horribly wrong. The whole town would be awake before Valia was anywhere near it. He reached the paling and peered around the corner, relieved to see the gates a few dozen yards away. He dropped the reins on the ground and ran towards the gate. The four soldiers there were all staring down the main street, faces awash in the flickering glow of the fire he had just set.

"Quickly!" he shouted. "We must save the war engines!"

The nearest one turned to face him. "And who are you?" he

sneered.

"I'm the High Princess of what does it bloody matter!" Starling yelled back, pointing down the cobbled street without taking his eyes off the soldier.

When he did look to where he was pointing for the first time, his mouth fell open. A full quarter of the war engines were ablaze, with still more beginning to take a flame. Beyond that the temple was burning like a torch against the night sky.

"They must be saved!" he repeated after shaking himself. "Fetch water!"

Three of the soldiers were already running down the street towards the fire and it took the fourth only a moment to abandon his post for the good of the war engines.

Starling watched their backs for a moment before turning to the gate where the batten was in place in its cradles. He put his shoulder under one end of it and pushed up with his legs and the huge timber beam shifted upwards. He strained against the weight of it until his legs were straight, but he was a pair of finger-widths short of clearing the cradle.

"Oi!" a shout came from down the main street. "Stop that! What are you doing?"

He dared a glance along the street and saw that bloody guard again. He had turned and was trotting back towards the gate, reaching for his sword.

Starling strained to lift it a little more, pushing up onto his toes to make the extra height.

"Stop!" the guard was running now.

Starling's eyes flashed between the batten and the approaching soldier.

One final heave and he had cleared the cradle. He twisted away from the gate to allow the batten to fall to the ground as he reached for his sword. The soldier was almost upon him.

Then, with a crash of hooves on timber, the gates were thrown open. A huge horse was still pawing at the air where the gates had been a moment ago, and a heartbeat later, the soldier died under the crushing hooves of Valia's mount.

The invading army poured through the open gates like a flood. Valia swung her sword as she ploughed along the street, cutting down the few soldiers that had been trapped in her path.

"No mercy!" Valia shouted. "Kill any who stand in your way!"

She reached the market square where the war engines were set in rows. Many were already ablaze at the furthest end of the cobbled space, but many more were untouched.

Two Eastern sparth bearers appeared from a side street and Valia only just managed to swat the point of the weapon away as she went by. It grazed her shoulder but did not penetrate her leather armour. Behind her, Marlon struck one with his sword and the other fell beneath his mount's hooves.

They reached the edge of the square where the fire was at its highest and Valia turned.

"We must hold the square!" she shouted as small skirmishes broke out where soldiers and militiamen had emerged to confront the attackers. "Where are those bloody archers?"

A moment later, with the road cleared, a second wave of riders charged in. These were Dachen's archers. Fifty of them hurried past the fighting men and formed a line that stretched from one end of the square to the other. They nocked and drew arrows, wrapped in cloth and dipped in oil as four other riders rode along the line with burning torches held up. They touched each arrow in turn, lighting the oil. The archers released their arrows as soon as they were lit, pulling more from loaded quivers even before the first had struck home. Back and forth, the torch bearers rode, lighting arrow after arrow, and volley after volley struck the wooden war engines in the square.

A group of fifteen soldiers, mostly Eastern men, had formed a defensive line, and had managed to establish a position at the corner of the square furthest from the gate. They pushed forwards down the road to allow a bucket line to establish itself. Sparths flashed in the firelight.

An Eastern man in robes, perhaps one of the engineers, was waving men into the square, urging them to douse the flames with the buckets they were carrying.

Valia saw them and snarled. She glanced behind her and saw Marlon close by and Acastes, Kapaneus and Abbil approaching.

"Marlon! We need to stop them!" She pointed with her sword to where the frantic engineer was directing the men with the buckets.

Without waiting to see if they were following, she urged her horse forward. With fires blazing to her right and a defensive wall of sparths and shields ahead of her, she held her sword high and charged.

Starling rode through Dargenmill towards the burning temple. He pulled Nirmaya's horse behind his own, glancing down dark streets and alleys between buildings of stone and timber. Soldiers ran past him in twos and threes as the town awoke to the fact that it was under attack.

"Nirmaya!" he shouted, having long abandoned any attempt at stealth.

Two soldiers in mis-matched armour ran past him, heading back towards the market square and the precious war engines. They did not even glance at him; the threat lay elsewhere.

"Nirmaya!" he shouted again

Glimpses of the temple through the buildings had figures silhouetted against the fire, running this way and that as they struggled to deal with the blaze.

"Starling!"

He spun in his saddle, relieved to see Nirmaya in the street.

"I've been looking everywhere for you," he blurted in relieved exasperation. "Get on your horse!"

"I'm sorry," she replied, climbing into the saddle and sagging against the horse's neck. Her face was streaked with tears. "It wasn't meant to happen that way."

"It doesn't matter. We need to leave. Now!"

He turned his mount and handed Nirmaya the reins of her own. "Now!"

At the last moment, before impaling her horse on the bristling sparths ahead, Valia veered to the right. Her horse jumped a flaming crate and landed at the edge of the square, safely away from the long blades of the Eastern soldiers.

The first man she met was carrying a bucket of water. He froze in wide-eyed terror and her sword sliced into his shoulder, shattering his collar bone and all but severing his arm. The bucket crashed to the ground as the man fell with a dull moan. She pushed on past the fallen man and found the robed engineer pressed against the wheel of one of his war engines. She turned her horse side-on and split his skull down to his chin. The explosion of blood was black in the firelight, and she snarled, eager to spill more. The fifteen men who had formed up in the street were holding Acastes, Kapaneus, Abbil and Marlon at bay with their tight formation of shields and sparths. She turned on them and drove into their exposed backs with a ferocity that shattered the formation in moments. Her friends were quick to fall upon the defenders as they struggled to turn their sparths at such close quarters, and the fight was over quickly as they fell beneath the hooves of the mounted attackers.

"We need to pull back!" Marlon shouted. "The whole town has awoken!"

Valia glared at the fires that surrounded her, her horse dancing and wild-eyed.

"Burn everything!" she shouted before lurching back towards the main street where dozens of soldiers were forming up.

Among the soldiers there were a small group of Heavy Infantry. They looked uncertain, barking questions at the militiamen and Eastern soldiers. Valia brought her horse to a stop, a dozen paces in front of the formation and glared at them with unrestrained hatred.

Then she levelled the point of her sword at them and bellowed with rage.

The archers called out that their arrows were spent. Only a few maddeners and a clutch of basic arrows remained in separate quivers to cover the retreat if need be.

"Time to go, I think," Dachen declared as Adeyemi wiped the blood from his impanga. The soldiers of Dargenmill who had come out to the defence of their town in ones and twos had fallen quickly. But now shouted orders could be heard and the soldiers were rallying to form a more cohesive defence.

Jon arrived at Dachen's side; his round shield had an arrow protruding from it. He appeared to notice it for the first time and chopped it off with the silver-skull pommelled sword he carried.

"Are we done?" he asked with a jaunty, gallows smile. "I'd love to stay a little longer, but I have an appointment with a large breakfast."

An arrow hissed between Jon and Dachen and vanished into an open window. There was a short, choked scream followed by the dull thud of a body hitting floorboards and the tell-tale sound of a crossbow releasing a bolt. They both flashed a glance in the direction the arrow had come from, and found Elan, standing at the edge of the square, scanning the buildings behind them.

"Sound the retreat?" Dachen said quickly, and Jon nodded. But before he could give the order, a terrible sound filled the night.

An inhuman shriek echoed through the town.

The ear-splitting sound brought a momentary pause to the fighting.

Valia saw the soldiers ahead of her turn. The Heavy

Infantrymen looked uncertain in the silence, glancing all around.

A cold wind whispered along the street, carrying dust and the smell of fear. A sound, like rushing water rose in the distance, growing louder with each passing heartbeat.

Valia stared down the street, past the Eastern soldiers and town militiamen; beyond the small cluster of Heavy Infantrymen to where the street was obscured by darkness and a pallid, rising mist.

Valia's mount pranced, nostrils flaring as its animal senses prickled.

The Heavy Infantrymen had their backs to her now and were edging backwards from the threat that even they could sense.

She saw it. A silhouette against the burning temple; unmistakeable by its size and form. It raised a trident above its head and shrieked.

Then, from the shadows came an outpouring of fluid darkness as hundreds of Shar filled the street in a heaving, loping mass.

Valia stared in disbelief as the Shar approached. The militiamen fell to their knees and the Eastern soldiers laid down their sparths, bowing their heads. The Heavy Infantrymen locked shields and gripped their huge, curved swords in bloodless fingers.

"Valia! Retreat!" Marlon shouted as he rode past her, breaking the trance.

She hesitated for only a heartbeat before pulling her mount's head towards the gate and heeling it into action. She joined the throng of retreating Hunters, Sisters, and Eastern archers in retreat. She saw Adeyemi sharing Dachen's horse up ahead, and Elan on the back of Jon's, all charging towards the gates to escape the horde of Shar.

Valia risked a glance over her shoulder to see the small group of Heavy Infantry tossed back like flotsam against a dark wave, their screams dying in moments. But when the flood reached the waiting militiamen and Eastern soldiers, it broke around them and flowed by, leaving them untouched.

"Maddeners!" Dachen shouted, and his archers twisted in

their saddles, even as their horses raced through the gates, to un-leash a salvo of Ago-Camdi-tipped arrows; the fire-silver that seared the flesh of the Shar.

The agonising shrieks of those struck by the arrows chased Valia through the gates and onto the road beyond.

"Ride!" Starling shouted. "Turn left at the end of the lane and the street to the gates is not far."

Nirmaya did not reply, but the terrible shriek had given her new urgency.

They hurried down the narrow lane until they reached a junction where they turned towards the main thoroughfare. Illu-minated at the end of that lane by the fires in the market square they saw the flashing shapes of riders leaving for the gates at speed. Several bodies lay at the end of the lane in their path; but Starling kept his eyes on Nirmaya's back.

She urged her horse to jump over the corpses and landed on the cobbles of the main street. She was swept away in the rush and vanished from his field of view.

He pushed his horse to follow, but something in the chaos ahead startled the animal and it pulled up short, sending Starling head-first out of his saddle. He landed on one shoulder and his head cracked onto the cobbles beside the dead soldiers.

The last thing he saw before he lost consciousness was his horse, being swept away in the rush towards the gates.

The sun rose on Dargenmill, illuminating the tendrils of smoke still rising from the temple and the market square. Samut Masahara splashed through ashen, grey puddles left after the ef-forts to save the war engines from complete destruction.

"How could this happen?" he demanded of the soldiers in the square.

No-one answered.

He searched the square until he found one of the Eastern

engineers, inspecting a damaged catapult. He strode across towards him, splashing the hem of his brown robe with sodden cinders.

"How many can be recovered?"

The engineer tilted his head and swept an arm across a section of the square. "These are beyond repair; the wood has lost all integrity."

Masahara spat.

"Many more will need material replaced," the engineer went on. "The rope burned fast. Lamp oil was used to soak the engines."

"Lamp oil? Lamp oil did this?" Masahara spread his arms to take in the destruction. "It would take barrels to do this."

"Or around twenty casks." The engineer picked up the scorched remains of a cask. The metal bands fell away as the blackened staves crumbled. The engineer held up a scorched cask head for Masahara to see. The branding was still visible.

Masahara took the piece of wood from the engineer and stared at it. Then he nodded to himself before throwing the cask head onto the ground, to stride away in the direction of the temple.

Ramash Suun screamed as the burned rags were cut from his body. He was writhing on the table when Masahara entered the second level of the damaged temple.

Masahara pressed his nose and mouth into the crook of his arm against the stench of burned flesh.

"Will he live?"

The physician who was trying to strip the remains of Suun's robe from the scorched flesh glanced up at Masahara with a weary expression. "He may yet survive."

Masahara swallowed hard and approached the spread-eagle man on the table. Four soldiers were attempting to hold him still as he thrashed against the physician's efforts. Suun's body was black and charred along his entire right side, with bloody, raw strips where his robes had needed to be pulled away. His groin was burned away leaving him emasculated. Masahara saw that the soldier holding the right wrist was struggling not to vomit as the blistered flesh tore beneath his grip.

Suun's face was a blackened mess with the right eye seared shut, while the other rolled in its socket with every terrible scream.

"You should let him die," Masahara managed to say against the rising urge to be sick.

That frantic eye found Masahara and stared at him as spittle drooled from between ruined lips. The physician did not answer but offered Masahara a brief look that left no doubt that this would not happen and began applying a thick unguent to the right shoulder. The eye turned away as Suun began howling in agony once more.

Starling came to, woken by the sounds of movement nearby. He was face-down and cold. The sun was up, and the smell of burned wood was heavy in the air.

He shifted a little to ensure that no bones were broken and was relieved to find that he had sustained no injuries beyond cuts and bruises. He opened one eye and found himself staring into the dead eyes of one of the soldiers his horse had failed to get past. He jerked back and winced as his shoulder protested at the sudden movement.

Voices nearby told him that the people of Dargenmill were searching the bodies.

"Those men should never have died," he heard a voice that he was sure he recognised. "We were meant to be gone before the Khalim-Shar arrived. That was the deal."

Starling crawled over one of the bodies to get a better view into the main street. His hand came to rest in a pool of blood as he peered past the carnage.

Silman!

He was standing with another Infantryman, arguing with an Eastern man dressed in brown robes. "Now I have to explain the loss of eleven Infantrymen."

"Then explain it however you wish, otherwise join them in death!" the robed man replied, unfazed by the huge men towering over him. "I did not expect the Khalim-Shar to arrive so early, but neither do I question the whims of a God!"

"Movement!" a voice cried out nearby, and Silman looked in Starling's direction. "A survivor!"

Starling clamped his bloody hand over his face as two soldiers trotted over in his direction.

"Are you injured, man?" one asked as they reached him.

Starling nodded, keeping his hand over his face, aware that Silman was watching.

"Can you walk?"

Starling nodded as strong arms lifted him to his feet.

"Get him to the infirmary," one said, leaving Starling with the other. The soldier helped Starling into the street on unsteady legs.

Silman was still watching him. Starling bowed his head and moaned.

"Easy, easy," the soldier said. "Take your time."

Starling was helped past Silman, the Infantryman and the robed Easterner. He could almost feel their eyes on him.

"Where are you taking that soldier?" the Infantryman demanded.

"To the infirmary," Starling's attendant replied.

"Very well," the big man said. "See that you do."

The soldier at Starling's side muttered to himself before continuing.

"Daelen," Starling heard Silman say. "Let them be."

Starling allowed himself to be led away and waited until they had turned down a side street.

"I need to rest," he said, sliding from the soldier's grasp to sit on a wooden step.

"You have lost blood, friend." The soldier had a look of deep concern on his face; a young man, no older than Starling himself.

"I will be fine," Starling replied. "I can get myself to the infirmary from here."

"Are you certain?" The soldier sounded unconvinced.

"I am. Thank you…"

"Armil," the young soldier said.

"I am St….Stellio," Starling said, offering his free hand.

"If you are sure, Stellio," taking the offered hand.

"I owe you a jug of wine for sure, Armil."

The man laughed and trotted away. "I will hold you to that," he shouted over his shoulder.

Starling waited until the soldier had rounded a corner before standing up. He winced and rolled his shoulder.

He needed a horse.

He wiped the blood from his face with his sleeve, surprised by how much had come away, and grateful that it was not his own. He turned to make his way to *The Gilded Throne* and walked straight into the steel breastplate of a Heavy Infantryman.

A huge hand clamped around his wrist, and another pinned his free arm to his side. The young Infantryman looked down at Starling.

What had Silman called him? Daelen?

"That is a great deal of blood for so little a wound," Daelen said. "In fact, I would go so far as to say that the blood is not your own."

Starling struggled, but he was held fast.

"I know you," Daelen brought his mouth close to Starling's face. "Do you not remember me?"

Starling shook his head.

"That day you came to our camp on the road to Ulan-Balsan. I was there, I remember you, thief."

"Ah, now, you have no proof…"

"Spy," Daelen said. "A spy could do a great deal of damage to a campaign."

"I am *not* a spy," Starling insisted.

"You were injured in battle," Daelen inspected the blood-smeared cheek. "A shame if you are discovered."

He spun Starling and clamped his arms to his side. A knife appeared at Starling's cheek, and before he could protest, Daelen sliced the flesh.

Starling gasped, as Daelen released him.

"The cut is clean and shallow," the big man said. "It will heal and remember; the ladies love a scar."

"What?" Starling managed as he felt the cut with gentle fingers.

"We all do what we must, little man," Daelen muttered. "I hope that Fate favours you in this."

Starling watched the Infantryman vanish down an alleyway, too shocked at what had happened to think. He slumped back down onto the wooden step and took a series of long, deep breaths, his cheek hot with fresh blood.

He remembered the Element in his pocket and his hand darted to his breast. He relaxed when he felt it through the cloth of his coat and leant back against the door above the step. It shifted behind him and he sat forward again.

He stood, feeling wearier than he had for as long as he could remember.

"Hello?" he called out, pushing the door open a little further.

There was no reply.

"Hello?" A little louder this time. "Is there someone home? I am not a thief." He rolled his eyes at that.

His hand went back to his pocket, and he retrieved the Element. He had it wrapped in a square of cloth. He dragged a chair over from the table at the centre of the room and took it into the little kitchen. He placed the chair beside a tall cupboard and stepped up onto it. The cupboard top had a thick layer of dust.

Good.

He placed the little wrap of cloth on top of the cupboard and returned the chair to the adjacent room. Then he left the dwelling and closed the door behind him, glancing about to ensure he had not been seen.

The weary procession of riders reached the encampment late in the afternoon. They had not been pursued beyond the paling and gates of Dargenmill, but the back of Valia's neck prickled still. Granger was waiting at the edge of the encampment to greet them. Several Eastern soldiers were rushing forward to help the wounded and to take the exhausted horses to be fed and watered.

She dismounted and dropped her horse's reins, striding past Granger without a word. Marlon arrived moments later and lifted the reins, handing them to one of the Eastern men with a nod of gratitude.

"What happened?" Granger asked. "Was Nirmaya successful?"

"The gates were opened," Marlon nodded.

"Casualties?" Granger asked glancing at the dismounting soldiers as they arrived.

Marlon sighed. "We lost a few. Injuries were light."

"Were the war engines destroyed?"

"Some, perhaps." Marlon scratched beneath his eye-patch before looking back at Granger. "The Khalim-Shar is here."

Granger was silent. He held Marlon's gaze for a long time and started to nod.

At last, he spoke. "How big is its army?"

Marlon shook his head. "I could not tell you. We ran as soon as we saw the Shar coming. Hundreds; thousands. I did not wait to count them."

"Of course," Granger said, placing a hand on Marlon's shoulder. "You must be tired. Come, there is warm food by the fire."

"Thank Fate!" Jon declared, overhearing the end of the conversation as he stomped through the trees. "My stomach thinks my head's been cut off!"

Marlon watched the fletcher trudge towards the cooking fire

as Acastes and Kapaneus arrived at his side.

"We must not tarry for long," Marlon warned. "We should leave for Kor'Habat without delay."

"At last!" Kapaneus clapped his hands together and looked to his friend.

Acastes glared back with a sour expression before spitting on the forest floor and walking off towards his tent.

Dargenmill was being turned upside down. Every house; every barn; every stable was being searched.

Starling remained out of sight, terrified that they were searching for him. Earlier he had seen Captain Silman and the Infantryman Daelen, leaving town on horseback. He was still shaken from his encounter with the Korathean soldier and touched the crusted blood on his cheek, wondering how it was that he was still alive.

He was pressed into a doorway in a narrow alley near *The Gilded Throne* when he heard a voice call out.

"Stellio! Stellio! What are you doing?" It took him a moment to remember that 'Stellio' was the name he had used earlier. He peered out from the doorway. It was Armil.

"What are you doing there?" Armil asked as he approached.

Starling puffed out his cheeks. "Just resting. What's going on? Who are they looking for?"

"Not who; what," Armil replied.

"Oh," Starling felt a wave of relief flow through him.

"You must be the only one not searching for it," Armil said.

"For what?" he asked.

"The jewel; a black jewel. The Khalim-Shar says that it is somewhere in this town."

"What?" Starling's hand went to his coat pocket before he could stop it.

Armil saw the involuntary movement and his eyes narrowed. "Stellio, what…?"

Starling pulled a handkerchief from the pocket and touched his wounded cheek with it, checking for blood.

Armil relaxed, and chuckled. "I thought *you* had it for a moment."

He laughed again, and Starling joined him until the smile pulled at the cut on his cheek. He winced and pressed the handkerchief to it. A fresh spot of blood had oozed from the scab.

"I am sorry," Armil apologised. "No more jokes until you are healed."

"Yes," Starling agreed with a pained sigh. "No more jokes."

They were silent for a moment before Armil spoke again. "So," he said with the tone of someone not sure of the response he was going to get. "Do you like wine?"

Starling looked back at him and lifted one eyebrow. "Is a fish keen on water?" He smiled and at once regretted it.

Armil stifled his laughter and took on a grave look. "No more jokes. This is serious business."

He led Starling through the streets of Dargenmill towards the temple. Many soldiers saw them and paid them no heed, and Starling began to relax. They reached a stone building across the street from the foot of the temple and Armil retrieved a key from under his leather breastplate and unlocked the door. They entered and Armil shut the door behind them, locking it again.

"Upstairs," the young man said, and led the way.

The stairs creaked as they ascended them and soon, they were in a large room on the upper level of the building. A table surrounded by four padded chairs adorned the middle of the room while the walls were lined with shelves, each holding jugs and casks in a variety of sizes. One wall was stacked with little wooden casks laid in neat rows and covered in dust. The room was heavy with the aroma of wine and Starling breathed it in and sighed.

Armil opened a shutter and allowed the light to stream in. Starling could see the temple and the damaged upper levels as well as the team of workers already attempting to affect repairs.

"I look after these for a precious stone merchant when he is away on business," Armil said, choosing a clay jug from a high shelf and taking it down. "This is his personal collection."

He took two cups from another shelf and blew into them to clear the dust.

"Doesn't he mind you drinking from it?" Starling asked, reaching out to touch one of the casks.

"Don't touch that!" Armil exclaimed, and Starling pulled his hand back. "It's a *collector's* peculiarity. The dust should not be disturbed until the cask is tapped."

Starling watched Armil fill the two cups. "He will know that *that* has been touched."

Armil shrugged. "I top up the jugs with cheap wine, or water. He cannot *really* tell the difference. This is merely to impress his clients."

Starling took the offered cup and breathed in the heady vapours. He took a sip and could taste the quality. He hoped that the merchant was as coarse as Armil suggested or else he would be found out soon enough.

They sat in the cushioned chairs and leaned back to enjoy the wine.

"When did you arrive in Dargenmill, Stellio?" Armil asked after a long while as he filled the cups again.

"Only very recently," Starling replied.

"I had not seen you before," Armil said, nodding. "Tell me, is he what you expected?"

"Who?"

"The Khalim-Shar!" Armil said, full of enthusiasm. "He is not what I expected."

"How so?"

Armil shrugged. "I expected a God to look more like you or I. Taller perhaps; I don't know. But why should a God look like that?"

"A God can choose whatever form it likes," Starling replied, burying his face in his cup.

"What put you onto this path? Why did you choose to join the Servants of the Arrival?"

"I did not choose," Starling replied, wiping his lips, "I was chosen."

Armil's eyes widened with approval and he nodded, full of enthusiasm. "It was the same with me."

"Tell me," Starling said, feigning interest but happy to have diverted the conversation away from himself.

"I am from western Dasar," Armil began, "the only child of a farmer. I was fourteen years old when the Jendayans came and we were forced to abandon our land. I watched the battle at Ara Dasari from the refugee camp east of the Temple Canal, certain that I would die. I watched the soldiers fall in their hundreds, and then I saw the Shar simply scatter." He took a long drink of his wine. "We thought that we had defeated the enemy," he grunted.

"The real enemy was still with us. When we returned to our land it had been taken. A Dasari noble with tenuous links to the Kodistai had claimed our land, and that of many others, for himself. We were destitute."

"I am sorry," Starling said as he watched Armil drain his cup.

"One day, I found my father. He had hanged himself from a tree." Armil filled his cup again and leaned across to fill Starling's.

Starling was silent. His memory stirred and an image boiled to the surface of a mother, wilted at the end of a rope.

He shook his head and the memory retreated.

"Some years later," Armil continued, "I met the very merchant whose wine you are enjoying. He took me in and helped me find my way in those difficult years. Now, he had a slave; a Jendayan man who had sworn to serve my master as a penance for the crimes of his people. He always carried a small book of wisdom and sayings and I would see him reading from it from time to time. He would translate phrases for me when he was sure that he would not be seen by the master. One has always stuck with me."

Starling leaned forward and listened.

"He said that 'the edifice built upon the backs of the poor will crumble when they rise'." Armil smiled into his cup. You see, the poor bleed and the wealthy fill their pockets further." He looked up at Starling. "We did not defeat the Shar at Ara Dasari; they let us go. They gave us a chance to put things right. We are putting things right."

Starling was trying to form a suitable response when they became aware of a rising commotion outside.

They stood and edged towards the open shutter to peer out. The street was filling as people gathered at the foot of the temple while a man in brown robes stood atop the first of the terraced levels. Starling watched as the robed man held up his hands for quiet.

"What is he doing?" Starling whispered.

Armil shrugged in response. "I don't know."

"Servants!" The man called out. "Our time has come."

Starling did not recognise the man but could not ask who it was without showing his ignorance and raising Armil's suspicion. He was sure that the man was Eastern, from the accent, but that was all that he could discern.

"As promised, the Khalim-Shar has come to us with the means to remake our world!" the man declared.

A cheer went up and a woman shouted from the crowd. "Where is Suun?" she asked. "He should be sharing this moment with us."

There was a rumble of assent from the crowd.

The man continued. "Ramash Suun was injured in the attack upon our town. He lives but is much weakened. I, Masahara, will take his place beside the Khalim-Shar as we press on to victory!"

Another cheer.

"You who stand before me remain faithful to Khalim-Shar, but be on your guard for those who lurk in shadow like snakes, biting at the ankles of the righteous!"

Starling slunk back from the window a little. Then he saw a naked, elderly man being led out onto the terrace in chains. He was weeping and begging as the soldiers threw him onto the stones at Masahara's feet.

"This man had in his possession the *Anaki*, the black jewel that the Khalim-Shar demanded be given over to him. This man refused; choosing instead to hide it and keep it for himself."

Starling felt the blood drain from his face and his mouth went dry as a sense of dread filled him.

What had he done?

The crowd hissed and Masahara went on.

"The *Anaki* has been returned to its rightful place, and the Khalim-Shar approves of the efforts undertaken to return it to him. And still, we find more traitors in our midst; those who would destroy what we have worked to build!"

Starling watched in horror as Lucerna, the lamp oil merchant, along with his two hapless guards were dragged out in chains. Their naked bodies were covered with signs of torture. Then the two young buyers, Victus and Infelicis appeared. They had both been gelded, and put up no fight as they were dragged, barely conscious out onto the terrace.

"No, no, no," Starling muttered as the bile rose in his throat.

"What is it? "Armil hissed.

"Spies are everywhere!" Masahara declared. "But hear me; none shall escape the wrath of the Khalim-Shar!"

The crowd roared as the Khalim Shar walked out onto the terrace. It dwarfed Masahara, who fell to his knees in supplication.

The elderly man tried to shrink away but the Khalim-Shar pinned the ankle chains to the ground with the butt of his enormous trident. The crowd fell silent as the huge creature reached down and took the ankle chains in its enormous talon, then lifted the writhing man like a doll, dangling upside down.

"This is a new age!" the Khalim-Shar shrieked, its voice

coarse and grating. "There can be no mercy for those who stand in my way!"

With that, the Khalim-Shar swung the man over its shoulder by the ankle-chains and smashed his head on the edge of the stone terrace like a melon. The explosion of blood and gore splattered those nearest and sent the rest into a frenzy of cheering. The body was thrown to the ground and a half dozen Shar fell upon it to tear it apart.

Lucerna was already screaming when the Khalim-Shar drove the centre point of the trident into his belly. The creature lifted the writhing body high before throwing him to yet more eager Shar.

Starling could not watch anymore. He pressed his back to the wall beside the window and slammed his head back against the plaster over and over again as more screams emanated from the temple. "No, no, no! What have I done?" he moaned through gritted teeth as tears streamed down his cheeks.

"Stellio? What is it?" Armil said again, staring at Starling with questioning eyes.

Starling stifled a cry as another scream erupted from the base of the temple.

"Stellio? Are you one of them?!"

Starling opened his eyes to see Armil resting a hand on the hilt of his sword.

"Armil, no," he began, but his new friend was already nodding his head, having made his decision.

"You are a spy," Armil breathed. "A traitor."

"Armil?" Starling pleaded as tears began to flow more freely. "I trusted you!"

Starling stepped towards the young man even as he pulled the dagger from his hip. Armil tried to draw his sword but the slender blade had already pierced his ribcage just below the armpit where the leather armour stopped.

Armil gasped, and his body went rigid as the dagger burst his heart.

"Armil, I'm sorry," Starling wept as he laid the dying man onto the floorboards. "You have to believe me. I'm sorry."

The young soldier's legs spasmed once, then twice, and the life went from his eyes and a final breath sighed from his body.

Starling pulled the blade free and pounded on the dead man's chest with a fist until he could summon no more strength. He collapsed, sobbing beside the man he had been sharing wine and stories with moments before.

Somehow, he fell asleep, and when he awoke it was dark outside. He retrieved the key from Armil's body and escaped into the night; his mind filled with guilty horrors.

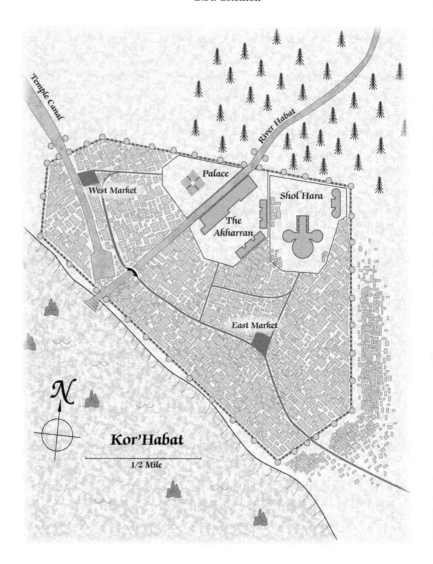

PART TWO: KOR'HABAT
CHAPTER 15

The sprawl of tents and makeshift shelters around the walls of Kor'Habat were terrible to see. For over a mile to the south and east, people clustered together in squalid camps. Children sat, listless in the filth; dead eyed and drained from hunger and remembered horrors.

Easterners who had fled their own homes for the safety of the west now found their sanctuary denied to them by fifty-foot walls. Veiled women bowed their heads as the men passed. They were covered from ankle to wrist in grubby clothing, head and faces covered with a gauzy fabric that left only their haunted eyes unmasked. Charms and polished stones glinted through the grime and ankle bracelets tinkled as they walked. A proud people viewed through the cracked prism of despair.

Pashwar and Dashiya had fallen. All that remained of their once proud people huddled in forlorn groups, starving and exposed.

Food had become increasingly difficult to buy and anything that once crawled or scurried had long since been eaten. The land was dead; sterilised through need.

The relentless sun of early summer scorched what little grew and dust, like smoke and misery, filled the air.

"They leave these people to starve outside their walls," Dachen lamented, as the refugees became alerted to their presence and closed in with hungry, pleading eyes. "There must be a hundred thousand people. No, two hundred!"

"We will see about that," Kapaneus murmured. "Acastes, we must do something!"

A few of the ragged men had started talking amongst themselves and were eyeing the horses, licking their lips.

"I am not master of this city," Acastes grumbled and urged his horse to quicken its pace to the gate.

The low stone wall, which had once marked the boundary beyond which no vagrants could set camp, was gone. The stone had been stripped for use in the ramshackle shelters which now hugged the great walls themselves. Even the ditches held people. These trenches had been a defensive measure centuries ago but were now filled with detritus.

Acastes, Kapaneus and Dachen approached the enormous gate that was situated between huge flanking towers. They had left the rest of their small army fifty miles to the east whilst they had come to Kor'Habat to negotiate and share news.

They arrived at the gate with a cluster of beggars pawing at their legs. Acastes swatted them away while Kapaneus banged on the heavy wood of the gate.

After the second attempt, a voice rang out from the ramparts above. "Who goes?"

"Acastes Fol'Denes, you bloody arse!" Acastes shouted. "Open the sodding gates before I catch pox from these bloody vagrants!" He kicked at the nearest beggar.

There was a long silence before an uncertain reply floated down.

"I will need to ask Hatar Fol'Brandam."

"Fol'Brandam? Hatar Fol'Brandam?" he bellowed. "Who put that arse in charge of anything?"

Another pause. "The Hatar is Steward of Kor'Habat while the

Kodistai is unwell."

Acastes pulled on the reigns of his horse and it took a few steps back. "Look at me," he shouted up to whomever was on the rampart. "Do I look like a peasant or an invading horde to you? Open the bloody gate!"

A moment later they heard the massive battens being slipped from the gate and it inched open. The desperate people around the horses tried to force their way in, but a dozen Heavy Infantry were quick to push them back and hold them at bay until Acastes and his companions were inside. Then the gate slammed shut again behind them.

The street that led from the gates was crowded and noisy, and the sound reverberated within the stone walls, pressing down on the people within.

Kapaneus leaned close to Dachen so that he could be heard. "This is the greatest city in the world," he declared. "It has stood for many centuries and will stand for many more."

"Where is the view?" Dachen replied. "In Lokhara, mountains can be seen to the north, and plains to the south and west."

Kapaneus laughed. "There are views."

They rode on and at last the street gave way to an open market where stalls selling everything from silk to dried fish were arranged in rows.

"This is East Market," Kapaneus said above the noise of the hawkers. "To the right; Shol'Hara. To the left; the *Sky* Bridge to the western part of the city and the palace."

"'*Sky*' Bridge?" Dachen asked.

"You will see," Kapaneus assured him with a wink and a smile.

Dachen nodded, and they pressed on through the crowds. At last it came into view, soaring over the River Habat in a single arch, supported in turn upon eight vaulted pillars. Two hundred yards long and soaring to twenty-five yards high at its centre, the bridge rose higher than the walls themselves.

The pillars could not be seen from the bridge, but soon the

river came into view as the road curved upwards, taking them higher.

"You see?" Kapaneus said, pointing ahead. "A bridge to the sky!"

Dachen stared up the enormous slope of the Sky Bridge and saw only a cloud-streaked sky until they neared the apex.

"Shol'Hara; the Akharran; the Kodistai's palace; 'views'," Kapaneus said with a laugh while Dachen gaped at the city vista. "I told you; the greatest city in the world. You are standing on a bridge that is three thousand years old. As solid as the day the Kodistai, Brahim Fol'Ashmar, placed the final stone in place." He laughed. "An army of slaves did the rest, I imagine."

The prince laughed at the wonder of it and looked back over the eastern quarters of Kor'Habat. The patchwork of dwellings and businesses were broken only by the sprawl of East Market, then continuing until hazed by smoke and distance to wash up against the enormous city walls. His eyes traced the sweeping defensive structure from flanking tower to flanking tower until he found the many-domed city within a city that was Shol'Hara. This was where he was told the Heavy Infantry were bred, and he wondered at the beauty of the sweeping architecture that served such a callous end. Copper, turned green by the elements appeared to glow in the sunlight, punctuated by the glint of coloured glass and the soft sheen of polished marble.

Stark against the flowing lines of Shol'Hara stood the colossal austerity of the Akharran. Hard and grey and broken only by the tiny dark shadows of distant windows. Dachen could have believed that it had been hewn from a single block of granite, its lines were so clean. Like a cliff, the Akharran plunged into the dark waters of the River Habat that ran, arrow straight, through the city and under the Sky Bridge. Steep walls to either side bound the vast river to its course, all the way to the crashing waterfall where it left the city and joined the sea.

The palace itself rose from a forested park that formed an

abrupt barrier against the press of lesser buildings. It had the form of a seven-layered ziggurat, each terrace hanging with gardens and banners, a proud proclamation of power.

Then West Market and the inland lake of the Temple Canal harbour and the waterway itself punctuating the city wall. To the south and west the glittering Adorim Sea stretched to an indistinct horizon, the water foaming where it washed over the shallow reefs.

Soon they were descending the western side of the Sky Bridge back into the claustrophobia of the busy streets. The palace vanished behind the buildings to either side until a long, sweeping turn had the seven-layered edifice come back into view at the end of the long, wide street.

"That looks like Suun's temple," Dachen observed.

Kapaneus shrugged. "This is far grander, and the seat of real power and influence."

Acastes had not spoken since they had entered the city.

"Is it true, Acastes?" Dachen asked with a wry smile.

"Is this the greatest city in the world?

But Acastes did not answer, fixing his eyes instead on the palace ahead as a duellist faces an adversary.

The wall around the palace grounds was broken by an ornate archway of carved stone. Beyond that, manicured lawns and ornamental trees declared that this place was forever untouched by the tribulations that plagued the world outwith the walls. A small herd of black deer raised their heads from the juicy tips of grass to watch the travellers pass but were untroubled by the presence of men.

They had reached the bottom of the broad steps that led up the centre of the north-western side of the palace before anyone greeted them.

"Times must be grim indeed if Acastes Fol'Denes has scurried back to the safety of these walls. I confess; I thought you dead!" A loud voice brought them to a halt.

Acastes looked up to see Rogan standing above them, hands on hips on the second level terrace of the palace. The Hatar was dressed in a light ceremonial armour that gleamed in hues of copper and gold.

"Thought it, or wished it?" Acastes replied.

"It matters little," Rogan said with a shrug.

"Steward of Kor'Habat, I hear," Acastes said with a sneer. "A fine title that you have awarded yourself."

"Not so," Rogan declared. "It is a position granted to me by the *Council of Hatars*."

"Council of…" Acastes guffawed. "You jest of course; no such body exists."

"It exists now," Rogan replied.

"Under whose authority?" Kapaneus demanded. "Only the Kodistai has the ascendancy to create such a body."

"Alas," Rogan said, "mindful of his own frailty, he has done just that. The Kodistai was left with no choice since no heir *worthy* of that name is positioned to replace him."

Acastes placed a hand on the hilt of his sword and started up the broad, weathered steps, with Kapaneus and Dachen close behind.

"Where is Chapok?" Dachen demanded as he ascended. "Where is my brother?"

Rogan laughed. "You have a presumptuous tone for one so far from home, and so reliant upon the charity of his neighbours. A little humility would serve you well."

The three men reached the second level terrace and faced Rogan, who made a show of looking down at Dachen before speaking.

"I apologise, of course," he said, starting to bow. "It is customary for me to lower my head beneath your own, as a show of respect." He stopped, well short and sneered at Dachen. "But to go lower than you have fallen, would require me to slither like a snake, and I still have my dignity, *Prince*."

Dachen glared back at him. "Chapok has abandoned his people," he spat. "Left them to live like animals in the field. As you have abandoned yours. Where is the dignity in that?"

Rogan looked away without comment, directing his attention back to Acastes. "Why have you come here?"

"We have news from Dargenmill," Acastes replied.

"Out with it then."

"No," Acastes murmured. "I will deliver it to your *Council of Hatars*. They all need to hear what I have to say."

Rogan was thoughtful for a moment. "Very well. Although I have a man not long from delivering news of Dargenmill."

Acastes stepped in close. "Then by all means, ignore mine. But I *will* deliver it."

Rogan glared back and narrowed his eyes. "Then return at sunset," he said. "The council will see you then."

Rogan hurled a chair against the wall of his chambers. It shattered and knocked a water jug from a side table as the pieces fell.

A moment later, Captain Raims burst into the room.

"Hatar?" he said, seeing the broken jug and splintered chair.

"How is he still alive!" Rogan raged. "How is he even here?"

"Hatar, who?"

"He threatens everything! It is my destiny to lead my people; mine! He abandoned them long ago, and yet he comes back now to piss on everything I have achieved!"

Captain Raims said nothing.

"Bastard!" He hurled another chair at the wall, and it suffered a similar fate to the first.

Captain Raims remained mute while his Hatar calmed himself. Rogan filled his lungs with air and steadied his hands on the surface of the large desk. At last he spoke.

"That man; Captain Silman," he said as his breathing slowed. "Has he reported to anyone but me?"

"I do not believe so."

"Good. Make sure he speaks to no-one and have him sent to me immediately." Rogan rounded the desk and sat in the only remaining chair in the room.

He watched Captain Raims hurry from the room, and waited for his return, running through his plan again and again in his mind.

Finally, Raims returned with Captain Silman.

"Thank you, Raims," he said. "That will be all."

Raims flashed a contemptuous look at Captain Silman before saluting; right fist on his left breast and walking from the room.

"I would offer you a seat, but…" Rogan gestured to the broken chairs across the room.

Captain Silman stood rigid as if on parade.

"Please, relax," Rogan said, and Silman eased his pose a little. "Tell me again what you saw in Dargenmill."

Silman cleared his throat. "They have fortified the town," he replied. "They are aware of the advancing Shar but believe that they can defend themselves."

"And the eleven men you lost on the road?"

Silman swallowed hard. "As I said; we were attacked by an advance party of Shar and eastern soldiers," he lied.

"Have you reported this to anyone else?" Rogan asked.

"No, Hatar."

"Are you certain?"

"I swear, Hatar, I…"

"I do not doubt your word, Captain," Rogan assured him. "I only wish you to be certain of it."

Silman nodded and swallowed hard again.

Rogan leaned forward and rested his elbows on the table, placing his chin on clenched fists. "Because I need you to change your story."

The room was illuminated with lamps set into the walls and a dozen ornate chandeliers hanging from the ceiling. Tables arranged in a crescent filled much of the room and a large brazier burned at the centre.

The Council of Hatars had gathered to hear from Acastes Fol'Denes.

Acastes entered, flanked by Kapaneus and Dachen, past the guards at the wide doorway, and came to stand in front of the brazier. He looked around the semi-circle of a dozen faces in front of him, recognising most. Rogan was sitting at the centre of the gathered men, his expression unreadable.

Chapok was there too. The bodyguard, Jangbu was standing close behind his King. He scratched beneath his eye with a smile. Acastes saw Dachen stiffen out of the corner of his own eye, remembering the small wound inflicted upon the Prince on the docks at Banihat.

"Welcome home, Acastes Fol'Denes," the grey-haired Hatar Bravik Fol'Gannity said. "Would you care for a seat?"

Acastes shook his head. "What I have to say will not take long," he replied.

Rogan gestured for Acastes to speak.

Acastes took his time, relishing the drawn out pause and the clear irritation it was causing Rogan. He surveyed the Council of Hatars. Most of these men should be retired, he thought to himself. With the exception of Rogan, only Gilean Fol'Maddon and Bravik Fol'Gannity looked fit to take to the battlefield. Gilean's topknot was fair, which hid the grey in his hair, but his face was etched with lines that he had earned through both battle and age. Bravik, on the other hand, was smooth skinned but the hair he had kept to signify his rank was streaked with strands of silver.

"There is an army approaching," he began. "We have seen it. The town of Dargenmill follows a deluded cult, started by the madman, Ramash Suun. They have gathered an army of thousands. Together with an army of Eastern soldiers and an untold number of Shar, they are marching on Kor'Habat as we speak."

"King Chapok?" Hatar Gilean Fol'Maddon asked. He leaned

forward and squinted which only accentuated the lines on his face. "Could this be true? We have heard tell of Eastern men and Shar moving together in small groups to the North and East. Could an army have gathered at Dargenmill."

"A shameful thing for me to bear if true," Chapok said, and his jowls shook with his head. "But I doubt it is so. A few traitors there may be, but whole armies? No, my people are loyal to me."

"Do not be taken in," Dachen warned. "He is but an exiled King of a scattered people. Khumjang; Shibatsu; Lhaksang; do you speak for all those peoples, or only those of Tianpok whom you have abandoned outside these walls?"

Jangbu stiffened and Chapok held up a restraining hand.

"They have built war engines," Acastes went on. "We attempted to destroy them at Dargenmill, but we were forced back when the Khalim-Shar arrived to defend them."

"War engines?" Bravik Fol'Gannity said.

"Dozens of them," Acastes replied.

"And, what of it?" Rogan muttered.

"You were at Hadaiti, were you not, Hatar?" Acastes said, addressing Bravik. "You saw how those engines crushed men like insects."

"The walls of Kor'Habat have never fallen," Hatar Gilean Fol'Maddon said with a dismissive wave. "Not in three thousand years. Weapons meant to kill men will barely scratch the stone."

"You are wrong," Dachen warned. "If my brother is to be at all honest with you, he will tell you what our engineers are capable of."

"I saw what they were capable of," Bravik murmured. "Saw men butchered in their hundreds. Can those engines breach our defences?"

Dachen held the Hatar's gaze and said, "I believe they can. But it is not too late to prepare."

"Go on," Bravik said.

"Out there, on the plains," Dachen pointed east, "are engineers still loyal to their people. We can build engines of our own to defend the city from the Shar."

Rogan leaned forward. "What are you suggesting?" he asked.

Dachen smiled. "Your battlements are fifty feet high; ask any apprentice engineer about the advantages of height in a battle for range, and he will tell you that you hold the dominant position here. But you must act quickly. Protect that Eastern wall."

Acastes nodded in agreement while the Hatars exchanged worried looks.

"Rogan, you have faced this Khalim-Shar," Acastes said. "Do not make the mistake of throwing men alone at it. We will need those Eastern engineers too."

"We will think on this," Rogan said at last.

"Do not 'think' for too long," Acastes warned. "You have thirty, perhaps forty days before that army reaches Kor'Habat."

"And those people on the plain will need protection, and food," Kapaneus added. "How can you stand to leave them out there while your stores are full?"

"A lengthy siege may require those stores," Hatar Gilean Fol'Maddon replied.

Kapaneus laughed. "The Khalim-Shar does not have the patience for a 'lengthy siege'," he said. "Let them in; fill their bellies and arm them. Anyone too young or too sick to hold a weapon should be treated with no less empathy."

"These are strange times, Kapaneus," Hatar Gilean Fol'Maddon said. "Men fight alongside the Shar. How can we trust those people out there? They are not all our own; Dashiyans eager for revenge; Pashwaris with memories of wars long lost. Tell me; how many do you ride with?"

Acastes answered for him, "Eight hundred; give or take."

"And you would have us throw open our gates to you too, I suppose," Gilean went on. "Hundreds of men loyal to a renegade prince; Shar-hunters known for their disdain for Kor'Habat, and a band of merry wenches? Oh yes, and of course 'Valia of Hadaiti' at your head. Yes, Kapaneus, we know with whom you ride. Our eyes are not so blind."

"You follow a woman now?" Chapok laughed with delight. "Oh brother, it is a mercy that our father is already dead, or the shame would certainly have ended him."

Dachen stepped forward but Acastes grabbed his shoulder in a meaty fist to stop him. Jangbu smiled and touched the flesh under his eye.

"*She* does not command *me* or the men loyal to me," Dachen spat.

"Of course, little brother, of course," Chapok teased.

"I did not come here to exchange insults," Acastes said. "I have said what I wanted to say; now it is up to you to decide on the path you will take."

The Hatars muttered amongst themselves whilst Chapok and Jangbu leered at Dachen

"Thank you, Acastes," Rogan said. "I trust you will be able to make yourselves comfortable here in Kor'Habat."

"I know my way here," Acastes replied, and turned to leave, with Kapaneus right behind him.

Dachen offered his brother a final acid glare before following the big man out of the room.

Rogan waited whilst the Hatars muttered amongst themselves after the trio had left.

"We have much to consider," Bravik said.

"Before we make any decisions," Rogan said, "I have one more deposition that you should all hear."

"Whose?" Gilean asked.

"That of a man whom I sent to Dargenmill in early spring. He has some," he hesitated, "compelling testimony." He raised his head and his voice for the guards on the door to hear. "Show him in!"

Moments later, Captain Silman entered the room and stood at

rigid attention in front of the Hatars.

"This is Captain Silman Fol'Ghealten; a fine soldier of excellent standing," Rogan said. "He will make Hatar one day, of that I am certain."

Silman saluted and stood a little prouder.

"Tell the council what you found in Dargenmill, Captain." Rogan said.

"The town is much grown, and fortified, Hatar, with a large militia," Silman reported.

"Any Eastern soldiers, Captain?" asked Rogan.

"Yes Hatar, accompanying many Eastern refugees. The town offered them shelter."

"I see. Did you see any war engines?"

"I saw some devices, strange things. Defensive weapons to be used in the event of an attack by the Shar."

Rogan glanced at each of his peers in turn. "And the cultists?"

Silman managed a chuckle. "A strange bunch, Hatar, but harmless enough."

Bravik leaned forward and asked, "Did you see any Shar in the town, Captain."

Silman puffed out his cheeks. "No, Hatar."

"Any sign that they were mobilising an army?"

"No, Hatar. As I reported, there is a large militia, but this appears purely defensive."

"Did you experience any aggression from the militia?"

"None, Hatar."

"And yet," Rogan interrupted, "I sent you with twelve men, and you returned with one."

"Yes, Hatar," Silman replied. "We were attacked on the road as we returned."

"Who by!" Gilean demanded.

"Shar-hunters," Silman replied. "And Eastern soldiers."

There was a loud murmuring as the Hatars growled curses.

"And who was leading these attackers?" Rogan asked.

"I would know her anywhere, Hatar. It was Valia; the 'Bitch of Hadaiti'."

Rogan let the news settle on the minds of his fellow Hatars. "And yet you escaped," he said.

"My men did not die cheaply, Hatar," Silman replied, his chin set firm with pride. "They killed four times their number to beat Valia."

The Hatars nodded amongst themselves.

"The Sons of Shol'Hara are not so easily defeated," Gilean declared to the general approval of the others.

"But it was only a small part of her army," the captain went on. "She has thousands more, including Eastern men and engineers."

"We must prepare," Bravik said. "That woman has been a burr in Korathea's boot for too long."

The Hatars nodded in agreement, murmuring assent amongst themselves.

Rogan allowed this to continue for a few moments before speaking again. "Are you lying to us?" he asked, rising from his seat.

Silman stuttered, suddenly unsure. "No, Hatar."

"If you are providing us with false intelligence," Rogan warned, "you will be punished."

Silman's mouth worked silently.

"Any action we take based on inaccuracies in your statement will be paid for in blood," Rogan warned. "Your blood!"

"Hatar?" Silman managed, "It is as I..."

"Very well," Rogan said before Silman could say any more. "You are dismissed."

Silman offered a weak salute and turned to leave wearing a dazed expression.

"A little *harsh*, Rogan," Gilean observed to the muttered agreement of the others there.

Rogan shrugged and smiled inwardly. *Good, Silman is* their

man now, he thought.

Rogan sat down again and said, "Perhaps. But what do we make of it? Why would Acastes Fol'Denes lie to us?"

"Valia," Bravik sneered. "She twists the hearts of men."

More agreement. These fools were so easy to play.

"But why warn us at all?" Rogan asked. "A fortified eastern wall can only hamper their attack, if that is what they plan."

"They will attack us from the west!" Gilean banged on the table. "They want to tie up our resources on one side of the city, while they prepare to assault the other."

"Agreed," Bravik said with a nod. "Your Majesty, with respect, we need those engineers."

Chapok spread his hands. "I will see it done," he said.

"Our defences should be concentrated to the west," Gilean added.

Rogan watched them plan the defence of the city for a few moments before he spoke again. "What of Acastes? We have him here, in the city. He should be arrested."

"And Dachen with him," Chapok added.

Gilean nodded. "And the 'Bitch of Hadaiti'?" he asked. "What of her and her army?"

"A negligible force," Rogan said, shaking his head.

"But if she is welcomed into the city, we could have her neck in a noose where it belongs."

Rogan smiled. "You have a devious mind, Gilean," he chuckled.

Rogan watched as the council planned the defence of the city and the end of both Acastes and Valia. When the attack came, the blame for the misinformation could be placed squarely at Silman's door; after all, had the Hatars not taken the captain's words as truth, even when Rogan himself had expressed doubt? If the attack indeed came from the east as he expected, there would be time enough to move their resources from the western half of the city. By then, of course, Acastes would be an unpleasant memory and Rogan's destiny would be realised.

The Glaive had changed. The inn where Acastes had spent so many carefree evenings exchanging inflated tales of heroism with hunters and soldiers alike had become a sombre place.

A few of the patrons recognised him and raised a cup in greeting, or else slapped him on the shoulder as he walked past them towards a free table in the corner of the large room.

"What news from the East, Acastes?" a man asked.

"I do not wish to sour your wine, so I will leave that unanswered," he replied without stopping.

He sat, waiting for Kapaneus to join him, positioning himself in the corner where he could see the whole room. Dachen took the remaining chair and sighed.

"I confess," the prince said. "I feel a certain amount of guilt knowing that I will enjoy a warm meal and a soft bed tonight, while my people are hungry and sleeping on the ground."

Acastes accepted the jug of wine from the serving girl with a wink and offered to fill his companions' cups. Both declined.

"The king looks to be well fed," he said, filling his own cup to the brim.

"Chapok has always looked after his own interests," Dachen sneered. "He was never meant to lead."

"In my experience," Acastes replied with a grin, "that is a prerequisite for any leader."

"Then you have poor leaders," Dachen replied, in no mood for humour.

"And Jangbu?" Acastes said, "Your animosity goes beyond that little scratch beneath your eye."

"One day I will kill that man," Dachen muttered, but offered nothing more.

"You really should try the wine," Acastes said, offering again to fill Dachen's cup.

"I'll take water," he said, waving to the serving girl to request some.

When the jug arrived, Kapaneus accepted the invitation to drink. Acastes offered the serving girl a copper mark for her troubles and a winning smile, which made her giggle as she left.

"You really are a boring pair," Acastes complained. "Look at Kapaneus there, sipping water and watching over me like an anxious mother duck. No; grandmother duck!" He laughed at his own joke.

"I watch over you," Kapaneus said, "because you will not watch over yourself."

Acastes snorted. "I was trained in the Akharran! I do not need a nanny."

"He makes a fair point," Dachen said. "Why do you watch him? Acastes looks as though he can look after himself."

Acastes raised his cup towards Dachen in approval. "I'll drink to that," the large warrior said and drained his cup.

"Do not be fooled by his manly exterior," Kapaneus replied with a spark of mischief in his eyes and smiling to himself. "Within that meaty chest beats the heart of a child, and worse still is the tiny brain encased within that thick skull. Look, Dachen, look within those pretty blue eyes and you will barely see any glimmer of intelligence. Take that serving girl for example; he winks at her and she smiles back. Emboldened, he offers a copper mark for which he is rewarded with a shy giggle. Now, as the great man drinks more, he will become freer with his money, rewarding every little smile, every flick of the hair with more coin. But he is not alone in the room; not the only man with eyes for her, and she knows that she can get into their coin purses with both hands behind her back. Who can blame her? The wages here are terrible, and so she works the room; unspoken promises to men who will soon be too drunk to stand, let alone indulge in any feats of imagined passion. She is plucking you like a lyre, and you sing so sweetly, never realising that you are being played."

Acastes stared into his wine in the sullen silence that followed.

Then he brightened. "I bet you five silver marks that I bed her before morning," he said with a grin.

Dachen recoiled in disgust while Kapaneus banged the table twice.

"Accepted!" he declared.

Then Kapaneus saw a man walking across the room towards their table; a man he knew; a hunter from several years ago that he and Acastes had worked with in Dasar.

"Orin?" he said, standing to greet his old friend.

"Twenty Heavy Infantry; two minutes away. I heard your name mentioned," the newcomer breathed, slipping into Kapaneus' vacated seat.

Acastes and Dachen were on their feet in an instant.

"Out the back, through the storeroom," Kapaneus urged, and the three men hurried from *The Glaive*, leaving Orin to sip on Acastes' wine. Moments later, a captain of the Heavy Infantry entered the room with a dozen Infantrymen at his back.

The huge captain made his way through the common room of *The Glaive*, staring at every customer in turn. He reached Orin's table and stopped, glaring at the silent Shar-hunter. The captain dipped his finger into one of the cups and tasted the contents.

"Water?" he asked. "Wine, and two cups of water? Where are your friends?"

Orin pointed to one seat then the other. "That there is Garvil, and that there is Anders. Lost those two fine men four years ago tonight; a Shar in Arbis Mora. If you don't mind, Captain, I'm trying to enjoy a drink with old friends; relive past glories; toast their memory."

The captain sneered. "You toast the memory of your friends with water?" he gestured to the two unattended cups.

"Captain," Orin replied in horror, "Garvil and Anders would have been *appalled* if I'd wasted *wine*. They're dead."

The captain considered the response, staring at the lone man at the table.

"I'm looking for Acastes Fol'Denes," he announced. "He is with two companions, including an Eastern man. Anyone here seen him?"

He was met with silence.

"Search the building," he said at last. "They're somewhere nearby."

CHAPTER 16

"It has been eight days," Valia murmured. "They are not coming back."

Marlon grunted. "We are running short on food," he said. "Even Granger cannot make what we have left taste good. If Kor'Habat will not open their gates to us, perhaps we should take a ship west."

"I'd sooner starve than set foot on another boat," Valia replied.

Adeyemi joined them at the edge of the woodland and sank down onto the fallen log that they were sitting on. Below them, down the gentle slope, the road to Kor'Habat etched a dusty line through the dry grass into the distance. Three days ride to the west would take them to the great city; the place they had hoped to make a stand against the Khalim-Shar. That felt like a childish dream now.

"The portents are bad," Adeyemi said at last. "I saw two ravens chasing a hawk and it cried out three times; a distressed hawk only calls twice in alarm."

Valia glanced sideways at the big man and shook her head.

"You fear for your friends," Adeyemi said, "as I fear for mine."

"Kor'Habat cannot be trusted," she grumbled. "They were fools for believing otherwise."

"Kekoa is looking for you," Adeyemi told her. "You are late for your lesson."

"Tell him I will be there shortly," she replied after a pause.

"Tell him yourself," he replied. "I am not your servant."

Valia scowled as she stood, but Adeyemi was paying her no heed; his mind was elsewhere.

She walked away towards the encampment to find Kekoa. Resuming the language lessons had provided a distraction from the burning desire to ride east again to throw herself at the enemy in a bloody, snarling act of finality. His soothing manner was all that kept her from the abyss of insanity; of that she was certain.

She passed the section of the camp where the Sisters had their tents erected. Nirmaya was there, sullen beneath a silver oak. Starling had not returned from Dargenmill, only the man's horse had escaped the town, and there was an argument to be made that the animal had greater use than its rider had ever had. Still, she sulked. Red-haired Maidra was running fingers through Nirmaya's hair and glared at Valia as she passed by.

What had she done to deserve that woman's ire? Of course, it had been Valia who had let Nirmaya go on that foolish mission in the first place. Starling was gone, and the young woman moped like a child instead of contriving an act of revenge. Sorrow was such a wasteful emotion.

The Eastern soldiers performed their drills in a series of clearings. The sparth bearer, Sangye raised a hand in greeting and she nodded in return. Most of the other Eastern soldiers ignored her. The fat one, Yeshe, paused his drill to glare at her with open hatred. There was a time when the Eastern disdain for any woman who was anything but demure had amused her. Now she just did not care. Even when Sangye slapped Yeshe on the backside with the flat of his sparth to get his attention, she felt nothing, and no righteous pleasure at the brawl that ensued.

Granger was poring over his books, lost in the stories he had recorded. Apart from the evening meal, she had barely exchanged a word with him for days, nor even made eye contact. His books were everything to him now.

She found Jon, sitting beside Elan as the jade-skinned man fletched arrows. Jon tried to keep up and emulate his Lythurian companion, but from his expression, he was failing.

The alchemist, Tsering, was grooming the pony that usually carried the urns of fire-silver, muttering to himself. He raised his eyes to meet Valia's and offered a toothless smile. She nodded a wary greeting and quickened her pace.

Shar-hunters sat in small clusters or alone, waiting for news with the air of the condemned. Abbil watched her pass with dark eyes as he whittled a short length of wood; the shavings at his feet were pale and deep but the task appeared to lack purpose beyond keeping his hands occupied.

Olgoi Kinbataar, the erstwhile leader of Ulan-Balsan's ruling conclave paced in front of his tent, flashing a guilty look in Valia's direction before resuming the nervous pacing.

Such a strange and disparate band of fools she had found herself among, Valia thought.

Kekoa was beside the small stream that they had been meeting at since setting up camp here.

"An hour, Kekoa; no more," she said as she slumped down onto the dry grass.

Kekoa was silent for a long time.

"If my master is dead," he said at last, "will you accept me as your servant for my final year of penance?"

"What? No," she replied. "I have no need of a servant."

"I must complete ten years of service to those I have wronged," Kekoa went on. "Any less will not absolve me."

"Time cannot buy absolution, Kekoa. You should learn to live with your mistakes; they make you who you are."

Kekoa sat back and smiled. "That sounds like something from those wretched texts I was forced to read as a youth," he said.

"Really? And what would those 'wretched texts' say about this? An army of Shar behind; an intransigent enemy in front; and a broken army in the middle. We cannot beat the Khalim-Shar alone, Kekoa; we need Kor'Habat if we are to have any chance of winning this. Even then…"

"So, you need to win a battle that is not a battle before the battle can be won?"

"One day," Valia replied, "you will give me a straight, bloody answer. In truth, I do not care. This will be my last; I have no interest in emerging from this; none at all. I only want to leave this life with every last scrap of anger spent." She sighed. "I am so tired."

"Then, no new words today," Kekoa said. "Offering teaching to a student whose mind is not receptive is akin to pouring water into a lidded pot. But think on this; is the enemy to the west a People or a man? If the People can be left intact, then leave it as such and face the man. Attacking the People to reach the man only hardens the People against you."

Valia pinched the bridge of her nose and lay back on the grass. *So tired.*

There was a call in the distance.

"Rider approaching!"

She rolled over and pushed herself up onto her feet without a word. Striding back to the other side of the encampment, she saw others moving towards the edge of the woodland. They had heard the call too and were eager for news to break the monotony of their days. She found Marlon at the front of a growing crowd. Between their position on the low rise and the road, a rider was making his way across the dry plain leaving a drifting trail of dust in his wake.

They watched in silence as the rider drew nearer. It was clear that he was alone and had seen them. He raised a hand in greeting.

"Do I have the honour of addressing 'Valia of Hadaiti'?" the man asked as he dropped down from his saddle.

He was young, and tall with a friendly smile beneath pale blue eyes.

"Who wants to know?" Marlon replied.

"I have a message from Acastes Fol'Denes," he said, his smile never shifting.

He put a hand into his coat and the loosening of steel in many scabbards caused him to stop where he was.

"It is only a letter," he insisted, easing a folded and sealed sheet of parchment from his pocket.

Valia stepped forwards and took the note from him, breaking the seal to read the message within.

"What does it say?" Marlon asked, keeping his good eye on the messenger.

Valia finished the note before reading it out load.

"Valia," she began. "We have arrived to a warm welcome. Do not delay in bringing the army to Kor'Habat. I have the personal guarantee of the Council of Hatars that your pardon will be honoured in full. Signed; Acastes Fol'Denes."

A collective sigh rippled through the gathered crowd, and many hurried away to spread the news and start breaking camp.

"Acastes gave this to you?" Valia asked, scanning the letter again.

"He did, my lady."

"You saw him write this?"

"Write it, sign it, seal it and place it in my hands," the messenger replied with a smile.

"What is your name?"

"Darisantus, my lady," he replied. "My friends call me Dari."

Valia nodded. "Well, Darisantus," she said. "If you are lying to me, I will stab you in the heart."

His smile slipped, and he shuffled back a little way.

"Break camp!" Valia ordered and strode away to gather her belongings.

"You still owe me five silver marks," Kapaneus insisted.

"That was not a fair bet," Acastes grumbled. "I've been in a cellar ever since we agreed on it."

"You lack commitment," Kapaneus replied before being hushed into silence by his friends.

Footsteps on the floorboards alerted them to a presence above. A little dust fell through the cracks above their heads as a table was dragged across the floor, and slivers of light scythed down into the gloom as a rug was pulled away. The trapdoor above was pulled open and a friendly face peered down into the hiding place.

"Good morning, my lords. Would you care to take breakfast in the arbour?"

"Fate, Dorigal!" Acastes exclaimed. "How long do we need to hide in this dank hovel?"

Kapaneus had led them to this house that night the Heavy Infantry had come for them and Dorigal had not hesitated to help. The fact that Dorigal would face a death sentence if any of them were to be discovered did not weigh heavy on Acastes' mind; he was hungry, bored, and furious with himself. He ascended the small ladder leading out from the under-floor space.

"The Infantry are all over the city searching for you," Dorigal said as he offered Acastes a hand.

"It's been six days," Kapaneus said, clambering out of the hole and dusting himself down. "They must assume by now that we have escaped the city."

He turned and helped Dachen from the hiding place.

"Come and eat," Dorigal insisted, arranging chairs around the table he had moved moments ago. He was a slender, balding man with wiry arms and large hands. He unwrapped two loaves and set them on the table with a pat of butter and a pot of honey. "Use the chamber pot in the next room and I will take your offerings out to the privy myself. Cannot risk you being seen."

"You tell us that every day," Dachen said around a mouthful of bread.

"And every day it is no less true," Dorigal replied without hesitation.

"Is there any word of Valia yet?" Kapaneus asked, tucking into the bread while Acastes made his way to the adjoining room.

"A rider was seen leaving the morning after you arrived here," he replied. Then he rolled his eyes as the sound of water hitting a chamber pot with force caused him to cast a shout over his shoulder. "Don't splash the Pashwari rug!" He shook his head in disbelief before continuing. "I have a man in the refugee camp keeping an eye out for her arrival should she be foolish enough to come here."

Acastes re-appeared, buttoning his flies. "We do not have time for this," he scowled. "The Khalim-Shar is marching on the city as we speak; have they at least started on the defences?"

Dorigal nodded. "Some of those Eastern fellows have been brought in from the camps outside. Fate knows what they are building on the ramparts, but it is taking a lot of wood to do it. The iron foundries too, are working day and night."

"That is something, at least," Kapaneus said before taking himself to the next room.

Again, the sound of water upon porcelain and Dorigal groaned, "Don't splash the Pashwari rug!"

"We need to get out of this city," Acastes said.

"And I am investigating avenues of escape," Dorigal replied. "But Kor'Habat is sealed tight."

"This is why they still search for us; they know that we have no way out."

Kapaneus returned and Dachen left his chair to go and use the chamber pot.

"I know," he said before their host could speak. "The rug."

Dorigal spread his hands and nodded in thanks. He waited in silence and listened to the tell-tale sounds from the next room. He looked pleased.

"There is another option," Dorigal ventured.

"If you are going to say what I think you are, then do not bother," Acastes muttered.

"There are enough men in this city who will stand behind you," he said anyway.

"No."

"The Kodistai is dying."

"The Kodistai is *always* dying!"

Dorigal put a finger to his lips

"The Kodistai is always dying," Acastes repeated in a quieter voice.

"This time, there is little doubt; he is barely awake."

"Then he is the fortunate one," Acastes sneered.

"Do not let Rogan take this city for himself," Dorigal urged. "I have devoted my life to this, as have others."

"I did not ask you to!"

"And I did not ask you to piss on my rug, yet here we are."

Acastes was silent for a long time as he pondered Dorigal's words.

"It was only a few drops," he said at last, which raised a chuckle from his companions, then he grew more serious.

"We cannot split the city in two when the Khalim-Shar is at our door."

"Then unite it, Acastes," Kapaneus urged, slamming his fist into his palm. "It is time."

Acastes rose and made his way back into the cellar without a word. Eventually his two companions followed, and they all listened as the rug was pulled over the trapdoor and the table pushed back into place. Acastes slumped down onto the bedroll he had been given and turned his face to the wall.

The army had moved as one for three days, but impatience had got the better of some. As soon as the city of Kor'Habat had appeared from the haze of the distant horizon, most of the Eastern men on horseback picked up the pace. Those on foot were left behind to watch with envy. Some of the hunters too, vanished into the dust, eager perhaps for the comforts of the city.

"What do you say, Yeshe?" Sangye said. "You may finally get that whore you have been dreaming of."

Yeshe scowled. "I would not lie with a common whore!" he spat.

"That is wise, my friend," Sangye joked. "She would be forced to charge you double."

He patted his belly and pointed the Yeshe's ample waistline.

The soldiers laughed, and Yeshe heeled his horse and urged it ahead.

Sangye looked around at his companions to share the joke.

"Did I not tell you he was eager?" he declared, urging his mount to keep up with Yeshe's, and perhaps torment the man further.

Valia felt no such urgency, and so tarried at the back with her companions.

Darisantus, the messenger, was keen to be away now that the city was in sight but Valia insisted that he remain close. Those over-eager riders were slowed when they reached the edge of the refugee camps around Kor'Habat. Throngs of people gathered around them to beg for food or ask for news.

"Stay watchful," Valia murmured as they entered the crowd. Desperate people surrounded the horses, pulling at the riders' legs and swamping those on foot.

"Get back," Valia shouted, inching her sword from its scabbard to show the gleaming steel.

A hooded man was walking through the crowd, angling his approach to meet Valia. She watched him as she kicked at the grasping hands below. People cried out in a rising cacophony, begging for help. Ahead, the gates crept open as the huge winches within were wound by the gatekeepers.

The hooded man was close now and Valia pulled her sword free, heeling her horse forwards.

Heavy Infantry poured through the gap in the gates to drive back any who tried to find a way inside to safety. The Eastern soldiers were ushered through and Jon cursed.

"Bugger this! I need a bloody drink!" he said, urging his horse through the crowd to reach the gate before more refugees could block the way.

Olgoi glanced at Valia before urging his own horse forward, shooing away the people who were crowding around them.

The hooded man lifted his head a little so that Valia could see his eyes.

"It's a trap," he mouthed, and turned away again.

Valia pushed her sword back into its scabbard and watched as the soldiers streamed into the city.

"Darisantus!" she shouted above the noise and steered her mount to his side.

"Yes, my lady," he replied.

"Where will I find Acastes?"

"In *The Glaive* I would imagine," he replied with a smile.

"Has he drunk it dry of ale yet?" Valia shouted, leaning closer.

Darisantus laughed. "He was certainly trying his best when last I saw him," he answered.

Valia nodded. "Do you remember what I told you?" she asked.

"I beg my Lady's pardon?" the young man said, leaning closer to hear her over the noise.

She pulled out her dagger and drove it into his chest to the hilt.

"He prefers wine," she hissed as he gaped in horror. "It's a trap!" she yelled, and the young man slumped forward on his saddle, eyes wide with shock.

She pulled him backwards and wrenched the dagger from his heart, pushing the dying man from his saddle as she shouted.

"It's a trap! Do not enter the city! We have been betrayed!"

The Heavy Infantry turned their weapons on the soldiers who had already passed through the gates and drove them deeper into the city. At once, the gates began to ease shut and those who could backed away to avoid being taken. The refugees screamed in panic at the sudden show of force and people fell and were trampled in the rush to escape.

She pulled her sword free and made to charge the retreating Infantrymen but the crowds in front of her blocked the way.

The gates boomed shut and Valia glared at the city walls, howling with rage. Then she turned her mount to the south and rode with anyone who could follow her.

As the gates started closing behind them, Sangye struggled to stay on his horse. The Infantrymen who had been holding the refugees back moments before had turned on him and his fellows. There had been a cry from behind, he was certain of that.

He managed to turn his mount in the crush and urged it towards the narrowing opening in the huge gates.

Yeshe was there ahead of him, yards away from the gates.

"Yeshe! Run!" he cried.

But Yeshe did not try to escape. Instead he drove his fist into Sangye's chin and knocked him from his horse. The last thing Sangye saw as he fell into the forest of legs, was Yeshe's satisfied grin.

Olgoi Kinbataar tried to discern his surroundings through the coarse weave of the sack that had been placed over his head. He was sweating, and the sack stuck to his brow, causing his skin to itch. He shook his head to shift the sack but could do nothing to alleviate the terrible prickling.

He was seated on a hard chair in a dim room. His hands and feet were bound, and he could feel cold stone beneath his naked feet.

"Hello, Olgoi."

The voice was familiar to him, and he saw a shape move against the light through the sackcloth.

"Hatar," he began, trying to strike a tone of hurt and confusion. "I was coming directly to you when I was taken at the gate."

"Of course you were," Rogan replied.

"I swear, it is the truth!" Olgoi insisted.

"No doubt you intended to return my gold to me,"

"Hatar?"

"You will never believe who walked through the city gates, only a few days ago," Rogan said. "Acastes Fol'Denes. I told myself that I must surely have been mistaken; Acastes Fol'Denes was dead. I had paid good money to ensure that he was dead; to a man who insisted that he had the means to see it done..."

"Hatar," Olgoi replied. "I made the mistake of hiring men who were not up to the task. They are dead now, of course. In failing me, they failed you and I could not allow that to stand. I tried many avenues, even contriving a conflict between him and one of his own companions. I have taken the matter into my own hands now and will do the deed myself. After all, a task of such importance and delicacy should be dealt with by someone possessing tact and skill; not the amateurs who failed to deliver on their promises. As recompense for late delivery of the task, I will insist upon a deduction, by half, of the balance owed once completed."

There was a short silence.

"A deduction?" Rogan asked. "By half, you say? That is a generous offer indeed, Master Olgoi. I am most grateful for your generosity."

Olgoi could hear the sarcasm in Rogan's tone and adjusted his offer.

"Of course, shall we say, for your trouble and understanding, substitute the gold marks for silver?"

"*Silver,* you say?" The comment was no less heavy with mockery.

Olgoi bowed his head. "Hatar, forgive me, I have failed you this time. But I guarantee on my honour and the honour of my father's name that I will not fail you again."

"In that, you are correct," Rogan replied, and Olgoi made out the shape of his captor as the big man moved around behind him. "You will never fail me again."

Olgoi felt a heavy rope drop over his head and settle on his shoulders. Then it was pulled tight.

"Hatar, my Lord," he began, but was hauled up out of his chair by the rope. He gagged, searching for the floor with his toes, kicking out in the gloom to find some purchase. He arched his back and thrashed as he felt his windpipe squeezing shut and ragged gasps of air rasped over his tongue. He barely noticed the stream of urine running down his leg or the emptying of his bowels; only the horror of the fading light; the helplessness of the bound man hanging by the neck. His head felt swollen; fit to burst, and the cry his aching lungs yearned to release remained stifled under the noose.

The unfeeling darkness, when it finally came, was a welcome surrender.

In the seven days they had been in hiding, Dorigal's home had been searched twice by Infantrymen. The three fugitives had endured the heavy footfalls above while the homeowner had engaged the soldiers in light-hearted banter. There had been a moment when Dorigal had served tea at the table above and chatted away as Acastes and his friends hid beneath the boots of their pursuers.

Acastes' patience was wearing thin.

Hurried footsteps had all three men reaching for their swords. The table scraped away above them, and the rug was kicked into a heap

A moment later, the trap door was lifted and Dorigal appeared, looking down at them.

"What is it?" Kapaneus asked, seeing the look of deep concern on the man's face.

"There has been an incident at the gate," he said. "Come, we must talk."

They climbed out from the tiny basement and stared at Dorigal as the man paced across the kitchen.

"Valia arrived not an hour ago with her army," he began.

"Don't you mean *my* army?" Dachen asked.

"Does it matter?" Dorigal replied. "She arrived with a force numbering in the hundreds. My agent reached her in time to give warning but not before the gates were opened to the head of the army. At least seventy men and women have been captured. Valia and the rest of the army have fled, possibly to the south."

Acastes punched his fist into his open palm.

"At least she is safe for now," Kapaneus said, rubbing his chin in thought. "What of the captured soldiers?"

Dorigal looked from one man to the next.

"The word is out that you have until sunset to surrender yourselves," Dorigal replied. "After that time, the prisoners will be executed."

There was a long silence before Kapaneus spoke again.

"Where are they being held?" he asked.

"The Akharran."

"I will surrender myself," Dachen murmured.

"Don't be a fool, Dachen," Acastes warned. "They will not exchange seventy lives for one."

"They are my people," Dachen insisted.

"And ours too," Kapaneus replied. "Even if we surrender, there is no guarantee that Rogan will not go ahead and execute them all anyway."

"I am willing to take that chance."

Acastes shook his head and said, "They will want all of us."

"I could tell them that you escaped the city," Dachen suggested

"You will be tortured," Kapaneus warned. "They will find out soon enough that we are here, and you will give us up; Dorigal too, in time. Surrender is folly."

Dorigal nodded in agreement.

"We should be rallying support for Acastes," he said. "We should move before sunset and we should move quickly. I have been sowing rumours in all the right places over the past few days. You will find more support than you think, Acastes; in the Akharran in particular. Rogan has hand-chosen those he knows to be loyal to him to enforce his rule upon the city. The infantry-men on the streets and guarding the gates are those most likely to offer him their allegiance. Those remaining, un-posted; well, where their loyalty lies remains to be seen. But there is talk of un-happiness at the way Rogan has insinuated his way into power."

Dachen looked from one man to the next. "How is it that you command so much loyalty in this city, Acastes?" he asked.

The three other men exchanged looks and nodded in silent agreement.

Acastes sighed and said, "Because I am the son of the Kodistai. I am the sole heir of a dying ruler and stand to inherit ultimate power in Korathea."

Dachen gaped. "You are heir to the throne? Then why do you not command that those prisoners are freed!" he demanded. "Why have we been hiding in a cellar when you have this au-thority?"

"Because I do not want it!" Acastes spat.

Kapaneus nodded. "And there are those who would gladly take it from you if you will not grasp it," he warned.

"We have dedicated our lives to defending the bloodline," Dorigal murmured. "The time has come for you to choose; as-cendancy or exile."

Acastes slumped into a chair and buried his face in his hands.

"How many did we lose?" Valia asked.

What was left of the army was scattered along a stony beach, silent and despondent.

Adeyemi was nearby, staring out to sea, clutching that pouch he wore around his neck.

Only Tsering looked happy in his surroundings, exploring the rockpools at the edge of the water and poking under stones with a stick.

Marlon slumped down beside her onto the flat rock.

"Around sixty of Dachen's men and a half dozen Sisters. There are hunters missing too but there is no telling if they are in the city or not. Jon was inside the gates for certain, and no-one can find Elan." He sighed. "Almost all of those taken were on horseback."

Valia nodded. "Typical. We needed those horses."

Granger, Abbil and Nirmaya joined them as the sun neared the watery horizon.

"We have food enough for two days," Granger announced, his faced etched with worry. "After that, we will be going hungry unless we can resupply somewhere."

"Where?" Abbil grumbled. "Every homestead for miles around has been stripped bare. I have not seen so much as a rabbit for days. Kor'Habat was our last hope."

"It was the last hope for many," Granger sighed, wringing his hands as he glanced northward.

"What will happen to those people at the walls if the Khalim-Shar attacks?" Nirmaya asked.

"*When* the Khalim-Shar attacks," Valia whispered.

"There is nothing for them where they are," Abbil said. "No food, no sanctuary."

"Why not travel west?" Nirmaya asked. "Why not move to Dasar away from danger?"

Granger sighed again and said, "They put their faith in the walls of Kor'Habat to protect them. They still cling to that hope. Besides, the only way into Dasar is through that city."

"Not so," Marlon replied. "There is a bridge to the north across the River Habat."

"'Rascal's Crossing' is fifty miles away," Abbil laughed. "Three days on empty bellies to the bridge, and then how much longer beyond?"

"Better than starving where they lie," Marlon argued. "Or waiting for an army of Shar to tear them to pieces."

"Then they will provide a distraction while we fall upon the backs of the Shar!" Valia sneered.

"We cannot leave them there, lying like bait," Abbil replied, appalled. "They are people just as we are. They are not to blame for their predicament."

Valia spat onto the pebbles of the beach.

"Then they have every right to fight," she scowled.

"The women and children too?" Abbil asked.

"Better that than being slain like sheep in the field!" Valia replied.

Granger cleared his throat and interrupted the dispute.

"There has to be another way," he said.

"Perhaps a settlement could be negotiated," Abbil suggested, keeping a wary eye on Valia's glowering expression. "Some supplies in return for the refugees leaving Kor'Habat. Surely they would be willing to part with a little food to have their walls cleared of people."

"Who would negotiate such a thing?" Valia sneered. "They tried to kill us today; have you forgotten?"

"They could speak for themselves if encouraged."

"'Encouraged' by whom?"

"I could do it, Valia," Nirmaya volunteered, and all eyes fell on her. "I could urge the refugees to move and take them to Rascal's Crossing; and to negotiate with Kor'Habat."

"Why would you do this?" Valia wondered.

Nirmaya chewed on her bottom lip before saying, "It feels like the right thing to do; isn't that enough?"

Abbil shook his head.

"There are too many Easterners there who will not listen to the words of a girl," he said, and under her acid glare hurriedly corrected himself. "Woman! The words of a woman." He scratched at his beard. "I will come with you."

"Nirmaya," Granger said, "If you are to do this, take the Sisters with you. Those people will need protection on the road north."

"We will stay and fight!" she said in defiance. "I will urge those people to move, but I will not go with them. The battle will be here."

Granger placed a hand on her shoulder and looked into her eyes.

"To help people requires great sacrifices. You will have your chance to fight the Shar, but please; do this for me, and for those people."

When she eventually nodded in agreement, he turned his attention to Abbil. "And you, Abbil? Will you go with them?"

Abbil grumbled a little but nodded after a few moments' thought.

"We should be careful not to associate ourselves with those captured yesterday," he said. "Although word of Acastes, Kapaneus and Dachen would be welcome."

Granger nodded. "We cannot help them now, whatever fate has befallen them," he said. "We will know in time. Marlon?"

Marlon had grown quiet and was staring out to sea. He turned to face them and managed an evasive shrug.

"What about the rest of you," Nirmaya asked.

Valia drew her sword and checked its edge in the dying light.

"We will wait to give the Khalim-Shar the welcome it deserves."

Dachen approached the open gates of the Akharran, a fortress within a fortress, enclosed by walls thirty feet high. Beyond the gate lay a vast courtyard and the austere buildings that housed the Heavy Infantry. He held his hands wide to show that he was unarmed for the benefit of the waiting soldiers. The sun was setting, blood red over his left shoulder and the armour of the Heavy Infantry in front of him gleamed in the day's last light.

He walked through the arched gateway and heard the Infantrymen close rank behind him. Ahead was a vast courtyard in front of the imposing building beyond; a grey block of granite built with no thought for artistic flair and at least as high as the city walls. Two smaller buildings with pillared frontages occupied the other side of the courtyard. Smaller than the huge monolith they may have been, but they were each bigger than any single structure in Lokhara.

Braziers atop poles roared with yellow flame and released streams of sparks into a dimming sky.

Heavy Infantry and Eastern men loyal to Chapok formed a horseshoe into which he was shepherded. The circle closed at his back. At the centre, the forlorn shapes of his shackled men sat in rows with heads bowed.

There were also four stakes set into the ground. Three of them were occupied by Sangye, Pemba, and Kanchun; one remained empty. Dachen recognised them at once as garrotting posts. A loop of rope snaked around the throat of each of the condemned and passed through a hole in the post from where it could be twisted and tightened.

Chapok was seated on a chair which in turn was set upon a platform to raise his head above those of his subjects. He was smiling; greasy-lipped, and victorious.

"I have come to offer myself in return for the lives of my men," Dachen declared.

A blow to the small of his back had him sprawled in the dust, winded. He rolled to face his attacker and saw Jangbu, twirling his sparth and grinning as he prowled.

"Kneel before me," Chapok sneered.

Dachen rolled onto his front again and forced himself to stand on unsteady feet. "Never."

Another blow and he collapsed against the vacant post. He struggled to push himself upright again using the rough wood for balance. A huge Korathean man, resplendent in gleaming armour and blue-green cape stepped into the circle. He regarded Dachen for a moment before speaking.

"Where is Acastes?" he demanded.

"Rogan, why are you doing this?" he asked, recognising the Hatar at once.

The butt of Jangbu's sparth struck him in the ribs and Dachen went down again. Once more, he struggled upright.

"They escaped the city," he said, wincing as he felt his bruised ribs with his fingers.

"That is a lie," Rogan replied. "No-one has left the city; they are still here."

"I cannot help you. I was promised that my men would be freed if I gave myself up to you."

Rogan turned to Chapok and shrugged. "Do as you will with them," he said, and strode away to a waiting horse. He offered Dachen a final, defiant glance before riding out of the Akharran gates and into the city

Dachen returned his attention to Chapok.

"If you have any honour, Chapok, you will release these men."

"Then put your own neck in the noose and we will discuss the fate of those loyal to you," Chapok commanded.

Sangye shook his head.

"No, my prince," he whispered. "Do not do it."

Dachen looked from one to the next; all three men were silently urging him to disobey.

He took the loop of rope that passed through the post and opened it, pushing his head into the noose.

"No!" Kanchun shouted from the other end of the line.

"Now, free my men," Dachen winced as his hands were bound to the post at his back.

"After your ignominious death," Chapok replied. "I will give those who recently swore allegiance to you the chance to recant. If they do this, then they shall live. Those beside you have been in your service for too long and are tainted beyond redemption."

Dachen twisted his head to the side and counted his three faithful warriors. Then, beyond he saw Yeshe, among the circle of soldiers; smiling and eager.

"You will witness the fate of your men before your own noose chokes your worthless life from your body," Chapok said with a gleeful smile. Then he nodded and Jangbu made his way round to stand behind Kanchun.

Jangbu passed a short stave through the loop of rope at the back of the post and started to turn it.

Kanchun tensed, bracing himself for what was to come, fighting tears of terror that welled in his eyes.

"Kanchun!" Dachen called. "You are a true son of Tianpok! Your brothers will know of your honour; your father will greet you without shame in the afterlife! Chapok! Stop this!"

The rope began to bite as the slack was taken up by the twists in the rope.

Kanchun tensed every fibre in his body as he fought the coarse, biting hemp. A short, agonized cough escaped his throat as his windpipe was crushed by the tightening noose and a dark stain spread from his groin.

"Chapok!" Dachen shouted. "Stop!"

Cold water struck Jon in the face, at once soaking him and bringing him to full alert. He shook his head and looked at the shackle around his right wrist, holding it fast to the arm of the chair. The flesh was raw from his initial struggles, but that was not what had caused him to lose consciousness; the large nail through his left hand had done that.

The wooden block his hand had been nailed to was dark with old blood and bore the marks of many such nails before this one. He had been beaten on his way to this room and stripped naked by his captors. His clothes lay in a bloody heap in the corner under his round shield and leather armour. The silver skull that topped the hilt of his sword leered out at him from the pile.

He took a few long, ragged breaths while his torturer carried the empty bucket to the corner of the room. The huge man was whistling a tune as he returned and pulled up a chair of his own to sit face to face with his victim.

The torturer was bald with rotting teeth and breath like meat left in the sun too long.

"I have all night with you before you hang from the city walls in the morning," he said, leaning close and giving Jon an evil grin. "Like I said before; I will start gently and get more creative as we progress to morning."

He lifted Jon's little finger and raised it from the block. Jon groaned, fighting the urge to move his hand against the large-head-ed nail. He stifled a cry as the torturer bent the finger back and it pulled from its socket with a sickening pop.

"There, see," the man reassured him. "Nice and gentle."

Jon stared at his finger, protruding at a grotesque angle, and steadied his breathing.

"I'll never play the lyre again," he managed to say with a manic grin.

"Oh yes, good." The torturer looked pleased. "Fight the pain with humour; show me what a brave soldier you are. It is rare, but I do enjoy it so. All the sweeter for me when you are crying for your mother and begging for death. Now," he said, lifting Jon's ring finger, "where is Valia?"

John laughed. "You know that I could not possibly know that. I was well inside … *BASTARD!*"

The next finger popped from the knuckle and remained pointing skyward. His cry of agony turned to a bitter laugh and then a guttural growl.

"How could I know that?" he shouted, using the pain from his fingers to channel his anger. "She's out there somewhere. Go and find her yourself and give her my regards. You're just doing this because you enjoy it, you sick bastard!"

The torturer smiled back once John had finished shouting at

him.

"When all of the fingers are done on both hands," the torturer explained in a calm voice. "I will start cutting them off." He stood and walked to the table at the side of the room and retrieved a large set of shears. He pushed the points of the blades into the small brazier at the side of the table and returned to his seat. He glanced back at the shears and smiled. "So that you do not bleed to death. It seals the wounds," he explained. "After that I will show you what agony *really* is."

Jon's head lolled forward, and he teetered on the edge of unconsciousness as he felt his middle finger being lifted from the wooden block.

Kanchun's head lolled, doll-like when Jangbu allowed the coils to loosen and removed the stave from the loop of rope.

The hemp had torn the flesh around Kanchun's throat and blood oozed from his nose. Dead eyes bulged from purple, swollen flesh and the body sagged as low as its bonds would allow.

"Chapok! You coward!" Dachen screamed. "Stop this now!"

"Is that fear, brother?" Chapok replied. "You have seen how this traitor has died and fear for your own life."

Dachen fought against his bonds. "You were supposed to free them! It is me you want to kill. So, kill me now and be done!"

Chapok laughed. "No, brother. It is right that you should watch your men writhe on the garrotting post before joining them in death. Jangbu; if you please, a little slower with this next one."

Pemba braced himself, lips moving in a whisper while Jangbu moved behind him and placed the spar into the loop of rope. A tear trickled down the condemned man's cheek as he waited.

"Pemba, forgive me," Dachen called out, but Pemba did not reply, intent on whatever mantra he was uttering to make ready for his death.

Dachen's own vision blurred with tears as he looked skyward.

The creak of the tightening rope around Pemba's neck filled his ears and he was barely aware of the approaching hoofbeats...

Jon had bitten the inside of his mouth when his forefinger hand been snapped back, and the taste of his own blood brought a surge of bile into his throat. He coughed up the watery vomit and stared at his ruined hand.

"Thumbs," the torturer said as Jon settled again, "are far trickier I find. I prefer a simple clamp to crush the nail. The pain can be quite exquisite."

He held the little device in front of Jon's face.

A knock at the door interrupted the explanation and the torturer sighed in annoyance as he turned.

"Come!" he called out.

There was no answer and the door remained shut but a moment later there were three louds raps that echoed from the stone walls.

The torturer groaned in irritation but sauntered over to see who had disturbed his work.

Riders erupted through the Akharran gates and charged the circle of soldiers in the courtyard, breaking to left and right before the enormous horses could trample the startled men. The clattering of hooves on the stone flags resounded from the walls in a deafening clamour that drowned the shouts of the riders. Swords flashed in the fiery light of the braziers as the horsemen encircled those gathered for the executions.

"Who do you stand with?" a voice sounded out, echoing in the courtyard. "Who do you stand with? Acastes Fol'Denes! Acastes Fol'Denes; the rightful heir!"

"Kapaneus?" Dachen called out in the confusion.

The foot soldiers were pressed into a huddle in front of the garrotting posts at the centre of the circling horses. A few of the riders had dismounted and were working to free the manacled soldiers.

"Stop them!" Chapok shouted, jumping from his raised platform to get nearer to the sanctuary of his own soldiers.

Dachen felt his bonds being cut and he pulled the rope from his neck as fast as he could once his hands were free. He felt a surge of exhilarating relief as he stepped away from the post. Pemba stumbled away, gasping for breath with Sangye supporting him.

The cluster of soldiers that Chapok had forced his way into in his terror was heavily outnumbered by the circling riders.

"Stand with Acastes!"

Dachen saw Acastes for the first time, sword held high and resplendent in his polished armour as Infantrymen began emerging from the buildings of the Akharran.

"It was not locked," the torturer declared in annoyance as he pulled the heavy door open.

There was a strange thump and the torturer took a few backward steps into the room. When he turned it was with a look of complete shock, with an arrow sprouting from the centre of his chest. He took two steps towards Jon and fell to his knees. Behind him stood Elan, bow in hand.

Jon stared in disbelief. The pain must surely have addled his brain.

The jade-skinned man walked into the room and took in Jon's predicament. Elan unscrewed the bolt on the manacle holding Jon's right hand until it was almost open; then he paused. He inspected the contorted left hand, nailed to the block.

Elan gripped the little finger of Jon's left hand and pulled it out as he laid it flat again. Jon howled in pain and fought to free his right hand so that he could punch the Lythurian away, but he was held fast. Elan worked each finger one at a time to howls of anger and agony.

"You little bastard!" Jon shouted as Elan retuned to the manacle. Another turn and Jon's right hand was free. He stared at his swollen left hand and the heavy wooden block that he was attached to. The head of the nail was broad and flat.

Elan moved to the table and raked through the various torture devices until he found a pair of slender shears. He returned to Jon's hand and in a moment had cut the head of the nail from its shank.

Jon grimaced as he tried to lift his hand free.

"Brace yourself, Jon," he murmured to himself and shut his eyes. "One, two…"

Before he could utter another word, Elan had grabbed his wrist and pulled his swollen hand over the nail.

"SON OF A WHORE!" he bellowed, taking a wild swipe at Elan with his right fist.

Elan stepped away and avoided the wayward blow with ease. He gathered Jon's clothes, sword and shield from the floor and placed them on the chair the torturer had previously occupied. Jon staggered to his feet and muttered vague thanks to his rescuer who stood and waited, head cocked to one side listening to a distant, rising clamour.

"Sons of Shol'Hara! Soldiers of the Akharran!" Acastes declared as Infantrymen spilled from the vast, granite barracks. "Stand with me!"

The Infantrymen had appeared, still buckling on their armour, ready to fend off an invasion. Instead they found themselves in the middle of an insurrection whose factions were yet unknown.

"What is this?" an Infantryman shouted. "Where is the Steward of Kor'Habat?"

"Rogan has lied to you!" Kapaneus shouted over the noise. "He has seized power in the city and wages war against our allies. The Shar army is coming! We must stand as one!"

While Acastes spread word among the Infantrymen, the newly liberated Eastern men were arming themselves from the bundles of sparths deposited by some of the riders.

"Chapok!" Dachen shouted in rage, lowering his sparth. "Face me, brother!"

The tight rank of sparth-bearers that had formed around King Chapok closed a little tighter. He had around thirty men around him while Dachen's men numbered more than fifty.

"Do not make me do this, Chapok!" Dachen called. "Show yourself!"

Jangbu stepped from the back of the defensive formation and placed the butt of his sparth on the ground.

"Will you face me, *Prince* Dachen?" he sneered.

Dachen glared at Jangbu and spat in the dust in front of him. "The coward sends another to fight in his stead. So be it."

"I have bested you before, young prince," Jangbu laughed, "and I will gladly do it again. But be warned; defeat upon this field means death."

Sangye appeared at Dachen's side but the Prince placed a firm hand on his shoulder and pushed him back.

Jangbu laughed. "Brave. I could take you both if you wish it."

Dachen lunged as the final word left Jangbu's lips. The jab was parried but he used the momentum to spin, sliding a hand to the midpoint of the sparth and jabbing the pointed butt at Jangbu's head. Jangbu ducked and rolled, coming up onto his feet in a defensive stance with a blood-thirsty smile on his face.

"Too slow, little prince," he laughed, and attacked Dachen, whirling the sparth about him like a quarterstaff.

Dachen met the attack with blinding speed, dancing across the dust and spinning as defence turned to attack and back to defence. Sparks flew when metal struck metal as the long blades flashed in the firelight. To either side, soldiers held their positions; facing each other across the duelling ground while the two men fought.

The tell-tale sound of hundreds of boots marching in quick unison signalled the arrival of yet more Heavy Infantry. They entered through the open gates with shields held across their chests and swords bared. They broke left and right as squads took defensive positions across the exit from the courtyard; hundreds of men drawn from all parts of the city.

Moments later, Rogan rode through from the rear and reined in his horse in front of his men.

"What is the meaning of this?" he roared.

Acastes rode to meet him and pulled his own horse to a halt some yards away. "I claim my right to succeed the Kodistai," he declared. "I am his sole heir and rightful successor!"

"You have no proof!" Rogan shouted for all to hear. "It is hearsay; no more."

"Yet you try to have me arrested! You condemn innocent men to death! Allies in our fight against the Shar; you are a traitor, Rogan!"

"Enough!" Rogan shouted in rage. "Seize them!"

The Infantrymen locked shields and advanced past Rogan towards Acastes.

Behind Acastes, a thousand more were spurred into action.

Dachen was barely aware of the confrontation a hundred yards away at the gate. The speed of Jangbu's attacks was taking every grain of concentration. He ducked, and the blade scythed over his head followed an instant later by a downward strike with the pointed butt, then a slicing motion that glanced past his shoulder.

Jangbu was fast; the finest warrior in the Eastern kingdoms, and he knew it. He brimmed with confidence, parrying Dachen's attacks with ease and striking back with terrifying speed and accuracy.

A blow struck Dachen on the knuckles and he released the sparth with that hand. Jangbu was quick to attack again, and this time Dachen lost his grip and watched as the sparth tumbled away.

His opponent paused and smiled.

"Defeated again, little prince," he said, bringing the point of the sparth to Dachen's chest.

Sangye stepped forward but Dachen held up a hand, eyes still locked on Jangbu.

Dachen inched forward and pressed his chest against the point. He glared at Jangbu for a moment as if daring him to drive it home. Then he turned, rolling as he moved forward to push the sparth aside. He dropped low and rolled over in the dust to reach his weapon again and swung it at Jangbu's ankles. Jangbu jumped to avoid the blade and counter-attacked with a downward swipe that struck the ground where Dachen had been a moment earlier.

The fight resumed with a new ferocity. Dachen fell back, barely aware of the shallow cut that appeared across his chest as he evaded a killing blow, nor the cut on his arm from when he had been the blink-of-an-eye too slow in parrying an attack moment earlier. He was numb to the pain; he was one with the sparth, a mind guiding a weapon. He reacted without thought, acted on instinct and the memories of thousands of hours of training and practice.

But Jangbu fought like a hurricane; speed, power and fury driven by pride and hate, always a little quicker, always a little stronger.

Pockets of Infantrymen loyal to Rogan formed among the gathering sea of bodies. Fights broke out which led to steel being drawn and soon Infantryman fought Infantryman upon the very soil where they had once trained together.

Those who had chosen to follow Rogan were forced towards the gate where they joined the ranks of their fellows.

The mounted soldiers formed a line and advanced on the growing ranks at the gate. Still more soldiers poured from the buildings and were forced to decide in a heartbeat who they would support; Rogan, the Steward of Kor'Habat or the newly revealed heir to the Kodistai's throne, if he was to be believed at all.

There was still a reluctance to fight their brothers, even though blood had already been spilled in those early clashes. Calls to hold back and sheath weapons sounded out in the chaos and two opposing armies formed up mere yards from one another.

Chapok watched the fight from behind his defensive soldiers and saw the developing stand-off between factions of the Heavy Infantry.

"Kill him," he urged, watching Jangbu and Dachen hurl themselves at one another. "End this," he said, pushing another sparth bearer forward.

The startled man stumbled forward and found himself very much in the fight. He struck out at Dachen who deflected the blow and countered with a strike that slashed the soldier's throat. Blood sprayed from the wound and the soldier fell back, but Dachen had been distracted for that one, short heartbeat and Jangbu pounced.

The point of the sparth speared into Dachen's shoulder and he lost his grip on his own weapon. Jangbu drove Dachen back on the pointed blade until he stumbled onto his back, then lifted the sparth to drive home into Dachen's chest.

At the last possible moment, Jangbu leaned back as an arrow hissed past his chest. Dachen lifted a foot and kicked upwards, throwing Jangbu back as he rolled away.

There was a scream from the gathered soldiers and Chapok stumbled from their midst. The arrow that had been meant for Jangbu had struck the King instead, entering his left eye and exiting at his temple. He collapsed onto his hands and knees with blood pouring from his ruined eye.

"My King," Jangbu cried out, throwing down his sparth.

At once, Dachen's men closed on Chapok's and the Eastern men stood facing each other, awaiting orders.

Chapok cried out as Jangbu touched the arrow and he waved the man's hands away. Dachen stared at his stricken brother even as he was helped to his feet. He knew that strange arrow; it was one of Elan's.

He looked back in the direction he judged the arrow to have come from, and found Elan standing, with an arrow nocked, watchful and ready. At his side was Jon with his sword and shield in hand.

Chapok cried out again and rolled onto his back in the dry, bloody dust. Jangbu snapped the shaft of the arrow and threw it aside. He bared his teeth and glared at Dachen, breathing hard.

"Sons of Shol'Hara!" a shout went up, resounding within the walls of the Akharran; it was the voice of Acastes. "Men of the East! We face a greater threat than that which you see before you. The Khalim-Shar is coming! Unite or fall!"

"Under whose banner?" an Infantryman from Rogan's side called out.

Acastes now saw that the banner of the house Fol'Brandam, a castle against a low, yellow sun had been raised. He looked back over his shoulder and saw the Eastern men who were facing each other in the courtyard. He looked at the men who had rallied behind him and were confronting their brothers from the Akharran.

He saw Rogan, sitting proud upon his horse with an army arrayed about him.

"Every banner!" Acastes called out. "And none! Stand together as men! Defenders of our lands and lives! Defenders of the ones we love! Raise banners from here to Eritania, each a different hue, I do not care, but stand!"

He stared down at the Infantrymen as he rode along their line, then fixed his eye on Rogan. "Kill me for a charlatan if you will, but know this; When the Shar come, and they will, would you sooner have my sword arm in the grave or at your side?"

There was a silence within the Akharran that echoed.

"The time for games is past, there is too much to do!" he shouted. "What will it be?"

Rogan glared back at Acastes for a long time before he finally nodded. He turned his horse and steered it through the gates of the Akharran.

His men followed, breaking ranks with cautious watchful eyes on their brothers across the gap.

Kapaneus arrived at Acastes' side and watched the Infantrymen leave. "You never cease to amaze me, Acastes," he said at last.

Acastes grunted. "Just wait and see how much wine I drink tonight," he replied, and breathed out for what felt like the first time in an age.

Behind them, Chapok was being lifted, crying, onto a litter. They watched the king being hurried from Akharran, surrounded by his soldiers.

Left to stand alone in the centre, one man, Jangbu, glared at Dachen with unrestrained hatred.

Dachen turned his back on the man and walked away, surrounded by the men loyal to him, to nurse his own wounds.

CHAPTER 17

The twelve men who made up the Council of Hatars gathered in their chamber late in the night. They each wore the topknot associated with their rank although the hair of each was streaked with varying amounts of grey.

"We condemned them on the word of your man," Bravik said; the accusation in his voice was clear.

"*My* man?" Rogan replied. "You were all just as keen to believe him if it meant justice being done on the 'Bitch of Hadaiti'. Do not lay that blame at my door."

"Valia is the least of our worries," Gilean argued. "With her being outside the city, a more immediate problem is currently locked inside the Akharran with half of the bloody Heavy Infantry!"

"Really, Rogan," Hatar Morgarth Fol'Garras scolded, "was it wise to leave him there?"

Rogan leaned towards Morgarth who was far enough away to avoid being struck, and growled, "He had several thousand men at his back. Just be grateful that they are contained while we consider our next move."

"How could he command their loyalty so quickly?" Gilean asked. "He has barely been in Kor'Habat in years."

Rogan nodded. "There have been rumours for many years of an heir to the Kodistai's throne," he replied.

"We have all heard them. *Is* he the Kodistai's heir?" Bravik asked.

"He has certainly been protected," Rogan muttered. "Held back from the frontline at Ara Dasari; spared active service and constantly followed by that blasted Kapaneus."

"But he is of Shol'Hara," Gilean said, spreading his hands.

"A bastard then at best," Rogan agreed.

"But, without evidence, he can lay no claim," Bravik said. "And the Kodistai himself has never spoken of an heir."

"We also have the word of your Captain Silman implicating his companions in an attack upon the Heavy Infantry," Gilean added.

Rogan looked up in annoyance at having Silman's statement pinned to him again. "I will question Captain Silman again myself. His recollections of the attack may have been clouded. It happens in battle. For now, I suggest we continue constructing our defences and keep the gates to the Akharran firmly shut. Perhaps with time his claim to the throne will ring false in the ears of his followers."

The Hatars nodded in agreement and concluded the meeting, going their separate ways.

Rogan remained alone, staring out at the night sky as though the answer lay in the stars.

Dachen walked along the edge of the Akharran training ground and watched the Heavy Infantry spar. The enormous soldiers swung their training swords with enough force to break the bones of lesser men.

"Has the two-hundred-year peace softened us, Sangye?" he asked of his companion. "When did we come to rely on the strength of others to protect our people?"

"How is your wound, my prince?" Sangye replied after a long moment.

Dachen's right arm was strapped across his chest and his

shoulder wrapped in linen bandages.

"My shoulder will heal quickly," he replied. "But my pride will take a little longer."

"The fight was not fair," Sangye insisted. "You were unbalanced by King Chapok's actions."

Dachen smiled. "It is not the fight with Jangbu that has left the deepest cuts; rather it is the loss of our lands. Could it be that we had lost the ability to defend ourselves? So long without conflict has left us wanting."

Sangye shook his head.

"No, my prince," he replied. "the Great Tournaments ensure our readiness."

Dachen scoffed. "Games? Every four years? Is that enough to keep an army honed? For centuries, the Lesser Kingdoms fought Khumjang, in defence and attack. Khumjang never had the strength to fight on three fronts and so our kingdoms survived. We were jackals biting at the heels of a tiger; not strong enough to face it down alone but wise enough to know that when the tiger turned to face one, another would strike from behind. That balance kept us strong."

"And millions died over the centuries," Sangye replied. "Surely the peace has served us better. And we proved ourselves to be fine warriors at the Great Tournament at Myampor; equal or better than Khumjang's own. You should have been champion at the last games."

"Perhaps," Dachen said without conviction. "But Jangbu beat me then as he did yesterday."

"He fights without honour," Sangye insisted. "A fine warrior, no doubt, but cruel with it. Perverted."

"How befitting then that he has found his way into my brother's service," Dachen muttered, wondering at the circumstances that had brought the warrior from Khumjang to Tianpok to stand at Chapok's side.

"The fletcher is coming." Sangye alerted Dachen to Jon's

approach.

"Good morning, gentlemen," Jon said with a grin and nodded at Dachen's shoulder. "I trust that is not your dominant hand; only, the whorehouses are all outside these walls, and well..." He made a vulgar hand motion and chuckled.

Dachen ignored the obscene gesture and instead pointed to Jon's own injury.

"You should certainly know," he said in response.

Jon held up his swollen left hand. "Still, less of a hindrance than my wife," Jon grumbled.

Dachen laughed. "One wonders why you ever married," he said. "I hear you denigrate this poor woman daily, yet none of us has ever seen her. Is she a figment of your imagination?"

"Count yourself a lucky man," Jon replied. "And no, she is no figment."

"Then, where is she? You have been away from home for so long, perhaps she has left you for another man."

"Then whoever he is, he has my sympathies," Jon muttered, "and my heartfelt thanks."

Dachen rolled his eyes. "Is Acastes' claim true?" he asked. "*Is he the heir to the Korathean throne?*"

Jon shrugged. "Acastes? Heir to the throne? Doesn't seem right," he replied, looking unconvinced. "I don't know what to believe. All the same, it got us all out of a tight squeeze, wouldn't you say?"

"Indeed," Dachen agreed, then quietened as a dark expression took hold of his face. "Too late for Kanchun..."

"I am sorry about your man," Jon murmured in a rare show of compassion.

"A fine and loyal warrior; he will be missed."

"Hello," Jon said, in a brighter tone and nodding towards the training ground. "What have we got here?"

Acastes had entered the large square and was dressed in the light clothing favoured by the Infantrymen for sparring purposes.

Those men who were training paused their bouts to watch, and a stillness spread across the vast courtyard.

Acastes picked a man at random and squared off opposite his reluctant opponent. They circled for a few moments before Acastes attacked with the heavy, wooden training sword. The Infantryman parried the blow but did not counterattack, returning to a defensive pose when Acastes paused.

Acastes attacked again and the soldier defended, edging backwards under the raining blows.

"Attack!" Acastes shouted, spreading his arms wide as his opponent recovered into a defensive pose once more.

"Fight!" Acastes yelled.

The man made a reluctant lunge which Acastes deflected with ease before a crashing blow to the arm knocked the sword from his hand, and he backed away.

"Will no-one fight me?" Acastes challenged all within earshot.

The soldiers stared at the ground.

"I command you to fight me!" Acastes yelled, attacking another soldier.

The man defended several blows before the training sword struck him in the ribs and he went down on one knee, winded.

Acastes threw his wooden sword on the ground and stormed from the courtyard.

"They will not fight their king," Dachen observed. "They believe, even if you do not."

Nirmaya led the small party on horseback through the sprawl of refugees. The Sisters had stayed far enough away to not be seen from the city gates since leading a small army of women could well identify her as an ally of Valia, and that would have got her killed. Fiery-haired Maidra was at her side now, glaring at the crowds that were being drawn towards them. The stench of human waste was not masked by the smoke from innumerable fires that smouldered within the vast encampment and each breath brought a fresh urge to be sick.

Abbil rode just behind, hunched down in his saddle.

"Keep your wits about you, girl," he muttered. "These people are not to be trusted."

"They are desperate, Abbil." Maidra scolded. "Would you be any better?"

"Not *these* people," Abbil replied. "It is those behind the gates I am concerned about."

The huge gates of wood and strap iron were shut ahead; closed against the threat of infiltration by throngs of the destitute as they sought a meal and safety. The false hope offered by the great walls of Kor'Habat kept the ruined peoples rooted to that squalid place, and if they did not move soon, they would die there, yards from sanctuary.

Nirmaya dismounted and banged on the gate, before exchanging looks with Maidra and Abbil as they waited, until the shout of, "Who goes?" was heard from the battlements above.

"I have come to negotiate for the resettlement of these people to the west of Kor'Habat," she shouted up to the soldier above her.

There was laughter from the top of the wall.

"Who put a girl in charge?" the soldier called out.

"Hear her proposal, fool!" Abbil shouted. "Or the blood of thousands will be on *your* hands when the Shar come."

There was a pause.

"Very well," the soldier replied. "I will send word to the Steward, but I do not hold much hope of him giving time to this; he is a busy man. Wait where you are. Make yourselves comfortable."

There was more laughter as the soldier vanished from view.

Nirmaya sighed and climbed back into her saddle to find two filthy women staring up at her. Their dresses were stained and ripped in places, but they both wore defiant expressions.

Both carried swords at their hips.

"Are you Nirmaya Suun?" one asked.

Nirmaya glanced at the gate, wishing that the woman had a quieter voice.

"Is it true that you ride with Valia of Hadaiti?" the woman persisted.

"Why do you ask?" Nirmaya replied.

"We heard that you led an army of women; the *Sisters*," the other said.

Nirmaya looked from one to the other.

"Do you have a quarrel with her," Nirmaya asked, eyeing the swords they carried.

The first shook her head.

"No. We would join her," she said. "I have my husband's sword. He died of fever two weeks south of this place. We were fleeing our home."

"This sword was my father's," the second woman said. "I can fight. *We* can fight."

Nirmaya watched as one by one, women approached. Widows and mothers who were tired of hiding; tired of running; tired of putting their safety in the hands of others; tired of waiting for men to act!

"Will you have us?" the first asked. "We would join the Sisters; we have nothing left."

"I…" she began, but then stared as word rippled through the camps and women came; in ones and twos, holding swords or axes, each had a story of pain and sorrow etched in lines and grime across their faces.

But each held a shared knowledge that they would never be cowed again.

Together, they had strength.

The small fishing village was perhaps half a day's ride from Kor'Habat. The settlement had been deserted ever since the flood of refugees from the south had swept the inhabitants northward with raw tales of the approaching horror. Four days since the ill-fated attempt to enter Kor'Habat, news trickled in from scouts and small groups of exiles.

That news was never good.

The Shar had landed in Pashwar too and had swept west into Dashiya all but unchecked. Hunger had driven Valia's small army to this village where they had found the means to feed themselves for a while. The first catch glittered as it thrashed on the deck of the small fishing boat that had returned to the stone pier.

"Is that it?" Valia asked, unimpressed by the efforts of the Eastern soldiers.

"I only said that I was raised in a fishing village," a soldier protested in a heavy accent. "I am no fisherman, and these waters are shallow; perhaps if we search further out to sea in the deeper waters."

"These reefs are no more than a nursery for the deep waters," Granger said in defence of the Eastern man. "But it is a start. How many boats are still out?"

"Six," came the reply, "but we are soldiers, not fishermen."

"I hate fish," Valia grumbled as she turned and stormed from the pier into the village.

Granger hurried to follow her. "The men are doing their best, Valia," he scolded. "A word of encouragement now and then would not go amiss."

Valia grunted and quickened her pace. They passed the old apothecary where Tsering had been ensconced since their arrival. A strong smell emanated from the building and Granger held his breath as they passed the building. He could not fathom what the old alchemist was doing with all those powders and unguents, and there was no point in asking. A crazed laugh and a knowing wink were Tsering's preferred answer to any question, and in a way that was more unnerving than ignorance alone. Granger struggled to keep up with her until they reached the old tavern where a temporary command post had been established. Marlon was inspecting a large map spread across a table while Adeyemi pointed to an area on the parchment.

"What did you find?" she asked.

Adeyemi looked up from the map.

"I travelled two days to the south," he said. "I met small group of people from the town of Kernhalt. They say that their town had planned to surrender to an advancing army but that *they* had chosen to leave."

"How big an army?" she demanded. "Did they say?"

Adeyemi nodded.

"They said ten thousand," Adeyemi replied with a frown. "Mostly Eastern men but some Dashiyans and Pashwari; Shar too."

"They told you this?" Valia asked.

Adeyemi managed a half smile.

"They were afraid of me at first, but soon realised that I am just a man." He shrugged. "So now Dashiyans and Pashwari fight for the Shar?"

"Perhaps they had no choice," Marlon suggested. "Swear fealty to the new master or die."

"We all have a choice," Valia scowled. "Too many choose poorly."

Marlon bit back a response and looked down at the map instead. "How long does that give us?" he wondered.

"That depends on how eager they are to reach Kor'Habat," Granger suggested.

"They will want to arrive with the Khalim-Shar," Valia said. "Two armies become one."

Granger puffed out his cheeks. "And we are in the way of one of those armies."

Valia stared at the map and traced the line of a road that led south from their position.

"What do your *portents* say about this, Adeyemi?" Valia murmured.

"I do not look for them," he replied, unaware of the scorn in her voice. "My time grows short and I would sooner not know."

"We have time," she said, ignoring Adeyemi's ominous tone. "This area is forested; it is Arkam's wood, is it not?"

Marlon squinted his good eye and nodded. "Yes, it is," the man agreed.

"It has not rained in weeks," Valia murmured. "It will be tinder dry. We wait until the army is within the trees, and then we burn it."

"Burn Arkam's wood?" Marlon replied. "Are you mad?"

Valia's eyes gleamed with imagined fire.

"We block the road and burn them all."

"Ten thousand men?" Marlon asked. "With their cooks, farriers, smiths and washerwomen? *Burn them all?*"

"They have all made their choices," Valia murmured, staring at the map.

Marlon stormed from the room but Valia barely glanced at his back.

After a long silence, Granger spoke. "Valia," he began. "Have you spoken to Marlon?"

"Of course I have," she snapped.

"Then have you listened to him?" he asked.

"What foolishness is this?"

"Valia, you need to talk to that man. He risked everything for you."

She glowered at Granger for a moment before replying. "We are *all* risking everything, Granger. We are at war if you failed to notice."

"You are stubborn, Valia," Granger scolded. "And you have lost the art of listening, that is for certain."

"Listening to whom?"

"Anyone who offers advice," he replied.

"I hear your *advice*," she sneered.

"Then perhaps it is yourself you should hear!" he snapped back at her.

"What is that supposed to mean?"

"I am sorry," he apologised at once, "but you need to speak with Marlon. The eye of a friend is often the best mirror."

Valia shook her head, glancing from Granger to Adeyemi and back to Granger again.

"I swear, you speak in riddles simply to vex me," she scowled and shook her head. "Very well," she said at last. "I will talk with him.

She walked from the room into bright daylight and set about looking for Marlon. She had a good idea as to where he would be.

Tents filled every gap available between the simple houses of the village as the population had risen to four times its capacity. The ringing of a hammer on steel guided Valia to the smithy where she found Marlon working beside the blazing heat of the newly rekindled forge.

He was shirtless under the leather apron and sweating from his efforts. A crude blade was taking shape beneath his hammer, glowing yellow and cooling through shades of orange until he plunged it into the forge once more. Several cold pieces lay on a bench awaiting his attention.

She lifted a jug from the window ledge and poured the water into a cup.

"I forgot to tell you; they have caught some fish," she remarked in an apathetic tone after swallowing a few mouthfuls of water.

"Then we will eat," Marlon replied above the ringing of his hammer.

"I hate fish," she replied, taking another long drink.

Marlon paused. "It is better than starvation," he observed.

"Barely," came the muttered reply.

Marlon turned to face her. "Those people outside the city would not see it so."

"They are a distraction, nothing more," she replied. "When

405

Nirmaya fails, and the Shar have their eyes fixed upon those people, then we hold the advantage."

"How so?"

"Their backs will be turned, and we will crush them against the walls of Kor'Habat."

"And the innocent with them," Marlon muttered. "Even if we survive the burning of Arkam's wood, we will still be hopelessly outnumbered!"

"Then we should not give our lives cheaply," she snarled.

"With thousands of innocent people killed; used as bait to distract the enemy."

"Do you not understand," Valia said. "There is no escaping this war."

"But they did not bring this upon themselves."

"Nor did I!" Valia retorted. "No amount of tenderness will defeat the Shar."

"*Tenderness?*" Marlon gaped. "I have no tenderness in my heart for those creatures. My own brother was among the first to fall to them; have you forgotten about Foley?"

Valia looked away, unwilling to meet his gaze and he went on, his voice a sad murmur.

"Little wonder that you have forgotten the dead already when you have such little regard for the living."

Valia groaned. "And how does mourning the dead help the living?" she demanded. "You of all people must see that our resolve must be unshakeable; our determination absolute."

Marlon took three slow steps to the bench, which was littered with cold steel, yet unfinished. He lifted one.

"Do you see this?" he asked. "This steel is hard. It will hold the keenest of edges and it will cut deep." He placed it on the anvil and brought his hammer down upon it.

With a peal that split the air, the unfinished blade shattered, scattering fragments across the ash and dust of the smithy floor."

"That is what becomes of a blade that is too hard!" he roared, startling Valia with his passion. "I can make swords of steel so hard that they never lose their edge; but they *shatter* every time without fail, Valia!" He glared at her as his shoulders heaved with every laboured breath. At last his shoulders relaxed and his voice softened. "Steels needs temper just as courage demands compassion. Where are you Valia? I thought that I had found you. Every day that you were lost, I felt you, drawing me nearer." He shook his head. "Now that you are here, you have never felt so distant." He tossed his hammer onto the bench and sank down onto the low wall surrounding the forge. "What happened to you?"

She stared at the grey steel fragments on the ground and eventually her eyes found his.

"I learned that there are fates worse than death," she replied without emotion. "I saw people, drained of all empathy or goodness using their stolen influence to take what they desired. I see now that *right* and *wrong* are illusions; there is only *struggle*. Everything I try to hold close to me is torn from my grasp. If I am not allowed keep a single thing that I hold dear to me then I choose to release it all. I give it all away for the chance to strike at those who would attack me. Revenge is all I have left. I have tried to fill the void and failed. In my moments of weakness, I have tried to embrace those gentle things that others hold so naturally, but always they slip from the grasp, or are torn from it. Mine must be a different path to contentment. I will find balance in death when my last breath escapes me atop the bodies of my enemies." She raised a clenched fist before her and glared at her old companion. Her voice became firmer. "I have been hardened beyond feeling. I am vengeance, Marlon. I am the blade; I am steel."

She lowered her fist and held Marlon's eye for a long moment before walking away towards the sea. Marlon watched her vanish into the throng of soldiers and tents, and a single tear rolled down his dusty cheek.

The Steward of Kor'Habat had not deigned to meet her in

person, but a clerk sent to speak with her had been charged with reaching a bargain. In the end, twelve carts loaded with flour was all that Kor'Habat would spare for them.

Twelve carts of flour for over two hundred thousand people. An insult. There had been fights when the bags were distributed; blood was spilled, and several people had been killed as desperation had unleashed a madness in the starving refugees.

That was behind them now, and the road north lay ahead.

"At this rate it will take four days at least to reach the crossing," Abbil grumbled. He was walking beside his horse while three skinny children sat on its back, wide-eyed and hollow-cheeked. "And two full days to get these people over the bridge."

Nirmaya looked back down the ragged procession as it snaked away back to the south and the hazy walls of Kor'Habat. Camps were still breaking and waiting to join the road.

"So many people," she breathed. "How are we meant to protect a column over twenty miles long?"

"The Sisters have grown in number," Abbil observed. "How many have come to you? A thousand or more?"

"Most can barely hold a sword," Nirmaya replied. She chewed her lip for a moment. "Granger had never intended for me to protect these people. He wanted me out of the way; to protect *me*."

"I am sure that was not his intention," Abbil assured her.

"He does not think that the Sisters can fight the Shar."

"Have you ever faced one?" he asked.

Nirmaya sniffed. "Not yet," she muttered. "But I will, and I will prove my worth to her."

"To whom?"

Nirmaya glowered ahead at the road, while Abbil chuckled.

The huge walls of Kor'Habat were punctuated by flanking towers, positioned every 200 yards. The towers offered the only access to the battlements and could be sealed off to isolate any would-be attackers should they successfully scale the wall. Any force reaching the top of the wall would then be within range of the bowmen on the towers, and vulnerable to the volleys of arrows that would surely follow. Each tower rose twenty feet higher than the walls themselves and were forty feet across.

This restricted access to the battlements meant that the materials needed for the defensive war engines had to be hauled up the side of the walls using a system of ropes and pulleys. Engineers worked day and night on top of the towers, constructing the fiendish mechanisms under the Eastern engineers' guidance in a race against time.

"It could be worse," Kapaneus observed. "We could be hauling timber up that wall."

Acastes drained his wine cup and filled it again from the jug. They were sitting at a small table outside one of the smaller buildings in the Akharran.

"It would be better than this prison," Acastes glowered.

"Hardly a prison," Kapaneus remarked.

"We are locked in," Acastes scoffed. "Define for me a different prison."

Kapaneus laughed. "You have wine in place of shackles."

"And a captor who refuses to negotiate."

"You have half the army in here with you," Kapaneus insisted. "Rogan will negotiate."

Acastes sighed and stared into the dark wine. "The life of a Shar-hunter was a simpler one was it not?"

Kapaneus nodded and sat back in his chair. "If one could ignore the constant threat of death," he replied.

"At least we were free. Travelling wherever we wanted; listening for tell of another Shar to kill; discerning fact from fancy from the gossip and hearsay of travellers and merchants. The race to be there before another hunter could take the commission, the thrill of the hunt. The wine and the women."

"You have wine here," Kapaneus observed.

"But you are no full-bodied maid, my friend," Acastes grieved.

His friend chuckled as Acastes went on. "I did not want this, you know. Of course, you do; I have told you often enough. In coming here, I have sown discord among the Heavy Infantry; driven a wedge into the midst of the Sons of Shol'Hara. Perhaps I should renounce my claim and unite them once more. Kor'Habat needs unity as it never has done before and my coming here has divided it."

"It is your *right* to be here," Kapaneus insisted. "Your blood is as much a part of this great city as the stone of its walls. The strength of your line has held Kor'Habat, undefeated for a thousand years. If you fail, then so does the city."

Acastes stared into his wine. "What banner did Rogan ride in under?" he asked.

"Fol'Brandam," Kapaneus replied. "A prohibited symbol."

Acastes nodded.

"Old but not forgotten," he said. "The Fol'Gannity crest is of crossed swords across a broken shield, the Fol'Maddons marched under a winged ram's head and the Fol'Garras' under the three golden cups. My family banner displays an armoured fist against a field of red. Of course, I have taken the name of my mother's line since the Kodistai is of no family, and of *all* families. I am fatherless.'

"Centuries ago, the Kodistai of the time could see how the bloodlines would divide the nation and how pride in symbols stood in the way of a truly *united* Korathea. A new banner was needed to bind all families together. The Korathean banner is one of plain blue-green; a blend of sky, land and sea; a new banner that all could rally beneath; family squabbles could be forgotten.

"The Kodistai has no name. His family disowns him, and he becomes the one and only true Korathean, with no ties to any line. Referring to the Kodistai by his given name carries a heavy price and many have paid it. A simple slip of the tongue can send a law-abiding Korathean to the top of the wall, with a short drop and sudden stop to follow. Such is the price of unity.

"That Rogan can raise his family banner at all shows how divided we have become. Men are willing to fight for a bloodline again, not their homes or their loved ones or their nation, but for a *line*. You are no better of course. You are a true believer, as was Doroman and countless other deluded souls in your secret society."

"What is the point in this history lesson? We are sworn to protect the heir," Kapaneus replied, clearly irritated by Acastes' tone.

"You are sworn to protect the *bloodline*." Acastes replied. "If I were a gibbering fool, would you still put me on the throne? If I was a madman? Yes, I think that you would. You would erase Acastes Fol'Denes and name me Kodistai, tethering me to that blasted palace and all its confounded politicking. You could still visit the inns and taverns as you please, and for a few coppers buy the companionship of a willing maid. Not me. Acastes would be dead and the Kodistai would sit, sullen and alone in his stead. This is the curse of the *bloodline*."

Kapaneus regarded his friend for a moment. "The wine has made you maudlin," he said at last.

Acastes filled his cup again.

"Then I will drink until I come clean out the other side," he muttered, returning his gaze to the work on the battlements.

CHAPTER 18

Nirmaya led the procession of refugees towards the bridge over the River Habat. The journey had taken even longer than she had feared, and after six days with little to eat her belly felt hollow and raw. She allayed the stabbing cramps with water, but that would not work for much longer. Some of the pack horses had already been slaughtered, their cargoes left at the roadside and their bones stripped bare. There were just too many mouths to feed.

What flour they had been given had not gone far, as expected, but even a morsel of that bland bread would have been a welcome feast. They had scoured the woods and countryside for berries and mushrooms as they travelled, which had slowed their progress further, but the little tidbits had kept low morale from dragging them to a standstill.

Scouts sent ahead had declared Rascal's Crossing safe, but Nirmaya still eyed the trees to either side as the forest closed around them. The road became narrower as it rose into the foot-hills of the Lesser Cascus mountains; soft soil giving way to grey rock beneath their feet.

"We should be at the bridge soon," Maidra said. "Then it is downhill into Dasar."

"How many will not make it that far?" Nirmaya pondered.

"Some of the old are refusing to eat; they say that they will not take food when children go hungry."

Nirmaya nodded. "How many have died?"

"I would hate to count the exact number, hundreds though. The sick and the old are faring badly." Maidra replied. "Their loved ones do not have the strength to bury them. They cover the bodies with stones and branches, say their words and move on."

"They have lost so much," Nirmaya agreed. "Dignity in death is the least of it."

"Will there be any more dignity to be found in Dasar?"

Nirmaya shook her head. "At least they will have Kor'Habat between them and the Shar army."

"Can Shar not use bridges?" Maidra retorted. "Dasar is no safer than anywhere else outside those walls."

"Perhaps you are right," Nirmaya murmured in reply as she scanned the trees ahead.

"What is it?" Maidra asked.

"We will be lucky to get half of these people across the bridge before nightfall," Nirmaya replied. "I do not like this."

Maidra smiled.

"You worry too much," she said. "In a week we will have full bellies and these people will have been led to safety; by you."

"I hope you are right," she murmured in reply, never taking her eyes from the murk of the forest.

"I *am* right," Maidra insisted, placing a hand on Nirmaya's shoulder.

Nirmaya gazed back at her friend and lover, and sighed.

"What would I do without you?" she said at last.

Nirmaya awoke in the dark. The faint crackle of a fire was the only sound from outside the little tent she shared with Maidra. She pushed back into the red-haired woman's embrace, longing to feel the warmth of bare skin against her own, instead of leather armour.

The silver ring felt reassuring on her finger as she rubbed it with her thumb. The metal felt a part of her now, warm against her flesh.

Not for the first time, she thought of Starling. Not because she would substitute Maidra's arms for his, but because she had always teased him with her choice. For all his insufferable advances and innuendo, he had been a good friend in the end, and she hoped that he had not suffered in Dargenmill.

Despite herself, she missed the fool.

With great reluctance she extricated herself from Maidra's arms and slipped out into the cold night. One of the new Sisters was warming her hands over a fire as she kept watch, and she jumped back from the flames the moment she saw Nirmaya.

"Warm yourself," Nirmaya whispered. "It will soon be morning."

The woman relaxed and nodded in thanks.

Nirmaya made her way through the tents and huddled bodies towards the bridge, Rascal's Crossing. By nightfall fewer than half of the refugees had managed to cross. Abbil and four hundred of the Sisters were already on the western side, but Nirmaya had wanted to see the last of them into Dasar.

The stony road narrowed further until it reached a gaping chasm, black in the faint starlight. Nirmaya peered into the darkness and could just make out a silver ribbon of water two hundred feet below. The wooden bridge was wide enough to take a single cart, no more, and spanned the fifty-foot gap into Dasar.

She started across on the ageing boards which creaked under her weight and she had to remind herself that tens of thousands had crossed the previous day without incident; it was not likely to fail under her weight alone. All the same she quickened her pace until she felt the reassurance of stone beneath her feet and walked into the encampment.

She found Abbil, standing by a large fire in a wide clearing.

"You could not sleep either?" she murmured.

"All this rich food has given me heartburn I am afraid," he

joked.

"I will have a word with the cook," she replied.

Abbil looked up at her and smiled. Even through the thick beard, she could see that his cheeks were hollow.

"You have lost weight," she remarked.

"I had it to spare, girl," he replied. "You did not."

She smiled, surprised that she had felt no anger at being called 'girl'. Perhaps she was going soft, or perhaps the care in his voice had weakened her guard.

"I knew ladies in Kernhalt who would have starved themselves as much to get into a wedding gown," she replied. "It is no terrible thing."

"How many of those ladies follow you now, I wonder?"

Nirmaya offered a tight-lipped smile. "They have lost everything, those women, most of which can never be returned. Most of them cannot fight either, they are as much a burden as a help."

"You give them a sense of purpose," Abbil said. "That is all we can ask for in life."

"I hope that it is enough."

"They are choosing to not stand idly by to be battered by events. In war, one must do what one can to survive, not wait for others to come to the rescue. Have the courage to seize what you need to survive." He grasped the air in front of him and then was silent for a moment before continuing. "I had a family once, you know. A wife and two children."

Nirmaya looked at him in surprise. She had never heard him speak of family, and to her shame she had never asked.

"Where are they now?" she asked.

"They died when the Koratheans came to take Dashiya," he said, staring into the fire. "I was attending a meeting of villages in the area when they attacked. We were meeting to discuss how best to defend ourselves," he laughed at the bitter irony. "I knew nothing of the attack until I saw the smoke on the horizon as I returned home. It was a warning to Hadaiti; surrender or suffer more of the same."

"Fate," Nirmaya breathed. "You must hate Korathea."

He shook his head.

"I did for a time, with a passion. Even after the battle of Hadaiti saw the Heavy Infantry crushed and sent running, I hated them. I had seen them fall and that should have been the end of it, but hatred has a way of lingering in the heart. I would have followed them to Kor'Habat to crush them once and for all." He paused. "And then the Shar came. I realised that all men, and women," he added as he remembered his company, "had a mutual enemy, and that no matter how I despised the fact, there was a common cause we all shared. We, as people had a purpose that was the same, from Eritania to Kylyptus and beyond; to live. Such a simple thing, I know, and while I will never forgive the men who murdered the woman I loved and the children she bore me, I have a duty to share this one purpose with them."

"Then you are a better person than I," she said.

"Not at all," he replied. "I can see that you will do great things. This bridge, Rascal's Crossing, you know how it earned its name, don't you?"

"I don't," she replied, intrigued.

"Well, they say that the only people willing to make the long journey north just to pass into Dasar, rather than the obvious route through Kor'Habat, are deviants and rascals, eager to hide their movements from the great city. 'Honest folk go through Kor'Habat while rapscallions and rogues take the secret route,'" he mimicked the voice of an outraged noble. Nirmaya laughed and he went on in a more thoughtful tone. "But I feel that one day soon, it could be renamed, 'Nirmaya's Crossing', in honour of your courage and selflessness. These people will remember what you did for them."

Nirmaya sighed. "That is a lovely thought but…" a sudden scream cut her off.

"That came from across the bridge," Abbil scowled, drawing his sword as he turned towards the gorge.

Nirmaya was already running, and every pace brought a rising urgency in the cries from across the bridge. A throng of desperate people were rushing across the wooden boards when she reached it, carrying children or bundles of belongings. A man at the front of the rushing crown stumbled and fell, only to be crushed by the careless feet of those behind him, which brought still more people down.

More screams and the cry of 'Shar!' sent an ever-growing mass of terrified people onto the bridge, choking it with a press of bodies. Nirmaya tried with all her strength to push against the tide and make her way onto the bridge but was forced back before her feet could reach the boards.

She staggered out from the crush and glanced across the gaping chasm in time to see a jet-black shape lunge from the trees and plough into the terrified refugees.

"Maidra!" Nirmaya yelled against the clamour. "Maidra!"

More dark shapes bolted from the trees, tearing at whatever was within reach with claws that gleamed in the firelight, and all around them people screamed in terror.

Suddenly, Maidra was at the far side of the bridge, wide-eyed in horror. She held her sword against the oncoming attack, her red hair plastered to her cheeks with sweat or tears, Nirmaya could not tell. The woman was casting her eyes this way and that searching for threats, searching for escape, searching for Nirmaya.

"Maidra!" Nirmaya shouted out over the deafening roar of the panicked crowd, and somehow the woman found her in the storm. For a moment their eyes fixed upon one another across the yawning gulf between them. Maidra was shouting something, but her voice was lost in the chaos and Nirmaya was powerless to reach her, so close, yet an ocean away.

"Maidra!" Nirmaya screamed as a black shape burst from the trees and engulfed her fiery-haired lover with its powerful forelimbs. Nirmaya screamed again but this time there were no words, just a primal howl.

Still the people fled onto the bridge, pushing those in front in desperation. Someone fell from the edge and vanished, screaming into the darkness.

Then, a sickening crack signalled one of the timber boards giving way under the strain. More screams as another splintering crack saw another flailing figure dropping down into the gorge. More sounds of stressed timber could be heard over the screams as Nirmaya sank to her knees. Maidra's broken body lay bloodied across the gulf with the sword still gripped in dead fingers.

"Maidra! No!" Nirmaya cried.

Then a loud retort brought a momentary hush to the running crowds and there was a short intake of breath as one of the main beams failed. The bridge sagged to one side, and the screams resumed. More desperate than ever. The people clamoured for the safety of the west bank in a frenzy of self-preservation. The tortuous tilt continued to steepen until, at last, the whole bridge collapsed, sending a hundred or more screaming bodies into the abyss. Still more were pushed over the edge by those who could not see that the bridge was lost. The terrified shrieks echoed up from the depths and rang in the air for long, terrible moments.

Perhaps they were the lucky ones.

Across the gap, the Shar continued the slaughter, and many people jumped into the gorge rather than be butchered by the Shar.

"They are lost!" Abbil shouted, "We must leave! Now! There may be more on this side of the river. We must go!"

Nirmaya had a final glance across to Maidra's body and turned away.

She wiped the tears from her cheeks with the knuckles of a clenched fist before following Abbil down the slope.

She had failed those people; every last one.

"We should have gone around these woods," Ishaan complained to his friend, scratching at the untidy beard with his thin fingers. "These trees could hide a thousand men and we would not see them until they were upon us."

The tall pine trees rose, arrow-straight from the dry forest floor which was deep with needles and old leaves from the parched undergrowth.

"The Eastern scouts found only a few woodcutters ahead," Manush replied, wheezing a little from the mild exertion. He was a silversmith by trade and doubted that he would ever get used to these long marches, even if he lost more of his impressive paunch. "And why add a week or more to our journey? The sooner we are done with Kor'Habat, the sooner we can return to Dashiya and our wives."

Ishaan chewed his lip as a Shar overtook them on the road, then leaned close.

"But fighting alongside Shar?" he murmured to the older man.

Manush watched the powerful creature as it prowled along the edge of the column of soldiers.

"If the Easterners have learned to tame them, then I see no reason not to have them in our army," he said. "You are young, Ishaan; you do not remember the Korathean Empire when it came to take Dashiya for itself. I remember the flayed men hanging in cages for all to see at the roadside. I remember every artisan in my village; the blacksmith, the bowyer and the fletcher, having their hands cut off for refusing to serve the invaders. We beat them at Hadaiti, eventually, with the help of the Eastern engineers, and now we will finish what we started and crush the Korathean snake once and for all!"

"I was a boy, for sure, but I remember what they did. Is this new army any different?" he glanced around to be certain that no one was eavesdropping and lowered his voice. "I heard that villages that resisted were slaughtered. I heard that the bodies were fed to the Shar."

Manush shrugged. "King Rashun decreed that we should welcome the Eastern army. Any fool who disobeys the King is deserving of no less."

Ishaan looked ahead at the column of soldiers, snaking through the trees. There were perhaps two hundred men ahead of them, mostly Eastern soldiers, but he could pick out Dashiyan armour in the procession too. He glanced back and saw the loose formation vanish over the crest of a gentle rise, and he knew that the line went on for over a mile.

"An army of ten thousand men will not take Kor'Habat; not with those walls." he murmured.

Manush smiled. "I heard the commanders talking last night," he replied. "We will join a larger force to the south of the city. They have war engines and another thirty thousand men."

"War engines?" Ishaan asked. "Like those used at Hadaiti?"

A self-satisfied smile spread across Manush's face. "And if they can smash Heavy Infantry, they can bring down walls," he said.

A call to halt sounded out from the front.

"What is it?" Ishaan asked as they shuffled to a standstill.

Ahead, the Eastern soldiers were lowering their sparths towards the trees that surrounded them. Ishaan placed his hand on the pommel of his sword. A pair of Shar chittered in excitement before darting into the woods. They had sensed something.

A tense silence followed, broken only by the slowing footfalls of the soldiers behind.

A wisp of smoke drifted over their heads and the smell of burning wood came with it...

A sudden shriek echoed through the forest and a moment later a rope was pulled from the packed dirt of the road. The rope went taut above them and for a moment nothing happened. Then the tree to which it was attacked started to topple.

Ishaan pulled his sword free and backed away as one after another, ropes sprung from the ground and the creak of failing timber filled the air.

"It's a trap!" Manush yelled as the first trees crashed down onto the road in front of them, crushing a man who was too slow to react.

A clay pot sailed over Ishaan's head, trailing smoke from a burning rag in its top, and smashed against a tree, raining burning oil onto the dry forest floor. All around him fires were catching as more pots smashed in the parched leaf litter.

A dozen trees had already fallen, and still more teetered as ropes went taut.

"Those trees are cut through!" Manush shouted, pointing to the deep wedge at the base of the nearest stem. The cut had been hidden with dead branches, but the fresh cuts were clear.

"Those woodcutters!" Ishaan shouted back over the noise. "They laid a trap for us!"

A Shar lurched onto the road screaming as lilac fire erupted from an arrow in its shoulder. The creature thrashed in agony, knocking men to the ground as it tried to shake the arrow free.

The fire was taking hold of the forest and Ishaan realised that they were trapped. Several burning trees lay in a tangled heap ahead of them as well as to the rear. The only way out was into the forest which was well ablaze already.

"Into the forest!" Manush urged.

Ishaan followed his friend into the trees, shielding his face from the heat with his arm. The smoke was already choking him, and he tried to hold his breath until clear air could be found. He stumbled into a small clearing and gasped for breath. He could see other soldiers doing the same, staggering through the woods in either direction. One man ran screaming through the trees, alive with flames until an arrow ended his suffering and he tumbled into the dry undergrowth, setting the scrub alight where he lay. Then the hiss of more arrows in flight brought Ishaan to a standstill.

"Manush!" he shouted, turning back to find his friend.

But Manush was already on his knees with an arrow in his chest.

The older man looked up from the shaft in his sternum, his lips quivering.

"Run!" he gasped, and then slumped forwards onto the ground.

Ishaan ran, stumbling through the trees. A Shar crossed his path, and was struck by two arrows, one after the other. The creature fell, thrashing in agony as the arrows spewed pale flames from the entry wounds. The screams drowned out the terrified cries of his comrades and cut through him like an icy blade.

Then he saw the enemy for the first time.

An enormous warrior appeared from the smoke-filled air and took the head from the writhing Shar with a single stroke of a massive sword.

Then the soldier turned on Ishaan, a snarl of purest hatred visible behind the cheek-plates of a battered helmet. He fell to his knees in terror, dropping his sword and raising his hands in submission.

"Mercy!" he begged.

The warrior advanced and drove the huge blade into Ishaan's throat. Shock overrode his every thought, and all he could do was stare down at the sword that had pierced him. A boot to the chest freed the sword and he collapsed onto the forest floor. Through fast dimming eyes, he saw his killer stride away to cut down more of his comrades with a sword that shone blood red in the light of the growing fire.

It was a strange thought to have as he died, but he was certain that the huge warrior was a woman.

Valia removed her helmet and placed it on the table in the tavern of the fishing village. Her scars were pale against a face that was blackened with soot. She washed the crusted gore from her hands using a jug of water and a small basin and dried herself with a towel. Outside it was dark, and the tavern glowed in the light of a solitary lamp.

"When that lamp burns dry," Granger said from a gloomy corner, "there is no more oil."

Valia glanced up at him and shrugged.

"It was necessary," she replied.

"You were successful?" he asked.

She nodded.

"Thousands dead and the rest have scattered. Even if they do regroup, they will be a much lesser force." She took a drink of water and sank into a chair. "The trap was sprung too early. The Shar sensed our presence. I would sooner have drawn more into the noose."

"It was a bold plan," Granger said. "Sending men disguised as woodcutters to weaken the bases of the trees."

"*They* taught me a few things about bringing down trees," she said as Marlon arrived at the tavern.

He paused at the door before entering, then nodded a greeting at Granger and made his way to the basin where he washed his hands without a word.

Granger glanced from one to the other.

"Prisoners?" he asked.

"None," Marlon replied, and stared at the back of Valia's head.

"We can barely feed ourselves," she muttered. "I will not waste resources on the enemy."

"Are you certain there is no ale in those barrels?" Marlon asked, striding behind the bar and checking the empty casks as he had done half a dozen times before.

They remained stubbornly empty.

"Did we suffer many losses?" Granger asked.

Valia shook her head.

"Minimal," she replied. "The fire did our work for us."

Granger nodded. "The horizon still glows with your handiwork," he said. "One wonders how long it will burn."

Valia worked at the straps of her leather armour to loosen them.

"I would burn the world if I had to," she scowled.

"Yes, and all of us with it," Marlon murmured.

"Still no word from Kor'Habat," Granger said, eager to steer clear of another argument. "Nirmaya should have reached the Habat crossing by now, so there is one thing to be grateful for."

"What of Acastes and Kapaneus? Dachen and his men?" Marlon asked.

"Also, nothing." Granger answered. "But their bodies are not hanging from the walls as far as I know, which is a good sign. What am I thinking? You must be famished. There are a selection of stews awaiting you and the men."

"A selection?" Marlon asked, cocking his head to one side.

Granger shrugged. "I find that it helps pass the time when you are away," he replied. "A distraction from darker thoughts." Then his voice grew more distant. "I know now how those soldiers' families must have felt, waiting for news. If I had my time again, I would tell their stories instead."

"Let me guess," Valia groaned. "Fish?"

Granger ignored her as he snapped out of his musing and went on with great enthusiasm. "Seaweed, cooked just so to remove the salt, tastes remarkably like cabbage."

"I doubt that," Valia muttered to herself.

And she was right.

Captain Silman entered the Hatar's chambers and passed Captain Raims who was leaving. Raims winked and aimed a kiss at Silman on his way out, chuckling as he left.

One day soon, Raims, he thought to himself.

Silman's sneer faded as soon as Hatar Rogan Fol'Brandam turned to face him.

"Hatar," Silman saluted with his right fist pressed to his left breast.

"Have you been approached by any of the Hatars?" Rogan asked without acknowledgement.

Silman shook his head. "No, Hatar."

"Are you certain?" Rogan persisted. "Not by Fol'Gannity or Fol'Maddon?"

"No, Hatar," Silman repeated.

Rogan's shoulders relaxed. "Good," he said. "You need to leave the city for a time. Questions have been raised about your testimony."

Silman's mouth worked in silence for a moment before he could speak. "Hatar, I told them what you wanted me to say. It was not *my* testimony, but *yours*."

Rogan glared at the captain. "I would watch my tongue, in your position, Captain. I could have you dangling from the city walls within the hour."

"Please, accept my apologies," Silman said, cowed. "If I am to alter my testimony in any way, please tell me how."

Rogan walked to the open window and stared out over the city.

"Things have moved on since you gave your deposition. Acastes now has twelve thousand men with him in the Akharran; and I need those men! The story you told was a gambit that has not paid off and your presence in Kor'Habat clouds the issue further. You will be rewarded for your loyalty, Captain, but for now your place is outwith the city."

"Where will I go, Hatar?" Silman asked.

Rogan smiled.

"I will not send you east," he said, and Silman breathed out a sigh of relief. "West. There is a caravan of refugees crossing into Dasar. I need you to watch them for me and send news if it is warranted. Take twenty men with you and do not return until called upon."

Silman swallowed hard. "Hatar, I would sooner be in the city if the Shar attack," he ventured. "This is my home; I would be ashamed if I were not here to defend it."

"There is no shame in following orders, Captain," Rogan replied as he began sifting through papers on his desk to indicate the meeting was over.

"Hatar," he said, and saluted again.

Silman left the room feeling cold. He had made Masahara a promise. If he were to reap the reward on offer, he needed to be in the city when the Shar attacked.

He *would* have his prize...

CHAPTER 19

The gates to the Akharran creaked open for the first time in six weeks. Inside, Acastes waited, flanked by Kapaneus, Jon and Dachen. Twenty paces behind them stood twelve thousand Heavy Infantry behind a wall of shields. The show of strength and defiance earned a nod of acknowledgement from Rogan.

"It has been a long time since I set foot in the Akharran," he said.

"You'll love what we've done with the place," Jon replied.

Rogan signalled to the men ranked behind him to hold their positions and approached Acastes with arms open.

"I have no weapons," he assured him.

"Well, we're armed to the bloody teeth," Jon declared, easing his sword from its scabbard.

"There is no need to be defensive," Rogan replied. "My men will not take another step; as long as *your* men hold their own positions."

"We have every reason to be defensive," Jon scowled back. "I have a whole fistful of broken fingers worth of reasons to mistrust you, snake!"

Rogan held Jon's gaze for a moment and smirked. "Does this Shar-hunter speak for you now, Acastes?" he sneered.

"No, he does not," Acastes replied. "Although I tend to agree with his sentiment; you are not to be trusted. You lie with the same ease with which you draw breath."

Rogan smiled to himself and ran his eye across the ranks of Heavy Infantry behind Acastes.

"What lies have *you* spun to rally those men behind a mere Shar-hunter?"

"A bloody *great* Shar-hunter," Acastes corrected him. "You should have tried it instead of hiding in the city with the other politicians. If you, and those like you had at least attempted to be soldiers, we might not be preparing the city for war. You failed Korathea. You are failing her still." He nodded towards the soldiers behind Rogan and the banner they held. "Your power games will see you hanged if we survive the attack. Raising that banner is as good as treason."

Rogan sighed and stepped closer to enable him to lower his voice. Jon edged his sword from its scabbard again and Rogan stopped.

"We have been led by nameless men for too long," he murmured. "The Kodistai is of no house; he has no heir."

"No heir?" Kapaneus asked. "You are looking at the Kodistai's heir, you fool."

"The Kodistai is a small man," Rogan replied. "We have bred the strength out of our leaders. I may be a fool, but I can see that Acastes was not sired by *that* runt."

"For hundreds of years, the houses fought amongst themselves for the right to rule Korathea," Kapaneus said. "They murdered, butchered, and poisoned their way to power and sat atop the palace until a new, younger, less scrupulous bastard could topple them."

"It kept us strong," Rogan argued.

"It held us back!" Kapaneus snapped. "When at last the houses agreed to stop slaughtering each other, the Empire could grow and flourish. The Kodistai is of no house for a reason. The bloodline was chosen for a reason."

"That bloodline has become feeble," Rogan replied. "It is

time for a new line to succeed it."

"You want a return to the old ways?" Acastes asked. "You have resurrected your old banner and hold it above an army sworn to defend all houses under a single Kodistai? How long before we see a dozen banners in the city; a dozen factions vying for power again? You may rule the roost for a time, but you will be toppled by a Fol'Gannity, or a Fol'Maddon in time, or any number of others."

Rogan laughed.

"And if they are strong enough to do so, I will welcome it," he replied. "Better that, than to persevere in mediocrity with a diminishing line of ever more fragile leaders! The Kodistai's line has ended. It is a failed experiment and now it is time for strength again."

"You are so certain that the line has ended," Kapaneus laughed.

"Show me evidence to the contrary," Rogan challenged him.

"Oh, yes," Kapaneus replied. "Fine words from a man who keeps us hemmed in here. Give me the freedom to leave the Akharran and I will give you your proof. Or do you fear what you might learn?"

"He has only half of the army," Acastes said. "He will not risk releasing us."

A smile spread across Rogan's face.

"True, I command *over* half of the Heavy Infantry," he said. "But that banner you despise so much has brought an unexpected boon. I also command over ten thousand Eastern men." He looked at Dachen, who had been silent until now. "Perhaps you can tell them why, *Prince*."

Dachen looked at the banner of House Fol'Brandam; fortress, silhouetted against a yellow sun in a red sky.

Without thinking, he began to whisper the words of the prophecy he had scorned for so long.

"'When the shadow casts its darkness from the north and the third King of that name passes from the world, cities will fall, and fires will burn high. Look to the west, for the sun shall rise there and bring with it a Saviour. And he shall turn you on your heads.'"

"Wait," Acastes laughed in disbelief. "They believe that you are their *saviour*? That really is too much, Rogan."

"No more ridiculous than the notion that you are the Kodistai's heir," Rogan replied.

"A fool's prophecy," Dachen declared. "They will abandon you as soon as another fits better into their delusion."

Rogan shrugged. "Perhaps," the large man said. "But until then I have their sparths at my back. They are not *Heavy Infantry* to be sure, but useful as a distraction if need be. Their slaughter will not sadden me."

Dachen tensed at that and was about to reply when Acastes spoke again.

"Why are you here, Rogan?" he asked. "You did not arrange this meeting to goad or threaten us, surely."

"Indeed not," he replied. "Although both have their merits. I have come to gauge your loyalty to Korathea, if not to me."

"Go on," Acastes said with a wary edge to his voice.

Rogan nodded.

"I have received word of an advancing army," he said at last. "From Dargenmill."

"The Khalim-Shar?" Acastes asked.

"The Khalim-Shar," Rogan confirmed.

"How far out?"

"A week at most. Tens of thousands of Eastern soldiers, assorted militias and mercenaries. Hundreds of Shar too; perhaps even thousands."

"And war engines?" Kapaneus asked.

"Dozens of them," Rogan nodded. "War is coming to Kor'Habat whether we are ready or not."

"The defences look well prepared," Jon said. "We have engines of our own on the walls."

"Yes, we do," Rogan agreed. "Although most have been constructed on the western wall." He shook his head. "Some believed that the attack would come from the West. We have time to remedy that, however."

"So, you believe us now?" Kapaneus said.

"I would not have started preparations had I not," Rogan replied. "There is another army approaching from the south; several thousand men and dozens of Shar. It appears that they were attacked on the road and are much diminished."

"Valia," Kapaneus said, nodding his head.

"We do not know who attacked them," Rogan replied. "Only that they will arrive at our walls with a bloody nose."

"Of course you know who it was!" Acastes barked. "An army capable of inflicting losses on a force numbering in the thousands would not go unnoticed by you. You know who it is, and you know that you owe her an apology!"

"Apology?" Jon added. "You ought to kneel on hot coals and kiss her on her bare arse for what you have done. She could have been a powerful ally and yet you do everything in your power to bring her down."

"He fears her," Dachen said.

"I do not fear that *woman*!" Rogan spat.

"Then you bloody well should!" Jon warned.

"Enough!" Rogan snapped. "An army approaches as we speak. I came here to talk; to broker a peace between us that will bring Kor'Habat together to face the Khalim-Shar."

"Not strong enough on your own, Rogan?" Kapaneus taunted him. "Are you not 'the sun that rises in the West'?"

"Your jibes will not protect you against the Khalim-Shar," he retorted.

"It is late in the day for you to show concern about the Shar," Kapaneus said. "You have left this to fester for almost a decade, and now realise that you do not have ointment enough to treat the wound."

"*You* were the Shar-hunters, not me. It was not I who failed."

"Oh, that is rich, coming from…" Kapaneus began.

"Stop!" Acastes shouted. "Do you bring terms, Rogan? Or are you here to trade insults?"

Rogan glared at Kapaneus a moment longer, before forcing down his anger. "You will be offered a full pardon, in exchange for your loyalty," he said at last.

"Pardon for what? Loyalty to whom?" Kapaneus snapped.

"Would you like a list?" Rogan sneered.

"Yes, I bloody would!"

"Kapaneus!" Acastes blurted. "Please." He held his palms down in a calming gesture and took a series of slow breaths. "We have committed no crimes," he said. "That must be acknowledged in full. There can be no pardon where there was no crime. I do not accept your mercy since I do not accept the charge. There has been no trial other than whatever you and the Hatars have concocted in your own fevered imaginings. There is more! My loyalty lies with the Kodistai, no-one else; that must also be made clear and shouted from the wall tops if need be. I do not serve *you*!

"And there is one more thing, Rogan," he snarled, "if you want these men of the Akharran to fight at your side; one more thing. You will stop your pointless attacks on Valia. Your machinations will end, and she will be given the freedom that she earned at Ara Dasari. The Kodistai pardoned her for her actions against the Empire. She redeemed herself in his eyes and your refusal to accept that fact borders on treason. She will be free to enter the city; free to fight beside me if that is what she chooses, and your feud will end! You will not raise a hand against her, or you will face *me* across the battlefield!

"Now, take my terms to your *Council of Hatars* and chew on them. Wash them down with whichever fine wine you have grown accustomed to and return with your answer. Better men than you have a war to prepare for, so do not tarry!"

Rogan glared back across the narrow space. His sword hand

went to where his weapon should be, and finding nothing there, he scowled at Acastes instead.

"You may have just signed your own death warrant, Acastes," he warned before turning away and striding back to his own lines beyond the gate.

"Send ale, if you would be so kind!" Jon called out to the Hatar's back. "The Akharran runs low."

Valia stared at the map on the table in front of her as though force of will alone could draw a winning strategy from the parchment.

Small pebbles were arranged on its surface showing where the various factions stood relative to their position: To the north stood the walls of Kor'Habat and those who would hang her if given a chance. To the east, the Khalim-Shar at the head of an army that numbered in the tens of thousands.

Approaching from the south came the remains of the army she had tried to burn. The survivors had regrouped and were half a day away at best. They would almost certainly attack in the morning if Valia remained in the fishing village.

And to the west lay the sea, and they had only a few fishing boats with which to move four hundred men...

There was no escape to be found on the map.

"If we leave after dark and follow the coast south, perhaps we can skirt past the army and get behind them," Marlon suggested. "They are unlikely to give chase. They must join with the Khalim-Shar's army. I do not believe that they will waste time on a few hundred men."

"We stand a good chance of passing by unnoticed," Granger agreed. "If we leave soon and travel through the night."

Valia grunted. "And if we are discovered, it will be a slaughter," she muttered. "Strung out with our backs to the sea, the enemy with the high ground? No."

"East then," Marlon suggested. "And turn south once we are

far enough inland to avoid detection."

Valia shook her head. "We risk being caught between two armies," she warned.

"How far away is the Khalim-Shar, Adeyemi?" Marlon asked.

Adeyemi stirred in a dim corner of the room. He was clutching the pouch he wore around his neck, squeezing it with pale knuckles.

"Two days," he muttered, before settling back into reticence.

"Time enough to avoid meeting them before we turn south," Marlon suggested.

Valia grunted. "I will not run anymore; we risk being attacked on two fronts. I would sooner decide the terms of battle than form a scrambled defence," she said, staring at the map. She lifted the small stone that signified their own small army and held it up in a clenched fist. "It is time to make a stand."

"Valia," Granger urged, "they outnumber us by more than ten to one. We have no cover, no strategic advantage, and no element of surprise. I have witnessed many such battles, always with the same outcome. They are called 'last stands' for a reason."

"So be it," she replied.

"Perhaps we could appeal to Kor'Habat again?" Granger suggested.

Valia swept the map from the table, sending the small stones clattering to the floorboards

"'Appeal to Kor'Habat?'" she shouted. "They tried to kill us! Acastes! Kapaneus! Jon! Dachen! All dead because we trusted Rogan Fol'Brandam to hide us within his precious, bloody walls."

"We do not know that they are dead," Granger reasoned.

"Then, where are they?" she replied, banging her fist onto the table and cracking the boards. "Sitting in *The Glaive*, sipping ale and cuddling whores? They are gone, Granger! Dead! Murdered by the very people they were trying to save, and I say damn them all! They do not want our help; they do not deserve it. I will not fight for them anymore. I will give you a 'last stand' to add to your histories. I will make a final stand that will send tremors from Jendaya to Khumjang. Watch it from afar and then run to Kor'Habat and pray to Fate that they do not hang you from their walls for sport! Why can't you see it? The self-interest of a few, greedy bastards is what will bring the world down around us. Aided and abetted by the gullibility of common people too pig-witted to see that they are being bent over and buggered daily by those who claim to protect them.

"I tried Granger! I really did! I tried to do the right thing and to fight for the good things of this world. But the world kicked me in the teeth for my troubles. I do not even know who the enemy is anymore. Tomorrow I will fight men who follow the Khalim-Shar. Think on that. Fools line up to serve a master who would just as soon eat them alive!

"Do you know what? I actually admire the Khalim-Shar. That's right. I *admire* it. It wants something and takes it. At least the Khalim-Shar is honest. People, on the other hand, are duplicitous, deceitful beings, even to themselves. They say that they want to be free and then sell that bled-for right to the first arsehole to arrive on their doorstep with a winning lie.

"The Khalim-Shar is welcome to this world and every senseless fool on it, from the lowliest peasant to the highest ruler. 'Rulers' more than any of them. They are meant to be the best of us; the finest, risen to the top through merit and effort, but I can tell you beyond any doubt that they are the lowest form of scum that ever walked the land. Self-interested, manipulative, untrustworthy and false. But this I trust," she drew her sword and held it up in the fast receding light.

"Steel does not lie." She pushed the blade back into its scabbard and strode from the room. She was seething as she left, and it took her a few moments to realise that there was a crowd watching her.

Gathered in the dusty courtyard were the Eastern men who had sworn allegiance to Dachen, along with the few remaining

Shar-hunters. Valia stopped and stared at them.

The Eastern man, Lhoma, was at the front of the crowd, leaning on a sparth that shone red in the dying light.

"We will fight with you, Valia," Lhoma said to murmured agreement. "If you will have us at your side." He clenched his jaw. "Prince Dachen trusted you, and we trust you too."

Valia surveyed the gathering in front of her. Every single soldier was surely there. Four hundred men ready to die in a battle as pointless as life itself.

She almost laughed at the absurdity of it.

"Then we should prepare," she said, nodding her head. "Tomorrow we will paint the dawn red!"

Nirmaya looked south-west, down the gentle slopes leading to the lush valley below. She could just about discern the course of the Temple Canal as it cut through the fertile farmland and hazed into the distance at either extent. The canal was ancient, built to link Kor'Habat to the deep waters of the Adorim Sea, avoiding the jagged reefs that protected the city from a sea-borne invasion. It was also the only way into the city from the west.

The road ran parallel to the canal, skirting fields of unripe millet and wheat, but she knew that it would curve southwards to meet it in a little over ten miles. Silent behind her was the mass of refugees she had led here. They huddled, exhausted and starving in sullen clusters. Since the attack at the bridge, their number had been halved, but still they extended beyond sight down the road and spilled onto either side. Every horse or mule that they had left with from the shadow of Kor'Habat had been slaughtered to get them this far. What could not be carried on weary backs had been abandoned at the roadside.

"How many have died to reach here?" she murmured, trying to take in the scale of the tragedy.

"There was no other way, girl," Abbil sighed, placing a hand on her shoulder.

"There must have been another way," she replied.

"Yes, and that way was closed to you by the Steward of Kor'Habat," he insisted. "You have saved tens of thousands."

"I lost tens of thousands more." The Sister turned to look at him. Abbil's face was gaunt behind the wild hair and beard that held more grey with every passing day.

"They were taken; not lost," he assured her. "The guilt is not yours, so brush it from your shoulders or it will crush you."

She managed a sad smile in return for his encouraging words. "Follow the road and wait for me where it meets the canal," she said.

"You have the inventory?" he asked.

She patted her breast pocket.

"Are you sure I cannot come with you?" he said after a pause.

"I will take three of the Sisters with me," she replied, shaking her head.

"Those millers can be tricky buggers," he warned.

"I can handle a few mill owners, Abbil," she insisted. "You just need to get these people to the canal, and I'll be there with barge-loads of meat and grain."

"In exchange for everything these people have left to barter with," Abbil said shaking his head.

At her hip, three pouches hung, heavy with rings of silver and gold; precious bands of age-dulled metal that held more sentimental value to their owners than would ever be redeemed in coins.

"I saw you put your own ring in one of those pouches," he noted. "That was special to you."

"As Granger said, to help people we must all make sacrifices," she replied, and offered the warmest smile she could muster. She glanced at the pale skin where the ring Maidra had given her had been since she had arrived at Ulan-Balsan, and quickly looked away. "She would have wanted me to use it. 'Not bands of silver, nor bands of gold have strength to bind the heart.' I will never forget her."

Abbil embraced her and she returned his gesture, planting a kiss on his cheek. She was sure that he blushed a little as he cleared his throat and stood back.

"Any man would be proud to have a daughter as bold as you," he said. "Stay safe, Nirmaya. I will see you tomorrow."

She turned and made her way along a narrow track that ran between two fields. This was the most direct way to the Temple Canal. From there she would follow the canal, bartering at every mill and grain store on the way until she met with Abbil again to the west. Better that, than marching a hundred thousand desperate people across fields of young crops; that would do little to ingratiate them with the farmers or the millers...

Afreda, Lorica, and Faylinn were the Sisters she had chosen for company. They had been with her since her time in Kernhalt and were loyal and dependable. Of course, they were more than just company; the pouches that they all carried held the bulk of her bargaining power and if the gold and silver were lost to thieves then the outlook would be bleaker still for the refugees.

The vast canal carved a broad, languid swathe through the land to the north-west of the city. It ran arrow straight for a hundred miles before curving to the west and the Adorim Sea beyond the reefs that protected Kor'Habat from seaborne attack. It was bounded on both sides by fertile fields and busy mills and flotillas of boats operated on the torpid waters. It was the only way into the city from this western side and huge, distant flanking towers stood in defence of the vital and precious waterway.

Huge, elongated barges loaded with grain moved east, pulled by teams of horses that clogged the dusty towpath.

"So much food," Faylinn remarked as they were shooed from the path by an angry barge master. "We are saved."

"We should try that mill," Nirmaya said, pointing to the lazy, turning sails on a stone building to the west.

The group hurried towards the mill, stepping aside to avoid

another pair of horses dragging a barge in the direction of Kor'Habat. They found the large mill to be set within a stone courtyard a hundred yards from the canal. Carts were being filled from huge stores flung open to spill their bounty. The air was dusty with chaff and ripe with the smell of labouring men and horses.

"Please sir," Nirmaya asked of a passing worker. "Where will I find the mill owner?"

"Master Trevayn," the main called over his shoulder as he hurried past. "Up them stone steps and turn right!"

Nirmaya nodded at his back as he vanished from sight and shook her head. "Wait for me here," she said to her companions. "I will see what *Master Travayn* has to offer us."

She waited as a cart full of sacks of flour went past and headed for the steps. At the top, she turned right and reached an open door.

"Master Travayn?" she called.

"Come, come," a soft voice called from within.

Nirmaya entered the room and found an elderly, rotund man at a desk with his balding head down, scribbling frantic entries onto the pages of a large ledger. Another man pushed past her holding a bundle of papers in one hand and mopping his brow with a handkerchief in the other.

"Lewin!" the man at the desk barked. "The manifests go on the second shelf. And those figures had better be legible this time or you'll be back cleaning the stables so fast you won't have time to say 'bookkeeper', let alone be one."

"Master Travayn," Nirmaya repeated when she was sure her presence had not pressed itself on the man's mind.

"What? Yes?" he said, looking up in agitation.

"My name is Nirmaya Suun, good sir, and I have travelled from Kor'Habat, in the hope of securing a deal with yourself, to buy flour and oats. You seem to have a great deal of both."

She offered a warm smile, but he stared at her as if she were speaking a foreign tongue. He shook his head.

"Sorry, who are you?" he said, squinting to focus on her face.

"Nirmaya Suun," she replied. "I am looking to buy rather a large amount."

The words took some time to register, but when they did, he shook his head and waved her away.

"Out of the question. Lewin! What is the consignment number for that barley shipment?"

"Master Travayn!" she said more forcefully. "I have spent the last two weeks on the road with tens of thousands of refugees. They are hungry and I am looking to do business with you."

Again, Master Travayn took a few moments to fully comprehend what she was saying. He sat back and gave her his full attention at last.

"I thought you said that you were from Kor'Habat?" he said. "All stores are being moved *there* as we speak."

"Sir, we will take whatever you can spare," she said and stepped forward. She opened one of the pouches plucked out a collection of rings and small items of jewellery. Gold and silver gleamed and a few precious stones glinted in her hand.

Master Travayn looked from her hand to her face and back to her hand.

"A suspicious man might think that you had stolen those," he said.

"What? No," she protested. "Those people are starving. *I* am starving. This is all we have, but it is valuable as you can see."

She lifted one of the gold bands and bit it, holding it towards him so that he could see the indents.

He gave her a pitiful look in return.

"Either way," he replied, "I have nothing to sell. The Steward has declared that all stores are to be moved into Kor'Habat. That is where the food is; you should return there."

"They won't let us in," she protested in a tone that was more pitiful than she had intended.

"I *am* sorry," he said. "I have heard that things are bad in the East. He scraped his chair back and walked to the back of the room. He lifted the lid of a wooden box and took two large loaves from it and put them in a small flour sack.

"Take this," he said, hurrying back to push the sack into her hands. "It is not much, but all the grain and all the flour *must* go to Kor'Habat. Take care, child." He offered her a look of genuine concern as he shepherded her out of the door. "Don't go getting yourself into any trouble."

"How will this feed a hundred thousand?" she asked, but the man was already away.

She returned to the courtyard feeling suddenly weak and exhausted, and broke the news to her companions.

They heard the same story at every mill and every grain store.

All supplies were being loaded onto barges and shipped into Kor'Habat.

Late in the afternoon they were trudging past a ramshackle mill. The sails hung listless and broken, and there was no activity in the courtyard.

"Abandoned," Afreda said, spitting onto the towpath.

"We may have more luck at the next one," Lorica murmured.

"There is so much," Faylinn almost cried as she watched another barge laden with sacks of flour ease its way through the sluggish water of the canal.

Nirmaya opened the sack again and tore off four more hunks of bread, handing them out as she did so. They devoured the chunks, sharing guilty glances as they thought of their friends starving on the road.

"We are no use to them if we can barely walk ourselves," Nirmaya scolded. "Now eat, and I will not hear a word of remorse from any of you. Clear?"

They nodded and finished eating, just as a man called out from the courtyard of the mill.

"You there!"

Nirmaya turned to face him, dusting crumbs from her lips.

"Wait here," she sighed.

The man ambled closer.

"Are you looking to do business?" he asked.

"I am," Nirmaya replied. "We thought this place was abandoned."

"This place? Nah," he replied. "I use it for storage."

She watched the man approach. He was nothing like the other millers she had met that day. He was unshaven and shabby with oily hair. His clothes looked uncared for; a once-fine waistcoat gone to holes that were never sewn; shoes with shoddy stitching.

"You buying?" the man asked.

They walked into the courtyard to get a better look.

"That store is full of barley," he said, nodding at one of the large doors. I got oats and flour at my other mill along the way"

"Wait here," Nirmaya murmured and then stepped towards the man. "What is your name?" she asked.

"My name?" he looked surprised by the question. "Skully," he replied. "People call me Skully."

"You are different from the other mill owners, Mister Skully," she said, glancing around the large courtyard. "May I see the barley at least?"

"Well, as my dear old mum used to say, 'it takes all sorts'," he replied. "Come this way, My Lady."

He offered her an arm, which she declined and walked alongside him to the wide-open doors of an empty store. Every one of her senses was screaming out for her to walk away; run away, but desperation drove her on. If there was even a slim chance of this man having any flour or oats to sell, then she had to take it.

"My office," he said by way of explanation as he ushered her into the gloomy space.

She squinted into the dark, her hand closing on the leather-bound grip of her sword.

"Fate smiles on me indeed," a voice sounded from the darkest corner of the room. "It *is* you."

A shape moved out of the gloom and came into view.

She recognised the man at once.

Silman!

"It's a trap!" she screamed, tuning to run, but the entrance to the courtyard was already blocked by the massive shapes of four Heavy Infantrymen

Lorica dashed for the gap between two of the soldiers, but it closed as she ran and the huge fist that struck the side of her head knocked her to the ground. She did not get up.

Afreda lunged at the nearest Infantryman but her sword skidded off the unyielding breastplate and she had to drop to her knees to avoid the broad, curved blade that was swung at her in return. She drove her blade upwards towards the gap in the armour at the Infantryman's shoulder and felt the blade bite soft flesh.

The soldier yelled out in pain and spun, ripping the sword from her grasp. The weapon clattered to the ground and she rolled away as a huge blade struck the cobbles where her head had been.

Afreda dashed past the injured soldier across the courtyard.

"Run!" Nirmaya screamed as the Sister neared the towpath. "Find the Sisters!"

Afreda paused to look back, face ashen and eyes wide with fear.

"Run!" Nirmaya screamed again.

She turned again, just as one of the Infantrymen hurled a dagger at her. The narrow blade struck her in the shoulder, and she howled in pain, stumbling across the towpath and into the dark water of the canal. She vanished from sight with a splash just as Nirmaya reached the men who blocked her path. At the last moment she dropped to the ground and slid under the legs of the soldier in front of her. She drove her sword upward into his groin and felt the blade bite and slide against bone. A strangled cry was all that came from the man as she pulled the blade free again.

She did not have time to see him topple before another kicked her in the ribs.

She felt them crack and a heartbeat later, red-hot needles of pain were stabbing at the left side of her torso. She tried to draw breath, but none would come. Blood pounded in her head as she fought for air and she feared that she would suffocate. At last, when she drew in her first, ragged breath, it was as though the air was fire itself, bringing waves of agony to her damaged side.

Through eyes hazy with tears she saw that Faylinn had been caught and Lorica was unmoving on the ground.

Silman came to a halt at her side and kicked her onto her back, which brought more pain than she had ever felt.

"Fish that bitch out of the canal, and clean up this mess," he ordered. "I'm going to enjoy this. Oh, yes I am."

Afreda clung to the edge of the canal, scrabbling for cracks in the stonework with numbing fingers and pulling herself along.

She had been lucky when the dagger had struck. She had fallen into the canal where the stonework had been eroded away to form a small hollow in the retaining wall below the waterline. After pulling the dagger from the back of her shoulder, she had squeezed herself into the gap and pressed her face into the sliver of space above the water.

The Infantrymen had been directly above her; she could have reached up and touched a boot at one point, but had fought the overwhelming urge to flee, and remained perfectly still so as not to ripple the water's surface.

They had given up, assuming her drowned, and now she was edging along, away from danger and towards help.

A barge slid by and she remained unnoticed, clinging motionless to the stone.

At last she felt that she was safe enough to leave the water.

She tried to climb but her arms had no strength left in them and she slipped back down.

She cried. Cried for failing to get out of the water; cried because she had run away; cried for her friends.

She tried to calm herself. There would be somewhere along the canal that was easy to climb from, a broken section of stonework or a sandbank.

Suddenly a hand clamped onto her wrist and she felt herself being hoisted from the canal.

She snarled, and struck out, hitting the arm of whoever had grabbed her.

"Steady there." She heard a bemused voice. "I can put you back if you want to stay there."

She focussed on the man in front of her. He was tall, broad-shouldered and smiling. The smile was warm, not the cruel grin of someone who meant to harm her. His clothes were dusted with flour, as was his face and hair, so much so that he looked faded and pale.

"There's a barge coming," he said as she stared at him, as though speaking to the hard-of-thinking. "Don't want you to get crushed against the wall." Then his face grew serious. "You're bleeding."

"Tell no-one you saw me," she said, stumbling away along the towpath. "Please. Do not tell the soldiers. Please."

Afreda staggered on, hearing him call out behind her but she could not make out the words. Her ears rang with the sound of Lorica's breaking skull, over and over again. Staring eyes filling her vision.

She had to find the Sisters.

She had to find Abbil.

Nirmaya trusted him and so did she, but he may as well have been half a world away.

Lorica's body lay in the corner of the room, brown eyes staring at nothing. Blood was crusted in her ears and nose and the flies that had already found her crawled across her face and into her mouth.

The soldier Nirmaya had stabbed in the groin was sitting in a pool of blood, groaning as he slipped from consciousness.

"Sorry, Laramor," Silman said. "There's no coming back from that. Die quietly though, there's a good lad. Should never have let yourself be bested by a girl." He hesitated. "Wait, are you going to soil yourself? A man's bowels can give out at the last, you know. Hate that smell. Daelen, drag him to another room, I think his bowels are going to give out."

One of the Heavy Infantrymen stepped forward, looking pale. He swallowed hard and then took the fellow's arms to drag him through the door and across the courtyard. No doubt to find somewhere peaceful for him to die.

Silman sat in a chair across the large table from Nirmaya. He had emptied the pouches of rings and jewellery onto the table, where they formed an impressive pile.

"Where did you steal these?" he asked.

Nirmaya looked away. She had been stripped naked and tied to the chair and she could feel his eyes roaming over her body. She felt with her thumb for the ring Maidra had given her, but her finger was bare. She looked down to where the rough cords bound her hand to the arm of the chair and saw only a pale mark where it had been.

"I suppose it makes no difference," he mused. "A thief is a thief. They all end with a short drop from the wall. You are special of course, leading an army through Korathean territory in a time of war. That sounds like treason to me. I think I might deliver you back to Kor'Habat when I am done with you."

A loud bang and muffled scream made her start. Another bang as the nail was driven home through Faylinn's hand and into the wood of the heavy table in a gloomy corner of the storeroom. She was sobbing now through a gag to muffle her cries. Bent over the table with both arms stretched out in front of her.

A tear rolled down Nirmaya's cheek as two loud thumps

signalled the second nail being driven home and she fought down the urge to cry. Faylinn did not cry out this time and all Nirmaya could hear was her breath, rasping past the gag.

"Do you want to watch?" Silman asked. "See what's in store for you?"

Nirmaya shook her head.

"Shame," he said after a moment.

Skully, who had been skulking in the background stepped forward.

"Begging your pardon," he said, "but you said that I could be first."

The Infantryman who was fussing with his armour behind Faylinn paused.

"Of course," Silman agreed. "You fulfilled your part with distinction."

Skully gave an eager nod and made his way to the table, loosening the buttons of his flies as he walked.

"You will be first," Silman declared.

His eyes were wide with lust as he dropped his trousers and positioned himself behind Faylinn. The rasping breath stopped as she waited.

Silman nodded to the other soldier.

Skully paused, and his salacious grin faded just as the Infantryman behind him drove a long dagger upwards between his buttocks.

The shock on his face was visible even in the gloom. He gasped, raising himself onto the tips of his toes as though that would lift him from the blade. The Infantryman jerked it free and flicked the blood and excrement from his wrist with a look a distaste, leaving Skully to stagger a few paces and then collapse, wide-eyed and gasping for air.

"Take him somewhere to bleed out quietly," Silman ordered. "I can't bear the whimpering. Now, where were we?"

Kekoa bowed his head and sighed. The inn was dark, save for a solitary candle that had been found at the back of a drawer.

"Is it worse for a man to betray an oath or to abandon his friends in their hour of need?" he asked.

Valia shrugged. "Men who are true to their word are a rare thing in these times," she replied, running a stone along the edge of her sword. "Stick to your oath. Live to fight another day, perhaps."

"Your words are intended to salve my conscience, and I thank you for them, but it is a betrayal all the same," he said. "*Ten years to lay down the sword and serve*, is what I vowed, and I intend to fulfil that promise."

Valia paused in her task and looked up. "If you want me to grant you permission to fight, consider it done. If you want to join us, then you have my blessing. I will not command you to throw away your life and nor will I command you to leave. If there was an easy way out of this, we would all take it. There is not. And I would sooner not die with an arrow in my back, running from the enemy. I give you leave to do whatever you want. You once offered to give me your final year of servitude? Well I accept; now do as you please. That is my first and only command to you."

Kekoa sank down onto the chair opposite her.

"You have not made my choice any easier," he murmured.

"In the end, we are all the same," she said, looking down the edge of her sword. "One life in a howling cacophony of voices; all trying to be heard, desperate to be remembered. Fleeting, and soon forgotten. Take what pleasure you can and leave while you still have some wits about you, is my best advice."

"You must know that I yearn to take up arms and join you," Kekoa groaned into his hands. "But my oath…"

Valia pushed her sword into its scabbard and glared at Kekoa.

"Stay, and your oath will be cut short in any case," she glowered.

"Leave, and I will have wronged you once more."

"You want me to make a choice for you; well I will not!" she snapped. "I have chosen to face those bastards because there is no other choice that does not risk my dying as I run. I would stand alone against them if I had to because that is what I choose to do; to fight! I long to have their blood on my sword and I cannot see beyond that moment. You made a ten-year oath? Well, I cannot see beyond sunrise. Tell me what you want to hear, and I will say it. There are so many battles to be fought, Kekoa, do not add your own conscience to your list of enemies, for it will fill your mind with doubt and bring you down. Decide, and live with the consequences. But harden yourself and decide quickly."

"The flesh is soft and fragile when living, but hard and rigid in death," Kekoa offered. "Thus, hardness is a partner to death, as softness is to life."

"It is *softness* that has left us standing where we do," Valia retorted. "There is no place for it now."

She rose and strode from the room, leaving Kekoa alone with his thoughts.

Valia stared to the east and saw the faint lightening on the horizon that signalled the approaching dawn. The village was all but empty now. The inhabitants were moving to the clumps of trees to the north where they might take shelter from the volleys of arrows to come.

"What do you think you are doing?" Valia asked, incredulous.

Granger stuck the spike of the sparth into the dust and leaned on the shaft.

"I once used a spear to push a Shar from the walls of Ulan Balsan," he replied. "I don't imagine you ever heard about that."

"This is no place for you, historian," she said, shaking her head. "Take your books and leave."

"My books are strapped to a pack-horse and will head north when the time comes," he replied. "I only hope that they fall into responsible hands."

She shook her head.

"You should take the old alchemist and go," she said, tugging at the straps of her leather armour.

"Ah," he replied. "I think that Tsering means to stay too although I admit it is difficult to tell. He appears to be very pleased with himself though."

Sure enough, the old man ambled past, grinning from ear to ear. The pack-horse he was leading had large mesh bags fashioned from old fishing nets hanging against its flanks. Inside the mesh were dozens of clay lamp-oil jars, and a bundle of paper tubes.

"What is in the jars?" she asked.

"Not lamp oil, that is all I know," Granger replied, smiling back at the alchemist. "And the Ago Camdi is finished; the bowmen have all that was left."

Valia grunted. "So long as they know to use it only on Shar. Those arrows are not to be wasted on men."

"They know," Granger said. "They are disciplined men; as good as any I have seen."

"They will need to be," she replied.

Granger sighed.

"Valia, I do not think you realise the significance of their willingness to stand with you, a woman. You show them none of the respect that they would expect in the Eastern Kingdoms."

"They are not *in* the Eastern Kingdoms," Valia replied.

"No, but a lifetime of custom and convention is not shed in a day," he said. "You have earned the respect of men who have been brought up to believe that women are less than them."

"I am pleased to have enlightened them," she replied.

"Better late than never, I suppose," he observed, ignoring her caustic tone.

Valia cocked her head to one side.

"What is it," Granger asked.

"They are coming," she said without emotion. "Take up your

position and do not die cheaply."

The sun rose and Valia watched its arrival with the serenity of the condemned.

That final, tranquil walk to the gallows once every ounce of fear and indignation had been hurled at uncaring and intransigent prison walls. Only peace awaited, and it was in sight, within reach.

One final outpouring to empty her of all she was, and she would find rest at last.

At the edge of the trees, Kekoa sat cross-legged on the ground to greet the sun. Golden fingers touched his face first and brought an easing of the tension in his posture. His shoulders sagged a little and his hands relaxed.

Across the dry field the enemy came into view. The tips of sparths and lances first, and then eventually the men who carried them. They stretched across a formidable width of the horizon; mostly foot soldiers, but a few hundred on horseback too.

"Six, seven thousand," Marlon murmured from her side.

"Their lines are shallow to exaggerate their numbers," she replied. "No more than five."

The unmistakeable shapes of Shar prowled across the front of the army; low, sleek and powerful.

"Twenty-five Shar at least," Marlon observed.

"They will use the men first," Granger said, fidgeting in his ill-fitting leather armour. "*They* can be replaced."

"The bowmen have the last of our horses," Valia said. "I hope they make their presence felt."

"They will," Lhoma assured her.

"Every Shar killed today is one less for Kor'Habat to deal with," Marlon observed.

"We should leave them be in that case!" Valia grinned. "Send the order, Lhoma. No Shar to be harmed in the battle. Only target the men."

"It is a strange time to regain your sense of humour, Valia,"

Marlon said.

Valia's expression turned dark again. "What makes you think I am jesting?"

There was a brief silence.

"What do the portents say, Adeyemi?" Marlon asked.

The big man shook his head, staring at the enemy, a few hundred yards away across the field.

"I do not look anymore" he replied.

"All our futures may be short," Valia said, "but we alone can choose how we leave this world, and how many we take with us."

"I will not die today, friend Valia," Adeyemi said as though it were obvious. "Soon, but not today."

Granger walked to the pack-horse he had tethered to one of the spindly trees and pointed it north. He slapped it on the rump and shouted, which sent the animal galloping off with a startled whinny. Strapped to its side were bundles of books wrapped in oil cloth.

He watched with a wistful expression as the animal receded into the distance.

"Your histories?" Kekoa exclaimed as he joined the group at the edge of the treeline. "Is it too late to write that I stood with you at the end?"

"I never doubted that you would," Granger replied.

Valia sighed. "You fool, you should have followed that damned horse," she said. "Fate knows, it has more sense."

Tsering shuffled past them with a bundle of those paper tubes in his arms. Valia saw now that each one had a short stick protruding from one end.

"What are you doing, Alchemist?" she asked.

Tsering turned and smiled, showing off a row of jagged teeth. Then he laughed and set about pressing the sticks into the ground with the tubes leaning towards the enemy.

"Valia," Marlon said, nodding towards the field. "They wish to talk."

She looked and saw three riders entering the field. The central rider was flanked by sparth bearers.

"Perhaps they wish to surrender," Valia muttered. She strode out across the dry grass towards the riders, conscious of Marlon and Lhoma at her side. They took some time on foot to reach the riders who had long since stopped midway across the gap.

The man between the Eastern sparth bearers was western for certain; Dashiyan from his armour. He regarded Valia and her companions with a look of both pity and derision.

"Surrender," he said, shaking his head. "Swear fealty to the Khalim-Shar and join us on our march to victory and a new world!"

"We'd sooner fight," she replied, approaching the man in the centre. The sparth bearers lowered the points of their weapons until they were level with Valia's chest.

The man sighed.

"If you cannot muster three horses to ride out to hear terms, then you must know that you are doomed," he said.

"We thought we'd take yours," she replied, grabbing the nearest sparth in one hand and drawing her sword with the other. She hauled on the sparth, half unseating the rider and pulling herself to within striking distance in the blink of an eye. Her sword severed his left arm above the elbow and bit into his ribs. He grunted as he toppled from the saddle and Valia already had the reins in her hand.

Valia heard the central rider's sword ring as it cleared the scabbard, and she parried his first and only attack before Marlon stepped in to drive his own sword upwards into the man's torso. Lhoma meanwhile had hurled his own sparth like a javelin and thrown the last horseman from his saddle with the long, pointed blade in his chest.

"Quickly," Valia urged as she took the reins of the nearest horse. "Before the first volley of arrows."

They left the dying men where they had fallen and rode back

across the field with the sounds of the enemy mobilizing at their backs.

"You could have bloody warned me!" Marlon yelled, but Valia did not hear him. Only the roar of her own rushing blood and the rhythm of the charging horse reached her.

They made the cover of the trees a moment before a volley of arrows hissed through the branches, thudding into trunks to either side.

"Cover!" she yelled, but her small army was already huddled in ones and twos behind the meagre stems of the little woodland. She dismounted and handed the reins to a bowman who had his back pressed against a slender tree.

Another volley hurtled through the stems. A grunt of pain emanated from an Eastern man as an arrow struck him in the shoulder, just a yard away from Valia. The man sagged against the narrow tree, clenching his teeth against the pain. Without a word, Valia stepped forward and snapped the head from the arrow where it protruded, then pulled the shaft free. The man growled in his throat and breathed a deep lungful of air, nodding in grudging thanks.

They weathered the volleys with only a few casualties, until the enemy had either grown tired of wasting arrows or had run out. Either way, Valia heard the shouted orders carried across the field for the men to advance.

Valia walked forward to get a clearer view. Eight distinct columns approached on foot with mounted men away out on the flanks. The sparth bearers made up the centre four columns while swordsmen made up the others to either side.

"Those sparth bearers will attack head on," Marlon murmured from her side. "The swordsmen will attack our flanks while the riders circle to fall on us from the rear. There are too many of them." He turned to her and softened his tone. "Valia, I will be with you at the end. I will follow you into the Soul Keeper's embrace. You will not be alone."

Valia held his gaze and nodded a terse acknowledgment. There were things she would have liked to tell him if she had thought there was any point to it, or if she could find the words. Time had run out.

"The Shar are not moving," Granger murmured.

"What?" Marlon snapped in irritation.

"The Shar," he repeated. "They have remained at the back with the archers."

Marlon squinted past the approaching army and saw that Granger was right. The rows of bowmen were interspersed with the waiting shapes of expectant Shar. One sat a little taller than the rest, raising itself onto its hindquarters for long moments as it watched.

"Fate!" Marlon hissed. "The Khalim-Shar!"

"Another one?" Granger asked, trying to discern the distant shape.

Valia laughed, a bitter sound. "Smaller than the Khalim-Shar at Banihat," Marlon muttered, shaking his head. "There is a an-other!?"

"And why waste your own kind when you have fools to do your bidding," Valia sneered. "Either way, they will eat well this day."

Ahead, the front ranks of the approaching Eastern soldiers lowered their sparths.

Tsering pushed past Valia and knelt, unhurried on the ground behind the sticks he had pressed into the soil. Kekoa was with him, carrying a net bag full of clay jars.

"What are you doing, Kekoa?" Valia asked.

"I could not leave, and I cannot fight. But I can help. Ahui hohrai," he said with a smile.

Valia nodded.

"Ahui hohrai," she replied. "Until our paths cross again."

Tsering struck a flint and steel over a small torch to light it as the approaching army broke into a trot.

"Form up!" Valia shouted. "Defensive formation! Bowmen, protect our flanks!" Then she lowered her voice and directed her glare at Tsering and Kekoa. "Move out of the way."

Tsering laughed as the army charged from twenty yards. Without taking his eyes off Valia he touched the torch to the back of one of the paper tubes and swept it across the line of sticks.

The tubes hissed for a moment before streaking away towards the approaching men. A heartbeat later brought a series of loud retorts and blinding flashes from the midst of the charging ranks. White fire fountained from sudden billows of smoke and the fervent roars were fast replaced by screams of agony. The front line fell into disarray with men crashing into their fellows in their attempts to dislodge the fragments of searing fire which stuck to their bodies and faces.

Kekoa handed Tsering one of the pots and the old alchemist lit a short string at its stopper. He cradled the pot in a sling, watched it burn short for a few seconds, and then hurled it forwards. The pot sailed towards the onrushing enemy, trailing a ribbon of smoke and then ruptured in mid-air with a loud crack, showering white fire onto the enemy.

Valia was rooted to the spot, watching in dismay as the orderly lines descended into mayhem. Another loud crack shook her from her stupor, and she glanced at Marlon to find his eyes fixed upon her. She nodded, then charged towards the broken formation.

She was unaware of her friends beside her as they joined her in battle; she only saw the enemy. Flashes above hinted at more of Tsering's clay pots raining fire on the ranks beyond, but she focussed only on those in her path. She poured everything into her attack, giving every ounce of strength to her great blade. Immersed in the enemy; cleansing herself with their blood; washing away her despair and her loss.

The mounted bowmen shot their burning arrows into the bodies of men as the Shar watched from the distance. The arrows, with their Ago-Camdi tips had been meant for the Shadows, but the Shadows wanted no part in this battle, happy to send men to die for their cause.

Screams of agony as searing lilac fire erupted from the bodies of those struck joined the cries of the dying and the clamour of clashing steel.

Valia let the music wash over her as she struck a man's head from his shoulders. Her hands and arms were wet with gore; she could taste the blood that had splashed across her face past the cheek plates of her helmet.

A sparth raked across her leather-armoured midriff as she twisted to avoid it and she brought her sword down onto its bearer, severing his arm at the shoulder.

She saw Adeyemi; unarmoured, swinging his great impanga beside her and dancing between the sparths of the enemy. Marlon's shield was split and yet he held onto it as he pushed forward.

She sensed the enemy encircling them; knew that Tsering's pots had grown silent and that the odds were always too great to beat...

Kill one more before succumbing; just one more to even the score. The exhilaration of vengeance realised filled her to bursting.

Her sword still thirsted; demanded the taste of flesh.

Let death take her in a wave of her enemy's blood...

They were surrounded. A few hundred could never defeat five thousand and their numbers dwindled around her as the enemy closed in. She did not care; this was her design.

Was she screaming?

Was it anger or joy?

She glared at the Shar in the distance where one stood tall among its fellows.

She drove towards it, hacking at the soldiers in her path.

She could not hope to reach it, but it was far better to die trying.

Men fell like stems before her scythe, and she cut them down;

for Surilya; for Truman. She hurled herself at them for Lushara Bedein.

Had Lushara ever been real? Or just a figment of her strained imagination?

Was anything real?

She felt the impact of weapons and bodies as they hit her, but there was no pain. Had the weapons breached her armour? Was she wounded? Those things did not concern her. There was no feeling now, only the fight. Woman and blade had become one, one in form and purpose. And then the wind came; it would carry her forward; it was a silver wind, howling past and driving away her enemies, sweeping them up in a maelstrom of flashing blades.

Perhaps she had laughed; she was not sure, but the wind was with her. It gleamed and shone in the light of the dawn and turned her enemies to dust. This was sweetness; this was life; the crowning, final moments of an embattled existence.

The wind was not silver! It was steel. It had come for her; to lift her.

The steel wind would bear her to oblivion and the end of care, and she rejoiced.

The battle was soon over, and the field was strewn with the broken bodies of the dead and the dying.

Acastes wiped the blood from his sword with a rag and tossed the soiled cloth to the ground. The Shar had fled from their position as their army had been destroyed under the weight of the Heavy Cavalry and only a few deserters could be seen fleeing into the distance.

Dachen had brought a hundred of his own men; mounted bowmen who had chased down the fleeing cavalry. They were still rounding up men from the defeated army who surrendered without hesitation.

"I thought you were dead!" Marlon exclaimed, sinking to the ground, exhausted.

"No, my friend," Acastes replied. "Merely without good wine, which is very nearly as bad."

Marlon forced himself onto his feet again. "Valia," he said, searching the bloody field for her. "Where is Valia?"

Jon dropped down from his saddle and helped Marlon to keep his balance. "We will find her, old friend," he said, taking Marlon's weight on one shoulder.

The ground was littered with bodies and broken sparths. When the Cavalry had swept in on their armoured horses, the foot soldiers had stood little chance. Those who had ducked below the broad swords of the Heavy Cavalry had been crushed beneath the hooves of their mounts. No armour could offer protection from the weight of those mighty war-horses; twenty hands at the withers and draped in steel plate. It was no ordinary horse that was needed to bear a son of the Akharran into battle.

Kekoa arrived, breathless at Acastes' side and bowed his head.

"I am thankful that you are alive," the smaller man said.

"Nonsense!" Acastes laughed. "You had hoped me dead so that you could weasel out of your obligations."

Kekoa ignored the barb and caught the helmet that Acastes tossed at him.

"Search the area for survivors!" Acastes barked. "And find Valia."

Kapaneus was already on foot, picking through the carnage, kicking at the ravens that had already landed on the heaps of bodies.

"I have found her!" he cried, taking long strides across the dead.

She was on her back, her sword still clutched in the limp fingers of her right hand. Her armour was stained deep red with blood and gore and her hands were slick with it.

Kapaneus eased the helmet from her head.

"Be gentle," Granger urged as he rushed over to the scene.

Kapaneus took only a momentary glance at the ill-fitting

armour hanging from the old historian before returning his attention to Valia.

Her cheeks were pale where they were not covered with blood and the old scars were an angry pink against the bloodless flesh.

"Is she…" Marlon began in a whisper, but he could not bring himself to finish.

Granger hushed him. The old man held his ear to her face for a while and then pressed his fingers against the side of her neck. He looked up.

"She is alive," he breathed. "But only barely."

"She is bleeding," Marlon's voice had a desperate edge. "Remove her armour."

"Not here, there is nothing we can do. She needs to be taken to Kor'Habat," Acastes declared from his saddle. "To Shol'Hara."

"She's a soldier," Marlon protested. "Not a breeder!"

"Perhaps. But she is also a woman." Granger said. "And Shol'Hara will know how to care for her like nowhere else."

"If she survives; you may not," Marlon muttered, calming himself, but made no further protest. He watched as Valia was lifted from the butcher's floor by four men and rushed to support her head as it lolled back.

"There are wagons coming," Acastes said. "Take her, quickly."

Marlon allowed another soldier to take Valia's head and he watched her being carried away. "Where were you?" he said at last, his eyes still on Valia.

"What?" Acastes murmured as he returned his attention to Marlon.

He forced himself to look at Acastes. "Where have you been? It has been weeks since you entered Kor'Habat. We thought you were dead; and we have been starving out here!"

"There is much to tell you, Marlon," he replied with a wry smile. "But I suggest we do it over a platter of meat and a jug or six of wine. Kekoa! Get this man a horse."

Kekoa nodded and hurried through the battlefield. Several of the enemy cavalry horses were ambling, aimless among the dead, nibbling on the dry grass where it was not covered with blood.

Dachen rode in from the edge of the battlefield.

"We have captured over a hundred men," he declared drawing his horse to a stop. "Most are Western men, but my own countrymen are among them too." He spat onto the ground.

"Thank you, Dachen," Acastes replied.

"Valia lives?" he asked.

"She is injured, but alive," Marlon said. "A little longer, and we would all be dead."

"Adeyemi," Granger said. "He assured me that he would not die today. Perhaps there is something to these portents of his."

"Where is he?" Dachen asked.

Granger pointed to the edge of the battlefield, to where a dark figure sat on a pile of bodies.

"I will go to see if he is injured," Dachen said, but was distracted by the arrival of Lhoma, who was leaning on his sparth for balance and nursing a wound to his side.

"My Prince," he said. "You are a most welcome sight." He tried to bow but Dachen moved to his side and helped him upright again.

"Hold your head high, Lhoma," he said. "You stood where others would have crumbled. Have your wounds seen to, I cannot afford to lose good men to little cuts."

Lhoma moved his hand to show a deep gash in the armour and blood oozing beneath.

"Any hole I cannot see daylight through can be survived," Dachen said, gesturing for two of his men to come and help.

They led Lhoma away towards the approaching wagons and Dachen turned back to where Adeyemi had been sitting. But the big man was gone.

CHAPTER 20

Nirmaya was shivering when she woke.

The hull of the barge was cold and damp against her naked flesh, and the sound of lapping water outside suggested to her that they were still moving.

Her wrists were bound with coarse rope that had worn her flesh raw where it touched and congealed blood crackled when she moved. Her mouth was dry, and the bulky gag had soaked up any moisture her body had been able to muster. She inspected the backs of her hands through eyes that were gummy and sore. The nails had gone between her bones and she was certain that only the flesh was damaged, but even small movements sent spikes of agony up her arms.

He had not shared her with the other Infantrymen, and he had not cut her throat when he was done.

Faylinn!

That memory was burned into her vision.

Nirmaya was still alive. He was not done with her yet.

The barge she was in was full of sacks of grain or flour; she could not tell. She only knew that the air was so dry and dusty that she would surely die if she did not get a drink of water soon. Breathing became harder the more she gasped for air and as her throat closed in panic, she groaned as loud as she could.

Footsteps above.

A hatch was thrown open and a moment later a large figure dropped in through the square of blinding light.

"Good morning my little flower," Silman leered. "Your bonds truly suit you."

Nirmaya tried to scream against the gag but the weak whimper she managed was soon replaced with hopeless sobbing.

Silman walked over the sacks, stooping beneath the deck above his head. He lifted her with ease and took her a few paces to a small, empty crate. He dropped her without warning and Nirmaya landed on the boards with an impact that took the last of the breath from her lungs. The pain was still better than the touch of his hands.

"We will soon be in Kor'Habat," Silman said as she struggled to draw breath. "If you make a single sound, this crate goes into the canal and you will drown before anyone can fish you out."

Nirmaya looked up at him and he smiled.

"Remember," he said, pulling a lid over the crate, "not a sound."

She jolted with the first thump of the hammer as it drove the nail into the lid. The memory of iron being driven through her hands. She squeezed her eyes shut and tried to lock out the noise of the hammer until at last, she was left in silence.

Naked and alone in a crate barely big enough for her curled-up body. Her thumb found the groove in her finger where Maidra's ring had been and rolled the missing band against her skin.

Perhaps drowning would be a release.

Abbil looked around the old mill's storeroom, both eager for, yet fearful of every sign or clue.

When Afreda had found Abbil and the refugees, she had been almost catatonic. It had taken a long time to find out from her what had happened at the mill, but so much was still unknown. He was dreading what he might find.

"There is blood," he said. "Someone was dragged from here, and from there."

A dozen of the Sisters had joined him as well as twenty men from among the refugees.

"Abbil!" Gemmilia, one of the Sisters called, and he made his way towards her voice across the courtyard.

"Lorica and Faylinn," she said when he arrived.

Abbil squinted into the gloom of the room she had led him to, and saw the bodies dumped against the wall. Faylinn was naked, and her throat had been cut. Abbil saw the wounds on her hands and knew at once what had happened to the poor woman before the end.

"An Infantryman too," he said. "And another man. What happened here?"

"Afreda said that they had been attacked by Heavy Infantry," Gemmilia said.

Abbil bowed his head for a moment. "But where is Nirmaya?" he whispered.

"The barges are all headed for Kor'Habat," one of the men among them said. "She must have been taken there."

"For what?" Abbil replied. "Asking to buy food is not a crime."

"We should follow them into Kor'Habat if that is where they are," Gemmilia declared.

"No!" Abbil said. "The entrance will be guarded, and we could never hope to sneak in with such numbers. I will go alone."

"I will not abandon Nirmaya!" the woman replied. "She is my sister and I will fight for her as long as I draw breath."

"I do not doubt that for a moment," he argued. "But do you know the city?"

She shook her head with some reluctance.

"I know Kor'Habat as I know my own face," he lied. "Return to the refugees and let me go and find her. I have friends in the city who see everything; know everything. I *will* find her."

Gemmilia would have seen him blush had his beard not

covered so much of his face, but instead she accepted the lie with a reluctant nod.

"Go back and lead the people to Ara Dasari," he urged. "It is their best hope."

Soon Abbil was left alone, staring along the canal. Five miles to the south-east lay Kor'Habat and an entire city of hostile soldiers. He puffed out his cheeks and started walking along the towpath.

Fate! He was hungry.

Nirmaya pressed her face to the narrow crack in the wooden crate to draw in some fresh air. The gag tasted bloody now, and she could feel her lips crack when she tried to flex her painful jaws. The cramped space was hot and muggy, and reeked of urine. Her head pounded with an ache that she knew was the result of breathing the same air for the past hour or more.

She could hear a growing bustle above deck and realised that they had entered the docks in Kor'Habat. Voices grew more distinct and then she felt a gentle thud as the barge bumped against the dock.

Soon, she felt the crate being lifted. A sliver of light shone through the crack in the wood and she resisted the urge to make a noise; thrash about in the crate to alert the dockers. She believed Silman's threat and had resolved not to die yet.

She heard his voice but could not make out the words, then heard the jingle of coins as they changed hands. She waited, trying to squint through the tiny crack but could see nothing. Then she felt the crate being placed on something solid and listened to the soft footsteps nearby. A moment later, the crate tilted, and the tell-tale rumble of wooden wheels on cobbles had her bouncing in her tiny prison.

Where was he taking her? The Akharran?

Why the secrecy if she was a prisoner of the Heavy Infantry?

After what felt like an age, the cart stopped and there were more voices that she could not quite discern. She waited, flexing her aching joints as much as she dared and as much as she could in the small space.

She was moving again; this time being carried. She heard the scrape of boots on stone and laboured breathing nearby. The light vanished and she was plunged into total darkness. Footsteps echoed and she could imagine stone walls to either side. A door creaked open and the crate was dumped on a level surface again.

A short silence ended when the lid was pried open. Nails squeaked against timber and the dry wood cracked until it could be lifted away.

She squinted up into the dim light and saw Silman looking down at her. A second, cruel face leered into the box and Nirmaya tried to shrink away...

"Remember!" Silman warned. "She is not for your other customers; only me. At least, until I am done with her."

The other man nodded while he grinned down at Nirmaya, displaying broken rows of rotten teeth. He licked his lips as he reached out to touch her with twitching fingers.

Silman clamped his wrist in an iron grip. "She is not for you either, Claytan," he growled.

Claytan tore his eyes from Nirmaya's naked body and flicked a nervous gaze at Silman. "As you say," the man replied as last. "She is yours and yours alone."

"Do not forget it," Silman cautioned. "Now, have the boy wash her; she stinks." The captain vanished from view and she heard his heavy footsteps echo away.

Claytan rubbed his hands together, fingers twitching in excitement. "Boy!" he shouted, making Nirmaya recoil further.

"Oh, don't cry, little one," he said in a soft tone that held no reassurance. "We're going to take good care of you." Another figure arrived on the opposite side of the crate. "We're going to treat you right."

They reached down towards her and she screamed into the gag.

Valia felt cool sheets and a warm breeze when she woke. She took a moment to gather her senses and tried to remember where she was. Was this how it felt to be dead?

She opened her eyes and saw the soft billows of gauzy curtains to either side. She was in a large room with smooth, pale walls and an open door. She tried to sit up and the pull of fresh cuts on her arms urged for caution. The smell of food assailed her and at once she felt hunger like she never had before.

"You were almost dead when they brought you here," a voice startled her. The speaker had been so still and quiet at her bedside that Valia had not noticed the thin, elderly woman sitting there holding a book. "But it was not due to your wounds. I was certain that you had given up on life. It happens, you know."

"What happened to me?" Valia asked. "How am I here?"

"None of those cuts was life threatening, although your armour took quite a beating," the woman mused. "You must be hungry. I will have cook prepare a meal for you." She closed the book and placed it on her lap. She clapped her hands twice and a young girl appeared at the door and nodded, then vanished again.

"Where am I? Who are you?" Valia asked again.

The woman wore her greying hair in a tight bun high up on her head. The line of green jewels that ran from the top of her left ear all the way to the lobe told Valia that she had been a *Haram*, and had borne six boys, '*to the glory of the Empire*'.

A feeling of dread settled in Valia's belly as she realised where she was. Childhood fears she thought long buried were stirring on the edges of her mind. This was the life she had fled a long time ago and sworn never to return to. She had been born to be a Haram herself and owed her great size and strength to the bloodlines that Shol'Hara curated with such diligence. Had she been born a boy, the Akharran would have moulded her into a member of the Heavy Infantry, but as a girl she was seen a womb, nothing more.

"I am Magdalen, child," the woman replied. "I am *Dam'Hara*;

the Mistress of Shol'Hara."

"I know what Dam'Hara means,"Valia scowled.

"Indeed," the Dam'Hara said with a patient smile. "You are not the first runaway to return to us."

Valia pinched the bridge of her nose and took a moment to gather her thoughts and memories. "I did not return," she replied, swinging her legs off the side of the bed. "I was brought. Now bring me my clothes and I will leave again."

The Dam'Hara sighed. "You are quite safe here, child, you know,"

Valia glared at the woman. "The last time I entered this confounded city, they tried to have me killed."

The Dam'Hara stood up and looked down her nose at Valia.

"You are in Shol'Hara," she declared. "The machinations of those witless fools in Kor'Habat cannot reach you here. I give you my personal guarantee."

Valia took little reassurance from the Dam'hara's words but eased back down onto the bed anyway, feeling her ribs with tentative fingers.

The Dam'Hara relaxed her own pose in response. "What is your name, child?" the Mistress asked in a softer tone.

"Valia. My name is Valia."

"No, no," Magdalen whispered shaking her head. "Those cheekbones; your strength; the fire in your belly. You are a child of Shol'Hara." She sat back and sighed. "A pity that you did not pass that fire on. Or have you? Have you borne children outwith these walls?"

Valia shook her head.

"That is all I could ever be to you and this place," she muttered. "A womb; not a woman."

"A 'Mother of the Empire' is no small thing," the Dam'Hara replied with a hint of hurt in her voice.

"What Empire!" Valia retorted. "It is gone! Swept away. And soon Kor'Habat will be crushed too because of blind fools like you!"

"Normally, I would have a girl beaten for speaking to me like that," she sniffed. "But in the circumstances, I will allow your little outburst to pass."

Valia almost laughed. "There is nothing you can do to me that I have not suffered already," she scowled. "Do your worst."

"Yes," the Dam'Hara agreed. "Your scars tell me as much. A shame: I am certain that you were pretty, once. But your flower has long since bloomed and withered."

"Do you think that your insults hurt? Are you trying to goad me, old woman? Wounded or not I could snap your neck in a heartbeat, so do not test me."

"Such fire!" the Dam'Hara laughed with delight. "You truly were a loss to Shol'Hara. '*Valia of Hadaiti*'; I have always known that you were one of ours."

Valia settled back onto the bed, irritated with herself for allowing her anger to get the better of her.

"Sadly, it is not *fire* we lack now, but *wisdom*," the Dam'Hara said as she stood, placing her book on the chair. She walked to the nearest window. "Men have neither the wit nor the foresight to rule. They have but two uses: fighting and fornicating. Precious few excel at either, and those who do at both are the stuff of myth and legend." She chuckled. "Our Kodistai does not have enough sense left in his aged body to die and so we are at the mercy of fools who vie for power like ravens squabbling over the soft parts of the carcass." There was a long pause. "What is it like out in the world, child?" she asked with a wistful edge to her voice. "In my seventy-two years I have never set foot outside of Shol'Hara; and I doubt I ever shall."

A tap at the door signalled that the girl had returned with food for Valia. She looked barely ten years old and yet was tall and broad-shouldered already. Valia could not help but feel sorry for her; a few more years of washing dishes and serving Harami before she herself was reduced to bearing children, '*to the glory of the Empire*'. She placed the tray on the table beside Valia's bed, curtsied and left. The smell of the soup and warm, crusty bread had Valia salivating in a heartbeat.

"You do not approve of us," the Dam'Hara said without turning from the window. "But these girls will live their lives in luxury. They will not be abused or blemished by the world outside, as you have been." She turned to face Valia and held her gaze for a long moment. "Eat," she said at last. "I will return soon, but for now; eat and rest."

Claytan and the boy hung Nirmaya from her bound wrists in the centre of the square cell and left. A metal hook suspended from the ceiling held her at a height that allowed her feet to touch the cold stone of the floor.

Shaking from the cold, she looked around the cell. The stone walls were unbroken save for a small, barred window set high on one wall, and a lamp that burned in a sconce opposite, above a low, narrow cot. She could see no movement beyond the iron bars but tried to scream for help anyway.

The bulky gag in her mouth absorbed most of the sound and after a moment she bowed her head in silent defeat.

The boy returned, carrying a bucket of water, with a large rag over his shoulder. He placed the bucket on the floor beside her and reached up towards her face. She recoiled from his hands until she realised that he was removing the gag.

The wonderful relief had her thanking the boy before she could stop herself. He shied away from her gaze and scooped some water from the bucket with a ladle. She drank from it when he held it up to her lips, almost choking in her eagerness to swallow it. The water tasted muddy, but she did not care.

At last she focussed on the boy who was avoiding her gaze. He looked no more than fifteen years old, and a long scar was visible across the left side of his close-shaven head.

"What is your name?" she murmured to the boy, but he

turned away.

He took the rag from his shoulder and dropped it into the bucket, soaking it with the cold water. Then he started to wipe her down, starting with her face.

"Help me," she whispered, but he did not reply.

He washed her arms up to the wrists and then worked down, wiping the grime from her shoulders, her back and her breasts. He did not speak at all and did not look her in the eye.

"What is your name?" she asked again, but this time the boy shook his head and uttered a low moan.

She felt the cold cloth wipe down over her buttocks and thighs. She clamped her legs together as he tried to wipe her groin and he made a pitiful sound as she twisted away.

"No," she said, and he flashed a guilty glance at her face.

He managed a weak smile before continuing down her legs with the cloth. Perhaps whatever had caused the injury to his head had left him the way he was now, for he did not have all his wits about him; that much was clear.

"We can help each other," she whispered. "We can be friends."

The boy replied with a vigorous shake of his head and slunk out of the room with the bucket. A moment later he returned with a bundle of coarse cloth. He laid it out on the cot and Nirmaya could see that it was a simple gown of some sort.

He pulled a stool from under the cot and placed it at her feet, then hurried from the room, pulling the door shut behind him. She heard a heavy bolt slide home.

For a moment she stood in the silence, waiting.

When nobody else came, she stood up onto the stool and lifter her wrists from the hook. She groaned as she lowered her aching arms and stepped down from the stool. She glanced at the door before making her way towards the window, which was well beyond her reach, even if she had stood on the little stool.

"Hello?" she called up.

She waited, but the only thing she heard was the trickling of water.

"Hello?" she called a little louder.

The bolt slid back from the door and it swung open. Claytan strode in as she spun and before she could move a single step, he had grabbed her and flung her face down on the cot.

She heard the loud crack of the switch across her buttocks before she felt it, but when it came the pain took her breath away.

Claytan grabbed a fistful of her hair and wrenched her head back.

"There is nobody there to hear your call, girly," he hissed into her face, his breath heavy with the stench of decaying meat. "So best you just lie quietly and wait until you are needed."

He pushed her face back down into the thin mattress, and she waited for the next blow.

But it never came. She heard his footsteps recede, and then felt a presence beside the cot. She dared to look through tear-filled eyes.

The boy was there with a knife.

She recoiled against the stone wall, but he grabbed her arm and before she realised what he was doing, he had cut the rope from her wrists. A momentary surge of hope vanished with the boy as he scurried from the room and bolted the door behind him.

She sobbed into the mattress until the cold drove her to pull on the coarse gown. The fabric was rough against the fresh welt that Claytan had left.

Then she curled up on the cot and waited.

Adeyemi stood alone at the edge of a large wood as evening came. The view from the rise was glorious, with wisps of high cloud glowing against a darkening sky.

He opened the pouch that he wore around his neck and felt inside. Only two seeds remained.

He plucked one out and held it up to stare at it in the dying light.

"Tomorrow, I die," the large man whispered. The tiny seed fell from his delicate grasp and landed on the dry ground. He flexed his shoulders and looked east.

"If a man cannot run from death, he should embrace it," he murmured, running his fingers across the jagged scars that ran through the precise, delicate whorls on his cheeks. "Even I cannot fail in this."

CHAPTER 21

The bolt slid back, and the door swung open.

"Get up!" Claytan barked. "Your owner's here."

Nirmaya sat up, wincing from the pain it caused her.

"Move!" her captor shouted.

Nirmaya stood and waited, not sure what she was meant to do next.

"Well, this way, girly," he urged, stepping away from the doorway and gesturing down the hall beyond.

She steeled herself and walked towards him, edging past as he made way for her. He stank of cheap wine and had surely not bathed for a fortnight. In the hallway beyond she walked past a dozen other doors like her own and wondered who was imprisoned behind them.

"Up those stairs," he ordered.

She started up the cold, stone steps that led to a wider, brighter hallway. There were no windows, but there were large clusters of lamps suspended from the high ceiling which cast an even glow along the hall.

Lurid tapestries hung from the walls, depicting vivid scenes of a carnal nature; women being coupled with beasts or else being bound and beaten. She tried not to look at them.

A muffled cry from behind one of the doors she passed made her shiver.

What kind of a place was this?

Claytan told her to stop when she had drawn level with a large, closed door.

"Now, knock," he said.

She stepped forward and lifted an aching hand. She glanced down the hall.

"If you're thinking of running; don't," Claytan warned. "There's no one to hear you down here, and every door is locked and guarded. Some girls try to run; but only once..."

She could feel his eyes on her as she knocked on the door, trying not to let him see how much it hurt her hand.

"Come," said a voice from within.

Claytan nodded for her to enter with a cruel grin. She opened the heavy door and walked in.

Inside, Silman was sitting in a large chair, drinking wine. She could see a large bed, as well as a table.

"Close the door," he said.

Nirmaya shut the door behind her.

"Do you know where you are?" he asked.

Nirmaya shook her head, staring at the floor.

"This is a very special kind of brothel," he explained. "It caters to a certain taste. Do you know what I mean?"

She looked past him to the table where heavy manacles rested, along with various other items she dared not inspect too closely; knives and tongs whose purpose she did not wish to know.

"Cowards, you mean," she said with less defiance than she had hoped.

"Oh, good," he laughed. "You still have some spirit left, even now. I will enjoy breaking it completely before leaving what is left to whoever can pay the silver mark to have you. Now, pull that heavy curtain across the door; it helps to muffle the cries."

An hour later, Nirmaya was dragged back to her little cell by one of the guards and dumped on the cot. She was able to pull the bedpan out in time to vomit, and lay gasping on the floor. The cold flagstones did little to sooth the fresh cuts on her back the whip had inflicted, but it was all she could do. She lay like that until the boy entered the room with a bucket of water and a tray with bread and a bowl of soup.

She sat up and tried to catch his eye.

"What is your name?" she asked.

The boy flinched.

"Please, help me," Nirmaya implored.

He gestured to the bucket and then made a rubbing motion on his chest.

"For washing? Thank you."

The boy lingered a moment.

"My name is Nirmaya," she said in a gentle tone. "What is your name?"

The boy edged closer, his eyes flashing between the open doorway and her. He opened his mouth wide and Nirmaya gasped.

"Who did that to you?" she whispered in horror.

The boy glanced out the door.

"Claytan?" she asked, and the boy nodded. "Claytan cut out your tongue?"

She recoiled as the boy scurried from the room. The door banged shut and the bolt slid home.

"Help me, please!"

Valia awoke, and for a moment was sure that the voice had been a dream.

"Please," it came again. "Don't let them take my baby!"

She raised herself up onto an elbow and squinted at the open doorway. "Who are you?" she asked as the stranger staggered in. A woman in a grey nightgown.

Before the intruder could answer she was bent double by a spasm that had her gasping for air. She leaned back against the wall and slid down onto the floor, clutching her swollen belly.

"You should not be here," Valia insisted, forcing herself from her bed. "Where are the midwives?"

"No!" the woman pleaded. "It is a boy; I know it is. He will be taken from me."

Valia tried to force the stiffness from her back as she crossed the room.

"The baby is coming?" she asked in a hesitant whisper.

The woman doubled over again and groaned through clenched teeth. Her dark hair was plastered across her face when she recovered a few moments later but was either unaware of it or did not care enough to push it aside. Valia knelt and reached out to wipe the sweat and matted hair aside and reveal the weary face behind it.

Barely more than a girl.

"You should not be here," she said again as gently as she could.

"Help me," the young woman begged.

"I can't. I do not know how."

"They will take him!"

"They won't take your baby," Valia assured her as another contraction took the breath from her.

Valia patted the woman's hand through the wave of pain, unsure what else to do.

"I will call for help," she said, making to rise.

"No!" The hand that clamped around Valia's wrist was like a vice. "Please, no."

She stopped and stared at the bloodless knuckles, shocked at the strength in those fingers.

"What can I do?"

"I don't know," the woman replied shaking her head. She loosened her grip and started to sob before the pain swelled again.

"What is your name?" Valia asked when at last the contraction ended.

"Lily," she replied after gulping down great lungfuls of air and sagging back against the wall in exhaustion.

"You need help, Lily. I do not know what to do."

"They will take him," she groaned.

"Who?"

"The Akharran," she replied. "They take them all."

"Only when the child is older," Valia smiled, wiping the sweat from the woman's brow with her hand. "When he is big and strong. They won't take your baby."

Lily's breathing quickened and she pitched forwards, landing on her elbows and bringing her knees under her. "He's coming," she managed, before dragging in a ragged breath and screaming through gritted teeth for what felt to Valia like an eternity. Then she inhaled again and screamed against the agony within her.

"You should lie down," Valia urged, but Lily shook her head as she gasped for breath, remaining as she was on her elbows and knees.

Valia watched the young woman steady her breathing, bracing for what she knew would come.

This was battle. A battle against the agonies of the body and the doubts and fears of the mind. The enemy hurled its clamour of dread and pain against the wall of her fortitude in a litany of callous waves, and she faced them without armour; stripped bare of all but her nature. Another test in an age-old war for the one thing more precious than wealth or status; the treasured prize valued above all others. She fought for life, but not her own. She struggled against the bane of her gender to gift the world a new life, unsullied by the evils of the world, and with it a single hope for the future.

Another spasm of pain took her as the battle reached its climax. She bit back a scream and pushed again, driven by a primal instinct older than memory.

She gasped. "I feel his head. Take him!"

Valia lifted the nightgown with trembling hands and saw at once the dark whorls of matted hair on a tiny head emerging into the world. She reached out as Lily pushed again and the child was suddenly free. Lily collapsed in an exhausted heap, leaving Valia to stare with shock and wonder at the bloodied new-born in her hands; unmoving.

Valia held her breath. The child's flesh was pale and grey beneath the smears of blood.

Fate *no, that struggle could not have been in vain. Fight!*

At last the baby drew in its first breath and a crackling cry declared that Shol'Hara had a new daughter. The soft skin was suddenly pink and alive, the baby flexing her limbs in a new and unfamiliar world. Perfect and pure in her innocence.

"It is a girl," Valia said in sudden relief, laying the baby on her mother's chest, conscious of the cord that still linked them.

Lily was at once changed. No longer the terrified girl who had entered Valia's room; she was a mother now, and her tears were those of joy. She wiped the blood and vernix from the baby's face with the hem of her gown and kissed the tiny forehead.

"Hello, little one," she cooed over the baby's cries. "You have a fine voice, do you not?"

"Lily!" a voice from the door declared. "What were you thinking?"

Two midwives bustled into the room and fussed around the new mother and her baby.

"We have been looking everywhere for you!"

Lily paid them no heed, even when she was lifted into a wheeled chair and rushed from the room. Her world was in her arms at that moment and nothing could break the spell.

Valia sat back on her heels, feeling utterly exhausted, but there was a spark in her mind that she had thought was long extinguished. A scintilla had been kindled by the first, precious cry of a new and pure soul, and had then grown into an ember.

That ember was hope.

Adeyemi had been watching the approaching army all day.

He pulled back as they approached, learning the pattern of

their movement. The ragged remains of the force from the south that he had fought the previous day had reached this larger army and been absorbed into it. Now, thousands upon thousands of Eastern soldiers and Western Cultists moved together in loose formations along the weathered road. Then came the war engines; huge, arcane contraptions dragged by teams of horses, rolled across the landscape on wheels as tall as men and bigger.

So, they had repaired much of what had been destroyed at Dargenmill, Adeyemi realized.

A procession of wagons and carts followed with the smiths and cooks who kept an army equipped and fed. Shar meandered through the vast convoy, ranging ahead to taste the air for enemy scouts. Smeared with a concoction of mud and tree resin, Adeyemi knew that they would not sense him on the wind.

But they would taste his flesh before the day was out.

The column stopped, and the soldiers began to strike camp as the light faltered. Tents sprung up in the fields to either side of the road, and teams of men headed for the trees to collect wood.

The Shar were not accompanying these men, Adeyemi noticed.

That was where he would begin.

With a sharp tug he snapped the leather thong around his neck and tossed the empty pouch on the ground.

His days were done.

He started down into the shallow valley, using the trees for cover to skirt around to the south. He freed the impanga from its sheath on his back, dashing with a silent tread through the woodland. Evening was coming, darkness would follow and for him there would be no more dawns, but he would help his friends this one last time. They would never know, but what did that matter? Most of his life had been spent in the shadows, serving his people in ways that could never be brought out into the light.

That he had been given so many days after his great failure was a blessing; a chance to put his mistakes to rest and find redemption in this distant land.

He could hear them now and so he slowed his pace, moving like a whisper towards the enemy.

Axes cut at the trees and men joked together about wine and women. They were close now, and unaware of his approach.

His impanga split the first man's head down to the shoulders. The second had just enough time to draw breath before Adeyemi had taken his head off with the heavy blade he swung with such efficiency.

He crouched behind an old stump as two more of the foraging party approached. They were full of stories about the whore houses of Kor'Habat and their lurid plans for the ladies there. They were both dead within a heartbeat of each other.

He broke the neck of the next man he encountered, laying the twitching body on the dry leaves before the life had even left the startled eyes of his victim. He moved in silence, taking cover when needed and striking from the shadows before his victims knew he was there.

This was what he was born to; the Queen's own assassin; protector of the throne; defender of the *Blood*.

The blood!

A memory flashed in his mind.

The blood on the tiles!

His failure!

The bodies of infants!

He was already upon his next victim and would have cut his throat if not for the terrified eyes staring back into his own with a spark of recognition.

He was jolted from the trance.

"You?" Adeyemi managed to say before the Shar leapt from the shadows and knocked him from his feet.

He rolled and came up in a low crouch just in time to cut down the second Shar as it lunged. He had severed a forelimb and a moment later had removed its head. The first, he deflected as he rolled but felt the cold of its claws as they sliced across his chest.

He resumed the dance and came up in an attacking pose, lunging at the creature as it shrieked. The terrible sound ended as he took its head, but he knew that there would be more after that cry of alarm...

Within moments the gloomy forest came alive with the keening sound of approaching Shar. He abandoned stealth and stood tall in the forest. Then he gripped his impanga and ran towards them with a cry that could be heard for miles along the shallow valley.

Valia had refused to wear the garments offered to her.

The skirts and dresses worn by the Harami were something she had sought to avoid for most of her young life and she was not about to change now. Striding through Shol'Hara in a nightgown, she was eventually able to find her own clothes, in a bin outside the laundry, marked for disposal.

She washed them herself and hung the simple woollen garments from the window ledge of her room to dry in the warm evening air. While she waited, she set about cleaning her armour.

It was crusted with dried blood and criss-crossed with cuts. Most of the gashes were shallow, but the few that had breached the leather could be matched to the fresh wounds on her body.

"You have an appetite for sure," the Dam' Hara remarked as she entered the room, seeing the empty tray. When Valia did not reply she went on, "I understand you had an uninvited guest this morning. She is fine, incidentally. Both she and the baby are strong and well. A small panic, no more. It happens at times, especially a Haram's first."

"I need a leather-worker," she replied, poking a finger through one of the holes in the armour.

"Or you could wear the clothes provided," the older woman suggested, a little taken aback.

Valia grunted. "I have no need of silk or lace," she replied.

"But this armour is damaged."

"Leather is seldom worn here," the Dam'Hara said and then quickly tilted her head and smirked. "Well, sometimes if the mood is right. But I doubt you would survive a battle in it."

"Never mind," Valia replied, rinsing the gore from the cloth and setting about working on a new section. "You have beeswax at least, surely."

"I am sure the apiary can provide some."

Valia worked in silence for a long while, absorbed by the task. "And I will need a smith to look at my sword," she said. "I must be ready."

The Dam'Hara chuckled. "My dear, it has been too long since you were among us," she chided. "There are no smiths in Shol'Hara. The only men that are allowed here are those deemed worthy of siring the next generation of Infantrymen. Those and the Eunuchs, of course. There are six thousand of the finest, breeding-age women in Shol'Hara. We could not just let *any* man in, now could we?"

"I need to find my friends," she said with a sudden urgency. "I need to find Marlon Padar and Granger. Where is the historian? How far away is the Khalim-Shar?"

"You need to rest," the Dam'Hara said in a soothing voice. "You are inside Shol'Hara, within the walls of Kor'Habat. There is no safer place in the world."

Valia hesitated. "How many children are here?"

The Dam'Hara shook her head in confusion.

"How quickly could you get them out if you had to?" Valia asked.

"Now you are being foolish," the Dam'Hara scolded.

Valia leaned forward and fixed the woman's gaze. "No, Dam'Hara," she said through clenched teeth. "It is you who is the fool."

Adeyemi felt his head being lifted and then left to drop

forwards again. He was hanging from his wrists and his arms ached from the pressure.

"I thought you people were just a story," came a voice with an Eastern accent. "Yet here one stands before me."

Adeyemi opened his eyes and found a man looking up at him. The man was from the Eastern Kingdoms for certain, and wore a simple, brown robe. His lips held a smile that did not touch his cruel, dark eyes.

With some effort, he lifted his head and saw that he was in a large clearing. At the centre, a fire was burning, casting a dancing orange light on the faces of the soldiers who were gathered around in a wide circle. Shar lay on the ground, pools of midnight around the periphery, their glassy eyes gleaming with reflected fire. Adeyemi took some of his weight on his legs to relieve the pain in his shoulders.

He chuckled. The sky was dark but was surely not yet midnight. Whatever these fools planned to inflict on him would be short lived. He would soon be dead; his days were used up.

"Spy," his captor murmured as he circled Adeyemi. "Scout. Messenger. What news would you have taken to Kor'Habat? What false hope would you have shared?"

Adeyemi spat the blood from his mouth and tested his bonds.

"Do not leave us yet," the man teased. "We have so much to show you."

A murmur ran through the gathered soldiers, and they began to part, opening a path that led into the darkness.

The Shar around the periphery of the clearing raised their heads, some rising to a low squat, and turned towards the gap in the crowd of soldiers.

A Shar entered the circle and shook its head in agitation. The creature raised itself onto its hind legs for a moment before dropping down onto the powerful front limbs and began pacing around the fire. This Shar was different; he could see that. The posture it held was an awkward blend of beast and something that yearned to be more. The Shar lifted itself onto its hindquarters before dropping down again to cower. The other creatures chittered with excitement.

Then a new figure emerged from the darkness. The Khalim-Shar.

Enormous and silent it strode into the clearing, towering over the soldiers. The Khalim-Shar walked as upright as any man and carried a huge trident in its right talon. The other Shar in the centre of the clearing cowered away from the Khalim-Shar, shrinking away on the opposite side of the fire.

The Khalim-Shar regarded the other creature for a moment before turning its head towards Adeyemi. The huge creature closed the gap between them in two, long strides and bent down to bring its head level with his own. Its tongue darted out and flicked around Adeyemi's face, tasting his scent, his fear.

"*Messenger*. What news from Kor'Habat?" it hissed with a voice of grating steel.

Adeyemi said nothing.

"You are a beaten people," it said, standing tall again. "You cannot hope to stand against me. The age of the *Shar* is at hand and it will last for eternity. I am the new order. I alone have the power to hold dominion over this world. One Khalim-Shar!" it shrieked and hurled the trident across the clearing.

The huge weapon struck the cowering Shar in the shoulder, pinning it to the ground with two of the trident's points. The Khalim-Shar had closed the gap between it and its victim even before the first scream emanated from the stricken creature.

The Khalim-Shar lifted its victim into the air and held it aloft for all to see.

The flesh oozed around the wounds, as the Shar worked to free itself but the Khalim-Shar slammed it onto the ground before it had a chance.

"One Khalim-Shar!" it declared with a shrill, grating call, clamping the screaming beast's head in its huge claws. Every razor talon dug into the writhing flesh, sinking into the dark substance as the agonised screeches grew ever more desperate.

The Shar thrashed in the Khalim-Shar's grip until at last, it lay still. The Khalim-Shar stood and held out its many-clawed hand for all to see.

A black jewel glistened in the light.

Adeyemi leaned forward in his restraints and gasped.

"The *Anaki* belong to me," the Khalim-Shar hissed, and turned to face Adeyemi. "You have seen one before?"

Adeyemi stared at the jewel; identical in every way to the one that had been stolen from him. That strange thing had given him hope; it had given him life.

He watched as it vanished into the flesh of the Khalim-Shar's palm.

The huge creature arched its back in ecstasy and uttered a low moan.

Behind it, the Shar stirred. The stricken beast was still impaled on the trident, but its flesh had begun the process of ejecting the foreign object.

With a sudden explosion of movement, the Khalim-Shar lifted its victim with the trident and dumped it on top of the fire. Sparks erupted in a glittering plume as the creature thrashed in agony. The Khalim-Shar pressed down on the trident, forcing the bubbling flesh deeper into the coals and hissed at the dying Shar beneath it. The shrieking went on for longer than Adeyemi thought possible, and the Shar around the fire cowered as their kin was roasted.

When at last the creature lay still, the Khalim-Shar pulled the trident from the blistered char and paced around the fire.

"That one dared to rise, when there can be only one Khalim-Shar," it hissed. "Ten thousand men it lost in battle outside the walls of Kor'Habat. Its failure sealed its doom." It stopped in front of Adeyemi. "Open your eyes and mark this well, *messenger*."

It strode towards the edge of the clearing and the soldiers

parted to reveal a new area, devoid of people. In the dim light of the torches there Adeyemi could see a large shape in a shallow depression.

That shape was a Shar; bloated and deformed. When it moved, it was slow and uncoordinated; it tried to stand but staggered sideways, eventually coming to a halt when it sensed the Khalim-Shar. Its head lowered as its master squatted low and held out long talons. The bloated Shar twitched and spasmed; its limbs kicked out, scraping at the ground and kicking up plumes of dust.

Adeyemi was sure that it was dying, but the Khalim-Shar had not touched it, only extended its hand over the creature's head. A pitiful whimper came from the throat of the beast as its body contorted and bulged. In the light of the torches, Adeyemi watched the Shar pull itself apart. The flesh flowed like melted wax, reforming into new shapes that were remaking the creature.

There was no longer a single Shar.

The solitary shape became two, fused together and struggling to break apart. The two shapes contorted in their efforts to tear away, pulling at the flesh that joined them.

At last they were free of each other. They stumbled away, snapping their bony jaws in irritation and gaining confidence in their movements with every passing moment.

The Khalim-Shar raised its arms above its head as Adeyemi gasped in horror.

"One Shar becomes two!" it declared, and the other Shar shrieked their tribute to the Great Shar. "We can never be defeated!"

Adeyemi sagged.

The Shar could multiply!

That single wisdom that had given people hope was now ashes in the wind. Their number was no longer finite.

Adeyemi raised his head as the Khalim-Shar stopped in front of him. With the flick of its razor talons his bonds were cut, and he collapsed onto the ground.

The Khalim-Shar bent down and placed its mouth close to his ear.

"Take this message to Kor'Habat, *messenger*," it hissed. "The Khalim-Shar is their God now. Surrender and serve me, or I will turn their city to dust."

Adeyemi found himself staggering along a path through thousands of soldiers who watched him pass. Some jeered, some spat but none attempted to hinder him.

Then he saw that familiar face again, etched with concern and fear as they locked eyes when Adeyemi stumbled past.

"Little Bird?" he murmured to himself. "Was that you?"

A few hours later and Adeyemi stumbled west on faltering legs, glancing back at an impossible sunrise.

How could a man whose days had been spent still walk and breathe?

The magic of the Khalim-Shar?

His enemy had granted him more time in order to carry this message. He was *its* servant now, doing *its* bidding. He was a slave to its power; bound by it.

Reborn into the service of the Great Shar, Adeyemi struggled on.

CHAPTER 22

Abbil was still doing his best not to look like the awestruck peasant in the big city. After leaving his companions behind he had been helped into Kor'Habat by a friendly barge master in return for unloading the cargo. Abbil could now start searching for Nirmaya, although he had no idea where to begin.

No one he spoke to had seen her arrive, either alone or in the custody of the Heavy Infantry. He was hungry and did not have a single copper mark to his name. The only thing of value he carried was his sword, and he would die before selling that.

He slumped down, exhausted onto a doorstep, and watched the people of Kor'Habat going about their days. Did they even know what approached?

A coin clattered onto the ground at his feet. He took a moment before realising it was meant for him. He picked it up and turned it over in his hand.

"Wait!" he protested. "I'm not…"

But his benefactor was gone. Vanished into the crowd.

Did he really look so wretched that people would think him a beggar?

He stood again. Pride would not allow another such insult. But all the same, a part of him considered that a copper mark would buy a meal if nothing else. He hurried to the nearest inn and slapped the coin onto the counter.

"What will this get me?" he asked.

"Not very drunk," the innkeeper replied, regarding the lonely coin with a sour expression.

"Food, man!" Abbil replied. "I mean food."

The innkeeper slid the coin over to the other side of the counter and it vanished into his apron. He walked to the kitchen hatch and slapped the shelf twice. A few moments later he returned with a bowl of meat and potatoes, and a wedge of bread.

He watched as Abbil wolfed it down.

"Been a while, has it?" he asked.

"Hmm?" Abbil replied.

"Since your last meal, I mean."

Abbil sighed as the food settled. "Do you know what is happening out there?" he asked with more heat than he intended. "Beyond your walls?"

"Alright. No need to take offence," the innkeeper replied. "Now unless you've got any more of those copper marks…"

Abbil sighed.

"I apologise," he said. "I'm looking for someone; a girl. A young woman," he corrected himself.

"Plenty of brothels down Porters' Lane," the innkeeper suggested. "But you'll not get much with an empty purse. *Charm* isn't a currency much in use down Porters'."

"Not like that! I think she was brought here. Perhaps by the Heavy Infantry."

The innkeeper raised an eyebrow. "Then you should try the Akharran. I believe they have resolved their differences for now, although I can't see *that* truce holding long."

Abbil shook his head, unsure what the man was talking about. "No one in the docks has seen anything like that," he reasoned. "Is there nowhere else a young woman might be taken?"

"Young women go missing from time to time," the innkeeper said. "They usually find them in the end, face down in the canal. If the Heavy Infantry have her, and she is in the Akharran, then *you* won't be getting her out."

Abbil thanked the innkeeper and walked back out into the street. He stared up at the sky as though the answer lay in the clouds. This city was bigger than he had ever imagined.

"Where are you, girl," he murmured.

He was suddenly aware of a large man beside him and his hand went by reflex to his sword.

"There is no need," the man said. He was young, and very big.

"Can I help you, son?" Abbil asked, taking in the size of the young man. Heavy Infantry for sure; even without armour, his size gave it away.

"There are places worse than Porters' Lane," he said.

"What? Who are you?"

"Sometimes women are taken to these places. Sometimes it's boys; sometimes girls so young it would break your heart."

"I'm looking for a young woman," Abbil urged, sensing that this young soldier knew something. "Her name is Nirmaya. She could only have come here a day or two ago."

The man nodded and handed Abbil a scrap of paper where a crude map had been scrawled.

"You will also need this," the man said, handing Abbil a small pouch that jingled with coins. "This place is not cheap, and there is no sign above the door to welcome you. It is secret, and it is well guarded. You will need that sword."

"What do I say to them when I get there?"

The young man hesitated. "Tell them Silman sent you," he said after a moment's thought. "Tell them you want his girl."

"*Captain* Silman? I know that name. Who are you?" Abbil asked, staring at the young man's face.

The stranger managed a weak smile. "Just someone trying to do the right thing," he replied, and walked away into the crowded street.

Granger joined the other men on the wall above the gates

at the edge of one of the two flanking towers. The centre of the forty-foot wide space was occupied by an enormous *Hatiyara*; a crossbow that could send spears the weight of a two men over two hundred and fifty yards. With this elevation, it could throw them even further. Acastes, Marlon and Dachen were staring out over the remains of the warren of ramshackle buildings, beyond the ditch that separated the flared base of the city walls from the plain. The dregs of Kor'Habat had once lived there, and then the refugees had driven them into the city. Eventually even the displaced people of the Eastern Kingdoms had left, and at last the plain was silent.

"Any word from Valia?" he asked, peering over the stone battlements.

"She was recovering, last I heard," Acastes replied. "But Shol'Hara is impregnable to the likes of us. News will come when the Dam'Hara is ready."

Granger nodded.

"I have not thanked you for retrieving my books," he said. "I feared I would never see them again."

"Very careless, allowing your pack-horse to wander off with them while you played soldier," Acastes said with a wry smile.

"Ah," Granger laughed. "But I will be quite heroic in my writing. I believe I slayed a dozen men; twenty, even!"

"Make it thirty, why not?" Acastes joked. "Who will know?"

Granger looked skywards and searched the blue expanse. "There is usually someone," he replied with less humour.

Acastes shrugged. "Just remember who came to your rescue," he said.

Granger nodded. "It will not be forgotten, Acastes," he murmured. "I only hope it was not in vain. Any sign yet?"

"They will be here by nightfall," Marlon grumbled.

"And we will be ready," Dachen said.

Granger looked back at the huge mechanism behind him, as well as the stack of steel and timber bolts at its side. "Is this a duel we can win?" he asked.

Dachen smiled. "At the Great Tournament at Myampor, Sangye destroyed Khumjang's weapons in only four rounds," he informed them. "That man could put a bolt through a keyhole without rattling the lock."

"Well," Acastes murmured. "That certainly sounds impressive. But this is no tournament."

"There is a man on the road," Marlon interrupted them, as he squinted against the noon sunshine.

They all stared east along the road that led away into the distance, and sure enough, a distant figure was making its way towards them. The runner stumbled and fell, only to regain its feet to keep on moving.

"Adeyemi!" Dachen breathed, rushing to the ladder.

"How could it be," Acastes said, shading his eyes from the light.

"It is him," Granger agreed. "I would recognise that stride anywhere."

The figure loped along the road on unsteady legs.

"Open the gate!" Acastes shouted and waited for the order to be carried out.

The sound of meshing gears turning against one another signalled that the massive gates were easing open as Adeyemi approached.

The moment he could squeeze through, Dachen was running to meet his friend.

"Is he being followed?" Acastes asked, staring beyond the exhausted man.

There was no sign of a chase and soon Dachen had helped the man through the gates, which eased shut again behind them.

Granger was already on his way down the ladder when Acastes and Marlon turned to follow. The wooden ladder led into the open space of the barbican from where a door led onto the battlements to either side. Spiralling stone steps took them down through the tower to ground level.

Adeyemi had collapsed on the cobbles and lay on his back, gasping for air. His eyes were wild with panic and exhaustion.

"Water!" Dachen called out.

An Infantryman arrives with a bladder a few moments later and Dachen held it to his friend's lips.

"Drink, my friend," he said, supporting Adeyemi's head.

Dachen looked up at his companions with a worried expression. "I have never seen him like this," he said, shaking his head, and then to Adeyemi. "You are safe now. Take your time."

Adeyemi spluttered as he took on too much water but managed to steady his breathing.

"The Khalim-Shar is coming, friend Dachen," he coughed. "With an army of thousands."

"We know, friend," he assured him. "We are ready for them."

"No," Adeyemi replied, fixing Dachen with a stare. "You are not."

He sagged back down onto the cobbles and squeezed his eyes shut, before drifting into unconsciousness.

Nirmaya sat on the cot with her knees up under her chin and her arms wrapped around her legs. Every scrape of a boot, every creak of a hinge had her on edge. Silman would be back.

She knew that their first encounter had been a taste of worse things to come. Silman had rushed, eager to quench the thirst he had harboured for so long. The longer he had her, the more he would enjoy it. She tried to dispel the recent memories from her mind, but they persisted.

She could hear no sounds from the city, so assumed that she was either deep underground or else in a very quiet district. Even if she could escape her cell, would there be other locked doors to get past? Or guards?

She was unarmed, alone and entirely at their mercy.

The bolt slid back and startled her, but it was only the boy with a tray. A cup of water and a bowl of that foul soup she had been served before. Nirmaya stood up and took the tray from him, placing it on the floor. A quick glance at the open door had her heart racing, but she resisted the urge to run. That would get her nowhere.

"Stay a while, please," she said, and he hesitated as he turned. "Will you stay and talk to me? I mean, listen for a while." She felt silly now.

The boy flashed a sideways glance at her and then stared at the floor.

"Do you like it here?" she asked.

The boy stood motionless for a moment before he gave a quick shake of his head.

"There aren't any other boys your age here, are there?" she said. "Do you have any friends?"

Again, the pause and the quick shake of the head.

"I don't have any friends here either," she said. "Perhaps you and I could be friends. Would you like that?"

The boy turned his head towards her and managed to hold her gaze for a heartbeat, with a weak smile, before his eyes darted towards the door.

She took a step towards him.

"Friends help each other, don't they?"

He flashed another nervous glance at her as she stepped closer still. She reached out and touched his cheek.

With a terrified whimper, he stumbled away towards the door.

"I'm sorry." She tried to calm him, but he was gone before she could say another word. The door slammed and she heard the bolt slide home.

"Stupid! Stupid!" she berated herself, flopping back onto the small cot.

She heard a snap and realised she had broken one of the wooden slats beneath the thin mattress. She lifted the filthy bedding and inspected the damage. One of the slats had indeed broken, a crack that followed the line of the grain in the wood. She worked it free and held the slat in her hand. The wood tapered to a sharp point like a dagger.

She stared at it for a long time before sliding it into her sleeve, then sat back down on the cot to wait.

Abbil reached what he was certain was the correct door; a heavy, wooden affair with strap iron riveted across it. There were no signs or markings, just a small aperture at head height that was sealed from within.

He banged on the door and waited. Evening was fast approaching, and the sky was growing dim above him.

The aperture slid open and a pair of eyes glared out at him. "What do you want?"

Abbil cleared his throat. "Silman sent me," he lied. "I'm here for his girl."

"Piss off!" came the abrupt reply and the little hole slammed shut.

Abbil banged on the door until the aperture opened again.

"I thought I told you to piss off!"

"And I told you that Silman sent me," he growled. "Let me see the girl!"

There was a short silence before the guard on the other side of the door muttered, "Wait there," and shut the aperture.

Abbil waited, not knowing what he was to do if he was asked to elaborate on the lie. A passer-by scowled at him and he glared back in response.

Then he heard sliding bolts from the other side of the door, and it opened on silent hinges.

"Come in, then," the guard said, standing back from the doorway.

Abbil went in and the scruffy doorman glanced out into the alley before closing and bolting the door again. "Leave your sword with me," the man ordered.

Abbil hesitated for a moment before unbuckling the belt and handing over the weapon. The guard leaned the sword against the wall and gestured along the wide hallway for Abbil to go. When they reached a doorway to the left, the guard opened it.

"Wait in here," he sighed, and closed the door behind Abbil when he was inside.

He was left in a simple waiting room. A few comfortable chairs and table with a wine jug in its centre. Paintings of lurid scenes adorned the walls, and a life-size stone carving of a naked woman on her knees with her head bowed filled one corner.

He smelled the wine and decided that he was not that thirsty after all.

Her heart was already pounding hard when she heard the bolt slide back.

Claytan entered the room carrying a long stick; the same one he had struck her with when she had first arrived. He waited for her to come to him, watching her every movement with lecherous eyes.

"Looking forward to having you myself once the good captain is done with you," he said, and licked his lips. He reached forward with the stick and lifted the front of her simple gown, laughing when she pushed it back down.

She paused and gripped the hem of her rough garment with her left hand. He watched as she lifted it, teasing him with the sight of her thighs. He swallowed hard and watched until her hand reached her groin, where she stopped.

"Go on, girl," he breathed, tongue darting out to moisten his dry lips. "Just a little higher."

She inched the hem upwards to reveal the soft curls of her pubic hair.

Claytan's shoulders sagged a little and he swallowed hard again.

Nirmaya lunged.

She dropped the wooden spar down her sleeve as she had

practiced and gripped it hard as she swung her right hand. The point pierced the side of his neck and he stumbled back as she pressed forward. His attempted cry of alarm was no more than a pitiful squeak as his throat filled with blood. He tried to grab her round the neck with both hands, but she drove the wooden dagger deeper and his strength faded.

Blood pumped from the wound as she twisted the spar. His lips curled in a spasm of agony and he gasped a final ragged, bubbling breath.

Nirmaya pulled the piece of wood free and left the body to sag against the wall. Her hands were slick with blood and she wiped them on the loose cloth of his nearest trouser leg. She looked at the crude weapon she had used before tossing it onto the floor. He had a belt-knife which would be far better.

She was shaking when she pulled the man's knife from the sheath but steadied herself before glancing down the dim hallway and was relieved to see that it was deserted.

She would need to be quick. Silman would grow suspicious if she did not appear at the door in the next few minutes. She hurried to the first door beyond her own, eased the bolt back and opened the door. A frightened whimper told her that there was someone inside.

"Sshhh," she whispered. "I am not here to hurt you, but I will need your help if we are to escape."

A shape rose from the little cot and edged towards Nirmaya. A girl, barely twelve if that.

Horror vied with disappointment. She could not fight her way out with a child at her back.

"My name is Nirmaya," she said. "Are all of these cells full?"

The girl nodded, and Nirmaya urged her to follow. Young women, girls and even boys were behind each door; always alone; always terrified.

How could such a place exist in the city!?

There were over twenty prisoners in all: slaves to the

perversions of those men up the stone stairs. Nirmaya began the ascent, stepping as lightly as she could and gripping the knife in her trembling hand.

She reached the door to the room where Silman had used her and hesitated. She desired nothing more than to cut that man to ribbons but attempting to do so would only attract the guards, and so she continued down the wide hallway to the foot of another flight of stairs. She glanced back to find more than twenty pairs of frightened eyes looking back at her.

Not one of them made a sound. They watched her and waited for her cue.

She only wished that she had a better plan.

Further down the hall was an open door. When she reached it, she peered in to find a room similar to the one that Silman had had her brought to before. The chamber was unoccupied, but there was a table, laden with the tools of some hideous trade; tools they would need to use if there was to be any chance of escape.

"You better have a bloody good reason for being here, old man, or they'll be fishing your bits out of the canal until winter."

The man in the doorway was wearing a loose robe and slippers and held a heavy cosh in one hand. Behind him stood a guard with one hand on the hilt of a sword.

"Captain Silman," Abbil replied. "The Heavy Infantry have relaxed their dress code since I fought them at Hadaiti."

"Who let this fool in?" Silman glowered to the guard behind him.

"He knew about the girl," the guard stammered. "Said you'd called for him."

"Idiot!" Silman spat. "You think I would tell anyone else about my arrangement here? You wait until Claytan hears about this."

"Tell me about this 'girl'," Abbil growled, taking a step forward. "Only, I do not like the stories I hear about these places."

Silman squinted and said, "I know you. You were in Ulan

Balsan. A bloody Shar-hunter."

"If you have hurt a hair on her head..." Abbil warned.

"Who are you; her father?" Silman asked, stepping towards Abbil. "Good. I'll do her in front of you. That can be your final memory."

Abbil regretted handing over his sword at the door, but only a fool would enter such a place unarmed. He always carried a short sword tucked up the back of his leather cuirass.

"What makes men like you think that they can act in this way unpunished?" he asked, shaking his head.

Silman stopped and gestured for the guard to come and take Abbil. The guard drew his sword and stepped past the huge Heavy Infantryman. Abbil waited until the man was at his side before pulling his hidden blade free. With an upward stroke he slashed at the guard's face and felt the grate of steel on bone at it sliced into his jaw.

The guard screamed and dropped his sword, clutching his face as he stumbled back. Silman lunged at Abbil, swinging the small club. Abbil stepped back but was unbalanced by the table and was forced to throw his body over it in an awkward roll to avoid Silman's attack. The wine jug was swept from the table and shattered in a blood red swathe across the stone floor.

Abbil heaved the heavy table over and onto Silman's feet. The captain howled in pain as the guard managed to pick up his sword again. He was still clutching his bleeding jaw with one hand, hissing bloody bubbles through clenched teeth. Abbil rounded the table as Silman struggled to free his crushed toes and attacked the guard. The injured man swung his sword in a clumsy arc that was easily parried and died with Abbil's sword in his chest.

The man fell, wrenching the sword from Abbil's grasp just as another guard rushed in with a sword at the ready. Abbil grabbed the guard's wrist and used the man's own momentum to swing him round. The guard pitched forward, and his head slammed into the bowed head of the kneeling, stone sculpture. His skull cracked, leaving a bloody splash on the pale stone.

Abbil turned to the door as another guard arrived to block it with a sword in his grip. The guard was distracted by something down the hall. A rising clamour of many voices, rushing closer, had him turning attention away from Abbil.

"Stop!" the guard shouted, and a moment later was swept away by a mass of women in rough robes. They fell upon the stumbling guard and stabbed at him with the tools they had found. He screamed as they plunged slender blades into him, slicing and stabbing at his flesh in a whirlwind of pain.

One of the women had reached the door at the end of the hallway and had pulled the bolts back, throwing it open onto the streets beyond, and freedom.

"Nirmaya!" Abbil shouted as he saw the young woman standing up from the bloody corpse.

She turned her beautiful, blood spattered face towards him and a relieved smile started to spread across it.

Then her eyes went wide, and she screamed his name.

Silman drove the sword into Abbil's back, piercing the thin, leather armour with the force.

"Abbil!" Nirmaya screamed again.

She took a step towards him as the other women and girls rushed out into the city.

"Run, girl," Abbil gasped as Silman struggled to stand behind him. Nirmaya hesitated, and Silman pulled the sword free, for Abbil to sink down to his knees.

"Nirmaya, run!" he sighed and then smiled. "*My girl.*"

Abbil pitched forward onto the stone floor.

"Abbil! No," she cried.

Silman bellowed in anger, taking a painful step towards her. She screamed back at him and fixed him with a look of purest hatred. She longed to attack him right there, to feel the blade pierce his belly; his throat; his eyes. She wanted to take her time; to make him suffer; to tear him apart, piece by piece while he screamed in agony. But there were more guards coming; roused by the commotion.

"I am not done with you, Silman," she yelled through her tears. "I am not finished with you yet!"

Silman roared back in defiance. He was hurt; she could see that he was barely able to stand, but she could not hope to challenge him now.

She turned and ran towards the open door while Silman raged at her back.

She ran out into a city in panic. A city under siege.

CHAPTER 23

"*C*an *you hear her call?*" *her father asks, hurrying as best he can along the track. Alisha follows until he holds up his hand.*

"*I can hear it,*" *Alisha whispers.* "*Where is it?*"

Her father points with his stick into the boughs of a red birch tree.

"*The nest is on that twisted branch,*" *he says in a low voice.* "*Near the tip, beneath that cluster of new leaves.*"

A flash of yellow as the little bird hops from twig to twig gives away its position.

"*Yes.*"

"*She is calling to her mate,*" *he says.* "*The chicks are growing hungry. Do you hear them too?*"

"*Yes,*" *she says, suddenly concerned.*

"*If he does not return soon, she will need to leave the nest unguarded.*"

"*Where is he?*"

"*I do not know,*" *her father says, shaking his head.* "*Perhaps he has been forced to travel further afield for food. The yellow-throated thrush feeds its chicks only on a specific type of caterpillar, the parents must work hard to feed themselves as well as their growing young.*"

"*What will happen if he does not come back? What if he has been killed by a fox or a hawk? Will the babies starve?*"

Her father smiles to allay her distress. "*This is the natural way of things,*" *he says.* "*But the female will need to make a difficult decision soon. She could wait and guard the nest in the hope that her mate returns in time, or else leave the young at the mercy of predators to find food by herself. Neither choice comes without risk, and she cannot know how long it will be until the male comes back to the nest, if indeed he does at all."*

"But her babies will die if she waits too long," Alisha says.

"It is a terrible choice to have to make," he says, watching the little bird fluttering around its nest in agitation. "Life often presents us with such choices; fear and uncertainty can overwhelm us at times, and we must be on guard against acting in haste. Patience can bear fruit just as often as action, but always weigh the options offered." They watch for a few moments longer until he says, "We should go. We can return tomorrow."

"What if it is too late?" she asks with wide, tear-filled eyes.

"We may yet see them fledge, Butterfly" he smiles. "Trust in the wisdom of the mother; she will do what is best."

The morning was warm and clear, and there were the beginnings of a festival atmosphere in the town of Bardiya as preparations continued for the five days of celebration to follow. Somewhere within that fog of revelry, Alisha would be veiled and married; transformed from girl to woman and with that, shackled to a life she had never once pursued or desired. The thought of living out her life as the wife of Unjen Yuddha filled her with dread and revulsion. Unless she chose to leave that fate behind her.

She paused from sweeping the street outside her gate and leaned on the broom handle, staring west. Beyond the shingled rooftops the distant sea blended into sky on an intangible horizon, no more certain than the future she sought beyond the haze. The uncertainties of the ocean frightened her as much as the certain future that had been laid out before her in Bardiya, but at least an uncharted destiny held a possibility of hope.

Even now it felt unreal. Even the knowledge that Dyansh had readied the boat; smuggled food and water onto the vessel in small bundles each day so as not to arouse suspicion, could not make it palpable in her mind. She had sat with him as he had calculated how much fresh water they would need; how much food to carry and which supplies would not rot; how much they could catch from the sea and cook daily. The numbers had washed over her without settling as though this was another's adventure. She was coming to realise what anchored her mind in this life she was seeking to escape, and it was guilt.

Tau.

How could she leave her brother? Such a benign and simple spirit.

But there was no room for another on the little vessel, and Tau would not understand the coming hardships even if there had been. He was safest there in Bardiya with a life he knew and understood in his way.

That knowledge did not ease the wretched claw that was clenched in her chest.

She finished sweeping with even less enthusiasm than the task merited and made her way back into the house. Her mother was sitting in the kitchen and glowered at her over the needlework that occupied her hands.

"I am adding some beads to your wedding veil," she muttered. "You did not make a good job of it; this should be your task after all."

"I thought I had done enough," Alisha replied. "I don't want it to be too heavy."

"Stupid girl!" her mother snapped. "It's a wedding veil; it is supposed to be heavy."

"Sorry, mama."

"You don't deserve this, you know?"

"Mama?"

"The wife of a *captain*," her mother sneered. "You don't deserve such an honour. I was cursed to be a miner's wife, and this just falls into your ungrateful lap. Where is your brother?"

"I think he is in the workshop," Alisha murmured as the sting of tears pricked at her eyes. She blinked them away.

"Go and fetch him, he has not had breakfast. Why must I endure this? Does he not have the wits to know when he must eat?"

Alisha left without a word and made her way to the workshop. Tau was sitting at the bench, looking at his reflection in a small tray. She looked over his shoulder and smiled at the distorted image in the unfinished surface. Tau grinned and tilted the tray to make their faces warp and bulge. Alisha wrapped her arms around his shoulders and hugged him.

"You will be alright, won't you, big brother?"

He made a gentle moaning sound in response.

"Perhaps when things get better here…" she trailed off, knowing that what she was about to say was a lie, and in any case was a lie for her own benefit. Tau could never understand what she wanted to tell him.

The Emperor Butterfly cocoons remained unchanged on the lintel of the workshop window and for a moment she wondered if the creatures within dreamed of wind beneath their unformed wings.

Alisha's eyes wandered to her father's walking stick; the one he had spent so long crafting. She lifted it from the bench and caressed the horn handle.

'The change that cannot be overcome should be embraced.'

"Should I embrace the change, Tau?" she asked. "Or should I force my own? I wish papa were here."

Tau did not respond other than offering her a blank stare via his reflection in the silver surface of the tray.

"We should go for breakfast," she said at last and walked him back to the house.

They ate in silence and after washing up, Alisha made her excuses and went to her room. The tension in the kitchen had become unbearable, and she was grateful to have the time to ready herself for what had to be done. She gathered a few changes of clothes, a hairbrush and mirror, a belt knife, and the purse of silver coins she had saved, and wrapped them all in a heavy blanket.

She lay listening to the familiar sounds of the house that she had known from her very first memories. The shutters being opened as her mother went about airing the house; the gurgle of a drain; the gentle ticking of warming shingles expanding under the sun. Distant voices carried through the streets and a murmur of industry grew with the day.

'Change happens by action or inaction, the true gift is in knowing which is ours to control, and which we must embrace.'

She sat bolt upright; decision made.

She took the bundle from the foot of the bed and placed it on the windowsill. Then she walked out of her room and through the kitchen towards the open door.

"Where are you going?" her mother demanded.

"Just for a walk, mama," she replied, heart suddenly racing.

"You have too much to do here," her mother demanded. "Your auntie is coming at midday and we will complete your dresses. You have two ceremonies in two days and there will not be time once the festival begins."

"I will not be long," she lied.

"You had better not be trying to visit Dyansh," the woman called out in warning. "It is not seemly for a girl who about to take the veil, let alone one about to be married."

"No, mama," she said and hurried away before her mother could argue further.

Alisha reached the cobbles of the street and circled around to the side of the workshop where she hopped over the low wall. Treading with as much care as she could she made her way to the side of the house and to her open bedroom shutters. The bundle awaited her on the sill.

As she gathered it up to her chest, she saw Tau, standing at her bedroom door watching her. She tried to muster a reassuring smile but the hurt in his eyes snatched it from her.

"I'm sorry," she mouthed, and turned away before the tears

could fill her eyes.

She hurried away with an aching heart, struggling to skirt the void of sorrow that threatened to swallow her. She buried her face in the bundle to soak away the tears and tried to push Tau to the back of her mind for now at least. She knew that she had to be brave or else all would be lost. The street sloped down towards the docks, carrying her towards the sea. Her stride became more confident the further she walked and soon the mast of Dyansh's boat came into view.

The tide was in and the vessel was sitting high in the harbour. Avoiding eye contact with the people she passed she made her way around the market stalls and hurried towards the far corner where Dyansh was waiting for her.

He sighed with relief when he saw her and motioned for her to toss him the bundle. He stowed it under a grubby tarpaulin without a word and then held out a hand, gesturing for her to climb down onto the boat.

There was not much space, with so much already aboard, but she managed to settle down at the stern. She stared at Dyansh, wide-eyed and breathless. Her heart was pounding in her chest.

This was it.

"Are you ready?" he asked, looking every bit as terrified as she felt.

She nodded.

Dyansh stepped across the boat and reached up past her to the cleat holding the stern line. He coiled the rope and stowed it in a gap between the hull and a small cask. Then he skipped forwards to the bow line and reached up to undo the hitched rope.

A boot clamped down on his fingers and he cried out in pain.

"My hand!" he shouted. "You're standing on my hand!"

"What have we here?" A soldier leaned over and looked down into the vessel. Alisha stared back at him in shock.

"You're crushing my hand, Mohanish!" Dyansh shouted, almost at the point of tears.

"Oh?" the soldier said, feigning shock. "I *am* sorry. I did not see you hand there." He leaned a little harder on Dyansh's fingers for a moment before releasing the boy who fell back in a mixture of pain and relief.

"What are you two up to?" Mohanish demanded.

"Fishing," Dyansh replied. "We're going fishing."

Mohanish inspected the boat. "Running a little low in the water for a fishing trip I would say," he said, unconvinced. "What's in the boat, boy?"

"Nothing," Dyansh retorted. "Leave us alone."

"Oh," Mohanish said, unclipping the whip from his belt, "you may want to be careful how you speak to me, boy. Just ask your father."

Dyansh did not take the bait and glared back at the soldier above them.

"Get out," Mohanish ordered. "Get up on the dock."

"No!" Dyansh growled.

Mohanish let the whip uncoil onto the stones of the harbour.

"Get out, or I will take the skin from your back," the soldier spat.

"Please," Alisha dared. "We don't want trouble. Please let us go. We only want to go fishing."

Mohanish turned his head towards her.

"Who do you think you are talking to, *girl*?" he spat. "Both of you, get out of the boat, now."

Alisha used the ladder to step up onto the harbour and stood with her head lowered and her heart racing. She felt a greasy nausea rising within her as she felt their plan unravel. Mohanish jumped down into the boat before Dyansh could follow and started kicking at the bundles under the tarpaulins. Rice and beans spilled out and he whistled through his teeth.

"Well, well. What could you be doing with all this food?" he said with a delighted grin.

Dyansh lunged towards the man and pushed him back, the

sudden move had Mohanish toppling backwards over the edge and into the water with an almighty splash. At once Dyansh leapt for the cleat and even with his bruised fingers had the rope free in a heartbeat.

"Alisha! Quickly!" he shouted, pushing the boat away from the wall.

Alisha took a moment to come to her senses, but when she did, she leapt into the boat. Mohanish returned to the surface, gasping for air and flailing with his arms.

The harbour exit looked so far away, and the little boat crept towards it at a snail's pace. Dyansh set the sail but in the shelter of the harbour there was no wind. He pulled a long paddle from the bottom of the boat and worked to put the boat away from the chaos behind them. One of the men from the market had jumped into the water to save Mohanish from drowning and the shouts and cries became a cacophony.

Dyansh strained at the paddle on one side and then the other, easing the boat towards the exit where the harbour walls narrowed. Soon the tide would have them dragged out to safety, but more soldiers had arrived on the harbour walls behind them.

"Dyansh!" Alisha screamed in horror as a Shadow emerged from the crowd and loped along the harbour wall, tracking their movement to the exit.

Dyansh redoubled his efforts and heaved on the paddle, edging through the wide gap. The sea beckoned beyond the harbour and Alisha felt the boat quicken as the ebbing tide pulled them to freedom.

The Shadow came faster and faster as they slipped past the last of the stonework. The creature did not slow, even as Alisha felt a surge of relief at their narrow escape.

They were free!

She could not restrain a small yelp of delight as the Shadow reached the end of the wall, but in a heartbeat her delight turned to horror. The Shadow leapt from the harbour and sailed towards the boat, an impossible, spirit-crushing jump that stole back the yards they had made; eating up every inch of freedom gained.

The creature landed on the boat with a crunch as the thwart splintered under the weight and sharp talons bit into the wood.

Alisha screamed and tried to back away but in the tiny vessel there was nowhere to go. Dyansh swung the long paddle at the Shadow from the other side of the mast but the wood splintered against its black hide. The Shadow swung its head back and forth as though terrified of the water it had found itself surrounded by and then swiped at Dyansh. He stumbled back and fell overboard.

"Dyansh!" Alisha screamed.

She looked back towards the harbour and saw another boat being prepared for pursuit. The Shadow rounded on her and tasted the air with its tongue. A low chitter emanated from its throat as it edged closer.

She stood up in the stern and watched it, transfixed. Shouts from behind washed over her and she knew that it was all lost. She fell backwards into the water and allowed the ocean to take her.

CHAPTER 24

The fireball sailed in a lazy arc towards the walls. Acastes, Kapaneus, Marlon and Dachen watched it trace a line across the night sky.

The ball fell short, smashing through the ramshackle lean-tos and tents that occupied the plain beneath the walls. Fires took hold within the abandoned encampment, but the huge ball rolled itself into the ditch and came to rest as the others had done, just another bundle of oil-soaked leather and rags.

"They do not have the range," Acastes declared. "The fools cannot reach us." He laughed as he looked out at the pinpricks of torchlight out on the dark plain. The clouds had occluded the stars and blocked out any light that would have illuminated the landscape.

"No," Dachen replied. "They are *finding* their range."

"How so?" Acastes scoffed.

"The counterweights will be light," he explained. "They are marking distance and will calculate accordingly."

Acastes looked unconvinced.

"That sounds like babble to me," he murmured.

"All the same, those engineers could place one of those missiles in a winecup, based on a half dozen throws."

Acastes sniffed.

"Can we reach *them*?" he asked, a little less sure of himself.

Dachen nodded.

"Sangye, what do you think?" he called over his shoulder.

The Eastern soldier shrugged. Behind him were two huge contraptions resembling massive crossbows. There was also an enormous, long-armed sling with a large counterweight, much like the mechanisms out on the field. On every flanking tower, and spaced along the battlements, war engines waited to repel the enemy. Piles of ammunition, in the form of huge bolts or boulders, filled those spaces not taken up by the weapons themselves or the soldiers who waited between them.

"It is difficult to find range in the dark, but I could try," he said.

"Do not let them get too comfortable," Dachen replied. "We had better stand clear."

The four men stepped aside as Sangye and his small team worked on the *Hatiyara*. The engine had limbs like a crossbow, but incorporated a baffling array of bundled ropes, pulleys and ratchets.

Sangye called out his orders accompanied by the sound of ropes creaking under tension and the metallic clink of ratchets locking.

"Run a torch along those cheeks to soften the grease," he barked. "That will earn some extra yards." He motioned to the four Infantrymen who were standing, watching from the edge of the flanking tower. "Help get this bolt in position. Place it with care; that cable will cut you in half if she jumps the trigger."

The four massive men heaved the long shaft of the bolt into place, stepping back as soon as it was nestled between the hardwood cheeks. Sangye gauged the wind with a wet finger and made small adjustments to various handles that had the bewildering machine moving by tiny increments.

"Stand clear!" he called, moving to the back of the mechanism. He kissed his forefinger and touched it to the butt of the enormous bolt.

A terrifying 'whoosh' followed and Sangye raced to the edge of the battlements, squinting into the darkness to follow the projectile. All that was visible was the pale, cloth streamer used to keep the bolt's flight true, fluttering from its base

A distant thump was followed by cries of alarm and Sangye giggled.

"That woke them up," he declared, hurrying back to the war engine. "Wind that windlass, and this time give her an extra two notches. Warm that grease; hurry, they know that we have them. Before they can move their catapult!"

Another bolt was placed on the *Hatiyara* by the four Heavy Infantrymen, who were sweating in their plate armour. The broad point of the bolt gleamed in the torchlight as Sangye touched the butt of the shaft. He hesitated.

"This wood is wetter than the last," he said. "Was this wood seasoned?"

"I doubt it," one of the Infantrymen replied. "Most of the wood was only felled a few weeks back."

Sangye rolled his eyes and moved his hand to a small windlass beneath the trigger. He gave it two gentle turns that had the engine moving an almost imperceptible amount, then he released the trigger, before rushing to the edge of the battlements again, and waited in the silence that followed.

A distant, splintering crash declared that Sangye's bolt had flown true. He bowed as they cheered on the battlements, soaking up their praise with a theatrical modesty

"Hah!" Acastes laughed. "Even Rogan enjoyed that." He pointed to the flanking tower on the opposite side of the gate to the south-west. He waved, but Rogan ignored the gesture

"There is movement out there," Marlon murmured, but he was not heard over the loud congratulations being cast about the tower.

"There is another war engine," he said with a little more force, and this time his companions heard him and turned to look.

A distant eruption of flame illuminated the enormous *Lamo Phenka* catapult in the gloom, and then it launched. The long, lazy sweep of the throwing arm accelerated the sling around its end, hurling the burning objects towards the city walls.

Screams that carried on the night air that made Marlon's blood run cold, as he was struck by an awful realisation.

"Those are people," Kapaneus gasped as the writhing, burning shapes sailed overhead to slam into the stone buildings beyond. "They are throwing people at us."

"Sangye," Marlon murmured, breaking the stunned silence. "Destroy that engine, now."

Sangye nodded, wide-eyed and pale, and rushed back to the war engine behind him.

Adeyemi sat upright as soon as he sensed the presence.

"Granger!" he said as his eyes adjusted to the lamplight. "You startled me."

"You are not yourself, Adeyemi," Granger joked. "The man I know should have heard me at the end of the hall."

Adeyemi sat up and cocked his head. "They are here," he said.

Granger nodded and sat beside Adeyemi's bed in the Akharran infirmary.

"A show of strength for now," he replied. "They will probe the defences and look for weaknesses."

"Can the walls be broken with those engines?" Adeyemi asked, wide-eyed and sitting higher still as though making ready to run.

Granger shook his head.

"Rogan is certain that the walls will stand firm. Even if he is wrong, they will not fall tonight, so please, lie back and rest. I only came to ensure you had everything you need. Something to drink? Are you hungry?"

Adeyemi glanced at the tray beside the bed with the food yet untouched and shook his head.

"I will leave you to rest," Granger said as he stood to leave.

"Friend Granger, please do not go." He placed a hand on Granger's arm, and the old man sat down again.

"What is it, Adeyemi," he asked.

The big man sighed, rubbing his face with those long-fingered hands.

"Friend Granger, I should be dead," he replied.

"You are lucky, but you are also strong."

"No," he said, shaking his head. "The Khalim-Shar has given me life. It has gifted me more time."

"It chose you to carry a message," Granger insisted. "Please, try not to give it more meaning than that."

"No," Adeyemi persisted. "I should have died last night, before the day ended."

"But you did not."

Adeyemi lay back and sighed. "You once told me that you knew what I was; knew what I had been, from these," he touched his cheek and traced the ruined whorls of scar tissue.

"I know many things that others do not," Granger nodded.

"You have travelled far?"

"In a manner of speaking," the historian replied.

Adeyemi touched the ragged scars that overlaid the careful patterns.

"Then you know that I failed," he murmured.

"You were an assassin," Granger nodded. "This much I know. You served your queen without question, defending her line. At times, no doubt you would be called upon to kill for reasons you could not understand. Perhaps you were asked to kill people you would rather not see dead."

Adeyemi chuckled, but the mirth was shallow and short lived. He waggled a finger at Granger.

"You see more than you should, Friend Granger," he said. "What magic do you use?"

"No magic," he replied. "I know the nature of our kind well enough to understand how we make our choices. There was a time in my life that many might consider to be 'magical', but developing a deep understanding of nature and having the means to manipulate the rules that define our existence is not magic, even if it appears that way."

"Then how do you explain my being alive?"

"I do not understand, Adeyemi. You live because you do, you were spared to carry a message. Call it 'luck' or 'good fortune', it makes no difference. If I stab you in the heart, right now, you will die; why question that?"

"I have outlived my days already," he replied sagging down onto the bed. "I doubt that you could kill me, even if I allowed it. Even if I begged it of you. The Khalim-Shar owns me now."

"*Nobody owns you*," Granger exclaimed, grasping Adeyemi's arm.

Adeyemi lay silent for a while before he spoke again.

"For my failure," he said. "I was given a handful of days; seeds of pin-wheat. All that I could hold in a single hand and place into a bag. '*A handful of grain; such will your days be numbered.*' I have carried those seeds with me ever since I left my home. Ever since I was sent away.

"As each day ended, I discarded a single one, counting down my life from a small bag that grew lighter with every spent day. I was certain that the black jewel could defeat the curse, but it was taken from me before I had a chance to test it. I would have died in the Khalim-Shar's camp; my time was done, but it saved me. The Khalim-Shar used its own magic to undo the curse and give me one more day to deliver its message. Perhaps I will die soon, or perhaps it has more yet for me to do. If I wake in the morning then I am bound to its will, can you not see?"

Granger was shaking his head.

"You are a superstitious People for one so wise in other matters, Adeyemi. Those seeds were never counting down your days and you owe nothing to the Khalim-Shar. It is all just a trick on the mind, making you believe the impossible. You have woken to a day you did not believe you would see, and are looking for ways to explain that, replacing one delusion with another.

"You tell us that the Shar can multiply now? If so, that is not *magic*. I do not know what you saw, and I do not doubt that it is true, but there will be another explanation. Whatever power the Khalim-Shar used to produce that trick cannot be used to hold you in its thrall unless you allow it. You are the same man you were yesterday, and the day before that and every day that led you here now. You will wake tomorrow, a little older and with any luck, a little wiser. We will fight the Khalim-Shar, and we may die, and we may live, but there is no power that the Khalim-Shar holds over you that you have not created in your own mind. I have seen this played out in the lives of those who allow their will to be enslaved by others, more times than you would believe. I *know* where this leads to unless you can break free from the delusion!"

"No, no, no," Adeyemi almost wept. "You are wrong."

"I am *not* wrong, I am right!"

Adeyemi sat up and clutched Granger's arm again and stared at him, his face lined with anguish.

"Then why am I afraid," he whispered as a tear ran down his cheek. "Why am I afraid?"

All night, the hail of bodies rained on the city's south-eastern quarter. Screaming shapes, ablaze against the night sky and thudding into stone to end the torment.

The *Lamo Phenka* catapults launched in darkness and pulled back before the engines atop the walls could strike at them. Sangye had tried, but for over twenty bolts he had loosed from the *Hatiyara*, he had only managed to hit a single other target.

The burning bodies were a warning. The catapults could have hit the city with more damaging ordnance, but the terrible missiles were meant to instil fear and to chip away at the resolve of the defenders. Word would spread through the city and people would begin to doubt the strength of the walls, and there was no room for doubt in war.

An hour before dawn, the catapults went quiet, pulling back out of range of the *Hatiyara* that could have reached out and smashed them once seen. Sangye lay slumped against the side of the *Hatiyara*, physically exhausted from his efforts and sickened by his repeated failure to break the engines that had caused such suffering.

Daylight also brought the enemy encampment into clear view.

The Khalim–Shar's forces held the plain from the sea to where the eastern road vanished from site. Orderly rows of tents formed blocks of tan, broken by clusters of war engines and separated by picket lines with thousands of horses. Smoke curled up from cook fires at regular intervals, and beyond the tents, a throng of carts and wagons hazed into the distance.

Closer to the walls were the remains of the catapults that Sangye had struck the night before. The pivot was smashed on one, leaving the throwing arm sagging at a useless angle and the counterweight stones scattered on the ground. The other had been abandoned with a broken frame on one side.

Acastes' eyes burned from lack of sleep and his legs were stiff after the long vigil. He rubbed his whole face and stifled a yawn.

The archers and Heavy Infantry who had been stationed on the walls overnight were replaced with fresher faced men as they went to steal some much-needed rest.

"Someone is coming," Kapaneus said, pointing out across the plain.

"Eight riders," Marlon replied. "Perhaps they are coming to discuss terms."

"And four Shar," Dachen added.

"They have discussed terms with us before," Marlon chuckled.

Dachen looked puzzled but Marlon shrugged away the unspoken question.

"Rogan is already on his way," Acastes noted, seeing the Hatar vanish down the ladder of the adjacent flanking tower.

"You should go too," Kapaneus urged. "Rogan does not speak for Kor'Habat."

"Rogan Fol'Brandam speaks for Rogan Fol'Brandam," Acastes observed. "Have Kekoa bring my horse."

Acastes and Kapaneus caught up with Rogan, Captain Raims and the twelve extra Cavalrymen he had taken as escort as they rode out to meet the enemy party.

"Your presence is not required here, Acastes," Rogan stated, keeping his eyes ahead on the approaching party.

The Shar were spreading out as they drew nearer, and the Cavalrymen mirrored the move. An Eastern man in simple, brown robes waited with his escort and nodded in greeting.

"My name is Samut Masahara," he said with an affable smile. "The advocate of the Khalim-Shar, your new ruler, king and God. This is Senji Dayivar, commander of the Khalim-Shar's armies; undefeated and undefeatable on any field."

"Pah!" Acastes scoffed. "I must surely have imagined crushing an army of yours just the other day."

"A small party was lost," Masahara agreed, glancing to Senji Dayivar for confirmation. "But I assure you, their number will not be missed. As you can see, we have an ample supply of men to take their place. And once your city has been taken, we will have many more. When the people see the power and majesty of the Khalim-Shar, they will gladly kneel before him and rally to his cause, or they will die."

"You will not take Kor'Habat," Rogan spat. "Those walls have never been breached."

Masahara looked from Acastes to Rogan and back again.

"Who is it that speaks for the city?" he asked.

"I do!" Acastes and Rogan said in unison.

"I, Rogan Fol'Brandam have command of the armies," Rogan declared, and Acastes scoffed.

Masahara's smile slipped before returning, a little wider. "Interesting," he muttered as the two enormous men glared at each other. "Still, I am certain that we can find common ground, the *three* of us."

"These are the terms demanded by the Kodistai of Korathea," Rogan declared. "Leave the field of battle and return to the Eastern Kingdoms. Leave all property and citizens as you found them. Do this now, and we will not pursue you. You will not be driven into the Ashkelit Ocean and we will not demand reparations for the outrages you have already committed on our soil. Do this now, and the Kodistai has promised to allow you to leave in peace."

Masahara smiled at the commander at his side; Senji Dayivar. The military man held no emotion in the gaze he returned.

"Interesting," Masahara murmured. "The Khalim-Shar will not accept those terms. You must accept him as your new ruler, and your God. You will submit to him, or you will die."

"You are on the wrong side of the city walls to make such a bold threat, little man," Rogan sneered.

"As were many thousands of your people our scouts found crossing the river to the north," Masahara said in calm manner. "We returned those yet living. Perhaps you noticed them last night?" He traced his finger in an arc in the air above them.

"What?" Acastes demanded. "What did you say?"

"They were happy to be returned to the *safety* of your walls. You really do not care for your people," Masahara admonished.

"What hold does it have over you?" Kapaneus asked from behind Acastes. "That creature you follow; what has driven you to kill your own kind in its service?"

"When one serves a God, one does not question that greater wisdom," Masahara replied. "If you were to stand simply in his presence, you too would feel the limitless power and wisdom."

"And you?" Kapaneus continued. "Senji Dayivar. What makes a soldier abandon his oaths to follow a monster?"

The soldier did not reply but held Kapaneus' gaze for a long time.

"You too will abandon old oaths and allegiances," Masahara assured them. "If you survive the days to come, you will also kneel before him. You cannot stop this new dawn from spreading its radiance."

"When I meet it on the battlefield," Acastes scowled, "I will take its head. You, I will hang from the city walls for the ravens."

"Your intransigence dooms many to die," Masahara sighed.

"Who, may I tell the Khalim-Shar, is to blame for this needless slaughter?"

"Tell that foul beast that Acastes Fol'Denes looks forward to meeting it," he declared. "I have been killing its kind for sport for some years now. Did you know that they scream when they die?"

Masahara returned a sad smile.

"As do men, Acastes Fol'Denes," he replied. "As do men."

The first volley arrived soon after they had re-entered the city.

Teams of horses had hauled twenty of the enormous *Lamo Phenka* catapults forward into position where the wheels were chocked, and the slings loaded with their ordnance. Some launched plain boulders while others sent massive urns filled with burning pitch into the air.

Acastes flinched as a burning shape tumbled over his head just as he reached the top of the flanking tower. The huge clay urn shattered against the roof of one of the buildings below, spraying burning pitch across the flat rooftop. All along the south-eastern edge of the city, fires were taking hold. Screams rang out, echoing from the stone walls.

A series of huge bolts shot out from the various flanking towers and arced towards the enemy catapults, trailing cloth streamers that marked their flight. They all missed, but Acastes knew that the operators needed time to find their range.

"Reload!" he shouted. "Hit them before they hit us again!"

He could hear the winches being wound behind him as he watched the enemy engines. The long arms of the catapults on the field tipped back against their counterweights as teams of winchmen worked to reset the weapons.

This was not battle as Acastes knew it; this was a race between men to set their machines into motion.

A series of heavy thumps signalled that the weapons on the flanking towers had at least won this leg of the race and he watched the bolts streak towards their targets. A cheer rang out when one struck home, smashing the throwing arm of the *Lamo Phenka*. The counterweight dropped and swung in its cradle, useless.

Another bolt flew true and hit the frame that supported one of the massive arms and it collapsed under its own weight. The cheer directly behind him told him that it was Sangye who had landed the blow.

Moments later, another volley sailed overhead, but lower this time. To his left, a boulder smashed into the battlements and swept an Infantryman from sight in an instant. Moments later the boulder crashed into the buildings below the wall sending up a shower of dust and debris.

"Clear the battlements!" Acastes shouted. "Clear the battlements!" He turned to Kapaneus. "Spread the word. Only the *Hatiyara* teams are to stay, there is no point is having our men picked off while we stand and watch. Clear the battlements!"

Kapaneus nodded and vanished down into the tower. Moments later he was running along the wall to the north-east while another soldier ran in the opposite direction, over the gate, to carry the order.

"No sign of Rogan," Marlon remarked as another bolt hissed by on its way towards the line of enemy war engines.

Acastes glanced across the gate to the nearest flanking tower and saw that the Hatar had not returned to his position.

Rogan rode at speed along the main road through the city. He left the shouting and chaos of the burning quarter behind him, to find a different sort of panic. People had gathered in the streets, and East Market was thronging with city folk peering with nervous expressions towards the gates and desperate for news.

Rumour could travel through a city quicker than his horse could run, and already there was a growing hysteria.

"Have the gates fallen, Hatar?"

"Do the walls hold fast?"

"The fire will destroy the city!"

He ignored them all and pushed on, scattering those who yet lingered in the road. The palace came into view as he crested the arch of the Sky Bridge over the River Habat before he dropped down into the city again. He pushed on towards West Market where the road curved east again towards the Palace. He glimpsed the huge catapult that rested at the edge of the market square; the first that had been built as a demonstration to the teams who had gone on to build the engines on the flanking towers. The timber structure stood, idle and un-manned, a mile and a half from where it could have been put to use. The palace came into view again at the end of the wide, cobbled boulevard and he pushed on towards it.

He was out of breath by the time he reached the long hall that lead to the chamber where the council of Hatars sat.

"Raims," he said as the young captain approached. "Do you have the document?"

"I do, Hatar," Raims replied, lifting a large, leather binder up towards Rogan.

"Hold onto it for now," he said, taking a series of long, deep breaths and wiping the sweat from his face with a handkerchief.

He strode into the chamber to find seven of the other council members already present. To his relief, Bravik Fol'Gannity was not among them. That man had his own designs on seizing power, and Rogan could well do without his interventions.

"What news from the battlements?" Gilean Fol'Maddon asked.

"The walls hold, and the fires are under control," he replied. "Their engines can barely reach into the city without our own crushing them. We can hold them back as long as we have the materiel to throw at them."

The Hatars nodded in satisfaction amongst themselves.

"But there will be a time in the coming days when we need to fight them with steel," he went on. "And for that we need to have a single commander. We need to bring the men of the Akharran under one banner."

"That banner would not happen to be your own, would it?" Gilean Fol'Maddon asked, steepling his fingers and peering past them.

"You know that I am the best man for this task," he replied. "Give me full command of the armies and we will overcome this enemy."

"We all command the army at the Kodistai's pleasure," Gilean replied. "The *Kodistai* remains in *full* command as long as the *Kodistai* draws breath."

Rogan clenched his jaw in irritation.

"How long since he was conscious?" he scowled. "How long must we be led by a man who does not remember his own name; a man who has been on the brink of death for so long that I fear he does not know what it is to live any longer, yet does not know how to die?"

"You aim to usurp power from the Council?" Hatar Foaran Fol'Armen murmured in accusation.

"No!" Rogan barked before he calmed his tone. "Forgive me, I have been awake for a very long time."

"As have we all," Foaran replied.

"I am not asking for any of you to cede your rank or title," Rogan assured them. "I only want to have your permission to have our armies put under my command for the defence of the city. We cannot be convening in these chambers every time an order needs to be given. An army needs a single commander; that is a doctrine that cannot be denied."

"And why should it be you who takes on the mantle?" Gilean asked.

"I have fought them before, at Banihat," he replied. "I know the enemy better than any of you."

"You were *defeated* at Banihat, as I recall," Foaran muttered.

"And I know the enemy better for it." He held out his hand and Captain Raims offered him the leather binder. "I have a prepared document in this binder. The seven men in this room now will give a majority if you all sign it. That majority will give me the ability to defend this city from an enemy that not one of you has even seen."

"And what of Acastes and his claim?" Gilean asked. "Your document is worth nothing against his claim on the throne."

"He has nothing," Rogan replied, shaking his head. "He has no proof, only hearsay. We have the sanction of the Kodistai. You have the power to allow me to defend Kor'Habat. And you have the power to prevent that very defence."

The Hatars were silent for a long time. They looked to one another or stared into their hands for insight.

At last, Gilean Fol'Maddon stood up and pressed his fists to the heavy table.

"Bring your document," he murmured. "I will sign it."

At last Rogan strode from the room, feeling light-headed. He had done it!

He *would* rule his people, as was his destiny.

He saw Bravik Fol'Gannity coming down the long corridor towards him and smiled.

Bravik slowed as Rogan strode by.

"What have you done, Fol'Brandam?" he called out to Rogan's back. "What have you done?"

A loud cheer went up as another of the enemy war engines was broken by a direct hit. The celebration was cut short by a fiery urn of pitch exploding against a *Hatiyara* on the battlements. The screams of burning men replaced the jubilant sounds and sharpened the minds of the defending army.

"We have the advantage of height," Marlon muttered. "But they have greater numbers."

A massive boulder bounced once before slamming into the base of the tower. Marlon felt the impact and took an involuntary step back.

Kapaneus puffed out his cheeks. "The walls can take it," he

assured Marlon.

"My bloody nerves can't," Jon said as he arrived beside them.

"The walls have never fallen," Kapaneus said as he watched another boulder sailing towards the wall.

"I wish I shared your confidence," he replied. "How long can we keep this up?"

"The smiths and carpenters cannot produce bolts as fast as we can shoot them," Dachen said as the impact of another direct hit sent a shudder through the stone beneath their feet. "But then, I doubt that theirs can either."

They stood in silence for a moment as the duel played out; huge stones and burning urns crashed into the battlements while the defenders hurried to cripple the enemy catapults. Both ends of the field were already littered with detritus and the stench of smoke from the damaged quarter of the city was heavy on the air.

They watched one of the *Lamo Phenka* catapults release a boulder at the end of a long, lazy sweep of its throwing arm, a moment before a huge, iron-tipped bolt shattered one side of the frame. The boulder bounced only yards from the gates and crashed into the steel-reinforced timber.

The boom was like that of an enormous drum.

Acastes ran to the edge of the tower and peered over.

"The gate is sound," he reported. "It took a small forest to build those gates and it will take more than a few pebbles to bring them down."

"Would that do it?" Marlon asked, pointing out across the field.

A huge weapon was being dragged forward by a team of horses. It came to a stop some way behind the line of *Lamo Phenka* and went still while the horses were unhitched and led away.

Dachen took a step forward and peered into the distance. The new engine was massive, with four enormous limbs forming a diagonal cross. At the centre was an aperture that a large man could easily climb into. He nodded, and the colour drained from his cheeks.

He dry-swallowed.

"Sangye?" he called, "Do you see that?"

"Yes, my Prince," came the exhausted reply after a brief pause. "*Thulo-Hatiyara.*"

"Can you reach it?"

A longer pause.

"I think so, my Prince."

"Then do so. Now! Acastes, have every weapon you possess targeting that engine!"

"Why that engine alone?" Acastes asked, too piqued at having been given an order to read the urgency in Dachen's voice.

"*Hatiyara!*" the prince shouted pointing to the engine that Sangye was urgently priming. Then he pointed out onto the plain. "*Thulo-Hatiyara!* That means," he struggled for words in his frustration, "much more *Hatiyara!*"

Acastes hesitated for only a moment more before calling out his orders.

The massive limbs in the distance were already beginning to curl back.

Starling worked the winch, watching the horses as they were led past him and out of range of the city's defences.

The idea had not occurred to him that Kor'Habat would have Eastern engineers to build weapons of their own, and so it was with a mixture of relief and terror that he had watched the huge bolts streak from the battlements towards the Khalim-Shar's army.

If Kor'Habat stood firm, he had hope of escape. Not for the first time, he considered running for the city, but the certain knowledge that he would be stopped, either by an arrow in the back or an arrow in the chest kept him rooted to the ground he stood on. He was caught up in a lie, first woven to save his skin when he had found himself alone in Dargenmill, now worn halfway across the continent as he tried to return to his friends. Slipping away on the long march had proved impossible with the ever-present Shar in their midst and now he found himself attacking his own best sanctuary, surrounded by men he had found it increasingly difficult to hate.

He glanced at the three other men who turned their own winch handles, pulling stout ropes through a system of pulleys to draw the massive limbs back. They were men, just like him, brought to this place and time by twists of chance and providence, and held there by fear. Some he even dared to call, friend.

Rope creaked under the immense tension, and the marker on his own line inched towards the predetermined stop. His arms ached from the effort and he was breathing hard by the time another team of men heaved the enormous bolt onto the bed of the weapon. A dozen yards long and as thick as his waist, with an iron tip, grey against the pale, fresh wood. Starling wondered if the lump of timber would ever leave the ground. The engineer called out his orders in the Eastern tongue and Starling watched as the massive projectile was worked into position with brute force and long levers.

A ground-shaking thump and a shower of dust startled Starling as a smaller, but not insignificant bolt from Kor'Habat thudded into the ground a few yards away. The bolt then somersaulted over his head, tumbling towards the waiting ranks of men and scattering them like dolls with the force of its impact. Another incoming projectile missed by a wider margin but there was an urgency to the engineers' calls now that they knew the defenders could reach them.

With final adjustments made, the engineer shouted for the chocks to be set. Heavy mallets were used to drive wedges under the wheels to hold the engine steady, and then it was ready to release. A sharp pull on a heavy rope triggered the massive catapult and the limbs leapt forward in unison.

A plume of dust leapt up around the *Thulo-Hatiyara* as it threw an enormous bolt towards the city. There was a sharp intake of breath from Dachen and everyone paused in whatever they were doing to watch the missile streak across the gap. A huge serpentine streamer chased it towards the city.

The bolt struck the base of the flanking tower on the other side of the gate with a peal louder than thunder. A moment later they felt the shock of the impact through their boots. Many of those who had been standing on the tower nearest the impact collapsed as the stone lurched under their feet.

"They will not miss again!" Dachen shouted. "Sangye! We *must* destroy that engine!"

"My Prince," he called back as the *Hatiyara* crews recovered from their shock and leapt into action again. "It is at the extent of my range."

"Find more!" Dachen demanded.

Sangye nodded and turned back to his crew.

"Bring more grease," he shouted. "And warm it well! Work that winch as though your life depends on it! We have to destroy that weapon!"

Starling worked at his winch to the metallic tune of the ratchet pawl bouncing over the teeth of the turning gear. Tears of desperation ran down his cheeks and were lost in grimy sweat. If the gates were breached, then the city could well fall.

The rope's marker reached the stop and he stepped back. A single stroke from his sword on the taught line would cripple the engine. One simple act could save the city and his friends.

He could save Nirmaya. She would never know what he had done.

Would they kill him at once, or would they have some terrible torture for his act of sabotage? He sagged under the weight of his own self-pity, but he knew what he had to do. A new projectile was being hauled into position as he eased his sword from its scabbard.

Sangye kissed his fingertips and touched the butt of the bolt, with his eyes shut.

He released the trigger and felt the rush of air as the tension in the ropes whipped the limbs forward.

He opened his eyes, and stood to see the streamer, fluttering into the distance...

"Cover!"

Starling turned and saw the bolt arcing towards them and pushed his sword back into the scabbard as he dived for the only protection within reach. He hit the ground and skidded under the bed of the huge engine. The incoming bolt dipped at the very last moment, having lost its momentum and struck the ground only yards in front of their position. Somehow it missed the limbs as it tumbled through them and landed another fifty yards behind amongst the soldiers who were still reeling from the last.

A sharp ache from his shin told Starling that he had struck something as he had dived for cover. A quick glance showed him that it had been the chock from behind one of the wheels at the front of the weapon, and he had knocked it loose.

He scurried out under the bed to exit behind the back wheels as the engineer shouted his frantic orders. Starling crawled over the chock as he exited, dragging it back with his knee.

The crew were so eager to get the missile away that no-one noticed his clumsy exit, and a moment later the rope was pulled to release the trigger.

The engine sprang to life, all four limbs lurching forwards.

The massive weight shift pushed back on the wheels and those that Starling had freed rolled back, turning the engine as the huge missile was thrown forwards. The projectile left its cradle and at once the butt was flung sideways, ruining the flight.

The engineer cursed as he watched the huge bolt's erratic

tumble end well short and well wide of its intended target.

Starling breathed a sigh of relief before he hurried back to his position at the winch.

A cheer went up from the battlements as the huge weapon had somehow gone awry. Sangye pushed his crew clear and worked at the winch himself to draw back the heavy rope. He smeared grease on the bed and cheeks that would hold the bolt and then ran a torch along them. When the Infantrymen lifted the missile into place, he warmed that too with the flames of the torch. He shut out the world and worked without a word, running through every check he could in his mind.

He knew that he could not get any more distance by altering the angle of the weapon and the ropes already creaked under the tension they held; any more would break them.

He closed his eyes and kissed his fingertips. He was about to touch the butt of the bolt when he paused. He glanced at the concertina of fabric that would keep the flight level.

He pulled out his belt knife and slipped it into the folds. The heavy cloth split against the sharp edge of the blade, and soon he pulled out a thick wad of the folded fabric and threw it on the stones.

He nodded and touched the bolt with gentle fingertips before releasing the trigger. The bolt scythed through the air, trailing a short streamer that had unfurled as soon as the air caught it.

"Fly true, fly true, fly true," he mouthed, watching the fast vanishing bolt and willing it to hold its line.

There was silence as the bolt arced across the plain...

Starling worked the winch once the engine was back in position and the chocks had been well driven under the wheels.

He had bought a little time, nothing more. This time, he would have to cut the rope.

"Cover!"

He turned again to see a bolt curving downwards towards him. He stepped back just in time as the bolt struck the engine almost in the centre. Bundles of ropes under huge tension exploded out in loose spirals and timber splintered from the impact. The broad-bladed tip buried itself in the bed of the weapon and an axle snapped. One of the limbs whipped around as the whole thing came apart, sailing over Starling as he fell backwards. The limb crashed into the engineer, crushing him with the impact.

Starling gasped as he crawled away. Men were screaming all around, bloodied and broken by the flying fragments, but he was still alive.

Somehow, he was still alive!

Sangye could not stand.

The emotion had drained him of the ability. He was hoisted onto the shoulders of the Infantrymen in his crew and they paraded him around the flanking tower with cheers of celebration.

Dachen breathed a sigh of relief and Acastes shouted a joyful curse at the attacking army.

"There is someone coming forward," Marlon said as he laughed along with the celebrating soldiers.

"Perhaps they have come to surrender," Acastes declared, before shouting over the walls. "You bastards!"

Marlon's smile began to slip. "I do not think so," he murmured.

"It is the Khalim-Shar," Kapaneus breathed, and the triumphant mood on the flanking tower began to dissipate.

A huge figure, twice as tall as a man strode out onto the plain, leaning on a trident as it walked. It paused and stood as silence fell on the battlements of Kor'Habat.

"Man the walls," Acastes managed to utter before the Khalim-Shar raised the trident above its head and shrieked a long and harrowing call.

"Man the walls!" he shouted. "Man the walls! They are

coming!"

The Khalim-Shar shrieked again, and the army at its back began to move.

CHAPTER 25

Starling joined his regiment with his heart pounding in his chest.

The men were busying themselves with the three breaching ramps assigned to them. Wheels, twice the height of a man supported the huge platforms that lay flat on an open frame of sturdy timber. Over fifty feet long and thirty feet wide, the platforms resembled nothing more than over-sized carts, but with these the invading army hoped to reach the battlements of the city. Starling tried to gauge the length of the ramps against the height of the walls, but at this distance he was wasting his time. More importantly, he had to find a way to get into the city without being killed and find his friends… That felt like an impossible task now.

Perhaps they would see him on the battlefield and call the whole thing off!

He almost laughed out loud.

Captain Gillain was shouting his orders to get the devices ready. At the rear, twenty men lifted the flat bed of the platform as they had practiced so many times. The frame lifted a little and an audible thud signalled that a support had dropped into place, holding the bed where it was. Another heave, and the bed lifted a little further at the rear. Every lift tilted the bed a little more until poles were needed to push the bed higher and higher. Soon all three were erected with the once-level beds were tipped up close to vertical. These would form the ramps that would lean against the huge wall and give the soldiers access to the battlements, if they made it that far.

Starling ducked behind one of the front wheels to take his position inside the left side of the framework that had been hidden by the bed until now. Down the centre ran a broad walkway that separated the two sides and had been revealed as the bed had been lifted. He waited while the space around him filled with men who he was to fight alongside; two hundred and fifty in all. Farmers, farriers, bakers and smiths; few of them were soldiers, but they had all bought into Ramash Suun's dream. If any of them had harboured doubts before, fear of the Khalim-Shar had ensured the misgivings were buried deep.

The air was ripe and clammy in the area behind the protective shield they had erected. Nervous grins were exchanged, and bravado was loud where real courage lay silent.

"I hope there are enough whores in the city for all of us," a man behind him declared. "A conquering army deserves a proper welcome."

"They're *all* whores to a conquering army, Seril," his companion replied. "We'll take whatever we like; *whoever* we like. What say you, men?"

The cheer was cut short by Captain Gillain at the rear of the siege ramp.

"Hold steady, lads," he called from the back. "There's no rush to get there first, but don't you linger when in range of their engines. When we get close enough, the engines can't touch us, but their bowmen can so hold the line and you will be sheltered. Remember the ditch and you won't get stuck. Get stuck, and you won't be feeling under any skirts tonight, so stay alert." There were a few jeers. "They will throw everything they have at us, but keep the ramps close together and we will weather the storm. Tonight, all drinks are on the Kodistai!"

There was a cheer of approval, but Starling could not bring

himself to join in. His heart was pounding so hard that he feared it would burst.

"Stay close to me, Stellio," the man to his right said. "I dreamt that I was sitting on the Kodistai's throne last night. It's a sign, is what it is."

"I'll bear that in mind, Marrick," Starling replied.

He looked to left and right. Dozens of siege ramps had been erected, and behind the wooden defences thousands of men huddled, ready to push the contraptions towards the walls. Shar prowled behind them, waiting for their chance to feast on the flesh of the people of Kor'Habat.

A shout went up from somewhere at the front of the line of newly erected ramps.

"This is it, men!" Captain Gillain called out. "On my command! Brace!"

Starling placed his hands on the timber frame and leaned into in.

"Forward!"

As one, ten thousand men leaned into their task. Starling pushed as hard as he could and the enormous wheels began to turn, rolling with increasing ease over the rough ground. Once moving he fell into slow, rhythmic strides, aided by the sound of a single, large drum beating out the pace.

Dust rose in choking clouds, drying his parched throat even further as they advanced on the walls of Kor'Habat.

Marrick fished a small wineskin out from under his armour and uncorked it with his teeth. He spat the cork out and took a long drink.

"Drink this," he said, passing it to Starling. "A bit of fire for your belly."

Starling took a swig and felt the burn of Dashiyan *rakshi* in his throat. He coughed and handed the bladder back to Marrick, who drained it and dropped it on the ground.

The drums picked up in pace and Starling felt the ramp lurch forwards as the soldiers added more urgency to their advance. In the distance, a horn wailed out from the city battlements, frightened and weak where the drums boomed with strength and confidence.

"We're in range of the war engines now, Stellio," Marrick declared, and clenched his teeth as he pushed.

Starling could not see ahead past the ramp, and his mind filled the void with images of flying boulders, everyone a moment from crushing the ramp that shielded him. He felt an impact through his boots as something hit the ground ahead. He glimpsed a huge lump of masonry tumble between the two ramps to his left, missing both.

Then a crash, followed by a terrible screaming told him that someone nearby had not been so lucky. He dared not look to either side, instead he closed his eyes and pushed.

Another crash followed by the screams of men being crushed under the weight of stone and timber.

The pounding drum grew more distant with every step and soon he could not hear it for rushing sound in his ears. He stumbled and managed to hold on to the timber spar in front of him. He was dragged for several yards before he was able to find his feet and avoid being trampled. He righted himself just as a huge bolt skewered down through the ramp to their left. The whole thing stopped dead and soldiers were flung forward against the frame, but most were not injured and poured out from the broken structure to seek shelter behind the neighbouring ramps.

Suddenly there were the ragged remains of tents under his feet. They ploughed on through the remnants of the huge, tented settlement, the massive wheels rolling with ease over the detritus.

Then the arrows came, thumping into the timber above Starling's head in a hail of steel-tipped shafts. His legs burned from the effort and his lungs ached for air as they rumbled on. He almost did not hear the cry of "Wall!" from the men at the front, but a moment later they bumped over the remains of a low, stone wall.

That was the point at which he could slow down; he remembered that much. With relief he sagged onto the wooden spar in front of him as the whole structure bumped to a standstill. The war engines could not reach them here, but the bowmen could, and those men at the edges were exposed already. The man to Starling's left cried out as an arrow sprouted from his hip. Starling leaned away from the open side, aware of how vulnerable he had become.

There was no time to rest.

From the back of the ramp, two groups of eight men ran out carrying lengths of timber to span the ditch. They held the long sections above their heads for protection from the arrows, but some still fell.

"It's not straight!" At the front, a soldier was peering through a slit in the ramp. "The left span is not straight!"

Captain Gillain was suddenly beside Marrick, having run down the central walkway.

"Get that span straightened," he shouted.

Starling realised that the order had been directed at himself, and Marrick was pushing him past the injured man to his left before he could protest.

They emerged into a storm of dust and arrows. The ramps to either side of them bristled with shafts, and already some were lurching forwards again across the spanned ditch. He followed Marrick without thinking, covering the yards to the ditch in a dozen strides. An arrow hissed past his head as he dived under the crooked span.

"Help me move it!" Marrick shouted, pressing his back up against the underside of the span in an effort to lift it. "Left! It needs to go left!"

Starling pushed up against the span and felt it move as arrows thumped into its upper surface. They eased it sideways until it was straight. Marrick nodded, red-faced from the strain; then his eyes went wide.

"Marrick?" Starling shouted above the noise.

His companion gasped in pain.

"Bastards," the man murmured, as he slumped onto the grass beneath the newly placed span. A bloody arrow remained where it had penetrated the timber.

Starling stared in shock at the steel point. A drop of blood fell from the arrow and a moment later the ramp rumbled over the planks above them.

Marlon watched the advance as it came. The wooden structures that he had seen rising from the plain in the distance now stood tall enough to reach the top of the fifty-foot walls. Dozens of the things rumbled closer in an advancing line that stretched over five hundred yards in width. The ramps themselves formed a giant shield in front of the soldiers who pushed them, and already the timber bristled with arrows. For a quarter of a mile in each direction along the sweeping walls of the city, bowmen released volley after volley at the onrushing army. He watched the first of the devices to reach the wall. The ramp arrived at speed, with the soldiers under it running all the way from the ditch they had crossed. At the last possible moment before crashing into the wall, the ramp dropped forward and was driven into the ground under its own weight. The momentum caused the ramp to topple forward towards the wall until it thudded onto the stone battlements. Men poured out from between the now useless wheels

After their mad dash across the plain those men were now easy targets for the bowmen, but from their mis-matched armour he could see that they were not professional soldiers. They had been sacrificed to get the ramps up, and now a black wave of Shar was racing towards the city.

The bowmen turned their attention to the onrushing Shar, releasing volley after volley.

"Save your arrows!" Marlon shouted, but his voice was lost in the roar.

The first of the soldiers reached the tops of the ramps and jumped onto the battlements to engage the defending army. Marlon watched from the safety of the flanking tower as the Heavy Infantrymen defended both the battlements and the bowmen. The soldiers who reached the top of the walls were sent tumbling, dead or dying back down to the plain.

"Burn the ramps!" Acastes was shouting. "Bring oil! Burn the ramps!"

Archers on the flanking towers worked to stem the flow of soldiers on the ramps, and skirmishes raged all along the battlements. The untrained soldiers were no match for the men of the Akharran, but the Shar had reached the ditch, and were pouring forward in a dark tide.

"Those bloody Shar are getting close!" Jon shouted.

Catapults had moved to within striking distance again and fiery missiles sailed overhead into the city to add to the chaos.

"Burn the ramps!" Acastes bellowed again, and at last buckets of oil were being poured down, onto the wooden structures.

The first of the Shar raced up the ramps, topping the wall in seconds. Archers scattered as scything claws slashed at them, cutting through the light armour and slicing into bone. The Infantrymen formed up in squares of half a dozen or more, driving against the Shar with shields locked together. Some of the creatures were overwhelmed, but as more reached the battlements the balance shifted, and the infantry struggled to deal with the ferocity of the attacks.

At last, a flaming arrow struck one of the ramps, igniting the oil that had been poured onto it. The flames spread across the ramp, and men screamed, burning as they fell. A few of the Shar shied away from the flames, but many more charged through, erupting over the wall with even greater fury.

One by one the ramps were set alight, but until they burned through and collapsed, the Shar were able to scale them. Hundreds surged through dust and flames, shrieking over the cries of dying men. Insane bloodlust drove them onto the wall and into the bristling steel of the Heavy Infantry.

Marlon cursed and made for ladder that led down to the wall below.

The sounds of battle called to Valia through the open shutters of her room. Distant shouts blended into a dull roar, punctuated by echoing impacts as the war engines hurled their ordnance at the walls. Her body still ached from her injuries, but they were superficial, and she had survived much worse in the past.

Still alive.

If she had believed in Fate, she would have cursed that fickle mistress.

A soulful wail drifted over the battle chorus as a baby cried from somewhere within Shol'Hara. Valia wondered what the future held for those children. She had been one herself, many years ago; a child whose destiny had been written from the moment of birth. But destiny could be changed; a chart rewritten. Lushara had done just that and perhaps the Khalim-Shar would do the same for this new crop.

She tightened the final strap on her leather armour and buckled her sword to her hip. Striding along the broad, marbled hallways towards the Dam'Hara's chambers, she kept her eyes fixed ahead. She dared not glance into the rooms to either side, where Harami lounged behind gauzy curtains, eating and drinking with a languor that only barely resembled living. Willing slaves within a system that had reduced their identities to nothing more than a series of amenable wombs.

A tray-bearing eunuch bowed to her as she strode past the open door of a large atrium. Water from a fountain tinkled from within and blended with the gentle sounds of laughter of the Harami. The whole place was built on a foundation of soporific comfort that eased its charges from birth to death without ever allowing life beyond what was necessary for its own continuation.

She reached the door to the Dam'Hara's rooms and paused.

When she was last here, she had been a girl; frightened of her future. Today she would not be cowed.

Valia knocked twice and entered the room.

The Dam'Hara looked up from her desk in surprise. "It is customary to wait until summoned before entering these chambers," the mistress chided.

"I rejected your customs many years ago," Valia replied.

"Has basic civility fled the outside world too?" the Dam'Hara asked.

Valia stared back at her. "Have you not heard? Civility died along with morality and decency. I believe that you hastened their demise from within these walls with your dreams of empire."

The Dam'Hara closed the ledger that she had open on the desk and started to rise. "I am not sure what you are thinking, child," she began.

Valia drew her sword in the blink of an eye and brought the tip to rest on the Dam'Hara's desk. "Call me 'child' one more time!" she growled. "I dare you!"

The Dam'Hara sank back into her seat and regarded Valia with narrowing eyes. "Why have you come here?"

Valia lowered the sword and held it at her side. "You have thousands of children and babies in Shol'Hara," she said. "If the gates fall and the Shar break through, how do you plan to escape?"

The Dam'Hara smiled and sighed, regarding Valia over steepled fingers. "You know what it is to be alive again," she said.

"What are you talking about?" Valia retorted. "I have come here to warn you to make ready."

"I have seen this before, of course," the Dam'Hara chuckled.

"Seen what?" Valia almost shouted in exasperation.

"You were almost dead when you were brought here."

"And you take much pleasure in telling me so," Valia growled.

"But it was not from wounds sustained on the battlefield, no," the older woman went on. "You had given up on life. It is not uncommon for Harami to try to take their own lives, nor any person for that matter. Loss of a child during birth or failure to produce a son can drive a woman to despair, you know? They often seek solace in a physic we call 'Bliss', or else open a vein to take away their sorrow. When a woman faces death with longing it can be a moment of catharsis, a purging of the spirit. Did you, *welcome* death, on the battlefield, Valia."

Valia stared back at the woman. "What do you know of '*welcoming death*?" she demanded. "You who has never faced it."

The Dam'Hara stretched out her right hand and turned it palm up. "That scar is older than you," she said.

"You tried to take your own life?" Valia asked, seeing the pale scar that ran the length of the Dam'Hara's wrist.

"I lost my first child," she replied with a sad sigh. "A boy. He was a fine little brute. But the birth was complex; he was stubborn and would not turn. By the time the midwife freed him from my womb, it was too late. My little warrior never drew breath."

"I am sorry," Valia murmured.

"I sank into a terrible depression, of course. I did not eat or drink for days. Then I decided that death was better than the pain of living and took a fruit knife to my arm. I had given up." She stood and walked towards one of the shelves. "I welcomed my own death like a meadow thrush welcomes spring." She pulled a ledger from the shelf and leafed through it. "I survived, of course. A eunuch found me in my bath, wallowing in my own blood, and I was saved. I had given myself over to the Soul Keeper, but I was not wanted there yet." She placed the book on the table and pointed at a series of entries on the page, then pushed it across the desk towards Valia. "Six boys and three girls followed, '*to the glory of the Empire*'. I was reborn; renewed. Giving myself over to death and then being restored to life had renewed my sense of purpose. I see that in you now."

Valia closed the ledger.

"Perhaps you are right," she murmured, unwilling to make

eye contact with this woman who could see into her soul. "Perhaps you are wrong. But if I have a purpose, today, it is to protect the children of Shol'Hara from the horrors beyond the walls."

The Dam'Hara returned to her chair. "They are still '*beyond*' the walls, are they not?"

"Yes," Valia replied. "All things are beyond the walls; until they are not."

"The gates will not fall," the woman dismissed the notion. "They have never fallen."

"They have never stood against a Khalim-Shar or Eastern war engines," Valia cautioned.

The Dam'Hara leaned back in her chair and waved a hand around her.

"Do you see these ledgers?" she said. "They are a record of every pairing and every birth within these walls. They date back over centuries, millennia. *You* are in there, as is your mother, your father, and their parents, and theirs. A hundred generations; more perhaps, and there is room on the shelves for a hundred more. You want to break Shol'Hara out of bitterness; replace courage with fear. You would have us run where your ancestors stood their ground? What gives you the right to march in here with your *outland* manners and boorish threats?"

"Dam'Hara, I have seen what lies out there. I know, with absolute certainty, that nothing is truly safe or immutable. I have made so many mistakes in my life and holding my silence here would be just one more."

"Well," she sniffed. "At least you can admit that you are fallible at times. This is one of those times."

"You have no plan," Valia sighed, shaking her head.

"To evacuate Shol'Hara? Of course not. And no intention either."

"Even the children?"

"*Especially* the children! They are safest here!"

"No one is safe, Dam'Hara," Valia replied. "You will see that in the end."

She turned and walked out of the room. Perhaps she had found purpose again.

Marlon split the head of the Shar the moment it topped the battlements and it tumbled back down the scorched ramp, vanishing into smoke and dust. To his right, Acastes and Kapaneus worked side-by-side on the defences. A dazed soldier had managed to reach the top of the ramp and stumbled from exhaustion as he drew his sword. Acastes drove his square shield into the man, knocking him back before thrusting his sword into the man's chest. The heavy, curved blade punched through the light armour and burst out of his back.

A Shar leapt onto the battlements and lunged at Kapaneus. He drove up with the short sword in his left hand and skewered the creature's head as he tumbled back under its weight. Pinned under the shrieking, thrashing beast, he could not bring his long sword into use. Acastes turned from the crumpling soldier and drove his sword into the Shar's flank, heaving it off his friend. Kapaneus was quick to strike its head from its shoulders the moment his right arm was free.

"Pay attention, Kapaneus!" Acastes shouted.

His friend nodded his thanks and turned to face another Shar as it clawed its way over the ramparts.

Heavy Infantry poured onto the walls via the steps in the flanking towers, but Shar were slipping through the defences and leaping down onto the rooftops below.

"They have entered the city!" Kapaneus called. "We need more men on the walls!"

Jon lunged at a Shar as it tasted the air in anticipation. The creature lashed out at him, but he was able to block its claws with his shield. His counterattack missed, and he stumbled as his foot caught on the boot of a dead Infantryman. He held his shield up as he fell and felt the impact from the Shar's powerful forelimb as it slashed at him. A moment later it was over him and he was staring at his own distorted reflection in its obsidian eyes. Before it could strike, an arrow hissed over him and struck the Shar in the head, right between its dominant eyes. A moment later, lilac flames flared from the bubbling flesh and the creature shrieked in agony, thrashing on the stones. Jon rolled to his feet and stepped close to end the torment before glancing behind him.

Elan already had another arrow nocked and he aimed and released in a heartbeat. A screaming Shar tumbled from the top of the ramp before it had a chance to step onto the battlements.

More bowmen followed; Eastern men with short bows and quivers filled with arrows.

"Thank you, Tsering!" Acastes laughed as the pitiful shrieking of burning Shar replaced the frantic cries of men.

Marlon severed the head of a Shar that was writhing in torment with flames erupting from its flank and saw all along the wall that the bowmen had stemmed the flow of the creatures.

"Dachen!" he called as the man arrived on the wall. "I thought you had left us."

"I had an errand to run," he replied, taking the hand offered by Marlon.

The bowmen shot their arrows at the approaching Shar and had soon pushed them back away from the ramps. The creatures recovered once the Ago Camdi had burned out, but they were hesitant in racing towards the ramps again.

A terrible shriek carried over the plain towards them and the Shar turned their heads from the wall. They loped away, back towards the army in the distance. Tens of thousands of men still waited across the field; only a fraction of the army had joined this fight.

"We are not done yet," Marlon cautioned.

"The walls held fast," Acastes replied. "They will hold again."

Marlon sank down onto his haunches to regain his breath. He looked up at Dachen.

"Tsering?" he asked.

"He has not slept since we arrived," Dachen nodded. "He found all he needed in the apothecaries of Kor'Habat, but the city treasury might not enjoy receiving the bill."

"Money well spent!" Acastes declared.

"He warned us to use it wisely," Dachen cautioned. "The additives are rare and expensive."

"Whatever he needs, he can have," Acastes assured him.

"Acastes," Kapaneus said. "There are Shar in the city. They will need to be dealt with."

Acastes nodded. "They are trapped now. We will hunt them down and kill them." He looked around at the men on the battlements. They were nursing wounds or else helping wounded comrades. "Kor'Habat has won today!" he shouted. "We will defeat them again! And again, until they have nothing left to send at us! Victory!"

A cheer was raised by the men nearest. The cheer began to spread as all along the battlements and on the flanking towers, the defenders realised that they had beaten their enemy.

"Victory! Victory! Victory!" they chanted.

The triumphant chorus was raised and carried across the south-eastern quarter of the city. Voices lifted in celebration echoed from the stone walls until 'victory' assumed a name.

"Acastes! Acastes! Acastes!"

The adulation settled on an unwilling heart, and in that moment, Acastes was king.

Starling stared into the glowing coals of the cooking fire.

He felt someone nudging his shoulder and turned to see who it was. It was Captain Gillain with a bowl of hot stew.

"Eat, lad," he urged him. "You did well today."

Starling accepted the bowl and thanked the man.

"Was I doing well when you pulled me out from under that wooden span?" he replied, poking at the stew with a spoon.

"You got the ramp into position; that's all I asked of you," Gillain replied.

"Yes, and then I hid."

"We were never meant to breach the walls," the captain sighed. "You wonder why they held back thirty thousand Eastern soldiers, professional men, whilst we charged at the city? We were expendable, lad. The city was not going to fall today."

"Then why?" he asked.

Captain Gillain shrugged.

"It is not for us to question the generals, lad. Perhaps they wanted to probe the defences."

"A pointless waste," he murmured "Captain, I lost friends to-day. I never intended to form friendships here, believe me," he laughed. "But it's hard to train and travel with men and not form a bond."

"You sound surprised, lad," the captain teased. "Is this your first time meeting people, eh?"

Starling soaked up the captain's laughter. "It's just," he muttered, "not what I expected."

"Here comes Tulley," the captain said, patting Starling on the shoulder. "See? They're not *all* dead."

Captain Gillain left as Tulley sat near Starling, tucking into his own bowl of stew.

"Boiled boots and arseholes again," he remarked, chewing on a piece of gristle.

Starling shrugged. "Who else survived?" he murmured.

Tulley spat the gristle into the fire where it sizzled in the coals. "Not Scolly, I know that for certain," he replied, digging through the stew for something recognisable. "Fernelly got crushed under his own ramp. Tammis; arrow in the eye. Lhagho burned, poor bastard. Marton might live, but he'll not get far with no legs. Might just be you and me from the old squad. Still all the more whores for us, mate."

Starling picked out what looked like a piece of turnip

and tasted it. It could have been turnip, but it was hard to tell; everything looked and tasted grey.

"I have people in the city," Starling said. "Friends. Whichever way this goes, I hope that they are safe."

"I'd keep that quiet if I were you," Tulley warned, and after a long pause, "Family, is it?"

"A few old friends," Starling replied.

"You got any? Family that is?"

"Last I heard, my father was still alive," Starling replied. "But he can rot for all I care."

"Want my opinion, Stellio?" Tulley nodded. "A soldier's better without one; a family. This is your family," he gestured around him. "More brothers than any man could ever need."

"Have you always been a soldier?"

"Soldier. Militiaman. Sell-sword. I've done it all," Tulley replied. "I can't even remember my father's face, and the last time I saw my brother, I'd cracked his head with an axe. Nah, you're better off without them. Even my mother up and left before I was old enough to talk, so don't let anyone fog your wits with all that talk of 'blood and bonds'. Your own are just as likely to let you down as anyone else, so choose your friends wisely."

Starling stared into the fire. "It wasn't her fault she let me down," he whispered.

"What's that?"

"My mother," Starling said. "It wasn't her fault."

"This sounds like a story worth hearing," Tulley said, leaning close.

"I have never spoken of this," Starling shrugged. "And I am not sure why I feel that I should now."

Tulley leaned in closer still. "War does that," he confided. "No soldier wants the burden of secrets with him in the grave."

"Perhaps," Starling acknowledged, and flicked an errant coal back into the fire with the toe of his boot. "My father is a powerful man. Was a powerful man; I don't know. But with great wealth and influence came arrogance and entitlement. He would often beat my mother; I have no idea why. I was too young to understand but perhaps she was the way in which he could take out his anger at his own personal failings. I would hide under the kitchen table when he beat her, or else under my bed. She would smile at me, even as she lay on the floor, as if that should be enough to reassure me. How rotten has a man become when he punches his own wife?"

"Could nothing be done to stop him?" Tulley asked.

"He spread rumours about her." Starling went on. "She was sick; she was hysterical; she was losing her mind; insane. She would not leave the house for days after the beatings and so was never seen bearing the marks. But I saw them.

"No one would have believed her once he had established the narrative in his favour, and no one would have believed a boy's word against his. So, it went on, year upon year and all the time, he garnered the best wishes of the townsfolk, wishing him well in his ordeal, until she broke. I found her hanging in the cellar. She had looped a rope over the rafters and stepped from a chair to take her own life."

Tulley whistled through his teeth, and Starling continued. "The outpouring of sympathy onto the *great and generous man* was something to behold. Of course, he filled her place in his bed almost before her body was cold. He could do whatever he wanted because of who he was. No one would ever doubt his integrity; not openly at least. That is not the way the system works.

"Anyway, I spent my adolescence trying my absolute best to get back at him; to infuriate him and somehow ruin his reputation, when I should have simply put a dagger in his heart. I actually enjoyed the games I played, and I think that's why I persisted for so long trying to sully his good standing with my own bad behaviour," he chuckled. "It really was tremendous fun. Eventually, I just ran away."

Tulley nodded and patted his young friend on the knee. "Feel better now?"

Starling smiled. "Yes," he nodded in mild surprise. "I do believe that I do."

There was a long silence before Tulley spoke again. "Hey, remember that attack on Dargenmill? The one they say 'Valia of Hadaiti' led?" Starling nodded. "Well I overheard a few of the scouts talking; and they got her. Kor'Habat, the Heavy Infantry or whoever got her when she arrived at the gates."

Starling looked up in surprise.

"What do you mean, 'got her'?"

"Killed her," he replied. "And killed her friends; hundreds of them. An Eastern prince and a hundred Shar-hunters. Killed the lot, they say."

Starling swallowed hard. *Nirmaya?*

"They killed everyone who travelled with Valia?" he said, dumbfounded.

"So they say," Tulley replied. "One of the Hatars has seized power now that the Kodistai is dead." Tulley looked unsure. "Maybe just dying, I'm not sure. Anyway, the city is controlled by this Hatar, and he ordered them all to be killed. Good riddance, I say, after what they did in Dargenmill."

"That can't be right," he whispered.

Tulley spat out another lump of gristle.

"Kor'Habat has always been a brutal place, Stellio," he said. "They'd hang you from the walls for looking at them funny. The stories I've heard about the things they did during the expansion would curl your hair. They don't care about anyone but themselves. Korathea; their Empire; it was all just a way to fill their coffers at the expense of you and me. They deserve to die. I almost hope that they don't surrender; they need wiped out; a clean slate. Know what I mean?"

Starling stared into the coals, only vaguely aware that Tulley was still talking. His ran his finger along the scar on his cheek and tried to remember Nirmaya's face. She came to him in a fleeting glimpse of that disparaging look she had favoured him with so often. He could almost feel her hair running through his fingers in that one act of passion she had gifted him so long ago, now reduced to an ephemeral, vanishing memory.

His heart would have broken had a cord of rancour not coiled around it and bound it tight.

He wanted the city to burn. He wanted the walls turned to dust.

He had never known pure hatred before, but the taste roused in him a hunger for vengeance that overwhelmed his senses.

Kor'Habat would pay.

CHAPTER 26

By evening of the second day since escaping the city, they reached the place where the road met the canal, and the refugees who waited there. Nirmaya was accompanied by six of the young women she had helped free from that awful place in Kor'Habat. They had nowhere else to go, and the city could never be home again; not least now that it was under siege. The pain of that place was too acute. Those new companions were all that had kept her from curling into a ball of self-pity, recoiling from the human touch that now made her skin crawl. Their expectations had not diminished when they had broken free into the seedy streets of the city. Now that she had led them from their cells, they still looked to her for direction.

What next? How do we rebuild?

She did not know, of course, and she would have confessed as much in an instant had that admission not surely have crushed them. Not only these few slaves, but the tens of thousands who had trusted her to deliver them to safety.

The sprawl of the shabby encampment extended up the gentle slope to the north of the waterway, filling the paths between fields and vanishing into the distance.

Nirmaya addressed a large gathering as the light faded. A fire blazed at the centre of the clearing and she could see the worried expressions on their faces cast into stark relief by the firelight.

"I know that this is not what you wish to hear," she started, ready for the accusations that would surely come as she was found to be an imposter. "But I have failed to secure the food we so desperately need. No doubt Afreda has told you what happened on the canal." She offered the Sister a thin smile. "If not for her courage, I would not be here now."

"Abbil is dead," she went on, feeling an awful tightening in her throat. "He died to save me from my captors. I will never forget him."

"What about the food," a man said from the crowd. "There's plenty on the canal. We can buy it from them."

Nirmaya sighed. "Everything I was given has been taken," she replied, and waited for the anger to come.

"That was all we had!" a woman shouted.

"How will we buy food now?" another asked.

"I know that," she said, forcing calm into her voice.

"We have to eat," a woman insisted. "I have no strength left and my children are so thin."

"We can work," a man suggested.

"They don't need labour," another replied.

"Then what do you suggest we do; eat grass? Those barges are filled with meat and grain."

"Where are they taking it?"

"Kor'Habat! They take everything!"

"We should take it back!"

"Wait!" Nirmaya shouted over the rising voices. "Wait, please. Listen to what I have to say."

The flaring tempers eased as she appealed for calm. She looked around the fire, and hollow-cheeked men and women stared back. Her thumb found the shallow, fading mark left by Maidra's ring and she stole from the memory a little of the red-haired woman's fire.

"Those barges are indeed full of food. But it is going to Kor'Habat where those merchants will demand a fair price for what they own. If we take it from those barge masters, they will go hungry instead of you."

"I can live with that!" a man shouted, but Nirmaya went on.

"Kor'Habat is under siege from the east!" she shouted, and the growing buzz of anger subsided. "The Khalim-Shar has attacked the city and they are filling their stores with everything they can get their hands on. The barge masters would usually enjoy Kor'Habat's protection, but I see no Infantry here. Every man is defending those walls and all within them while we have been abandoned to the wind. This is what we do: The Sisters, along with any man or woman willing to wield a sword, stop every barge from here to Ara Dasari, and we take a tithe. One quarter of all cargoes passing through the canal will be taken from those barges." She paused to let it sink in and then with more force said, "No harm will come to the barge masters or their crew. We take a quarter, no more, no less and we leave them to continue their journey."

'Have the courage to seize what you need to survive.'

Is this what you meant by those words, Abbil? she wondered

"If Kor'Habat will not protect them," she went on, "then Kor'Habat can pay the levy, and if every barge master demands it, they cannot refuse. The barge masters get paid and we get fed."

"We are to be thieves?" a man said from the back.

"We are at war," she replied. "We are to survive!"

A general murmur spread around the fire. The crowd broke up into pairs and small groups, muttering amongst themselves in small, animated clusters.

One by one they turned to her and nodded their assent.

Nirmaya looked from one to the other, a smile spreading across her face. "We will make enemies in doing this, but together we are strong. This is the last night you sleep with empty bellies. Tomorrow, we will eat like the Kodistai himself!"

Granger knocked on the open door and peered into the

room. Adeyemi was staring into the darkness outside the window of the Akharran where he had been recovering.

"May I come in?" he asked from the doorway.

Adeyemi turned his head towards the door and nodded.

"I have something for you," Granger said, stepping inside. He was carrying a large, flat object wrapped in cloth.

"The siege is over?" Adeyemi asked.

"A brief cessation in hostilities I am afraid," Granger replied. "We have not yet heard the last from the Khalim-Shar and his armies."

Adeyemi almost laughed. "We cannot defeat him, friend Granger," he said.

"Not without a weapon you can't," Granger said, unwrapping the bundle. He unfolded the cloth to reveal a large flat piece of steel. "It is a new impanga. I had it made by the smiths today, as best I could at least, having only a passing acquaintance with its design."

Adeyemi turned and stepped towards Granger's outstretched hands. The blade shone in the dim lamplight and he held his hands over it as though afraid to touch the steel. At last, he gripped the handle and lifted it from the cloth. He felt its weight, turning away to move the large, flat blade through the air.

"Do you approve?" Granger asked. "It can be modified, of course."

Adeyemi paused as he caught sight of his reflection in the polished steel. He felt the skin on his cheek with his free hand, tracing the whorls and jagged scars with gentle fingers.

"Do you know why I carried the impanga?" he asked, moving his fingers to touch his image in the steel. "It is a tool of farmers and labourers. It is used to clear bush, split wood, cut open fruit. This is not the weapon of a warrior."

"You do not have to accept it," Granger began.

"But I am not a warrior," Adeyemi nodded. "I am not worthy to hold the weapons of my people, nor yours."

"The best measure of a man's worth is not his own judgement, but that of his friends," Granger assured him. "And your friends hold you in the highest regard. Your courage..."

"It is easy to have courage when one knows he will not die," Adeyemi interrupted him. "My life now lies at the mercy of the Khalim-Shar's whims."

"That is not true," Granger argued. "That creature has no hold over you except that which you give it. There is no magic that can hold you to a path, nor portents to tell what lies upon it. You are, and you have always been, in control of your actions. The courage is your own, that strength your own. We need you."

Adeyemi returned to the window and stared out at the field of stars.

"Thank you for your gift, friend Granger," he said. "I shall miss your wisdom."

Granger sagged. "In time, I hope that you will see it for the truth that it is."

He turned and left the tall man to his introspection.

A small courtyard separated the main gates of Shol'Hara from the city beyond. The tangled cherry trees had long since lost their blossom and now the dense foliage cast a deep shade over the benches. Managed beds of orange and mauve flowers on slender stems filled the spaces between the winding paths and bees moved from bloom to bloom searching for precious nectar.

"You received my message," Kapaneus said, sitting on the bench beside Valia.

Valia nodded.

"Have you recovered? You look eager to take the fight to them," he noted, seeing her leather armour.

"How many days has it been?" she asked. "Three?"

"Yes," he nodded. "And the army is still camped on the plain."

"They will not leave soon," Valia sighed.

"Kor'Habat has food enough for the winter and beyond. We

will see how strong their resolve is when the cold winds start to cut across from the sea."

"They will not wait that long," Valia assured him.

"I tend to agree with you," Kapaneus said. "And every day they grow a little stronger."

Valia raised a quizzical eyebrow.

"How so?" she asked.

"The Shar can multiply," he said after a pause. "Adeyemi witnessed the Khalim-Shar causing a Shar to split in two. Granger is certain that they will need a great deal of food to fuel this, but they have that in abundance."

"What?"

"The refugees that Nirmaya led away from the city were taken before they could reach safety according the reports from outside the walls. They have thousands of prisoners to feed on."

"I thought Granger assured us that this was not possible?" she growled. "He said that they could not multiply!"

Kapaneus shrugged. "We now know that they can."

"We should ride out and attack before they can grow any more in number," she said, rising to her feet. "We need to end this before it is too late!"

"They have upwards of thirty thousand soldiers, war engines and hundreds; possibly thousands of Shar. Facing them in the open would be a terrible gamble. In the city we hold the advantage."

"For now," she replied. "How long before they have the numbers to swamp us? Who commands our armies? How many can we field against them?"

Kapaneus winced. "Rogan commands a little over half of the Heavy Infantry," he said. "Fourteen thousand men, plus thousands of Eastern men, while King Chapok can muster around eight thousand of his own warriors. There are of course another few thousand assorted militia and Shar-hunters to add to that."

"Rogan commands *Eastern* men?"

"It is complicated," he chuckled. "You would not believe it."

Valia nodded, deep in thought.

"You said Rogan commands half the Infantry? Who commands the rest?"

Kapaneus hesitated before replying. "Acastes."

"Acastes?" she said in surprise. "Half of the Infantry follow Acastes?"

"Twelve thousand men."

"I have nothing against Acastes," she chuckled, "but why would twelve thousand men choose to follow him over one of their own Hatars?"

"Because they believe that he is heir to the Kodistai's throne."

Valia laughed out loud, walking away for a few paces before ambling back as her mirth abated.

"Who told them that? Acastes?" she asked. "He certainly holds himself in high regard, but the Kodistai's heir?"

"I told them," Kapaneus replied, "although many suspected it already. There have been rumours for some time."

"Rumours spread by Acastes, no doubt," she said with a shake of her head.

"Valia, I need your help," he urged.

"Oh? Do you need me to spread *rumours* for you?"

"No," he replied, ignoring her cynicism. "I need you to open a gate for me, in Shol'Hara."

"Why can't you do it yourself?"

"Valia, I am neither a eunuch, nor an Infantryman who has earned the honour of entering Shol'Hara. I would never get in there. Besides, I need to be on the other side for the gate to open."

"Now you have me confused. Go on," Valia said, curious to hear what he had in mind.

He glanced around to be sure that no one was listening and leaned forward.

"There is a tunnel," he said in a low voice, "that links Shol'Hara to the Kodistai's palace."

"A tunnel?" she asked. "That would need to be, what; half a

mile long?"

"Indeed," he replied. "And pass under the River Habat. It exists, although it has been a long time since it was last used. It is flooded but is being pumped out as we speak. For it to open, I need to operate the lever on one side, while a lever on the other side is pulled at the same time. This is why I need your help."

Valia thought for a moment. "Could this tunnel be used to move the children out of Shol'Hara if the walls are breached?"

"It would take time," he said, nodding, "but it could be done."

Valia sat down again and looked at him. "Tell me what you want me to do," she said.

Captain Silman limped along the narrow street that led to the apothecary. He had burned the little scroll that the Shar had brought him, but its message had been clear. This was his chance to prove his loyalty and earn his reward. Even since that blasted creature had emerged from the shadows in the room that he rented in the dock quarter, he had been on edge. The Shar had delivered the note and vanished out a window just as quickly as it had appeared, without ever threatening him. Still, every dim corner of the city held crawling flesh in his mind's eye now.

The pain from the broken bones in his feet had abated over the past days, but the effort of walking again was bringing it back with a vengeance.

He could hear the tinkle of glass jars from a basement vent at ground level, and a sulphurous smell burned his nose when he bent down towards it. He entered the shop and the apothecary looked up from his counter.

"I am afraid I am closed, it is past midnight," the thin, elderly man said.

"Please," Silman replied, grimacing in pain. "I cannot bear it any longer. I can pay well for your trouble."

"In that case," the apothecary said. "How may I be of service? Something for the feet?"

"You are very perceptive," Silman replied, hobbling towards him. Perhaps if you could see the problem."

The thin man walked around the counter and ushered his customer towards a chair.

Silman placed a hand on the apothecary's shoulder for support as he made to sit. Then he pulled a dagger from his belt and drove it into the man's sternum. He twisted the blade, feeling bone grate against the steel as his victim gasped in shock and pain.

He pulled the blade free leaving the dying man to drop to the floorboards. He bent down to wipe the blade on his victim's tunic, then made his way to the door behind the counter. Stairs led down into a well-lit basement from where a strong smell that burned his nose emanated. Leaning on the handrail for support, he went down, one step at a time, wincing at every single one.

A long bench ran the length of the room, filled with smoking vials and boiling jars. The stench was awful, and Silman raised a hand to cover his mouth and nose as someone stirred at the far end of the basement room. An old man turned to face him, wisps of grey hair hanging in lank strands from his blotchy head and wizened chin. A jagged toothed smile spread across the old man's face and he muttered something that Silman could not understand.

"You must be Tsering," he said, lifting a jar of cloudy, yellow liquid. "What are these foul-smelling concoctions?"

Tsering replied in the Eastern tongue and Silman threw the jar against the far wall. The pottery smashed, raining its contents on the floor.

"Strange that with all the warriors in the city, *you* should be seen as a threat," he went on, sweeping another cluster of jars onto the floor.

The liquids fizzed and bubbled where they mixed on the flagstones. He walked towards the old man and pulled the dagger from its sheath.

"Captain!" A voice from the stairs caused him to turn in

surprise.

"Daelen?" he said. "What are you doing here?"

"I cannot let you do this, Captain," Daelen replied, placing his hand on the pommel of his sword.

Tsering started to edge across to the far end of the room.

"Don't you move!" Silman growled, turning to point the dagger at Tsering. The sound of a sword being drawn dragged the Captain's attention back to the young soldier.

"Daelen," he urged. "This is our time; our moment."

"No," Daelen replied, shaking his head. "It was never meant to go this far."

"We agreed!" he spat back. "You are a part of this; you cannot back out now."

Daelen descended the final two stairs and approached Silman. "Ever since you killed the clerk at Banihat to conceal your own error, I have known that you would need to be stopped." Daelen murmured. "I had hoped that your own greed would bring you down, and I have stayed close to hasten your fall if given the chance. But you have reached a point where I cannot stand by and watch any longer."

"Why come alone? You are no match for me."

"You would only seek to implicate me," Daelen said. "Try to shift the blame from yourself to save your own neck. No, it is my duty to end your madness alone, and I believe that you will find me more than a match for you."

Silman spread his hands and smiled. "All I have is this dagger," he replied. "You come to fight me with a sword and full armour? Where is your sense of fairness or justice?"

Daelen took a stride towards the Captain, raising his sword in an attacking stance. Silman stepped around the table, putting it between them.

"Think hard on this, Daelen," he urged. "You could yet have more power than you ever dreamed possible."

"At what cost?" Daelen spat, lunging across the long bench.

Silman staggered back to avoid the scything blade, grimacing at the pain it caused him.

"You are injured." Daelen stated. "This will be easier than I had thought."

Daelen vaulted the bench and swung his huge, curved blade in a downward arc. Silman ducked to the side and the sword crashed into the shelves behind him, sending glass vials tumbling to the stone floor. He stabbed at Daelen with the dagger but could not reach the younger man as he spun away.

Tsering moved with surprising speed, scampering towards the foot of the stairs. Silman hurled the dagger at the fleeing alchemist but the slender blade struck the handrail and stuck fast.

"You made a deal with the Khalim-Shar, you scum!" Daelen shouted, attacking again.

Silman dodged backwards with Daelen's blade missing by a hair's breadth at first and then slicing across his chest. A shallow wound, but he knew that he could not evade a killing blow for long. Then his back was against the shelves in the corner of the room and there was nowhere left to go.

Daelen advanced and pressed the point of his sword against Silman's throat.

"I should have known," Silman mocked, "when you would not take your turn with that bitch in the mill, that you had no balls between your legs. A disappointing man in every way."

Daelen leaned in and punched Silman in the teeth with his free hand. His lip burst from the impact and he sagged, dribbling blood and broken teeth down the front of his shirt.

"Look at me," Daelen said, using the tip of his sword to lift the captain's bloody chin.

Without warning, Silman swung his arm towards Daelen. He released the jar his hand had fallen upon on the shelf and smashed it against Daelen's head.

The soldier staggered back from the shock, wiping a milky liquid from his face. Then he began to scream as his flesh bubbled.

"My eyes!" he cried out, hands trembling as he tried to wipe the liquid from his face. His flesh smoked and blistered and Silman stared in shock.

The captain hobbled to where his dagger was stuck fast in the wooden handrail. He took his time, returning to Daelen. The young soldier had sunk to the floor and was pawing at the dissolving flesh on his face. Silman felt bile rising in his throat and looked away from the groaning man on the stone tiles. He sheathed the dagger and instead picked up the sword that Daelen had dropped and held it against the side of the young man's neck. A moment later he drove it home, ending the misery he had inflicted.

Silman used the sword to sweep the tables and shelves clear before smashing a lamp on the wooden desk. The oil sprayed out in a burning blue swathe that leapt to life as the fire took hold. Silman hurried to the stairs as smoke filled the room. He glanced back through the flames to the body of the young soldier and grimaced before turning to escape the growing inferno.

Hatar Bravik Fol'Gannity was seated at the Kodistai's side when Acastes entered the room in the small hours of the morning. A few clerks waited at the bedside while an apothecary tidied away his vials and potions.

"If you have come to find favour in his valediction, you are too late," Bravik murmured.

Acastes looked from the Hatar to the wraith on the grand, pillow-strewn bed. Bravik slid a sheet of parchment from the silk sheets and hid it from view.

"Is that why you are here?" he replied. "I imagine you had hoped that he would sign that document you have there, naming you successor to the throne. And now it is too late. You tried until the very end; your persistence is to be admired."

Bravik's expression betrayed his guilt.

"I have at least watched over our Kodistai in his final days," he sneered.

"As the vulture watches over the lame deer," Acastes noted.

He walked towards the bed and looked at the body that lay there; thin and grey and wasted.

"You never came to him in life, even when his health was failing," Bravik accused. "Why come now in death?"

Acastes leaned down and placed a hand on the Kodistai's forehead, feeling the cooling flesh under his palm.

"Perhaps if he had acknowledged me," Acastes murmured.

"Perhaps your claim has always been a lie," Bravik shot back.

Acastes stood straight again. "It has never been *my* claim, Bravik. If it consoles you at all, I would rather have it forgotten."

"You have the power to renounce it."

Acastes laughed. "And leave you in charge? Or Rogan? You must be mad."

"Your very presence here weakens Kor'Habat," Bravik roared, getting to his feet. "make your claim; present your proof or leave the city! The Heavy Infantry is divided when we need them united!"

"Our common enemy unites us, Bravik!" Acastes spat. "Perhaps your presence on the walls would do greater good than you have managed trying to squeeze a final signature from a dying man."

"You are not the man to lead us," Bravik growled.

"I am twice the man you are, Bravik, by any measure you care to choose. I hope to see you defending the walls from the next assault, if your arm still holds any strength after so long wielding a pen!"

Acastes gave the body of the Kodistai one last glance before storming out of the room. The old man's death could change everything for him. Or it could change nothing. Acastes only had to choose.

The sky was still dark when Dachen was driven from his bed by sleeplessness. The sound of marching boots in the courtyard alerted him to a change of guard. He washed his face and left the small room to make his way down the gloomy stairs. Outside, weary faced Infantrymen streamed past him, eager to find the sleep that had eluded him.

Eastern men too, were filing out of the Akharran gate and Dachen felt a small spike of pride that his people had put their shoulders to the wheel in Kor'Habat.

He craved hot tea, and so made his way across the massive courtyard to one of the many large dining halls where a wisp of smoke from the chimney suggested he might find some. Sure enough, there were a few clusters of men drinking and eating, either preparing for duty or taking precious moments to relax before retiring to bed.

He found what he needed in the kitchen and carried a steaming cup of tea to a table near a group of four Eastern men. They lowered their heads at once when they recognised him, and he acknowledged their mark of respect.

"Are you fresh from the walls," he asked, "or preparing for duty?"

"We have finished our spell on the wall, Highness," one of the men replied. "A quiet night."

"Long may it continue," he replied. "Tell me, which Kingdoms do you hail from?"

"Bhatsal and Dhonu are from Shibatsu," the soldier replied. "Hiransh is of Khumjang; although we do not hold that against him." The men laughed and slapped Hiransh on the shoulder as he groaned at the joke. "My name is Tirtha, Highness, and I am from a small village near Lokhara."

"Lokhara!" Dachen replied. "The finest city in the four Kingdoms."

There was an awkward silence as the men stared into their cups.

"It will be again, Highness," Tirtha replied.

Dachen nodded.

"We will win our homeland back," he assured them. "And we will do well to help defeat the Khalim-Shar here in the West. You give me reason to be proud."

"Even King Chapok is taking to the walls today," Tirtha remarked.

Dachen looked unconvinced. "Are you certain?" he asked. "He has not yet recovered from his wound I hear, and he is far from being the soldiering type."

"I overheard two of our men as they left not an hour ago. Chapok will join them defending the gates today."

Dachen laughed. "How well do you know the king?" Dachen asked. "He prefers silk to armour."

"I was among the men who found him after the fall of Lokhara," Tirtha said, not engaging in the mocking of his king.

"Oh?" Dachen's interest was piqued.

"Four days after the city was razed, we found him, or rather, he found us," Tirtha went on. "He walked into our encampment, without a scratch. He showed no fear but led us to safety and secured the ships we needed to cross the ocean. He is a great king, deserving of our admiration and loyalty."

Dachen sat in silence for a long time.

"Four days after the city burned," he said at last, his voice slow and deliberate, "you found King Chapok, in your encampment? He was unhurt and without a mark?"

"He was by every measure, a king," the man replied.

"That man is my brother!" Dachen snapped back. "He could not survive a single day without servants fawning over him. Four days in the wilderness? The Khalim-Shar let him go!" He leapt to his feet, spilling the tea across the table. "Rouse every man you can find and send them to the gates!"

Dachen ran out of the dining hall and into the training ground.

"To the gates! To the gates!" His voice echoed off the walls of the Akharran. "We are betrayed! To the gates!"

The Heavy Infantry had been taken by surprise. Seeing the approach of supposed allies had not roused them to urgency and it had taken Chapok's men under a minute to kill all thirty men at the gate. Throats were cut as guards were lowered, and not a single cry of alarm had escaped the hapless Infantrymen. Size was no match for guile.

The last to die was still gasping at the end of Jangbu's sparth. The point of the wide blade had been driven through the steel breastplate and into the man's chest. The steel squeaked as he pulled the blade free and the Infantryman fell to his knees.

"Open the gates, Yeshe," Chapok ordered from the shelter of the gatehouse doorway and the plump soldier motioned for others to help him. Chapok glanced up at the battlements, eager to be done before the alarm was raised by the opening of the gates. A jewel-encrusted patch covered his ruined eye and he scratched at the scar on his left temple as his men rushed to follow his order. He would have that bowman skinned alive when he caught him, and his green hide hung upon the wall of his palace. And what a palace it would be once he had helped the Khalim-Shar take the West. The Eastern Kingdoms would be his to rule; a single kingdom under King Chapok.

Shouts from above told him that the movement of the gates and drawn the attention of the soldiers above. He glanced at the barricades over the flanking tower doors and smiled. The nearest stairs were two hundred yards away at the next tower, and the gates were already beginning to move.

Inside the gatehouse, six of his men turned the huge, horizontal wheel that lifted the great counterweights and opened the gates. Chapok was reminded of a horse in an awful mill he had been forced to visit with his father. He had watched the dumb beast walk in circles, powering the mill while the King had spoken with his subject. A nail placed in the animal's path had soon found its way into the hoof, and Chapok had giggled when it stumbled and fell.

The sound of approaching horses pulled his mind back to the present.

How had they mustered already?

"Hurry!" he ordered. "Lock it open and break the wheel."

Those hoofbeats were awfully close now, and he suffered a moment of doubt until he glanced out through the open gate.

The horn sounded from the battlements; frantic blasts to rally the defences.

Out of the darkness, the Shar army rushed past him and into the city that could not be breached.

CHAPTER 27

Rogan led the Cavalry towards the invading army of Shar. The first of the soldiers, who had attempted to form a hasty defence, were already a ragged, disjointed mess. The Shar were too fast and too strong, and all but impervious to the arrows that were rained upon them from the battlements.

Heavy Infantry and Eastern sparth bearers alike were falling back against the onslaught that had already reached halfway to East Market. Shar flowed down the main thoroughfare, spilling into side-streets and alleys to wreak their bloody havoc.

Two hundred Cavalrymen ploughed into the black mass, crushing those men still standing, too weary to or too slow to make way. Rogan brought his sword down onto the head of the nearest Shar as his horse pawed the air in front to hold the creatures back.

Dark shapes darted away off the main street into the deeper gloom of the narrower lanes.

"Raims!" Rogan shouted to the captain at his side. "Fall back to East Market. If we hold the market, we can form barricades and hem them in to the east of the city!"

"Hatar," Raims replied, turning his mount against the flow of riders and forcing his way back the way he had come.

Rogan pushed on amid the press of horses and men, a wall of armour and flesh pushing towards the gate.

"We must seal the gates!" he shouted. "To the gates!"

"Man the war engines!" Hatar Gilean Fol'Maddon shouted as he strode along the battlements. "Aim for those formations!"

The vast army of Eastern soldiers was approaching the city, and Gilean Fol'Maddon was determined not to allow them an easy walk. The first hint of dawn was now touching the eastern horizon but there was no birdsong with it, only the shriek of hungry Shar.

Gilean felt a curious thrill that he had not felt since his first campaign as a young Infantryman in Eritania. His armour had been looser then, of course, but the fear-tinged exhilaration of battle reminded him what it was to be alive. He could have laughed; he had only ascended onto the walls to inspect the soldiers, but now found himself at the heart of the defensive effort. The gates had been opened, that much was clear, but the 'how' and the 'why' of that would have to wait until they were sealed again

The volleys of arrows had done nothing against the Shar, with the creatures pouring forwards, bristling with shafts, undaunted and unharmed.

"Let the Infantry deal with those Shar at close quarters!" he shouted as the catapult crews sprang into action. "We will give those soldiers a taste of Kor'Habat's hospitality!"

"They are out of range!" a soldier called out from the flanking tower above him.

"Then let them come to us!" he shouted back.

An over-eager crew, further along the wall, released the long arm of their *Lamo Phenka*, which sent a barrel of burning pitch streaking through the darkness. The barrel hit the ground well short of the marching formations and sprayed fire across the dry plain.

Then, screams from within the nearest flanking tower alerted him to the danger coming from within the walls.

"Seal the doors!" he shouted. "If they take the walls, they can turn the engines on the city, and we are as good as lost."

Acastes rode his horse across the front of the defensive formations of Heavy Infantry. From East Market the road curved away in the dim light towards the gates. More men poured into the market as he shouted his orders.

"Form barricades in every street to east and west!" he shouted. "Seal them in and we can force them back to the gates!"

Detachments of soldiers broke away from the main force, vanishing into the warren of alleys that pervaded the city.

"Acastes!" Dachen called as he rode into the market. "The apothecary is in flames. The Ago Camdi is gone! Sabotage, I am certain."

Acastes swore. "How much is left?" he asked.

"I have a hundred bowmen with a handful of maddeners each," he replied.

"Tell your men to make them count. We will worry about the apothecary later. Have them take high positions above the barricades. And make sure every man wears his mark. Let us not fight friends at a time like this."

Dachen touched the strip of blue-green cloth around his arm. He nodded and rode back towards the Akharran.

"Marlon!" Acastes called when he saw the Shar-hunter approaching. "The gates have fallen. We will try to block their advance from here. Put yourself wherever you can do the most damage."

"I need to find Valia," he replied. "She is still in Shol'Hara."

"Do what you must," Acastes declared. "I have a battle to win!"

Rogan steered his horse to the north-east and hurried away, just as a rider approached from the south.

"That's Captain Raims," Acastes murmured to himself. "That's Rogan's man."

Hooves clattered and slid on the cobbles as he arrived, throwing up his visor to expose wide eyes.

"Hatar Fol'Brandam has ordered barricades be erected in the streets!" he shouted. "The Shar are through the gates and moving freely through the city."

"Already done, Raims," Acastes replied with a smug grin. "Go back and tell your master *that*!"

Raims glanced back the way he had come and then to Acastes.

He did not reply.

On the battlements, the flanking towers were over-run by Shar. Screams echoed from within the tower walls as the stairwells were lost. They had never been designed to protect the walls from within. The doors flew open to the battlements and the black creatures swarmed out to attack the defending soldiers.

Gilean swung his sword with a practiced ease that he had never lost, but he was tiring fast with both the sheer numbers of Shar and his years colluding against him.

"Rally! Rally!" he shouted, trying to bring the soldiers still standing to his side.

A *Hatiyara* on the tower nearest to him released its ordnance, but he was too consumed with his own survival to see where it landed.

Moments later a soldier tumbled, screaming from the tower as the Shar took the higher ground. Gilean grabbed a shield from a dead Infantryman and parried an attack from another Shar. He hacked back at it and roared as he felt the blade bite. He stepped back and saw the creature stumble, then watched in horror as the wound on its shoulder knitted before his eyes.

He had not believed the stories, until now.

He glanced out across the plain where the vast formations were moving closer. The war engines were lost, and the battlements would soon be taken too.

How was this possible?

Then he saw, at the head of the army, a giant figure, striding across the plain towards the open gates.

He had not truly believed in the existence of the Khalim-Shar either.

He threw the shield onto the stones and gripped his sword with both hands.

"Come on then, you bastards!" he yelled, before throwing himself at the nearest Shar, resigned to giving his life in the defence of his beloved Korathea.

Valia strode through the Opal Rooms towards the large Atrium at one end. She remembered being a serving girl to women such as those who were cowering from her now. She remembered the abuse and threats she had endured from a woman named Chesa. She remembered her mother; mind ruined by the drug, Bliss. She remembered that all of this could have been hers if only she had lowered herself to be used by the Empire.

"Get out of my way!" she roared at one of the Harami who had started begging her to help them.

The woman stumbled to the side and Valia reached the massive plinth at the centre of the atrium. Shallow water surrounded the monument with carved urns at each corner trickling water into the pool. The statue of a woman, babe in arms stood upon the block, with the words 'Mother of the Empire' chiselled into the stone discs that adorned each side of the plinth.

Each disc was easily two strides across. She drew her sword and banged the hilt on the stone of the nearest one. Three sharp raps.

She listened, and over the trickling of water and whimpering of frightened women, she heard three echoing taps in return. She stepped around the plinth to one of the other discs and reached up to the urn high up to its left. She pulled down on the handle, and after a moment it shifted. The urn moved a little at first and then tipped towards her with ease.

An echoing thud emanated from within the plinth. She stood back.

The huge disc began to roll to the side with a painful grating sound. The water of the pool drained away into the widening gap and splashed down the stairs that were revealed as the stone rolled away. Kapaneus jammed his torch into an empty sconce and grinned at her from the gloomy tunnel.

"I must be quick," he said, stepping out into the atrium, "My presence here will not go un-noticed for long."

The gates were lost; there was no escaping that simple fact.

Rogan pulled back what was left of his Cavalry as the Eastern sparth bearers poured into the city in well-disciplined order. The Khalim-Shar strode into the city behind a regiment of a thousand men and shrieked in triumph as Rogan retreated.

Ceding ground to this enemy was the most painful thing he had ever done. He felt sick; violated, as he watched the invaders pour into his city. But he would have it back, by whatever means necessary. He was destined to rule Korathea, he was certain.

East Market was already defended by a wall of shields and he saw Acastes at the head of the army.

"The streets!" Rogan shouted. "You must barricade the streets!"

"It is in hand, Rogan," Acastes replied. "Take your leave now, your place is at the palace."

"What is that supposed to mean?"

"You want to rule?" Acastes sneered. "Go, take your seat and rule. Hide in the palace as rulers do."

Rogan glared at Acastes, aware that every soldier within ear-shot could hear the conversation.

"I know about your games," Acastes went on. "I know about the document you have from the Council of Hatars. Well, now is your time to seize power. The Kodistai is dead! Run, run to the palace. *I* will defend the city."

"The Kodistai…" Rogan began.

"Dead. Go and rule now while you can, Rogan! See if it is as sweet as you had dreamed."

An ear-splitting shriek pulled their attention to the road again. The enemy had arrived at East Market.

Pemba pulled his last maddener from his quiver. He was a hundred yards or more to the south-west of the market square, strung out in a thin line with his fellow bowmen.

He nocked the arrow and watched from the roof above the barricade. The headless bodies of six Shar lay at the feet of the soldiers there and each smouldered from a single point where the maddener had struck home. In the gathering light of dawn, the Shadows could be seen darting this way and that in the narrow alleys trying to find a way through the barricades. He saw one of the creatures slink around a corner and fixate on the barricade below him. Frustrated at finding its way blocked again, it chittered in agitation and loped forwards. The Shar accelerated until it reached the upturned cart and stacked furniture of the barricade and leapt…

Pemba sighted down the arrow as he drew the string back. A single drop of oil fell from the tip of the arrow and the small chunk of Ago Camdi within before he let it fly. He watched as the arrow and Shar converged in mid-air.

The creature hit the cobbles screaming. Lilac flame burst from its flank where the arrow had entered, and the Infantrymen fell upon it to take its head as it thrashed in agony.

One of the soldiers saluted in thanks.

Pemba held up his empty quiver and shrugged.

The soldiers braced themselves as they realised that their one true advantage was gone. Pemba watched as the next Shar to leap the barricade killed one of the soldiers and injured another before it was stopped. Another cleared the barrier before they had fully recovered, and then that point of defence was gone. Pemba could hear the screams of dying men all around him and he realised that without the maddeners, the soldiers were being over-run.

He looked down to the street below and a Shar slunk by, followed by another. He was trapped.

Across the alley was another flat-topped building, but he would need to manage an eight-foot jump to reach it. He paced back to the far end of the building and ran. Pemba leapt from the flat, tiled roof and sailed across the gap. He made it, but with only a finger to spare, and the scrape of his boots alerted the Shar below. They shrieked and chittered as he ran again, desperate to put some distance between himself and their razor claws. He sprinted across the flat roof to the next gap and jumped.

He knew at once that he would come up short and reached out with his hands. The edge of the roof slammed into his upper arms and chest and his bow skidded away from him across the tiles. Winded, he clawed his way back up as a Shar stared up at him, pacing in the alley below.

He gathered his bow and took a deep breath before running again, this time aiming for a roof that was a little lower than the one he was on. He landed on the tiles and felt them sag beneath his feet. A moment later, the supporting beams collapsed, and he tumbled down in a shower of tiles and splintered wood.

Someone screamed as he crashed onto the floorboards, and as the dust cleared, he realised that a terrified family were huddled, staring at him from the corner of the room.

He struggled to stand amongst the debris, testing his body for damage.

"I am an ally," he coughed, aware of how his Eastern appearance may have been construed. "The barricades are falling. You must move to safety."

The man nodded, wide-eyed as he pulled the two children and the woman closer to him.

"Now!" he urged them.

Marlon entered the courtyard at the entrance to Shol'Hara where two guards blocked his way.

"Halt!" one shouted as he rode towards them.

"Open the bloody gates!" he shouted.

"On whose authority?" the Infantryman shouted back.

"What is wrong with you, man?" Marlon growled dropping down from his saddle. "The city is under attack."

"And?" the other soldier sneered. "What business do you have in Shol'Hara?"

"*My* business is none of yours," he replied.

A scream from beyond the courtyard interrupted the argument and both Infantrymen drew their swords. They stepped forward, looking past Marlon to the edge of the courtyard.

He turned and saw the Shar too. The creature took a few sinuous strides towards them and paused.

"You go left, you go right," Marlon instructed. "I'll go down the middle. On my mark. Ready?"

The Shar lunged before he could say another word. He sidestepped as it leapt, and swung his sword at its nearest forelimb. He had mis-timed the strike and the cut was shallow, allowing the creature to turn and leap again. This time it landed on one of the Infantrymen, wrapping him up in its sinuous limbs. The man's scream died as his head was ripped from his shoulders in the powerful, bony jaws of the Shar. The beast dropped the gory prize on the cobblestones and slashed at the second Infantryman who was rushing towards it. The talons scraped across his steel breastplate in a shower of sparks and his curved blade sliced across its body. Marlon darted in close and struck the Shar's head off with a single blow.

The Infantryman was still staggering from shock when Marlon rushed towards the gate. He was aware of the man's protests as he lifted the batten but ignored them and soon the gate was open, and he was inside Shol'Hara.

"The gates have fallen," Valia said as Kapaneus pushed past her.

"What?" he gasped. "How? Are you certain?"

Valia spread her hands. "I hear fighting in the streets beyond Shol'Hara," she replied, "so unless you have finally taken to fighting amongst yourselves, I would say that the enemy have breached the defences."

"Then we must hurry," Kapaneus said after a moment, and rushed out of the atrium and through the Opal Rooms

Valia hurried after him.

"If you want to live," she called out to the Harami, "follow that tunnel and do not stop until you are on the other side!"

She caught up with Kapaneus who was striding down one of the wide, airy halls.

"The Dam'Hara's chambers?" he asked. "I have only a map in my head for reference."

"This is the way," she confirmed.

A eunuch almost walked into them as they rounded a corner and he looked from Valia to Kapaneus with growing alarm.

"Go to the nurseries," she ordered. "Have the nurses take the babies to the Opal Rooms and find the tunnel within the atrium. Follow it to safety. They will need lamps." The eunuch's mouth moved without sound. "And speed!" she shouted, startling the man to action.

"What are you doing?" Kapaneus asked.

"I will not leave children to the Shar," she replied and hurried on with Kapaneus in her wake.

"There are thousands in Shol'Hara," he argued. "If the gates have indeed fallen, we do not have the time to evacuate the entire complex."

"Then we will do what we can," she replied. "Here we are."

They stopped in front of the large doors leading into the Dam'Hara's rooms. Kapaneus turned both handles and pushed the doors open. His shoulders sagged when he saw the dim room, filled with ledgers from floor to ceiling. He strode deeper into the room and went to the nearest shelf.

"What are you looking for?" she asked.

"A ledger, I think," he replied, running his finger along the bound edges of the books.

"Take your pick," she muttered.

A door at the back of the room opened and a woman walked out, carrying a lamp. "What is the meaning of this?" the Dam'Hara demanded. "Who are you?"

"My name is Kapaneus Paras," he said, stepping back from the shelf with a guilty look.

The Dam'Hara glared from Kapaneus to Valia. Valia shrugged.

"And what are you looking for at this time of the morning?" the Dam'Hara asked.

"A record, Dam'Hara," Kapaneus replied. "An entry in the books of a child born here twenty-four years ago."

"Name?"

"Kapaneus Paras, Dam'Hara," he replied.

"Not yours, you bloody idiot," she snapped. "The child."

Kapaneus apologised, and tried again, looking for all the world like a scolded child. "Acastes Fol'Denes."

The Dam'Hara eyed him for a moment before speaking again. "The old fool is dead then, is he?" she sighed. "This way. You are in the wrong room."

The rhythmic pounding of thousands of boots echoed down the wide, cobbled street. The gathering light brought the invading army into full view as they marched, unhindered towards East Market. To either side of the main street, the sound of fighting ebbed and flowed as the barricades fell. Short screams signalled that the Shar were winning in the narrow alleys.

"Archers stand ready!" Rogan called, watching and waiting for the Eastern soldiers to come into range.

Ranks of bowmen nocked arrows and waited while formations of Heavy Infantry stood ready to receive the sparth bearers' charge when it came. Eastern soldiers joined the defenders to stand against their countrymen, but in nowhere near the same numbers.

"Reinforce those exits!" Acastes ordered, sending more soldiers to seal off the two roads that led away from East Market, to Shol'Hara and the Sky Bridge. "If the Shar have breached the barricades then we are vulnerable at the flanks!"

"You should have sent more men," Rogan snapped. "then the barricades would have held!"

"I did not have '*more men*'!" he retorted. "*You* stood them down when you gave Chapok a part in defending the city!"

"It is as much my fault as yours, Hatar," Dachen said as he joined them at the front of the army. "I should have known."

"And you, *Prince*?" Rogan sneered. "Can you be trusted?"

The sound of marching came to an abrupt stop and cut off Dachen's reply as all eyes were drawn to the enemy ranks.

They watched as the men parted to allow the huge figure of the Khalim-Shar to walk to the fore. The Khalim-Shar stopped and brought the butt of the trident down onto the cobbles three times. The sound rang through the streets, echoing from the ancient walls and brought a hush to the city.

"People of Kor'Habat!" it called out with a voice that chilled the blood, a sibilant hiss of rusted iron hinges. "I have been merciful this far. Surrender your city and live under my shadow or stand against me and see everything you love turned to dust and ashes. I am a *compassionate God*! Submit to me!"

Rogan turned in his saddle to the nearest bowman.

"Is it in range?" he asked.

"Yes, Hatar," the man replied. "I could hit that in my sleep."

"Good," he replied, then raised his voice. "Archers! My answer if you please! Loose!"

A thousand arrows streaked up into the sky in a shallow arc towards the Khalim Shar.

The creature watched the hail of shafts rush towards it until at the very last moment it crouched and held a powerful forearm up to cover its head.

Most arrows hit the cobbles, and a few found their way to the soldiers behind the Khalim-Shar, but dozens found their mark. The Khalim-Shar stood, bristling with arrows, and shrieked in fury. It ran the trident down its arm, snapping off the shafts that had struck there, and screamed that tortuous note again. Then it ran towards them.

Behind it, the Eastern soldiers charged, but the Khalim-Shar was closing the gap far quicker than they ever could.

"Archers! Loose!" Rogan shouted as he heeled his horse in the ribs. A volley of arrows hissed overhead and arced towards the enemy as he watched the Khalim-Shar race closer. "Infantry! Close ranks! Forward!" he shouted, "For Korathea!"

The front four units moved through the ranks of archers to take up their positions and locked shields.

"For Korathea!"

The Khalim-Shar arrived at speed, swinging the huge trident and clearing the front row of men like a scythe against grass. Bones shattered within the buckled armour and the screams of broken men replaced the defiance of their battle cry.

The Khalim-Shar struck again, screaming with the voice of a thousand tortured souls and crushing the Infantrymen before they could get close. It towered above them as it killed a dozen men with each swing of its trident, impervious to the arrows that struck it.

Then the Eastern army arrived at full charge.

The Dam'Hara led them to the back of the room and pulled aside a dusty tapestry to reveal an age-worn, wooden door. She took a key from her belt and unlocked it. The hinges grated as she put her weight to the ancient timber, but it swung fully into a dark space beyond. Taking a lamp from its hook on the wall, she beckoned for them to follow.

"This is as old as any part of the city," she said following worn stone steps downwards into the gloom. "Built before the walls of the city themselves."

The stairs brought them to a small chamber from where five other passageways radiated.

"What is this place?" Valia breathed as the Dam'Hara lit more lamps for them to hold.

"The tomb of my predecessors, amongst other things," she replied. "A safe place for precious secrets."

She walked ahead along one of the narrow passages until they came to a low-vaulted chamber with a solitary bookshelf at the far end and a table and chair at its centre. She selected a single, large volume from the middle shelf and handed Kapaneus the ledger.

"I will need that returned, young man," she said.

"This is it?" he asked.

"What is it?" Valia said, still unsure what the Dam'Hara and Kapaneus were talking about.

"The proof we need that Acastes is heir to the throne," Kapaneus replied, leafing through the pages of the big book.

"You cannot be serious. I thought you were joking," she laughed in surprise.

Kapaneus shrugged.

"It is not uncommon for a Kodistai to come to Shol'Hara to sample her delights," he said. The Dam'Hara rolled her eyes and added. "Usually, however, any offspring that result from these unions are not suitable for the Heavy Infantry. Acastes has more of his mother in him, I think."

Valia stared from one to the other. "And you have known all this time, Kapaneus," she muttered. "That is why you have followed him; guarded him."

Kapaneus nodded. "I am one of a small secret society here in Kor'Habat, sworn to defend the bloodline of the Kodistai. It has maintained the peace for over seven centuries. Trust me, a glance at any history text will tell you how bloody the preceding two thousand years were."

"Peace?" Valia laughed. "Korathea has spent the last two hundred years expanding its Empire by force! You have a very strange way of defining '*peace*'."

Kapaneus shrugged as he laid the large book on the table and opened it. "To maintain peace within the Empire at least. Far from perfect, I know. In fact, it was one of *my* people who released you from your cell in the Akharran," he said. "Do you remember?"

Valia gaped. "You ordered that?" she whispered, remembering the hopelessness she had felt when Rogan had condemned her to die. She never could thank the shadowy figure who had led her to the river, and escape. "I had all but forgotten."

Kapaneus returned his attention to the ledger and Valia turned away to inspect the room.

She looked about in the dim light and something caught her eye. A mural set above the passage from which they had entered the room.

"What is that?" she asked, stepping closer and holding her lamp high.

The Dam'Hara moved to Valia's side while Kapaneus lost himself in the pages of the ledger.

The paint was faded with age, but the image was still clear.

"An ancient work," she said. "Perhaps the telling of a story long forgotten."

"I have seen this before," she murmured, recalling the first time she had seen this as a sketch in a book gifted to her.

"Those are Shar," she said, pointing to the left side of the scene.

"Are they?" the Dam'Hara said.

"Yes, they are," Valia breathed, losing herself in the painting.

The Shar cowered at the edge of the work; one of their number was half-lost from sight as it was swallowed by the shadows of a gaping crack in a rockface. Central to the sculpture was a figure with sword held high as it drove the Shar to their doom, towering over the army at its back, just as Kekoa had sketched in his book. Now though, she could see the army for what it was; she could see the colour and detail in the armour and in the weapons; the slender, curved swords of an army she had herself fought against.

"The Shar have been defeated before," she whispered. "But not here, not us. I had forgotten."

"What do you mean?"

Valia stared at the mural in silence, struggling with the many pieces of an ancient puzzle.

"The giant is a mystery," she said at last, "But those soldiers are Jendayan!"

"There is much knowledge here that cannot leave these walls," The Dam'Hara murmured but Valia was too lost in her own thoughts to heed the warning edge in the woman's voice.

"Now why would Shol'Hara have a Jendayan painting in its cellar?"Valia muttered to herself before a new sound intruded on her senses.

"I have what I need," Kapaneus declared, slamming the ledger shut and startling both women. "What is it?" he asked, seeing Valia's silent intensity.

Valia cocked her head and hushed them.

"The Shar," she hissed. "We must evacuate Shol'Hara, now!"

She hurried up the stone steps and through the Dam'Hara's quarters. Out in the hall she saw that nurses were already carrying infants towards the Opal Rooms. The sounds of battle growing nearer had erased any doubts they would have held, and now at last they were moving.

"What is the meaning of this?" the Dam'Hara demanded, catching the arm of a passing nurse.

"I ordered it,"Valia said, urging the young woman away. "You would not listen to reason."

"How dare…" she started but was cut off by a shout from down the hall.

"Valia!" It was a man's voice and the Dam'Hara looked apoplectic at the intrusion of yet another uninvited guest.

"Marlon?" Valia said, looking up.

He was standing at the end of the corridor, sword in one hand and shield in the other.

"Valia," he said again in relief. "I have been looking everywhere for you."

"You found me, old man," she replied as he hurried towards her.

"Have I?" he asked with an edge of caution.

She sighed and managed a half-smile, placing a hand on his shoulder when he reached her. "I have been distant, I know," she said. "I have treated you harshly of late; at times."

"When you were lost…" his voice trailed away. "And when I found you, it was as though you were not there at all."

"And I am sorry," she said. "But for now, we need to get out of Shol'Hara. There will be time later."

Marlon cleared his throat. "The gates have fallen," he warned.

"I know," she replied. "But there is a way out." Then she turned to the Dam'Hara and said, "I have found my sense of purpose again, Dam'Hara. I will give you this one victory, but do not try to hinder me."

CHAPTER 28

"We must fall back to the bridge!" Acastes shouted.

"I will not!" Rogan replied, spitting blood from his mouth.

"We are fighting on three fronts, Rogan! The Shol'Hara road is almost lost. If the enemy encircle us, then we are doomed. But we *can* hold the bridge!"

Dachen nodded in agreement from the saddle of his horse, resting the butt of his sparth on the cobbles. Blood ran down from the blade, dripping unnoticed onto his hand.

Rogan clenched his jaw and glared across the market square to where his soldiers were being pushed back, inch by inch.

"How did they take our flanks so easily?"

"We cannot defend the warren of alleys that make up this city!" Acastes shouted. "The Heavy Infantry are only of use in the open field, where they can move as one. The Shar excel in tight spaces!"

Rogan roared with impotent fury, raising his voice to an uncaring sky.

"I will not surrender the city! I will not abandon Shol'Hara and the Akharran!"

"To kill the viper," Dachen offered, "one must sometimes let it strike. At full stretch, it is vulnerable."

"We can hold the bridge!" Acastes urged. "We have two

thousand men in reserve, waiting in the Akharran. We pull back now and have those men fall upon the enemy's flanks as they follow.

Rogan curled his lips back in anger.

"Every inch we give up now will cost us ten times the men to take back!" he replied.

"At least we will have men," Acastes retorted. "We are losing this fight!"

Rogan took a moment to survey the battle in the vast market square. They were indeed losing, and the enemy were encircling their position with the surety of a snake crushing its prey. On the ground, the bodies of the fallen were fast becoming a morass that would impede any progress that they made, and all but cut off their escape. The cacophony rang from the walls and flooded back into the market, growing in intensity as he watched; filling his mind with a featureless landscape of sound that threatened to take his senses.

He growled and shook with anger, but his mind cleared.

"We hold our ground!" he shouted and urged his horse forward. "Raims! I want three hundred Cavalrymen on the Shol'Hara road ready to attack the flank. The Infantry *must* hold the road to keep our passage clear."

Raims saluted and set about relaying the Hatar's orders.

Rogan turned and glared at Acastes.

"I will not abandon my people!" he spat.

Ganindhra could see the encroaching darkness in that part of his mind that could see beyond his prison. Life was being extinguished in great swathes.

He was powerless to help now, a mere shred of what he had once been. He could only watch in captive horror.

"Help them!" he called out, but only silence returned his call.

On the Shol'Hara road, the Heavy Infantry sealed the alleys

and lanes, forming shield barriers against the Shar and skirmishing with the Eastern soldiers who harried them. The main battle raged a hundred yards away from Rogan where the road reached the edge of East Market. He sat at the head of the column of three hundred Heavy Cavalry, readying his mind and taming his fear.

He pushed his visor down and raised his huge sword. Behind him he heard the nervous clatter of hooves as the riders drew their own weapons.

A gentle nudge with his heels and his great, armoured warhorse stepped forward. He sensed those behind him following his lead.

"Men of the Akharran!" he bellowed. "Sons of Shol'Hara! For Korathea!"

He urged his horse to charge and it responded beneath him.

A roar followed.

He raced towards the enemy along a corridor held open by the Infantrymen to his left. He could see the Khalim-Shar behind the lines of Eastern Soldiers. It turned to face him as he bore down on the incoherent boundary of the two armies where they intertwined in a dance of death.

A horn.

Three short blasts.

Rogan saw his men respond to the command. Those endless drills in the Akharran courtyard giving a reflexive nature to their movement. They moved back as one, drawing the frontline of Eastern soldiers with them and stretching the ragged formation.

The Khalim-Shar shrieked as Rogan reached the newly exposed flanks of the enemy, bringing his heavy blade down on the first man he could reach. The sword cut through the man like sunlight through mist.

Rogan felt the jolts of impact as his horse ploughed through the ranks, and he swung his sword again and again, killing with every stroke.

The Khalim-Shar raised its trident and screamed again, and

Rogan felt the speed of his initial charge begin to lessen as the men in his path sapped the energy he and his horse had carried.

The point of a sparth scraped against his shield and he brushed it aside, splitting the head of the man who wielded it.

As he slowed, he became aware of the Khalim-Shar striding towards him through the waiting ranks of men. He glanced back and found only a handful of Cavalrymen behind him. Further back, and onto the Shol'Hara road, Shar had burst through the Infantry's defensive lines and had hit the Cavalry from the side even before it could reach its objective.

He was isolated.

Rogan brushed the thrusting sparths aside as the enemy closed around him. Then, his horse screamed as a blade found a gap in the armour and he felt it stumble beneath him.

He fell in silence, feeling the dull ache of his horse crushing his right leg. His ears rang with a growing tinnitus that resolved into the clamour of the battle. He opened his eyes to find the Khalim-Shar staring down at him with black eyes. He saw his own face reflected in their glassy surfaces, distorted and pale. He felt for his sword, finding it just within reach. His hand closed around the leather-bound grip and he swung it up in a wide arc towards the Khalim-Shar.

The Khalim-Shar parried the blow with the butt of its trident and shrieked down at its prey as the sword clattered away across the cobbles. Rogan watched, helpless as the Khalim-Shar raised the trident above him. He held his breath, staring at the gleaming tip of the central tine that hung above his chest.

Then, the roar of men and the thunder of hooves caused the Khalim-Shar to hesitate. A dozen arrows struck it in the chest and Heavy Cavalry swept past, clearing the sparth-bearers away like dry leaves. The Khalim-Shar stepped back, snapping the shafts of the arrows before another volley struck home.

"Hurry! Free his leg!"

Rogan struggled to focus on the man dragging him away as

he felt the weight lift from his leg.

"Acastes?" he murmured. "Why?"

"You do not deserve a noble death; you sack of turds!" the man replied before turning his head and shouting. "Take him to safety!"

Rogan felt himself being lifted, and he glimpsed Acastes shouting his orders to Captain Raims.

"We *hold* that bridge, Raims; do you hear me?" Acastes seethed through clenched teeth. "Signal for an ordered withdrawal! We are pulling back."

The Khalim-Shar allowed the Eastern soldiers to press on in pursuit, turning instead to the north-east, and the walls of the Shol'Hara.

Pemba exited the ground floor of the building ahead of the terrified family.

They were not alone in fleeing the Shar. There were others, running for their lives and away from the advancing horror. They were running towards the river, Pemba was certain of that, although how anyone could navigate this maze of alleys and lanes was a mystery to him.

He followed the young family as they hurried away through the stone buildings with their children bundled in their arms. Glancing back over his shoulder he could see more people exiting the buildings and running. A young man ran past him, sprinting in wide-eyed terror down the alley. A dark shape moved with alarming speed across the narrow junction just yards ahead of Pemba, and the young man was gone. He dared to look down the alley as he dashed across the intersection and glimpsed the Shar, tearing at the flesh of its lifeless victim. He quickened his pace, moving with the terrified people and hoping he could find his way back to friendly lines.

Jon and Granger pushed their way through the throng. The

surging mass of people heading for the Sky Bridge had choked the road, and as the crowd was forced ever closer together their progress became slower. Soon they were shuffling along among the press of bodies.

Granger carried the book-stuffed saddlebags over one shoulder and was labouring under the weight.

"Let me take one of those," Jon said over the noise, and lifted the bag onto his own arm. "Just remember; I want my own chapter, and it better bloody well flatter me, you hear?"

"If we survive this, you can have an entire volume," Granger replied as the crowd jostled him.

"A tall man, with a slender waist and a midriff you could crack walnuts on," Jon declared as they edged onto the bridge.

"A man who drew admiring eyes from ladies, and the jealous glares of men," Granger added.

"A hero, unmatched in his lifetime; a lifetime that I hope will extend well beyond today," Jon laughed.

Granger stumbled and grabbed his companion's shoulder for support. "You have a stout heart, Jon," he said once he had found his footing again, "and you are a good friend."

"Careful," Jon warned. "You might make me blush." He glanced around the crowd as it edged upwards along the arched bridge. "I have not seen Elan since yesterday. Where does he get to?"

Granger shook his head. "Elan is not the man he once was. So much of his *self* has been erased, and yet in strange ways, he is more."

"What happened to him, Granger? Why is he the way he is? One moment he is looking me in the eye with what I swear is recognition, the next, it is as though I am smoke. What made him that way?"

"Lythurians are a complex race, Jon, and Elan has experienced something neither of us could ever comprehend" Granger replied by way of explanation. "One day, if we survive this, I will take you to their homeland. You will understand then."

Jon turned as they crested the huge arch of the Sky Bridge and looked back towards East Market. From their vantage he could see the battle, indistinct in the distance but still visible. Sounds of fighting carried to them over the city. Then, horns sounded, cutting through the clamour, clear blasts carrying a simple message to the 'Sons of Korathea'. Jon froze, and listened as the sound of thousands of men shouting with a single voice boomed across the rooftops.

"They are retreating," Jon breathed. "The Heavy Infantry are falling back."

Again, the boom of unified voices as the Infantry moved as one, edging backwards and away from the onslaught.

"They are abandoning the eastern side of the city," Granger replied, shaking his head in disbelief. "They hope to hold the bridge."

The crowd surged with renewed urgency as that realisation dawned on the people of Kor'Habat, and a wave of fresh panic rippled through them.

"What about Shol'Hara?" Jon asked. "Valia is in there!"

"We cannot help her now," Granger replied as the press of bodies drove them over the crest of the bridge. "But Shol'Hara is a fortress within a city. It will hold for a time. I hope."

Nurses hushed wailing babes, holding them close as they hurried through the Opal Rooms towards the tunnel.

"How many?" Marlon asked as a pair of Harami rushed by, holding the swaddled bundles of new-borns in their protective arms.

"Harami; children; nurses," Valia replied. "Thousands."

"And you plan to move them all through that tunnel?" he said, pointing at the opening in the plinth.

"As many as I can," she said.

"Even after everything, you are still willing to protect them," Marlon chuckled. "Valia is back after all."

"They are innocent," she muttered. "For the most part at least. Even if I detest what they stand for, I cannot bring myself to leave them to die. And the young have not yet had the chance to choose otherwise."

Kapaneus hurried across the room.

"The Infantry are in retreat!" he warned. "Hurry; it will not be long before the enemy are at the gates of Shol'Hara."

Valia clenched both fists and pressed them to her eyes.

"We need more time!"

A sudden thump emanated from outside Shol'Hara and the ground shuddered. The room fell silent for a moment before the women started rushing towards the tunnel with renewed urgency.

"The war engines," Marlon murmured. "They have turned them on us."

Another impact and the women began screaming in fear as the Dam'Hara called for calm.

"You are safe within these walls!" she insisted, but her voice fell upon deaf ears and the sense of panic only grew.

"There is no more time," Kapaneus insisted as Valia walked towards one of the wide, airy windows.

She stared out across the gardens towards the gates as a boulder tumbled through the air from atop the city wall in the distance. The boulder grew as it neared until it skimmed the top of Shol'Hara's defensive wall and thudded into the lawn. A shower of soil and dust was thrown up into the air and Valia found herself taking a reflexive step back.

"Hurry," she breathed. "We need to go faster."

The bulk of the Heavy Infantry marched at speed towards the Sky Bridge and the western part of the city. A tight defensive formation of two thousand men backed along the main thoroughfare to cover the withdrawal, moving as one with shields locked together.

In the warren of alleys and lanes to either side of the wide, cobbled road, Eastern soldiers still loyal to Dachen had spread out to prevent the Shar from encircling the retreating army. They moved in a cautious line as best they could through the maze of buildings, keeping a watchful eye on the shadowy corners and dim doorways. They crossed the road to the Akharran behind the two thousand strong reserve force of Infantrymen as it hurried to the main road. They looked a pitiful number.

"Watch those rooftops!" Dachen called out. "And hold the line. Let nothing get past you!"

He had only just finished speaking when a Shar burst around a corner and lunged at him. The point of his sparth sunk into its shoulder and it impaled itself on the steel, but the impact knocked Dachen from his feet and he fell backwards onto the packed dirt of the alley.

He felt the shaft of the sparth slide through his weakened grip as the Shar drove towards him. He kicked out at its snapping maw to fend of the attack. The bony jaws snapped shut over an ankle and he slammed his free foot into the creature's face. He kicked again, feeling the vice-like grip tighten to the point where he was sure his bones would be crushed. Dachen twisted the sparth, hoping a jolt of pain would deter the beast from tearing his foot off, but the blade slipped free from the oozing flesh.

Another sparth was driven into the Shar's flank, and the creature suddenly released its grip on him to face its new attacker.

Then another blade skewered it from the other side as soldiers rushed to the aid of their prince. A moment later, Sangye arrived to strike its head from its shoulders with a single stroke.

"Prince Dachen!" Sangye said with a look of grave concern on his face. "Are you injured?"

Dachen flexed his ankle.

"I am not," he replied, and accepting Sangye's help he returned to his feet, then shouted for the benefit of all within earshot. "Stay alert! Do not find yourself stranded or alone! Protect each other's flanks!"

They edged backwards, holding their sparths low and ready for attack. Shar tested the line as they moved through the buildings, but it held. The distant thrum of marching feet and bellowed commands floated over the city from the main thoroughfare, and Dachen flexed his fingers to ease his grip. He cast a glance over his shoulder and glimpsed the top of the vaulted bridge through a gap between two houses, and then it was lost from sight again.

"The bridge is near!" he shouted, and heard the news being passed down the line.

Soon he found himself in the open with the river at his back. To the north-east, the grim block of granite that was the Akharran rose above the featureless walls surrounding it. Two hundred yards to the south-west, the bridge beckoned.

He watched his men spill out from the close-packed buildings onto the cobbled strand and beckoned for them to make for the crossing.

"Go, Sangye. You lead them, I will follow at the rear. Get them across the bridge."

Sangye nodded and hurried away.

Acastes stood ready to lead the counterattack. The frontline edged closer as the rear-guard gave ground to the oncoming enemy.

A hundred yards.

"On my signal, Raims, give the command."

"Yes sir," the captain replied.

"I hope to Fate those reserves are in position, or this will be a short-lived rally," Acastes murmured.

"The walls!" someone called. "They've turned the engines."

Acastes looked to the distant ramparts and saw the tumbling shapes of boulders hurtling through the air.

"We are out of range," Acastes reassured the Infantryman. "You are quite safe."

"Perhaps," murmured Captain Raims, "but the reserves are

not."

Acastes looked again and traced the trajectory of the missiles. "Give the order!" he barked. "Get them out of there."

Raims flashed a glance at the trumpeter, who at once gave the signal; two short blasts, followed by another two and then a pause before repeating the call.

The boulders struck in the near distance, the sound of the impact arriving a heartbeat later. Screams followed, and Acastes knew at once that the manoeuvre was doomed to failure.

"Charge!" he yelled, urging the Infantrymen forward.

The roar of voices and thunder of footfall swelled in the wide thoroughfare and the rear-guard broke away from the retreating army and back towards the advancing enemy.

Another volley was in the air before the Infantrymen had reached the Eastern soldiers and Acastes could only imagine the disarray in the ranks of the reserves two hundred yards distant. He forced his horse into the fray, bringing his huge sword down onto an enemy soldier. The blade of a sparth scraped against his shield and he brushed it aside, urging his mount forwards to trample his enemy.

His horse screamed in agony as a sparth found its way through the armour and he pulled his feet clear of the stirrups to free his legs as it fell. He rolled and came up onto his haunches in time to deflect a blow with his shield and drive the point of his sword into his attacker's chest.

The Heavy Infantrymen towered over their enemies, but the reach of the sparths and their speed whittled away the advantage.

Acastes heard a rush of air above his head and turned in time to see an enormous bolt cut an Infantryman in half with its broad head. He turned and brought his sword down in an arc that shattered a defensive sparth and split its bearer's head in two.

Another bolt hissed overhead, then a boulder. He glanced up to see the lazy sweep of a *Lamo Phenka* arm as it swung back and forth in the distance over the rooftops.

"They have engines in the street!" he shouted. But behind him, his forces were already in disarray.

Dachen limped towards the Sky Bridge. His ankle ached. Perhaps the Shar had done more damage than he had thought. Another two hundred yards and he would be at the crossing. He paused to rest, leaning on his sparth for support.

"Little prince." He heard a voice from the gloom of alley and glanced up to see his men receding into the distance.

"Where are you, little prince?"

"Who is there?" he demanded.

A shape emerged from the shadows and took form at the edge of the cobbled strand.

"Pemba," Dachen said.

Pemba offered an apologetic smile while behind him Jangbu leered. The blade at Pemba's throat gleamed, wet with blood and Jangbu looked eager for more. The weapon had a curved blade at each end of the handle and a short stabbing point protruded from the centre of the knuckle guard.

"Let him go," Dachen said, bringing his sparth up into an offensive posture.

"Why would I do that?" Jangbu replied.

"Your quarrel is with me."

"*Quarrel*? You think this is a *quarrel*?" Jangbu sneered. "I have no argument with you, little prince. A low-born such as me could never quarrel with a spoiled pup of your stature."

"Then do as I say and release him!"

Jangbu looked to the sky as though considering his response. "Very well, little prince," he replied, and pushed the point of the blade into the side of Pemba's neck.

"No!" Dachen shouted, too late.

Jangbu released him, and Pemba fell to the ground with his hand pressed against the wound. Blood pumped out between his fingers as he struggled to stem the flow.

"Sorry," Jangbu said, and reached behind his back for another of the double-bladed weapons so that he held one in each hand. "I did not know that you wanted him alive."

"You will pay!" Dachen spat as Pemba crawled along the cobbles, smearing blood in his wake.

Jangbu flexed his shoulders and carved a series of flashing arcs through the air with the knives. He paused to lick the blood from the tip of the blade he had used on Pemba.

"So sweet," he leered. "The blood of the defeated. One can almost taste the despair, and yours will be sweeter still..."

Dachen lunged, driving the point of his sparth towards Jangbu's head. The warrior ducked to one side and slapped the blade away with one of his own weapons, spinning on one foot and stepping low and fast towards the prince. Dachen danced back, favouring his uninjured foot and sweeping the sparth first one way and then the other. Each strike was brushed aside with ease as Jangbu advanced.

"You are already injured," Jangbu noted. "This will be too easy. Here, let me even the odds a little."

He tossed one of his weapons to the ground and assumed a defensive stance. "Come, champion of Tianpok; show me what the *lesser* Kingdoms have to offer."

Dachen tried to ignore the jibe, focussing instead on the man in front of him. He could do nothing beyond the fight if he lost now; everything else was trivial.

He lunged and Jangbu parried the blade, a finger's breadth from his chest.

"It almost saddens me," Jangbu declared, ducking a sweeping blow that would have taken his head from his shoulders had he been slower, "that I have to kill you so soon."

Jangbu moved forward to get inside the cutting arc of the sparth and Dachen responded by driving the butt towards his attacker's face. Jangbu caught the shaft in his free hand a moment before the prince kicked him in the chest. As he stumbled back,

Jangbu slashed at the exposed knuckles of his opponent.

Dachen felt a coldness in the fingers of his left hand, but no pain.

"I wanted you to see the fall of this new home of yours," Jangbu gloated. "The sight of Lokhara in flames is something you can never behold; the sounds of your women screaming will never reach your ears. I will accept the consolation of being able to take you down, piece by piece."

Dachen glanced at his wounded hand, aware that something was amiss.

Only his forefinger remained untouched. His middle finger was cut to the bone and the other two had been severed from the first knuckle.

Still no pain; only cold. The prince stepped forward with the sparth gripped in his right hand only.

"Come and take the rest," he urged, with a numbing indifference engulfing both his body and his mind.

A boulder hit the manicured lawn only a few yards from the building, sending a shower of sods through the un-shuttered windows of Shol'Hara. Another crunch from beyond the veil of dust and smoke signalled the attack on Shol'Hara had begun.

"They have turned the bloody engines!" Marlon cursed. "They are using our own weapons against us!"

"Hurry!" Valia shouted. "Get into the tunnel and move swiftly."

The building rang with the sound of screaming women and wailing infants, and panic vied with fear on the faces of the nurses and Harami.

"Dam'Hara?" Valia called out. "How many more?"

The elderly woman looked up from the child she was lifting from a basket to put into the arms of a waiting nurse.

"Too many," she replied. "We have only just begun."

Valia cursed and looked around her. "You! Eunuch!"

A startled man stared back wide-eyed.

"Can you hold a sword?"

His eyes went wider still, and he shook his head.

"We cannot wait much longer, Valia!" Kapaneus urged from beside the tunnel entrance. "We *must* collapse the tunnel behind us, or it will give the enemy a direct route into the palace itself."

Valia watched the stream of women hurrying down the steps and vanishing into the gloom of the passage below.

"You have what you need, so go now," she retorted.

A moment later a scream carried to them from a distant corridor and brought with it a wave of new frenzy as the women rushed for the safety of the tunnel.

Marlon was aware of a weight within his armour that he had not noticed before. The Element he still carried for its safekeeping, suddenly did not feel so safe in his possession. Was it vibrating?

"Valia," he said, leaning close. "We need to leave. The Khalim-Shar is here."

Dachen spun the sparth in his hand and spat a bloody stream of saliva onto the cobbles.

Jangbu grinned, crouching as a wolf awaiting its prey.

"I am told that you are the best that Tianpok has to offer," he mocked. "Little wonder that your kingdom fell so quickly. Before you die today, will you wail, I wonder, as your women did? Scream as your city's children screamed?"

"You crow like a rooster, Jangbu," Dachen replied. "But you are just that, and your head will be on the block when you have outlived your usefulness."

Jangbu ducked and lunged, forcing to Dachen to leap back. The prince's lower back came up against the low wall that separated the strand from the river channel, and he had to dart to the side in his attempt to maintain a safe distance from the gleaming blade in Jangbu's grasp. But Jangbu was too fast, and in a flash had grasped the shaft of the sparth and had it pinned between them as he pressed Dachen against the wall.

Dachen released his own weapon to grapple with his opponent and keep the razor edges of the curved blades away from his neck. His left hand was wet with blood and weak and very soon Jangbu had a blade tip inching towards Dachen's throat. Dachen's back ached as he was forced backwards over the wall. Below him the river oozed, cold against the stonework that channelled the river through the city.

"Let me bleed you slowly," Jangbu hissed as he pushed the blade close enough to prick the skin.

Dachen pushed back with all the strength that he had remaining.

But it was not enough.

He felt the blade pierce his flesh, cold and sharp like frost. Dachen's vision blurred as he strained against his opponent, but he had no more fight to give.

Through the haze of his blurring vision, he saw Jangbu's eyes suddenly widen, and felt his grip loosen...

Jangbu staggered back and turned. Dachen saw the discarded dagger lodged in the armour of the man's back. Pemba was standing with a hand pressed against the wound at his neck, pale and weak from blood-loss.

"Flee, my prince," he uttered through ashen lips.

Jangbu roared in fury and lurched forward to drive his own weapon into Pemba's chest.

Dachen sagged against the wall, blinking to return some clarity to his eyes. Jangbu pulled the blade free and turned again to face the prince.

"Now we finish this," he scowled. "You *will* die today."

Dachen held himself upright against the wall as his legs buckled beneath him.

"Not by your hand," he murmured, as he turned and pitched forward into the water below.

Her father eases himself into the chair, leaning the walking stick against the bench as he always does. He rubs his ruined knee and winces from the pain. His notices Alisha's look of deep concern and his grimace turns to a smile at once.

"Does it still hurt, papa?" she asks.

"Only a small discomfort, Butterfly," he replies. "Nothing to worry about."

"Will you still be able to take me and Tau for a picnic?"

He leans forward in his chair and fixes her with a serious expression.

"Just try and stop me," he says, then he leans back again and smiles. "The wild cherries in the South Meadows will be ripe by now. We may even find Dewberries if the birds have not beaten us to it."

At the mention of the wild fruits, Tau stops the game he is playing with the polished tray and places it on the table, still in the sun's path. The reflected light on the wall goes still.

"Has there ever been a boy who loves fruit as much as you do, Tau?" his father laughs.

Tau laughs with excitement.

There is a tremor; a deep rumble they feel through the floor as much as they hear it. The reflected light shivers on the wall and Alisha's father is on his feet in an instant.

"The mine!" he gasps.

He rushes from the workshop, heedless of his stiff leg, leaving the walking stick against the bench.

"Papa?" Alisha manages to say as her heart is clutched by fear, for she has known this feeling before. But he is gone.

She knows that he has gone to help, but the selfish part of her wants him to stay and hold her hand. She holds Tau's hand instead, and together their strength is more than doubled.

Not long after the first tremor, a second, more violent quake is felt.

The mines claim the lives of the trapped and the rescuers alike. This day is a black day for Bardiya, but there were far darker times yet to come.

Alisha awoke in her own bed, and for a long moment could

recall nothing. Memory crept into her consciousness with ruthless clarity and the insidious weight of dread pressed down on her chest.

She sat up and saw Tau staring at her from her open door and tried to force a smile. His expression was unreadable, and the thought that he may have considered her actions a betrayal crushed her heart further.

"Tau," she started, but did not know what else to say.

"Alisha?" her mother's voice sounded from the kitchen, laced with fear and anger. "Are you awake?"

Alisha swung her legs off the bed and saw that she was wearing her nightclothes.

"Alisha!" her mother appeared at the doorway, eclipsing Tau. "What have I done to deserve this?"

Alisha sagged and stared at the floor as her mother marched into the room.

"You could have drowned, you stupid girl!" her mother berated her. "You are lucky that those men were quick to follow you. You were rescued by Naran. Now I have his wife holding this over my head as though it is to *her* that I owe the debt. How will I ever walk tall in Bardiya again. Get dressed, girl. Get up. You must do the right thing now and face what you have done. You bring me nothing but shame! What have I ever done to deserve this? Am I cursed?"

"Dyansh?" Alisha asked, ignoring her mother's ranting.

"Yes, he will be punished too."

She sighed. At least he was alive; at least there was some hope.

The whole town had congregated in the town square by the time Alisha was marched there by her mother. Captain Yuddha was standing at the centre of the crowd, puffed up and imperious. The two Shadows lay nearby, malignant pools of night on the unblemished cobbles.

At the edge of the crowd, Dyansh stood between two soldiers. His hands were bound in front of him and his face was ashen. She tried to catch his eye, but his gaze was fixed on the ground.

"People of Bardiya, this is a sombre day indeed," Yuddha announced. "Our laws are what separate us from the animals in the field; they cannot be taken for granted. They must be enforced. Punishment is that most unpleasant of tools with which we must dissuade would-be offenders from breaking those laws. To be effective, punishment must be swift and decisive."

"They are only children," someone called out. "They have learned their lesson."

"And what if their attempt to leave should embolden other children?" Yuddha countered. "What then if *children* see our laws as frail things to be ignored on a whim? No! The law is clear on this and there can only be one censure, and that censure is death."

Alisha's knees went weak and a cold terror washed over her. Her mother put an arm around her waist and pulled her close or she would have collapsed where she stood.

"Children!" she heard above the ringing in her ears. "Children! They're children!"

Dyansh's mother collapsed into the arms of the woman next to her and wailed.

A whip snapped over the heads of the angry crowd, silencing the protests. The soldier cracking the whip was Mohanish, the same who had confronted them on the dock; and his grin was unmistakeable.

"But I believe that justice should be moderated by fairness," the Captain assured them.

"Yes!" someone called. "Show mercy. They are only children."

A muttering of approval ran through the crowd.

"The girl was led astray!" Yuddha declared. "This much can be accepted. It is a mitigation in her favour and has been taken fully into account. The boy will bear the full brunt of the punishment for *both,* as he rightly deserves!"

Dyansh sagged and was held up by the soldiers at his side. Alisha sobbed, struggling to reconcile her relief and horror as both threatened to overwhelm her.

Another crack of the whip to silence the stirring crowd as cries of 'mercy' rang around the square. The Shadows stirred and Yuddha continued.

"Mercy? Yes. The Shadows administer a cruel and agonising end. The boy's age has been considered, and he shall be shown the mercy of the rope."

"No!" Alisha rushed forward and prostrated herself on the ground at Captain Yuddha's feet. "Please, I beg you!" She wept. "Let him live. I will do anything; anything. I will marry you; I swear it. I will be a good wife. Please let him live. I will do as you say."

Yuddha looked down at the girl grovelling on the cobbles with a mixture of discomfort and disgust.

"Foolish girl," he murmured. "Those things were never in your gift to begin with."

"Please," she begged, her voice wretched and weak.

"Garrotte him," Yuddha ordered.

"No!" she cried.

The townsfolk stirred, but as their protests grew, the Shadows were at once on their feet and snapping at the fringes of the crowd. Dyansh struggled against the soldiers to either side of him in panic even as the rough rope was passed over his head.

"Mama!" he cried, but his mother was motionless on the ground. "Mama!"

He was forced onto his knees and a soldier grabbed his hair to hold his head still. Mohanish had abandoned his whip for a baton which he passed through the loop of rope at the back of Dyansh's neck.

"Dyansh!" Alisha got to her feet and made to run to him, but Yuddha pulled her back.

Mohanish turned the baton to twist the rope and soon it was biting into Dyansh's flesh.

Tears streamed down the boy's panicked face and his trousers went dark with urine as the rope tightened. The Shadows chittered with excitement, tasting the air and finding death upon it.

Alisha screamed his name as her mind recoiled from the horror. This was not real. It could not be real. No such terrors were real; only in the awful fantasies of nightmares.

The soldiers struggled against the strength of the boy as he fought with every fibre to break free. Mohanish gritted his teeth and doubled his efforts on the baton as it crushed the child's windpipe, forcing the twists tighter and tighter. Dyansh's mouth worked in silent agony until his body spasmed and the final sparks of life flared and went out forever.

Alisha was howling with despair, sobbing as she begged for a life that was already lost.

At last his body was thrown to the Shadows who tore at it with a savage craving, crushing bone and tearing flesh. His blood spread across the pristine cobbles to the mournful howls of a People grieving the loss of another son; lamenting the loss of their own fortitude and the death of hope.

Captain Yuddha released Alisha at last and she sank to her knees in the square. She would have welcomed death in that moment, had it been offered, but that mercy had been withheld from her.

Her being was rocked by a tremor she could feel resounding through her core and her world collapsed around her.

She was trapped… and alone in darkness.

CHAPTER 29

A castes fought as he retreated.

The damage inflicted on his ranks of Heavy Infantry by the war engines at such close quarters had been devastating. He stumbled backwards over the heaps of gore that littered the road, desperate not to become another bloodied corpse on the stones.

The Sky Bridge reared up behind him, leading upwards with the false promise of safety beyond the gentle arc.

He grabbed the edge of Captain Raims' armour as the man lost his footing and stumbled.

"We cannot hold them!" he shouted, pulling Raims upright again.

"We can hold them on the bridge; with barricades if needs be," Raims called out over the noise.

Acastes risked a glance over his shoulder. They were almost at the bridge and soon the enemy would be fighting up the slope. A small advantage to the Heavy Infantry, but he was ready to take anything on offer.

For a moment he thought that the enemy had encircled them when he saw the tips of several sparths coming in from the strand along the river, but flashes of blue-green against the soldiers' armour marked them as Dachen's men.

There was, however, no sign of the prince himself.

"I beg you, help them!" Ganindhra beseeched across a landscape of dying minds, calling out beyond the mortal realm to have his pleas heard and felt. "The time for standing idly by is long past. Too much has been lost already!"

He fought against the throne that bound him to the soil, roaring in impotent fury in the gloom.

"Help them, Athusilan!"

The violent bouncing of the cart and the pain induced by every movement brought Rogan back to full consciousness. He forced himself up onto his elbows and grimaced as he took in his surroundings. Panic was rife everywhere he looked.

"Stop the cart!" he shouted. "Stop now!"

The driver had veered right, away from the chaos of West Market, and glanced over his shoulder as he hauled on the reins.

"My orders were to take you to the palace, Hatar," the man said, despite the cart clattering to a halt.

"You have new orders," Rogan replied. "Find me a man who can operate that." He pointed towards the huge catapult that rested at the edge of the expansive market.

"Hatar?"

"I need someone, anyone who knows how it works!" Rogan barked.

"I know how it works," an Eastern soldier declared from the road. "I can operate the engine."

Rogan turned and scowled at the speaker. While most of these Eastern men looked much the same to his eye, this one he was certain was one he had seen in the company of Acastes in the past; one of Prince Dachen's men.

"What is your name?"

"Sangye, Hatar," the man replied.

"You say that you can make it work?"

"I can. But it is a little far from the fight."

Rogan nodded and set his jaw, then pointed into the distance to where the arc of the Sky Bridge was visible above the rooftops.

"Can you hit that bridge?"

Sangye sucked air in through his teeth and shook his head.

"Not from here," he said. "But give me horses or men to move it up the road a little, and you can tell me which cobble you want me to crack."

Rogan nodded as he considered his options. "You will have men," he promised. "But if that swagger is misplaced, you had better hope the Shar get to you before I do."

Sangye smiled in response. The Hatar began barking orders from his position on the cart as though he was sitting astride a warhorse.

"The city is ours, Stellio!" Tulley called out in delight. "Did I not say it would be so?"

Starling followed the man through the open gates of Kor'Habat and found a city wreathed in smoke and dust. The clamour of combat rang from the encircling walls, swirling like a broth that filled and choked the streets. Bodies were everywhere that he looked, lying in cruel contortions atop one another where they had fallen.

Death had shown no favour and attacker lay with defender in mutual ruin.

"Death to Korathea!" Tulley yelled, raising his sword and shield high. "Take what you can, Stellio," he urged. "Those Eastern men have left us rich pickings."

With that he darted into a low building. There was a scream from within, evidence that there were still those in hiding from the invading army within the buildings that had not been crushed by the war engines. Tulley emerged a moment later, stuffing a silver plate up beneath the leather armour that covered his torso. He sheathed his sword to make the task easier even as he vanished into the next doorway.

Starling stared in disbelief at the carnage. Doors were being smashed by the looting army and those residents of Kor'Habat who had not already fled were being flushed out into the streets and corralled into terrified huddles. A hundred yards from the walls the buildings were intact for the most part, and he began to recognise the many landmarks he had come to know over his many previous visits.

'*The Stunted Willow*'; the inn where a lusty serving maid had made a man of him at the age of fifteen. The bakery from where he had stolen sweet loaves when he was visiting as a young boy. The upmarket armoury where his father had bought Starling's first, real sword.

Strange that he had not thought of his father until now. The governor of Kernhalt was surely dead, and yet Starling could not bring himself to feel any sorrow for the man who had been part of the millennia-old system of corruption and decay that had seen Nirmaya murdered.

What was that Eastern proverb that Armil had shared with him?

'*The edifice built upon the backs of the poor will crumble when they rise*'.

He looked around him and saw the common folk of Korathea taking back what their labours had built. They were joined by those from Dasar and Pashwar eager to avenge the years of theft and oppression suffered at the hand of Kor'Habat.

A man burst out from a doorway at Starling's side, wild-eyed with terror and wielding a sword he held in a clumsy, shaking grasp. Starling reacted without thinking, brushing the blade away with a stroke before driving his own into the man's chest.

He glared into his eyes as shock turned to fear turned to grim acceptance by slow degrees. Then life fled the crumpling body as it hit the bloody cobbles.

Starling felt no remorse.

Kor'Habat wielded the power it did because fools propped it up with their own indifference to what befell those outwith the cossetting walls.

He was haunted by a fleeting vision of Nirmaya's reproving frown before he swept it away. He howled an animal strain, then plunged deeper into the city to be among those who would destroy the old order for its crimes.

The huge block of masonry sailed from the sling and arced towards the bridge.

"Sangye!" Jon called out as he arrived at the huge war engine. "What are you doing?"

"Saving this side of the city!" Rogan bawled from his position on the cart. "Stay back you fool!"

"There are still soldiers on that bridge!" Jon protested. "They need a chance to fall back."

The projectile glanced the side of the bridge and a heartbeat later a loud crack reached them from the distant collision.

"That should give them warning," Sangye murmured as Rogan cursed.

"You missed, you fool! Get that engine reset! You must hit the central arch!"

"Now, Valia!" Kapaneus screamed. "We have to leave now!"

Valia hurried the terrified women past her as she edged further from the safety of the tunnel. The flow of women from the corridor beyond the wide, arched doorway had stopped, and the Dam'Hara was urging those who had made it on from the back.

"Valia!" Marlon shouted just as the first of the Shar burst into the room, skidding on the polished granite floor. She lunged at it and hacked one of its forelimbs off before it could recover from the slip. The scream was cut off when she followed through with a second blow that severed the head.

"Dam'Hara!" she urged. "Move!"

The woman turned, but a moment later a second Shar was on her. Sharp claws stabbed into her back and stole the breath from her lungs. She collapsed under the weight of the attack and did not move again.

With a growl, Valia rushed at the Shadow which managed to recoil from her flashing blade and dart sideways. Marlon was there to drive his sword into its flank which gave Valia the precious heartbeat to attack again. A moment later, it was dead.

"We must go!" he said, grabbing her arm. "Now!"

She nodded and followed him towards the dwindling group of women gathered at the tunnel entrance.

"How many are through?" she asked, glancing back towards the entrance to the chamber.

"I do not know," he replied. "but we can do no more for them."

The last of the Harami were entering the tunnel when an agonizing shriek filled the room and the Khalim-Shar strode through the archway. It stopped and drove the butt of its trident onto the stone floor with a sound that rang like the breaking of a world.

It turned to face them and tasted the air with its serpent's tongue, lips black and drawn back from the bony ridges of its mouth.

"You cannot hide," it hissed, a slow and deliberate utterance.

"Valia, we must leave now," Kapaneus murmured, transfixed as he was by the Khalim-Shar's stare.

"Run. I will find you," the Khalim-Shar breathed, a whisper that echoed from the walls.

"Valia?" Kapaneus said.

Valia took a long steady breath. "We could end this now," she whispered.

"Valia, no," Marlon breathed, knowing at once what she intended to do.

But it was too late, and he was too far away to stop her.

Valia took only a moment to steady her racing mind before she charged at the Khalim-Shar.

Ganindhra raged against his prison. From the waist down he was fused to his throne, his legs indistinguishable from the base of the chair.

"Athusilan!" he bellowed. "Athusilan!"

An ellipse of blinding light appeared and then vanished, and Athusilan was suddenly there.

"Brother!" Ganindhra pleaded, leaning towards the God and reaching out his gnarled hand. "Help them, please!"

"Why do you call out to me when you know I can do nothing?"

"I call to you because we are brothers."

"I took an oath," Athusilan replied, shaking his head but unable to meet the eyes of his kin.

"We are the last! We are all that remains," Ganindhra implored. "Help them. Help *me*!"

"It is not meant to be."

"I release you from your oath!" Ganindhra insisted. "So much has been lost already. I release you, brother. I release you!"

Athusilan was silent for a moment. He made to speak but instead spun on his heel and stepped away. A glaring breach in the air opened and was gone in an instant, taking Athusilan with it.

"They're trying to bring down the bridge!" Acastes shouted. "Fall back! Fall back!"

Any semblance of an ordered withdrawal had crumbled when the first block had glanced the side of the stone structure. The impact had shaken the once solid surface beneath their feet and now the Heavy Infantry were in a full rout. Acastes was near the apex of the bridge when he saw the huge arm of the catapult lurch into motion again.

"Move!" he bellowed over the deafening roar of battle and panic, pushing forward against the backs of the men in front of him.

The *Lamo Phenka* had released boulder from its sling and

Acastes watched the exorable flight as it arced towards him. His world slowed. He threw himself forwards, feeling the rush of air of the massive stone passing in silence, a hand's width above his sprawling body. He struck the cobbled surface of the bridge at the same moment it lurched upwards to meet him. He felt the breath driven from him with the impact as the floor of the Sky Bridge shook, making his body bounce up before falling again onto the hard surface that was shifting under his chest.

He heard screams of terror but for a moment had forgotten why that could be, his own sense of self-preservation having over-ridden all other concerns. He was sliding but could not be certain why. His reeling senses had lost all notion of up or down and he only knew that his legs were now dangling over thin air.

Reflex alone had him grabbing for purchase with his hands even as the bridge crumbled beneath him. The ancient arches that had spanned the river as they had the millennia had been broken and a city cleaved in two. Men screamed as they fell, vanishing into the water of the River Habat almost a hundred feet below where their armour dragged them to their collective doom. Chunks of aged masonry sent spray soaring in all directions and the river swallowed every trace of that mortal endeavour it was fed.

Acastes' fingers slipped in the rubble and dust but there was nothing to slow him, nothing to hold.

A gauntleted hand clamped over his wrist just as the last of the support vanished from under him. For a moment he just hung there watching the great chunks of masonry as they tumbled into the river among the frail bodies of his fellows.

"Reach up!" A voice broke through to him.

He looked up to see who had spoken.

"Raims?" he murmured.

"Acastes! Reach up!"

Acastes shook his head to clear it and swung up with his free hand to grab a hold of the Captain's own. Raims grimaced from the effort of holding the big man, pouring every ounce of his remaining strength into the task.

At last Acastes was able to get a foothold in amongst the broken masonry and edged up a little higher. More hands pulled him up until he found himself lying on the shattered edge of what remained of the Sky Bridge. He sat up and looked across the gap. The last few Infantrymen were being driven from the eastern side and fell into the water where they vanished below the surface under the weight of their armour.

Acastes backed away from the edge, glaring across at the Eastern soldiers who had drawn to a halt on the other side of the 70-foot gap.

"Thank you, Raims," Acastes muttered as the shock cleared from his mind.

Raims had collapsed exhausted on the cobbles beside him.

"You won't tell Rogan, will you?" Raims replied, gasping for breath.

Acastes placed a hand on the captain's shoulder and managed a weak grimace in return.

Then a cheer went up from the defenders that Acastes could not fathom; revelling in such a crumb of victory whilst swallowed by a sea of defeats almost made him laugh.

Valia charged across the polished marble floors, oblivious to the shouts behind her. Her eyes were fixed on the enemy ahead.

She could finish it all here. Now.

The Khalim-Shar stood erect and screamed in defiance as Valia closed the gap between them. Then a black tide washed into the vast room through the wide, arched entrance as dozens of Shar poured in.

Too late, she realized her mistake and tried to turn back. Her feet slipped on the polished floors and she stumbled as she turned and put her hand down to steady herself. She looked up and saw Marlon being pulled back towards the tunnel by Kapaneus. A glance as she rose again and the Khalim-Shar was raising its trident over a sinuous shoulder.

She ran, knowing that she could not cover the distance in time.

Marlon shouted her name, stumbling backwards into the gloom of the only escape route behind him as Kapaneus struggled to pull him to safety.

Every step she took was interminable. Valia was deafened by the rushing of her own blood and she could no longer hear his voice but could see the panic written stark across his face, her name upon his lips, imploring in the silence and the horror.

She felt nothing, but her vision jolted upwards and knew that she had been struck.

She fell to her knees and looked down at the bloody tip of the trident protruding from the leather armour below her chest.

No pain. She was numb.

She looked up and saw Marlon's anguish as he was dragged away by strong arms around his own. In his eyes was the promise that he would have rushed to her side even then, given his life so that she would not have died alone. But that sacrifice was denied to him and he vanished from sight, despair etched plain on his face in a silence that deadened her name as he called it.

The black tide enveloped her.

Blinding, white light.

Then, nothing.

In the shadows of his living prison, Ganindhra leaned back in his throne. A deep rumble emanated from his chest as he bowed his head and closed his emerald eyes.

"It is done."

EPILOGUE

Alano felt a shiver run down his spine despite the warmth of the air and the sun on his back. A shadow had encroached on the serenity of his thoughts, and he knew that something terrible had happened.

"What is it, my love?" Casilda asked from the open door of the cottage.

"Nothing at all," the man replied with a warm smile, and reached out for her from his seat on the bench.

She took his hand and moved to stand behind him, placing her hands on his shoulders to work at the muscles there. He allowed his head to drop forwards as she eased the knots with her thumbs and groaned with a mixture of pain and relief.

"You have brought many things to this marriage, Alano Clemente," she said at last, "but dishonesty has never been one of them."

He nodded and placed his hands on hers at his neck. "I was away too long," he replied.

"You did what had to be done, and I recall giving you my blessing," Casilda assured him. "Besides, I could not have you moping about, staring at your sword all day."

"No. I think that is why I left them so readily. I missed you; I missed my home. It was too easy."

"You should have stayed?"

He sighed, "I don't know."

In the distance, a small group of jade-skinned children were playing in a meadow. One of them looked towards the adults as though sensing their eyes upon them and waved. Kellan's son, Layall.

Alano waved back. "They are not safe," he said.

"Even here?"

"Even here."

"What can be done?"

"I do not know," he replied, shaking his head.

"You will do the right thing," she assured him, giving his shoulders one, last squeeze before turning for the cottage.

'*The right thing*', he wondered. Why was it so hard to see what that was?

Adeyemi reached the top of the low rise and looked south. A haze of black smoke rose from the distant horizon, a stark reminder of what he had left behind.

He pulled the new impanga that Granger had gifted him from the sheath at his back and stared at his reflection in the lustrous steel blade. It was hard to look into his own eyes.

"You feel it too," he asked. "It is guilt."

His companion did not reply.

"Do you feel anything at all?" he went on. "Or are you just here to judge me?"

Elan looked north towards the mountains.

"You understand that I could not stay? I could not face the Khalim-Shar with the power it holds over me. I am split between two realms, that of the living and that of the dead. My life is not my own."

Elan removed an arrow from his quiver and checked the fletching before placing it back where it had been.

"I have no soul and you have no mind," Adeyemi sighed. "Perhaps together we make up a whole man."

After a moment's silence, Adeyemi sighed and looked north to the rising mountains and then west to the gentle plains. "West, I think," he decided. "That path looks easier; do you not think? A future waits over every horizon, but I would meet it with the softness of grass beneath my feet if I could choose."

Elan did not answer but followed the dark-skinned man as he set off again towards their choice of unknown futures.

In the still, evening air, Senji Dayivar walked up the slope of the enormous bridge. Smoke occluded much of what should have been a spectacular city vista. The air cleared as he went higher, and soon the stepped pyramid of the Kodistai's palace came into view over the unseen river. The Akharran and Shol'Hara too rose above the sooty air in defiance.

He stopped short of the chasm that lay ahead; the shattered stone of a once-proud bridge was jagged in the gloom, reaching to span the gap but falling short. Kor'Habat had not yet fallen in its entirety.

"You should be wary of opportunistic archers on the north-west bank."

Senji turned to find Masahara making his way up the slope behind him.

"They will be resting," he replied. "They know that they are safe."

"Safe?" Masahara asked. "I hardly think that they are safe. Safety will be theirs when they declare fealty to their new God, not before."

"They will fight us to the end," Senji sighed.

Masahara shrugged. "So be it," he said.

"And when this continent has fallen, do we cross the sea to the next?" Senji asked. "Will I ever be allowed to return to my home?"

"Why don't you ask him yourself?" Masahara replied and looked back down the slope of the bridge into the sooty depths of the city.

Senji could hear it now; the rhythmic clang of the trident on cobbled street, growing louder with every strike. A dark shape took form from out of the darkness and the Khalim-Shar strode out into the dying evening light. It walked past Senji and Masahara and stopped at the very edge of the broken stonework. A part of Senji willed those stones to give way under the weight and send the creature into the water below.

Were those strange nubs at its shoulder blades more prominent?

"You doubt your purpose?" it hissed.

"No, Khalim-Shar," Senji exclaimed in guilty horror, and went down on one knee.

"Yet you long for home."

"I...I miss my wife, it is true," he stammered, "but I will do what was agreed to hold her safe."

The Khalim-Shar made a high-pitched grating sound that Senji took for a chuckle.

"Your allegiance comes at a price, I see," it said.

"No, great one," he managed. "I am yours."

"Witness true devotion!" the Khalim-Shar went on, and Senji realised that another had followed the creature onto the broken bridge. "I will have this zeal from all, in time."

The newcomer wore brown robes that covered the wearer's head in a deep hood and hung down to kiss the cobbles. Masahara could not hide his displeasure and looked away from the figure to stare at the dimming sky.

"Show your face," the Khalim-Shar urged. "Do not be ashamed of what you have endured in my name. Wear your scars with pride that others may see the strength of your faith."

Senji swallowed hard as he saw the ruined hands of Ramash Suun emerge from the sleeves to reach up and pull back the hood. He could not look upon the man for long, and turned away, feeling sick to his stomach.

The head and face of Suun were a twisted mess of scar tissue. A single eye stared out from the blistered features, darting from the cobbles to the Khalim-Shar and back to the cobbles with a nervous glee. Much of what had once been lips had been burnt away, to reveal his teeth in a sickening parody of a grin.

"You will build me a new temple, Suun," The Khalim-Shar declared. "One so great that the old Gods will tremble in their crypts."

"Yes, Khalim-Shar," Suun replied, his pink tongue darting to wet what remained of his lips.

"I will be unrivalled! The old enemy has grown weak."

"Yes, Khalim-Shar," he breathed.

The Khalim-Shar turned back to face that part of the city that had eluded him for now and screamed his challenge into the darkness.

The mood in *The Glaive* was sombre.

No one was celebrating their salvation; too much had been lost; too many had fallen. A ruined bridge was all that stood between what remained of the defending army and the might of the Khalim-Shar and all its followers.

An animal scream floated out across the city and a silence fell upon the common room for a short time before wine and ale won back the attention of the drinkers.

Granger and Jon sat in silence as the argument ran itself full circle again.

"We still hold the western city," Kapaneus said as he watched Acastes drain his winecup.

"How long before they roll those war engines to within range and pound what we hold to dust?" the big man replied.

"We need leadership," Kapaneus insisted. "Hesitate now and Rogan will take the throne, and he only has his own self-interest at heart."

"The *throne*? We are beaten, Kapaneus. We lost. The throne is lost."

"The chair itself may yet be at risk, but not the position, not the title. You are still the rightful leader of the Korathean people.

You are the rightful Kodistai."

Acastes laughed.

"What '*people*'?" he replied with a bitter laugh. "Yesterday, I was nobody's ruler, now I am to be a ruler of nobody. Those not yet dead will scatter or else join their fellows in the ashes. The city has been carved in two and the walls did not even need to fall. No, the enemy marched in through open gates! We defeated ourselves. The Khalim-Shar does not need an army to break mankind, we will do that for it!"

An empty wine jug smashed against the wall not far from them.

"Wine!" Marlon shouted as he stood swaying as though against an unfelt wind a few tables away.

Granger hurried to his friend's side and steadied him as a serving maid arrived with a nervous smile and a full jug of wine.

"He has had enough," Granger murmured, but Marlon snatched the jug anyway. "Come and sit with us, Marlon," the historian said and nodded to the serving maid who hurried away.

Granger shepherded the staggering man back to the table where Acastes and Kapaneus still sat and deposited him into a chair. He had barely taken his own seat when Sangye hurried across the common room to join them.

"Prince Dachen has been found," he said in an urgent whisper. "He is injured but he lives!"

"That is good news indeed," Granger sighed. "A welcome word at last."

"A pearl within a midden," Acastes murmured.

Marlon muttered something unintelligible as he poured wine into a fresh cup, splashing some onto his hand but paying the spill no heed.

"He was in the river," Sangye went on. "They were searching for survivors after the bridge fell and he was floating on the surface, hurt but alive."

"A hundred Infantrymen were not so lucky," Acastes said,

glaring into his own cup.

"Air pockets trapped under the leather armour kept him afloat," Sangye reported in excited tones, until an acid glare from Acastes silenced him.

"He was indeed lucky," Granger said. "Fate smiled on him today."

"Another ruler without a People," Acastes declared, raising his cup. "There is much of it around, it would seem."

"These are dark times," Granger said, leaning forward and placing both hands on the table. "Adeyemi has vanished; Elan has not been seen for some time. Abbil, Nirmaya and the Sisters, Starling?" He shrugged. "Shar-hunters and Infantrymen we knew well have fallen. *Valia* has fallen." The last was said with a note of disbelief and he caught the eye of each man at the table as the reality set in. "But we still cannot abandon hope."

"Hard to believe she is actually gone," Jon murmured, staring into his mug of ale. "But we've been here before."

There was a long silence before Granger spoke. "Tell me again what you saw, Kapaneus."

Marlon growled, sullen and swaying in his seat.

"In Shol'Hara?" Kapaneus said. "It is as I told you before, she ran to attack the Khalim-Shar and was overwhelmed. We were too far away to help."

"You dragged me away," Marlon slurred, focussing on Kapaneus with a look of unrestrained hatred.

"You would have died too," Kapaneus replied. "There were too many of them."

"The last thing you saw," Granger urged, eager to avoid a new argument. "What was the last thing you saw?"

"Before retreating into the tunnel and collapsing it?" Kapaneus asked, shaking his head as he stirred the awful memory. "Valia was down. Wounded mortally. The Shar swarmed over her. The last I saw," He laughed. "A trick of the mind."

"What did you see!?" Granger's voice sounded intent.

"Light." Kapaneus said. "Bright as the sun but gone in a heart-beat. I saw light."

Granger nodded, scratching at his chin. "Marlon," he said, placing a firm hand on the man's arm. "You told me once before, when Valia had been taken in Kylyptus, that you could *feel* that she was still alive. You *knew* she was when all others told you it was not possible."

"I watched her die," he murmured before lifting his head and growling through gritted teeth. "I watched her die! How many times must I say this?"

"But do you still *feel* her?"

"She's dead! Even Valia could not survive that!" he shouted, banging his fist down onto the table and spilling his wine. "I watched her die! And I could do nothing to save her!" His whole body shook with pent up anger and sorrow and he balled his fists on the table, squeezing his eye shut as tears fought through.

Granger leaned closer, despite the danger and spoke in an urgent whisper. "Do you still *feel* her?"

Marlon trembled with such ferocity that Jon moved to put himself between the grieving man and the historian.

Suddenly, Marlon stopped shaking and sighed into the hush.

"I do not understand. She is so distant." He shook his head as sought to order his jumbled thoughts and then fixed Granger with a sudden, lucid gaze. "She lives!" he breathed. "Valia is alive!"

'*When the shadow casts its darkness from the north and the third King of that name passes from the world, cities will fall and fires will burn high. Look to the west, for the sun shall rise there and bring with it a Saviour. And he shall turn you on your heads.*'

From **THE PROPHECIES OF TIANPOK.**

ABOUT THE AUTHOR

B. R. Crichton lives in Perthshire with his wife, Lesley, and three children, Sandy, Laura and Douglas. He was born in Bulawayo, Zimbabwe, but moved to Scotland in 1992. His various jobs have included barman, youth-worker, and tree surgeon/arborist.

Follow on Twitter: @BRCrichton

Facebook.com/brcrichton

www.brcrichton.com

Lightning Source UK Ltd.
Milton Keynes UK
UKHW011016021220
374440UK00003B/88

9 780993 489426